The Gaming Room

Paul Ver Bruggen

Cover design by Scott Gaunt – scottgaunt@hotmail.co.uk

ISBN: 9798650427186

PublishNation
www.publishnation.co.uk

To Carina,

who taught me that women are far more interesting

'The market is rigged, the market is always rigged, and the rigging is in favour of the people who run the market. That's what the market is. It's a bent casino. The house always wins.'

David Hare

'Money is human happiness in the abstract; and so the man who is no longer capable of enjoying such happiness in the concrete, sets his whole heart on money.'

Arthur Schopenhauer

'It's just like a magic penny
Hold it tight and you won't have any.
Lend it, spend it and you'll have so many
They'll roll all over the floor.
For love is something if you give it away,
Give it away, give it away
Love is something if you give it away
You end up having more.'

Song lyrics by Malvina Reynolds

Prologue

I picture Theo Law in his younger days. Apart from the many adrenalin-fuelled moments he experienced on the trading floor, he liked nothing more than playing Texas Holdem with his well-heeled mates. He loved the tension that lurked beneath the surface of frivolous banter; the dick swinging face-offs for high stakes; the way the game played out almost as a ritual.

Deal two cards each face down – *the hole.*

A round of betting.

Deal three shared cards face up – *the flop.*

Another round of betting.

Deal a fourth shared card – *the turn.*

More betting.

Deal a final shared card – *the river.*

Make the best five-card poker hand possible from the two cards in the hole and any three of the shared cards – *the rose.*

A final round of betting.

Turn over the cards in the hole – *the showdown.*

He also liked that you didn't always need the best cards to win. Many games ended when someone simply bet enough that the others folded. Good as he was at this kind of hustle, he used it sparingly and usually when he had excellent cards. That way, it kept everyone guessing.

And he often had excellent cards. Too often, some might say. More recently, the mood of the regular game had shifted. There was less banter, more tension. The other players had begun to suspect that something more than luck or calculated risk was involved in Theo's success, though they couldn't see how that might be the case.

One evening the mood darkened further when one of them – let's call him Ed – lost a large amount of money to him, large even by City trader standards. It didn't help that they'd all had a lot to drink, as well as a couple of lines of coke.

'It's been going on too long, Theo.'

'What has?'

'Your run of luck.'

'What are you saying?'

'That maybe something else is happening here.'

'Such as?'

Silence.

'*Such as?*'

'Such as…you're not being…a straight arrow.'

'You saying I'm a cheat, Ed?'

'You used the word, I didn't.'

'That's a serious allegation. How am I cheating?'

Ed shook his head, shrugged, took a deep breath.

'I'm not sure…'

'Well, there you are – *you're not sure.* Do you want to apologise?'

'No, I don't want to *fucking apologise* – I know you're cheating.'

Theo had reached across the table and grabbed him by the throat before the others managed to restrain him.

'I'm just good at cards, *you fucking asshole!*'

There was no denying Theo was good at cards, but some of the others were convinced he was also very good at cheating. So good they couldn't work out how he did it.

Chapter 1

Rome, November two thousand and something in the teens. An adolescent year, a year that thought it knew more than it did and gets itself into all sorts of trouble. It seems like a fitting place to start, a good measure of how far I'd come. Many years before, I'd been a junior member of a large finance team from various European and American banks, arranging loans for the Italian government via its central bank. This was pre-crash and early-boom, so there was plenty of easy money around. Which was just as well because a corrupt political system and a thriving black economy – the *Nero,* as it's called – meant that the government needed to borrow lots of it.

I remember getting a taxi from the airport and giving the chirpy Italian driver what I thought was 30 of the new euro currency – a 20 and a 10. He held out two 10s and gave a big shrug.

'Hey, with these new notes, it's an easy mistake to make...'

'Of course – I'm sorry...' I replaced one of the 10s with a 20, together with a tip, as an apology. It was only later I realised how he'd conned me out of the extra 20 euro, and my outrage at having been stung was completely out of keeping with the scale of the crime: the money man mugged; the deal maker duped. But then, I was ignorant of all sorts of sharp practices that have since become second nature to me.

I ponder this as I sink into the sumptuous leather of the large Mercedes that has been sent to collect me. No cheap Fiat and chiselling driver this time. Next to me in the back is my escort, a senior official of the Vatican Bank, who is suited, booted and Acqua di Parm-ed – I'm a Terre d'Hermes man myself – in that fussy Italian style. He's extra-smiley and solicitous, asking me in very decent English if I had a good flight and saying how much the Cardinal is looking forward to seeing me. The 'Cardinal' in question is Cardinal Mancini – the grande capo of the Vatican Bank, who's obviously equally at home with God and Mammon, as well as being the Pope's right-hand man.

Because my business this time is not with the Italian state but with the Vatican. I have journeyed from one curious hangover of Medieval Europe – the City of London – to another. What a bizarre age we live in, the richest of times, the poorest of times. We've never been better off, we've never wanted for more, which is certainly true of the Vatican. To cut to the chase, the place is stony broke. Or rather it has no cash, no liquid, which if you're a business amounts to the same thing. And not only the Vatican, but the Church itself, or the Holy See, as it's known. It could be the result of a decline in donations from the faithful, what they call 'Peter's Pence', but I doubt that's the case. It could be some toxic investments, which is not difficult in these days when toxic investments have become the norm. After all, the system is as heavily polluted as ever. Whatever the reason, before you know it you're joining the queue with the rest of the poor men of Europe, of which there are many these days, going cap in hand and looking for someone to bail you out.

At least, I think that's what's happened. I don't know for sure; it could be far more complicated. Why else would they ask to see me, if not because all the more conventional channels of raising finance have failed or are unavailable? That's usually why I get the summons.

Meanwhile, the limo is on the Appian Way and I'm marvelling at the ancient tombs that line this, the oldest of the roads to Rome. My escort, a Signor D'Angelo, is asking me if I know the city very well, which I don't, and extolling its wonders, although he's got his work cut out on this occasion. The temperature may be mild for November but it's pouring with rain, the traffic is bumper to bumper and there's an irritating over-use of the horn, as if this is India rather than Italy. He also outlines the programme for my visit: an initial meeting with Cardinal Mancini, followed by dinner evening with His Grace and another Cardinal, and then breakfast with their *two* Graces and a group of Vatican finance people. It promises to be quite a party. I stare at the torrential rain, the traffic and suddenly the darkness descends and I tumble into a black hole of depression, where I flail around cartoon-like in mid-air before plummeting into a void.

4

This takes me by surprise; I am ambushed by it. I am doing exactly what I love to do. I'm making vast sums of money sourcing vast loans from unconventional sources. Not via the traditional banking system, nor even the shadow system, as it's known – that tangled web of unregulated funds and investment operations that contributed to the biggest financial meltdown in history – but from the shadow of the shadow system; something even more off-shore, off the radar, invisible as dark-matter. But more of such arcane matters later. The point is I don't indulge in your regular financier's fare. This is deal making of the highest order, if I do say so myself; each one carefully crafted, a work of art. And in the process of doing it I'm being treated like an A-list celebrity, a man who, if he can't exactly turn water into wine or heal the sick like that other Vatican favourite, can work the odd financial miracle. It should make me feel very happy, or at least more pleased with myself.

Then I recall that these sudden eruptions of anxiety – or panic attacks, as we now like to call them – are what happened before I started taking the anti-depressants. Matters have simply resumed where they left off now that I've stopped taking them. It'll be all right, I tell myself, as I begin to feel a cold sweat, a chill in what is an overheated vehicle.

I even remember my techniques for preventing the free-fall into nothingness: grasping at any kind of human contact, like branches on the way down; encouraging the most banal form of conversation; thinking of my favourite things - raindrops on roses, whiskers on kittens; a few lines of coke (something I've been doing my best to resist) or great sex (something I've been doing my best to have more of).

'So many must-sees in Roma,' I say out of desperation.

'Si, Signor Law, so many *must-sees,* si.'

'But before that I *must see* the Cardinal.' I force a smile along with the jest.

'Si, the Cardinal, si.' Despite the fact that Signor D'Angelo returns the smile, I can tell he doesn't envy me the experience.

*

5

Venice, October 1728

*Let me begin by making one thing clear. If I have my way –
and in the more important matters it has often been the case –
I will carry on playing at the tables until the very end, until they
carry me out and lay me in my Venetian tomb. Gaming is what I
have always done and I see no reason to stop now, simply
because of a slight physical indisposition. Of course, down the
years my style has chang'd in many ways. I long ago
abandon'd the somewhat ostentatious rooms of London and
Paris where I lov'd to make a grand entrance, swaggering and
literally swinging bags of gold, taking on all comers. Now I can
be found here in the more genteel surroundings of the Ridotto,
the best gaming salon in Venice, where I have little to prove and
take a more measur'd approach. I choose my opponents
carefully and play either cards or dice, depending on my mood
or whether I can claim the Banker's chair. The game of Pharo is
my favourite and has prov'n extremely profitable down the
years. Hazard, Piquet, Brag and Primero I will also play quite
happily. Indeed, if the odds are right, I will play anything. I will
wager on who will next enter a room or who will be the first to
leave. The nature of the game is of little consequence, as long
as the odds can be calculat'd. That is the key to my success –
the shrewd calculation of odds. In a game of chance, I leave as
little to chance as possible.*

*But do not think of me as a compulsive gambler, a slave to
the thrill of the wager. On the contrary, this is my profession; it
is how I make a living, as a humble merchant of the gaming
room. I remain calm and inscrutable to the outside world, my
face betrays nothing, and all the while I do large, complicat'd
sums very quickly in my head, calculating the odds of turning
over certain cards or rolling certain numbers on a dice. It is an
ability I have had since childhood and it is all but effortless.*

*Certain factors have help'd me. I am fortunate to have liv'd
in times when very few understand the true power of science
and mathematics. Even for the so-call'd educat'd, life is still
subject to mysterious, unfathomable forces. You are what you
are born to; the rest is govern'd by the will of God, by Chance,
Fate or Fortune. And most poor fools, many of them rich, bring*

6

the same blind faith to the gaming table, hoping that Lady Luck will smile upon them that evening, that they will somehow divine the right numbers when all they need do is calculate them.

'Greetings, il Duce,' says the conte di Bellini. He is passing through the sitting out room on his way to one of the many gaming rooms. 'Is the richest man in the world feeling lucky this evening?' He speaks in his best English, which is surprisingly good. As a Venetian noble, he is wont to speak in French, but I have told him I am pain'd by the very sound of that language and he is happy to indulge me.

I incline my head. I am wearing my short grey wig, but am otherwise in my preferr'd black velvet. 'As always, my dear Count, as always,' I reply. 'What separates us from the gondolier, pray, but luck?'

The Count gives a wry smile. He likes these little jokes. First of all, he knows that I am not a duke, although it is fair to say that I am treat'd like one in the Ridotto. Unless of noble birth, the players here must wear masks, an item of dress much favour'd by the Venetians. But I am grant'd the privilege of going unmask'd if I so wish, due to my great renown and ability to attract much business.

Secondly, the Count also knows that I am no longer the richest man in the world, although it was almost certainly true a few years ago. Indeed, many still think I have immense wealth hidden away – a double-edg'd sword in that it earns me great favour, but no interest and keeps my numerous creditors in hot pursuit. In fact, I am now worth little more than what is on the table in front of me – in liquid terms at least.

And thirdly, the Count is in jest because as a Banker at the tables here, a position that can only be held by a noble – and occasionally someone as favour'd as myself – he no more believes in 'luck' than I do.

The Ridotto is my sanctuary, practically my home. Although I have rooms near the Rialto, I am usually here during the day, in the 'sitting out' room on the piano nobile, with its tall windows overlooking the Grand Canal. I write my increasingly desperate letters to Katherine, my estrang'd partner – we were never married, so were all the more wedd'd to each other – as well as to Europe's rich and powerful, among whom I have ceas'd to figure. And now, as you see, I also pen my memoirs, which means that much of the time I do little but sip hot chocolate, while staring into the past or watching the play of light upon the canal and the boats ply back and forth like so many exotic water fowl.

In the evenings, I play at the tables, sometimes against the bank, sometimes in a small, discreet group. Few of the wealthier visitors to the Ridotto can resist the opportunity of indulging in dice or cards with 'the richest man in the world'. Instead of concentrating on the run of play, many press me on questions of finance or my experiences in France. Others, in league with creditors no doubt, hope I will let slip some clue as to the whereabouts of the vast fortune I am suppos'd to have secret'd. All of which makes my winning that much easier. I go on calculating the odds, while diverting them with scandalous tales from the French court: the amount of wine that the French Regent wou'd consume at a single sitting – four bottles was not untypical; the number of mistresses kept at any one time by Cardinal Dubois – five, as befits a man of his holy eminence... But more of this glorious excess anon.

'My game, I believe. Thank you, a pleasure as always to share a table with your Lordship.' Another noble lord contributes to my meagre pension fund. They come from all over Europe, from Britain, Spain, the Hapsburgs and even France, where my name is nothing more than merde. They are drawn to Venice by its history, its beauty, its decadence and now of course myself, John Law, its most famous emigrè.

Ah Venice, La Serenissima, where wou'd I be without you? Hang'd by the French or bor'd to death by the Dutch or English. Here, though an outcast, I am welcom'd as another lost soul in life's masquerade. Venice embraces the exile. She is the model of tolerance, too old and wise to bully, the enemy of Absolutism, which has been my own worst enemy. I love her art, her architecture, her music. (On Sunday I heard the most splendid concert by Father Antonio Vivaldi – or il Prete Rosso, as he is known, the Red Priest, for his red hair.) They restore to me that sense of glory I once knew and have now lost, and for that reason alone, La Serenissima is the perfect place for me.

Until now, when the weather turns cooler and a clammy mist creeps off the water, engulfing the city. Now, as the evenings draw in, it is as if the dead walk abroad, laying their cold hands upon every shoulder, freezing the Venetian soul. It is a memento mori, a sad reminder that life is not all sunshine and fine wine. I begin to cough and wheeze, as I did last winter. The searing pain returns to my chest, a pain I had thought was gone for good. I shou'd leave of course and return in the spring, like a swallow. But where wou'd I fly? To France and my lost lov'd ones? Or back to that glorious time in Paris when I first met Philippe, duc d'Orleans.

*

If St. Peter's and the Vatican Museum are the stage – and what a stage, surely one of the world's grandest – then the Vatican City is the back end of it, an array of levers, ropes and pulleys that keep all the scenery in place. We enter via an unassuming gate and it's a measure of Signor D'Angelo's status that the Swiss Guards only hold us up momentarily before waving us past. The limo purrs on through the gardens, cheerful with colour even in the November rain, to the guest quarters, where I check in and freshen up. This grand house looks as if it's seen better days, but before I have much chance to take it in I'm swept off to the administration building, the Palace of the Governate, to meet with the Cardinal.

The halls are marble-clad but his office is restrained, austere even, certainly when compared to the public galleries. He has an extremely large desk, but there is little by way of adornment, save for the Vatican crest, a large framed photograph of the Pontiff and the obligatory crucifix or two, one hovering over the seating area. And this is where we sit and exchange courtesies and where a young aid, a priest from the look of him, offers me tea, coffee or water – or something stronger if I prefer.

'Coffee's fine,' I say, 'thank you.'

The cardinal is not what I expected. For a start, he's American – *Italian*-American, but more Stateside in manner than European. And he's a big bear of a man, with an unruly mop of grey hair and a general appearance that's more stylishly business-like than ecclesiastical. He wears a dark grey lounge suit – I note the Armani label – and a crimson shirt with a white collar buttoned at the neck. (The crimson colour is the one thing that denotes his cardinal status.) He could be a corporate executive making a small concession to dress-down Friday.

'Mr. Law,' he says, 'good to meet you.'

I should have checked with D'Angelo, but I'm not sure how to address him. I offer, tentatively, 'Your Grace...' but he smiles an un-American smile, his teeth being stained with nicotine: 'Please – call me *Michael*.'

'And please call me Theo,' I reply.

'As in Theodore, I assume?'

'Yes.'

'A name that means *gift of God*,' he says. 'Are you a gift of God, Theo?'

'I'm not sure – probably more of a loan.'

He chuckles at this. 'Very good. Do I detect the faint trace of an accent? Do you mind if I smoke, by the way?'

'No, I don't mind. Your house, your rules, Michael – and yes, you do detect a very slight accent. My mother was American, from the Mid-West, Michigan. I spent some time there as a child.'

I can never say this without picturing that child running, tumbling down one of the giant dunes on the northern shore of the lake. The happiest time of my life, I've since come to realise, and this despite the fact that my parents had recently separated.

'Ah *Michigan*. I always think of the line from that old Simon and Garfunkel song: *Michigan seems like a dream to me now...* But now I *am* showing my age...I'm also a Mid-Westerner, from Chicago originally...'

He lights a cigarette and so we go on trading pleasantries and generally bonding for a few minutes around our US heritage, as he shows me how human and down-to-earth he is, despite the hotline to heaven. Then we get to the business in hand.

'You come very highly recommended,' he says. 'As much for your discretion as your financial connections.'

'In my business the two go hand-in-hand.'

'It's absolutely essential in this case.'

'It always is.'

'There's only so much I can tell you,' he says.

'Or you'd have to kill me, right?'

He chuckles again. 'This is the Vatican, Theo, not the mafia – although that is of course the other eternal institution this country is home to.' More chuckles. 'No, it's because I only know so much myself. We're still trying to work out what's happened.'

'Which means?'

'Which *means*' – he draws on his cigarette, blows out a jet of smoke – 'there would seem to be a very large hole in the Bank's accounts.'

'The same is true for a number of banks just now.'

'And in most cases there's an obvious reason, but with us there isn't. We've done our best to be prudent – especially since the Calvi scandal in the '80s – and we escaped the worst, er, excesses of the more recent crisis, I'm glad to say. Of course, it's tough in this current climate. Of course, we're all expecting another crisis. Of course, the Holy See and the State struggle to balance the books.' He lowers his voice. 'And – between these four walls – it doesn't help that His Holiness is a new kind of pontiff, one who seems intent on giving most of our material wealth away...'

I smile. 'I thought the gentleman who set the whole thing up in the first place favoured a similar approach.'

Michael manages only a tight smile before continuing. 'Anyway, this - this is different, this looks as if something highly illicit has occurred. We think we're victims of some sort of very smart cyber fraud – a virtual bank robbery, partly due, I suspect, to our lax security systems – which is being addressed, I hasten to add. It's a desperate situation. Substantial funds have disappeared without trace and we must assume – in part, anyway – that it's...'

He pauses. 'I'm trying to think of another way of putting it, but I can't – an *inside job*.'

'Right.'

11

'So you understand how critical your discretion is and how we couldn't possibly go the traditional route to make up some of the shortfall – even if we could find someone to our satisfaction. Such er transparency is not the Vatican's style in normal circumstances, let alone these. You do understand?'

'I do,' I say, while thinking that even among the representatives of God on Earth, when it comes to banking, the line between the licit and illicit is a very fine one these days. And that's so much the case that the sins of the crooked banker Roberto Calvi, to whom Mancini referred, seem minor by comparison. As head of a Vatican-sponsored bank in Milan, he became known as 'God's banker'. Hundreds of millions of dollars disappeared on his watch – much of it the Vatican's – and he landed up hanging by the neck from Blackfriars Bridge in London. The original verdict of suicide was later overturned – the method was a touch theatrical, even for an Italian – and with so many powerful factions, from the Church to the mafia, lining up to settle with him, the whole case remained as murky as the River Thames over which he was found swinging.

In fact, it even crosses my mind, briefly, that this may not be a job I should dirty my hands with. Apart from the financial scandal – which, despite Michael's best efforts, might well draw the public eye – there's also the quicksand of internal politics to consider. However, I swiftly overcome my reservations: the financial rewards will be substantial. And dirty hands are a speciality.

'Discretion is guaranteed, Michael,' I add. 'The funds – if I can arrange them – will reach you through a complex web of accounts that even I have trouble following – and I created it. You will never know the ultimate source of the loans.'

'And you must never tell me – or anyone else for that matter.' He chuckles once more and I'm beginning to realise it's a double-edged sort of habit, a good or a bad sign, depending on the context. 'In which case, even the Church might have to display some mafia-like tendencies…'

*

12

Perhaps, because I am suddenly engulf'd by the memory of those early, heady days in France, I have decid'd not to start at the beginning, but to leap forward to our most dramatic of first meetings with Philippe. Katherine and I had been in Paris for some three months and were already frequenting its best gaming salons, making where possible their richest habitués a little less rich. That evening we were in the fashionable salon of Madame de Chateauneuf, which was much atwitter, our hostess inform'd us, due to the presence of one of the most powerful men in France – Philippe, duc d'Orleans, Louis XIV's nephew and to everyone's outrage, fascination and envy, a notorious libertine. As usual, Katherine and I made a striking couple: I, tall and imposing in black velvet, she, blond and elegant in creamy satin. Less showy and flamboyant than the French, we stood out in our foreignness, and if that alone fail'd to gain attention, my bags of gold did the rest.

I first saw Philippe sitting at the head of the largest gaming table in the room, playing the role of Tailliére or Banker. He was flank'd by two exquisite courtesans and repeatedly bestow'd lingering kisses on their bare necks and shoulders. He look'd every inch a Bourbon, a shining reflection of the Sun King himself when he was younger. His periwig was by far the largest of the evening; he wore a royal blue velvet jacket, edg'd with the finest lace and studd'd with diamonds that sparkl'd in the candlelight. His face was fleshy but handsome; his cupid lips and cheeks heavily roug'd. Here was a man, I thought, who was us'd to indulging his every whim and appetite whenever he pleas'd. What I cou'd not have known then was that this mask of frivolous excess hid a more serious side of his character, one that yearn'd not only to rule France but to rule it well.

When Madame de Chateauneuf had made the formal introductions, I ask'd in my faltering French if we might join Philippe's table, saying by mistake 'son grandesse le duc' – 'His Bigness' – instead of 'son altesse' – 'His Highness'. Thankfully, Philippe smil'd, patt'd his well-padd'd belly, and everyone else was permitt'd to find it most amusing. He announc'd that he had already heard of the tall Scotsman with the bad French, the bags of gold and the beautiful wife and wou'd welcome the opportunity to relieve me of all of them –

starting with the gold, of course. This provok'd more courtly laughter all round at my expense and I inwardly vow'd to finish the evening at his – as well as improve my French.

Meanwhile, Katherine treat'd His Highness to a look of some disdain and address'd the whole table in the kind of French that need'd no improvement. (She only translat'd it for me in detail later.) She said she made it a rule never to be the prize in any wager or to suffer the indignity of being referr'd to in the third person, as if she were not present or not worth addressing directly. 'It wou'd indicate a lack of refinement and good breeding on the part of that person, wou'd it not, Sir?'

The table held its breath again before Philippe smil'd, rose to his feet, and bow'd low towards her. 'Madame, it wou'd and ill-bred as I am, I humbly apologise if I've caus'd you any offence.'

She inclin'd her head to him, smil'd and curtsied in return 'And I not so humbly accept your apology, Your Highness...'

Oh dear, this was not a good start, I thought, and in the cause of moving swiftly on from our second embarrassment of the evening, I suggest'd that we had rudely interrupt'd the game for long enough and that they shou'd continue forthwith. Thankfully, everyone agreed, including Philippe, who indicat'd two chairs across from himself where we shou'd sit.

The table was playing a simplified form of Pharo – or Pharaon, as the French call it – a favourite of mine, as I have already intimat'd, and often the most advantageous for the Banker. Players select three cards apiece and can choose to make a stake – an agreed number of gold louis d'or – on each card; the Banker lays down two cards – a 'loser' and a 'winner'. He pays the players whose select'd cards show the same number as the 'winner'; the suits are irrelevant.

The cards are discard'd after each round until the pack is reduc'd to the final three. At this point each player, including the Banker, has to bet a double stake on the face value of the three cards left and in which order they will appear. If there is no winner, the stakes are carried forward to the next final round, when they must be doubl'd at least. Pharo can quickly become a very rewarding – or very expensive game.

14

In order to simplify matters, I decid'd that I wou'd clear the field as soon as possible and leave just myself and the Tailliére. I rais'd the stakes at every opportunity and lost a number of rounds deliberately to the Bank, feigning the occasional anxious look at Katherine, so as to boost Philippe's confidence. Not that he need'd it. He was a good counter of cards, if not a calculator of odds, and was doing extremely well in the role of Banker, despite the distractions of his brace of nymphs – and Katherine, to whom he paid several overweening compliments, in a clear attempt to make up for his earlier breach of good manners. (Even with my lamentable grasp of the language, I cou'd tell as much.)

After a couple of hours, only the two of us remain'd. We had gone through three consecutive runs of the pack without a conclusive outcome and the pile of louis d'or on the table had grown extremely large. Philippe had drunk a good deal and look'd highly flush'd but still seem'd supremely confident. He was perspiring heavily and remov'd his gem-studd'd coat. The fondling of the ladies had stopp'd – they were now part of a large crowd gather'd round the table, including Madame de Chateauneuf, who from her expression was inwardly urging me to lose and so avoid upsetting 'son altessse le duc', lest he never grace her salon again.

We were now at the end of the pack. To gasps from many of those watching, Philippe doubl'd the stakes and I respond'd by doubling them once more; the small fortune on the table had grown to around three thousand livres. Still overheat'd, Philippe remov'd his periwig, the final prop of his Bourbon pride, to reveal a fine head of auburn hair. We each nominat'd the face value of the last three cards and their order. As Banker, Philippe went first; he chose Ten, Queen and Five. I was oblig'd to name at least one different card and selected Ten, Five and Three. (I knew the Queens had gone, but was less sure of the Threes.) The cards were turn'd over one at a time to more gasps from the onlookers. Ten…Five – Philippe cou'd not win, but would I? – Three!

There was a tense moment while Philippe continued looking down at the cards. When he look'd up he was wearing his broadest smile yet. The room relax'd and broke into excit'd chatter. Katherine kiss'd me softly on the cheek.

Philippe held out his hand – shou'd I kiss it or shake it? I did the latter. 'I admire a man, even a foreigner, who can remain so calm when taking risks of such magnitude.' As his ladies return'd like ministering angels, he pour'd me a large glass of wine.

'I can assure Your Highness that I never take risks of any magnitude. My game is all a matter of Science.'

'Ah, Science! I am a man of Science myself,' he said, without irony. 'I drink to Science – it is our only hope. That and nightly fornication.' He emptied his glass, and kiss'd each of his ladies, before continuing: 'Monsieur Law, however you us'd your Science tonight, I fear you may have gone some way towards bankrupting France.'

'I thought His Majesty, your uncle, had already achiev'd as much,' I smil'd, while fearing that the bounds of politesse might have been overstepp'd yet again. But my fear was unfound'd. Having just endur'd a gaming rite of passage together, Philippe and I cou'd allow each other a degree of candour.

'Alas, you're right. Despite all the conspicuous wealth and finery you see around you, France is a pauper, thanks to my uncle. What he has not spent on wars, he has spent on palaces, and what he has not spent on palaces, he has given to the undeserving rich, like myself. None of which puts anything in the national coffers – and, in this instance, puts it in the pocket of Monsieur John Law.'

'Then it's only right that I shou'd help restore those coffers,' I said. 'I can make France the most prosperous Nation on Earth.' Again, I had the table's attention.

Philippe laugh'd. 'I doubt if even you have enough money to help France, Monsieur.'

'Oh but I do.' I request'd an attendant bring me pen and paper and then ask'd Katherine to write the following (lest my poor French ruin the drama of the moment): 'Je promets de payer le porteur Cinq Livres' – 'I promise to pay the bearer Five Livres' – 'This she duly did and I hand'd it to Philippe.

'But this is just a piece of paper,' he frown'd.

'No, Your Highness,' I said, 'it is a piece of Science.'

*

Surprising I know, but I've somehow managed to forget about all the panic attacks, my main reason for taking the anti-depressants in the first place. I've forgotten how terrifying they could be at their worst, and the migraines that often went with them - the fact that I couldn't go out of the house, couldn't even get out of bed at one point. I suppose I've needed to suppress the thought of them in order to go on functioning. Unfortunately, it isn't enough to stop them happening again and when they do, it's in the most unlikely situation and all the more shocking for that.

I manage to stay on top of things during the dinner with cardinal Numero Due – Cardinal Capello. This is a sombre affair. Unlike Mancini, Capello *is* an Italian, but one who seems to be crossed with a dour Swede. He dresses more traditionally than Numero Uno. His English isn't up to much, or at least he's not very happy to speak it. And he has nothing of Mancini's jovial bluster. Perhaps, he's not trying to pretend it's anything other than a very depressing situation – that even after some major re-structuring, sizeable loans are about to fall due and there's not much in the kitty to pay for them. And anyway, debt default hardly makes for entertaining dinner conversation, no matter who's round the table, although I am left with a good idea of how much money I have to find for them – which I have to tell you is an almost indigestible amount. I will need to approach some of my major league investors, as I prefer to call them.

As if to atone for this dip in mood, Mancini proposes a treat. The curtain has fallen on the front of stage; one of the greatest shows on Earth is over for the night and the last of the Chinese tourists have been bussed back to their hotels for Puttanesca and Chianti. I can experience, if I wish, that most privileged of treats: a private tour of the Sistine Chapel and anywhere else in the Vatican Museum I choose to go, as well as St. Peter's. There will be nothing of the usual throng that reduces what should be a sublime experience to the level of shopping in Oxford Street or Fifth Avenue the week before Xmas. 'No one but you and the guide,' says Mancini. 'Oh – or perhaps the odd cleaner or maintenance person...'

He introduces Claudia Ferrari. I don't ask if she's any relation to the car family, but she does look a little er racy for a Vatican guide. (Not that I've known another to make the comparison.)

'Would you like the full tour, Theo?' she asks in the kind of silky Italian accent that would soften the hardest of hearts, and – I can't help thinking – harden the softest of members. I immediately notice every curve of Claudia's body, as if I'm some horny, hormone-driven adolescent or been incarcerated for years. Why this sudden lechery, I wonder, this surge in the libido? Is it another symptom of coming off the anti-depressants? If so, Claudia could be a shop dummy and I'd be probably be feeling the same.

'Thank you,' I say, 'the Sistine Chapel and the Raphael Rooms will be more than enough for me.' I'm glad I've had a quick look at a guide on my way over, as a bit of background to my discussions with Mancini.

A warm wave of her perfume laps around me, not unpleasantly. And of course there's the make-up – far too much of it, like so many Italian women, though in her case it's finely done. She's a Madonna in a Renaissance painting.

And she's a good guide to all those Madonnas, though I can't say I get the most out of this uniquely privileged experience. To be the only two people in the Sistine Chapel; to be able to take in *The Creation* and *The Last Judgement* in that singular calm is something that should verge on the transcendental. And yet I continue to be distracted by the swell of her breasts and the syncopation of her derrière, which act as a more powerful form of transcendence.

Maybe, it's all that flesh on display, I'm thinking. Not Claudia's, she's modestly attired, but on the walls, on the ceiling – everywhere I turn. It's overwhelming. Flesh floating through the air, despite its solid and substantial nature; flesh falling to Hell and rising to Heaven. It's a cascade of the carnal, a Niagara of nudity.

'This represents the acme of High Renaissance art,' Claudia purrs. 'And for all its divine inspiration, it puts Man, in the

18

corporeal sense, at the centre of everything, some at the time said too much so. The human body becomes a Neo-platonic ideal. Man will rise again and have eternal life but in a perfect, transfigured form.'

Neapolitan? Isn't that an ice cream? 'Of course...absolutely...' I'm wishing I'd studied Art History rather than Economics and been able to impress Claudia – or even understand what she is saying.

And the riot of sacred images continues in the Raphael Rooms. Prophets, saints, virgins, angels, cherubs and Christ himself come at me from every direction, while Claudia talks about Raphael and his rivalry with Michelangelo and how he died before this great cycle of frescoes was complete.

'I think he's my favourite painter,' she says, as we stand before *The School of Athens* in the Stanza della Signatura – the Pope's Study. The painting depicts a gathering of all the greatest minds of antiquity.

'This is him at the height of his powers. Please notice: the ease of his composition, the clarity of his forms and the naturalism of his subjects. These people are *real.*'

She looks at her watch. 'If you like we can go into St. Peter's. It will still be partially lit. I love it at this time. It's awesome...' The word seems out of place for a Vatican guide, but then again, *she's* out of place for a Vatican guide.

'Let's do it,' I say. And we do. Down a network of marble-clad corridors, with that sublime syncopation going before me, and emerging via a small door to find ourselves under the dome. Or is it the very canopy of Heaven? She's right: it *is* genuinely awesome – not in the 'cool', devalued sense of the word, but in the original, wide-eyed, jaw-dropping, sink-to-your-knees sense of it. *Oh. My. God.* If you don't believe in Him – and I for one don't – at this point you're obliged to invent Him.

Why haven't I been here before? I ask myself. I didn't visit during my previous business trips – I had no time, and especially no time for churches. A Euro-tour in my youth included Florence and Venice but not Rome and since then it's been the Far East (Thailand etc), the Far West (California) and the Far South (South Africa and Argentina), awesome in their way, but somehow I'd missed this one.

And I share this sense of wonder with Claudia, and she with me. There is, I decide in this ridiculous fit of horniness, more than a hint of the come-hither in her smile. Definitely. And in the tender way she says: 'Theo...Theo? *Theo?*'

Because suddenly I lose it again. I'm exposed, vulnerable. I'm trembling and cold sweating – with what? With fear – fear of what? Of the void, of course, of that enormous gaping void, no doubt evoked by all this space around me. Of everything. Everything is out to get me, every icon, every statue, the munchkin cleaners around the pulpit, the two old monks kneeling at a side altar – the only others in the whole basilica, it seems. Claudia in particular is a huge threat, plotting my downfall, my death, in league with either Mancini or Capello, who have decided I'm not the man for the job, after all, but I already know too much. The Church has not survived all these centuries by letting its enemies live. I will wake up a cold corpse next to that hot body – there is no doubt about it.

I must get out, get away but I don't really know where to go without her.

'Can we leave, Claudia?' I say finally.

'Yes, of course...' She's confused, concerned or just appalled by this melodrama. We've been engaged in a major flirtation – or at least I imagine we have – and now we're back to being strangers, cool and stiff as the marble statues that surround us.

'Are you okay?'

'Yes. I just need to go back to the guesthouse. Thank you. I just need to...' – *escape the black hole*, I almost say, but that would sound too silly – 'go back...thank you...'

*

It wou'd be marvellous to recount that this meeting with Orleans was a matter of pure coincidence, but like luck at cards or anything else, it wou'd be mostly a myth. Katherine and I had gone to Paris with the express intention of making contact with him and we knew that like us, he wou'd frequent its best gaming salons. It was only a matter of time until our paths cross'd, although the instant ease of our rapport did come as something of a surprise even to me.

But why, you may wonder, was I so keen to meet Philippe duc d'Orleans? And more to the point, why bother to go to France at all, uncomfortable as I was with its language, its culture and its whole political system? The answer is simple: in my native land – and by that I mean England and Scotland, for they had recently become one with the Act of Union – I was a want'd criminal, a fugitive. And that which had reduc'd me to this unwholesome state was the outcome of a duel I had fought – not figuratively at the gaming table, where I am always a likely winner, but literally, in a field near Bloomsbury Square, where I was less than confident of surviving, let alone winning.

I had never fought a duel before and the first thing I discover'd was that my mind, usually so full of scheming and dreaming, became a complete blank. I cou'd not remember who I was or what had brought me to this miserable point. As for any notions of swordsmanship, what few I possess'd, they too had disappear'd. The perfunctory fencing lessons as a boy, the studious avoidance of practice and arm'd service, the preference for developing my natural ability at the gaming table – none of this had prepar'd me for that drizzly November morning, when I stood in the field and star'd into the grim face of my opponent, Edgar 'Beau' Wickham.

His was a face I had known in almost all its phases: smiling, laughing, leering, sneering, often thoughtful, but never, until that moment, grim. It was a handsome face, a pretty face even, for he appear'd somewhat effeminate and in truth preferr'd boys to the female of the species. We, my gaming companions and I, thought him the most foppish of us all. The idle second son of a forgotten Earl: genteel, amusing, waspish, always penniless, always having to sing – or rather sting – for his supper. Yet, as a member of the merchant class, I realise now that I deeply envied his highborn indifference to the acquiring of things, to the desperate scramble up the social ladder in which most of us are oblig'd to engage. And where I envy, I usually befriend.

Yes, my opponent was my friend, or had been until a few hours before. And as we prepar'd to do battle on that chilly morn, making mock thrusts at the air with our swords, striking martial poses, it occurr'd to me for the first time that for all his effete ways, he was also a very fine swordsman. Gone were any signs of foppery. Here was the season'd warrior, squaring up manfully for the fight, while it was I who look'd out of his element and wish'd to slip girlishly away.

I remember the raucous cries of the rooks, my head pounding from too much liquor, my stomach churning from sheer terror. Having check'd to make sure we wore no protection under our thin linen shirts, our seconds withdrew. Mine, David Stair of Edinburgh, squeez'd my arm, a gesture of either good luck or goodbye, before joining the small group of onlookers: our fellow gamesters who had come to see this particular game play'd out to its sorry conclusion.

Our referee, a raddl'd lawyer coax'd into the role with several bottles of his favourite port, gestur'd for us to face each other and pay the ritual courtesies – the offering of the sword, the gracious bow. He then limply wav'd his handkerchief and beat a hasty retreat, as if he himself might be call'd upon to join the fight.

Even now, each cut and thrust of our encounter stands out distinctly in my mind like so many beads upon a counter; and I have count'd them a thousand times in the suicidal hours before dawn, when one seems alone with all the world's worries. Suffice to say that my fears were instantly confirm'd. I was the poor, wee lamb to Beau's snarling wolf. He fix'd me with his cold, blue eyes and with thrust after thrust – that I either dodg'd or parried – he ran me round that field until my chest heav'd and the sweat pour'd from me.

At which point I realis'd something else about my friend Beau: he was not just waspish – he was extremely cruel.

Already exhaust'd, I lower'd my weapon briefly, only to have him slice into my arm just above the elbow. I saw the blood seeping through my shirt, felt its warm trickle upon my skin, even before I recoil'd from the pain of it. He will not only kill me, I thought, he will first slowly, painfully disable me; I will suffer the death of a thousand cuts.

Still he came on, dancing while I lumber'd and flail'd at him wildly, as if I wield'd an axe not a sword. Then, with a deft flick

22

of his wrist, he dash'd the weapon from my hand, which had little strength left to hold it. I slipp'd and fell on to my side, clutching my wound'd arm, and look'd up to see Beau, standing over me, pois'd to perform the coup de grace. Or so I thought.

For then it happen'd, that which my nightmares have turn'd upon ever since: Beau smil'd. At the time, I was sure it was a pitiless gloating, so ferociously had he fought. Ever since, I have known what it truly was – a conciliatory gesture: 'The game is over,' he was saying, 'we can be friends once more.'

Thinking I was about to die, I reach'd for my fallen sword with my good hand. As Beau lower'd his weapon a little – on the verge of ending our contest, I later realis'd – I lung'd from the ground in one swift movement and drove mine into his chest. He ceas'd smiling, dropp'd his sword and clutch'd at his wound, trying vainly to staunch the blood that spill'd through his fingers. Shock'd and disbelieving, he sank slowly to his knees, look'd down at his chest and then at me.

'Law, you fool,' he said with a bewilder'd expression, 'you have killed me…'

*

If Claudia has said anything to Mancini about my odd behaviour the night before, he certainly doesn't mention it when we meet the next morning. He asks if I enjoyed the tour and if Claudia had been a helpful guide. (Is that a knowing gleam in his eye or is my twisted imagination still at work?)

'Yes, of course,' I say. 'Thank you, Michael, it was a truly memorable experience.'

Cigarette in hand, he waves my thanks away and we move on to our remaining business. In fact, there seems to be little reason for me to meet Cardinal Capello again, plus the three members of his senior finance team, except to confirm figures and timelines. There's also a sense that he's letting me know whom he can trust in this less than trustworthy organisation, which can't be an easy call when everyone seems so deeply committed to the cause of Mother Church. Perhaps he's been tipped off by Himself.

23

At the end of this meeting there's a final exchange with him before I head for the airport. I'm like a doctor discussing a high-risk course of treatment with a seriously ill patient.

'Michael, are you sure you've explored all the more conventional options in Milan?'

He is.

'Are you sure you want me to go ahead?'

He is.

In other words, I don't want him calling me a couple of weeks later to cancel the deal after I've already made considerable efforts to set the wheels in motion. I also want him to read between the lines: even if I realise that the Vatican is not so far removed from a multinational corporation, dedicated to turning a profit, my investors are not what you'd call natural partners for the Pontiff.

But he seems to get it. 'Look at my eyes, Theo – they're wide open.' (In fact they're half-closed from the cigarette smoke.) 'My overriding priority has to be the financial stability of the Holy See – *whatever it takes…*'

Mancini has Chicago-street smarts, I decide. Yes, he wears the cardinal's crimson and has the jolly demeanour of Santa Claus, but beneath it he's a hard-ass. Indeed, I get the distinct impression he may have run a racket or two in a former life – closer to a Godfather than a man of God.

Once I'm convinced that there are no misunderstandings, that I have a genuine greenlight, I head for my limo and the airport. From there, I tell myself – trying to stiffen my still wobbly state of mind – I will go straight back to London to broker a deal that may not only be one of the best of my life but will also save the Church of Rome from ruin.

At least that was the plan, and it wou'd have happened had it not been for a message I received on the way.

There's no escort with me this time, so I have the back of the limo to myself. I stretch out and start scrolling through emails, twitter feeds and sundry e-junk. (It beats thinking about the more important stuff.)

Among all the work messages, there's a personal one, which is unusual because I try to keep the personal and business sides of my life separate – and anyway, there's much less of the former these days.

The sender signs herself Diana Lennon. She says she's a writer and a dealer in antiquarian books, living in Venice. She has recently been given access to an old Venetian manuscript, which appears to have been written in the early 18th century by a Scotsman called John Law. She believes that he's a distant ancestor of mine; that I might well be his only living descendant. If I'm interested, she would very much like to show me this manuscript, which I may want to consider acquiring.

I am stunned by this. The power of the internet never ceases to amaze. That this woman has been able to identify and track me down is impressive and worrying enough in itself, never mind the fact of the manuscript. For yes, although I have not heard the name John Law for many years – from when my parents were still alive – he is indeed my ancestor and there is on my family tree a direct line to him, like the London to Edinburgh rail link.

Of course, I'm intrigued, but it shouldn't stop me going straight back to the UK and telling Ms. Lennon that I'll come to see her and the manuscript at some later date i.e. when this deal is sealed. But for some reason I don't go straight back to London. Instead I think: well, I'm already in Italy – I can go back via Venice, can't I? I can spend a few days there, send the emails I need to and get the team back in London on the case. Meanwhile, I can go to see Diana Lennon and the manuscript and – what the hell – hang out in the most beautiful city in the world for a few days, even if it is November.

And the more I think about it, the more I like the idea. I'll change my ticket. I'll book a hotel. The thought of it immediately lightens my leaden mood, cheers me up. Indeed, I'm almost buzzing with the spontaneity of it all. Isn't that what being super-rich and successful is all about – spontaneity, self-indulgence? Occasionally, anyway, as an antidote to all that toxic control freakery.

I reply to Diana Lennon. I tell her she's got my attention, and that I just happen to be in Rome at the moment and can stop by in Venice on my way back to London. Send me your address, I say. Let me know when it will be convenient to come and see you in the next few days.

And as we approach the airport, for the first time in many years I start thinking about my distant ancestor, John Law. I try to recall what he was famous, or rather, infamous for. And it doesn't take me long to remember some of the things my father said about him: that he coined – ha-ha – the word 'millionaire', that he created the world's largest financial bubble, that he was the world's biggest fraudster, an out-and-out charlatan, a sociopath, a criminal. How could I have forgotten? He sounds exactly my kind of guy.

Chapter 2

Venice, October 1728

It is no coincidence that I shou'd finally have start'd these memoirs on the anniversary of this duel. As you will see if you choose to bear with me, the intervening years have been every bit as eventful. I have mourn'd Beau's death – many were to say his murder – almost daily. Yet you will think me mad when I tell you that he has not remain'd entirely among the dead. He – or someone who resembles him, for there are some odd aspects to this creature I do not recognise – has paid me several visits during these turbulent years, appearing so real that if I were not always paralys'd by fear, I am sure I cou'd reach out with my hand and touch him. He often wears that ambiguous smile of his. He displays his ghastly wound, like some medieval Christ. He stares at me with those piercing blue eyes. He never speaks, although I have often pour'd out my innermost thoughts to him. In short, he haunts me. Either that or I have haunt'd myself all these years. My guilt has taken on his morbid form the better to torment me. Or there is something else, something even more horrible in me that struggles to manifest itself. Still the answer eludes me, but like a religious devotee before the altar – godless though I am – I long for this mystery to be reveal'd.

In fact, it was not long after his death that the ghost, for want of a better description, put in its first appearance and in the most uncomfortable circumstances imaginable. Duelling is unlawful in England, but few are ever severely punish'd for it, not least because they are usually people of influence – only a gentleman can afford the luxury of an impugn'd honour. If a duellist is prosecut'd at all, the plea of manslaughter is often enough to ensure clemency and the accus'd is let off with a stern warning or at most a short prison sentence – assuming, that is, that the family of the deceas'd does not bring an action against him.

I had never met any of Beau's family. Indeed, I had assum'd them all to be either dead or lock'd away, mad or senile, in some dilapidat'd rustic pile. Not so – the Wickham clan was very much alive and its influence and resources were considerable. (Why had Beau always claim'd to be so reduc'd in circumstances, I wonder'd?) As it turn'd out, the very active desire of his family to avenge their scion's death, together with my own self-flagellating sense of remorse and a judge who was both malicious and corrupt, was enough to make my already bad situation much worse.

Immediately after the duel, I became little more than a pale spectre of a man myself and shook and whimper'd at the horror of what I had done. David Stair and the other second help'd me transport Beau's body to the local mortuary and found a doctor to tend to my wound. I eventually return'd alone and exhaust'd to my rooms in St.Giles, where almost immediately three men from the watch came to arrest me. My first mistake was to admit to them on the spot that I had fought a duel with Beau Wickham, when the shrewd response wou'd have been to deny being anywhere near him or Bloomsbury Square. What follow'd only serv'd to expose my foolish naivete even further.

I was taken to that foretaste of Hell in London, Newgate Prison. Although many bold authors have tried to describe this place from first hand experience – authors seeming to spend a lot of their time in conflict with the law – none in my opinion has manag'd to convey the full horror and misery of it, and I doubt I can do better.

A stench hangs in the city air at the best of times, but compar'd to Newgate it has the fragrance of finest French perfume. As the huge rusting gate clang'd shut behind me, I thought I wou'd vomit, but as things turn'd out, the smell was not the worst of the prison's evils. It was human waste of another kind that I was to find so disturbing. The prison's dark, cavernous interior was full of the most foul, ragg'd, verminous creatures that ever stagger'd, crawl'd or slither'd upon the Earth. They were huddl'd pathetically around several dying braziers or pac'd up and down in the effort to stay warm.

'Most of this lot'll be hang'd by Christmas,' I was inform'd by the charming turnkey who escort'd me. 'If they're lucky, that

*is – it's the only way they're ever leaving.' He waddl'd along
before me like a giant crow. His teeth and breath were ruinous;
he wore a preposterous black wig and a huge filthy coat in
which he carried the tools of his trade and the instruments of
his power, an array of jangling keys. He was a shambolic
demon presiding over the damn'd in his own little corner of the
Inferno.*

*'They might enjoy the best erection and climax they've ever
had, though,' he caw'd. 'Did you know that's what happens to
a fella when he's 'ang'd, milord? Shame it also gives you a stiff
neck...' He was a lexicon of cheerful, gallows humour and took
a sadistic pleasure in leading me through the most pestilential
parts of the gaol on our way to the 'gentler quarters', as he
term'd them. These were reserv'd for those like myself who
were able to pay for the privilege of being incarcerat'd.*

*As we walk'd, ghoulish figures loom'd up out of the shadows
to abuse me, assail me or just beseech me pitifully to help them.
Eventually I was mobb'd by them and start'd to push them
away. The turnkey took his time before wading in with his cosh
and beating them off. 'Manners! Manners, you scum!' he
shout'd. 'Show the gentleman some respect!'*

*He turn'd to me. 'Sorry, milord, they always gets a bit
excit'd when there's gentry about, but it's as I always say to
'em – the rope's a great leveller.'*

*'And what relevance has that to me?' I replied, finally rising
to his insolence. 'As yet, I only stand accus'd, not condemn'd to
be hang'd.'*

*He gave his sardonic grin. 'Whatever pleases your
lordship,' he said, thoroughly enjoying my discomfort. 'Do step
this way.'*

*After a number of gloomy passageways and more clanging
iron doors, we arriv'd in the 'gentler' quarters and what was to
be my room for the duration of my stay. This was little more
than a monk's cell, with a wooden pallet for a bed, a simple
table and chair, and a bucket in the corner. But at least it was a
room, away from the lowest circle of Hell, and for that I was
extremely grateful. After informing me that if I made a larger
contribution to the costs of my stay, my quarters cou'd become
much 'gentler' – and also include the services of some fine*

young ladies – my host withdrew and left me to contemplate my happy situation.

In fact, although I remain'd profoundly shaken by Beau's death, I was not yet unduly worried about the legal outcome; I certainly had no fear of having my neck 'stiffen'd' – or any of the attendant pleasures mention'd by my gaoler. Through David Stair, I had sent word regarding my situation to James Johnston, Earl of Warriston, a good friend at court who was close to King William himself. I was sure that his influence wou'd work quickly to my advantage and that I wou'd soon be back in the congenial surroundings of St.Giles or at the gaming table, discussing the whole incident as if it were a bad dream. In the meantime, my mind turn'd to other matters.

The duel had sober'd me in more ways than one and my exposure to the horrors of Newgate had already begun to take effect. I was drawn back to my many conversations with Beau regarding the huge changes occurring in the world at large. Gaming and carousing may have brought us together, but each of us had a more serious side to his nature from which the dice and drink offer'd easy diversion. (Wou'd it were as easy for me now.) Beau was very much the thinker, the philosopher amongst us and fuell'd by wine and whisky, wou'd debate with me late into the night, long after the gaming table had been put away and the others had retir'd richer or poorer to their beds.

In my own philosophy, I favour'd all things new and progressive: the work of Science – particularly that of Sir Isaac Newton – the retreat of religion, the increase in trade and commerce, the establishment of the new Bank of England, in which I plann'd to have substantial investments. I was sure that these things wou'd lead to a fairer, more prosperous society; one that overcame the kind of shameful waste of humanity that I had just witness'd in Newgate, but which was evident throughout the land, particularly in London. Much of the populace seem'd to languish in poverty and idleness, with little hope for improvement, lest it be of the moral or spiritual kind prescrib'd by their masters. But I saw the problem differently, materially. I saw that society lack'd one simple element for which the Christian Heaven had long ceas'd to be a substitute:

money – large amounts of it, so large that for practical reasons it cou'd only come in the form of paper.

As the son of a successful Scottish goldsmith and banker, I cou'd not avoid being school'd in matters financial, although I fundamentally disagreed with my father on many of the basic principles of his trade. For him, metal equall'd stability, and if a nation's economy was failing it was due to the idleness of its people rather than an insufficiency of its currency. But I was convinc'd that for our society to become more productive at all levels, we need'd to distribute money more widely – and I was determin'd to find a way to present this theory of money supply to both the King and the directors of the Bank of England.

Indeed, the establishment of the National Bank had already prepar'd the ground in which my ideas cou'd flourish. King William had need'd money to fight the war against the French and, following the fine examples of cities like Venice and Amsterdam, a Bank had been establish'd in London to raise it. Investors were guaranteed repayment by the Government and were given bonds or banknotes that cou'd be exchang'd at any time for gold or silver coins. Building on these foundations, I was determin'd to inspire the authorities with my vision of what was possible: if only we cou'd find a way to increase that supply of paper money without it losing value, we wou'd stimulate commercial activity throughout society. England wou'd become the most prosperous Nation on Earth...

Sitting in my cell in Newgate Prison, awaiting trial for the manslaughter of Beau Wickham, I was much comfort'd by the thought of these grand plans – little knowing that in England I wou'd never get the chance to present them, let alone realise them.

*

Once I've made the decision to go to Venice, there's no end to my rekindled interest in my ancestor, John Law. One of the first things that strikes me – as it struck me when I was first told of it – is that although we're separated by almost 300 years, we still share the same surname. As the family tree shows, with every successive generation we descended via the male line. I remember my father being very proud of this – '10 generations of sons who sired sons!' – though it's worth noting that none of those male heirs had ever gone anywhere near finance or banking again. According to the records, they'd been merchants, engineers, lawyers (my father), doctors and civil servants; all good bourgeois stock, but never bankers. It was as if the fall-out from the original Law's catastrophic failure had poisoned the ground where such a species could take root. Until I came along, that is.

I can't resist googling Law, even while I'm at the airport waiting for the flight. I get the potted biography. His early success as a gambler and financier; his imprisonment for murder and escape to Holland and France; his acquiring immense wealth and power under the Bourbon Regency; and his final disgrace and refuge in Venice, where he resumed his life as a gambler and died penniless. I would say it's a classic tale of rise and fall, except there was a fair bit of falling before he started.

The biog also tells me that when he was in Venice he set up shop in the Ridotto, a gaming room overlooking the Grand Canal. (I think my father had also told me this before I did my first Eurorail trip to the city, but I'd not paid much attention.) Another link and I discover that this is now part of the newly refurbished Hotel Monaco, right by the landing at St. Mark's. It looks comfortable enough for my stay and I book the best suite available for a minimum of three nights.

Because suddenly I have another idea. (I'm on a run, possibly approaching the manic phase.) I've been seeing someone, as they say. You could call it my first half-decent relationship since my divorce three years ago, even though it's only about two months old. In fact, this is one of the things that's prompted me to come off the anti-depressants. I'd first started taking them to help deaden the pain in my life, but now I don't want them numbing the pleasure too, as recently represented by one Joanna de Vere, my new inamorata – or *squeeze* might be a better description. It is, after all, the sweet waters of sexual gratification after a very long drought that I find so compelling; the old hormones are hopping again. Which is why the very sight of Claudia, my Vatican guide, must have awoken such lust in me – and why I decided to ask Jo to come to Venice.

I text her. 'Jo, will you join me in Venice for a romantic weekend? This weekend. Sorry for the late notice. Let me know. Tx'

She somehow finds time in her busy City lawyer's schedule to call within minutes and say she'd love to. It's great to hear her voice. She sounds so…fresh, so *young*. But then she *is* young, at least 20 years younger than me.

'I'll make all the arrangements and let you know the details. Hope you don't mind. I've been in Rome and decided to do it on impulse…' I think it best not to mention John Law and a manuscript at this stage.

'It's often the best way to do things,' she says.

'Have you been?'

'Where? To Venice? Not since I was in my teens.' (Not so long ago, then.)

'It isn't really the best time of year, but at least there won't be so many crowds.'

'I'm sure it's amazing whatever time of year – especially if it's with you.'

'I bet you charm all your clients with that kind of BS.'

'Yep – but there's no way I'd dash off to Venice to screw them senseless.'

I laugh; she laughs. I guess she's enjoying the sex too. But then I knew that.

*

I spent an extremely restless first night in Newgate; my head rac'd, my wound'd arm throbb'd and there was much screaming and shouting coming from the less gentle quarters. The next day I was visit'd by David Stair and James Johnston, himself an experienc'd lawyer in constitutional matters. (The latter look'd comically out of place in his courtier's finery and make-up, although I was grateful for the great waft of perfume that came with him.) He immediately deliver'd two pieces of bad news: first, the charge against me was not manslaughter, as we had assum'd, but murder; second, the case wou'd be heard in a matter of days by none other than Sir Slathial Scrote, whose reputation was as ugly sounding as his name. It appear'd that Sir Slathial was a sadistic monster who made up for the leniency he display'd towards those who had brib'd him, by hanging those who had not, irrespective of their innocence. Fac'd with these alarming facts – and this was by no means his customary counsel, he assur'd me – Johnston had no hesitation in advising a bribe; Stair nodd'd in consider'd agreement; and I instantly overcame any scruples to ask who wou'd do it and how much. Stair said he wou'd make an approach through a third party and let me know the outcome.

On the subject of representation, I insist'd – with all due respect to Johnston – that I wou'd find it difficult to hide behind an advocate in court; I wou'd rather speak for myself. Johnston said this was very noble of me, but as a defendant in a Crown case of this kind, I was not entitle'd to legal representation anyway, nor cou'd I testify. After a shock'd silence, I suggest'd that whatever sum was deem'd necessary to sweeten Sir Slathers shou'd be trebl'd, which despite our depress'd mood, brought smiles all round.

As for the charge of murder, Johnston suppos'd that the Crown wou'd try to show that what happen'd between Beau and myself was not so much a duel as a brawl and that I had struck first. It also look'd, he said, as if someone was putting pressure on the court to ensure that the maximum punishment was applied.

'Which is what?' I ask'd.

'Hanging, of course,' said Johnston.

'Don't despair, Law,' he add'd, as he and Stair depart'd. 'We'll just have to apply some equal and opposite pressure of our own, won't we? It's all part of the legal process...'

The next day Stair return'd alone with more unpleasant tidings. It turn'd out that the prosecution wou'd produce witnesses to testify that Beau and I often argued over money – which in one sense was true, as I have describ'd – and that Beau ow'd me hundreds of pounds – also true, but then he was in debt to everyone. Through these testimonies they hop'd to prove that I was extremely angry with Beau Wickham and had deliberately set out to kill him.

Stair also confirm'd that Beau's family had indeed press'd for the charge to be murder and had almost certainly offer'd Sir Slathial a large financial inducement to ensure that I was found guilty. 'Did you know,' he ask'd, 'that Beau's uncle is in fact the Lord Chancellor, Sir Herbert Cecil, one of the most powerful men in the realm?'

'I did not,' I said.

'It's strange that he never once mention'd him to any of us – why do you think that was?'

Stair spoke with the kind of soft, lilting Scottish accent that always put me in mind of misty glens and the distant sound of the pipe. But he was no Jacobite, and in fact was actively seeking political advancement in London under the patronage of powerful Unionist peers like Johnston. He very much support'd union with England and the Protestant succession of King William, while I was more aware of the dire financial implications for Scotland and much less enthusiastic. Even so, we had known each other since we were boys in Edinburgh and despite the differences in our political views, there was a strong bond between us for which I became increasingly grateful as this drama unfold'd.

'I think he had a very low opinion of his family and want'd nothing more to do with them,' I replied.

'Well, they are very determin'd to make up for the estrangement now that he's dead.'

The trial took place two days later at the Old Bailey. Mine was just one of many colourful cases, a lurid assortment of thefts, assaults, murders and coin clippings. (For those of you unfamiliar with English criminal law, the latter is a capital offence that involves cutting gold and silver from coins, melting it down and selling it abroad – another good reason, I thought, for the wider distribution of paper, lest the currency be clipp'd away.)

I felt like a mere spectator at the proceedings, which is a most uncomfortable position if you happen to be standing in the dock. I still wonder'd if Johnston had manag'd to purchase any influence over Sir Slathial, but all hope was extinguish'd when I saw how the latter was shamelessly leading the jury to a verdict of guilty. Sir Slathers was truly monstrous to behold: his face was blotch'd and swollen from drink; his neck disappear'd behind great sagging jowls, so that he resembl'd nothing more than an old bulldog that bark'd at everyone in the court. The whole jury, which look'd as though it had been specially transport'd from Newgate, seem'd in mortal terror when he growl'd and my own soul froze when he cast his ferocious gaze towards the dock.

There was a whole series of fake witnesses for the Crown, only one of whom I recognis'd – the proprietor of the gaming room. They all testified to the long-standing bitterness between Beau and myself, mainly due to his refusal to settle his gambling debts. My statement to the officers of the watch, in which I admitt'd killing Beau in a duel, was then read out to the court.

In my 'defence' Johnston had organis'd several fine character witnesses: two or three highly respectable acquaintances who said what a gentleman and all round fine fellow I was – a banker by trade (I don't think they meant in the gaming sense) from a successful banking family. A further statement of mine was read out, more or less dictat'd by Johnston, in which I said that no maliciousness was intend'd on my part. Beau and I had arrang'd to meet; an argument had spontaneously arisen; he had struck me first, hence my wound; I had had no alternative but to defend myself. I deeply regrett'd the outcome and wou'd carry the remorse with me to the grave. (One or two of the jury gave me a look that seem'd to indicate that I wou'd not have long to bear the burden.)

I thought it all sound'd plausible enough, but unfortunately it was not the play that Sir Slathers had been paid to write. He summ'd up by saying that all the evidence suggest'd that Beau Wickham had refus'd to pay his gambling debt and so I had decid'd to teach him a severe lesson. I had been intent on committing murder and through this most malicious of quarrels had done so; no high-mind'd claim to have fought a duel cou'd disguise this base motive.

It took our spineless jury all of three minutes to reach a decision. After the verdict of guilty was deliver'd and before the sentence pass'd, Sir Slathers rose to the occasion with a stirring peroration, deliver'd as if from the pulpit.

'As we all know,' he bark'd, 'the smell of depravity hangs around any gambling den like that of rotting meat around the slaughter house; even if he is not accus'd in law, the successful gambler is little more than a thief and a parasite. It is no wonder then that the man standing before you shou'd finally resort to murder in the attempt to extort his ill-gotten gains. Despite his distinguish'd background, upon which he has brought profound disgrace, he is in no respect a gentleman – he is the worse kind of cut-throat, driven by no nobler purpose than common greed...'

By the end of the session, one of thieves, two of the clippers and two of the murderers, one of them myself, had all been sentenc'd to be hang'd – or rather 'stiffen'd', as my turnkey had so eloquently put it.

We were return'd to Newgate in a filthy prison wagon, which lurch'd so violently we would have crack'd our skulls on the roof had we not been heavily chain'd to the benches. Back at the prison the turnkey and his strong-arm'd assistants were in good spirits. They liked nothing more than welcoming more poor wretches into the Order of the Condemn'd, especially if they includ'd gentry.

'A disgrace to his distinguish'd background, was what I heard,' said one.

'Don't worry, milord. We won't keep you 'anging around for long,' laugh'd another.

I was too dispirit'd to respond to their taunts. I cou'd hardly believe what had happen'd since that fateful evening with Beau, and yet like all tragedies, it seem'd to have its own implacable logic: transgression follow'd by retribution – and there seem'd very little chance of my escaping it. In fact, so resign'd to my fate had I become that it was a while before I even bother'd to open the seal'd note that Stair had sent. In this, he assur'd me that the Earl of Warriston wou'd immediately approach the King on my behalf in order to secure a pardon, and that this wou'd be accomplish'd 'within a matter of days'. He made it sound like a mere formality – the issue of a bill of sale or a letter of introduction – but by then I knew how much influence

Beau's family wield'd and doubt'd that Johnston cou'd prevail against the Lord Chancellor himself. At that point it was obvious that my situation had gone from extremely unfortunate to entirely hopeless.

As he remov'd my chains and lock'd me in for the night, the ever-cheerful turnkey inform'd me that the date for my execution wou'd be set the next day.

'They usually gives you a week or two, milord. Time to make your will – and satisfy some of your very last wishes.' He gave his most lascivious grin and left.

For hours I must have done little but stare at the dying embers of my meagre fire and the shadows of the guttering candle dancing on the bare stone wall. Through the tiny barr'd window a pale sickle moon disappear'd behind a bulbous cloud; it seemed like a symbol of my rapidly waning fortunes. Animal-like noises came occasionally from the main part of the prison and the sound of muffl'd voices drift'd up from other cells, but otherwise everything became oddly quiet, peaceful even.

It was then that I heard footfalls in the narrow passageway outside the door. At first, I thought it was the turnkey or one of his henchmen returning for more sport, but then the air suddenly turn'd colder and I felt a profound sense of dread and unease, as one might in the midst of the worst nightmare. I was aware of a presence, but not a human one. The figure of a man – was it Beau? – appear'd to step through the clos'd door and move towards me. It was difficult to tell exactly what he was wearing – a dark topcoat that might have been Beau's, yet was plainer – but as he came towards me, he pull'd back the coat to reveal the bloody patch of his chest wound. It was my dead friend, surely – or some ghostly version of him. Petrified, I saw that he held something in his other hand. Was it a weapon of some kind? Had this spectre come to deny the hangman a victim? No, it was a moneybag. He shook it. I heard the jingling of coins and it seemed as if he was offering it to me. Then, within seconds, the phantom, or whatever it was, had gone, disappear'd, moneybag and all.

Surely the events of the day had unhing'd me, and yet what I had just witness'd seem'd so real. I start'd to shake; I scream'd repeatedly and pound'd on the door: 'Let me out, for God's sake, let me out!' – which only brought loud abuse from the cells nearby. I have no idea how long this went on. Eventually, my hands grew sore, my voice hoarse and I subsid'd into exhaust'd silence. I fell back on the pallet and watch'd the door in terror, expecting the apparition to return at any moment, until eventually I drift'd into a merciful, dreamless sleep.

Daylight, even the insipid kind that is filter'd through prison bars, brought some relief, but I was determin'd not to face another night alone. I would fulfil one of my final wishes: I wou'd lose myself in lust, and for a few brief hours forget my sentence of death.

I ask'd the turnkey to find me a woman, which seem'd to brighten him considerably and bring out the honest tradesman: did I want her big or small, fair or dark, young or old, English or foreign? 'Some do like 'em old and ugly and English, milord, strangely enough. Must be something to do with their mothers, I expect...'

The cost was the same whatever – extremely high – but then how else wou'd I be spending my money in the future? Certainly not investing in the Bank of England. After much advice from my host – 'Now your Irish girls are the most wanton, I always say, on account of all the time they've spent in convents' – I chose young, dark, somewhere between big and small, and certainly not ugly; her country of origin I left to his expert judgement.

Throughout the day, I cou'd not help but expect some word from Stair or Johnston, but none came. In the evening, having eaten some of the toughest beef it is possible to chew – Lord only knows what kind of rations the less gentle enjoy'd – I was taken by the turnkey up a narrow spiral staircase to the bower of love, as he so poetically put it. This turn'd out to be a surprisingly well appoint'd room, with a large oak bed, crimson velvet curtains from floor to ceiling, an ottoman carpet and an elegant table laden with brandy and wine. Sitting up in the bed, bare-breast'd, raven-hair'd and in candle-lit chiaroscuro, was the most beautiful woman I had ever seen (a slight exaggeration that I was more than happy to indulge). With uncharacteristic discretion, the turnkey withdrew.

'Good evening, sir,' my courtesan purr'd, in her warm Irish brogue. She patt'd the bed beside her. 'Come and forget your troubles for a while.'

Which I have to say, I did. Women had prov'd little more than sport to me in the past – a poor second to gaming, and far less predictable. But Maggie, for that was her name, was dedicat'd to her trade and appear'd to enjoy our love making as much as I (although I am sure the London stage has been denied a remarkable acting talent).

After our first coupling – and while I took time to recover, I must admit – we drank wine and talk'd a little. She ask'd about my wound'd arm, the trial and whether I thought there was any prospect of a reprieve. 'Are you afraid of dying, sir?' she enquir'd.

'Of course I am,' I said.

'You will see the priest, won't you?' She seem'd as concern'd for my soul as she had just been for my body.

'No, Maggie,' I said, 'That will only disturb me further. I'll have no truck with priests of any shape or hue.'

'Then how will you make your peace with Almighty God?'

'I'm afraid I don't believe in Almighty God,' I replied.

She was visibly shock'd. She sipp'd her wine thoughtfully and push'd back her hair from her lovely face. 'Then what do you believe in, sir?'

I consider'd the question briefly: 'The power of money,' I said.

'Well, forgive me for saying so, but it hasn't got you very far.'

I smil'd. 'It has bought me a night with you for a start...'

We return'd to our love making for several more wonderful couplings. My fourth and final climax of the night was the most profound, and Maggie certainly match'd me for sound and fury. Afterwards, as we lay sat'd and exhaust'd, drifting into sleep, I recall'd the turnkey's words about hanging and climaxing. It was true, I thought, the imminence of death did seem to increase the pleasure of the petit mort immeasurably; it was almost worth dying for. I laugh'd out loud, but then began to weep like a child, and Maggie, who seem'd used to such things, held me very tight.

In the morning, I awoke to heavy knocking on the door. Stair burst into the room, accompanied by a thin bar of daylight. He wav'd a rolled up parchment, looking excitedly at me and then at the slumberous, wondrous Maggie, who sigh'd and turn'd so that her magnificent breasts fell towards me. Stair falter'd somewhat, but quickly regain'd his stride.

'Law!'

'Stair!'

'Sorry for the er rude awakening, but I have some very good news.' He hand'd me the parchment. 'The King has pardon'd you!'

I look'd quickly at the royal signature, then leap'd nak'd from the bed and hugg'd my dear friend. Maggie was finally rous'd by the commotion, as Stair began to explain what had happen'd. As luck would have it, Sir Herbert and the King had fallen out over – of all things – the propos'd Act of Union with Scotland! The King want'd it as soon as possible, but his Lord Chancellor was concern'd about various constitutional questions. This gave Warriston the opportunity he need'd to request my pardon, which earlier the King had refus'd.

'I never thought I'd hear myself say it,' said I, 'but Thank God for Scotland and lawyers – even Warriston, the rogue. More wine, eh Maggie? Let's make a day as well as a night of it, shall we? There's an extra fee for you...'

'However...' Stair's bright smile dimm'd a little. 'There is one small problem...'

'Which is what?' I ask'd.

'Beau's family has invok'd some ancient law. They have issued an Appeal of Murder...'

'An Appeal of Murder?'

'As the victim's heirs, they have fil'd a civil suit for murder against you and if it is upheld, even the King himself cannot by law pardon you a second time.'

'You mean, I am to be tried for murder again?'

'Yes.'

'I see. And if they win, cou'd I be hang'd?' Stair hesitat'd. 'Stair, cou'd I be hang'd?'

'Warriston says...yes...you cou'd be hang'd.'

Standing there nak'd, I suddenly felt ridiculous – and not a little cold.

*

Venice, La Serenissima, apparently. I wish I could say that her beauty is undimmed by the winter season – by the cold drizzle and the slate grey water; by the dark landings and buildings that loom out of the mist; by the sodden chill that seeps further into me with every move I make. I wish could say, as Joanna said on the phone, that the city casts her spell whatever the time of year. But I can't. As I climb aboard the Monaco Hotel's courtesy launch on the Grand Canal, I can only admit to thinking that my spur-of-the-moment decision to come here – and to invite Jo - was a little rash.

'Welcome to Venice, signore,' says the driver, wrapped to the chin in his large purple puffa, as if in a duvet. But he seems far from welcoming in mood, sullen even, and can manage only a weak smile. As we travel down the canal, it becomes clear that he's less inclined to point out famous landmarks – which anyway we can hardly see – and would rather tell me baleful tales of this being the worse November weather and slowest tourist season he can recall since the great *acqua alta* of nineteen-whenever.

'*Guardi!*' he nods into the gloom, sliding the steering wheel slowly through his kid-gloved hands. 'The city is already flooding.'

I can't see, of course, but I take his word for it. 'This is worse than usual?'

'*Si, molto, molto!* Very high tides. And today, no wind. But most days it blows very, very strong...' Then he throws one hand theatrically to the heavens. '*Cambiamento climatico!* How do you say?'

'Climate change?' I hazard and contemplate what I can make out of the passing palazzos. It seems it's not just a case of the buildings sinking, as was always the main threat to the city, but also of ice caps melting and the water rising. Later I'm to learn online that even in the 1950s, *acqua alta* occurred in the older parts of the city as much as thirty times a year. Now there

42

can be a hundred such incidents. Indeed, so bad has it become that after much public debate, construction started some years ago on a vastly ambitious and expensive barrier at the entrance to the lagoon, designed to stem the flow of high tide.

'*Si,* climate change. To live in Venice we will soon need to be…' He cups a hand over his mouth, breathes deeply.

'Frogmen?'

'*Si, si* – frogmen.' At last there's a full-blown smile from him.

I seem to be the only guest bound for the Hotel Monaco, certainly the only passenger on the boat. At first, I sit behind my driver in the small well-appointed cabin, but then decide to stand outside to get a better, if wetter, view of the city.

For the main artery, the canal seems spookily quiet, with few craft of either a pleasure or commercial variety and oceans of room on the water. Even so, with no warning, another motor boat, moving at much greater speed than ours, shoots out of a side canal in front of us and crosses our bow. The driver swerves to avoid him; I'm thrown across the deck, bang my head against the upright of the cabin and land up sprawling against the side of the boat.

The capitano is torn between hurling loud abuse at the stern of the offending vessel as it disappears into the mist and checking to see if I'm okay.

'*Scusi…scusi, signore.*' More curses into the mist, as I clamber to my feet, rubbing my temple and trying to steady myself against the rocking caused by the other boat's considerable wash.

I'm still feeling somewhat shaken and my head's still throbbing, when we reach San Marco. And yet, even with such discomfort – and in those murky conditions – I'm able to appreciate the magnificence of the famous view. Suddenly, yes, its spell takes hold and all is well; I'm glad I came.

Of course, my driver does his best to ruin it. As we near the landing, he points out the duckboards across the Piazza, most of which is already under water and resembling a large, shallow swimming pool.

A liveried porter, all obsequious greetings at the landing, immediately diverts me, taking my bag from the boat, asking is my head okay and ushering me into the smart white reception area of the hotel. In minutes I'm installed in the suite, gazing across at the hazy façade of a massive church, known as the Salute, and out to the lagoon, where a multi-storey cruise liner, the height of the highest Venetian dome, lurks like a monster in the mist. Even with this blot on the waterscape, the panorama is worth every euro.

Once I've settled in – I don't have much to unpack – I decide to head straight down to the room that was Europe's first casino, where the villainous John Law became a fixture in the last years of his life. This is situated on what's known as the *piano nobile*, the principal floor of a large house and usually its second storey. In Venice this means that the ground floor can more easily accommodate regular flooding.

In the case of this particular large house as was, the *piano nobile* would have overlooked the Grand Canal. I say 'would have' because I'm sorely disappointed when I get there. The room itself is impressive enough – grand in the classical manner, with fluted pillars and a high ceiling of gilded stuccowork. Unfortunately, in redeveloping the hotel, they have built out in front of it and robbed the former Ridotto of its greatest asset: the magnificent view that made it such a 'noble' floor.

I'm looking out of a tall window at a blank, white wall and rueing the loss, when my phone pings the arrival of an email. It's from Diana Lennon, giving me a number to call so that we can arrange to meet. I call it immediately.

'*Pronto*,' says a voice.

I don't risk any Italian, not even a ciao. 'May I speak to Diana Lennon?'

'This is Diana.' Another American; Italy's crawling with them.

'I'm Theo Law.'

'You're quick off the mark, Theo,' she says as if she's known me for years. (That's most Americans for you.)

'It's a function of a busy life, I'm afraid.'

'Ah…an old slouch like me wouldn't know about such things. You're here – in Venice?'

'Yes.'

'Where are you staying?'

'At the Monaco.'

'Like your ancestor, you couldn't resist the Ridotto.'

'I'm actually standing in it, as we speak. Sadly, it's minus the view.'

'I know – it's a great shame. Like everything else in this town, it's about maximising income from tourists.'

'When can we meet?' I ask.

'I'm out for dinner this evening, but why not come for a drink beforehand?'

Seeing as Jo isn't arriving until the following afternoon, this seems like a good plan. She gives me the address, a house in the Dorsoduro area. She tells me it's easiest to take a water taxi or vaporetto as far as the Rezzonico landing – too many small, twisty canals after that. From there it's a short walk to her place.

'The *acqua alta* will have subsided a bit,' she adds. 'We won't have another warning siren until the morning, when the tide turns. Even so, be careful. It's sometimes difficult to know where the walkway ends and the canal begins…'

*

I was to be transferr'd from one cesspit – Newgate – to another – the King's Bench (or his Arsehole, more like) in Southwark. There, I wou'd await a civil trial that might not begin for weeks, maybe months. I sat looking at my reflection in the small mirror I had been given to groom myself for my recent tryst. Like a severe pox, this whole unfortunate episode had begun to leave its mark on my strong but increasingly haggard features. It was a disease and I need'd to be rid of it as soon as possible, before the marks became scars and I us'd the looking glass to slit my wrists. It was time, I decid'd, to test the power of money even further.

I summon'd the turnkey to me, who thought I wish'd to request another night with Maggie before my departure. 'No,' I said, doing my best to sound imperious, 'as delightful as she is, there is something of even greater urgency. I wish to escape and I think it's best accomplish'd when I am being transport'd

45

to the King's Bench. You are the best person to arrange it, are you not?'

'I see, milord,' he look'd at me suspiciously from under his ludicrous wig – wou'd he turn out to have some scruples, after all? 'It took you long enough to work out history's most ingenious battle plan.'

'And that is?'

'Flight,' he said, and treat'd me to his most toothless smile - I had begun to have a grudging respect for this turnkey of Newgate.

We haggl'd over his fee, of course, but the arrangements for flight were simple. The turnkey wou'd ensure that I was transport'd alone, after dusk. On the way to Southwark, in a quiet street, the prison wagon wou'd be raid'd by a party of three mask'd men, who wou'd release me and take me to my chosen destination. I wou'd send word to Stair, and through him make arrangements to head straight for France and from there to Scotland, which – thanks to Beau's uncle - still lay outside English jurisdiction.

And as it was plann'd, so it happen'd. By the following evening, to my immense joy and relief, I was free. I had met up with Stair in Aldgate and was on my way to Calais, away from respectable English society forever.

I later discover'd that I had become somewhat notorious during this time. Lacking a war on which to report – the recent Peace of Ryswick had conclud'd nine years of conflict in Europe – the news sheets recount'd my exploits with great relish and embellishment. Apparently, I had escap'd from Newgate single-handedly and been spott'd riding towards Scotland with a mysterious woman. (That week several 'John Laws' and their paramours were arrest'd on the Great North Road.)

Meanwhile, Beau's family put a reward notice in the London Gazette, which read:

'John Law, a Scotchman, aged 35, lately a prisoner at Newgate, a very tall, black, lean man, well-shap'd, above 6 foot high, big high nos'd, pock-mark'd face, speaking broad and loud, made his escape while being transferr'd

from said prison to the King's Bench in Southwark. Whoever secures him shall have £50 paid immediately by the Marshall of the King's Bench.'

There were several things I took exception to in this notice, including 'big, high-nos'd', 'pock-mark'd face' and 'speaking broad and loud', a caricature of my refin'd Edinburgh accent. But perhaps its most upsetting aspect was the size of the reward itself: a paltry £50 – for he who wou'd soon become the richest man in the world.

Chapter 3

Venice, October 1728

Recently at the Ridotto, I have had what the less rational wou'd refer to as a run of bad luck. In other words, the laws of statistical probability do not determine that my calculation of odds will always result in my winning, only in my winning more often than losing, and just now there has been a little too much of the latter.

I have therefore ask'd the conte de Bellini if I may take the more lucrative Banker's chair for an evening or so, in the hope that it will help restore my good fortune. He was happy to grant my request, especially as we are to be join'd by a very rich French nobleman, none other than the young duc de Conti, the son of a once – how can I describe him? – bitter rival of mine, the prince de Conti, now deceas'd due to an excess of good living. (The elder Conti was a 'Prince of the Blood', one of Louis XIV's many bastards.)

As well as whoring and gambling, the Duc has no doubt come to the Ridotto for some sport at my expense. He will try to provoke me into some contretemps and in his youthful arrogance will expect to beat me at the card table, having some years before witness'd my downfall in the political arena. (I remember him particularly well at the banquet to celebrate my conversion to Rome in 1720, one of the grandest social events of that year, attended by the Papal Envoy, as well as the Regent.) Bellini of course, unaware of these intricacies, expects the Bank to triumph and trusts it will be of much pecuniary benefit to the Ridotto.

Among our group at the high table, only the Duc and myself are without masks. Numerous elegant ladies look on, making up for what they cannot convey with the mask'd portion of their faces by displaying as much of their fulsome breasts as decency will allow. The Duc and I acknowledge each other with cursory bows. He is not unlike his father in appearance; he wears a large periwig of luxuriant chestnut curls, framing thin lips and cold eyes that betray even less than a mask. I can only hope he twitches under pressure, as his father us'd to.

We have agreed to play Pharo, and as we settle at the table and I prepare the cards, the Prince turns to his pretty female companion. 'Goodness, my dear,' he trills, in a manner made fashionable by the young Louis XV, 'the Ridotto is not what it was. Mere commoners are now not only permitt'd to appear without masks but to play as Bankers. Whatever next?'

'Next,' I hear myself saying, rather rashly, 'they will be Bankers to the French Crown and even some of the lesser Nobility, like the Princes of the Blood.' I continue before he can respond: 'And as for my mask, I have only remov'd it in order to give Your Grace a sporting chance of reading my intentions.'

Conti shoots me a look and curls his lip. 'I know your intentions, Law. They are to avoid repaying France the millions of livres you stole from her.'

'Perhaps,' I reply, 'Your Grace might like to try and win some of those livres back...on France's behalf.'

And with these first skirmishes complete, we settle down to the real business of gaming.

Much to my surprise, the young Conti is not bad at selecting the individual cards. As he lays down each shining gold coin to place a wager, he knowingly makes a show of it, turning it in his long, beringed fingers for my benefit. It is a direct provocation - as only he knows and you will soon understand. In the final rounds, when choosing which three cards are left and their order of appearance, he begins to twitch – to my great relief – but is still reasonably accurate. Towards the end of the evening, we have been through many bottles of wine and as many as six runs of the pack consecutively, without a conclusive result – we have both chosen the right cards at different times, but fail'd on their order. There is a very large pile of gold coins on the table, so many that I see a look of concern pass briefly across Bellini's face, as he stands looking on. I feign concern in response and Conti, misreading my only significant expression during the whole game, decides things are running against me and raises the stakes heavily for this final round.

Almost the whole room is gather'd round us by now. Only Conti and myself are left in the running; we both nominate the face value of the three cards and their order. As Banker, I select Jack, Four and Seven; twitching like mad, he chooses Jack, Four and Eight. (I am sure all the Eights are gone.) The cards are turn'd over one at a time: Jack, Four – the room holds its breath, as do I – Seven!

As I scoop the pile of coins into the Banker's bag, Conti gives me a strain'd smile. The money is nothing to him, but he hates to lose before a crowd. He speaks to his mistress, whose breasts are now highly flush'd and have all but sprung from their moorings at the sight of so much gold, lost and won. 'Our friend Law is still a better gambler than he was a Controller of French Finances, my dear, but then the latter role obviously requir'd something a little more substantial than mere luck at cards ...'

I speak to the assembl'd company, as well as to him. 'It requires the ability to spot enemies who masquerade as friends - as you know only too well, Conti. In early 1720 your father, whom I had already made an extremely rich man, came to the Banque Royale and demand'd over 14 million livres in gold louis d'or in return for his shares in the Company. He knew it wou'd help destroy the System that I had set in place so as to benefit the whole of France.' I hold up the Banker's bag. 'This is little recompense for the millions she owes me!'

Any remaining sense of noblesse deserts him - the young Duc literally spits on the table in front of me: 'France owes you nothing more than that, Law, and your so-call'd System destroy'd itself, as do all things that are the work of the devil ...'

*

The overcast skies usher in an early dusk and the daylight's already failing as I leave the hotel. The flooding is serious enough for the concierge to issue complimentary waterproof boots. They're called 'goldons', he says. He holds out what he thinks are my size in front of him and grins broadly. They are bright transparent yellow plastic and cover the calves like rubber boots.

'Is this what all the locals wear during *acqua alta*?' I ask.

'No, these are more *alla moda, signore*. The locals wear...' - he pauses to think of the English – 'plastic bags. Much cheaper...'

I sit and pull the boots on over my shoes and trousers. I feel less *alla moda* and more a fashion victim, but as long as they keep my feet dry, what the hell.

He also gives me an umbrella and orders me a water taxi. Fully equipped for the trip, I head outside.

Diana Lennon was right: the water has receded and in places is almost contained by the quayside. The rain has stopped and the air feels fresher, calmer. Boats and gondolas rock gently at their moorings. Lights are coming on across the square and lagoon, and along the canal several large torches unfurl banners of naked flame. Everything flashes and sparkles, as if we're inside a great crystal cave or hall of mirrors, Venetian mirrors.

And in amongst this light show, people are out and about, real Venetians, it seems, as well as tourists. At the end of a grey day, there's more buzz and excitement than I expected. I want to toast this, my first evening in Venice as a grown up, toast it with a glass of Aperol or Prosecco or some other Italian brew. I think of heading to the famous Harry's Bar, just across the bridge from the Monaco, or the *bellissimo* Danieli Hotel, further down the waterfront, where I would have stayed, had it not been for John Law and the Ridotto.

But there's no time. I must wait for whatever aperitif Ms. Lennon has to offer, or I'll not get to see her this evening and I very much want to see her. My head has stopped throbbing. My mood is more buoyant, the opposite of the black ones I've been subject to over the last few days. Long may it last, I tell myself, as we drift past the elegant line of palazzos that form the banks of the canal. Some of these are lit up in gaudy colours, more Las Vegas than La Serenissima.

Before I left the hotel I looked up Diana Lennon online. (Never meet anyone you know nothing about is one of my cardinal rules.) However, although it listed several women of that name – an academic, a politician and a maker of jewellery among them – none fitted the profile of the woman I'm now on my way to see: a writer and dealer in antiquarian books in Venice. (So I'll be breaking one of my cardinal rules.)

By comparison, my own online presence is prodigious – a distinguished career in investment banking before I set up my own successful fund. (I'm particularly well known, it says, for having foreseen the crash and avoided the worst of its dire consequences.) This no doubt means that I'll be in the uncomfortable position of her knowing much more about me than I know about her. After all, she's already tracked me down as the most direct living descendant of John Law - and one thing she'll have established is that I'm in a position to pay a large sum of money for his manuscript, if indeed it is *his* manuscript. Should I be wary of a scam? Of course I should. But then I would be anyway; I've never forgotten that Italian taxi driver, and in many ways Diana Lennon sounds like someone who's gone decidedly native.

*

The System, as the system for managing France's finances became known, always arous'd strong feelings, for and against. Most of its main elements had in fact been formulat'd by the time Katherine and I first met Orleans in Paris, although it cou'd not be reveal'd in its entirety until its first stage – the Bank – had achiev'd some degree of success. Before then, the sheer scale of its ambition may have overwhelm'd even Philippe.

Not long after our encounter at Madame de Chateauneuf's, he invit'd me to visit him at the Palais-Royal, the Orleans family home in Paris – 'in order to explore more fully our mutual interest in the Science of Money', as he put it. The Palais was fairly modest by Bourbon standards, but it was more than comfortable enough for Philippe and his colourful menage, which did not include his wife, who spent most of her time at their chateau in St.Cloud. (Many of the more prominent nobility still attend'd the King at Versailles and Marly, but Orleans preferr'd to keep his distance from his uncle and the Court, not least because Paris afford'd him many more amusements.)

The afternoon I went to see him, he was in the company of a certain Dr. Homburg, who was introduc'd to me as a Doctor of Chemistry. I had expect'd Orleans to do little more than preside languidly over his own small court at the Palais. To my surprise, I discover'd that one of the larger rooms had been set up as a laboratory, where he and the Doctor were busily performing chemical experiments in a bizarre array of glass burners. The smells that emanat'd from the room were as atrocious as the two men were enthusiastic. They told me proudly that they were observing the interaction between different chemical substances, many of which had proven highly combustible, judging from the various burn marks on the walls and tables. In stark contrast to our first meeting in the gaming salon, Philippe went wigless and wore a grubby apron. He was extremely excit'd, as they were about to test a substance that they hop'd would be able to burn through metal. How this would prove to be of any use to anyone, I was unsure.

'Monsieur Law is also a man of Science,' Philippe told Homburg, a short plump man, with large tufts of grey hair at the sides of his otherwise bald head and a long scar on his left cheek – a laboratory war wound, no doubt.

He frown'd at me querulously over one his glass burners. 'And what is your area of enquiry, Monsieur Law?' he ask'd, in a Hanoverian kind of French that oddly enough I found easier to comprehend than the domestic version.

'The Science of Money,' I said.

'The Science of Money, Monsieur? But surely money is a matter of scarcity rather than science,' he sniff'd, displaying a rare wit for a Hanoverian.

'And the scientific method will turn that scarcity into plenty,' I replied, 'just as it will find the right combination of chemicals to perform all sorts of other miracles. For what is Science but a rational body of knowledge – a system – that enables us not only to understand the world but to impose our will upon it.'

Homburg mutter'd something about his money having a will of its own and carried on arranging his experiment. 'Please, don't mind the Doctor,' said Philippe, 'our investigations have reach'd something of an impasse today and it has left him a *little vex'd. I, on the other hand, am impress'd by your talk of Money Science, Monsieur Law, and want to know how it can be applied to the sorry state of French finances.'*

Since Katherine and I had first come to Paris, this was what I had been waiting for – the chance to explain my ideas, if not to the King, then to someone as close as to him as Philippe. I pitch'd straight into my argument. 'The theory is simple enough, Your Highness. As we know, the problem with France is that it is starv'd of money. The solution is to establish a National Bank that will issue a paper currency to increase the money supply. This will stimulate activity in the economy, which will become more productive and so encourage more investment and so on. France – and its National Bank – will prosper.'

'But France has tried this before under Louis,' he said. 'We have experiment'd in some small way with paper and the result was disastrous. The money was very soon worthless.'

'Quite so,' I replied, 'but only because it serv'd the exclusive needs of the monarchy, not the economy – therefore no one had any faith in it. Currencies like churches need a faithful following to survive.'

Philippe smil'd. 'It cannot have escap'd your notice that we still live under a Monarchy,' he said. 'The King's rule is absolute - Parlement merely ratifies it.'

'But that rule cou'd become more enlighten'd under a more enlighten'd ruler – if he were given the right financial advice.' I look'd at him meaningfully; he paus'd for thought.

'This is all very rational, Monsieur Law, all very scientific. However, there are other factors to take into account. Please - stay for an informal dinner this evening. I will show you the difference between Physical Science and the Science of Money...'

Dr.Homburg cut in excitedly. 'We are ready, Your Highness...'

He turn'd up the flame under the glass burner and we all three watch'd it begin to bubble. Very quickly the bubbling became a spitting and then a flaming torch. Within a few seconds there was an almighty bang and the glass explod'd, sending us diving for cover beneath the table.

Homburg swore loudly in German; Philippe smil'd and shook his handsome head. 'Sometimes physical substances can be just as intractable as people,' he said. And with that, the experiments were conclud'd for the day.

Given that Philippe's invitation was not extend'd to Katherine, it quickly became clear that the informal dinner in question wou'd be a very French affair, with courtesans only. (It wou'd have seem'd churlish of me to tell my host that Katherine was not in fact my wife, but then neither was she what he thought of as a courtesan.) I felt privileg'd to be seat'd next to 'son altesse', no matter how informal the gathering; on his other side was Marie-Louise de Sèry, his then paramour, who beam'd at everyone and was obviously making the most of her favour'd status. From where we sat, Philippe quietly took me round the table, with its assortment of extravagant wigs and frocks.

'Antoine Crozat, probably the richest man in France,' he said sotto voce. 'He has the monopoly of foreign trade, as well as vast estates... The prince de Conti, who is only here to annoy me. He's one of Louis' illegitimate sons – as well as one of my main rival's for His Majesty's favour... The marquis d'Argenson, our police chief, here to protect me, he claims, but in truth he cannot resist wine and women, which is perfectly understandable... Samuel Bernard, another rich financier, a Jew and thoroughly debauch'd – not that that has anything to do with his being Jewish... The Paris twins, never seen apart in public. They are among the country's wealthiest tax collectors – mainly, I suspect, because much of the tax finds its way into their pockets... The Abbè Dubois, my old tutor, a shrewd politician and a renown'd lecher... The duc de Saint-Simon – the only man here I wou'd consider a true friend; we have known each other since childhood. He thoroughly disapproves of my licentious behaviour and will quietly slip away before things become too unruly... And...aah...the exquisite Madame de Tencin – she presides over one of Paris' best salons and is a virtuoso of the boudoir – or wherever it pleases you to avail yourself of her charms.' Philippe was in a transport of delight. 'Such sensuality, Monsieur Law, such tendresse, such appetite, made all the more piquant by the fact that she is the sister of the

Cardinal de Tencin. _I fear that even a man of my stamina is not enough for her... Incidentally, I do believe she's unattach'd this evening – or are you, like Saint-Simon, notoriously faithful to your wife?'_

'If it means that like Saint-Simon, I have a chance of gaining your trust, then yes.'

Philippe laugh'd, then lower'd his voice. 'Entre nous, I cannot understand for the life of me why Saint-Simon does remain faithful, but in the case of Madame Law, who is as beautiful as she is formidable, it comes as no surprise. Please send my best wishes to her and tell her how well-behav'd I was this evening.'

'I will.'

He continued: 'Around this table are many of France's major creditors. As the King has become more profligate, they have become more powerful. The debts have mount'd and so have the rates of interest – to the point where the only option may be to label them all traitors and have them broken on the wheel...but then you'd be the first to point out that that is not very good for business. As with a woman, one can exploit a country only so far, I suspect, before she shrugs you off!'

Philippe finish'd his enormous glass of wine in one long draught and another was pour'd for him immediately. 'But what are we to do?' he sigh'd. 'These people will permit nothing that is not in their interest, whilst my uncle and his Financial Controller seem paralys'd by indecision. The English and the Dutch really have no need to wage war on us – they can simply buy us for a song.'

He turn'd to Crozat across the table. 'Monsieur Crozat, how much does the Crown owe you at the last count?'

Crozat look'd up from his soup; he was an old man with the face of a large fish. 'Much more than it or I, for that matter, can afford, Your Highness,' he shrugg'd. 'In the region of 10 million livres.'

'And if it were able to repay you tomorrow, how wou'd you like to be paid – in more government bonds?'

He snort'd at the idea. 'And have them devalued or cancell'd at His Majesty's whim? I think not. Nothing but gold coin will do.'

'And Monsieur Bernard? How would you like to be paid?'
Philippe ask'd.

Bernard agreed: by the same token, it cou'd only be gold.
Orleans turn'd to me. 'Monsieur Law, where does that leave
your issue of paper?'

I suddenly realis'd that I wou'd have to show more of my
hand than I had intend'd at this stage, but this cou'd be turn'd
to advantage. 'Surely, there is something more valuable to you?'
I ask'd Crozat and Bernard. 'Something that will be worth far
more than gold coins in years to come — and that you will not
have to transport by the cartload.'

They shook their heads and wav'd the notion away with
their napkins. Philippe look'd smug, as if the game were his: a
paper currency in these circumstances wou'd never work -
surely I must accept as much. 'And what wou'd that be,
Monsieur Law?' he prompt'd.

'Instead of cartloads of coins, Your Highness,' I replied, 'I
wou'd rather have shares in the company that mines and
produces the gold.'

Many of the guests had been listening to our exchange and
there was a ripple of nervous laughter, while they tried to work
out whether my reply was brilliant, absurd or just banal.

Philippe laugh'd as nervously as the rest. 'And where is this
company?' he ask'd me.

'I really cannot say just now, Your Highness. It may be
necessary to create it.'

How much Orleans understood of my cryptic vision at that
stage, I do not know, but he did not press me further on the
matter that evening. He simply told me that I shou'd write down
my proposals and that somehow he wou'd get them to the King
and his Financial Controller. If possible, he said, I shou'd
present them in person. This in itself was enough to put me in a
jubilant mood and made me determin'd to enjoy the rest of the
evening's entertainment.

The dinner itself was of course a feast. It featur'd most
things with wings and many with four legs, including the most
tender of suckling pigs, all accompanied by fine sauces and
unusual vegetables, like the spear-shap'd asparagus, which was
completely new to me. Finally, after a dozen or more courses,

the meal was round'd off with a series of sublime syllabubs, a sweet I find utterly impossible to resist. If this was an informal dinner, I cou'd not for the life of me imagine how lavish the full Bourbon banquet might be!

Afterwards, I hop'd there might be cards or dice, but Philippe's young mistress had other games in mind. She insist'd that everyone join in a séance, something that had become a regular feature of evenings at the Palais-Royal, I was told. Some of the guests – like the Abbè and Saint-Simon – look'd askance at this; others seem'd happy enough. Philippe inform'd me that he himself only participat'd 'in a spirit of scientific enquiry', although I guess'd that it excit'd Marie-Louise to be the centre of attention in this way and made her all the more amorous afterwards.

Certainly she put on a fine show as our spirit medium. Many of the candles were extinguish'd, leaving us in partial darkness; only our faces were visible and the women's ivory shoulders, with the odd gleam of diamond and sequin. We all held hands around the table and join'd with our hostess in calling to mind our dearly depart'd brethren. After such a meal, you can imagine what a symphony of farting and belching there was; soon someone began to snore, and I had enormous difficulty suppressing laughter as much as wind.

None of this, however, deterr'd Marie-Louise. She took a series of deep breaths and appear'd to go into a trance, from which she emitt'd several orgasmic moans and groans, before delivering in a deep strangulat'd voice a number of messages from visiting spirits. These seem'd to me either trite or trivial, until she announc'd that there was someone, an Englishman, she thought, asking for 'John Low', who had some connection with 'Lon-don'. He want'd Monsieur Low to know that he looked forward to playing a game of cards with him.

In the low light no one wou'd have notic'd my face lose its vinous flush and drain to a ghostly white, even though some of them look'd towards me when my name was mention'd. One was the fish-fac'd Antoine Crozat – and I was chill'd to the bone as he appear'd to metamorphose into the creature who had visited me that night in Newgate! There he was, as large as life – or rather, death – dealing cards on the table in front of him, his wound seeping blood. He look'd up at me with an ironic smile and eyes like blue fire, but I still cou'd not be sure if it was Beau Wickham. The next instant he was gone and Crozat was back, almost asleep.

I was devastat'd; it was all I cou'd do to stay at the table. I did not know if this was trickery, wine or a true haunting. Perhaps Madame de Sèry's powers were considerable. Or was it my own powers that had conjur'd this apparition? After Newgate and now Paris, I resolv'd to take a leaf from Philippe's book and approach the whole matter 'in a spirit of scientific enquiry' – or maybe that shou'd be 'a scientific enquiry into Spirit'.

Before I had the chance to ponder this any further, Marie-Louise deliver'd more messages from the other side, until she finally emerg'd from her trance and fell into Philippe's arms. Meanwhile, there were more shocks. I suddenly realis'd that a number of guests had taken advantage of the darkness to invoke something other than the dead. From what I could see, many of them were kissing, caressing and even undressing each other. Breasts were fully expos'd and fondl'd; likewise, male members. One woman knelt in prayer over the Abbe's swollen manhood and the Police Chief seem'd to have disappear'd headfirst up the voluminous skirts of his partner, no doubt in search of criminal cunny. A faint smell of musk began to mingle with that of stale perfume.

I saw Saint-Simon discreetly take his leave, as predict'd, and thought I shou'd do the same, especially as Philippe had begun to lavish attention on one of Marie-Louise's sizeable breasts – French fiscal policy was the last thing on his mind, I thought. Had someone put something in the syllabubs? I wonder'd. Had the visiting sprites had the effect of a potent aphrodisiac? If so, Madame de Sèry cou'd soon find herself the high priestess of a very popular new cult. I got up to leave, only to see before me the exquisite Madame de Tencin, with a face that had doubtless launch'd a thousand infidelities. Our eyes met; we smil'd at each other. For one moment, part of me - the lower part – want'd very much to stay. In something of a panic, the higher part made a curt bow and left, following the diminutive figure of Saint-Simon down the echoing halls of the Palais-Royal.

Once home, I woke Katherine and told her excitedly about Philippe's reactions to my proposals – <u>our</u> proposals. (At this point it seem'd unnecessary to mention the séance, the Beau-like apparition or the orgy that follow'd.) Afterwards, we made love with as great a passion as when we had first met in Scotland and become not just lovers but partners in a daring business venture. For if, like a poet, an artist of the gaming room can have a Muse, then Katherine Gregg was mine – and the System with which I propos'd to rescue France from bankruptcy was essentially hers.

*

Even though the water has receded, my plastic boots come in very handy on the walk from Rezzonico. Twice I have to wade along quaysides that are still swamped with canal water and at one point in the half-dark I narrowly avoid slipping into the canal itself. (This would not have been pleasant: as well as being extremely cold, the water looks like a toxic concoction and I'm sure a single mouthful would have proved fatal.) It doesn't help that I'm navigating via my phone. A young woman's voice with an Italian accent tells me to turn right, then left and in 20 metres, cross over the bridge. But there is no bridge. 'Re-calculating,' she says.

Then the phone starts to lose its signal and threatens to leave me stranded in this labyrinth of narrow canals and winding passageways. There's no one around to ask the way and the place is eerily silent but for the sound of my sloshing around on the flooded quays. In fact, I'm chastising myself for not having taken a good old-fashioned map from the hotel, when I suddenly emerge into a large square; the signal is restored and I realise I'm just one canal away from Ms. Lennon's. (I'm relieved that, according to her, it's only a 'short walk'.)

I cross the square, which is mostly free of water, walk over the next bridge and there it is, 'you have arrived at-a your destination': a fine old corner building that stands at the junction of two canals. The interior of the first floor – the high-ceilinged *piano nobile* – is illuminated enough for me to make out a combination of antique wood panelling and book-lined shelves. It looks warm and inviting and since the rain has started again, I want to be inside immediately.

It's just as well, then, that an American woman of a certain age wastes no time in answering the buzzer and letting me into the tiled vestibule. Several icons are displayed on its walls, including a Madonna and Child, such that it could be the entrance to a chapel or convent or some other religious institution.

And initially, I think the woman who introduces herself as Diana could vaguely pass for a nun or even a Mother Superior. She wears rimless spectacles, a baggy grey cardigan and her grey hair is cut in a severe bob. The look is dry, professorial, which makes her seem older than she is, I quickly decide. However, the dryness is redeemed by a large turquoise and silver necklace in the Native American style, visible through the open cardigan.

'Bravo, Theo, you *are* well equipped. I *love* the *acqua alta* boots – very fetching. They're very popular with the tourists.'

'I'm not conspicuous then?'

She laughs. 'Best leave them here with your coat and umbrella,' she says, and ushers me upstairs to the *piano nobile*.

'I normally drink a negroni at this hour,' she says, implying that different hours regularly occasion different drinks.

'Don't think I've ever actually had a negroni, but I'll drink whatever you're drinking, thank you.'

'Excellent - you're in for a treat...' She goes into a small well-appointed kitchen, while I stand in the doorway, watching her fix the drinks. 'No mishaps on the way here?' She puts ice into a jug and pulls bottles off the shelf like a skilled barista.

'Apart from getting lost and very nearly slipping into the canal, no...'

She shakes her head. 'As I said, *acqua alta* can be treacherous and it gets worse every year.'

'That must be very worrying.'

'It is, which is why so many are pinning their hopes on the new flood barrier – although it's certainly not without its critics, myself included.' She pours generous measures of gin, sweet vermouth and Campari into the jug and begins to stir.

'I take it you've heard of our *Modus Sperimentale Electromeccanico*? It's known as MOSE, which is not only an acronym, but a reference to Moses - he who parted the waters.' She puts the jug on a wooden tray with some glasses and takes out a couple of small plates of olives and salami from the fridge. 'Some *chiccetti*', Venetian tapas. Never drink negronis on an empty stomach or you *will* fall in the canal!' She suddenly peers at the side of my head, which has ceased to hurt but is still somewhat puffy and inflamed. 'Is that what happened earlier? Did you fall over drunk and hit your head?'

I smile. My hand goes lightly to my temple. 'This? No. I fell over on the motor launch on the way to the hotel – and I was stone cold sober, I'm afraid. Some other boat nearly collided with us. As museum's go, Venice is a dangerous place …'

I watch her give the jug one more stir. 'Anyway, in answer to your earlier question, I suppose I was vaguely aware of the barrier, but I've learned a whole lot in the few hours I've been here. It's quite something.'

'Oh yes, a 10 billion US and rising kind of something - like the waters,' she laughs. 'And this being Italy, it's been sinking into a quagmire of corruption before it's even been floated.'

Someone who at first sight appeared a little fusty is starting to seem savvy and street smart – or is that canal smart?

'Of course, there are those who say it's not rising water that's the problem, but the fact that Venice is sinking due to the sheer weight of tourists visiting it everyday. Let's go through, shall we?'

I nod at the tray. 'Shall I carry?'

'How gal*lant*. Thank you…'

We're soon settled and sipping our negronis in the large room I admired from the quayside. It has tall windows on two sides, each with a balcony overlooking a canal – though now it's dark, the water is nothing but shifting reflections of the streetlights. I see that most of the books in the room are antiquarian volumes, many of them leather-bound. The run of them is interrupted by more religious art, and the ceiling is painted with winged cherubs and angels hovering amid cotton ball clouds and the duck egg blue of the sky.

'What do you think?' she asks, nodding at my glass.

'Of the negroni? Oh, it's good, thank you.'

'Good...'

In fact, I've very rarely known such a mood of late without plummeting into a black hole, but as the drink – which packs quite a punch – takes effect, an exquisite sense of calm floods through me, a Grand Canal of alcohol. I'm happy, sitting in the company of this complete stranger, who somehow already seems very familiar. There are a few moments of perfectly comfortable silence between us, without my wanting to reach for my phone, until she says:

'The other thing about MOSE, apart from the staggering cost and delays, is that we don't actually know if it'll work, if it'll actually hold back the tide – at least, not without a large element of divine intervention. And if it does, it may prove an ecological disaster. It may destroy much of the marine life by preventing it from moving in and out of the lagoon. Besides, the high tide serves other purposes. It flushes the lagoon and prevents the build up of waste and pollution. The place might otherwise stagnate, asphyxiate.'

'So it's a case of asphyxiating, stagnating or drowning?'

'Yes,' she smiles. 'And that's even before we get to the impact of er welcoming 20 million tourists a year and their cruise ships. UNESCO tried to ban these toxic monsters but the city authorities, in their infinite wisdom, thought it would be at too great a cost to the local economy. As ever, money talks, Theo...'

'And bullshit walks, I think is the expression.'

'In this case, it performs a dance of death. Venice, I'm afraid, is a city in mortal danger.' She takes a solemn sip from her drink. 'Now, I suspect you're wondering about Mr. John Law.'

'Yes,' I say, 'but I'm also wondering about you.'

'What are you wondering?'

'You described yourself as a writer and dealer in antiquarian books.' I gesture around. 'I see the books but I'm wondering what it is you write.'

She shrugs. 'Oh, nothing of any great significance – the only thing you can make any money writing these days: crime fiction. I write under a pseudonym.'

'Would I have heard of you?'

'I don't know – do you read that kind of thing?'

63

I sip the wondrous negroni. 'These days, I'm ashamed to say I don't read anything that's not connected with the business of finance.'

'Well I hope you'll find time to read some of this…'

She reaches for the file that's been sitting on the table next to her chair and takes out a sheaf of paper.

'And you'll be glad to know that it's very much connected with the business of finance.'

'Is that it? My ancestor's manuscript? It doesn't look very antiquarian.'

She smiles. 'It's a photocopy. The gentleman who's in possession of the manuscript thought you might like to browse through it before seeing the original.'

'To whet my appetite?'

'Of course.'

'And you've seen the original, Diana?'

'Oh, yes – *and* had it authenticated.'

'You think it's genuine.'

'It's certainly of the right vintage, early 18th century, and found here in Venice, miraculously. Given the rising damp, this place isn't kind to antique documents, as I've discovered in my dealings with them down the years. But then, I don't know why anyone at the time would have gone to the trouble of forging such a thing.'

She puts the paper back in the file and passes it to me. 'Anyway, Theo, have a look and decide whether you're interested. There's no obligation.'

I open the file and look at the top sheet. It's a decent copy but I can tell that the script will take some getting used to. It's not going to be an easy read.

'This may have to wait till I get back to London.'

'Of course. But if you're at all interested you should at least see the original before you go.'

I flick through the pages. 'Have *you* read it?'

'I have, and as a writer of crime fiction, I'm impressed. I can't say whether it's a true memoir or not, but it is a crime story of sorts - as well as quite a steamy love story.'

'Sex and money. Gets my vote.'

She laughs. 'Well, it *is* written by a man – although I think the most interesting characters in it are the women, as is so often the case. But then I would say that, wouldn't I?'

Then she's looking at her watch and apologising for having to go off to dinner – a long-standing date with an old friend – and for going in the opposite direction to Rezzonico, which means she won't be able to accompany me. Our date seems over almost as soon as it's begun.

'Take care, Theo,' she says, as I reluctantly take my leave of her cozy palazzo and head off into the gathering fog. I'm bearing my umbrella and the photocopy of John Law's memoir, which she has put in a plastic bag to protect it from that rising damp. I tell her I will contact her the next day.

I must admit that I would have liked her company as far as Rezzonico. In my tender state, I feel secure in it for some reason, even though she's the mystery woman of Venice – perhaps *because* she's the mystery woman of Venice.

Despite the negroni, the journey back to the hotel is more sure-footed; I'm familiar with the route and the water level has receded further while I've been at Diana Lennon's. Even so, the misty quaysides and bridges spook me somewhat. At one point, I have a classic horror moment straight out of the film *Don't Look Now*. I think I hear footsteps behind me, but looking back, see no one.

This doesn't stop the strong feeling of being watched, as if the ghost of John Law himself were stalking me. It's a feeling that almost tips me over into my black hole, rather than the canal, and initiates another panic attack. Somehow, I pull back from the edge, and it's with some relief that I reach the landing and the comforting presence of several other travellers, real Venetians, their feet clad in black plastic bags, their heads withdrawn tortoise-like into scarves and upturned collars. While I stand there self-consciously in my yellow boots and wait for a water taxi back to the hotel, I ponder Diana's notion that women are so often the most interesting characters and why that might be true.

Chapter 4

Venice, October 1728

    The laggard Scottish spring seem'd finally to have burst into life on that April evening. The birds were piping away and the air was almost balmy as my carriage swept into the grounds of the Duke of Argyll's grand house on the outskirts of Edinburgh. (It had the usual rugg'd quality of Scottish houses, but with a fashionable dash of Frenchification, I am glad to say.) At the prospect of rubbing shoulders with the bewigg'd and brocad'd of the City, I had elect'd to defy the dress convention a little and thus stand out in the crowd (although my six feet four inches always gave me that distinction, anyway). I went wigless, with my long black hair tied back behind, and was relatively plainly attir'd in a black velvet coat and linen shirt, the better to appear the honest tradesman, the opposite of a fop.

    At the time of this soirée, I had been back home in Scotland for only a few weeks, having narrowly escap'd the clutches of so-called English justice. My position, however, was far from secure. There was a danger that English justice wou'd follow me through the propos'd Act of Union – which was looking more and more likely, given the hopeless state of the Scottish economy and its dependence upon England. For my native land was in a sorrier state than France even. There was widespread poverty, little trade, and the currency had been almost clipp'd to extinction. (In many places, I had been told, the most reliable medium of exchange was the 'oat' – a decent bowl of porridge would buy you most things.) To help save Scotland from Union – and indirectly myself from the hangman – I had put together a financial proposal for a new paper currency. This was bas'd – rather ingeniously, I thought – not on metal, which was in short supply, but on something far more widely available: land.

    Having publish'd this proposal, I had begun to petition some of the most influential figures in the Edinburgh parliament. Unfortunately, mine was not the only scheme on offer. Within days, I had learnt of another, bas'd on metal and devised by Dr.Chamberlain, widely known for his financial schemes in England as well as Scotland. As is the way with parliaments, the rival factions were soon taking sides: that led by the Duke of Argyll and the Earl of Roxburghe support'd my proposal, while the so-called nationalist faction support'd Chamberlain. Argyll, a portly old political campaigner whom I regard'd as a true Scottish patriot, had been candid with me. He had warn'd that my scheme cou'd well be disadvantag'd by the 'chequer'd career of its author'. This was not help'd, he had add'd, by the fact that since I had been back in Edinburgh, I was rumour'd to have made frequent visits to a notorious private gaming room – which he knew to be true, because he was often there himself.

To help dispel this dark cloud hanging over my reputation, he had very kindly offer'd to arrange a series of meetings and soirées within the first few weeks of the scheme's publication, in order that I might promote it personally to various key members of the Parliament. At the first one of these, held at his home, the Duke had assur'd me that he wou'd muster members of both factions and that Sir William Gregg, the Crown agent, would also be present. Gregg was almost certainly in Scotland to prepare the way for Union and his support wou'd be essential to the acceptance of any financial scheme. At that point, I had no idea where his sympathies lay, or if indeed he had any, although I was soon to find out.

At first, I spoke with several Parliamentarians from both sides, all of whom were keener to learn about my narrow escape from the hangman and my success at the gaming table than how I propos'd to Supply the Nation with Money. One of them, my supporter, Roxburghe, point'd out Sir William across the other side of the room – a typical looking upper-class Englishman, whey-fac'd and chinless, in a large wig of grey curls. If it is possible to dislike someone on sight, then this was such an occasion. It was partly his air of smug condescension, partly because he seem'd to possess much of what I had been denied since becoming an escap'd criminal – the arrant self-assurance that goes with being a member of the English Establishment. Fortunately, I was distract'd from these depressing thoughts by seeing his wife for the first time. She was standing next to him and was one of the few women present that evening in Argyll's grand reception room

Roxburghe must have read my expression. 'That's Gregg's young wife, Lady Katherine,' he said in a hoarse whisper. 'As forthright and intelligent as she is eye-catching, I can assure you, having exchang'd views with her on several current political issues. The woman does not wait to be ask'd.'

She certainly was eye-catching, not so much pretty as handsome: flaxen-haired, with a tall statuesque figure, taller than her husband, I not'd, and much younger: he must have been twice her age, fifty to her twenty-five. Strangely, because such things had never perturb'd me before, I cring'd inwardly at the thought of their coupling. Her features were highly mobile; she gesticulat'd with her hands, drawing vivid shapes in the air, as she spoke, which she did a lot, not waiting demurely to be ask'd, like most women in society, but leading the discussion, asserting herself volubly. I was instantly impress'd - and we had yet to exchange a word.

'And what are her political views?' I ask'd, trying to sound as if it was of no concern.

Roxburghe smil'd mischievously. 'Ah yes, that's the first thing one wants to know about any woman – her political views...and her reading habits, of course. Well, she doesn't seem that given to the Union. She has a rather low opinion of Scotland, thinks it will become a burden. She also feels that government shou'd be more – what was the word? – 'representative' and that women shou'd play a more active role in it – but then she is descend'd from the same family as Anne Boleyn, apparently, so I can understand her objections to absolutism, especially the male variety. Anyway, she's extremely high born but penniless, which is probably why she's land'd up with Gregg.' And he laugh'd again. 'Come, Law, let's introduce you to the Crown agent and his charming consort, shall we?'

As expect'd, Gregg was extremely patronising in manner and wou'd have look'd down his nose at me, had I not been a good deal taller than he; it was obvious that he wou'd rather not engage with someone he consider'd an interloper. Lady Katherine, on the other hand, smil'd broadly; her green eyes sparkl'd, like the emeralds she wore at her neck, and she spoke in a rich, throaty voice: 'Ah, the infamous Mr.Law. How very tall you are. Stand up too straight, Sir, and you might brush the chandeliers.'

'That is why, Madam, I have dispens'd with a periwig for this evening,' I replied. 'I have little need to aggrandise myself further.' And I gave Gregg's enormous periwig a mock-admiring look.

'And why you have the appearance of a rakish highwayman,' she smil'd, cutting me down to size. 'I hope you do not come to rob us, Sir.'

'Only if charm and wit are thieves, Madam,' I said, and her smile became a loud chuckle. How uninhibit'd, I thought, how utterly adorable.

Roxburghe persever'd with Gregg. 'Mr. Law has propos'd a scheme to help save the Scottish economy, Sir William.'

Gregg condescend'd to smile. 'A daunting, if not overwhelming task, Mr. Law. Which of the schemes is it, pray? There seem to be several in circulation.'

'Two to be precise,' I said. 'Mine is the one based on land value.'

'Ah yes – land.' He survey'd the room as if it were a landscape, before meeting my eyes. 'A little homespun, from what I recall. Forgive me, Mr. Law, but I hear you know your way around the gaming rooms, as well as His Majesty's prisons. High finance, however, is another thing altogether, surely?'

'Oh, I don't know, one meets some of London's best financial minds in Newgate,' I replied to everyone's amusement. 'And as for gambling, the nation's economy can be look'd upon as a kind of game. If we make sure as many people as possible have a stake to play with, the final pot will be so much the greater.'

Gregg looked unimpress'd. 'An interesting notion, Mr. Law: to reduce our noble kingdom, in all its power and glory, in all its richness and diversity, to a gaming table. I see you are a man of high ideals. However, there are – how shall I say? – overarching political considerations here that preclude the adoption of certain financial policies.' He was referring, of course, to the likelihood of Union. 'If I were you I wou'd worry less about Scotland's future and more about your own.'

And with this less than veil'd legal threat, he turn'd away to Roxburghe and began discussing the negotiations that wou'd soon be taking place between London and Edinburgh. The conversation was over; the door had been shut in my face. And another was about to open. 'I have read your pamphlet, Mr. Law.' I turn'd to Lady Katherine, as if to the warm sun after a cold wind. 'And I think it very well argued and professional and not at all homespun.'

'Thank you, Madam.'

'It is, however, flaw'd in one important respect. I agree with what you say about the nature of money and its supply, although I must admit to not having thought of it in that way before. And I am sure that the issue of a paper currency will stimulate commerce, increase trade and benefit us all, as you claim. However, I cannot agree with your proposal as to the use of land as security.'

If before I had been more interest'd by Lady Katherine's person – her green eyes, her blond hair, her handsome form – I was now fully engag'd by what she was saying. 'And why is that?' I ask'd.

'Well, you seem to assume in your scheme that the value of land will remain stable.'

'And so it will...for the most part,' I simper'd.

'But how so? In being us'd as security, it will naturally become more valuable and will therefore attract more investment, probably more than any other commodity. There will be speculation in land, which will in turn undermine your currency.' I went to speak, but she continued. 'Moreover, you treat land as a kind of constant, as if it were something almost abstract. But as someone who was brought up on it and whose family has owned great tracts of it for generations, I can tell you that it comes in many forms, some productive, some barren, some just to look at, and therefore its value varies considerably. Another destabilising factor for a currency, don't you think, Mr. Law?'

I was speechless at first and when I did finally say something, it was to ask for more of her views on the matter. 'Then...what wou'd you have us do, Madam, stick with metal and all its evident shortcomings? Or try tulips, like the Dutch?'

Again, her liberating laugh. 'Oh, I don't think so, Mr. Law, tulips are better in vases than banks and I agree entirely with your views on gold.' She touch'd the gold of her necklace. 'Much as I cherish it, I understand how its scarcity will limit the growth of trade and the spread of wealth. No, if a paper currency needs security, then it must be somehow' – and here she made a gesture with her hands, drawing something large and round in the air – 'grander than land and even more attractive than gold. It must have infinite potential to grow in value. Something big enough for a nation to invest with its hopes and dreams – as well as its money.'

'Hopes and dreams, Madam?'

'Yes.'

'But hopes and dreams are hardly solid enough to rest a nation's money on, surely? What kind wou'd they be?' I ask'd.

'How shou'd I know, Mr. Law? I'm not school'd in these matters. That's for an expert in the workings of money such as you to answer. But I will ponder the question and if I do have an answer, I will let you know...'

Unfortunately, at that point Argyll and several others join'd us. Lady Katherine immediately turn'd to talk to them and we were unable to resume our conversation that evening. I was reeling, breathless and had trouble speaking about my scheme or any other subject for the rest of the gathering. Roxburghe ask'd if I was all right. I had gone rather pale, he said – had Gregg's comments upset me? I made light of it and said that the English nobility always had a somewhat queasy effect on me.

But in truth I was in turmoil. It was as if I had been suddenly set adrift upon a wild sea, without charts or instruments. Absolutely certain of my bearings one moment, I was blown off course the next and sure of nothing, save this: Lady Katherine Gregg had not only demolish'd my theory, she had stolen my heart – and I wou'd either have it back or I wou'd have her.

*

Back at the hotel, I'm torn between starting to read Law's manuscript, dealing with various pressing business matters or just carrying on drinking negronis. Sad to say, I take the business option. I order room service and log on to the hyper-secure website I use for most of my business transactions.

Just as there are at least two banking systems – the regulated and the not-so-regulated – so, if you're prepared to pay a not-so-small fortune to the right digital wizard, there are different types of internets. One of them, the deeper or 'dark' one, flies well below the radar of official surveillance. It's a place where the most confidential and illicit of affairs can be safely transacted and where you can make contact with those who should not be contacted too frequently i.e. my investors. We have a minimal on-line relationship and as much as I can, I avoid meeting them in the flesh, which is fine. The less we know about each other, outside a strictly professional context, the safer it is for everyone.

Because – how can I put this? And perhaps you've already guessed it – I'm one of the world's most successful money launderers. Which is to say that I do it on a grand scale for some of the world's wealthiest business people. (Law enforcement agencies might refer to them in less flattering terms.) Billions of dollars of dirty money – the proceeds from crime and corruption, personal and corporate – flows around the world every day, probably more than the cleaner kind. It's 'washed' by people like myself through a network of bank accounts and off-shore tax havens that help it to find its way back into the mainstream banking systems, where it can be spent more openly.

Of course, these services do not come cheap. I may only charge a small percentage of the money I launder, but as the sums involved are vast this amounts to a sizeable sum in itself. Add to this a percentage of any profits that the money makes when legitimately invested, using the funds and the complex web of accounts I've created, and you're looking at a considerable income – not quite as large as most of my clients, perhaps, but serious enough.

Only I and one other member of my team know the exact route any particular illicit flow of money takes, and I do my best to keep that information stored in my head rather than on any hard drive. To say it's a thriving business is an understatement; to call it high risk is a euphemism. It's actually a dangerous game, and one that I could only have started playing in an almost unconscious way, incrementally, little by little, like tartar building upon a tooth, until it became too attached to me – and I to it – to fall away.

For now I am triangulated. The first of the three co-ordinates is my clients. There's no doubt that most of them suffer – and profit – from a deficit of decency, a lack of common humanity. I'd rather not know how they amass their enormous wealth, how they add all those zeros to the other zeros, but I've occasionally been given some strong clues. I read between the lines, put two and two together and, not surprisingly, none have so far turned out to be social workers or teach kindergarten. (Certainly not the Russians – *especially* not the Russians.) It is, therefore, not for business reasons alone that I have no wish to fall out with them.

Then there are the authorities – I've already mentioned them – the financial regulators and enforcers who represent hard-pressed governments eager to get their hands on these illegal funds and boost their revenues. But it's hardly that straightforward. Their attitude is two-faced, hypocritical. They preside at arm's length over the tax havens that shield the illicit money and their super-rich benefit from this enormous flow of capital. For fear of it going elsewhere, nobody dares stand in the way of big money these days, no matter how questionable its source. Money speaks all languages, of course, but more than ever it talks dirty.

On the other hand, they can't be seen to allow such criminal activity to take place on their own turf, among their own plebs. They make a half-hearted effort to pursue the major launderers and tax dodgers to extinction, and their measures appear to grow ever more draconian. Even though we all know it's a charade, a game of make-believe, and even though they're always a few steps behind, the smallest slip can have the anti-money laundering boys breathing down your neck and in their bumbling manner destroying the web you've so carefully spun over the years.

The final co-ordinate is my legitimate business, if anything to do with finance can be said to be legitimate: investment banking, asset management – high risk enough in itself if it is to yield the kind of returns demanded by my clients. It's a truism, I know, but in my experience the more people have, the more they want, and the less tolerant they are of those who fail to deliver it.

Which brings me on to *me*, he who sits in the middle of this unholy trinity. (Or is it a three-ringed circus, with me acting as ringmaster?) As well as being exhilarating and richly rewarding, it's also terrifying to be at the centre of so many moving parts. Because I glory in success, I live in abject fear of failure. No wonder that without my anti-depressants, I have a tendency to fall into black holes and become totally dysfunctional.

But enough of that for now – here I am running on alarmingly, revealing all my trade secrets, when I should be getting on with the trade itself. I log onto the site to answer various emails from the London office, but more importantly to see if there's been a reply to my messages regarding the Vatican proposal. Usually with an opportunity to move such a large amount of money, the response is fairly instant. One of the clients I've ear-marked for this deal was pressing me to shift tens of millions of roubles only weeks ago, but now there's a worrying silence. Why isn't he biting my hand off?

I feel somewhat uneasy about it – more of my resurgent paranoia, I assume, because there's probably an innocent explanation. I can easily approach another major player, but before I do, I decide to send a follow up message, stressing the urgency of the situation.

I'm just about to do this when there's a knock on the door – room service. Until now, I've forgotten how hungry I am, despite the *chichetti* I've consumed with Diana Leonard. I open the door to find that it's not room service at all – or at least not the kind I was expecting. It's a beaming Joanna, with her trademark mane of black corkscrew curls and porcelain complexion. She's still in her business suit, her coat is over one arm and the other holds her weekend bag.

'I raced to get a late flight – thought I'd surprise you with your Italian mistress.'

'You *are* my Italian mistress…'

Before I can throw my arms around her, smother her with kisses and sweep her off to bed, I notice the waiter behind with a trolley carrying my dinner. She gestures at the ice bucket from which an uncorked bottle I didn't order rises with priapic grace. 'I added some bubbly to the menu,' she giggles. Pop!

*

Such a thing had never happen'd to me before. I had reach'd the mature age of 35 years and never felt this way about any woman. Of course, I had enjoy'd the chase as much as any hound, but I always knew full well that once the quarry was caught I wou'd quickly lose interest. Women for me were not the ultimate destination of the journey, merely a bed for the night at some hostelry along the way. I had avoid'd the constraints of marriage, not even pursuing it for reasons of social advancement, and scoff'd at soft notions of 'romantic love', of being 'in love' or 'love sick', never thinking of the latter in any literal sense, until then. Before, no matter what walls had surround'd me, my mind at least had always been free to roam where it pleas'd, to ponder anything that took its fancy. But after that first encounter, whatever I did, wherever I went, I cou'd think of nothing but her; of how I might possess her and be with her forever – Katherine Gregg, another man's wife. It was indeed a sickness and one for which there seem'd no immediate cure.

My grand financial schemes – the castles in the air I had work'd so hard to construct, without too much hope, I admit, of seeing them built in the real world – were suddenly no refuge. She had shown them to be worthless, without substance and all with such effortless grace and intelligence. If I thought of them, I thought of her, whilst on another level I suffer'd the torment of frustrat'd desire for her person, her body, as well as for the fiery opal that I knew to be her mind.

'Fiery opal'? Do I sound ridiculous? Certainly I do, yet even after Beau's death and during my time in Newgate, I had not experienc'd such inner turmoil. I became indifferent to the parliamentary debates that took place and the arguments over

the two different fiancial schemes, in which before I wou'd have been an eager participant. Now it all seem'd petty and futile. The only palliative I could think of was to try to immerse myself in the cards and dice, but even that was fraught. If anything need'd a clear head, it was the gaming table. Yet I was constantly distract'd from my calculations and start'd losing the money I had won since my return to Edinburgh.

On one such occasion, two weeks later, only Argyll and myself remain'd at the table. He had won three games in a row and his grizzl'd, ruddy face had taken on distinctly self-satisfied glow. Even so, I guess'd there was also something other than cards on his mind that evening.

'I thought you shou'd know in advance,' he said eventually in his broad accent, 'Gregg's taking the leaders of the Parliament, including Roxburghe and myself down to London. It's a delegation, as he put it, to explore all the issues surrounding the question of Union.'

'So the deed has been done,' I replied.

He look'd uncomfortable. 'Law, you're suspicious by nature - it's by no means a foregone conclusion, I can assure you...'

I shrugg'd. What did it matter? My scheme was unlikely to be adopt'd and I wou'd have left Scotland soon enough. 'I hope he'll also be taking that insufferable Lady Katherine with him,' I said, feeling better for the mere mention of her name (that is how sick I was) and at the same time hoping that she wou'd be put beyond my reach.

'I didn't realise she'd upset you so much that evening.' He was reliev'd to get off the subject of the Union. 'Opinionated lass, isn't she? A real beauty though...' He grew wistful at the thought before continuing: 'No, no, she'll stay here I'm sure. Apparently, she hates travelling and this will be a short visit. We shou'd return within days.'

'And announce the Union.'

He look'd at his freshly dealt cards. 'The truth is that despite all the huffing and puffing' – the debate over mine and Chamberlain's schemes, he meant – 'it has been inevitable ever since the failure of the Americas' expedition.' He was referring to the loss of 2000 colonists and £400,000 – over half the country's capital – on a botch'd attempt to establish a Scottish

76

trading colony in Central America. 'People had enormous faith, as well as large investments in that venture and it turn'd out to be little more than an illusion.' He smil'd to himself. 'The whole notion that a bunch of mad, kilt-wearing Scots could forge a major trading route across the Isthmus, defeating Indians, Spaniards and deadly diseases on the way, now seems absurd. But at the time, we all believ'd it; all our hopes and dreams were pinn'd on it...'

'Hopes and dreams' – the very phrase Katherine had us'd, the gauntlet she'd thrown down, which I seem'd incapable of picking up. I had no answer to her question and yet there was no way I cou'd stop thinking of her. 'But if it had work'd,' I said.

'If it had work'd' – Argyll puff'd himself up, a proud Scot – 'it cou'd have mark'd the beginning of a trading empire to rival that of the English, the French and even the Dutch. Scotland wou'd have been rich – and so wou'd I.'

'It cou'd also have avoid'd the Union.'

'Yes...perhaps,' he mutter'd. 'Now, it's your bid, Law. Let's see if Lady Luck has completely desert'd you this evening, shall we?'

But I was less interest'd in Lady Luck than Lady Katherine. Argyll had given me hope that I might be able to see her alone in Edinburgh. I was so excit'd and distract'd by the whole prospect that I lost three more games before retiring for the night, leaving Argyll to count his considerable winnings. On balance, I think he had earnt them.

I spent the next few days feverishly marking time until Sir William depart'd for London, when I wou'd be able to pay Lady Katherine an impromptu visit. Looking back, I realise that I act'd like some ravening animal tracking its prey, calculating each move with instinctive cunning. My only defence was that I was driven temporarily insane by my 'sickness' and was compell'd to act as I did. In some way, I desperately hop'd that simply by seeing her again and being able to finish our conversation I wou'd be heal'd. Deep down, however, I knew this was impossible: I desir'd Katherine in a way I had not desir'd any woman and my only real hope lay not in any immediate cure, but in her reciprocating my passion.

Gregg had taken a grand house in Princes Street for the duration of his stay in Edinburgh, which was where I call'd on a stormy Friday afternoon in late April. The day before, he and the delegation had left for London, on the pretext of putting Scotland's case for independence to the English government – or at least that was their public utterance. Privately many knew the likely outcome of the meeting and that it wou'd create widespread unrest. The overwhelming majority of the Scottish people was against a legal Union with England and already regard'd the sharing of a monarch as an unnatural relationship for natural enemies.

I was let in by a maidservant, who show'd me to a well-appoint'd drawing room, with a large portrait of Sir William on one wall; he was standing proudly before a grand country house accompanied by two sleek greyhounds. (The fact that he had bother'd to transport the picture from London said much about the Crown Agent, yet Katherine must surely have found this combination of power, money and vanity highly attractive – or was it simply de rigueur for someone of her class?)

Within minutes, she appear'd. She look'd as handsome and elegant as I remember'd. She was dress'd in a rose-pink silk gown and was bare shoulder'd; her blonde hair was pinn'd up with diamond-studd'd clasps.

'Mr. Law – what a nice surprise! But I'm afraid my husband left for London yesterday.' She seem'd friendly enough, as she had been that evening at Argyll's. I was encourag'd.

'Madam, it's not your husband I've come to see - it's you. It may be somewhat importunate of me, but I was keen to know if you'd arriv'd at an answer to that question you rais'd at the soiree.'

'What question was that, Mr. Law?'

'The question of finding something big enough in which to invest a nation's – what was it you said? – hopes and dreams – yes, that was it. I must confess, I have wrack'd my brains and can think of nothing...'

She motion'd me to sit in a large armchair on one side of the grand mantel, where a fire burn'd brightly, while she settl'd on a finely upholster'd sofa on the other. How many times at the gaming table had I need'd to maintain an outward appearance of calm, while being barely able to contain the excitement within? Now, more than ever, this skill was essential.

'Ah yes – this is to do with how to ensure that a paper currency retains its value – shou'd there ever be a paper currency, of course.'

'Indeed. You suggest'd quite rightly that I dispense with the notion of land and pursue that of...something else, something grander...'

'Oh Mr. Law, I have put you to a lot of trouble, haven't I? I do apologise.'

'Don't apologise, Lady Gregg. I'm very grateful to you for taking the time to speak to me.'

She smil'd - was it genuinely fond or simply patronising? 'It's no great hardship, Sir, I can assure you. But more to the point, I think I do have an answer.'

'My God! I mean...do you?'

She arch'd an eyebrow. 'Does that surprise you, Mr. Law? That I, a mere woman, shou'd have an answer to such a serious question?'

If I'd been truthful and said yes, I sens'd it wou'd have got me nowhere except out the way I had come. So I said: 'I'm reliev'd that someone has an answer, no matter what their sex, Madam.'

Both eyebrows now form'd arches; she was doubly sceptical. 'Of course, it may not please you, Sir, but it's my best shot, as they say.'

'I'm sure it's a...perfect shot...' I think I was rapidly losing control of my tongue and my mouth had become unnaturally dry. Had this been a card game, I wou'd have been suffering untold losses.

'Well, I probably don't need to explain this to you of all people, but this is my reasoning, such as it is. We think of money in many strange ways, but it seems to me that the wealth of a nation is for the most part found'd upon how much it trades – not how much gold or land it has. That is why, for instance – and I'm sure you know – despite being small, Holland is so much wealthier than Spain. England has also learnt this to its great benefit, but Scotland I fear has understood it too late. Now, there is one place, I believe, where

trade will grow more quickly in the future than anywhere else, as colonists pour into it at an ever-increasing rate – and that is America. The prospect of riches to be found and trad'd primarily in America can become the security for your new currency…'

There was what seem'd an interminable silence while I took in both the answer and the manner of its delivery, which had all the facility and ease of drawing breath.

Extraordinary, I thought, an idea as brilliant as it is revolutionary. Sell shares in the future prosperity of the Americas…This will support the currency…which in turn will stimulate trade and commerce…which in turn will create prosperity…and so on – a most virtuous circle. The unbound'd promise of the future will secure the bounty of the present. Something in which people can invest their hopes and dreams, indeed, just as she had said. She was a genius. As I wou'd tell her.

'Madam, it's not an answer…'

'Oh, I am so sorry, Mr. Law…'

'It's the answer, the only answer. You're a wonder, an utter genius.'

'Oh, I doubt that very much, Sir.'

On impulse, I went across to the sofa and sat down next to her. Our eyes met instantly and there was a moment of wordless intimacy between us.

'Do you know what this means, Lady Gregg?'

'Not entirely, Mr. Law, no.'

'You have given me the keys to the Kingdom of Heaven. You have unlock'd the system that will enable me to fulfil my every ambition, Madam.'

'Well, I'm very pleased to hear it…'

'Of course, there is much to be done. There is still the small matter of persuading a government of the benefits of that system, which can only be implement'd on a national scale. In England I am an outlaw and Scotland will soon be England, as it were.' *At this she smil'd and her green eyes sparkl'd.*

'Holland has no real need of my help; the Austro-Hungarian and Italian states have no overseas interests, to speak of; Spain

is on the wane, far too deeply entrenched in Catholicism and gold. That leaves only one possibility – France.'

'France? You think the Sun King wou'd sponsor such a scheme?'

'The Setting Sun King' – again, the grin – 'even Louis XIV will not live forever and will probably die much sooner. France is competing with England for control of North America but is in desperate financial straits due to Louis' extravagance, and his finance ministers are always trying some new misguid'd scheme to raise money. Ergo, France it must be. However, there is something else I require from you without which none of this can succeed.'

Our eyes embrac'd once more; her shining expression cloud'd over. 'What more do you need, Sir? As you said, I've already given you the keys to your future.'

'I need you, Madam – as my partner in this venture.'

She was adorable in her confusion. 'Me? A partner? In a business sense, you mean? Sir, if you're looking for an investor, I must tell you I have very little capital of my...'

'In every sense – and I have no need of your money, Madam. I have ample sums for us both, and there will be much, much more, I can assure you.'

She grew stern. 'Mr. Law – what <u>exactly</u> do you want?'

'I want us to be lovers. I want you to leave your husband and come away with me.'

*

I first met Jo during the course of an unpleasant court case I was involved in. As it happened, she was the only pleasant thing to come out of it. I was being sued by an ex-client – another Russian – for withholding profits on one of his investments. She was in the team of corporate lawyers who were representing him. We caught each other's eye across the courtroom on the first day, but it never occurred to me that it would go any further than casual eye contact.

To be honest, I was too preoccupied with the legal proceedings, even if I *was* trying to give off an air of blithe indifference. (By contrast, my opponent sat looking like he'd spent all night sucking on a lemon and then had to eat it for breakfast.) His claims were mostly groundless and I could only assume he was flexing some of his mafia muscle to show me who was boss. However, it didn't stop him threatening me with all sorts of dire revelations about my business if I didn't pay him an outrageous sum of money in compensation. It was a form of blackmail, of course, but I knew it was a bluff; he had as much to lose by any revelations as I did, a fact that I made very plain in our off-the-record conversation before the trial. It was what in the end led us to an out-of-court settlement, negotiated in part by Jo, in which I paid him a whole lot less than he was suing me for. I thought it was a bargain, given the money I'd made out of him over the years. It was also a valuable lesson in client management - i.e. which ones to avoid - and it did mean I got to meet Jo.

She called me a couple of weeks later to ask if I would consider being represented by her firm in the future, should the need arise. (She obviously thought it would - perhaps she'd discovered the true nature of my business, although she hasn't said as much.) A week later we met to discuss this arrangement. She was even smarter and more attractive than I'd thought, the product of an expensive upbringing and education. Her recently deceased father had been an executive with a big oil company, so she'd done spells at various international schools and had the hybrid accent and polished persona to match. She herself said she felt like she was from everywhere and nowhere.

We had dinner and landed up having sex as well. It was my first time for a couple of years and all the more exhilarating for that – and I hadn't even stopped taking the anti-depressants by then. It probably compromised any chance of her representing me, but it didn't matter. I decided I'd rather have her as a lover than a lawyer – and see her, as I do now, sleeping peacefully next to me in this luxury hotel in Venice.

What a wonderful thing sex is, truly a gift of the gods. This is especially so when it's with someone you actually like and may even be falling in love with (oh, yes, and is a good few years younger than you). From the moment Jo appeared at the door all my worries were forgotten. I didn't send my email; I could think of nothing but wanting to be inside her. Dinner went uneaten; we only managed one glass of champagne, before we threw ourselves into some vigorous sex, followed by a dead sleep.

But marvellous as this was, this short-circuiting of the mind, I have now woken in a panic in the middle of the night and I'm not sure why. A noise in the hotel? Something outside on the quay or canal? The need to urinate? No.

Now, I look at this young woman, this angel who is heaven to have and to hold, and I feel like hell. I feel unworthy of her, guilty for laying my grubby paws on her, as if I'd sullied her in some way or forced myself upon her.

I'm so disturbed I have to get up. I go to the window, inch back the heavy brocade curtain, and peak out at the dark, shimmering surface of the canal. All is bleary, sub-aquatic. There's a heavy storm raging and great gusts of wind blow waves of canal water over the quayside and make grape shot of the rain against the window. (Is this what's woken me?) I think of how the sirens will be sounding again in the morning, warning of the perils of *acqua alta.*

I feel scared – of what? Of the flooding? Surely not. I've no clear idea what has spooked me, only a sense of vague foreboding; a sense that some kind of invisible presence has whispered in my ear and dragged me out of blissful sleep into this state of deep depression. It feels as if Jo and I are not the only people in the room, as if there's a third party, an intruder. But there isn't, is there? Or is there? I stand naked, half looking out of the window, half around at the room – at what? At something in the shadows, some faint, almost imperceptible movement or tremor in the air. I was hot when I woke and reeked wonderfully of our love-making. Now I'm cold and starting to shiver and I can smell something else, like rotting flesh, a waft of putrescence. Something or someone is moving towards me, I'm sure of it, but I can't see it. If I could move, I'd switch on a light and banish it, burn it out. Instead, I glimpse what I think is the shape of a head and my sense of panic that has curdled to fear now becomes out-and-out terror. I shrink away and sink slowly to the floor, so that my back presses against the curtains and my naked backside and balls rest disconcertingly on the carpet's thick pile. I put my face in my hands – I don't want to see whatever it is; if I do, I'll die. I let out a loud wail like I'm the siren for *acqua alta.*

*

For a woman in deep shock, Katherine Gregg certainly manag'd to retain her poise as she ask'd me to leave. She said nothing further and wou'd not even look at me. All I cou'd do was ask her to think about what I had said and to contact me. 'Please…I will be at my home in Lauriston.' Sir William seem'd to gaze down even more smugly as I was brusquely dismiss'd.

The next few days prov'd agonising. No news from London, no news from Katherine (why did I think there wou'd be?), no visits to the gaming room. On the fifth day of this purgatory the weather turn'd fairer, and I walk'd by the murky Forth, trying to contemplate my future. I wou'd not wait for the news from London, but wou'd leave Scotland within days and settle for a while in Rotterdam, where I had some business interests and the gaming was tolerable. From there, I wou'd consider the situation in France and work out how best to approach the French government with our – pray that it be <u>our</u>! – financial scheme.

Dusk fell and the lamps were lit; the evening grew chilly. Light from the fire danc'd on the far wall, as I sat writing in my study, frantically revising and reformulating the proposal document in an attempt to banish thoughts of Katherine. But how foolish was that? It was <u>her</u> proposal and so it only remind'd me more of her. My passion for my work and for her had merg'd, become one, and I felt I might collapse under their combin'd weight. Not even the pleasures of gaming cou'd save me now.

I heard the carriage draw up, and moments later the housekeeper knock'd at my door saying there was a young woman come to see me; she had not given her name. Having follow'd from the front hall, Katherine was there behind her.

Then she was in the room and everything took on the quality of a dream, almost like that of those ghostly apparitions I had witness'd, only far from chilling, quite the reverse.

84

We sat down opposite each other. She had remov'd her topcoat and wore a deep blue velvet gown, low cut and button'd at the front to the waist, where it open'd to reveal a fine lace skirt. She look'd flush'd and angry; I was sure she had been drinking. I went to speak, but she told me to say nothing; she had heard enough from me for now. She hat'd, she said, the presumption of most men that only they had anything worth saying – while women were only there to listen and applaud.

What was more, she hat'd my presumption that she was some commodity or a piece of property that cou'd be trad'd or acquir'd, if the price was right and the quality unsullied.

I protest'd that nothing was further from my mind - had I not us'd the term 'partner' in relation to...? But again she silenc'd me.

Most of all, she said, she hat'd herself, for being attract'd to someone who in many ways epitomis'd all the worst male traits. Vain, arrogant, selfish, putting their own interests before those of all others, especially if those others are women...

I thought she meant Sir William, but I was quickly disabus'd. 'Yet so powerful is the attraction between us, Mr. Law, that it appears I'm willing to risk everything to see you again...'

She got up and mov'd across to me. I thought she wou'd hit me, but instead she bent over me and press'd her lips - they burnt like fire - firmly against mine. I was sitting in an old but sturdy upright chair and as we went on kissing, she rais'd her skirts so as to sit astride me.

For all my own carnal desires and designs upon her, there was no doubt who perform'd the physical seduction. She unbutton'd my shirt, kiss'd my neck and chest. She reach'd down, deftly releas'd my swollen member and guid'd it into herself, the softest, warmest of vessels.

She stay'd for another two hours, in which time we retir'd to my bed and continued our love-making until our physical passion was spent. But it was she who seem'd to need to spend that passion all the more and in her frantic search for release, she appear'd heedless of whether she land'd up with child. When I rais'd the issue, so to speak, she said that as long as she was with Sir William it was the only way she <u>wou'd</u> land up with child.

'Don't worry, Mr. Law, seeing as he only likes women in so far as they have something in common with young boys, he'd be extremely reliev'd to be getting an heir. He wou'd never deny it was his own...'

This begg'd so many questions that all I cou'd say was: 'Please, why don't you call me John and I will call you Katherine. It seems only appropriate in the circumstances.'

She lay back amidst the hills of pillows and linen, smiling with satisfaction. Her hair was a golden halo; candlelight play'd across the satin sheen of her flesh. It was tempting to see her as some Botticelli Venus – and perhaps I did at first, but not for long.

'Come here, John...' When she pull'd me towards her again, this time it was to talk.

During that first brief encounter, I was not able to see the full picture of Lady Katherine Gregg, but what I did see was enough to realise that she was much more than a mere object of desire. For the first time in my life, I was coupling with a woman who was not simply a conduit of my lust, a servant of my pleasure, but a person in her own right. This may be no revelation for some, but for me, and I suspect many of my sex, it comes as a shock to look past the pretty (or plain) face, the shapely (or not so shapely) body and see someone who cou'd be a friend as well as a lover, who inspires trust as well as lust. This is not so much about seeing the flaws in the picture – the moles, the spots, the blemishes – as well as the line of beauty; it is about seeing past the picture entirely to the character beneath.

I learnt several important things about her that evening. As reput'd, she was indeed high born – from a branch of the Howard family, on Anne Boleyn's mother's side. Unfortunately, the family money had been squander'd through mismanagement of the estates, all mortgag'd to the hilt, and a father who was too fond of cards and claret, losing heavily at the former as a result of an excess of the latter.

Before long, there was a pressing need to marry Katherine off to a wealthy suitor and who better than a successful merchant, keen to buy his way into the nobility. Arise Sir William, leather magnate, supplier of half the tack and saddles *in England, pursuing an impoverish'd blue-blood, with little alternative but to put herself up for sale to the highest bidder, as if she were a thoroughbred filly. She had sacrific'd herself on the altar of her family's solvency and as a result – the luck of the draw, she said - she had land'd up in a loveless, childless marriage to an old tyrant who preferr'd social climbing to sexual congress (with women at least).*

'Is it any wonder that I embrace every radical cause, especially regarding women, and lend support to every underdog who comes within stroking distance?'

I imitat'd a bark. 'Ruff-ruff!'

'You're hardly an underdog, John.' But she strok'd me, nonetheless, as she threw back her head and laugh'd her intoxicating laugh.

'Nor are you, Katherine. It's time you took matters into your own hands.'

'Ah, and I have' – and she reach'd down and caress'd my dormant cock, making me groan with pleasure. 'But I suppose what you mean is run away with you to a new life of adventure in France. You, with whom I have been acquaint'd for all of a week. A man of dubious reputation – a gambler, an outlaw, a dabbler in finance and a womaniser, I'm sure – not that I'm inviting you to grace me with the detail, John Law. Do I need go on?'

'No. I am all of those things. But I am also planning a very serious business venture, in which I want you to be my partner, *not – how did you refer to it earlier? – a piece of property. I will draw up all the contracts that will guarantee your equal rights and interests in the business. For you, as a woman, it will be a far better contract than any marriage.'*

'I am pleas'd to hear it. One marriage has already been one too many for me.'

What else did I learn about Katherine that evening? That she knew how to laugh, that she had a capacity for happiness, that she was the equal, nay, the superior of any man – if not de jure, certainly de facto; that she was a passionate lover and – most significantly for me – that she was courageous – that she knew what she want'd and was not afraid to take it.

87

As she went to take her leave, she kiss'd me several times with lips that were even hotter than when she'd arriv'd, draining me of every last drop of passion.

'So that means you'll come with me?' I manag'd, having caught my breath.

'John, wou'd you enter into partnership with anyone who was rash and impetuous enough to give you an answer right now, when her whole body yearns for more of you? When I have finish'd reading a book, no matter how absorb'd in it I have been, how thrill'd and enthrall'd, I set it aside and inwardly digest it. Only then, when I've ponder'd it for a while, do I know if its quality is ephemeral, a passing fancy, or whether it has touch'd something deeper inside me; whether it has lasting value. When I have an answer – a far more important answer for me than how one might secure a paper currency – I will contact you...'

*

Jo is up out of bed and next to me, speaking into my ear. Her tone is comforting but has an edge, so that it cuts through my wailing and leaves me in no doubt that I need to snap out of my hysteria.

'Theo, *wake up*...it's all right. Everything's all right...'

And maybe I do wake up. Maybe I've been asleep and it's all been a bad dream – my getting up, going to the window and seeing whatever it was I saw or thought I saw.

She is half-crouching, half-kneeling next to me, pressing her naked body against mine, trying to prise my hands away from my face, to hug me, cradle me in her arms. I resist her at first, but then I breathe heavily as I decompress and submit to her ministrations. My face is wet with tears, I realise.

'You frightened the life out of me. What was it?'

I answer her question with another. 'Is it raining?' Surely the water has swept over the quayside and is creeping up the wall of the hotel by now.

'Is it what?'

'Raining. Look out of the window.'

88

After some hesitation, she stands, pulls back the curtain. Not water but daylight floods in, highlighting her nakedness. I look up at it: the white flesh, the dark mound, the underside of her perfect breasts. It's obviously later than I thought, not the middle of the night. How long have I sat here, delirious?

'There's a bright blue sky out there – one of the best views in the world.' She looks down, smiles at me. 'Does that help?'

'I'm not sure. I thought there was a terrible storm. Maybe there was.'

'Is that what upset you?'

I don't answer, can't answer – it's far too complicated. She suddenly looks concerned again. 'Is it me?' she asks. 'Am I the problem?'

I reach up, grab her hand and pull her back down to me, kissing her lips as if they're sustenance. 'Why are you saying that? Of course it's not you.'

I look across at the bed. Suddenly I want her again. Still holding her hand, I get up and lead her back over to the bed. We lie down, embrace and she immediately straddles me, as if she's keen to provide some form of therapy, even this most basic kind.

As she starts gently riding me, she gives me a saucy smile: 'Well, there's nothing wrong with this part of you...'

I smile too, but minutes later I lose it again. The monkey mind, silenced by my urge to have her, starts to chatter. Passion gives way to anxiety. I tell myself that this is nothing more than some kind of pity-fuck on her part. She knows what I know: that I'm hopeless, pathetic, past it. And anyway, I can't do this when someone else is watching – and I'm convinced someone *is* watching.

I shrink back to nothing and she has nothing to move upon. She stops, flops forward on to me, as I have flopped, her shock of hair spread around my head, her cheek against mine.

'I'm sorry,' I say. 'I just...'

'It's okay, Theo, you don't have to tell me what's going on.'

'I really don't *know* what's going on, Jo. But I think someone - or something – is trying to tell me...'

*

89

I wou'd of course have been only too pleas'd to give Katherine as much time as she need'd to make her decision. However, the pace of other events quicken'd more than I had anticipat'd. The next day news arriv'd from London, ahead of the returning delegation: Scotland was to go into Union 'within a week'. As it turn'd out, economic realities had play'd a part here too and not just because of the country's parlous finances. The rumour was that Argyll, Roxburghe, Hamilton and the others had been assur'd by the English that one of the financial benefits of Union wou'd be large back payments to the Parliament (i.e. its Leaders) for 'administrative duties in the service of the Crown'. In other words, despite all the fine words, my noble colleagues had sold out.

Immediately upon the news of Union, the streets erupt'd in protest. There were riots throughout Edinburgh and a host of heavily arm'd Redcoats descend'd on the city from the garrison, cracking skulls as they went. Alas, I cou'd not get to see Katherine before her husband's return and with Union imminent, I was forc'd to hasten arrangements for my immediate departure. I only just had time for a last visit to the gaming room, partly to hear Argyll and Roxburghe's stories and partly to top up my purse. In the heroic language of those who have surviv'd mortal combat, I was told that given the economic circumstances, the delegation had had very little choice but to submit to the wishes of the English government and had salvag'd what they cou'd for Scotland – and themselves.

There was condolence all round for the rejection of my scheme, which was deem'd 'chimerical' by the Chancellor. (Roxburghe jok'd that they wou'd have object'd to this description if anyone had known what the old boy meant!) Following this entertainment, we play'd Hazard and in one session, during which my mind seem'd astonishingly sharp and clear, I won over £2000 – a tidy sum, but a relatively small proportion of their ill-gotten gains from London. By then, I am sure that most of my Scottish friends were heartily glad to see the back of me.

The day before I was due to leave, I still had not heard from Katherine. I wrote to her, begging her to join me immediately at

Lauriston, and if not there, later at an address in Rotterdam. I sent her full details of the itinerary and more than enough money in the form of gold sovereigns and Dutch bonds.

By then, I was so distraught I had convinc'd myself that she wou'd not be coming with me. In fact, I had even decid'd that our liaison had merely been a ruse on her part to provide William Gregg with an heir. My stomach churn'd with anxiety; I cou'd neither sleep nor eat.

At first light, I rode to the coast and from there took a boat to Rotterdam, where I set up in some comfortable lodgings not far from the port. Three days of the deepest gloom and depression went by, match'd by the sullen Dutch skies. On the fourth day I went to a coffee house at midday and return'd a few hours later, feeling even more despondent. My heart all but stopp'd when I heard a woman's voice call out from the bedroom – 'John Law!' – and I rush'd in to find Katherine, sitting up in the bed, wearing only the scantest of underclothes. She had brib'd the maid to let her in, she said, so that she cou'd be there to welcome me – was that not resourceful?

I agreed it was, but before another word was spoken, we kiss'd and embrac'd and made love. Meanwhile, a soft purple twilight descend'd. I eventually got up and stood by the window, looking out upon a world that seem'd as right and replete as a Flemish still life. I was mov'd to address Sir William Gregg loudly across the sea: 'You, Sir Crown Agent, can keep Scotland – and I will keep your wife!'

Katherine spoke to me from the bed, her voice soft and sleepy. 'I'll be <u>kept</u> by no man, John Law. We are business partners, remember – or was that just a ploy to seduce me?'

A few moments later I went back to the bed. 'I think it's fair to say that you seduc'd <u>me</u>, Katherine Gregg...'

But she did not hear me. She had already fallen asleep.

Chapter 5

Venice, October 1728

Yesterday I was shock'd to discover how rapidly my health is declining. I took a short trip down the Grand Canal to visit a friend, the Venetian artist Giovanni Pellegrini, and the effort almost prov'd too much for me. Either that or what he actually told me was so painful that it affect'd me physically.

In 1720, when I was in Paris, I commission'd him to paint the vault'd ceiling of the Bank Royale. Poor Pellegrini was oblig'd to interpret my vision of a revitalis'd France, found'd not upon the Divine Right of Kings but Trade, Commerce and, of course, the Plentiful Supply of Money – Heaven brought down to Earth, or at least as far as the ceiling. To an artist who was used to adorning the insides of churches – he had narrowly lost the competition to decorate the cupola of Wren's new St. Paul's – adapting classical and religious imagery to the depiction of Money, Security, Credit, Book-keeping and Industry was undoubtedly a challenge. But he rose to it magnificently and watching his, our masterpiece unfold across the 130 foot ceiling fill'd me with such pleasure that I remember thinking that if I bequeath'd nothing more to France, I wou'd die happy.

And if not dead, I was certainly out of breath and wheezing heavily by the time I had walk'd down to the mooring at Rio San Moise. From there I took a gondola down the Canal to the church of San Stae, where Pellegrini was painting the Martyrdom of St. Andrew. It is the most exhilarating journey, especially on a bright autumn morning when the sun has burnt the mist off the water. To the sound of a host of church bells, tolling the Angelus, we wound our way serenely through the city: under the Rialto bridge, past the magnificent palazzos that line the waterfront on both sides – the Ca' d'Oro, the Ca' Fascari, the Grimani, the Pesaro and many others. These are the architectural fruits, not of peasants' toil, but of goods trad'd in far away lands; the triumph of the mercantile, such as I had proclaim'd with my ceiling at the Bank Royale.

The splendid façade of San Stae stands overlooking the Grand Canal. It is a new building and several artists including Pellegrini are still working on the interior. I found him in the Sanctuary, standing in front of his half-finish'd St. Andrew, mixing paints: gold, crimson, azure – a sacred palette, as he wou'd say. St. Andrew lay on his diagonal cross, looking remarkably sanguine for a man who was suffering the agonies of crucifixion. No doubt the jewel-encrust'd gates of Heaven were already winking at him.

'It seems like a fitting pose for the patron saint of the Scots,' I said.

Pellegrini smil'd and seem'd pleas'd to see me. 'Maestro, you look terrible.' He was ever straight with me

'Thank you, Pellegrini.'

He is a small wiry man, with a shock of grey hair, a straggly beard and large hood'd eyes, the colour of the dark wood of St. Andrew's cross. Perhaps, it is the macabre nature of most of what he paints that lends him his somewhat melancholic air.

We spoke of what was happening in the Venetian art world – who was in, who was out, who was commanding the largest fees and commissions. Despite being an artist, Pellegrini is extremely interest'd in money. Like myself, he keeps a weather eye on whose work might be worth buying – a rare talent indeed in a world where paintings are still acquir'd mainly for social and devotional reasons rather than as investments.

'This Antonio da Canale is creating quite a stir,' he said, sombrely mixing more deep crimson for bloody wounds. 'Does views of the city – nothing of an ecclesiastical nature, lucky fellow.'

During our time in Paris, Katherine and I had built up a large picture collection. The Venetian School had been well represent'd, and for many years I had tried without success to get them back to Venice. Now, while I could, I was ready to invest my surplus winnings in some new work. Pellegrini was my guide in this.

'Da Canale? Is he also known as Canaletto?' I ask'd.

'That's him. He'll be big...very big, mark my words.'
Pellegrini sigh'd and look'd sadder than ever.
'But you are big, Pellegrini,' I replied, trying to cheer him
up. 'Your ceiling, our ceiling in Paris is as much a masterpiece
for this new Age of Commerce as any cityscape!'
He turn'd away from St. Andrew to look at me. 'Then you
don't know?'
'What don't I know?'
The hood'd eyes were moist with emotion. 'Maestro, they
have paint'd over our ceiling.'
It was like a body blow. 'Paint'd over it? Who has paint'd
over it? I wou'd have been told, surely. Someone in Paris wou'd
have told me.'
Pellegrini shrugg'd and shook his head. 'A friend was there,
just recently. Saw it with his own eyes. Or rather, didn't see it.
I'm sorry, Maestro. When your company was clos'd down, the
authorities turn'd the building into a library and apparently
Commerce as Supreme Spirit was deem'd unsuitable to look
down upon the Acquisition of Knowledge...'
I cannot remember what else Pellegrini and I talk'd about
that day, if indeed it was anything. We were like a couple
grieving over our lost child – words were inadequate, so we
resort'd to the most mundane of exchanges. I made my way
down to the gondola in a daze, struggling to recall the detail of
Pellegrini's magnificent images, wondering why Katherine had
not told me in her letters of their destruction. Maybe she did not
know. If she did, she surely wou'd not have miss'd the
opportunity to inflict a measure of pain on me.
It was on the return journey I felt the bolt of pain in my
chest, accompany'd by such shortness of breath that as we
enter'd the shadow of the Rialto Bridge, I must have fallen
unconscious. Afterwards, the gondolier told me he was sure I
had died. If I did, I recall no Heaven's Gate, only dark oblivion
until he and an attendant from the Ridotto, with the assistance
of some fine brandy, reviv'd me and help'd me limp home from
Rio San Moise.

*

I suppose the time has come in these confessions – for that's what they're rapidly becoming – to talk about my marriage and divorce, from here on referred to as the M&D. If my career is a game of two halves – from the jobbing professional to the go-to-guy – my personal life is not dissimilar. Indeed, so profound was the impact of my marriage break-up, it's a case of my being not so much two halves as two different people: the person before it happened and the one afterwards.

I say this because unlike most marital breakdowns, mine didn't seem to happen over time. There was little indication that anything was seriously wrong, before it was. There was no growing apart or growing irritation with each other. There were no affairs, certainly not on my part, and I believed her when she said there'd been none on hers. It's true there was a physical cooling. We'd virtually stopped having sex for some time before the break up, but that was her choice after the birth of our child and for lots of good reasons. It wasn't ideal, by any means, but nor was it the cause of our split.

Angela was in her early thirties and I was four years older when we first met. The City was our natural habitat, the febrile air we both breathed. I was ambitious enough to be on the verge of starting my own fund; she was that rare thing at the time – and it's still uncommon now – a female commodity trader, a woman who'd broken into a rabidly male preserve by being much better at what she did than any of the loud-mouthed flash boys around her. (She told me her team had been imaginative enough to nickname her 'Cunt' when she first started. Rather than sue them for harassment, she said she simply showed them who the real cunts were.) She was small in stature, a bobbed blonde in a Chanel suit, but in nature, a whirlwind, a powerhouse, a firecracker. She was the highest earning trader on the floor, which was a large part of her attraction to me. And it had to be – apart from this obsession with coming top and the fact that she was extremely cute, she had no other obvious facets or interests. To be as good at her job as she was at her age, she'd made it her life to the exclusion of all else, and if we hadn't met on that Friday night in a City champagne and oyster bar, it might well have stayed that way. Instead, there was suddenly something else in both our lives – a relationship that wasn't the one we had with our careers.

Maybe it wasn't only to do with the change of priorities. Maybe, having proved her point in the dealing rooms, she'd gone as far as she wanted to in the City fast lane and was ready for a change. Whatever the reason, within a month of our getting together, she was already beginning to take her foot off the gas; to sense there was more to life than being a multi-millionaire by the age of thirty. She was going in later and leaving earlier; she was talking about how much her life had lacked during the years she'd spent as a trader.

For my part, I had someone who understood, even shared the mad world I worked in and was able to sympathise and advise. We both understood the anatomy of finance and the pain and pleasure associated with it, but we could also enjoy each other's anatomies as well. We went at physical intimacy with the same high-octane gusto that we approached our jobs. For a year or more we screwed ourselves silly at every opportunity. There were whole weekends when we hardly got out of bed, be it at my place or hers – we both had flats in fashionable Islington – or at the luxury hotels where we often stayed.

What made the sex even more exciting was that Angela appeared to orgasm very easily, often from the lightest of touches. If the mood took her, and it often did, the deft use of the flat of my hand or the subtle positioning of my thigh was enough to set her off – although she swore she'd never experienced this kind of thing before. This was very flattering for me, especially as not one line of cocaine or any other narcotic substance featured in the whole process. We were high on lust, pure and uncut.

Her passionate need was most acute in public places – bars, restaurants, trains, offices and lifts – particularly lifts. All we needed were two or three floors on our own and bingo! 'Now that's what I call an elevator pitch,' I said the first time it happened; she giggled in response. I never thought to check whether there were CCTV cameras present, but given the level of security in most City offices there must have been.

And there was sometimes another, more perverse twist to proceedings. On occasions she asked to be handled less than gently – given a firm hand on her ass (I've always preferred the American word, for some reason); spoken to sternly or taken roughly, without ceremony, always from behind. I was somewhat ashamed to see how readily I fulfilled her requests, but she always insisted it was her choice and that she was grateful for my obliging her. May my life always be full of such heavy obligations, I joked.

Perhaps I shouldn't have been too surprised to find that these polymorphous pleasures of hers went hand-in-hand with a fondness for porn that was much greater than my own – a tasteful but nonetheless hard-core variety that I thought was more to the gentleman's taste. By then, such things had become easily accessible on the internet and could be watched more discreetly. Yet early in our relationship, I discovered a whole collection of old DVDs and magazines at her flat, on open display beside the huge TV. She didn't appear the slightest bit embarrassed. On the contrary, she simply shrugged, said it was an interest of hers and asked me if I was shocked. No, I wasn't, I said, but in part I was and in part I wondered if it was just another way in which she was determined to outdo the boys at their own game. Not that I had any reason to complain. Many blokes would have said I'd struck gold. Those DVDs had taught her several pleasurable techniques – or rather techniques for pleasuring – and I was the beneficiary. At the same time, I couldn't help wondering how many others had benefitted from her expertise, especially as many of them were girl-on-girl

I quickly came to the conclusion that Angela wasn't someone who did anything by half. It should have been a warning, but it only made me adore her all the more. When she wasn't making a stack of money, even in a lower gear, or dictating the pace of our social and sex lives, she was giving me shrewd advice about the business. Without her, the fund would not have been so successful so quickly and I would not have made as many profitable decisions.

At this point, I hadn't told her who most of my investors were and she hadn't asked. I'm not even sure myself if I deliberately set out to tap into this particular vein of business. Most banks facilitate money laundering for wealthy clients, to a more active or passive degree, and I had found myself dealing with several very high net worth individuals – HENWIs as they're known – when I'd worked for a couple of years in the London and Swiss operation of a US bank. As regulations for many banks became more stringent, I saw an opportunity to help one or two of the wealthiest clients in an unofficial capacity. They were so impressed, they referred my services to their equally wealthy friends, also burdened with too much money, and so it went on from there. In certain golden circles, I rapidly became known for moving funds around untraceable networks and so taking the heat out of hot money.

Meanwhile, beneath all this working and playing hard, the tectonic plates of our lives were shifting. I wasn't at all shocked or dismayed when two years into our relationship, Angela said she had two significant pieces of news: the first was that she'd decided to quit her job; the second, was that she was pregnant. I proposed to her in an instant and in an instant she accepted.

We were married within a month, at Islington Town Hall. It was a small affair attended by close friends, mainly work colleagues. My parents had died a few years before and Angela was estranged from her family and wanted none of them there. In fact, she'd not had any contact with them as long as I'd known her – she'd refused even to talk about them – but it was only at the day of our wedding I realised just how little I knew about her background.

Although nothing about her polished manner suggested it, I knew she'd been brought up in Stepney, a rough part of the world even by the rough standards of East London. It wasn't far from where we now worked and lived, but in other senses it was a million miles away. And I knew she'd gone to university – an Economics degree at the LSE – where she'd made a big effort to 'refine' herself as she put it. But that was it. She told me little else and strangely enough, I liked it that way. I liked her being this high-achieving, highly sexed woman of little known origins, a blank canvas on which I could project whatever noble or scandalous features I liked. And anyway, I had enough pedigree for both of us – that unbroken bourgeois line, remember, stretching back to the distinguished, if notorious, John Law.

*

So I must hurry on with this memoir. Not only does death appear to be snapping at my heels, my story itself gains momentum as I near one of my major goals – an audience with His Most Royal Majesty the King, Louis XIV.

For that very purpose, one magnificent May morning in 1715, Philippe d'Orleans and I join'd Louis' Finance Minister, Monsieur Desmarets at the Palace of Versailles. Even with Philippe's support for my proposals, Desmarets had been reluctant to consider them. But having tried to no avail all the usual ruses to revive his country's finances – re-valuations, devaluations and the restructuring of debt – he had finally had little choice but to take an interest in what I was offering.

Desmarets was a tiny, hook-nosed fellow of mature years, fussing and sweating under a powder'd periwig and heavy frock coat; a man at his wit's end, if ever I saw one. He had summon'd us to a relatively small reception room in a corner of the palace and seem'd less than pleas'd to be there.

'His Majesty is attending a musical recital in the Labyrinth,' he announc'd peevishly in my direction, dabbing at his forehead with a large lace handkerchief. 'It is the only reason he ever comes here now: to enjoy the Gardens. Otherwise he prefers the relative seclusion of Marly.'

I cou'd see why. This monster of a palace was extremely public in parts, thronging like a market, but one where there was little or nothing to buy.

The nobility who remain'd there and the crowd of commoners who came to gawp at them seem'd to drift without purpose – for the only purpose Versailles had ever had was as a stage for Louis and now he had virtually desert'd it.

Philippe obviously enjoy'd the Finance Minister's discomfort. 'What Monsieur Desmarets is saying is that my dear uncle is a prisoner of his mistress Madame Maintenon – she for whom the word pleasure is a term of abuse. He is oblig'd to stay at Marly to atone for his earlier sins of excess and must sneak away, like a boy playing truant, in order to enjoy his Gardens.'

Obviously, Desmarets did not wish to be implicat'd in these profanities; he immediately leapt to the King's defence. 'Your Grace is very droll, but knows only too well that His Majesty has been profoundly sadden'd by the loss of his heirs – as I'm sure, are you yourself.'

'Indeed I am, Monsieur Desmarets, profoundly sadden'd.' Philippe chose to ignore the sting in the other's remark – it was of course the deaths of Louis' son, grandson and great grandson that had put him in line to be Regent. 'Anyway,' he continued briskly, 'we must seek out His Majesty before he returns to the seclusion of Marly. I take it he has already been given Monsieur Law's Proposals?' he ask'd. Desmarets nodd'd curtly in response.

I must confess that at that point I was somewhat distract'd from my Proposals – and even the prospect of seeing His Majesty – by the sheer sumptuousness of my surroundings. From an early age, I had heard tales of the court of the Sun King and dreamt of visiting Versailles. Now I was there and with a member of the Bourbon family, no less. So excit'ed was I that I immediately ask'd if we might go to the Gardens via the famous Hall of Mirrors, the scene of many of the most glittering occasions at the palace.

'But of course, Monsieur Law!' Philippe smil'd and clapp'd me on the shoulder, as if indulging a child. 'Even I, who have always felt fonder of the Bastille than this gild'd prison, cannot deny that it is a rare spectacle.'

We set off towards the Gardens, with Philippe as our guide. For a man who had done his best to avoid Versailles over the years, he certainly knew his way around the lavishly decorat'd rooms. Not that we saw them all, extending as they do over some 120 acres, but enough to appreciate the grandiose absurdity of Louis' vision. Everything proclaim'd the same inflat'd notion: Louis was not only the absolute ruler of France, he <u>was</u> France; the two were one and the same. If he was great, France was great. If he was happy, France was happy. If he suffer'd, France had to suffer. For the first time, I understood and shar'd Philippe's desire to see the end of his uncle's rule, which seem'd to have gone on longer than was good for his country.

At the Salon des Glaces we paus'd long enough for me to stand at its centre and be amaz'd. Here the silvering techniques stolen from the master glassmakers of Venice were put in the service of vanity on the grandest scale imaginable. I was dazzl'd – by myself: some twenty vast mirrors, floor to lofty ceiling, with hundreds of panels displaying an infinite number of my reflections, as if I stood inside an enormous gem. I tried to imagine the effect of a large soirée – the jewels, the sequins, the silks, the satins, the candlelight, the crystal of the chandeliers – a universe of stars and at its centre, Louis.

Philippe was suddenly there beside me, as if reading my mind. 'On the day of St. Louis,' he said, 'the sun sets straight into the Salon des Glaces, a perfect convergence of God, the Universe and the Sun King.'

He gestur'd around at the tables and chairs, all exquisitely carv'd and upholster'd in the finest silk. 'The furniture here,' he went on, 'was once made of solid silver. His Majesty had it melt'd down, together with the gold plate from the banqueting halls, in order to pay for his wars.' He let out a sigh. 'And now after all the glorious battles and grand palaces, what are we left with? A country where the most fortunate lie idle to the point of madness and the least die of starvation on derelict estates. France needs you, Monsieur Law, I am sure of that.'

For a few moments, we star'd at our multiple reflections, as if looking into a brilliant future. Then Desmarets, still standing in the corner, urg'd us on to our audience with His Majesty.

Minutes later, after yet another marble corridor, we emerg'd into the Gardens. Steep'd in the spring sunshine, with avenues and parterres fanning out in all directions, the grounds of Versailles were a celebration of all that was calm, order'd and rational; the triumph of Man over Nature and once again, of a particular man – Louis – over all else. Yet despite their formal grandeur, they were full of playful surprises: the 'Grand Canal', the Trianon – a pink marble palace in the Italian style – the Orangerie, the lake and many strange and exotic trees and plants, the like of which I had never seen. It was as if the King was teasing the visitor, saying in the most extravagant manner possible: you may think life predictable, but unexpect'd delights abound if only you look more closely.

One such delight was the Labyrinth, a network of paths between trees and high hedges that contain'd a dozen fountains, featuring large mythical beasts cast in lead. Having enter'd via a tall verdant arch, we soon became extremely lost. Monsieur Desmarets grew even more ill-temper'd and curs'd at every wrong turn; Philippe told me he himself had been in the Labyrinth only once before and that had been in pursuit of a very spirit'd young woman. Thankfully, the strains of the harpsichord and viol grew louder – a piece by Louis' favourite composer, Marais, Philippe inform'd me – and drew us towards our goal. Another turn and the path open'd up into a wide pav'd area, at the centre of which was the largest fountain of all, a fabulous unicorn, and a small tower, high enough to survey the surrounding paths and view with amusement the labours of the lost. Gather'd nearby were the musicians and the Royal party.

The three of us stood to one side for a while, until the music had finish'd and Desmarets, through much bowing and waving of his lace handkerchief, was able to attract the attention of one of the King's aides. I had seen several likenesses of a much younger Louis at the height of his power and was truly shock'd by how old and frail he now appear'd, even from a distance of thirty paces. He eventually crook'd a long bering'd finger to summon Desmarets and nodd'd sternly at Philippe, who told me to stay where I was until invit'd to approach. I was thus reduc'd to trying to read the meaning of a Royal dumb show, while Philippe and Desmarets tried to interest the King in granting me an audience.

The coolness between uncle and nephew was immediately apparent; nothing but formal gestures pass'd between them and they contriv'd not to look at each other. I began to realise that having Philippe as my sponsor at Court had been less than advantageous. Desmarets stood mutely for the most part, staring down at his lavender colour'd stockings, occasionally shaking his large wig and shrugging his shoulders. At one point Louis condescend'd to cast the royal gaze in my direction, but he squint'd heavily and in all probability saw nothing more than a large blurred object. It did not bode well and sure enough, within a matter of minutes he had dismiss'd both *nephew and Finance Minster with a wave of his hand and order'd the musicians to resume playing. We had been little more than a mildly irritating distraction from the main purpose of his visit to the Gardens and were shooed away like flies.*

Philippe return'd at once, barely able to control his anger. 'My uncle grows more and more sanctimonious, if that's possible. He feels there is little point in meeting you, Monsieur Law. He will not, he says, do business with a Protestant, nor will he sanction a paper currency which he sees as an invention of Protestant nations, like Holland and England, who set a greater store by Man's achievement than God's.' He shook his head in exasperation. 'What is more he is inform'd that you – like myself – are a gambler and a fornicator and not fit to participate in the government of France! Such hypocrisy beggars belief, even by his standards. I must apologise. I fear we have been wasting our time. We might as well go gamble and fornicate!'

Desmarets had linger'd briefly with the Royal party, but join'd us looking insufferably smug. (Heaven knows why – he had just lost his only chance to save his country from insolvency.) As the harpsichord and viol struck up once more, in a more fitting, doleful vein, we set off back through the Labyrinth, this time taking a surprisingly direct path. Philippe said little on the way through the Gardens and I suddenly realis'd that his hopes for the meeting had been even greater than my own. He had not only sought the acceptance of a financial scheme, but his own redemption in his uncle's eyes, and yet what had happen'd had only damn'd him further.

After our visit to Versailles he became convinc'd that Louis wou'd never name him as Regent – and from his silence over the ensuing months, I conclud'd that he blam'd this partly on 'Monsieur Low' and his financial scheme.

*

As much as it pains me to speak about the M&D, it seems to be one of many unpleasant things surfacing at the moment. I feel like a backwater canal in Venice that's long overdue a good dredging. Now it's finally being done, it brings up so much muck and creates such a stench, I'd rather it stayed where it was. Unfortunately, what with panic attacks and nightmares, I don't seem to have much choice in the matter.

Angela and I spent three weeks in Bali on a honeymoon - idyllic but for some emails from clients I couldn't ignore – and a few months later we moved into a large house in Notting Hill, in a street that used to be shabbily inhabited by drug dealers and was now the smart home of money dealers, like myself. (There goes the neighbourhood, Angela laughed.)

My cup of joy overflowed. A life that had seemed to be floating away on a balloon of personal success and excess, now had something to keep it firmly tethered to the ground: a marriage, a substantial family home and soon a family to go with it. I felt as if I'd finally grown up. I even decided to give up my monthly poker nights, a tradition that stretched back over 15 years. The members of the group had changed over time, but had always included those who felt minted enough to lose sometimes thousands of pounds to each other. Not that I often lost anything. I prided myself on being such a good card-player that if everything else went pear-shaped, I'd be able to join the professional poker circuit. Anyway, as much fun as it was, it became a thing of the past at that point and it's only more recently I've begun to miss it.

Angela embraced pregnancy with the same unbridled enthusiasm she brought to the dealing room. There were the pre-natal classes – which I was not allowed to miss, although pressure of work did prevent me from attending a couple of them. There was yoga, homeopathy, acupuncture, aromatherapy, hypnotherapy and every other alternative therapy known to woman. And there was also a Vegan diet, complete with muddy-hued vegetable juices and something called kombucha, fermented tea. (One sip was enough for me to decide to stick with fermented grape.) She became the complete designer hippy, a fully signed up Earth Mother before she was any other kind of mother.

Much to her surprise and disgust, she even re-connected with her own mother. It was a late Saturday afternoon in early April. She was some six months pregnant and had an impressive bump. We were sitting in our vast, shiny new kitchen. (How had I done without one all these years? I know – because I nearly always ate out.) We were discussing the possibility of buying a weekend place in the country, not too far out of London, maybe in Suffolk. I was hardly the world's most enthusiastic consumer, but by then, there was so much money sloshing around between us we'd have been silly not to put a lot more of it into property, either in the UK or somewhere else in Europe. Or both. Is it any wonder that the gods were about to piss on this domestic idyll?

The front door bell rang and Angela insisted on going upstairs to answer it, as if wanting to prove she could still skip around.

I heard her exclaim with uncharacteristic crudeness: 'How the fuck did you know I was here?' It was a much louder and rougher tone than I'd ever heard her use, more street than City trader, although it's often easy to confuse the two.

The reply was mumbled and I couldn't catch it. There then followed a lengthy but more hushed exchange, before the front door closed and whoever had rung the bell went away. Or so I thought. I was surprised when Angela came through to the kitchen with a woman who was obviously much older than she was dressed. At least, that was what immediately struck me - the contrast between the short, tight skirt and stilettos and the heavily lived-in face and hair, dyed blonde almost to extinction. As she stood looking round at our kitchen, with its quarry-load of marble and granite, I realized she was swaying very slightly, like a reed moving in the breeze.

'Nice place, sweetart. Very nice...posh Nottin' 'ill.' She fixed me with a glassy eye and broke into a broad, yellow grin. She was drunk but in a way an alcoholic is drunk – so habituated to the rhythms of the booze that it can almost pass as sober.

'Aren't ya gonna introduce us, Anj?'

'Don't call me *Anj*, Mum, please. This is Theo, my husband – Theo, meet my...mother.' The word had a dying fall.

I stood up, stuck out a hand. She didn't respond.

'*Theo*? That's a bit fancy. Always thought Anj would find someone a bit fancy. Still waitin' for the wedding invite, though...'

She had on a grubby beige raincoat, open at the front; a cheap looking handbag dangled from a gold chain on her forearm. She pulled the raincoat around her as if she was suddenly cold, suddenly exposed.

'Please to meet you, Mrs...'

'Call me, Maggie, Theo. Don't feel like a bin a missus anyone for years.' She drew herself up, swung round towards Angela.

'Anyway, it's one of the reasons I came, Anj.'

'What's that?'

'To tell you 'e's dead. Finally fuckin' dead.'

'Who's dead?'

'Yer father, of course. Who d'you think?'

Angela looked away, said nothing.

'I'm sorry, Maggie,' I said, trying to fill the silence.

'Don't be sorry, Theo. Nothin' to be sorry about. I'da finished 'im off meself years ago if I'd've 'ad the guts. 'ardly saw 'im, anyway. When he wasn't inside, he was off somewhere with some woman or uva sittin' on 'is face.'

'Mum, please...'

'Always loved 'em sittin' on 'is face. Pussy mad, 'e was. I used to sit on 'im for ages. One way of shuttin' 'im up.' She laughed. 'And when 'e wasn't doin' that, 'e was knockin' me around. But that's men for you.' She turned back to me. 'You're not that kind of man, are you, *Theo*? You'd go in for psychological torment, I bet, like most rich boys...'

'Oh, for fuck's sake,' said Angela.

'I tell you what, I could do with a drink. Aren't you gonna offer me one, Anj? And I don't mean a cuppa tea, sweetart.'

'I'm not your *sweetart* and to be frank, Mum, I'd rather you didn't stay for a drink of anything. You've delivered your news – now you can piss off.'

I'd sat down at the table again. She looked at me, as if appealing against her daughter's hostility. She sat down opposite, reached into her handbag and pulled out a pack of cigarettes.

'And I'd rather you didn't smoke,' said Angela. 'Apart from anything else, you may have noticed I'm pregnant.'

'Well, if I can't 'ave a drink, Anj, luv...'

'Mum – please leave.'

'It's no way to treat your mother, is it, Theo? She's no idea what I 'ad to do to protect 'er when she was small.'

'Mum! Please go! Please!'

'She's no idea. If she did, she might wanna thank me - or at least offer me a drink.'

Maggie put away her cigarettes and slowly got to her feet. She started to walk across the kitchen, but stopped to look at a large vase of tulips and daffodils on the work island.

'Beautiful flowers...' She looked round again. 'Beautiful place...' She looked at each of us. 'Beautiful lives...don't fuck 'em up...' It was as if the wicked fairy had cast a spell that was destined to fuck 'em up entirely.

Angela went out with her up the hallway. They seemed to be there for a while before I heard the front door close. She came back, alone this time. I immediately threw my arms around her and hugged her.

'Oh, *Anj*,' I said.

She looked up. There was a muted smile: the recognition and relief that everything was all right as far as I was concerned. And it was.

'And you know the worse thing?' she sniffed.

'What?'

'The only way I could get her to go was by agreeing to see her again. Jesus, I despise that woman.'

'Yes, but go easy on her. She's about to become a grandmother.'

The smile broadened.

*

No matter how much my grand plan had founder'd, the love between Katherine and I remain'd solid. Several times I ask'd her if she ever regrett'd our 'elopement'. But her answer was always no, and on one occasion, she said: 'Just as you escap'd from a prison, John, so did I. I feel liberat'd...'

Nonetheless, the strain on her of abandoning her former life and settling in Paris was immense. She had receiv'd many irate letters from Sir Crown Agent telling her that she was every kind of whore and I every kind of scoundrel and villain. He demand'd that she return to him immediately or he wou'd bring the full force of the law down upon us and there wou'd be all hell to pay etc. He sound'd like Menelaus, the betray'd husband of Helen of Troy, threatening to lay siege to us. We manag'd to laugh it off, but it was hard for Katherine, especially when her family join'd in the hue and cry.

Gregg had cut off their stipends and they were almost as insulting in their letters to her as he was. She was a disgrace to her noble family and forbears. She shou'd be whipp'd through the streets and made to watch me hang from the scaffold. Why they thought this wou'd encourage her to return to Gregg, I do not know. I observ'd that as is so often the case when love and money go head-to-head, money wins.

Katherine said their viciousness came as no surprise. She had never felt lov'd or cherish'd by them. From when she cou'd first remember, she had been treat'd with indifference – by her mother because the woman had lost the capacity to love; by her father because she was not a son. It was as if it were a matter of principle and wou'd best equip her for an indifferent husband.

And as for Gregg, it was not a broken heart that was paining him, but the humiliation of being cuckold'd – and it wou'd be the same for most men in his situation.

She echoed me wryly: 'As is so often the case when love and male pride go head-to-head, male pride wins...'

Meanwhile, it was my male pride that was smarting after my farcical 'audience' with the Sun King. We continued to visit the gaming rooms. Occasionally, I wou'd catch sight of Orleans and we wou'd acknowledge each other across the room, but it seem'd that he want'd no greater degree of familiarity. At one point, I wrote to him asking if we might meet to play some Pharo and discuss 'the Science of Money'. He replied in a courteous but formal tone that his calendar was full and, anyway, he thought he had contribut'd enough to my personal fortune.

'As for Money Science,' he add'd, 'for the time being it has become a matter of irrelevance to me.'

This dealt me a devastating blow; I was made to feel like a spurn'd lover. *Where do I go from here?* I ask'd myself. Without my patron, the answer was nowhere.

Thankfully, Katherine had a greater sense of direction.

'John, trust me, there's more than one way to gain influence within society, even French society. Yes, you may be fortunate enough to have a patron, but if that's not possible you can be your own patron...'

'How so?'

'You have money, you have a brilliant scheme – and most brilliant of all, you have me. We will set up our own court and cultivate all the elite of Paris. We will be our own Sun King and Queen. We will act as if everything we touch turns to gold...'

'Or paper, even...'

She threw back her head and laugh'd. 'Yes...*paper, even*...We will build such a reputation for success that when the System is reveal'd in all its glory – and that process must have all the quality of a plann'd seduction – the Bourbons will come begging to us to be part of it...'

'You are the Queen of Seduction, Katherine Gregg.'

'Affairs of state and affairs of the boudoir – who's to say they're not all one?'

I cou'd say that she applied feminine wiles to both, but that wou'd be to miss what was most important in all this and it had nothing to do with her sex: her intelligence. It was her intelligence that inspir'd me, truly the most seductive thing of all. If you cannot be at the centre of things, create your own centre – what a superb notion! She was like some all-conquering general on the field of battle, rallying her troops and outwitting the enemy with one clever stratagem after another.

No sooner had this been decid'd than we abandon'd our plan to move into a relatively modest house and instead set up home – or shou'd I say, 'shop'? – in a large and beautiful house in the Place de Louis le Grand, not far from the Louvre.

And so began our wooing of Parisian society on a lavish scale, with a series of elegant soirées and dinners. Paris loves extravagance and romance and we were able to offer both in large measure, albeit not yet on the level of Versailles. We made *love to the city's elite and they flock'd to us, drawn firstly by curiosity to the wealthy, mysterious Scotsman and his beautiful, aristocratic consort, who cou'd walk into any gaming room and leave with more income from an evening than most of them made from their rundown estates in a whole year. This social whirligig, with its endless parade of decrepit nobles and thrusting parvenus afford'd us much amusement, as well as having the more serious side of helping us gain the social and political influence that wou'd serve us beyond Louis' faltering reign.*

Katherine was the most magnificent hostess. If her background had denied her nurturing love and affection, it had at least gift'd her with the skills to navigate society at the highest level. Her poise, her wit, her calmness under pressure, as well as her physical beauty, disarm'd and charm'd even the most belligerent and Anglophobe – it help'd that I was Scottish at least - of our Parisian guests.

In fact, the problem was not so much cultivating general influence, which we did with ease, as deciding whom in particular to cultivate and where precisely to place our allegiance. Had it been cards or dice, I wou'd have known instantly, but the odds of power and influence were harder to fathom.

How wou'd Louis himself play the game? Who wou'd he nominate to take charge until his second great grandson Louis XV came of age? Wou'd it be Orleans, the duc de Maine or even the prince de Conti? Or was it possible that he himself might live that long? Under the embalming protection of his mistress, Madame de Maintenon, it was not out of the question. Like carts and carriages in the streets, Parisian society jockey'd for position and we along with them, without any of us really knowing which was the best way to go.

Except Katherine, it seem'd. She was certain that Philippe wou'd somehow win out and in order to learn what was going on with him, she suggest'd we invite the man I had describ'd as his closest friend, the duc de Saint-Simon, to our next soirée.

I doubt'd he wou'd come, but to my surprise he did, accompany'd by the wife to whom he was 'notoriously faithful'. It turn'd out that the tidal flow of high society – who was in and who was out – was his subject. *As well as being a good friend of the Royal family, Saint-Simon was the great chronicler of life at Court and took a keen interest in all that was new or unusual on the social scene.*

He was a personable if dishevell'd fellow in his early forties, with a dreamy, far-away expression, as if he ponder'd pale abstractions rather than the all too solid figures that inhabit'd the palaces and salons of the city. He spoke slowly, with a diplomat's care and precision, and I fancied that he play'd the diplomat's role in an increasingly fractur'd Court – that, and its conscience.

'Well, you and Madame Law are certainly making quite an impression.' *Katherine had taken Saint-Simon's wife off to meet other guests, so that he and I might have time alone.*

'The whole of Parisan society rolls at your feet and wants its tummy rubb'd,' *he smil'd, with the air of man who had seen it all before.*

He knows exactly what we're up to, I thought, but it does not stop him admiring it when he sees it done well.

'Oh, it's just my way of giving back some of the gold I've won from them at the gaming table.'

Now he laugh'd out loud. 'And it may even encourage them to return to the gaming table, so you can fleece them some more.'

'Precisely...'

I was already feeling a rapport with Saint-Simon, even if I cou'd not tell if he reciprocat'd. From our dialogue, it soon became apparent that he not only knew about my gaming activities, but my financial proposals and Orleans' approach to the King, although he cou'd not remember any of the details.

'Monsieur Law, forgive me, I am not very good with money. It is beyond me to understand my household accounts, let alone those of a whole nation.'

'They are much the same, Your Grace,' *I replied.* 'One just adds a few more noughts.'

He nodd'd at this, then grew more serious, if still somewhat abstract'd. 'As you may have gather'd,' *he all but whisper'd, as if Philippe stood beside us,* 'the duc d'Orleans has always been a man of many enthusiasms and passions. But to be truthful, it *pains me to see what has happen'd to him of late, how indifferent to the – how to put it? – higher pursuits he has become. Even I cannot reach him. I realise that I do not share his passion for Science – and as for this latest thing, the Science of Money, as he calls it, I'm not sure what he means by that. Yet at the same time, I hate to see him spurn the life of the mind and turn exclusively to indulging the, er, baser instincts. You have spent some time with him, Monsieur Law – what do you make of it?'*

It was as if he were testing my commitment to Orleans – or was he concern'd about my own 'baser instincts'? After all, he must have seen me that evening at the Palais-Royal.

'One of his passions is for ruling the country,' I replied. 'He is convinc'd that the King has denied him that possibility and he indulges his wound'd pride. For a man of his ability, it wou'd be a tragic waste if he allow'd this to destroy his self-belief.'

It seem'd that I had utter'd certain magic words and broken a spell: suddenly I had all of Saint-Simon's attention. 'Then I am not the only one who sees the qualities of leadership in Orleans?'

'Not at all. Many, including myself, think that the duc d'Orleans wou'd make a fine Regent – and as we know, he has legitimacy on his side.'

He frown'd and lower'd his voice even further. 'But what if that legitimacy is not grant'd?'

'Then it must be seiz'd,' I found myself saying, without hesitation.

Saint-Simon ponder'd his pale abstractions once more. 'Thank you, Monsieur Law. I will do my best to convey some of these thoughts to His Royal Highness – if he will listen to me. And meanwhile, I wou'd be greatly indebt'd if you were to approach him yourself and – how to put it? – re-affirm your interest in him.'

I was genuinely surpris'd, flatter'd even. 'Cou'd that make such a difference?' I ask'd. 'I am a foreigner and only recently in Paris.'

'Monsieur Law, you may be a foreigner and I may not be very good with finance, but I have observ'd the workings of power over many years and it is clear to me that a ruler without money – even an aspiring one – is much like a ship without a sail. It will make a very significant difference.'

He look'd around. 'You and Madame Law have already become important players on the stage of Parisian society. I think you shou'd now turn it to a higher purpose than elegant soirees, don't you?'

Saint-Simon took his leave shortly after our conversation and I realis'd it was not so much the chronicler's curiosity that had drawn him to us, as a more pressing and practical need: to secure support for his friend, Philippe, in any efforts he might make to become Regent. I cou'd only assume that the country's finances were in a worse state than even I had suspect'd and that Bernard, the Paris brothers and their ilk were squeezing the Crown harder than ever.

Even so, I was still in two minds as to how to proceed with Orleans. Was he someone who need'd to be court'd and woo'd, along with the rest of Parisian society? Or shou'd I keep my distance and let him find his way to me?

Katherine, of course, knew the answer.

Our plan had work'd, she said, after I recount'd my conversation with Saint-Simon. He had been sent by Orleans, who cou'd not be seen to approach us directly. He was asking for my help and I shou'd write to him again, this time offering more than a game of cards.

Which meant that Katherine wou'd write to him again in her most cogent French.

His Royal Highness
The Duc d'Orleans
Palais-Royal

14th September 1715

Your Grace,

It is some while since our visit to Versailles and the submission of my financial proposals to His Majesty the King. The memory of this episode has become increasingly painful to me, not so much because of the outright rejection of my scheme, which wou'd have been of immediate benefit

113

to France, but more because it seems to have mark'd the end of our own association.

I write to you in order to make it clear that I wou'd very much like that association to continue and that I believe it is in our mutual interest, as well as that of the French nation, to ensure that it does. To remind you of the essence of my Money Science: in answer to France's chronic shortage of money, the Government will endorse the establishment of a National Bank and the issue of a paper currency, the supply of which will be strictly controll'd by that Bank.

In case you are in any doubt as to my commitment to this project, let me assure you that I will use my considerable influence and resources to facilitate the setting up of such an enterprise. As you rightly suggest'd, even I cannot entirely underwrite the operations of the Bank, but I will make the proposition attractive enough to other major investors, so as to guarantee its overall viability.

The Bank, however, is not the only, nor the greatest of my ideas. I will produce another work of Money Science, something that will surprise Europe by the changes it will bring in France's favour, greater changes than those brought by the discovery of the Indies or the Americas. By this unprecedent'd work, any new French government will be in a position not only to relieve the kingdom of the sad condition into which it has fallen, but to make it more powerful than it has ever been, perhaps more powerful than any other. I will establish order in public finances, increase the productivity of agriculture, manufacturing and commerce, and the revenues of the King and the kingdom, while helping people from every level of society.

I have not yet set out this aspect of my ideas for Your Grace, but wou'd be happy to do so in some detail when next we meet. I therefore await with keen anticipation your summons to the Palais-Royal or wou'd be delighted to receive you here at the Place de Louis le Grand, in order that we might explore these matters further.

May I take this opportunity to reiterate my belief – a belief I think we share – that rational thought and the scientific method can as easily be applied to human affairs as to material reality. The world at large often appears an alien and forbidding place, but I believe it is only made so by the darkness of our ignorance. By contrast, Science is like a bright summer dawn that sweeps away that darkness and reveals that the demons and monsters conjur'd by our childish fears are nothing more than flickering shadows thrown upon the wall.

I urge your Grace to welcome that new dawn and help lead France into an era of power abroad and lasting prosperity at home.

I am, yours etc

*

Although I didn't press Angela to tell me more about her family, her mother's visit seemed to crack open a door that had remained firmly locked for many years. During the last few months of her pregnancy she started to describe the experience of living with a violent father and an alcoholic mother. The information came in fragments; I would never be given a full picture and I'm not sure she had one herself. (Since then she may have sought professional help in putting it together, but I have such little contact with her now, I don't know for sure.) At that stage, she thought therapy a waste of time, that in stirring things up it only muddied the water, made things worse, and I probably agreed with her. Now I think she was wrong. As I'm beginning to find out, things have a general tendency to turn muddy, whether you deliberately stir them up or not.

She elaborated on what Maggie had made passing reference to – that her father had served time for assault and armed robbery, that he was as violent at home as he was on the streets. When he was inside, she and her brother as young kids were told he was away working, and in some ways these times were the least miserable. (They were never what you'd call happy.) Yes, Maggie was more or less permanently drunk and brought home sundry men to share her bed. And there was no money, no food in the house and a constant threat of eviction. But at least Angela's father wasn't around to physically abuse her mother

115

and brother, and sexually abuse her. For, yes, though Maggie did try to protect her, she was too out of it much of the time to be of any use to anyone and when he wasn't in jail or off philandering, Angela's father was able to take full advantage.

I don't know how far this abuse went - Angela would say nothing further on the subject, which perhaps spoke volumes. But I'd certainly heard more than enough to know why she'd rejected her background, as well as explain her eccentric approach to sex.

Oddly enough, although I'm not exactly a natural counsellor or even a good listener, talking to me did seem to have some kind of therapeutic effect for her. It became apparent that until this point – the point when she was also about to become a mother – she'd only ever seen her family through the prism of her own experience, which was hardly surprising. Her brother had fled when he was 16 and she'd lost all contact with him. There'd been no one she could share it with, no one to give her any kind of alternative take on what had happened or even confirm that it had. Now, in speaking to me and seeing her mother again, she somehow found it in herself to feel some sympathy for Maggie. It wasn't much, a mere twinge at first, but to my surprise it seemed to herald a more forgiving attitude. A few days after her mother's visit, she said that she'd just begun to realise how much Maggie had suffered at her father's hands, perhaps worse than she had herself. Her mother had born the brunt of her father's violence and even though she was often badly injured, she'd refused to go near a doctor or the authorities for fear of the consequences.

There was one traumatic incident that was now particularly vivid for Angela, although she'd obviously managed to repress it for a long time. While she was recounting it, she began to cry - the first and last time I saw her do so in relation to this particular subject.

It was her thirteenth birthday. Her mother was relatively sober and had actually got it together to buy her a present: a proper bra and some make-up. Her father sneered at it, said Maggie was turning the girl into a tart, 'just like her mother.' Maggie snapped back that he couldn't stand to see Angela growing into a woman, because he preferred little girls. When he threatened to slap her, she said she'd go to the law and tell them how he liked to behave with his own daughter.

Angela remembered Maggie saying: 'If they put you away for that, you're not comin' out in one piece - if you're ever comin' out, you fuckin' prick.'

He said he'd make sure she was in no fit state to speak to the law or anyone else. That was just before he laid into her and knocked her around the room until she was unconscious.

I hugged Angela a lot during this period, but no more so than when she described this incident. She said she was fine; that her tears were all hormonal, but I wasn't convinced. A couple of days later, she told me that she'd arranged to see her mother again and was determined to get her into the best rehab in town. A few weeks after that, she was talking about buying her a flat in a decent area, perhaps near us. I even started to worry that the rapprochement might go as far as Maggie actually moving in with us, but it didn't come to that – at least not while I was there.

At one point, I wondered if re-living episodes from her appalling childhood would have a detrimental effect on the pregnancy. But she continued to thrive physically and it wasn't until the last couple of weeks before giving birth that she complained of feeling uncomfortable and said she was ready 'to evict the little bugger.' Unfortunately, this period when she needed my support coincided with something of a crisis in the business. One of my largest investors was threatening to switch to another fund and I found myself having to get on a plane to Geneva to persuade him and his advisors to stay with me.

What made the situation worse was that a few days before her due date, Angela suddenly went from being a woman who'd been in control throughout the pregnancy to one who'd lost it. She kept saying how frightened she was and that the whole thing felt very wrong.

'What's wrong?' I asked. 'Let's get you to the doctor.'

'I don't know. Something…' It was most un-Angela like.

She didn't ask me not to go to Geneva – she knew how important the meeting was – so I offered to cancel it anyway. But she really wouldn't hear of it – she insisted I go. She'd be fine, she said. Nothing would happen to her in 12 hours.

'But you said something's wrong.'

'I know, Theo...but it's not. I'm fine now, honestly...honestly...'

So I went to the meeting and if I was surprised when I got the call from her, I shouldn't have been. As I was being driven from the airport to the client's lakeside office, she'd gone into labour and was being rushed to the Lindo Wing at St. Mary's in Paddington.

'I know it's my first time,' she howled down the phone, 'but something feels very wrong, Theo...'

*

We had no reply from Orleans, but Katherine insist'd it was just a matter of time before we did. She thought that the King wou'd have to show more signs of decline before his nephew felt any great sense of urgency. Meanwhile, from what she knew of Philippe, he wou'd probably give himself over to much drunken debauchery. I was less cynical of him, but otherwise I cou'd not fault the logic of her argument.

And so we continued with our social whirl. As the economy deteriorat'd and hardship increas'd, even among the previously well-off, our extravagance became all the more notable. From my gaming, as well as my various business interests in Holland, I had amass'd a fortune of more than £300,000, which enabl'd me to spend at will, certainly on a level I wou'd not have believ'd possible of a Scotsman. This encourag'd either widespread resentment or admiration of me as 'a man of great substance', always an asset for someone who intend'd to establish a bank.

Our grand house had become a mansion to rival the 'hotels', the town houses of the aristocracy, in the Faubourg Saint-Germain. It was fill'd with gild'd treasures and sumptuous furnishings, mostly of Katherine's choosing, her aristocratic instincts having been re-awaken'd by the challenge of setting up a palatial home. The refinement of her taste was, I have to admit, an education for me. Her particular fondness was for the work of the great cabinet-maker Cressent and for long-case clocks by Toqueville. (Tick-Tockville, I quipp'd.) She acquir'd many books bound in the finest Italian calf for our library and Persian carpets of pure silk, whose intricate patterns had long held a fascination for her. There was at least one of these exquisite objects in every room, bringing the wide world to our feet, the exotic fruits of trade which wou'd increase a thousand fold under the auspices of the System. But beautiful as they were, these were not our most cherish'd possessions. That distinction was reserv'd for the drawings and paintings, which we usually select'd jointly. (As a young man, I had develop'd a knowledge of Flemish and Italian paintings with a view to investing in them at some point.) My ambitions start'd out as fairly modest. We bought a number of landscapes by little known artists and I want'd to commission intimate portraits of us both and perhaps one of us together.

But Katherine had bigger ideas. As Paris grew poorer, paintings became relatively cheap. Several agents, acting on behalf of hard-up noblemen, were seeking buyers for the works of well-known masters. It was an extremely good time to buy and although pictures were more akin to sacred objects than investments for Katherine, we soon had the beginnings of a fine collection: drawings by Michelangelo and Leonardo; oils by Titian, Raphael, Tintoretto and Veronese.

It was in the middle of this buying spree, and some four weeks after we had written to Orleans, that she became sick – a 'trifling malady', as she put it, but one that brought such fatigue upon her that she had to take to her bed.

More and more we were being invit'd to society gatherings – few of them as glittering as ours – but that week her sickness prevent'd her from going and I was forc'd to attend on my own. It was a sober reminder to me, if I need'd reminding, of how much I depend'd on having her at my side, not only during the occasion itself, but afterwards when we always compar'd notes on the social hugger-mugger of the evening.

In the case of Orleans, I shou'd have wait'd for him to reply to our letter, as she had advis'd me. Make him come to you, she said from her sickbed. That way you will set a firm precedent in your relationship and always be in the driving seat. It's like training a horse.

119

But Orleans was not a herd animal – he was a Bourbon and the nephew of the Sun King. Besides, by then my impatience had very much got the better of me.

I tried to contact Saint-Simon, only to find that he was visiting his estates in the South. I even consider'd our penning another letter, but knew it cou'd only seem like pathetic bleating after the last one. It became clear to me, if not to Katherine, that more decisive action was requir'd, some significant gesture that cou'd not be as easily ignor'd as a letter.

What decid'd me was the dramatic news that spread like wildfire through the city, so that every street urchin and fishwife knew within the hour – the King had been taken seriously ill and may not last the week. On that stormy morning in October, I resolv'd to present myself uninvit'd to Orleans.

I took a sedan to the Palais-Royal, it being relatively close to Louis le Grand. Even through the rain and the perfum'd handkerchief I held to my face to mask the stench of the streets, it was obvious there was a different mood abroad – one of tense anticipation, as if the whole city were holding its breath and on the brink of some great disaster. The Palais-Royal itself was oddly quiet: no one coming or going, no footman at the gate. In fact, I saw no servants at all. The place was like an abandon'd ship, adrift in a tempest. I walk'd down the long entrance hall, where lamps still burnt, past the ante-rooms, towards Philippe's apartments. Eventually, in a portico, I caught sight of a listless group of servants, playing cards. They look'd up briefly from the game, gave cursory nods, yet made no effort to detain me. As I enter'd Philippe's rooms, the reason became clear.

In the main drawing room I was present'd with the most unsavoury of scenes. What I assum'd to be guests from the evening before lay scatter'd across the embroider'd sofas and the magnificent Savonnerie carpet, singly or in pairs, male and female, lewdly entwin'd. All were asleep – or rather in a stupor – and in various states of undress, most of them virtually nak'd: several of the men wore nothing but wigs, the women little but scant underclothes. Bottles and glasses, many overturn'd, cover'd the inlaid surfaces of every table and cabinet, and a strong whiff of wine, mix'd with musk and urine hung heavily in what was left of the air. Here was the aftermath, not just of an *evening's entertainment, but of a bacchanalian romp, an orgy. No wonder I had not been challeng'd by the servants: to their weary eyes I had not been arriving, but going back for more – was I to feel flatter'd or insult'd?*

One of the guests groan'd, another mutter'd something incoherent in his drunken slumber, a third turn'd and roll'd off the sofa on to the floor, but did not wake. As if through carnage after a battle, I pick'd my way across the room and into the corridor that led to the bedchambers. I shudder'd to think what I might find in these, but cou'd not resist looking. In two of them there were more of the wound'd – a man and two women in one bed, two couples in the other. One of the women stirr'd, sat bolt upright and, with wild eyes and shaking breasts, laugh'd uproariously in my direction before falling back into oblivion. Further down the corridor I heard more noises – not laughter this time but a loud rhythmic moaning. I stopp'd at the open door of a third bedroom, the largest, and stood transfix'd. The shapeliest of young women knelt upon the edge of the bed, nak'd but for a short white bodice; she rest'd forwards on her elbows, her haunches held high. Behind her, facing me, but with his eyes clos'd from the effort, stood Philippe, an open silk robe embroider'd with the Bourbon crest, hanging off his shoulders. A hand gripp'd each of the woman's fine hips, the sweat dripp'd from him, as he thrust into her repeatedly, making her whinny from either pain or pleasure, I was not sure which.

Before I cou'd turn away she look'd up, saw me, and smil'd. Even in these somewhat informal circumstances and with her hair falling around her pretty face, I recognis'd Madame de Tencin from that first dinner at the Palais-Royal.

'Monsieur Law,' she pant'd, her voice thick with wine and lust, 'how nice of you to join us.'

Philippe open'd his eyes wide in surprise and I, suddenly embarrass'd, set off quickly down the corridor. Within seconds, he was out of the bedroom and bawling at me.

'Monsieur! To what do I owe this intrusion...this...coitus interruptus?'

There was nothing for it but to turn and face him. He stood by the door, attempting to muster some dignity: his chest puff'd out, his regal robe drawn hastily about him. Unfortunately, his ardour was still on prominent display and try as I might, I could not suppress a smile. He look'd down at himself, at his rampant manhood now slowly drooping and when he look'd up again, he was also smiling. We both began to laugh like schoolboys.

Only after some moments did he recover enough to speak. 'Monsieur Law,' he said, obviously drunk, 'you wou'd have been proud of me...I have won a considerable wager – who cou'd drink the most wine and still perform, still provide satisfaction...' He wav'd an arm wildly towards the bedroom. 'Of course, it's Madame Tencin I have to thank. She inspires me to greater and greater heights of passion. Amazing woman...'

He sway'd slightly and beckon'd me towards him. His tone was soft and appeasing: 'May I ask why you are here.'

'I sent a letter to Your Grace.' In the circumstances it seemed ridiculous to mention it.

'Ah, the letter, yes...'

'And what with the news this morning...'

He looked quizzical. 'The news?'

Of course, he may not have heard – or worse, he may have heard and chosen to ignore it. 'The King has been taken seriously ill.'

It took a few moments for this to register. 'Ah, yes,' he said wearily, and then he gestur'd for me to follow him into another, smaller room, a study that seem'd to have avoid'd the ravages of the rest of the apartment. A welcome (to me) shaft of daylight pierc'd a chink in the curtains and fell upon a large mahogany desk, pil'd high with letters, mine no doubt among them. From somewhere he produc'd wine and glasses. We sat down; he pour'd for us both. It was much too early for me, but I felt oblig'd to join him.

'I'll give you some news of my own in return, Monsieur Law,' he said after a long draught. 'The King has appoint'd a Regency Council to succeed him, if necessary. It includes myself, although I am not at liberty to name the others. Suffice it to say that I have little time for most of them. It is an insult to me, it is bad for France and I will have nothing to do with such an arrangement. Nothing.'

As wou'd often be the case with Philippe, he had drunk enough to leave most men comatose, yet was still coherent.

'Surely you wou'd have the greatest influence on this Council and...'

'I will have nothing to do with it!' he cut in, his features hardening. They soften'd again instantly; he look'd into his wine.

'Have you ever fought in battle, Monsieur Law?' he ask'd after some moments.

'Battle?'

'A military campaign...'

I shook my head. 'My main arena has been the gaming room, as you know.'

He smil'd. 'In battle one becomes like a child again – a child who is very lost and very frighten'd. You pray that you don't piss or shit in your britches or disgrace yourself by running away, while all round you in the chaos and the mud, men are screaming and dying from the most ghastly wounds. I fought in the Succession Wars against the mighty Marlborough. I was a fool. I want'd to show that a Bourbon cou'd do more than sit astride a horse – that he cou'd lead men into battle – unlike my uncle and most of his so-call'd generals, who behav'd as if they were spectators at a pageant. I fought in several engagements and after each I was commend'd for my valour – and do you know what the King's response was? Do you know how he reward'd me? He denied me any further command – not, as he told our family and the Court, to protect me from my own impulsive nature, but because on the battlefield I had outshone him – the Sun King. Ha! It is true – Louis is a great man, perhaps the greatest of men, and yet the greatest of men are often the most petty and spiteful.' He drank some more wine. 'Such contradictions, Monsieur Law. Where does that leave your Science and mathematical laws? '

This was not the time or place, I realis'd, to draw the distinction between predicting the behaviour of whole populations bas'd on statistical evidence and the vagaries of particular individuals. But at that moment I sincerely wish'd to share something with him, even if it was not to be the details of my System.

'I fought a duel once,' I said. 'It is nothing like fighting in a battle, Your Grace, but I star'd death in the face, nonetheless.

And I discover'd two things: first, that we shou'd make the most of what we have, while we still have it; and second, that there is one thing worse than losing one's life and that is taking someone else's - especially if it belongs to a friend.'

Philippe's eyes had clos'd but he open'd them again and look'd at me with genuine concern. 'You killed your friend?' he ask'd.

'I did.'

'I'm sorry, Monsieur Law. We do not have so many friends in this life that we can afford to kill them, even in a duel...'

Ever since the spectre's last appearance – at the dinner in that very apartment – I had done my best not to think of Beau Wickham and I worried that even this passing reference to him might be enough to summon the ghastly revenant who had visit'd me before. Thankfully, there was no one in the room other than Orleans and myself.

He suddenly perk'd up. 'Your letter was superb. One of the best letters I have ever receiv'd. I am impress'd by the brilliance of your ideas and excit'd at the prospect of hearing more of them.'

Before I cou'd be cheer'd by this praise, he clos'd his eyes again and sigh'd to himself. 'However...however...I currently have little use for them, Monsieur Law. I currently have little use for anything other than Madame de Tencin... and, of course, the odd jug of wine. I am sorry...'

'I understand. I will leave you in peace.' I went to stand up.

'And I had another letter, Monsieur Law. Several of them, in fact' – and he swept his hand theatrically towards the pile on the desk – 'from one Sir William Gregg, an agent of the British Crown, which, of course, now has jurisdiction over your homeland. He urges me to deport you and Madame Law. You, because you are an outlaw want'd for murder by the British Crown – perhaps, as you have just told me, of your friend, which is its own punishment – and Madame Law, because she is not Madame Law at all, but Lady Gregg.'

'Your Grace...'

'No explanation is necessary, Monsieur Law – although I wou'd love to hear the story at another time. Why wou'd I deport people who are bringing such joy to Parisian society *and for whom I have the deepest respect and admiration? Outlaw, murderer, gambler, adulterer and keeper of one of society's most beautiful mistresses. Very good for a fellow whom I thought was some kind of Puritan – you have shot up in my estimation. I told Sir William I had no intention of doing anything of the kind, especially to a woman who is descend'd from the family of Anne Boleyn, that most tragic Queen of England. It is understandable that she shou'd wish to seek a sanctuary in France. She – and you – are most welcome. I also warn'd him not to attempt to abduct either of you, because you both have the protection of the French Crown. It wou'd amount to an act of war...'*

'Thank you, Your Grace.'

And with that Orleans' head nodd'd forward and he fell fast asleep. He was snoring loudly, as I quietly withdrew.

*

Yes, I should have told the driver – my client's chauffeur – to turn around and go straight back to the airport, and that was my first thought, I promise you. But...I knew the next flight to London wasn't for a couple of hours and it would have taken me that long to organise an alternative route. I considered the idea briefly, but decided to spend the absolute minimum time at the meeting – just enough to resolve the situation with the investor – and then head back to London. Meanwhile, I'd stay in touch with Angela via the phone. I told myself that the sound of my voice would be every bit as comforting as my over-anxious physical presence.

As we pulled up at the office, I called her again. She was a lot calmer. She'd been told she wasn't dilated – I think I'd missed that antenatal class; the contractions had stopped and the pain had receded. She would stay at the hospital while they ran a few more tests but it was most likely a false alarm.

'Please, though, Theo, get back as soon as you can...'

'It's all right,' I laughed. 'I won't be hanging round - this guy's rude, even by Russian standards...'

Was it the same rude Russian who would sue me a few years later? No, but they shared the same super-rich asshole tendencies and I suppose I should have foreseen similar problems with him. I suppose I should have told him even then to crawl back under the rock he came from, one of those Swiss rocks that harbour so many super-rich assholes. It's a no-brainer, as they say, but that's employing hindsight. At the time, he seemed more than worth the trouble. (Or is that the rouble?) I was making huge fees out of his investments and he'd also been instrumental in encouraging other rich Russians to do business with me. If I was given to such corporate speak, I might have referred to him as 'strategic going forward' or 'pivotal'. Whatever. The trip to Geneva seemed like the logical thing to do – even in the context of Angela being about to give birth.

It was a beautiful spring day in the city of Luther, but what with the lake and the Alpine backdrop and that freshly scrubbed Swiss quality, it's the sort of place that's beautiful every day. Even so, I couldn't help thinking how much I preferred Italy – Italy, where they fleece you openly, brazenly on the street, or in taxis. Here in the soulless land of chocs and clocks, the crime is all white-collar and happens behind closed doors with a gold card and a sanitised smile. Somehow, it's less honest, and not nearly as much fun.

But I shouldn't carp. Switzerland's been good to me. It was and is the source of most of my business, a land of rich pickings. It enabled me to avoid the messier aspects of the job, to convince myself that my life was unsullied, clinically clean; that it was not a life at all but more a glossy lifestyle, in which the bathrooms are like ballrooms and the views across the lake to the mountains take your breath away. Even at that time, all those years ago, I knew it was wrong, I knew it was phony, but I was happy to be seduced by it. Now the difference is I'm not so happy to be seduced – by that or anything else.

My client's office had one of those breathless views across the lake. I say 'office' but it was more of an elegantly appointed living room in a palatial home, with one whole wall of glass, overlooking the water. An ugly man in a beautiful house with a beautiful wife – an Italian Swiss woman, I remembered from a previous meeting. She was there briefly when I arrived and gave me a discreet look of exasperation as she left the room to the three of us – myself, my Russian client (let's call him Boris) and a tall grey-suited gentleman, with rimless specs and the beady eye of a reptilian predator. I immediately assumed he was my rival and I was right.

Boris spoke brusquely to his wife in his thick Russian accent. 'This is Theo Law, my financial advisor in London. You may remember him, Gina. Do say hello...'

She stopped and managed a strained smile that seemed to indicate how much she needed to escape from her glazed cage on the lake. 'Hello, Mr. Law. Good to see you again.'

The atmosphere was fractious. I got the impression I'd come in at the tail end of an unpleasant domestic scene and my arrival was the only reason it wasn't still going on. 'I'll send in refreshments.'

'Thank you, refreshments would be most welcome.'

She closed the door loudly behind her.

Boris made a face as if he had very bad indigestion. There was a basic exchange of courtesies – very basic in his case – and he introduced me to his new financial director, Carl Schilling. Childishly, I wanted to say 'let's hope he watches the pounds and pence as well', but instead I tried to sound like a grown up and told them my wife was about to give birth.

'So you see how important you are to me, Boris,' I smiled, 'I left London just as she was about to go into labour.'

Any hope that this might evoke a little sympathy, and so give me some edge in our discussions, was quickly dashed. Boris let out a wry chuckle that somehow sounded like a sneer. 'Yes, Theo - or is it just a measure of how far a man will go to avoid attending the birth of his child?'

'You sound like someone who's gone a long way to avoid the experience himself.'

He shrugged. 'I had several children with my first two wives. Thankfully, they were traditionalists in such matters and asked me to stay well away.' Again, the sneering chuckle. 'I'm all for the conception stage, with the right woman, but the birth and death stages, I leave to the professionals...'

Done with these pleasantries, our conversation, or rather, negotiation proceeded in a chess-like manner. My new enemy, Mr. Schilling, explained the problem they had with my fund and why they wanted to withdraw from it. I defended its record, with much supporting evidence. They presented a detailed profile of an alternative fund that appeared to outperform my own. I pointed out its weaknesses; they played up its strengths.

At this stage it was something of a stalemate, and it had me looking at my watch and trying to work out how I might bring matters to a swift conclusion.

'Look,' I smiled, 'we can sit here all afternoon debating the indicators, but I'm afraid I have a baby to deliver.'

I directed my remarks to Herr Schilling, seeing as it was his machinations and calculations that seemed to be at the root of the problem.

'Of course, I'd be more than happy for you to leave the fund, if that's what you want. However, I'll have to insist that I also cease moving your money through my networks, certainly on the scale I've been doing.'

The financial director was impassive. 'But as I understand it, Mr. Law, very little of our money has gone through your network over the last year.'

I noted his use of the word 'our' – either corporate coinage or he had some of his own skin in the game. I looked across at Boris. Even though it was the subject about which we very seldom spoke, both of us knew that I was in fact shifting more money than ever for him. (It was all to do with the exceptionally high spike in the price of gas, he'd told me.) Suddenly a gap had opened up in the Swiss-Russian defence. Boris's expression alternated between the menaced and the menacing. I almost said 'check'.

He cleared his throat; his accent became even thicker. 'I didn't know the, er, two arrangements were linked in that way, Theo.'

'They weren't,' I said. 'But they are now.'

Herr Schilling seemed a little unsettled. This data had not been entered on the hard drive of his brain. He thought he'd managed to corral Boris' sprawling finances, but now he realised that some key elements were still off running wild.

He breathed deeply. 'Well…we may be unable to resolve this matter today…especially as you have to return to London so soon.'

'No, Carl,' Boris cut in, 'I think we can settle it now. We stay with Theo's fund. In light of what we've said, I'm sure he'll be doing all he can to improve the returns.'

'It's what I always do, Boris, you know that.' I wanted to add: 'checkmate'.

And then I was up and saying my goodbyes, and Boris was even wishing me luck with the 'delivery' and hoping I made it back in time, which was a relative first in the niceness stakes for him.

'We will speak, Theo.'

'We will.'

As I headed to the waiting car, Boris's wife appeared in the white marble entrance hall and made straight for me.

'Mr. Law, a quick word before you go...' There was more than a hint of urgency in her voice. 'I wanted to ask you' – she looked quickly back at the room I'd just left – 'if you were fully aware of what sort of business my husband is in.'

'I think so, yes,' I smiled. 'Oil and gas – and a bit of mining, isn't it?'

'Only in part – and if I've judged you correctly, the other part is something you would never want to be involved with.'

'I didn't think I was.'

'Oh, you are, believe me. I'd do some more research, if I were you...'

We heard a door open behind us; Boris emerged.

His wife raised her voice. 'Have a good trip back to London, Mr. Law. Perhaps, we'll see you there some time soon.'

*

I am not sure why I did not immediately tell Katherine that Philippe had been contact'd by Gregg. It was bound to come out sooner or later and some in our elevat'd circles must surely have already known. Even if they were still being discreet enough to refer to her as 'Madame Law', it wou'd only be a matter of time before those among them who resent'd our success tried to use it against us. On the other hand, this was Paris and I knew I wou'd gain as much prestige in society for having my 'mistress' pose as my wife, as I wou'd suffer

129

opprobrium for it. It might only become a problem at some later stage – when and if I achiev'd high office – and that prospect seem'd a long way off.

But whatever my thoughts on the subject, another matter swiftly eclips'd it.

Louis did not die that week, or the week after, or indeed the week after that. Under Madame Maintenon's matronly care he made a miraculous recovery, as if exercising his royal prerogative for one last time. He even took up the reins of government again: yet another futile devaluation of the coinage was order'd and the effect on the country's commercial life was reflect'd in the cold wintry gloom that descend'd on the city.

And for the first time since we had been in Paris – indeed, since we had been together – Katherine and I were also plung'd into depression and discord. This was not so much to do with the thwarting of our plans – Katherine was still convinc'd that Philippe wou'd take over the government at some point – but something even closer to home, to do with her 'malady'. As she reveal'd to me after she had woken that morning and had to rush from the bed to be sick, the 'malady' was a pregnancy.

Of course, I was sorry she was sick, but otherwise I was overjoy'd, if a little puzzl'd as to why she had kept the news from me for so long. Nor was I sure why, in telling me, she sound'd as if she had just been told to prepare for her own wake – was it not a cause for celebration?

'I don't see it that way, John.'

The issue of our marriage – or lack of it - having been on my mind, I said: 'Is the child being born out of wedlock a problem for you? We can be married tomorrow...today, even...'

But she wav'd this away like a bothersome fly. 'I have no wish to be married. That's not the issue.'

'Do you not want us to have a child together?'

She shrugg'd. 'Even a few months ago I wou'd have been happy with it. But something has chang'd since then.'

'You mean something has chang'd between us – you no longer...love me.'

'It has nothing to do with you, John. Not everything is to do with you. No, something has chang'd in me – I have no wish to be a mother. I don't mean that unkindly, but this is about what I

want. I have come to realise the importance of my role in the wider world – in our plans for the bank and everything else...'

'Of course, that's important...'

'I mean it's importance to me, John, to who I am. I know we'll succeed and I want to be part of it. I want to be part of the setting up and running of the bank, to play an equal and active role in our business affairs and the decisions we make. I am excit'd by the prospect and completely committ'd to making it happen...and, as a mother, I fear all that will take second place – I will take second place.'

This, I realis'd, was a return to the radical views on women she had been known for when we first met. Somehow, they had become submerg'd in the drama of our romance, our fleeing Scotland and our plans for the System. Now they had resurfac'd in a way I had not anticipat'd.

Yes, she had been a great help to me since we had come to Paris. Our plans were stall'd at present, but without her we might have had no plans at all and we certainly wou'd not be pois'd to realise them when the time was right. However – and this was what surpris'd me – I had certainly never seen her as taking an active, day-to-day role in the affairs of the bank, as and when it was establish'd, any more than I wou'd have her decide which cards I shou'd play at the gaming table. There were certain things that I regard'd as my domain and mine alone. She, of course, wou'd be my counsellor, my advisor, my lodestar, and I was sure that she cou'd fulfil that role whether or not she was a mother.

So I temporis'd. I reassur'd her, I told her she wou'd never take second place and that I wou'd do everything in my power to ensure that was the case.

She smil'd wearily. 'Oh, John...you don't understand the great paradox of women's lives, do you?'

'Obviously not...'

'Child getting and rearing' – and she spoke to me as if I was a child – 'are what have rais'd women to a subordinate position, since the dawn of history. We are cherish'd for it – we are punish'd by it, and I see no reason why that shou'd change for me, despite your best intentions.

131

'So, I'm afraid I will have to wish for another outcome. I was an only child, but by the time I was born, my mother was a dried-out husk. She had no feeling left for her daughter. It had all been drain'd from her like so much fluid that seeps from the womb during childbirth.' (I winc'd at the thought.) 'She told me that she had never want'd any children with my father – she cou'd not bear him near her. But he often forc'd himself upon her and she land'd up having two stillbirths and four miscarriages. Right now, I can only hope I take after her in that regard and that this pregnancy is as short-liv'd. I am sorry...'

I was render'd speechless. Katherine had suddenly reveal'd a level of heartlessness that shock'd me to the core. I see now that my reaction was more to do with a somewhat naïve understanding of how a woman cou'd or shou'd behave rather than anything exceptional in her. But at the time, I was apall'd by the idea that she wou'd want to rid herself of a child growing in her womb and I found it difficult to have any sympathy with her or her radical views. I even worried that she might do something to actually encourage such an event.

After her initial sickness had pass'd, she insist'd on attending every soiree with me, which was something she continued to do even when she was at the later, heavier stage of her pregnancy. This was much to the surprise and dismay of many of the guests, although others admir'd it a great deal – I cou'd see how the men certainly admir'd the fullness of her breasts – and told her she was 'intrepide' and 'courageuse'.

A doctor I consult'd on the subject of gestation inform'd me that in certain instances an excess of alcohol cou'd cause a miscarriage. Katherine had always drunk wine in moderation, but I began to observe her consumption carefully and on several occasions I went so far as to instruct the servants to refuse her more, for which she was less than grateful.

'I'll decide when I've had enough wine, John. Look to yourself – the more you drink, the worse your French becomes...'

I ask'd our servants to take particular care that she did not undertake anything physically strenuous; to be more protective of her than they wou'd normally be of a woman who was expecting. Charlotte, our housekeeper, a large ruddy-fac'd woman with a heart of gold and several children of her own, obviously thought I was fussing. She smil'd indulgently, before telling me that women, even expectant ones, were more resilient than men thought. She had work'd as a cook through all her pregnancies and they were all healthy. 'And let me tell you, Monsieur, there's nothing more strenuous than being a cook in a big kitchen. You're working in heat, carrying heavy pots...'

Meanwhile, my researches also reveal'd that there were certain herbal potions and poisons with names like Belladonna and Maculata, which when taken in mild doses, cou'd help bring on a miscarriage. I frequently scour'd the house for them, but cou'd find none.

Looking back on these events, it is only now I realise that I achiev'd nothing other than an erosion of that most precious of all commodities possess'd by lovers: trust. From that time on, I think I ceas'd fully to trust Katherine, even if none of my worst fears were realis'd.

Despite all my assurances that as a mother, there wou'd be no change whatsoever in her standing or status in our business affairs, she remain'd depress'd and miserable for most of her pregnancy. She refus'd to have any physical contact with me – even a caress was outlaw'd. She complain'd about the baby kicking, about the pains in her back and her general discomfort, all of which she blam'd on me, as 'the planter of the seed'. But she did not miscarry. The pregnancy was a healthy one and in the last month of her term I finally began to detect a softening of her attitude.

'You know the worst thing about this?' she said one evening, looking down at the considerable mound of her belly.

'What is that, Katherine?' The whole business had been the 'worst thing', as far as I was concern'd, but it was about to take a surprising turn.

She clos'd her eyes for a few moments, as if in silent prayer. 'I had plann'd to farm this child out to a group of nursemaids and to have as little to do with it as possible...'

She paus'd and I wait'd to hear what other arrangements for separation she had in mind.

'But now I know I've been fooling myself, that it won't be possible. That I will have no alternative but to lavish love and

133

affection on the child day and night and do everything in my power to make sure he or she has the happiest of lives.'

I was so pleas'd to hear her say it that I defied the physical ban and immediately kiss'd and embrac'd her. She took my hand and plac'd it on her belly, so I cou'd feel the child move – the first time she had done so.

'I cannot tell you how happy I am,' I whisper'd.

'Even though I've push'd you away for I don't know how long?'

'Oh, I know how long – I've count'd every agonising second...' It was good to hear her laugh again. 'Yes, Katherine, even so...'

*

Any concern that Boris's wife Gina had aroused in me was quickly replaced by my concern for Angela. I was speaking to her even before I was in the car, and the news was not good. She'd not in fact left the hospital. The contractions had started again and were far more severe and frequent. 'I don't want to alarm you, Theo, but there seems to be a bit of a complication...'

'What sort of complication?' I was very alarmed.

'Something to do with the position of the baby.'

I was asking what the hospital was doing about it, when I heard the voice of a woman in the background: 'We really need to go, Mrs. Law...'

'Look, they're about to move me, I should get off the phone.'

'I'm on my way back.' I looked at my watch. 'I'll be with you by 7.00.'

'Thank God...' She sounded breathless now. 'Did it go well?'

'Very well.' But what did any of it matter when there was a complication? I gave a nervous laugh. 'Promise you won't do anything until I get there.'

More panting and then: 'Promise...' She rang off.

My flight departed on time. The hour it took seemed more like three and the fifteen minutes it circled over Heathrow was an eternity. I watched the paisley patterns of the suburbs revolve beneath me and all the time I thought about the 'complication' and said a kind of silent prayer that amounted to a deal with God or Fate or Whatever was in charge of the whole thing, which was complete nonsense because I knew full well nothing was. 'Please, please let it be all right. Let every deal I've done come undone, but let them – *them* – be all right.'

I called Angela immediately we landed, nearly three hours after the last call, but her phone was switched off. There was an agonizing train journey into Paddington and as much of a sprint as I could muster to the maternity wing of the hospital, which was very close to the station.

Breathless, I asked the receptionist for Angela's room and was even more worried when she gave me directions to the operating room. Another woman, a midwife I assumed, met me at the door and attempted to explain the situation to a desperately puffed and panicking expectant father.

'Mr. Law…'

'Please…call me Theo.'

'Theo…'

She told me that the baby had turned in the womb in the final stages of the pregnancy, which meant the birth would be breech - bottom first. They'd done everything they could to try to reverse it but it hadn't worked. A caesarean was now the only option.

'And it's a good job you arrived when you did, Theo, because the baby's blood pressure has dropped suddenly and the operation's now an emergency.

'Am I allowed in?' I said this as if I was desperate to be there, but in fact part of me wasn't so sure it wanted to be.

'Of course. It's just as important you're there for a c-section as for a normal birth. Even though Angela won't be in pain, she'll still need all the support she can get. And by the way you'll be glad to hear we put a screen up so neither of you can see the actual operation – unless you really want to?'

'Er, no…thank you…'

'Good. Plus, there's another reason you're needed.'

'What's that?'

'After the birth, while we finish the procedure Mum's out of action.' She smiled. 'You'll be the one left holding the baby...'

As I was getting into the surgical gown, I thought how all Angela's enthusiastic plans for the birthing pool and a drug-free natural birth, without intervention, would come to nothing and what she feared most, the medical machine, would now take over.

And indeed, when I stepped into the operating room, that machine was in full swing. The staff moved in seamless formation – a practised routine for them, a horror show for us. The screen was already up across the bed, which meant Angela and I couldn't see each other until I was up by her side. I'm sure she thought I was a doctor under my mask, because she didn't react at first. She looked tired and drawn in repose, but when she realised it was me, her face became wildly animated, first by smiles, then by floods of tears.

I kissed her firmly on the lips – she tasted of a long hard day.

'Theo...I'm so sorry.' She gripped my hand.

'Why are you sorry?'

'I feel as though I fucked up. My body, I mean...' Her crying got louder.

I bent down, put an arm round her shoulder. 'Don't be silly, no one's fucked up. And this is so much easier...on you and the baby.' I breathed deeply. And me, I thought.

The team was now poised for action; there was a final check to make sure the epidural had taken full effect.

'Anyway,' I said, 'I'm the one who should be sorry - for going to the meeting.'

'You're here now.'

'I'm here now...'

How long did the operation last? Ten minutes? Thirty? An hour? I couldn't say. We existed in an intense, timeless zone, where every act seemed to be in slow motion and of great significance. We held hands tightly throughout, anxious spectators at a show we couldn't see. The midwife gave a bland and comforting commentary on the procedure. Finally, she said: 'She's here, Angela – a beautiful baby girl!'

Even so, we heard no crying, no disgruntled daughter announcing her arrival, and we were unable to see her until the midwife brought her round the screen to us. Nor was I invited to hold her, as trailed. Instead, she was immediately whisked away again and we were told that her blood pressure was so low she'd have to be taken to intensive care. She'd be fine, of course; it was just a precaution.

Angela started crying again and nothing I said could make her stop.

*

In that final month of her term – or 'sentence', as Katherine had referr'd to it – I was forc'd to make an unexpect'd trip to Rotterdam in order to settle a business matter. Before coming to Paris I had help'd set up a lottery for the Dutch, in which I retain'd a large interest. A dispute had arisen over my rights to the profits from this and I was keen to resolve it, not least because I still regard'd Holland as a safe haven for us, shou'd our position in Paris become untenable.

In her softer, more affectionate state, Katherine was extremely reluctant to see me go – our leave-taking was difficult – and the journey to Rotterdam was far from pleasant. Flat and bleak at the best of times, it was late November and the country north of Paris was shroud'd in freezing fog, every tree and hedgerow festoon'd with heavy frost. From my cold carriage, I look'd out at ruin'd farms and ragg'd peasants, looming like wraiths out of the mist, as they struggl'd to gather meagre supplies of wood. This was a land of scarcity, not because it was blight'd or infertile, but because it was unproductive, almost entirely lacking in economic activity. If I was losing sight of my ultimate goal in my dealings with Orleans and the Court, this pitiful scene gave me renew'd purpose.

Yes, I want'd power, influence and even greater wealth for myself - I cannot deny it – but I also want'd to breathe new life into this country, to infuse it with commercial vigour in such a way that the majority of the population wou'd benefit, even the labourer in the field. As we journey'd across Picardy, I became

137

more committ'd than ever to this objective, whilst doubting I wou'd ever be in a position to achieve it without Philippe.

Despite the same wintry conditions, Holland by contrast appear'd much more prosperous, the product not only of trade, as I have said, but of a sound system of banking. There had been a bank in Amsterdam for over a century and it had us'd metal prudently to finance trading enterprises in every corner of the world. In return, goods and money had pour'd into the country and the Dutch had become a people who appreciat'd the benefits of making a good profit.

Hence the attraction of a lottery. I had devis'd it for them and financ'd most of it. But now the good burghers of Rotterdam were complaining that my own profit was excessive, that I had us'd my knowledge of numbers and finance to set up a system to my advantage and 'to the prejudice of the Dutch People' – by which they meant themselves.

In fact, everything had been perfectly legitimate, devis'd along the lines of calculat'd risk on my part, as in a card game, and yet no amount of explaining cou'd convince my partners. They insist'd that I withdraw from the lottery and leave the country immediately. I was shock'd, but had little choice and agreed, on condition that they paid in cash everything they ow'd me. The negotiation took three painful days, but my legal position was strong and in Holland, unlike France, legality is taken very seriously. Flank'd by several heavily arm'd guards, I eventually depart'd for Paris with my carriage some 200,000 guilders heavier – a healthy fortune in itself, although I wou'd rather have had the good will of the Dutch, for now I was a double exile.

On my return that evening, there was some commotion in the streets and bells had begun to ring across the city. My coachman ask'd a passer-by what all the fuss was about. 'The King is dead!' he shout'd.

<u>*The King is dead*</u> *– finally. However, before I cou'd think much more on the subject, I was also greet'd with the news that Katherine was in labour. Although still far from an expert in such matters, despite all my researches, I thought this a little premature and said as much to Charlotte.*

'One cannot be sure of such things, Monsieur, especially with a first child...'

I rush'd upstairs and found Katherine sitting on the bed, clutching her swollen stomach and moaning softly. A smile of relief flicker'd across her drawn face.

'Oh John! Thank God, you've return'd. I've spent months wishing the babe dead and now I'm so scar'd that it will happen...I'm in so much pain. It's so much worse than I imagin'd...surely, there's something wrong...'

'There's nothing wrong,' I said.

'Yes, the baby's dying, I know it...' And she dissolv'd into tears.

I hugg'd her and whisper'd comforting words, only to find water pouring on to the floor, as if I had squeez'd it from her myself. Charlotte bustl'd in behind me with towels.

'The waters have broken, Monsieur, a sure sign...'

'The waters?' Had the pain forc'd her to lose control of her bladder?

'The fluid that surrounds the babe in the womb, Monsieur...it is releas'd when the birth is nigh...'

'Yes...of course...the fluid...' As Katherine had said about her mother all those months before and there was I, a witness to it.

'Anyway, this is no place for a man,' she said, ushering me away. 'The midwife will be here shortly...'

Yet before I cou'd leave, Katherine did in fact begin to urinate and she follow'd this by vomiting on to the floor. Charlotte seem'd to take this in her stride. 'There, there, Madame, 'tis very normal – evacuation at both ends, clearing the way for the babe to come...'

I look'd on, appall'd and powerless.

'Where is the midwife?' I ask'd.

Charlotte was helping Katherine off with her ruin'd shift. 'I sent the maid for her as soon as the pains start'd, Monsieur. God knows where that girl has got to...'

Reliev'd to be able to retire from the room, I set off in search of the maid and all but collid'd with her in the entrance hall. She had run in, flush'd and distress'd and cou'd hardly speak for weeping; then words came in a breathless torrent.

139

'Oh, Monsieur, surely you know...the King is dead...and the streets are full of people saying it is the end of the world and what is to happen with the heir only a boy and who is to lead us through these dark days?' – Who indeed? I thought – 'And I was coming along with the midwife and some drunken buffoon staggers into her and knocks her into the road and she falls in front of a passing carriage, which was not going fast because the road was so crowd'd and...'

'Is she all right?' I ask'd impatiently. 'Will she be coming?'

The girl shook her head and sobb'd afresh. 'I don't think she'll be doing much midwifing tonight, Monsieur...'

I had only a moment to contemplate this news, as well as that of Louis' death, before Charlotte was shouting down at me from the first landing: 'Please, Monsieur, there is no time to waste! We must get the midwife!'

I climb'd the grand staircase and explain'd what had happen'd; Charlotte immediately turn'd on her heels and head'd back to Katherine. 'Then I'm going to need your help, Monsieur...'

I had not felt such trepidation since I stood in front of Beau Wickham that fateful morn. Was it the fear of what wou'd happen to Katherine and the child after what she had just said to me? Or simply fear of what to most men is the great awful mystery of childbirth? Both, in all likelihood. All I knew for certain was that as I climb'd those stairs to help Charlotte bring more towels and hot water, I felt like a condemn'd man ascending to the scaffold.

When I return'd, Katherine was lying on the bed with her knees up under her shift. She did not seem to question my presence, nor did she ask about the midwife. All she cou'd say was 'Tell me I'm not going to lose the child, John. I'd rather die myself than lose it. Please tell me it'll be all right...'

'Of course, you're not going to lose the child, Madame,' Charlotte's voice of reason cut in. 'What are you thinking? It's almost here, you'll be holding the babe in your arms in no time...'

'But you don't know what I've said, the terrible things I've wish'd for...'

'I'm sure I don't, but the time for saying and wishing is over. It's doing what's requir'd now, Madame....'

140

As the labour pangs grew more intense and frequent, Katherine got up and mov'd around, with our help, or sat on a chair and then return'd to the bed, squatting back against the huge mahogany headboard. In this way she tried to ride the waves of pain, or 'contractions' as Charlotte call'd them, which apparently are the tightening of the womb, squeezing the child out into the birth channel.

At the height of these waves, Katherine wail'd loudly and utter'd the foulest language – in English, I am glad to say, for poor Charlotte had enough to cope with. She held my wrist or hand so tightly that it hurt for days afterwards, drawing blood with the very nails that had so often scor'd my back at the height of our passion.

The contractions continued for what seem'd an interminable period, during which Katherine became so distraught and exhaust'd that she sobb'd without pause. I began to fear that mother and child really were in mortal danger and that her perverse wish was about to come true. Even I, the infidel, utter'd a desperate prayer to myself that such a thing wou'd not come to pass.

Finally, having put a hand and then look'd between her mistress' legs, Charlotte announc'd that it was time for Madame to push as hard as she cou'd.

'Push? Isn't that what Madame has been doing all this time?' I ask'd, surpris'd.

'No, Monsieur, the passage from the womb is only now wide enough for the child to pass through...'

Charlotte and I now knelt on the bed either side of Katherine and with our arms around her shoulders, urg'd her to push – or 'bear down', Charlotte said, 'as if – excuse me, Monsieur – you are passing a large stool, Madame...'

Katherine duly push'd until she cou'd push no more, while Charlotte and I shout'd ourselves hoarse. We had reach'd our lowest ebb, when the housekeeper duck'd below the great orb of Katherine's stomach and came up with a broad smile.

'The head, Monsieur! The babe's head is there!'

Did I dare look for myself? I did, and saw between the widely stretch'd lips of Katherine's sex what seem'd nothing more than the moist skin of an apple – the very top of the child's crown, as it turn'd out.

With this news to spur her on and with Charlotte exhorting her to push some more, Katherine redoubl'd her efforts. And sure enough, I cou'd see the child's head begin to emerge. 'Yes!' I shout'd. 'Yes! It's coming!'

'Is it alive?' Katherine manag'd. 'Please tell me it's alive...'

'Madame, just keep pushing...'

Katherine now began to breathe more heavily and moan as if in the grip of some powerful climax, while Charlotte began to ease the child into the world, revealing the whole of its huge head and then its shoulders.

Then, all at once, the babe slipp'd out on to the sheets, like a fish bringing a bloody stream in its wake. And there she lay, my daughter, pink and glistening, fixing me with a stare, as if we had been long acquaint'd, before letting out a howl to wake the dead - or at least, alert Katherine that she had arriv'd and was alive.

'Thank God!' she cried, in a voice that was as broken and exhaust'd as she was.

Like Dante himself, we had all been to Hell and back, but now we were in Heaven. The umbilical had been cut and tied, the afterbirth deliver'd – more fluid! – and, for all Katherine's terrible misgivings, it appear'd that neither mother nor child had suffer'd any injury during the bloody struggle, in which I had play'd an active if reluctant part. I felt my researches into child bearing and now birthing were complete – or rather, as complete as I ever wish'd them to be.

Finally, we were able to give the babe to Katherine to hold, and I watch'd as she press'd our daughter firmly to her chest, giving her the most adoring look and what I imagin'd to be silent thanks that her wish of many months had not been grant'd.

'I wou'd like to call her Anne,' she said, 'if you have no objection.'

'After Anne Boleyn?'

'After my mother...'

I smil'd and nodd'd. It was obviously another of those womanly paradoxes.

As the dawn whiten'd, an atmosphere of exhaust'd calm pervad'd the room. Katherine slept peacefully and I had taken Kate from Charlotte, insisting that the housekeeper get some rest herself. Having open'd the curtain a little, the better to see the *child, I stood holding her by the window, in awe of her tiny perfection, admiring her every monumental movement. Outside, the city itself also seem'd swaddl'd in calm, and I cou'd not help but wonder who, if anyone, had taken up the reins of government and what that wou'd mean for our new family.*

As I did so, I look'd back towards the sleeping Katherine and was shaken to see standing beside her the pale, translucent figure of the phantom. He was there for a matter of seconds, that is all, but it was enough to see that he wore some kind of mask and was dress'd head to toe in ghostly white; there was no sign of his chest wound.

I watch'd him stretch a hand towards her, as if to wake her or – much worse – take her away.

'Katherine!' I said in warning, but he had disappear'd and she did not stir. Even so, I was compell'd to cross to the bed and check that she was safe, which she was – safe and beautiful, even after the rigours of childbirth. Still holding the babe, I leant over her, kiss'd her softly on the cheek – and wept from a mixture of fear and relief.

Later that morning, as I struggl'd to sleep, my head in turmoil from the events of the night before, a carriage with the Bourbon livery drew up in front of the house. To my astonishment, Saint-Simon was announc'd. He look'd as vague and untidy as ever, but beam'd when he heard our news.

'One life is taken, and another given – ah, the eternal cycle, Monsieur Law, congratulations!'

'Thank you, Your Grace.'

'Last night, it turns out, was significant indeed,' he went on. 'The duc d'Orleans persuad'd the other members the Council that he alone shou'd be Regent.'

I was stunn'd by this news. 'And how did he achieve that, Your Grace?'

'Through the judicious deployment of several hundred troops, Monsieur Law. As you said, legitimacy must sometimes be seiz'd. I came to say that in a week or so, when His Royal Highness has had the chance to consolidate his new position, he wou'd be grateful if you cou'd come to speak to him again about the' – he paus'd before saying the words – 'Science of Money…and your plans for a new bank.'

Chapter 6

Venice, October 1728

'*Buongiorno, il Duce. And how is the richest man in the world this morning?*'

'*I'm sure he is well, Count,*' *I reply,* '*but I am terrible...and getting worse.*'

The conte di Bellini feigns a pain'd expression. '*I heard you were not well,*' *he says, and gestures towards the gaming salon.* '*But not so unwell that you cannot play, I hope. After all, there is no better remedy for sickness than winning at cards, il Duce...*'

The Conte smiles, wishes me better and leaves. He likes our little jokes, although I do not joke about my condition, which is indeed deteriorating.

I am in my usual spot on this late October morn, sitting on the piano nobile at the Ridotto, sipping my hot chocolate, ready to resume my story. I feel excit'd, even happy at the prospect. My pulse quickens as I picture myself over 10 years ago, my best days still to come, bringing with them wealth and power beyond even my imagining. And all this due to one thing: my superior understanding of the nature of Credit.

Of all the figures on Pellegrini's ceiling – our ceiling – I made sure that Credit was the grandest, the most striking. More than Security, Industry and Money itself, Credit was the life-blood of my System. Only I recognis'd its true importance, whereas even the English and Dutch treat'd it cautiously, lending only to those who could already afford it, approaching it as the Puritan does the act of sex, as a necessary evil.

Only I embrac'd Credit without reserve, and understood it for what it is – a commitment to the future, a force for change that wou'd take us into a new age. By establishing first the Bank and then the Company I was able to provide money not only to lords and landlords, but to farmers, trades people, shopkeepers, artisans, those who have little to pledge but their future prospects. In this way, I turn'd the wheels of commerce until they had enough momentum to turn by themselves. And once start'd, I knew they wou'd never stop; that they wou'd roll over anything that stood in their way. This is in fact what quickens my pulse: not so much the thought that I was to grow richer and more powerful, but that I began a social and economic revolution and for a brief moment stood a whole society on its head.

I see myself, those 10 years ago, visiting the Palais-Royal once again. As advis'd by Saint-Simon, I had made no contact with Orleans for several weeks, during which time I heard little news of him, save that he had sack'd Desmarets and taken a new mistress, a Madame Parabère. (The gossip in Paris, of course, was mostly concern'd with the latter.) Seeing him in his new role came as something of a surprise. A greater contrast to the man who had presid'd over an orgy it was difficult to imagine. Now it was an orgy of administration he oversaw, an informal court where obsequious secretaries came and went, busily pulling the levers of government in a way that Louis wou'd never have permitt'd. In this sense alone, Philippe already represent'd a new era of leadership, as much bureaucratic as autocratic.

He receiv'd me in his full regalia — hugely bewigg'd, wearing an ermine-trimm'd velvet jacket with the Royal sash secur'd by large rubies set in gold. I bow'd low before him; he seem'd extremely pleas'd to see me and insist'd that everyone clear'd the court so that we might be alone. Once we were, he immediately undid the top buttons of his jacket, pour'd us wine and slump'd back on his 'throne', an extravagantly carved ebony chair, crown'd with the Bourbon crest.

He sigh'd heavily in what I was beginning to recognise as his more theatrical manner. 'Monsieur Law, have I done the right thing?'

'In seeing me alone, Your Royal Highness?' I said only half-jokingly, for I was not sure to what he referr'd.

'In becoming Regent,' he replied.

'Ah...most certainly,' I said, certain that it was the right thing for me at least. 'I hear Your Royal Highness acquitt'd himself like a true commander-in-the-field.'

He smil'd. 'My military action took everyone by surprise, it's true. Most of them had only ever seen a sword used ceremonially – they were scar'd out of their wits, which is not saying much at all...' And we both laugh'd, until His Royal visage suddenly cloud'd over. 'But I must tell you, Monsieur Law, I did not entirely carry the day. Certain compromises had to be made in order to secure enough support for the Regency. Parlement now has the Right of Remonstrance, which cou'd prove extremely troublesome, and all the major departments of government have Councils, which I am oblig'd to consult on important matters of state. So you see, my power is far from absolute, even if my idea of absolute power is far from that of the late king - God rest his soul.'

'Indeed,' I nodd'd.

'However,' he continued, his voice taking on a more hush'd tone, 'if I am to rely on the art of persuasion and negotiation as much as outright authority, there must be a select few I can trust implicitly. Saint-Simon is ill-suit'd to any specific role in government, but is a trust'd friend and advisor nonetheless. I have appoint'd the Abbé Dubois as my Foreign Minister. He was a tutor of mine when I was a boy – better at teaching the ways of the world than Latin or Greek, for which I am eternally grateful; he is a shrewd counsellor, as well as negotiator. Also, as you probably know, I have dismiss'd that fool Desmarets and appoint'd the duc de Noailles as Financial Controller. Noailles has many good ideas and great...energy.'

He paus'd to drink his wine and seem'd to be trying to gauge my reaction to this, although I wore only my card-playing expression. 'And I suspect he will need all of it,' he add'd, 'because the state of French finances appears to be worse than even we had imagin'd.'

'Is that possible?' I ask'd.

He nodd'd slowly. 'The country is bankrupt, in debt to the tune of over two billion livres, a conservative estimate, I'd say – which of course makes it even more important that you yourself are among my trusted circle...'

'I am deeply honour'd, Your Highness.'

Philippe wav'd this away. 'The honour is mine, Monsieur Law. Now to come to your letter, which was both inspiring and *intriguing. In it, if memory serves, you say that you will produce a great work of Money Science, greater than a Bank even.'*

'I did - and I will.'

'And I am very excit'd by that prospect and look forward to hearing about your scheme in great detail...'

'Thank you, Your Highness.'

He drank some more wine. 'Meanwhile, I'd be grateful if you were to share your ideas with the duc de Noailles at the very earliest opportunity. I'm sure you'll find him very receptive to everything you have to say.'

And before I cou'd reply, Philippe was on his feet and re-buttoning his jacket. 'In fact, let me introduce you to Monsieur le Duc right now...'

Why I felt so deeply disappoint'd by this, I am not sure. I did not seriously entertain the notion of Orleans asking me to be Financial Controller – apart from anything else, as a foreigner, I was not eligible. But I did expect him to take an immediate and personal interest in my Money Science and resent'd the fact that he want'd me to share it at this point with one of his time-serving flunkies.

Which was pre-judging Monsieur le Duc, I admit, but turn'd out to be a highly flattering assessment of his character. Desmarets had simply been incompetent, but Noailles compound'd that particular shortcoming with a dangerous arrogance. He was the consummate courtier – always a bad sign – full of false smiles and fine phrases, which he seem'd to hiss through thin lips rather than speak. How deeply honour'd and privileg'd he was to meet me...how highly His Royal Highness had spoken of me...how very astute a financier I must be...and how very much he look'd forward to what he was sure wou'd be our fruitful association. All of which made my stomach turn. Orleans, how cou'd you? I thought, how cou'd you do this to me?

'Naturally, my dear Monsieur Law, I have many ideas myself,' Noailles add'd.

'Naturally...'

'I plan an immediate reduction in the value of all government bonds and a revaluation of the currency, which will involve recalling all coinage, re-minting it and' – he was very

proud of this old ruse – 'appropriating a percentage of the gold as bullion for the government.'

It was all very depressing and my own false smile must have signall'd as much to Philippe because he began to look a little uncomfortable. 'Yes...well...I'm sure there's something in that, Monsieur Law, don't you?'

He was spar'd further discomfort by the fairy-like entrance of the woman I took to be Madame de Sery's replacement, Madame Parabère. She was small, but exquisitely form'd and walk'd swiftly, almost on tiptoe, which gave her the appearance of almost floating on air. She spoke in a soft high-pitch'd voice, saying that government was all well and good, but it had denied her the company of her 'sweetness' long enough. Orleans, who was obviously still in the earliest stages of infatuation with Madame P, went from being somewhat regal to having the demeanour of a large drooling puppy, jumping up its mistress' skirts. He made the most perfunctory of introductions, apologis'd for having to leave us and was promptly led off virtually skipping to the boudoir. Little wonder, I thought, that her 'sweetness' had had no time for the discussion of finances.

Over the next month or so I saw next to nothing of Philippe, but a great deal, unfortunately, of Monsieur le Duc. Revealing the full scope of the System to the man seem'd futile. It was all he cou'd do to grasp the notion of a paper currency, obsess'd as he was with the Treasury acquiring as much metal as possible. And although he smil'd appreciatively and applaud'd my financial acumen, the idea of establishing a National Bank that regulat'd the supply of paper money was completely beyond him.

As if this charade were not bad enough, matters suddenly took a more sinister turn. One morning when I arriv'd for yet another meeting with him at the Palais-Royal, he ask'd if I might join him on a short journey.

'Where to?' I ask'd.

'The Bastille.'

'The Bastille?'

Noailles' false smile grew broader. 'My dear Monsieur Law, relax...I am not arresting you.'

'I am pleas'd to here it,' I said. 'I have seen more than my fair share of prisons.' He cock'd an eyebrow, but said no more on the subject, except that we wou'd first be stopping off at the Convent of the Grand Augustins.

'To pick up prisoners?' I jok'd, tir'd of this coyness.

'As you'll see,' came the sombre reply, 'that is not such an absurd notion...

Out in the city there were distinct signs of spring. Trees were budding along the Seine, birdsong echoed around the courtyards and the breeze had grown mild and gentle. But if nature was turning clement, commercial life was still mir'd in winter. Due to Desmaret's and now Noailles' economic measures, more and more shops and businesses were closing, the theatres were dark and the city was beginning to resemble a provincial backwater. The only activity on the increase was begging, as more and more people found themselves without employment. Was Monsieur le Duc aware of this sad state of affairs? If so, he kept it to himself as he gaz'd impassively out of the carriage window.

*

Poor Jo – she goes away for a romantic weekend in Venice only to find she's in the company of a complete fruitcake. I decide that for her sake, if no other reason, I must make every effort to stay on top of things. While she's here with me, I'll live in the moment. I'll set all the sources of my anxiety aside: the black holes of depression, the Vatican deal (I'll not send another email), the feeling of being stalked or haunted or whatever, the re-living of my last months with Angela and Grace, our daughter. All this must be put out of my mind – or at least to the back of it – so I can be *present* and concentrate on her.

How difficult can that be? I ask myself, as we're having brunch in the Il Ridotto restaurant, which is next to the hotel. She's gorgeous, intelligent, great company – and young. Surely I can allow myself to be wrapped up in her for a couple of days. And yet I know, of course, that if simply saying things was enough to make them happen, life would be a kind of heaven on

149

earth, and it's not. It's more a kind of hell and I don't really expect my good intentions to have much of an impact, although I'll certainly try. Short of turning off my phone, I'll do everything I can.

We hardly ate last night, so we're both ravenous. We can't speak for tucking into a breakfast of prosciutto, bruschetta and scrambled eggs with more than a hint of parmesan. When we do talk, Joanna discreetly avoids the subject of my disturbing behaviour, and anyway, we're high on the view of the Grand Canal and the sparkling weather. It's a great day for sightseeing. We decide to book a motor launch with a guide. We'll go exploring and have lunch at the Cipriani.

Being at Il Ridotto reminds me of John Law, of course, another subject I must set aside while Jo is here. But this also proves far from easy. As we head for the quayside, negotiating our way through a large group of Chinese tourists, I receive a text from Diana Lennon. The owner of the manuscript is available for lunch – would I like to meet him? My immediate reaction is to put her off, but then I think, why not? It's the reason I decided to come to Venice and it could well add to the fun. Jo might find it interesting and it will give me an excuse to tell her about John Law. So I ask Diana if she wants to meet us at the Cipriani at 1.00 for lunch. My treat. (It's only later it occurs to me that demonstrating my largesse is hardly the best way to get a good deal on the manuscript, should I decide I want it.)

She texts back instantly: 'How very kind, Theo.' Even though I've had little contact with her, I can hear her sly wryness in these few words. She's the wiser, older sister; I'm the precocious baby brother slowly catching on to the real ways of the world. It's disturbing the effect this woman has on me. Nothing simple like sexual attraction, it works on some other, more metaphysical level, as if she's a guardian angel who's maybe the devil in disguise.

But no, I mustn't run away with such thoughts. I mustn't get side tracked. The moment, the moment, I tell myself, for fuck's sake, live in the moment, Theo…

I broach the subject of John Law with Jo. I tell her how I have an historic connection with Venice, through a distant forbear, who was here in the early 18th century. In fact, he's the reason we're booked into the Monaco, where he all but lived in what was then a gaming salon. To my surprise, she's full of interest.

'That's amazing, Theo – do you know much about him?'

'He was so badly behaved his life's been quite well documented. The devil has the best tunes, as they say…' She's even more intrigued, especially when I tell her about his manuscript and how I've arranged for us to meet its owner and the dealer who put us in touch, Diana Lennon.

She laughs. 'So I'm not your only reason for coming to Venice.'

'Do you feel insulted?'

'I feel happy to be with you – whatever your reason for being here.' She *is* gorgeous.

At the boat, our guide introduces herself as Marisa. She's a woman of a certain age, with large tortoiseshell glasses and heavily hennaed hair that contrasts wonderfully with her bright yellow puffa jacket. (Brightly coloured puffas are obviously the winter wear of choice this year, and indeed, Jo has this morning exchanged the navy-blue overcoat she wore last night for a dark orange puffa.)

Marisa has a big smile, very white teeth and English that is so good it could only be spoken by a foreigner. But for her liberal use of the words *allora* and *avanti*, you would never know she was Italian.

'*Allora*…I know how the British love to talk about the weather,' she says, 'but this is the season when we're obsessed with it too.' She pulls a sad face. 'There's a storm coming in later, so I suggest we make the most of the sun. And bring some waterproof boots. *Acqua alta* will return, I'm afraid…'

Before we embark, she offers us a choice of themes for the tour: the Major Churches, Art and Architecture, Titian and Tintoretto, Daily Life in the Renaissance, Backwaters, the Age of Decadence – her own particular favourite – or just something very general. She does them all – it's up to us.

Funnily enough, we both opt for Decadence.

'Good!' she says. 'It certainly brightens up a gloomy winter season. It's the story of the city's glorious decline during the

151

18th century, from which, you could say, it's never really recovered. Unless you think this Age of Mass Tourism represents another cultural flowering...' Again, the big open smile.

And she begins the tour immediately by pointing behind us, back towards the hotel. 'I think you're staying at the Monaco?' We nod.

'*Allora*...you may not know but it was once the Ridotto, a notorious gaming house, the world's first casino, frequented by the richest and most corrupt Venetians of the time, as well as similar types from all over Europe – Eurotrash, as we might now call them. It's said that when they ran out of gold while playing at the table, they wagered their courtesans. '

Jo gives me a wry smile. 'We do know about the Ridotto. Theo's ancestor used to be one of the er Eurotrash who frequented it.'

Marisa laughs and looks at me with renewed interest. 'Who was that?'

'A Scotsman called John Law. I'm a direct descendant.'

'Ha! Well, I *am* impressed. This tour always begins with John Law. I always say his arrival in Venice raises the curtain on the Age of Decadence. I hope you're not offended.'

'Not at all. It makes me very proud.'

We board the launch. 'I know what will be our last stop today,' Marisa says.

'What's that?'

'Your ancestor's grave – although I expect you've already made that pilgrimage?'

'No...never...'

'*Avanti!*'

*

The Convent of the Grand Augustins was itself built like a prison and hidden behind high stone walls, doubtless to keep the heathen without as much the Brides of Christ within. We enter'd via a long white corridor, lin'd with morbid icons and crucifixes, and came into a small hall, where guards were post'd along the panelled walls. The hall was shot through with bolts of sunlight from small narrow windows, one of which illuminat'd what seem'd to be a group of officials gather'd in conference around a long oak table at the far end. It was only as we drew closer I realis'd this was a tribunal or court: a man, flank'd by guards, on one side of the table, was undergoing interrogation by four imposing fellows in long crimson robes on the other.

Noailles was immediately welcom'd by the one I took to be the head of this court and the questioning halt'd while they spoke quietly to each other; Noailles then bade them continue. We stood off in the shadows, where he hiss'd with pride into my ear: 'Welcome to the Chamber of Justice, Monsieur Law.'

I took a deep breath, determin'd not to let him know how disconcert'd I was. 'Justice for whom?' I ask'd.

'For those who have profit'd illegally from France's economic misfortune. I thought that the convent wou'd add an air of sanctity to the proceedings, as well as being somewhat discreet, of course.'

'Of course.'

'This is only the second day of its operation,' he continued with enthusiasm, 'but already large sums have been recover'd for the Crown from corrupt officials and dishonest money lenders - or financiers, as they are known in more elevat'd circles.' He fix'd me briefly with his snake eyes, before gesturing towards the table where the 'accus'd' was shaking his head frantically and pleading with the men opposite. 'This man is a senior tax official who has been lining his own pockets. He can agree to repay his ill-gotten gains now, together with a substantial fine. Or he will be tortur'd until he agrees - and then the fine will be much greater.'

'To cover the cost of the torture,' I found myself saying.

'Indeed...' Monsieur le Duc chuckl'd at this, but only because he took it seriously.

'What of the evidence?' I enquir'd.

'Evidence?'

'Against these people. Evidence of their crimes.'

'Ah yes. In most cases their fraud is a matter of public knowledge, although it has been tolerat'd for years. We will also offer rewards to those who inform on such criminals. We

are starting with the big fish, but will move on to the minnows in due course. Such is the scale of corruption that the income to the Treasury will be considerable, enough to silence all talk of bankruptcy...'

And now this corruption wou'd become even greater by masquerading as justice, I thought. Nothing wou'd be reform'd, no change effect'd. The Crown wou'd simply extort as much as possible from 'such criminals' – in other words, its former agents and creditors – until there was nothing left and all confidence was destroy'd. As with the 'revaluation' of the currency, the effect wou'd simply be to drive money away. In the longer term the policy wou'd be disastrous.

Noailles was ready to leave and a shrinking feeling in my stomach told me that we were about to visit one of his 'big fish' – a guest of his in the Bastille. I tried to brace myself for the experience, but little cou'd have prepar'd me for what was to come, not even twenty years in Newgate.

The Bastille was not far and we were there within minutes. Once through the great iron gates, we were escort'd into one of the prison's enormous towers, where the bright spring day and all its hopes were extinguish'd like a candle. Not a splinter of natural light found its way into the foetid darkness of this Royal fortress. And although it was less crowd'd than Newgate and therefore less rank, I judg'd it an even more monstrous place in that all prisoners were in solitary confinement and denied any kind of physical comfort, no matter how much they cou'd afford to pay.

Our torchbearers led us down a series of echoing spiral steps. As we went deeper, the air grew fouler and the walls began to ooze a black slime as if all the waste of Paris were draining into them. We pass'd a number of poor wretches, incarcerat'd behind bars in filthy narrow cells, all of them seemingly too weak even to cry out to us. In fact, the only sound, apart from our own footfalls, came from a chamber at the far end of the passage: the prolong'd groan, I was to discover, of a man being stretch'd upon the rack.

Only Noailles and I enter'd the chamber, which had a high vault'd ceiling and contain'd what I assum'd to be other instruments of torture, thrown into ghastly relief by the sconces on the wall. In the middle was the infernal contraption itself, and spread upon it, chained hand and foot and nak'd to the waist, was the victim, suffering the agonies of being slowly stretch'd. A large, beard'd oaf in a leather jerkin was operating the dreadful device, while nearby a young fellow sat at a small desk with pen and ledger, as if he were a bookkeeper counting the day's takings – which I suppose in some bizarre way he was.

My impulse was to run from the room rather than be a witness to such barbarism, but before I cou'd do so, Monsieur le Duc, sensing my revulsion, took my arm in an iron grip and drew me closer to the grisly scene. His black eyes shone like bits of jet in the torch's flame. I think he was truly excit'd by the sight of the man groaning on the rack, whose face was contort'd like screw'd up parchment and whose fleshy torso dripp'd with so much sweat that it seem'd he had been dous'd by water.

'I believe you know him,' said Noailles. 'A Jew, so also a foreigner, like yourself, Monsieur Law...'

The implications of this remark were unpleasant in the extreme. But why shou'd I have known him? I thought, before I realis'd that even in these appalling circumstances his face seem'd vaguely familiar.

'Tell Monsieur Law our guest's name,' he said to the clerk.

'It's Samuel Bernard, the financier, Monsieur,' the young man replied, a schoolboy, anxious to please. Samuel Bernard – a man I had first met at Philippe's table and since then welcom'd at one of my own gatherings.

'And has Monsieur Bernard, the financier, agreed to repay the Crown as yet?' Noailles ask'd the bookkeeper.

'He has, Your Grace. Two million livres.'

Noailles nodd'd to the rack operator. 'Let's tighten the chain a little, shall we, until we're promised four million – in gold.' And he look'd at me with his viper's smile.

'Let us call it a tax upon his vast profits. Monsieur Bernard can afford it, I'm sure...'

'Is the Regent aware of this?' I ask'd Noailles.

'Of the Chamber of Justice or of this particular... interrogation?'

'Both,' I said.

'His Royal Highness thinks the Chamber of Justice a brilliant idea...and it was he who suggest'd we start by prosecuting Monsieur Bernard...'

I look'd away as the rack was turn'd another notch and thought of Philippe entwin'd with Madame Parabère and the dangers of delegating power to the unworthy.

*

The first part of our tour is all done from the launch. Just being on the canal is an exhilarating business: the sunlight flashing off the water, the bright little boats and gondolas, the gilded buildings etched against the blue sky. Such a contrast to yesterday when the city was submerged in gloom and drizzle and my mood was a sodden, sunken thing along with it. Now, while Marisa speaks so eloquently about the past, I have no trouble being present. We pause at several grand old palazzos, built by the City's ancient families. These, she says, were the patricians whose fortunes faded with those of the city and who surrendered their influence and palaces to the new rich, a brasher crowd, all money and no class or roots in the city's distinguished past.

She points out various architectural features and what they symbolise. She tells us stories of each family and its decline, and the inexorable decline of the city. As it cedes its overseas interests to the larger, stronger trading nations of Europe – the British and the Dutch – Venice's coffers are severely depleted. Her sea power wanes; she ceases to count as a serious international player and becomes the playground of Europe instead, morally as well as financially bankrupt.

As the city grows more corrupt, Marisa's language grows more colourful. How quickly La Serinissima embraces her new role. How happy she is to open her legs and play the highborn whore, to provide an exquisite breeding ground for venality, frivolity and sexual licence – all of which is epitomised by the annual orgy of fun that is Carnivale.

'I'm beginning to understand what brought John Law here,' I laugh.

'It was the perfect place for him,' says Marisa, 'He was such a notorious, mysterious figure…'

'Just like Theo,' Jo interjects to more laughter.

'He fell from grace so spectacularly, under the weight of such a grand scandal. It's not everyone who could have brought France, the most powerful nation in Europe, to its knees and sown the seeds of the Revolution. He loved Venice and Venice loved him back. Decadence breeds tolerance – or at least it has sympathy for the failure, the outcast, because it has become one itself.'

She speaks about Law with such authority that I'm about to ask if she knows of anything he wrote while he was in Venice. But I hear the ping of my phone, signalling the first email of the day. It's likely to be a reply from one of my investors. I resist looking at it for all of 30 seconds and then apologise for taking it out. (I don't know why - no one else does these days.) The mail's from an anonymous source and marked 'No Reply'. The words are all upper case, shouty:

'THEO, WE KNOW WHAT YOU'RE DOING AND WE'RE PUTTING A STOP TO IT. ENJOY VENICE. IT'S A BEAUTIFUL PLACE TO DIE.'

We've stopped in front of the Palladian façade of Ca'Rezzonico, the grandest palazzo of them all, not far from the landing where I came to visit Diana Lennon yesterday. (Was it only yesterday?) Marisa is explaining its origins: 'So here we have the greatest example…'

But I'm not taking it in. I can only think of the email. *Who* knows? *What* do they know? *What* are they putting a stop to? A beautiful place to *die*? What the *fuck…*'

And yet, I'm not sure why I'm asking myself these questions, because I probably know the answers.

'*Allora…*' Marisa is saying that the patrician Bon family started to build the palazzo but ran out of money and sold it to the arriviste Rezzonicos. Meanwhile, I grip the side of the launch and topple headlong into the deepest, darkest, blackest hole I've ever experienced.

*

Within days the work of Monsieur le Duc's Chamber of Justice had been made public knowledge. I look'd on appalled as many of the leading financiers were forc'd to pay large sums of money to the government in order to atone for their 'profiteering', which in effect had amount'd to lending more money to the state than the state cou'd ever afford to repay them. Most brib'd their way out of trouble, of course – hardly a major saving – but as resistance stiffen'd in some cases, so did the punishments. After suffering torture, many were imprison'd and Noailles, carried away on a wave of vindictiveness, insist'd on public disgrace and humiliation for several of the more prominent offenders. They were display'd in pillories outside Notre Dame with signs hung about their necks – 'This thief has stolen from the People of France'.

Even worse, Noailles' offer of rewards for information leading to the arrest of profiteers quickly creat'd a new mode of social intercourse: mass betrayal. Husbands and wives, parents and children, masters and servants, friends and neighbours, all inform'd on each other, not only for suspect'd fraud, but for hoarding coins that had not been exchang'd for revaluation - which meant almost everyone. And all for a small percentage of whatever gold was recover'd, for many their only likely source of income.

The talk at our dinners and soirées was of little else and quickly turn'd against the Regent and his Financial Controller. Katherine, who to everyone's surprise was back in the social whirl within a week of the birth, made the essential point. Did it matter how much money was being recoup'd for the nation? A modicum of trust between people was surely the mortar that bound society together and yet this was rapidly being dissolv'd by Noailles' Chamber of Justice. Soon it wou'd bring the whole edifice tumbling down.

As she was speaking, I cou'd not help recalling how the mortar between us had been severely damag'd during her pregnancy and I comfort'd myself with the thought that it was well on the way to being restor'd.

Saint-Simon appear'd one evening, looking as dishevell'd as ever, and join'd the chorus of protest and disillusion. He was full of apologies to me personally for the turn events had taken. 'I can assure you, Monsieur Law, that I was never in favour of the duc de Noailles' appointment. I have observ'd his plausible but poisonous manner over many years. Apparently, Dubois sponsor'd him heavily and Philippe listens more and more to his old tutor. Of course, I have voic'd my disapproval, but the clinking of gold flowing into our national coffers seems to have drown'd me out...'

I smil'd wryly at this. The more I saw of Saint-Simon, the more I lik'd him and thought he return'd the compliment. Yes, he cou'd be as slippery a courtier as the best of them and yet somehow, he stood above the court's petty jealousies and intrigues, and manag'd to cast an impartial eye over the whole tir'd tableaux. Once again, in his oblique manner, he seem'd to be summoning me to fight for a cause that he cou'd not quite define for himself but knew instinctively was right – a financial system that would relieve France of its damaging corruption.

That evening when the guests had depart'd, Katherine took our wakeful, fretful daughter from the nurse and we sat in the bedchamber before the fire. Within minutes she had manag'd to pacify the child with soothing words and milk from her breast. (She had dismiss'd the wet nurse early on and decid'd to feed Anne herself, rare for someone of her class.) I do not think I can remember a more wonderful sight – not Pellegrini's ceiling, or freshly print'd banknotes, or even a late summer sunset over the Grand Canal. Nothing compar'd to Katherine sitting there that evening, her face and shoulders as smooth as ivory, glowing in the firelight. She was still in her sequinn'd evening gown, the top of which she had unlac'd to feed the babe. I watch'd the child suckling contentedly, her face buried in the swell of her mother's breast, and marvell'd at this Madonna and Child. It seem'd to me a vision of tenderness and perfection.

Katherine look'd up at me. 'What are you thinking?' she ask'd.

'That I've never been happier.'

She smil'd, held out a hand, which I rais'd gently to my lips. What I said next was completely unpremeditat'd, coming as much as a surprise to myself as it did to Katherine.

'I want nothing more than this, you know.'

'Do I know?'

'Not the bank, not the company, not our so-call'd System, not this house full of treasures, none of it. We are what is important. Our little family. Ca suffi.'

She look'd puzzl'd.

'I'm thinking out loud, of course...'

'Clearly...'

'And I'm thinking we shou'd leave Paris. Go to some other part of France. Or perhaps to Venice, where I know they love to game.'

'Why wou'd we do that?

'For a peaceful, happy, family life, Katherine. Simply for that. I cou'd play at the tables, make all the money we need'd and more – and we wou'd cease to be involv'd in this sordid political drama, subject, as we are, to the whim of a Bourbon Prince and all the ghastly flunkies around him. Apart from Saint-Simon, that is. He's an exception. I wou'd miss Saint-Simon...but maybe he wou'd come to visit us...'

She had gather'd a more and more concern'd expression.

'John, are you serious about this?'

'I am. I realise it is very much on the spur of the moment, but I'm serious about our family – and I'm serious about not wanting to wait around for Philippe to allow me to implement my – our – proposals. From what I've seen of him and his court it's unlikely to happen. I think we're wasting our time...'

Anne had stopp'd feeding and gone off to sleep; Katherine went across the room, plac'd her gently in the bassinet by our bed and return'd to the fireside chair.

'Your happiness with our family is a great happiness to me, John, and of course I agree we shou'd come before all else. But that doesn't mean that we need to give up on our plans. I've watch'd you this nearly two years.' (Had it been that long?)

'You thrive on being in society; you love the cut and thrust of the court, just as you do that of the gaming room. You must remember they involve many of the same things: trickery, fakery

160

and calculat'd risk. You excel at all of them at the card table –
you must play the same game at court.'
I laugh'd at this – yes, I was very good at bad things like
trickery and fakery.
'And you love nothing more than winning. That's why you're
frustrat'd. You have the best of hands and you're not able to
play it. Well, let me tell you - I enjoy winning too, as much as
you do, maybe even more so, and I'm not willing to give up on
this game until we get the chance to play our hand and win it. If
Philippe is withholding his endorsement for the bank and that's
what's standing in our way, we need to work on him. I need to
work on him...'
'You?'
'Yes, John - me... It shou'd be as plain as the Roman nose
on your face. Philippe is most susceptible to attractive women
in general and I know, as only a woman knows, that he's
particularly susceptible to me...'
Is he? I thought. And is my nose truly that 'Roman'?

*

How thoughtless of me. I realise I've left Angela in tears,
post-caesarean section, while I stood at the bedside making
futile attempts to comfort her. Her worst fears had been
realised, not only in terms of the operation but also as regards
the health of our daughter, who'd just been rushed off to the
special care unit. She'd been oxygen-deprived during the birth
and we were later told she'd almost certainly suffer from some
form of cerebral palsy. The severity of it would only be
determined after the hospital had conducted a series of tests.

But even before we were given the full story, the effect on us
– particularly on Angela – was devastating. The fact that we
didn't know the full extent of the damage meant that she
assumed the worse. She blamed herself – I don't why. She
blamed me – then quickly took it back. *She* was the one who'd
failed, or at least, her body. She'd not eaten the right food.
She'd not taken the right vitamins. She'd not been fit enough. It
was the stress of worrying about her mother, of worrying about
me and the business... She made no sense, she went round in

circles; she worked herself up to a hysterical pitch, until she was all but up on the ceiling. The midwife and the doctor joined me in trying to bring her down and console her.

'No one's to blame here, Angela. Babies sometimes turn in the womb and get themselves into awkward positions – I'm afraid it just happens...And anyway, we think in the case of your daughter the effect is likely to be minimal...'

'But you can't say for sure.' Angela's weeping softened briefly.

'No, not at this stage...but experience is a good guide...'

Yet I sensed a certain reticence on their part, the faintest whiff of guilt perhaps, as if something else may have happened that doesn't 'just happen' – something that was somehow down to them. It was a question I'd return to afterwards, with upsetting consequences. But for now we had to wait until Angela had recovered enough for us to go and see our daughter.

'I'd like to call her Grace,' she said, as the nurses prepared to get her into a wheelchair.

'Fine,' I said, 'Grace it is. It's a beautiful name...'

When we got to the special unit, we found that 'Gracie', as she quickly became for me, looked far from damaged. Yes, she had an oxygen tube in her mouth and wires attached to various parts of her tiny body, but it didn't stop her appearing anything less than serene and remarkable. The fact that the miracle of birth occurs everywhere all the time doesn't make it any less miraculous, especially for first-time parents. Nor did it make us feel any less blessed, even though we knew then that she wasn't perfect in every way.

From the moment we first saw her we were both spellbound. She took on magical, fairy tale dimensions. She instantly became the focus of our relationship. As such, she brought us closer together - bound us together – but there would be a trade-off: we would each cease to be the other's priority. Our love for each other was relegated to second place, trailing well behind our love for her. If it came to it, we might make certain sacrifices for each other, but for her we'd make the ultimate sacrifice. If necessary, we'd die for her.

I think we were aware of this, even as we stood there, looking into the protective perspex bubble that prevented us from picking her up and holding her for the first time - and even before we were told of the full extent of her condition. Angela didn't have to touch her; the very sight of Grace calmed her as nothing else had. I squeezed my wife's hand and realised two things: that my relationship with her would never be the same - and that my existence needed no other purpose than protecting our crippled princess.

And then, as if we hadn't had enough drama for one day, there was further excitement. If only we could have laughed, it would have provided comic relief rather than a heightening of the tension. If only.

A nurse came quietly up to us. 'Angela,' she said, 'your mother's here to see you.'

'Where?'

'Just outside.'

'Can you let her in?' I asked.

'Er...it may not be a good idea...'

Angela was reluctant to leave Grace, so I followed the nurse outside. Maggie was standing in the corridor - or rather, she was swaying to and fro, brandishing a bottle of fizz.

'The proud father!' she slurred when she saw me, her face lighting up in tipsy slo-mo. 'I've come to wet the baby's head,' she said, trying to stand up straight and affecting a posh accent.

I'll not let you near the baby until you go through rehab is what Angela had told her a couple of months before. Well, she'd gone through rehab but I doubted Angela would be letting her anywhere near the baby as yet.

'Is it a girl?' she asked, struggling to focus.

'It is.'

'Thank fuck for that. Last thing we want is another little prick in the world...'

*

Katherine's wise words woke me, as if from a laudanum-induc'd dream. She was right. I had allow'd my frustration with Philippe to get the better of me. My love for her and Anne was genuine enough, but the rest was a turning away from the challenge, a desire for flight rather than fight - in short, a moment of weakness disguis'd as inspiration. And yes, now she had said it, I realis'd that we wou'd have much greater chance of success with Orleans if she approach'd him. The only outstanding question was how we wou'd get them together. Meanwhile, the mood abroad in Paris deteriorat'd rapidly. Hungry mobs prowl'd the streets and various pamphlets appear'd, attacking the Regent's government for incompetence and the repressive measures employ'd by the Chamber of Justice.

'I have seen,' said one, 'the Bastille fill'd with brave citizens, faithful subjects! I have seen people wretch'd under a rigorous servitude! I have seen them perishing of hunger, thirst, indignation and rage!'

Another, a verse entitl'd Puerto Regnante attacked Philippe personally, even accusing him of murdering members of his own family to ensure his succession. Katherine did a more than passable translation:

'A boy reigning:
A man notorious for poisonings
And incest administering;

Councils ignorant and unstable;
The Treasury empty;
Public faith violat'd...'

Both of these stinging attacks were alleg'd to have been written by a philosopher called Francois-Marie Arouet, later known as Voltaire. Although it wou'd not have been wise for me to meet him at that point, I must admit to feeling a certain affinity with this young man's anti-religious views and his championing of social and political freedom. Indeed, I saw my own ideas as being a disquisition on economic freedom, a subject that most philosophers, from the Greeks onwards, have neglect'd in favour of more abstract and elevat'd notions. In different circumstances, I wou'd have loved to discuss these ideas with Monsieur Arouet personally and explain how my System cou'd help alleviate what was perhaps the greatest cause of human misery and oppression: poverty. (Alas, no such discussion took place and eventually I too became a target for his poison'd pen, as well as that of several others, such as Montesquieu.)

After the first pamphlet, he was warn'd publicly by D'Argenson, the Chief of Police, that he risk'd severe punishment. Three weeks later, after the second, he was arrest'd and sent to the Bastille, where he was to stay for almost a year.

Even more depressing than this stifling of political protest was the 'news' I was given by Noailles. I cannot say whether this was pure mischief on his part or whether he want'd to demonstrate how much Philippe was in support of his work. Apparently, when the Chamber of Justice had fin'd the financier Michel Cresson for profiteering, he claim'd that he had already paid 100,000 livres to Madame Parabère in return for a guarantee of immunity. Noailles was obviously amus'd by this.

'And was Cresson pardon'd?' I ask'd.

'Of course,' he replied.

'So he did pay Madame Parabère?'

'His Royal Highness confirm'd as much to me, yes...'

So intensely bleak was my mood upon hearing all this, I decid'd that only a prolong'd gaming session cou'd relieve it. It had been a while since I had taken up the bags of gold and swagger'd into a salon, but we had been invit'd to Madame de Chateauneuf's that evening and it seem'd churlish not to attend. For some reason – a quaint Scottish notion of how rulers shou'd behave in public – I did not expect Philippe to be at Madame's gambling party. However, within seconds of our arrival, I sens'd the familiar buzz of excitement that indicat'd His Royal Highness was present, and as Katherine began her usual expert working of the room, I immediately swung my bags of gold in the direction of his table.

Some weeks had pass'd since I had spoken with Philippe, most of his time having been spent frolicking with Parabère and the rest cloister'd with his secretaries and councils. Did a faint flicker of embarrassment cross His Royal visage when he saw me? If so, it was extremely faint and quickly replac'd by a broad smile.

'Monsieur Law, how good of you to join us. At last, I have the chance to recover some of my losses. My lords, ladies and

gentlemen,' he announc'd to the table, 'please meet the greatest card player in all France – and I know that to be true because he is even better than me...' A titter of appreciation ran around the assembl'd company, none of whom look'd particularly intimidat'd by the prospect of my joining them.

Strangely enough, although I had become famous for my success at cards in Paris, there was still no shortage of gamesters keen to test their mettle against me – nor indeed of metal itself, it seem'd, for all its shortage about the kingdom. Gold was pil'd monumentally high in front of Philippe and his companions, who includ'd d'Argenson, Dubois and the fat, decrepit prince de Conti, head of one of the wealthiest families in France, whose son was later to pay me such a fond visit in Venice.

We began with a little Primero and mov'd on to some Brag, a relatively easy game to call with its accumulation of pairs and threes-of-a-kind. At first, the odds fail'd to run for me, which I put down partly to the natural flow of numbers and partly to my lack of concentration. I was unusually distract'd by the personalities around the table and their conversation, which rang'd from the carnal preferences of their mistresses to the feckless and rebellious nature of the mass of French people – at least, that was the prince de Conti's view. It was his and d'Argenson's remarks about the need to break more of the ringleaders upon the wheel and send the rest to the galleys that made me determin'd to pocket every last louis d'or in front of this porcine pair.

Meanwhile, Dubois, a competent enough player himself, it seem'd, observ'd that 'the famous Monsieur Law' – he pronounc'd it more as 'Low', with great emphasis – was obviously losing his touch now that he was up against 'some players of real substance.' Philippe's Foreign Minister had a decidedly predatory look about him – lean-featur'd and hook-nos'd, with large bright eyes that belied his grey wig and fifty-odd years.

'Do not underestimate Monsieur Law,' Philippe caution'd, 'it may well be a ploy to have us drop our guards...' I smil'd and rais'd everyone another twenty louis d'or.

166

By the time we had mov'd on to Pharo, the numbers were working for me, and as a consequence one or two members of the company were beginning to look a little uncomfortable. Conti was displaying what I later came to identify as the family facial twitch and rivulets of sweat ran down from under d'Argenson's wig, streaking his heavy powder. At one point I leant across and offer'd him one of my fine lace handkerchiefs, which he grudgingly accept'd, having misplac'd his own. Dubois went very quiet and Philippe adopt'd a look of what I would call calm resignation, as he watch'd the pile of gold before him slowly but inexorably diminish, despite his Tailliere's advantage. I felt as Beau Wickham must have felt that morning when we fought – toying with my opponents, wounding them at will, teasing them into defeat, except that unlike Beau, I was not about to drop my guard until the table was clear. In the end, as Katherine appear'd like an angel at my side, only Dubois and myself remain'd playing – and the bank had just been broken.

'Well, Monsieur Law,' Philippe sigh'd, 'it looks as if you have bankrupt'd me again. As a distinguish'd man of finance, what is your advice?'

My reply was rash and intemperate, a measure of the annoyance I felt towards him. 'If Your Royal Highness wishes to borrow a sum of money, I have heard that Monsieur Cresson is only too ready to oblige.'

'Monsieur Cresson?' Orleans feign'd puzzlement. 'I don't think I know a Monsieur Cresson.'

I persist'd in my madness. 'I do apologise to Your Royal Highness, but I was under the impression that he had recently provid'd a loan to Madame Parabère...'

Already subdued by the outcome of the game, the table seem'd to recoil at this remark.

There was a brief silence while Philippe finger'd the last of his louis d'or. 'Ah, that Monsieur Cresson. Yes, well...one is not responsible for the behaviour of one's mistress – for one's wife, yes, but not for one's mistress. In fact, irresponsible behaviour is what one often prizes most in a mistress.'

Everyone laugh'd, partly in relief and several of them, took a point'd look at my 'mistress', I notic'd – or did I imagine it?

'*Anyway, as you know only too well,*' he continued, '*the Crown takes great exception to anyone who seeks to exploit France financially – as did Monsieur Cresson, I believe,*' and he toss'd the coins on to my pile. '*My advice to you, Monsieur Law, is to make sure you are not among them. You seem to have acquir'd a good deal of our French gold and the Chamber of Justice may well be forc'd to determine its legality.*'

And on this chilling note, he and his party rose and took their leave, bidding a Royal adieu to all as they went.

I sat staring at the huge pile of louis d'or on the table in front of me – and the Fourteenth's face star'd implacably back, a hundredfold at least. Katherine reach'd across and gently squeez'd my hand.

'*Not a good idea to have accus'd him publicly, John – although he will respect you all the more for saying it.*'

'*If respect means setting me on the rack, yes...*' *I gave a rueful smile. In an insane moment, driven by frustration and intoxicat'd by my potency at the table, I had squander'd all the time and effort of the previous few years or more and was again cast out into the social and political wilderness. I doubt'd even Katherine cou'd get an audience with him now, let alone manoeuvre me back into favour.*

Yet, while I sat berating myself, one of Philippe's attendants return'd, bow'd low in his blue livery and spoke softly in my ear.

'*His Royal Highness requests the pleasure of yours and Madame Law's company at Marly next week. His Highness very much hopes that you can attend, not least because he wishes to thank you personally for finally curing him of his worst affliction – the urge to gamble at cards...*'

*

Perhaps, the worse thing about cerebral palsy, apart from its crippling effects, is the fact that you don't know how crippling those effects are going to be. It could be minimal – as the doctor had said – or it could be much worse. Tests and scans give some indication, but the real extent of it only becomes fully apparent as the child develops. The tests showed that there would probably be no mental disability, which was a relief, but that the movement of Gracie's legs could be severely restricted. There was no outright cure. We just had to wait and see how bad it was and what therapy or surgery could be used to alleviate it.

Meanwhile, there was the agony of watching and waiting to see her learn to sit, crawl, walk and speak. How did she compare with other kids? Was her development slower? What was the exact nature of the disability? All parents scrutinise and celebrate the early milestones in their child's development. First smile, first word, first step – they all seem so significant. But for us, for the first few years of Grace's life, those milestones became a morbid obsession as we struggled to read the runes of her condition.

What was as disturbing for me was to witness the effect it had on Angela. It combined with her mother's bad behaviour – in and out of rehab, but failing to kick the habit – to drive her into a deep depression. Sometimes I wished she could have expressed her pain more openly: given vent to it - thrown things around, shouted at me, at anyone, even Grace. But she didn't. The storm never seemed to break. There were just brooding clouds of silent despair, as each expensive doctor we engaged said more or less the same thing: let's wait and see – and meanwhile keep on with the stretching and massage. Poor Grace's legs were stretched and massaged to rawness, and it only contributed to our sense of helplessness.

It was partly for this reason I decided to launch a legal case against the hospital and pursue compensation. I thought it might make us feel we were doing *something* and help give Angela a focus for her pain. But I was wrong. She thought it was a waste of time; that we'd only go on reliving what had happened rather than moving on. And anyway, it wasn't as if we needed the money.

I pointed out that this wasn't about the past or the money. We would be reliving what happened everyday into the future, as would Grace. And the money was neither here nor there. It was the principle: the hospital should be made to acknowledge its responsibility.

But she wasn't interested, and I began to realise that something else might be going on: maybe it conflicted with her firm belief that if anyone was to blame, she was. Whatever the reason, something I thought would bind us even closer together gradually became a source of discord between us.

Surprisingly enough, given that my mind was not on the case much of the time, the firm did better than ever during this period. Far from taking his business elsewhere, Boris in Geneva channelled even more hot money through my network and into the fund. Indeed, there was so much of it that the system was in danger of overheating and needed careful management to avoid any serious mishaps. I also began to worry that I was becoming a little too dependent on him – too many eggs and all that – especially as he was also referring more and more clients to me. All roads were leading back to the rude Russian.

Of course, there's no escaping the fact that I should have known more about him and his business before we got to that point. I'd never followed up on what his wife Gina had told me in such hushed tones that day I'd visited him in Geneva. I'd convinced myself that I'd been too distracted by Grace's birth, but the truth was I hadn't wanted to know. Remember the golden rule: the less I know about my clients and they about me, the better. And anyway, I'd not ignored the issue entirely. I'd run some basic financial checks on Boris when he'd first come to me and established that his oil and gas credentials were solid. Even so, I finally had to admit it: now that he was my biggest client, it made sense to do some more research on him. Who knows what attention he was drawing my way now we were so closely associated?

The first trawl yielded little I was not aware of. Okay, Boris wasn't spotlessly clean, but then show me a Russian oligarch – or indeed any super rich personage – who is. He'd acquired his original business assets in somewhat dubious circumstances. There were even suggestions that he'd been responsible for the untimely deaths of some of his business rivals – car accidents, suicides and the like; that he'd had no choice but to leave Mother Russia. Again, all par for the course in the Mafia state. I joked with one of my team that it would be odd if he didn't have a few enemies lining up to take the odd pot shot at him.

How could he possibly have amassed such a fortune in post-Communist Russia and there not be someone trying to steal it away?

However, when we dug a little deeper, my smile began to slip. Boris had been married four times, and one of the discarded wives, two before Gina, had not gone quietly. She'd made several poisonous remarks to the media about their marriage. One was that he was physically abusive; two that he was a major philanderer, who went with whores and tried to make a whore of her, his own wife; and three – the one that made me flinch – that he was head of an organisation that trafficked girls and drugs. Not long after these pronouncements, the ex-wife had become ex, period. She'd apparently died at the hands of a burglar who'd broken into her apartment in Moscow to steal her jewellery – no doubt bought for her by Boris.

The researcher who brought me the good news about our best client – he knew nothing of the illicit business I did for him – gave me a look that didn't know whether to be amused or anxious.

'A woman scorned,' I shrugged. 'Probably all slanderous...'

'Yep...probably...'

But I knew there was more to it than that. I knew it was what Gina had alluded to that day – and it presented me with a moral dilemma that I could only wriggle out of by giving Boris the benefit of the doubt. If I had devoted any thought at all to his illegal activities, it was that they involved the corrupt practices of his oil and gas businesses in Russia and Africa. Yes, it was criminal but because he only ripped off other criminals in the main, I could live with what I saw as victimless crimes.

The crimes his ex-wife version 2.0 had accused him of, however, were of a different, much scummier order, and I couldn't understand why he would dirty his hands with them. Why take the risk? It didn't make sense. He'd probably been involved in that kind of thing when he was younger – when he was a sleazy little hoodlum in the Wild East of post-Communist Russia. But since then, since he'd become a relatively respectable businessman, I told myself it was only reasonable to assume he'd cleaned up his act and that his ex-wife had taken it all out of context. Only *reasonable* – right?

171

So that was it, conscience disabled – although it hadn't exactly been overactive down the years. I'd always prided myself on being a pragmatist, especially when it came to financial matters. In fact, it was after I'd checked the firm's revenue for the quarter that I decided to draw a veil over the issue. (The figures were impressive, the best ever.) I would stop worrying about it and return to worrying about my family, where there was plenty of scope for concern.

For instance, in her second year, it became obvious that our daughter had little control of her legs. While continuing to seek the miracle cure that maybe even money couldn't buy, we were doing our best to come to terms with the fact that she might never walk. Also, after a period of relatively good behaviour, my mother-in-law had gone AWOL. She'd managed to stay 'off the gargle', as Angela put it, for some months and had become almost human. She'd even stayed with us for a week, an experience that was much less painful than I'd expected. She seemed less caustic and spiky and took a genuine interest in her grandchild that passed as affectionate.

Then, when we were due to see her one evening and she didn't show – and there was no sign of her in the smart new flat Angela had bought her – we knew she'd hit the bottle and the streets again. She was probably sleeping rough, as she'd often done before.

Angela became very angry, as angry as I'd ever seen her, banging around the place and cursing her 'putrid fuckin' piss'ead of a mother'. I thought in part it was finally a vent for what had happened to Grace and saw it in a positive light, despite its foulness. (I must admit to discovering the snob in myself when Angela betrayed her ruffian roots in this way.) We reported Maggie missing, but still spent a frantic week trying to find her ourselves. We combed the streets of her once favourite haunt – what was at the time the seedy area around Kings Cross, preserve of tarts and junkies – but there was no sign of her. Then, nearly another week later, I opened the door to some vigorous ringing and she fell in.

'Whoops – I always was a bit of a doormat,' she cackled.

She reeked of many unpleasant substances, alcohol being the least of them. Her clothes were filthy and torn; her face

bruised and cut. As I stood paralysed, Angela swept past me –
to assault her, I assumed. Instead, she gathered her up in her
arms, as if she were Grace.

'Oh, Mum…we've been so worried about you…'

"'ave you, sweetart? That's nice of you…'

This was a surprising, even touching turn of events, and
prompted thoughts of blood being thicker than water etc. But I
couldn't help feeling that our whole situation had become
deeply depressing. In two years, as a couple we'd gone from
being footloose to shackled, from soaring eagles to caged birds
– and it was no consolation that the cages were gilded. Nor was
it helped by the fact that Angela and I had seldom made love
since Grace's birth. My formerly sex-crazed wife had become
almost frigid – and it wasn't down to the natural evolution of a
romance, when the lava of early lust cools into the bedrock of
something more enduring. No, there was nothing 'natural'
about it. This was a more brutal cut-off. Sex between us had
suffered a cardiac arrest and it wasn't responding to
resuscitation.

But I lived in hope. I decided we needed to get away for a
while and give physical intimacy the kiss of life - something
longer than just a holiday. I actually suggested we rent a place
in Florida, down near the Keys for a while. It would be partly
for pleasure, partly because there was a prospect of my doing
some business in Miami, one of the great money-washing
centres of the Americas. But we didn't go for it for either
purpose. Time away in the sun was the last thing Angela
seemed to want. She preferred to be in London, where the
bruised winter skies mirrored her own inner bruising, and
where she had, she said, an established support network for
Grace and her mother.

Following this last Maggie scare, I again suggested we go
away: 'Wouldn't it do us all good?' I wasn't including my
mother-in-law in the 'us'.

'It's the last thing I need right now, Theo – to have to up
sticks and go to the US.'

'I'm talking about an extended holiday, not emigration.
Apart from anything else, wouldn't Grace love to be in the pool

every day?' We'd found that immersion in water encouraged movement in her legs.

'We're happy with the pool down the road, at my gym.' (We'd discussed putting a pool in the basement of the house, but Angela hadn't wanted to suffer all the disruption.)

'*Okay*…If not Florida, then where *would* you go?'

'I don't need to go anywhere right now...and anyway, there's Mum to consider – I can't leave her to stew on her own.'

But I was all for leaving her to stew on her own. As it was, we were all stewing unpleasantly together – which was probably one of the reasons I leapt at the invitation from, of all people, Boris.

*

As quickly as it had come, the storm had pass'd and a shaft of sunlight had pierc'd the gloom in the form of a Royal invitation to Marly, that most priz'd of all invitations. But cou'd it be taken at face value? Or was it another Bourbon jest? Was I to be fet'd or merely fatten'd for the slaughter? I struggl'd in vain to make sense of Philippe's behaviour, to fathom his motives, and despite Katherine's daily reassurances, I still half-expect'd a summons from Noailles, not to the Palais-Royal but to the Convent of the Grands Augustins.

But no such summons came, only a written invitation from Philippe to confirm the verbal one. Even so, as the time for our visit approach'd, my misgivings persist'd. Orleans may have been easy to read and no match for me at the card table, but he was revealing himself as an expert at playing with others' emotions, as unpredictable as he was now politically powerful. I was unsure that we cou'd easily turn him to our advantage, but Katherine saw it differently. We need'd to make it clear to him that our plans were to <u>his</u> advantage, she said, and a visit to Marly was an excellent chance to do that.

'Besides,' she add'd, 'Marly is reput'd to be the most beautiful of all the Royal palaces. Invitations to those outside the Royal circle are unheard of. It's an experience not to be miss'd…'

And sure enough, as our carriage descend'd through the woods and we caught our first glimpse of the palace through a curtain of silver birches, I was the one who grew more excit'd. For Marly was indeed beautiful and seem'd to draw us on like some enchanted castle in a fairy tale. Seclud'd among hills around the Loire River, it consist'd of a small chateau flank'd by twelve pavilions – the chateau for His Royal Highness and the pavilions for his guests. These overlook'd an artificial lake, stock'd with scores of exotic carp – blue, red, silver and gold. A great cascade fell behind the chateau, running in sparkling torrents to the lake, around which were the most magnificent gardens. Apparently, the Fourteenth had plant'd over eighteen million bulbs at Marly and they all seem'd to be in bloom the day we arriv'd.

We had not been settl'd in our guest pavilion for more than half-an-hour when a servant appear'd and ask'd if I wou'd attend the Regent in the studio.

'The studio? Is his Royal Highness sitting for a portrait?' I replied.

He bow'd and smil'd. 'Not exactly, Monsieur. Let me show you the way...'

He led me down the splendid hornbeam passage that connect'd the pavilions to the main chateau and across a gild'd hexagonal-shaped hall to the door of this 'studio', which turn'd out to be a specially convert'd ante-room. Unsure of what kind of reception to expect from Philippe, I felt somewhat nervous as I stood waiting for the command to enter, although the scene that present'd itself to me when I did, banish'd all such feelings.

A bewigg'd Orleans in artist's smock was working at a large canvass. Across from him by a tall, half-curtain'd window, a young woman reclin'd on a velvet chaise-long. But for a hair band of pink May blossom, she was entirely nak'd and doing her best to hold her motionless pose, although I immediately notic'd a slight movement of her shoulders and the delicate tremble of her breasts.

Philippe was gently remonstrating with her. 'Now why are you fidgeting, my dear - are you cold?'

175

'No, Your 'ighness, just a bit stiff round the shoulders,' she replied in a coarse accent. She was no Parabère in class, but her form was every bit as delightful.

'Very well, relax a little...' He turn'd to me, set aside his brush and gave his warmest smile. 'Monsieur Law, what a pleasure it is to see you at Marly.'

'And what a pleasure and privilege to be here, Your Royal Highness.' I took his proffer'd hand and bow'd. 'I see you have exchang'd the laboratory for the atelier.'

'Yes indeed,' he said airily, very much the artist, 'I must admit to having grown rather weary of Science just now. Dr. Hoffman continues his experiments in Paris on my behalf, but I felt the need for some other form of endeavour, something to set the creative juices flowing...'

Which seem'd a cue to admire his work-in-progress. This in fact display'd a great deal of skill: to my inform'd eye, the proportions and perspective, the relationship of light and shadow, the variations in flesh tones were all perfectly render'd. I was much surpris'd and my voice must have register'd as much.

'The work is...excellent,' I said.

He rais'd a defensive eyebrow. 'For a Bourbon, you mean? For someone who is not meant to do such things?'

'For anyone, Your Royal Highness,' I replied.

'Thank you, Monsieur Law.' Encourag'd by this, he continued more airily than ever. 'Of course, I say I am tir'd of Science, but what is painting other than a form of scientific observation, a study of light and the way in which it falls upon an object?'

I agreed, and look'd from the study to the 'object'. She was even more alluring in her relax'd pose and had stretch'd out her long slender legs to reveal a neat triangle of pubic hair, the tone and texture of sable.

'An object of desire, on this occasion,' Philippe purr'd in my ear. 'Brigitte, my favourite chambermaid at Marly.' He nodd'd at her and she return'd a wanton smile that bespoke a far more intimate relationship than that between artist and model, even a nude one.

176

'Of course,' he said, taking up his brush again and lowering his voice to a lascivious whisper, 'I am preparing to embark upon a similar picture of Madame Parabère and am only practising with Brigitte, you understand. Please – you are very welcome to practise with her yourself. She'll be more than happy to accommodate, I'm sure. She loves all things...artistic...'

'Thank you, Your Royal Highness, I will certainly consider it...shou'd I decide to take up painting.' But again, my tone - and perhaps expression – had betray'd my true feelings, which were little short of dismay: when he was not seeking favours from the public purse for his mistress, I thought, he was peddling his chambermaids like a madam with her whores.

Sensing my reaction, he laugh'd and clapp'd me on the shoulder. 'Poor Monsieur Law, for all your own misdemeanours, you _are_ some kind of Scottish puritan, I do believe. I can tell you despair of me.'

'It is not my place to despair of you, Your Royal Highness.'

'Quite so.' His tone grew sterner. 'But it does not seem to stop you. At Madame de Chateauneuf's you act'd above your station, Monsieur!'

'But only because you had act'd beneath yours, Your Royal Highness.'

Philippe tried to shrug this off with a nervous laugh, but I knew that I had stung him. This was truly the end of our relationship, I thought, and I had only just arriv'd at Marly. Then I thought of Katherine's words – it will only increase his respect for you. We were about to test that theory.

He turn'd to Brigitte and ask'd her to leave us; he wou'd send for her presently, he said. She put on her robe and flounc'd out, pouting beautifully as she went. Philippe star'd in silence at his picture, while I wait'd to be dismiss'd as well – to be told to leave Marly and Paris or worse: the spectre of the Chamber of Justice loom'd over me once more.

After some moments he said: 'I think I remember telling you in so many words that in order to guarantee certain allegiances and thus the Regency itself, I wou'd have to make several compromises.'

I nodd'd.

'Well, the duc de Noailles and his Chamber of Justice qualify as such a compromise. Yes, I admit it has serv'd a financial purpose of sorts, but it is abhorrent to me, a tool of tyranny, and I have wait'd patiently for it to run its course.' He sat on the empty chaise-long, which still bore the warm imprint of Brigitte, and struck a reflective, even melancholy pose. 'As for Madame Parabère's indiscretion, it had already occur'd by the time I was told of it. And anyway' – he smil'd at his own frailty – 'had I known, I cou'd not have refus'd her, slave to love that I am.'

I smil'd in response. A slave who happily forges his own shackles, I thought.

'But I don't have to tell you, Your Highness, that – the delightful Madame Parabère's indiscretion aside – the financial affairs of the State and therefore the State itself are in crisis...'

'No, you don't have to tell me, Monsieur Law, nor do you have to remind me that we need a new initiative and that the new initiative shou'd be a National Bank. However, I have to remind you *that there is enormous opposition to it, not least because it wou'd be run by a foreigner, who, no matter how influential in Parisian society he has become, is still a foreigner, as well as a cardsharp whom many do not trust...'*

Touché, I thought. By calling me a 'cardsharp' – en Anglais – Orleans had return'd my earlier insult with interest. 'Your Highness, give me the opportunity to convince the doubters and naysayers...'

He rais'd a paint-stain'd hand to forestall any further discussion. 'Please, Monsieur Law...I really must continue with Brigitte. The afternoon light is simply not to be miss'd. We'll meet again at dinner...'

And so we did, when we join'd a small party that includ'd Saint-Simon and his wife, and of course Madame Parabère, who arriv'd later that afternoon. She held herself aloof from us at first, and giggl'd and chatter'd with her 'sweetness' as if there were no one else in the room. It was not until he explain'd that I was an extremely successful financier – 'a man of money par excellence' – that she start'd to warm to us. Money, or rather her love of spending it, turn'd out to be Parabère's favourite subject, apart from Philippe, and I quickly realis'd why he was happy to have her dip into the exchequer rather than finance her extravagance himself.

Our first day at Marly was a delight. The sun shone in a cloudless sky. We walk'd in some of the gardens, which echoed with the sound of birdsong and rushing water. There was the inevitable court gossip, but also brilliant talk of Art and Philosophy and I learnt for the first time of Saint-Simon's chronicles of life at court. Philippe wryly dismiss'd these as yet more tittle-tattle, if of the very highest calibre, and I gather'd that in the more recent reports, Katherine and I receiv'd more than one mention. At my request, Saint-Simon promis'd to share them with us.

In the evening, we play'd cards, the ladies includ'd, although not for money; Philippe announc'd that he had foresworn gambling, for which he was eternally in my debt, so to speak. As well as a mean hand of Black Lady, Madame Parabère play'd a fine harpsichord; the duchesse de Saint-Simon warbl'd wonderfully, like a blackbird in the gardens, and Katherine charm'd everyone with her wit, beauty and enthusiasm for everything at Marly, particularly the gardens.

How she miss'd extensive grounds, she said. Her family seat in Norfolk in England had had the most exquisite grounds and gardens, but of course the Paris house, grand as it was, had little by comparison.

Philippe, whom I had witness'd watching her throughout the evening – so much so that Madame P was beginning to show signs of peevishness – said he wou'd be very happy to give Katherine his own personal tour of the grounds and gardens of Marly, an offer that she was very happy to accept.

'I hope you will not think it ill-manner'd of me, Madame Law' – he was no doubt alluding to the incident that had occurr'd during our first meeting – 'if I demonstrate to you the superiority of the French formal garden over any type to be found in England.'

'If I do, Your Highness, I'll do my utmost to forgive you.'

This was met with amusement by the whole table, and Katherine's fleeting, knowing look in my direction confirm'd what had become obvious – that the tour was not an open invitation to us all.

179

Early next morning, before the day grew too hot, they set off through the gardens on foot and then proceed'd by carriage around much of the rest of the estate.

They were gone for several hours, during which time Saint-Simon introduc'd me to boules, a game with which I was unfamiliar, it not being play'd with cards. He prais'd my natural talent for the game and chastis'd me when I suggest'd we add an element of wager.

'Don't you think, Monsieur Law, that some games shou'd be play'd purely for the joy of playing them?'

'What? And exclude the joy of winning, and then the even greater joy of winning a fortune? I think not, Your Grace.'

He shook his head in mock-despair at me; I lik'd Saint-Simon.

When Katherine and Orleans finally return'd, they were wreath'd in smiles and full of good-natur'd banter. 'Well, His Highness has certainly won me over to the French style of horticulture. I'm now convinc'd that the English are inferior in every regard...'

'That is <u>not</u> what you said to me earlier, Madame Law,' Philippe laugh'd.

'And did you win <u>him</u> over?' I said to her sotto voce.

'Wait and see, John. Wait and see...'

I did not have long to wait and see, although at the time it seem'd an age. After dinner, Philippe took me aside.

'I've given the subject we discuss'd earlier some more consideration, Monsieur Law. I will likely need a few days to bring the Council round to our way of thinking, but I'm sure they can be persuad'd of its merits. Meanwhile, I suggest you make preparations for the establishment of a bank under your ownership and supervision – and within the week, I will issue a Charter...'

I had no chance to ask what had chang'd His Royal Highness' mind. Parabère and others were immediately upon us, talking about what she shou'd wear at the latest staging of a comedy-ballet by Moliere, Le Bourgeois Gentilhomme.

*

I was inclined to keep a low profile socially, especially as regards anything to do with business; I only attended such events when absolutely necessary. This usually meant some arcane ceremony or dinner in the City of London, a place where ancient ritual appears to be merely symbolic but actually facilitates some very real – and lucrative – financial dealing. This kind of rite has the opposite effect of a religious one, in which the mundane is supposed to be transformed into something of a higher order. In City ceremonies, the archaic mumbo-jumbo boils down to one thing and one thing only: money, and much of it dirty.

Ah, the British Establishment – what it cannot teach the world about hypocrisy isn't worth learning. And to think I used to feel privileged to be part of it.

Anyway, given that these City affairs only seemed to cater for middle-aged-to-ancient white men, I never took Angela and nor would she ever have wanted to go. But the invitation from Boris was something different. It turned out he was leaving Geneva and setting up in London. Or at least, he'd have a place in Central London, but had also acquired a very large estate in Wiltshire with a 16-bedroom Georgian mansion. Apart from the obvious reason for doing this – sinking lots of his shady capital into English property, an alternative to availing himself of my services – it occurred to me that he might want to play the English landed gent for a while. In fact, I'd always assumed that his affinity for all things English was one of the reasons he'd stayed loyal to me all these years – if you can apply a word like 'loyal' to Boris. But then again, perhaps I'm flattering myself. After all, I am half-American.

We were invited to celebrate his birthday, as well as his coming to the UK. We could arrive as early as we liked on the Saturday and sample the delights of the estate, which would no doubt be similar to those of a 5-star country club. In the evening, there'd be a 'banquet', no less, and dancing, and it was very much hoped we'd take the opportunity to stay overnight. Lord Boris was obviously keen to show off his new pile, and I was quite intrigued by the idea of some major Russian bling rubbing shoulders with the tweedy country set.

I could hardly refuse to go, anyway, and I stressed to Angela that the invitation was to us both. It might be big and brash, I told her, but it would not be boring.

Perhaps she felt bad about refusing to go to Florida or anywhere else. Perhaps it was enough that she knew how important Boris' business was to me. Whatever the reason, she agreed to come along without too much persuasion. She even said it was probably time she started taking an interest in the business again. And as for leaving the nanny to take care of Grace over the weekend, for the first time ever, it was not a major problem.

There were two beautiful things about our drive out to Boris' place. (Three, if you count the house itself, which possessed genuine bling-defying elegance.) The first was that it was a rare oh-to-be-in-England April day: a sky of Mediterranean blue, the grass an electric green; everything bursting into tender life. The second was Angela. Since Grace's birth, I'd grown so used to her making very little effort with her appearance that I'd forgotten how stunningly attractive she could be when she put her mind to it. Her blond hair was longer and she'd grown much curvier since the pregnancy. She may not have liked the extra pounds, but from where I sat she wore them well. In fact, I found myself stiffening at the sight of her next to me in the passenger seat. Would our finally being away together, just the two of us, conjure up the old black magic I'd hoped for from a Florida trip? We'd soon find out.

My excitement was also heightened by her buoyant mood and the sense that there was more chemistry between us than there'd been for many months. More recently, the subjects of Grace and Maggie had dominated most of our conversation, but that day we hardly talked about them. I told her some more about Boris. I confined the story to what a demanding client he could be, but how I appeared to have won his trust and now handled most of his investments. We discussed buying a weekend place in the country, which I thought was another encouraging sign that she was moving on from her depression. From there, I also managed to steer the conversation round to our relationship, particularly the sexual bit of it. How radical of me - isn't it usually the man who avoids the up-close-and-personal? And yet there was I making all the running in the intimacy stakes.

'It's really not because of you, Theo,' she said.

'I'm glad to hear it.'

'It's partly hormonal, partly to do with that screwed up background of mine. I'm afraid I'm either full on or completely off it. I should have apologised before now. You've been very understanding.'

I tried to give her a half-sympathetic, half-nonchalant look that said 'understanding' was my middle name and I could cope with the abstinence, no problem.

It obviously didn't work, because she laughed and ran her hand up my thigh. 'It's okay. I think there's a bit of a thaw coming. Something might just be flicking my ON switch...' And the hand moved up to what by then was a considerable erection.

'Oh, good,' I said. 'Boris' house probably doesn't have a lift, but maybe we can screw on his grand staircase?'

She laughed again – twice in thirty seconds was a record of late. 'Let's start in one of his four-posters – I assume they'll be four-posters?'

'I'll be making an official complaint if they're not...'

The estate itself was just outside Marlborough, behind a seriously high wall and massive front gate, complete with armed security guards, who checked our ID with polite thoroughness. We saw the house first from across the valley, as we drove down its long winding drive. It sat on a gentle slope overlooking a lake and a river. Its Palladian façade, with its grand pediment and columns, glowed a mellow ivory colour in the spring sunshine. It was the stuff of dreams, or certainly – aside from the helipad and chopper – of glossy period dramas.

'Wow! Can *we* have one?' Angela joked.

'Probably.'

She turned to me, surprised. 'Are you serious? Are we that rich?'

'More or less.'

I don't know whether it was the news of our wealth or the sight of Downlands, as the house was known, but she was left virtually speechless until we got there.

We were greeted with studied cordiality by the butler. (There *would* have to be a butler, and he *would* have to be called something like Bedwell, which he was.) There also appeared to be several footmen, who parked our car, carried our things and escorted us up to our vast bedroom, with its, yes, magnificent old four-poster of exquisitely carved oak and various other fine originals, including a Venetian glass mirror. Although we were sorely tempted, it seemed impolite to go at it there and then, especially as Bedwell informed us that 'Mr. Aranovsky' – Boris – was looking forward to 'receiving us' in the drawing room as soon as we were ready.

'Have Sir and Madam everything they require?'

'They have, Bedwell, thank you.' Apart from that quick shag on the four-poster, I couldn't help thinking.

My memory of the next 24 hours is a stormy weather map that whirls cyclonically around two events, neither of which I was actually party to. We found Boris with two other couples in the drawing room. (There was no sign of Gina, I realised.) One couple were obviously English toffs, the other – with her high-class hooker looks and his lowbrow manners – obviously Russian. Bling was indeed meeting tweed.

Boris made a great show of welcoming us and focussed an almost embarrassing degree of attention on Angela. Why hadn't they been introduced before? Why had I kept such a gem hidden away? It suddenly occurred to me that this expansive mood of his, coupled with the old-fashioned courtesies, almost enabled him to pass for charming. It could even go so far as to make him – as opposed to his immense wealth – attractive to women.

Far from wilting under the glare of this attention, Angela seemed to take a shine to it. You could say they established an instant rapport and even I was hard-pushed to know whether she was just going through the motions as a good guest or finding it a genuine pleasure. Certainly, it was convincing enough for the other women to shoot several loaded looks her way.

Others began to arrive. An international set radiating burnished health and affluence – a combination of Russians, Americans, English, French and even an Indian and a Chinese couple. Judging from those I spoke to, none were in finance, which at least kept the competition to a minimum. Boris had somehow contrived to organise a group from across the professional, if not social spectrum: a CEO of a major corporation, a prominent politico, an oil baron, a media mogul, a lawyer, a well-known actress, a very camp Lord and a very snooty Lady – indeed a Baroness, no less.

I didn't find out for certain what the Indian and the Chinaman did, but I got the distinct impression they knew what business I was in, since they both made reference to 'utilising' my services. (They each contacted me some weeks later to that end, but by then the landscape of my life had changed utterly and I wasn't sure I wanted their business - or indeed anyone else's.)

Angela and I more than pulled our weight socially. We walked with one group and swam and hung out in the sauna with another, where I found it hard to take my eyes off the gloriously enhanced breasts of the Russian super-hooker.

'Keep those peepers to yourself,' Angela smiled thinly, 'or I might just cancel our appointment with the four-poster…'

I'd asked Boris about Gina. He'd made an un-smiley face and said she was 'what's that fine English word, Theo? *Indisposed.*'

She eventually appeared at the cocktail hour. To me she looked a little – what's that fine French word? – *distrait*, and not a little dishevelled. I wondered if the cocktail hour had started much earlier for her. It was obvious that Boris had her under surveillance, quietly moving her around the room, trying to keep her out of trouble, as if she were a vulnerable queen on a chessboard.

The banquet more than lived up to its billing. The Georgian splendour of the dining room, with its Adams ceiling and blazing candelabra, combined with some eight courses and numerous vintage wines to produce an occasion fit for the Prince Regent himself. My own appreciation of it was dented by my being seated between the Russian hooker and the toffee-nosed Baroness, another of Boris' little jokes, no doubt, made all the more un-amusing by the fact that he'd seated Angela next to himself.

And what fun they appeared to have at the other end of the long table, while I struggled between the Russian devil and the deep blue Baroness, an unwholesome man sandwich, if ever there was one. While the Baroness brought a frosty condescension to any given subject, the hooker came on so hot, heavy and tactile that I began to suspect another Boris set-up, especially as there wasn't much less of those breasts on display in the dining room than there'd been in the sauna.

I somehow managed to keep my composure, but I was extremely relieved when we moved to the next stage of the proceedings. We were invited by Bedwell to go out on to the main terrace, 'where a pyrotechnic display will soon commence'. In a food and wine coma, we filed out into what had become the chilly April night. God knows how much of Boris' hot dosh went up in exploding mega-rockets. They floodlit the sky to the last movement of Tchaikovsky's Piano Concerto No. 1 and many delighted 'oohs' and 'aahs'. As a finale, the rockets grew more frenetic, while in the middle of the lake – on a pontoon that had been towed into place while we were at dinner – 'Happy Birthday, Boris' was emblazoned in flame.

I'd lost track of Angela in the excitement of the display, but once the smoke cleared and the torches on the terrace were re-lit, I saw her deep in conversation with Gina. After a few minutes, they disappeared together, and it was only much later I learned they'd gone up to Boris' office. I should have realised what was happening, but the wine had taken its toll and I was distracted by Anna, the Russian. She was determined to stick close and I'm ashamed to admit that she was looking more and more like someone I'd give anything to fuck. Perhaps, it was for that reason that when she suggested we head for the ballroom to dance – the final event of the evening – I allowed her to take my hand and lead me there.

On the way, she offered me a line of coke – the first sign of it at this otherwise determinedly respectable do – but I politely declined, and we had champagne instead. We'd been drinking and dancing for maybe half-an-hour when I felt a firm tap on the shoulder: Angela beckoned me grimly outside.

My first thought was that she'd overreacted to my less than erotic bopping with the Russian. (Okay, Anna's bopping was *very* erotic.)

'I'm leaving,' she said. She looked extremely unhappy, not at all in the mood to dance.

'What? We can't drive back to London now.'

'*We're* not. I've ordered a taxi. I don't want you to come with me. In fact, I don't want you to come home again – except to collect your things and move yourself out...'

'*What?* Angela, what are you talking about?'

She turned and walked quickly away. I was reduced to chasing after her, pleading and grovelling, as we went. 'Angela...please...what's going on? *Please*...'

We went through the main hall of the house and up the grand staircase to our room, where she collected her things. We went back down to the entrance, while I went on getting louder and angrier. Bedwell and the other staff discreetly ignored us.

Eventually, I grabbed her roughly by the arm and pulled her round to face me. 'What the fuck's happened? What's this about?'

'Take your hands off me!'

'It's not to do with the Russian woman, is it?'

She took a deep breath and managed to look down her nose at me, which for someone a head shorter was a measure of her contempt.

'Is it?'

'Is it what?'

'About the woman I was dancing with?'

'I don't give a shit about you dancing with that whore. And funnily enough, I didn't really mind being groped under the table by Boris. It was all quite titillating, as it happens...'

'He did *what?*'

'What I do have a real problem with is the fact that he's a major trafficker of heroin and women. Gina, his wife, showed me the evidence. She also showed me how you launder his toxic millions. You make all that shit happen, Theo. You're as guilty as he is. It's obscene. It sickens me. *You* sicken me. We're done. We're fuckin' done. Do you fuckin' 'ear me? We're fuckin' finished.'

As she spoke, her accent had gone from the Home Counties to Stepney. My mouth fell open but no words emerged and it remained that way as I stood at the top of the steps at the front of the house that suddenly seemed more a whited sepulchre than an elegant Georgian mansion. I watched Angela get into the cab. I watched its taillights recede down the winding drive until they disappeared.

I was aware of the thumping disco beat, a thumping headache, the chill wind on my face and Anna at my side, pressing those breasts against me. This time I accepted the offer of the coke. It was of course her I screwed several times that night in the four-poster, and she turned out to be the consummate professional.

Chapter 7

Venice, November 1728

Now November is upon us, with its sea drizzle and slinking mists, like a requiem for the year, and even for Serenissima herself. The whole city takes on a phantom quality. Few craft ply the canals; the quaysides and sinuous alleyways are almost desert'd, and all the sounds of daily exchange seem strangely mut'd and distant. The city has become another place, and yet I wonder that I am so affect'd by these seasonal changes. I have witness'd the dying of many years, but none has depress'd me as profoundly as this. It is as if I am in mourning. Each evening, I delay the lighting of the lamps, preferring to sit in the shadows. I indulge in bouts of morbid introspection and wou'd almost welcome a visit from my spectral friend, who perversely does not come. In fact, he has ignor'd me in recent years, leading me once more to dismiss him as a trick I play upon myself in my most anxious moments.

But there are other, even more worrying signs. I have been spending time of late away from the Ridotto at La Pieta, a nearby church attach'd to one of the great music schools of Venice. It is there that Antonio Vivaldi is not only Maestro, but composer and player of the most inspirational music. On the one hand, I tell myself that this is the only reason I attend: to hear his violin and the choir of young women singing the Gloria from behind the huge wooden grill. (Apparently, it is the only female choir in all of Europe, but due to some misguid'd notion of propriety we are not allow'd to see them!) On the other hand, if Vivaldi's music were the only thing that attract'd me, I wou'd attend his operas and other secular works, which I do not, so clearly I visit La Pieta for another reason – the first stirrings of religious devotion, I fear. Lately, I have caught myself following the Mass and mumbling the Latin prayers. All I need is to finger the beads and this picture of piety will be complete. It is all very upsetting.

Yesterday, for instance, was the feast of All Souls, when Masses are said for 'our dear depart'd brethren'. (That I now know such things is sad in itself.) I suspect I went along to La Pieta in the bizarre hope that I might somehow encounter the ghost. Not surprisingly, there was no sign of him. The young women sang the De Profundis and I sat contemplating the ghastly images of Christ's passion and his mother's grief that line the walls of the church, one of which was paint'd by Pellegrini (not one of his best).

I am puzzl'd. How can I now be drawn to such grotesquerie? What has happen'd that I find these lurid expressions of pain and self-sacrifice in any way ennobling when before they were utterly repugnant to me? I have no answer. All I know is that these images contradict everything I stood for and still do, despite what took place in Paris. For the System was found'd upon a contrary vision to that of the Christian faith. It encourages its devotees to put aside suffering and self-denial in favour of prosperity and personal happiness; to enter a world of trade, commerce and money; to engage in the pursuit of pleasure, rather than pain.

And on the fourth day of June 1717, it was in the pursuit of pleasure, prosperity and personal happiness for all that we first open'd the doors of our Banque Generale in the Rue St. Avoye – even if the crowds did not immediately flock to use its services. I cou'd not be sure who exactly my enemies were at that point – there were already numerous possibilities – but the vitriolic news sheets they issued on the streets warn'd away many potential customers. They denounc'd me as a murderer, a swindler and a charlatan who had cheat'd people out of thousands of louis d'or at the gaming tables and wou'd now do the same to anyone foolish enough to involve himself with the bank and its worthless paper.

This was bad enough, but worse was the fact that they also traduc'd Katherine. She was a high-born whore who, having desert'd her noble husband in England, had abscond'd to France with this low-born cur to live in sin and have his bastards.

Thankfully, she brush'd it all off with wry good humour. 'I'd rather be a high-born whore than a low-born cur, John. Some

190

*of the most powerful women in the world are high-born whores.
It's the only way we can wield any political influence...'*

*Even when I told her about Gregg's letters to Orleans and
apologis'd for not informing her of them sooner, she remain'd
philosophical.*

*'Well, Gregg said he wou'd do as much in his letters to me,
but it hardly matters. As many will be attract'd to our notoriety
as will be discourag'd by it.'*

'I had the same thought,' I said. 'This is Paris, after all.'

*She laugh'd. 'Yes, and I fancy it all adds to my allure, as far
as Orleans is concern'd. He probably thinks of me as he does
one of his courtesans – Madame de Tencin, for instance – and
is all the more excit'd by it...'*

*I smil'd at this, but I had to admit to feeling a twinge of
jealousy at the thought and the fact that Katherine evidently
took some pleasure in it.*

*'And as for its effect on the bank, John, we'll let the profits
speak for themselves...'*

*And they did just that. The scandal-mongering scar'd away
customers at first, but given the favourable terms they were
offer'd, it did not as easily discourage the investors who help'd
us capitalise the bank. This, of course, was the bait'd hook that
Katherine had dangl'd before Philippe at Marly and caus'd his
dramatic change of heart.*

*Through this scheme – as much of Katherine's devising as
mine – every member of the Council was able to invest in the
bank with heavily devalued billet d'etats and still receive an
early dividend, initially in gold coin. Philippe, who had a large
number of these bonds, benefitt'd more than anyone.*

*There was, of course, an element of risk in the approach –
exchanging good for bad – but we had long ago decid'd that
the bank's success wou'd depend not so much on money pledg'd
as on that most invaluable and intangible of financial assets:
confidence.*

*Not only did Katherine help me in the setting up and
financing of the bank, she also came up with various ingenious
methods of increasing that confidence. To encourage
commercial customers, we offer'd them free services and
discount'd their bills. They soon discover'd that their*

transactions were eas'd considerably through the use of paper, especially when money need'd to be dispatch'd to other parts of the country – given a swift set of carrier pigeons, they cou'd deposit it in Paris today and draw it in Lyons tomorrow. Within weeks, the trickle of customers became a stream, as people began to see the sense of using, not just the banking services, but banknotes that guaranteed a fix'd value on the day of issue, when all other monetary values fluctuat'd at the whim of the duc de Noailles.

What pride we felt – yes, pride! – when the bank issued its first note, upon which were some of the most potent words ever written, sign'd by myself: 'I promise to pay the bearer the sum of 100 livres tournois fix'd upon the day of issue...' Like a boy who had caught his first fish, I took the first one off the press home and wav'd it around in triumph. As I held it aloft, and Katherine held Anne between us, we waltz'd around the drawing room. 'I predict,' I said, 'that within two years this will be France's only legal tender...'

It was a bold prediction, but it rais'd our sprits considerably. Yet for matters to move that swiftly, we both knew that the trickle of customers wou'd have to become a torrent, and that wou'd require a grander gesture than free services and the discounting of bills. It need'd not just Philippe's investment – which had been clandestine – but a more public sign of his Royal approval.

Since the issue of the bank's Charter, I had tried to see him on several occasions when he was in Paris, but he had always made the excuse that he was far too busy with affairs of state. In fact, I knew from Saint-Simon that he had become more besott'd than ever with Parabére, if that were possible, whilst still indulging in his usual wild excess. It was hardly surprising that his duties as Regent were taking a poor second place. However, when I said that Katherine had miss'd him since our visit to Marly and suggest'd she accompany me, he agreed readily and even sent a carriage for us. We found him wigless, alone but for the company of a half-finish'd bottle of wine, and looking very sorry for himself.

The affairs of state, he told us, appear'd to him as a mountain of seemingly insoluble problems. Rapidly dwindling tax revenues, disagreements with the Papacy, a meddlesome Parlement, a demanding young Louis XV who insist'd on spending more time at Versailles or Marly than suit'd Philippe, a wife who had decid'd she want'd to spend more time in public – they were all conspiring to grind him down, and only wine and Madame Parabère cou'd relieve his misery. And of course a visit from us, his favourite couple.

'I was sad on your behalf to hear what the scandal sheets are saying about you.' He look'd more towards Katherine. 'I do hope it's not causing you too much pain, Madame Law… I of course will go on calling you <u>Madame Law</u> *and I'm sure others will follow suit.'*

'If it pleases Your Highness, you may call me Katherine…'

'Ah, a good solution for our private intercourse…' And he gave her what was either a sympathetic smile or a mischievous grin, I was not sure which. 'Sometimes, Katherine, when it suits their purpose, the French can trade as much in hypocrisy as the English. Please, let me apologise for my compatriots and assure you both that you continue to have my full support and protection.'

'That's very good to know, Your Highness,' I said, 'thank you.'

'And if I might be so bold, Your Highness,' Katherine put in, 'we were wondering if you might make a public demonstration of that support – to discourage our detractors, those people who wou'd like to see the enterprise still born.'

Orleans suddenly look'd wary, as if we were about to add to his mountain of problems. 'I see…you want me approach these detractors – to speak to them directly? Assuming I know who they are, of course.'

'No,' she said, 'nothing so crude. We have another request. You are already an investor in the bank, which as we know is a private arrangement. But we wou'd be grateful if you wou'd simply make a deposit there - in other words, become a customer.'

'A deposit?'

'Yes. Not because we have need of more funds, you understand – although one can never have too many - but to

help boost confidence, to set an example. Where you go, others will surely follow.'

We let him ponder this for a few moments, before I continued: 'I think Your Highness will find our rates of interest the best in Paris, not to mention the terms of our loans, which are extremely favourable.'

Still he ponder'd, as he pour'd us both some wine.

'On a relat'd subject,' he said, more brightly, 'I have in mind to begin some major renovations of the Palais-Royal. This very afternoon, I will be briefing architects and builders on my plans, which are fashion'd around my large collection of paintings, as well as several enormous pictures that I intend to paint myself – bacchanalian scenes of classical antiquity after Corregio.'

Katherine enthus'd. 'An excellent idea, Your Highness!'

'Thank you, Katherine. I knew you wou'd appreciate it. And when and if I come to execute these works, I wou'd welcome your advice on the mounting of the collection, for I know you are a collector yourself, as well as a woman of exquisite taste.'

'Thank you, Your Highness. I'd be honour'd.'

'There was, however, a more depressing note sound'd today, by the duc de Noailles, my Financial-Controller. He told me earlier that there is little money available for what he deems <u>inessential</u> public works. It will have to come out of my own family coffers, he says, which are themselves far from overflowing...'

I went to respond, but Katherine had already taken the cue: 'The bank of course wou'd be only too happy to support you in this project, Your Highness – once you become a customer...'

Philippe sipp'd his wine, turn'd and walk'd slowly away from us across the room, before turning back to face us. 'I will not make one deposit at the Bank,' he said solemnly, before breaking into a smile. 'I will make several.'

We both thank'd him effusively.

'And by the way,' he add'd, 'I had no idea that the Banque Generale was a – how shou'd I put it? – a <u>family</u> business.'

'Yes, Your Highness, Katherine and I are business partners.'

'How extraordinary! Well, if it's good enough for the Paris Brothers...' He rais'd his glass. 'Here's to you both,' he

194

beamed, his eyes firmly on Katherine, 'and your most formidable partnership.'

A week later, without warning, his carriage drew up outside the bank, attend'd by a contingent of heavily arm'd Swiss guards. Down he stepp'd, dress'd in some of his finest and most colourful silks, and personally supervis'd the unloading of many heavy coffers. The handful of customers present – enough to be a reliable source of this news – look'd on in unconceal'd interest, as pairs of flamboyantly liveried footmen carried the boxes through the banking hall to the vault. When Philippe follow'd on, I made a huge show of greeting him – I had never before bow'd as low and have never since – saying, as loudly as decorum wou'd permit, how extremely privileg'd we were to have him as a customer of the bank.

Over the next fortnight there were four more of these visits, each time involving the same entourage and number of coffers; each time drawing a larger crowd than before. The coffers were fill'd with louis d'or, except for the last consignment, which contain'd, to our surprise, nothing more than rocks. In one of these was a short note with the Regent's seal:

'Monsieur Law, it seems you have reliev'd me of a large sum of money once again. However, I thought a fifth delivery of coffers wou'd help boost confidence even further. What can I expect in interest for this last deposit? Yours etc.'

By return I thank'd him for his custom and told him that the Bank wou'd of course pay interest on the equivalent weight of louis d'or.

The effect of Philippe's visits to the bank was almost instantaneous. Customers were suddenly queuing to use our services and notes were issued as fast as we cou'd print them. The impact on commerce was mark'd. Crippl'd for so long by uncertainty and a shortage of currency, business slowly return'd to life. The city grew busier, many shops and theatres reopen'd. The gloom that had pervad'd the country gradually gave way to a sense of optimism, express'd to me personally at the many soirées Katherine and I continued to hold and reflect'd in the rising popularity of the Government.

With his recently discover'd enthusiasm for financial affairs, Saint-Simon declar'd that my paper money was like new blood

*coursing through the country's veins and the Banque Generale
was its newly pumping heart.*

*

It may be time to come clean, as they say, which is difficult
when you've been deluged in a shower of dirty money for as
long as I have. If I'm honest, I've been at odds with myself for
a while. I felt the twinge of this inner conflict even before the
break-up with Angela, and from then on it became a raging
headache. The anti-depressants allowed me to keep a lid on it
for a while, but the gremlin just bided its time and now it's out
and creating all sorts of havoc. Now I'm so badly conflicted it
will have to come down to a fight to the death between the two
sides.

On one side is the professional Moneyman who takes great
pride in the skills that have enabled him to amass a large
fortune. (Not even the divorce dented that. Angela wanted none
of my blood money, as she put it, just her share of the London
house.) But the Moneyman's not so much interested in the
actual size of his pile, his stash. It's more about his position in
the table; where he features in the rich lists. Before that, it was
his standing in the investment team, which had to do with
getting the biggest bonus. The fact is that the numbers don't
represent money *per se* so much as *winning* – getting the
highest score, as if he were playing a computer game. And he is
– modern investment happens mostly in virtual reality.

Of course, he always knew he'd never be in the major *major*
league – the owners of vast corporate assets with leviathan lives
all of their own; the Bill Gates' and Jeff Bezos' of this world.
Instead, he compares himself to his peers, to the other
successful Moneymen – the top fund managers, financiers,
hedge funders and market players, mainly in London and New
York. In this company, he's very much a contender and has
risen rapidly to somewhere near the top of the table.

Does he find it satisfying? Probably. Does it make him
happy? He wouldn't go that far. It's much more important than
that. It's to do with who he is, his identity, his DNA. He was
raised in a solid bourgeois family. He didn't have to fight his

way up; it's not about success against-all-odds because the odds have always been in his favour. It's more a sense of entitlement, coupled with the desire to excel, to be the best in class. He knows that if you're not the best, you're nothing. You're lost in that black hole.

He's not sure what drove his ancestor, John Law. Maybe he actually thought that as well as enriching himself he could save the sinking world by floating it on a sea of money. But if he was gripped by the burgeoning ideals of the Enlightenment, the modern Moneyman is at the other end of the line. All the ideals are threadbare. Nothing improves; there's no redemption. There's only winning.

Now, if there were just the Moneyman, I wouldn't have a problem. But it's not that simple. There's someone else, the one who's been breaking through while I've been in Italy, and I don't just mean via the panic attacks. This guy loathes the Moneyman. He sees him as a criminal among criminals; a sociopath, a scourge. The Moneyman has tried talking him round, seducing him with all the usual specious arguments. You know the kind of thing: venality turned to social purpose. The whole system is criminal, riddled with corruption. Every government is complicit, every institution bought and sold. Everything is part of the same money-go-round. He, the professional, merely gives it another spin and thereby keeps the whole world spinning. That way, he helps more people get a piece of the action.

Bull*shit* – more people get screwed. *Badly fucking screwed.* The other one – let's call him the Anarchist, for want of a better title –isn't buying it. He wants to bring down the Moneyman and destroy him. And not only him – he wants to bring down as many of the other criminals as he can, perhaps the whole rotten Establishment. He thinks they've had it their own way for too long. And he's as ruthless as the Moneyman himself.

There's no avoiding it – the fight is on.

Which is why when I get the email at Rezzonico it takes me a while to pull myself out of the hole. (Where will I land? In whose corner will I be?)

Both Jo and our guide, Marisa, register concern. Jo's seen it before, of course – and may have had enough of it – so she lets me take my own time. Marisa urges me to sit down, while the launch starts to tie up at the landing. I come up for air, take several deep breaths.

'Sorry…I get these bouts of giddiness. Probably to do with some medication I've been taking…'

Jo leans in close, puts an arm around me. Her smell alone – a heady of mixture of perfume, perspiration and youth – is healing.

'You okay, Theo? Was it something on the phone?'

'Yes…I mean no…sort of. It's fine. You go ahead to the museum. I just need to make a call.'

'Are you sure?'

'Yes, it's okay…I'll join you when I'm done…thanks…'

Marisa tells me I can stay on the boat as long as I want. They'll meet me in the museum, on the *piano nobile*.

'Thank you…See you in a little while...'

'*Avanti...*'

I remain sitting in the launch. Our skipper discreetly goes up on to the quayside and lights a cigarette. I think there's a chance my phone is being tapped, so I pull out another that's more heavily encrypted and allows me to call only one number.

It's answered immediately. I'm relieved it's the American male voice I expected. My digital wizard.

'How's it goin'?'

'I think they're on to us.'

'I doubt it.' He doesn't miss a beat. 'We'd know if anyone had even attempted to hack us.'

'I know, but I've had a very threatening message.'

'How threatenin'?'

'Telling me they've stopped us - that I'm going to die here in Venice.'

'I thought you were in Rome.'

'I was. I took a detour…'

'Anyway, it's a bluff. They might have got a whiff of something going down, but they're not sure what – and they sure-as-hell won't be able to stop it. They're just trying to scare you.'

I give a nervous laugh and use the American coinage: 'Well, I'm scared already.' As I'm speaking, I'm looking around at the craft on the canal and the people on the quayside – everyone and everything poses some sort of threat.

'I'm sorry, Theo,' he says eventually. 'You knew what could happen...'

'*Yes*, I know I knew...How far off are we?'

'Forty-eigth hours at most.'

The imminence of it shocks me and yet we've been working towards it for a long time. I *do* want it to happen - or at least, a part of me does: the Anarchist. "But nothing happens until I say so, right?' Silence. '*Right?*'

'Absolutely not. You're the boss.' It's true enough and there's no irony in his tone. Yet as I ring off, it feels anything but the case.

*

Today at the Ridotto, partly because of my coughing fits and the worsening pain in my chest, I am finding it hard to write. Extracting raw memories, then cutting and polishing them to the point where they sparkle with lucidity and wit is an exhausting business. It is far more demanding than the rigours of the gaming table, although they too are beginning to prove a challenge for me. The conte de Bellini has notic'd this recent lethargy at cards and has taken to bringing me hot chocolate lac'd with cognac to the table in the hope that it will raise my game.

'Il Duce,' he smiles, his eyes twinkling with mischief, 'the cards seem limp in your hands today. Maybe this will help stiffen their purpose...' Alas, it only leaves me feeling warm and befuddl'd, which is pleasant enough, but does little to enhance my gaming performance.

Later, he returns. 'I've decid'd you're in need of a treat, il Duce. I will arrange a little outing for you in the next few days. A change of scene will refresh you...'

I thank him. Again, there's the mischievous twinkle - or do I imagine it? Because I've guess'd what treat the Conte has in mind. He's like my corrupt gaoler in Newgate.

But apart from this general indisposition, in all seriousness there is another reason I feel distract'd and unable to concentrate. *It is four months to the day since I have heard from Katherine and I am beginning to think that our letters have somehow gone astray, or more likely, been intercept'd by the French authorities – or worse, that we have return'd to the time when she did not correspond at all. Then, her anger at what she had had to endure after my departure destroy'd what little feeling for me remain'd, and she preferr'd to maintain an accusing silence.*

It was at least year after I left Paris that she eventually permitt'd herself to write. At first, her letters were cold and formal, with no expression of sentiment or enquiry after my own situation, only the bald description of hers: the hounding by the government, the confiscations, the snubs, the insults, the fear for her and Anne's safety, the authorities' refusal to let them leave. They were being held hostage in France in the vain hope that I wou'd be forc'd to 'repay' millions of livres I did not have.

And I was set upon the rack of guilt - as she no doubt intend'd – knowing that she was suffering these punishments on my behalf and that the French were persecuting her because they cou'd not reach me. I offer'd to return, to suffer every indignity and hardship in order to be with them, but when I receiv'd her reply, it was worse than all the agonies of guilt. There were two reasons I shou'd not come. First, it was pointless; I wou'd be hang'd or broken on the wheel even before I saw her and Anne. And second, she did not think that she cou'd bear to set eyes on me again. Even with all that had happen'd, with my exile from France and our separation, nothing had cut me as deeply as those words. On the other hand, I cannot think that I deserv'd to be treat'd in any other way.

But then as her situation improv'd, so did the tone of her correspondence. There was no more warmth and affection, it is true, but she seem'd happier within herself. At first Philippe had abandon'd her, cut her off completely, but his attitude towards her had soften'd as he had become stricken by illness. Although he had pointedly ignor'd all my personal letters to him - as well as those that sought compensation for my losses - it seem'd that he had finally heed'd my request that Katherine

200

be grant'd a small pension. This was authoris'd six months before his death, just as Parisian society was beginning to re-open its doors to her. (I knew that Saint-Simon had work'd hard on her behalf, and anyway, as we have remark'd before, notoriety will always excite a certain curiosity among the genteel classes.)

At this point, I felt encourag'd to write to her more frequently. I told her more of my own news – about my futile efforts to regain some of our property, and the absurd letters from French lawyers demanding full reparations for the damage our System had done to France – a total of 5 billion livres, no less! I describ'd my life in Venice, and how empty it felt without her and Anne. How I long'd to be with them, watching our daughter grow up, affording her every possible comfort and advantage. I promis'd to do all I cou'd from my place of exile to provide for Anne's future, and in my most recent letter to Katherine, written over three months ago – and to which she has not replied - I explain'd how I need'd her help in this.

...As you know, I came to Venice almost entirely without means and those I have since acquir'd have been deriv'd solely from my efforts at the Ridotto's gaming tables. I do not know if the mental faculties always decline along with the physical, but certainly my gambling prowess is not what it was, and the relatively modest scale of my winnings reflects as much. The fact is that although it is enough for me to live in relative comfort, it will not amount to much of a legacy for Anne. This will require a larger capital sum than I am likely to accumulate in the near future, despite my best efforts, and I would like to suggest an alternative.

I believe I am right in thinking that some of our paintings were not among the goods and property confiscat'd by the authorities following my departure. Even if there were a large market for art in France, any attempt by you to sell some or all of these pictures wou'd only attract unwant'd attention. With my own resources I have tried to acquire several pictures here in Venice that

201

I might sell at a profit, but I fear they are of limit'd value and will realise very little. May I therefore suggest that a selection of our paintings and drawings – perhaps half – be sent to me? Works from the Italian and Dutch schools are beginning to fetch extremely high prices here. I wou'd have little difficulty in selling them and wou'd ensure that the money is put straight into trust for Anne. I hasten to add that the Venetian banks were among the first to be establish'd in Europe and there wou'd be no safer home for our daughter's inheritance, until such time that she is able to leave France and claim it. Please let me know your thoughts on the matter as soon as possible...

No sooner had I finish'd writing these words than the thought occurr'd to me that Katherine wou'd be unlikely to trust this proposal of mine; that she wou'd think it just another commercial venture, one last attempt to salvage some profit from the System, rather than a means of providing for our daughter. And indeed, on the evidence of what happen'd in Paris, she had every reason to feel as much. Perhaps, it was the need to convince her of my good intentions – as well as my genuine longing for her - that urg'd me to continue in the more intimate tone that had once been so natural to us.

...You may be surpris'd to learn that affairs of a material and monetary nature have not been my main preoccupation of late. My health has deteriorat'd – an incurable disease of the lungs, I am told – and much as I try to deny it, I have become afflict'd by an acute sense of my own mortality. Matters like my success at the gaming table or the rights and wrongs of the System seem to pale into insignificance. Instead, I find myself pondering the profit and loss of the heart – not just in relation to our daughter, but ourselves: the meaning of our time together and whether there is still the possibility of our caring for each other.

It is a shameful fact, Katherine, that in all my letters I do not think that I have even said sorry to you and Anne for the pain and suffering I have caus'd you on so many levels. Not least – and perhaps worst of all – was my failure to understand, honour and protect your natural rights as a woman, over above the existing legal or social rights, which I know you hold in contempt. So, let me correct that now and offer my most sincere and abject apologies. I do not deserve or expect forgiveness. In fact, I deserve nothing from you except your eternal contempt. Yet I ask if you might find for me in yourself a tiny fragment of the love that I still feel for you. For yes, to use what you wou'd call a fanciful image, the fire has burnt itself out, the smoke has clear'd, but to my surprise and wonder I discover that part of the grand house we built together is still standing. I cannot help but want to return to this ruin and live there again. Please, Katherine, tell me that you might join me, if not in a literal sense then at least in some corner of your heart.

Yours, with love, John

*

I must join the others. Better to be in company, I decide, though surely I'll be safe in broad daylight, in a public space like this? The skipper hurries over to help me out of the boat and onto the dock, where I do my best to steady myself, mentally as well as physically. I just need to get the Moneyman back in charge and I'll be fine. Remember, I tell myself, nothing will happen unless I say so. I don't *have* to do anything, and I may choose to do nothing at all. Now more than ever, I need to live in the moment: enjoy my time with Joanna, at the Ca'Rezzonico, the Cipriani, wherever. No past, no future. No regrets, no fearful anticipation. Just spending time and money enjoying myself - isn't that what I'm here for?

And yet…and yet as I head into the palazzo, a couple of crucial questions keep repeating in my head: how the hell have they got wind of something going down? And will they try to make me tell them what that something is?

I find Jo and Marisa on the first floor, in one of the magnificent staterooms overlooking the canal. Jo seems both relieved and surprised to see me; she obviously thought I'd given up on the tour. Marisa breaks off mid-exposition. 'Are you okay, Theo?'

'Much better, thanks. Please carry on.'

'*Allora...*' And she does in her theatrical fashion, her hands conducting an orchestra. As she's been telling Joanna, Rezzonico houses an incomparable collection of 18th century Venetian art – paintings and frescoes by Canaletto, Tiepolo, Tintoretto and many more. 'And by the way, Theo,' she says, as I join them, 'in Room 20, should we have time and we probably won't, is a painting of the interior of the Ridotto by Francesco Guardi. Above all others, the palazzo itself represents the triumph of the *nouveaux riches* over the ancient families of Venice - power that comes through money rather than birth and is all about vain display. The Baroque is inflated into the Rococo and embraces ever more ornamentation, ever more ostentation. The Age of Decadence is in full swing.'

We go through to the ballroom at the rear of the building where the lavishness rises to another level, literally – its height is double that of the other rooms, a grand fantasy on a classical theme. It's reached on one side by a vast marble staircase, lined with Ancient Greek statuary. The walls are decorated with architectural *trompe l'oeil* that make the room appear even larger. The ceiling is awe-inspiring: Apollo rides his chariot over Europe, Asia, Africa and the Americas. The power of La Serenissima may have been in decline, but here she – or rather the family Rezzonico – reigns supreme.

The room is so magnificent that even without trying I'm entirely swept up in the moment and forget that every tourist in the palazzo is intent on murdering me. Still, I'm grateful when, at one point in our tour, Jo discreetly squeezes my hand and whispers in my ear: 'As beautiful as this is, I'd rather be back in our hotel bed with you...'

Since her words go straight to my genitals, so would I. The prospect of lunch is a poor second, but it will have to do.

'I think it's time we headed over to the Cipriani,' I say. Marisa offers to drop us there in the boat and pick us up for the second half of the tour this afternoon, if we're still up for it. We are, of course - even if I'm more excited by the thought of going back to the hotel with Jo. (Given my current form, the thought of it is probably about as exciting as it gets.)

'*Allora*...we'll be visiting a secret Venetian gem - the building that housed the Casino Venier.' She gives us both a wry grin. 'In the 18th century, it was both a gambling salon – a much smaller version of the Ridotto – and a high-class brothel, probably more the latter...'

Outside, the sky is beginning to cloud over. A wind has sprung up; it feels cooler. 'Ah, as forecast, the storm is on its way,' Marisa says, as we head for the boat. '*Avanti...*'

It takes us back down the Grand Canal, past our hotel and San Marco, and round the Salute. We head across the wider waterway, the Giudecca, to the island where the Cipriani is situated. Another, much larger vessel is crossing the water from the other side. When it first starts to shift its course towards us, none of us pay much attention, not even our skipper. Only as it's almost upon us, does he take evasive action; only then do I think this is not just a figment of my paranoia. As our boat swerves sharply away from a disastrous – for us – collision, I expect it to overturn and pitch us all headlong into the water. It seems as if living in the moment is about to become dying in it.

*

Philippe was right. I cou'd not deny that the Banque Generale was a family business Nor cou'd I deny that Katherine's involvement in it had been, and continued to be, critical to its success. Her financial acumen was nothing short of remarkable – not just for a woman, but by anyone's standards – and her influence over Orleans had become much greater than mine. It was our ace in hand, helping us achieve our ambitions when all else fail'd.

As she herself became more aware of this, she grew in confidence. Her fears that motherhood wou'd stand in the way of her role as a businesswoman had not come to pass. On the

205

contrary, she felt empower'd by giving birth and claim'd it made her all the more ready to take up the challenges of the day-to-day management of 'our other child', the bank, a step that I still found hard to accept.

Because I finally had to admit the truth to myself: despite my best intentions, I realis'd I was growing resentful of Katherine, and it was more and more apparent that although we were partners, we were also becoming rivals. Or at least, that was my perception – perhaps, I was mistaken. Perhaps, as she might have said, it was merely my male pride that was bristling at her success, rather than there being any conscious effort on her part to outshine me.

I mull'd this over, as I watch'd her going though the accounts at the bank and issuing instructions to the staff, who were all male, of course, and cast furtive looks of protest in my direction. Who is Director here? they seem'd to be asking. I ignor'd them at first, but I knew that I cou'd not do so forever, any more than I cou'd go on ignoring my own discomfiture. Indeed, I was soon put in a position where I felt forc'd to assert myself.

Katherine was in the office and I was in the banking hall speaking to a prospective customer when a shock'd-looking Monsieur Ginot, the Chief Clerk, came to me with a stack of banknotes that a customer wish'd to exchange for gold coin. They totall'd three million livres – the equivalent of roughly two million louis d'or. Seeing as they had been present'd by a local moneylender, who did not normally deal in sums of three thousand, let alone three million livres, I immediately sens'd a device. But if the rogue expect'd to see me squirm and panic, he was disappoint'd. The outward appearance of card-playing calm was the order of the day, even if I felt a tide of panic begin to rise within.

Katherine must have realis'd that something was amiss, because she immediately came out of the office and stood at my side. From the look of concern on her face, she too knew that a damaging ruse was afoot.

'This is an extremely large sum of money, Monsieur,' she said.

He ignor'd her, look'd down his nose and sniff'd at the notes, as if they gave off some unpleasant odour. 'I'm much reliev'd <u>someone</u> thinks so' - even a woman was the implication – 'because all I see, Monsieur, are words on bits of paper...'

'Words that are pledges that will of course be honour'd,' I said, 'although we do not keep such large amounts of gold here.'

'Because they are not pledges to pay the bearer in gold,' Katherine cut in.

Again, he ignor'd her and spoke pointedly to me. 'Ah, how silly of me,' he sneer'd, 'and I was under the impression that this was a bank!'

He thought himself a clever fellow, this one, and in other circumstances, I wou'd have lov'd to tear up the notes, throw them in his face and throw him out the door, not least for his rudeness towards Katherine. However, I knew only too well what was at stake and remain'd a model of civility. She, on the other hand, felt no such constraint.

'Don't ignore me, Monsieur. I'm a Director of the Bank and I'll have you thrown out on your backside for your uncivil behaviour...'

'Please, <u>Madam</u>!' I turn'd to Katherine and gave her a look of such reproof that she was shock'd into silence; I turn'd back to the customer with a simpering smile.

'And so it is a bank, Monsieur, the Banque Generale, and one that deals mainly in banknotes the better to provide its services. But forgive me, we cannot exchange the notes today.'

'Then when can you exchange them?' he ask'd.

The other customers, those bearers of news, good or bad, were now attending closely.

'Tomorrow, Monsieur,' I replied, without hesitation. 'We just need time to transport such an amount, you understand.'

A look of triumph spread across his face. He spun round full circle to make sure everyone in the hall was still listening, which they were, of course. 'I understand, Monsieur Law, that if my gold does not appear tomorrow, this Banque Generale, so call'd, must consider itself defunct.'

He took up the notes. 'And, by the way' – he rais'd his voice – 'if you wish to at least keep up the appearances of being a *bank, I suggest you leave your harridan of a <u>wife</u> – or whatever she is - at home, where she belongs.' He turn'd again and left.*

'I pity any wife that a boorish imbecile like you might keep at home...' Katherine's loud abuse wou'd have continued had I not put my finger to her lips and given her another reproving glare, which she return'd as brusquely as she push'd my hand aside.

I took her firmly by the arm and led her back to the office, where, once the staff had made a discreet exit, we cou'd be alone.

She wrench'd her arm away from me. 'How dare you silence me like that!'

'How dare you embarrass me in that way!'

'How else was I to react? I don't know what's worse - allowing him to insult me or agreeing to pay him the gold.'

I took a deep breath and tried to regain what composure I cou'd. 'I'm truly sorry, Katherine, but you must realise that if we cannot produce the gold, the Bank will indeed cease to function - and that will remain the case until it is secur'd by something other than coin.'

'And <u>you</u> must realise that if you give way to a villain like that, whoever's behind this will do the same thing again and again until there is no bank.'

'Perhaps...but our immediate problem is that its reputation is still fragile. We have to demonstrate how strong we are, how well capitalis'd – and this is as good a way as any to do it.'

Katherine had calm'd down and seem'd to be listening to me. Her manner grew more conciliatory; she took my hand. 'I'm sorry too, John. I understand, of course I do – but his arrogance was more than I cou'd bear. I'm afraid I lost control.'

'And who cou'd blame you?'

'You do know that even with Orleans' deposits, we're well short of 2 million in gold?'

'I do,' I said.

'Then we must ask him for more.'

'Ask whom?'

'Orleans.'

'He hasn't got any more.'

'No...but the Treasury has...'

'The Treasury? Yes...yes, of course...*the Treasury*! It's rolling in gold!' I cou'd not help throwing my arms around her and kissing her full on the lips. 'And you're worth your weight in it!'

'We must pay him another visit,' she said, recovering from this onslaught.

I held her shoulders, look'd her in the eye, 'Let me go alone, Katherine. It's high time I made another attempt to deal with Philippe man-to-man.'

I thought she wou'd ridicule the notion, but her knowing smile told me that on this occasion she was happy to indulge my male pride. 'Very well...if he'll see you...'

'He will. I'll tell him the bank's survival depends on it. He has enough invest'd to want to save it...'

And I was right. My cris de coeur, as Katherine call'd it, met with his immediate consent to see me first thing the next morning. It was as prompt a reply as I had ever had from him, almost as if he had actually been expecting the request.

On my way to the Palais-Royal, I return'd to the question of who was behind this attack. Who wou'd have had the resources – and the nerve – to set it up? It was almost too much for one person to finance, unless extremely wealthy, and that in itself narrow'd my suspicions to one or two of the more powerful financiers who might have resent'd my banking operation. Bernard had undoubtedly been weaken'd by his confrontation with the Chamber of Justice, which left the Paris Brothers or more likely, the seemingly unassailable Crozat – and the owner unfortunately of the very overseas concessions I wou'd need if I were to set up a trading company.

Yet it might also involve others, those with political power, and here the possibilities were almost too many to consider. Save for Saint-Simon, I had to assume that all of Philippe's ministers and courtiers had reason to feel threaten'd by my relationship with him and wou'd have been very happy to see the bank fail.

Philippe was not an early riser; the only dawns he tend'd to witness were those that follow'd a long night of debauchery. Thus, when I arriv'd shortly after sunrise, fretful and anxious and having had very little sleep, it came as a surprise to find him not only up, but fully engag'd in the painting of the first of his bacchanalian scenes after Corregio – 'to make the most,' he said, 'of the precious daylight...' The latter was falling delightfully upon a tableau of near naked 'fauns' and 'nymphs', drawn from the ranks of the palace's many servants.

He was in as buoyant a mood as I had ever seen him. He laugh'd and jok'd with the servants, telling them to stand down, while he and I went off to talk about much less important matters than Art.

I at first made conversation on the subject of the latter, asking him how his portrait of Madame Parabère was coming along.

'Oh, _that_,' he said. 'It is abandon'd.'

'I'm sorry, Your Highness...'

'Don't be sorry, Monsieur Law. It is abandon'd because I have abandon'd her – a cause for much celebration. I am no longer her slave. I am liberat'd. I awoke as if from a spell – as in that English play by Shakespeare – A Midsummer Night's Dream, I believe it's call'd?'

'It is.'

'For some reason, one morning last week, I look'd upon her and saw not an object of desire but a woman plain and vain, who took advantage of my devotion to her. Well – no more. No more do I hang upon her every word, grant her every wish. No more is she the puppet mistress pulling at my heart strings. I am done with her – and what a bless'd relief it is.'

Before I cou'd ask if anyone had replac'd Madame P in his affections, he had mov'd on. 'So, to business. How can I be of help to you, Monsieur Law?'

I explain'd as briefly as I cou'd, without underplaying the gravity of the matter. I made it abundantly clear that this attack on the bank was likely to be the work of someone in his own circle. It was political as much as it was financial.

'How much money do you need from us exactly?'

'Two million louis d'or, Your Highness.'

He made what the French refer to as une petite moue, _as if he'd sipp'd from a faintly sour glass of wine._

'I will of course issue notes to the Treasury for that amount,' I add'd.

'Of course. What does Madame Law think?'

'About what, Your Highness?'

'About whether this shou'd be done.'

'If I am to be honest, at first, she thought we shou'd call their bluff, tell them to go hang.'

'Ah, Madame Law... what spirit, what intelligence...what beauty. You are a very lucky man, Monsieur Law...'

'Thank you, Your Highness.'

'I'm inclin'd to agree with her. It's a risk, but why not take it?'

'Well, with all due respect, Your Highness, that was before she fully understood the dangers of such a course of action. The risk is too great. The bank cou'd easily fail. We cou'd lose everything. You cou'd lose...much... She now agrees that we shou'd exchange the notes for gold. In fact, it was her idea to approach the Treasury via yourself.'

'She is a remarkable woman.'

I suddenly found I was playing the Katherine card again, even though she was not in the room. 'She wou'd be extremely grateful for the support of the Treasury....as wou'd I...'

He paus'd for thought, before delivering his verdict. 'When the duc de Noailles appears, I will have him order two million louis d'or from the vaults.'

'Thank you, Your Highness.'

'My pleasure. I have every faith in your Banque Generale, Monsieur Law...'

'Thank you, Your Highness...'

'And please convey my warmest regards to Madame Law. Tell her that together, we will discover who your enemies are and take firm action against them. Now I must away to my Bacchanal – as captur'd on canvass, you understand. I do believe that just now I'm finding flesh as attractive in the form of oil paint as it is...'

'In the flesh, Your Highness?'

'Ha! Indeed, Monsieur Law...'

To my surprise, when Orleans gave Noailles the instruction, the Financial-Controller put up only minor resistance. He *shook his head at the idea of exchanging my banknotes for two million in gold, but order'd it up immediately. Perhaps, like Orleans, he was finally recognising the benefits of the Banque Generale. With the improvement in trade and commerce, pressure on him had been greatly reliev'd, although he continued to pursue 'all manner of tax evading vermin', as he put it, through a much diminish'd Chamber of Justice.*

In fact, he boast'd of his latest conquest while we await'd the delivery of gold coin. 'Crozat, the richest man in France, will finally pay up rather than face the Crown's justice – and a pretty sum it is too – seven million in back taxes. For part of this, the Treasury has agreed to take back one of his many trading privileges.'

Noailles had my attention as never before. 'Trading privileges? Which ones?' I ask'd.

He smil'd. I am sure he thought I was simply taking a sardonic interest in another's financial pain, as he was wont to do himself. 'The Mississippi, I believe. Does it matter? They are none of them worth very much, in my opinion. I thought we were generous to take any in lieu of gold...'

But I did not hear the rest of what Noailles had to say on the subject. I was too busy thinking of the trading rights. I knew for a fact that they had been much less profitable than Crozat had expect'd; trade out of all the French territories overseas had been abysmally low, not least because they had seen little by way of investment. And yet, if the Mississippi rights had now become available, it cou'd not have been more timely. I wou'd do everything in my power to acquire them.

'Of course, my dear Monsieur Law' – Noailles was still smiling – 'it is because of the money from Crozat that the Regent was happy to lend such a large amount of coin to your Bank.'

'Lend?' I said. 'The coin is not a loan, Monsieur le Duc! It is exchang'd for banknotes, which are a form of legal tender.'

'Ah, legal tender, yes - I suppose we must refer to them as such...as long as they continue to enjoy public confidence, that is...'

Which must surely outlast your days as Financial-Controller, I want'd to say, but before I cou'd pursue our difference any further, a clerk announc'd that my gold had arriv'd.

Back at the Bank, Katherine seem'd genuinely pleas'd that the Treasury plan had work'd out, and laugh'd when I told her how much Orleans had prais'd her. 'What spirit! What intelligence! What beauty!...'

'What merde!' she jok'd. (I held back from saying that I suspect'd he had agreed to provide the gold as much to please her as to save the bank.)

'Fortunately, we caught him on a good day. I've never seen him so jolly.'

'And why was that?'

'I think because he's finish'd with his mistress Parabère.'

'Ha! Until he has the urge to bed her again. Probably later on this afternoon...'

'That long?' We were happy again, it seem'd.

Parting company with a large sum of money is seldom enjoyable, but it gave me a great deal of pleasure to hand over the two million in gold in exchange for banknotes, if only to see the glum expression on our tormentor's face. Never had a man been so unhappy to receive so much money!

'Tell whoever it is you serve, Monsieur,' I said, the look of triumph now all mine, 'that our bank and its notes are here to stay. This is just the beginning. I will, of course, be happy to exchange your louis d'or for notes again when coins cease to be legal tender...'

He gave me a rueful smile and went off with his cartload of gold, accompanied by several burly guards. One of these, I notic'd, bore a crest on his inner waistcoat – fleur-de-lis flank'd by lions rampant. I ask'd Monsieur Ginot if he knew whose it was. He look'd blank for a moment and then said that he thought it belong'd to one of the Princes of the Blood, the prince de Conti.

*

Somehow the boat stays upright and afloat. We're all badly shaken but we do *not* die in the moment. Once the launch has stabilised, we do our best to gather ourselves. We stare in disbelief after the vessel that very nearly rammed us, too shocked to say anything, let alone shout or swear after it. The skipper apologises profusely, his palms pressed together in supplication: 'Scusi...scusi tanto...scusi tanto...' In all their years on the canals, neither he nor Marisa has seen behaviour like it – not even from the gondoliers, who are more aggressive than anyone else on the water.

I say nothing about this being my second near miss since I arrived in Venice. I take Jo's hand. 'You okay?'

'Yes – you?'

'I'll be better once I've had a drink. I think we all need one.' I try to sound chipper but it's not how I'm feeling. I gesture towards the landing at the Cipriani. '*Avanti!*'

In fact, Marisa and the skipper graciously decline the offer of joining us; they'll head off for their own lunch. We agree they'll come and pick us up at the restaurant in an hour and half, so we can finish the tour.

'You're still shaking,' Jo says, as we walk up through the hotel garden. The clouds have thickened; the grey light flattens everything. I suddenly realise how hopeless I've become, trapped inside a life-threatening situation of my own making. 'What's going on, Theo? What's wrong?'

'Nothing – other than the fact that we were just nearly killed in some freak accident.'

'But it wasn't an accident, was it? Someone did it deliberately. Someone intended us some serious harm...' She waits for my answer, but there's none. 'Then there was the thing with the phone, back at Rezzonico.' Again, I don't reply. 'And what happened last night...and this morning? What was that all about?'

We walk on in silence. I assume she wants to put some distance between us; I wouldn't blame her if she did. Instead, she stops, puts her arms around me and presses me close. 'I'm so worried about you, Theo...' She kisses me hard on the lips; looks searchingly into my eyes, as if attempting hypnosis. 'Please tell me what's happening. I really want to help...*Please*...'

Should I tell her – or at least, give her some idea of what's going on? Do I even know myself?

I'm spared a decision by the sound of a polite cough behind us. Suddenly self-conscious, we turn to see Diana Lennon.

'*Sorry...*' She's wearing a black raincoat and some signature glasses with round black frames. They combine with the grey, bobbed hair to look very severe. Matron has caught us in the act.

'We're the ones who should be sorry.' I turn on a sixpence – or is it a dime? (My father was always impressed by how easily I moved – socially, emotionally, intellectually. Some might call it shallow, he also said.) 'We're behaving like a couple of teenagers.'

She laughs, and the matronly air is instantly dispelled. 'I try to behave like a teenager myself whenever I can.'

I laugh too. 'Jo de Vere – meet Diana Lennon, the lady who's trying to sell me the dodgy manuscript.'

'Good to meet you, Diana.'

'You too, Jo. How are you both – apart from in lust?'

'Actually,' says Jo, 'we're in a state of shock – or at least I am. On our way here, we narrowly missed being rammed by another boat...'

'Oh dear, I'm sorry. Didn't you have a near miss on the canal when you first arrived, Theo?' She looks pointedly at the graze on my forehead.

I nod and avoid eye contact with Jo.

Diana smiles wryly. 'Sounds as if he's a dangerous man to be hanging out with, Jo – I'd be careful if I were you. By the way, I'm merely brokering the manuscript deal. And as for it being *dodgy*' – she gives the word a mock-English vowel – 'I think Count Orsini, whom you're about to meet, will be able to reassure you on that front.'

'Last time I looked, Italy was a republic,' I say, trying to move things on from near misses. 'I thought Counts were discounted.'

'Ha! You're not wrong, Theo, but old habits and all that...'

She chats to Jo as we walk on to the restaurant. 'Poor you. As well as almost being rammed by a boat, you've had storms and *acqua alta* to cope with.' It starts to rain right on cue. 'Although I always think the city has a magical quality all its own in winter – something deeply melancholic. And, of course, there are fewer tourists. Well, a few fewer…'

'Deeply melancholic?' I say. 'It's downright sinister, if you ask me…'

The Count – as I will now always think of him – is already at the table when we arrive and stands to greet us. He's a personable man in his late sixties, perhaps older, immaculately coiffed and tailored. A full head of silver hair, swept neatly off his bronzed face; a double-breasted blazer of royal blue and a flamboyant shirt of blue, gold and pink stripes, its high collar open at the neck.

He's all flirtatious charm with Jo, breaking out of his perfectly modulated English into effusive Italian – 'Ah, bella donna! Bella donna!' – and holding her hand for longer than necessary. But he's just as touchy-feely with me, and I think it's fair to say he has us both instantly spellbound. Where I was expecting a moth-eaten antiquarian, as dusty and hide-bound as his books, here's a man oozing well-being and the *dolce vita* out of every pore.

He doesn't introduce himself as a Count, but as Piero Orsini. He and Diana seem very comfortable with each other. I picture them moving in the same sophisticated circles, stewards of what remains of the true Venetian culture, elegists of what's gone. Indeed, there's such an easy familiarity between them, I decide they may even have been lovers once upon a time.

At first, we talk about anything other than manuscripts: *acqua alta*, the current ratings of the restaurant and the Cipriani – much better in bygone days, of course, but still good – and, given that the Count is obviously a regular, his recommendations from the menu. When the waiter comes to take our orders, they greet each other like old friends and we all order what Piero recommends. (The wine is excellent and hardly the most expensive on the list. Not that it matters – by then I'm so desperate for alcohol, I'll drink anything.)

It's Jo who, after swiftly downing the first glass of wine – she needed it too – raises the subject of his title: 'Diana tells us you're *Count* Orsini.'

He gives Diana a fondly chastening look but doesn't seem too ashamed of the fact.

'Yes, it's true. I'm a member of an old aristocratic family. Some of us even claim a line back to ancient Rome – although I think that's a little fanciful myself.'

'But you're still old,' says Jo, with a nervous laugh. 'Er...as in the family sense, I mean.'

'Ha! As in *every* sense – not that I let it stop me behaving badly most of the time. We've certainly been around since the 12th century. Several of us became Popes – so we could behave *very* badly.' He laughs. 'It's not a job we've been offered since. More recently we were members of what's known as the *Nobilata Nera* – the Black Nobility.'

'Do the Orsinis practise the dark arts, then?' I polish off the first bottle and gesture to the waiter for another.

'Oh, that would be too interesting, Theo. I'm afraid it's far more prosaic. During the Risorgimento, the unification of Italy in the 19th century, the Papal States were overthrown and for nearly 60 years the Pope himself was virtually a prisoner in the Vatican. We and other noble families who were members of the Papal Court sided with him – we acted as a kind of papal guard. And to mourn the imprisonment of His Holiness, we kept the doors of our palaces black – so we became the Black Nobility.'

I recharge his glass. 'And does the family still act as a papal guard?'

'Not in any official capacity, no – the Papal Court and all its titles and positions were abolished in the late Sixties. It's now merely the Papal Household. But the Orsinis on the whole have remained very loyal to His Holiness' – he gives a wry smile – 'and I'm sure we'd spring to his defence if we felt he was threatened in any way...'

Is my paranoid imagination at it again or does the Count seem to address his last remark pointedly to me? He fixes me with his blue eyes – eyes that should have seen better days, but shine like they were just put in. Is it possible he knows of my meeting at the Vatican and is somehow involved? Is that why I'm here? Is this whole manuscript thing some sort of lure, some sort of trap? It's too absurd to contemplate, but that doesn't stop me.

He seems to read my thoughts. 'In fact, it was through my family that I first came across your forebear's manuscript,

Theo. I found it among the possessions of a very old aunt of mine after she died. She had married into the Bellini family and the manuscript was in the possession of her husband. It seems it originally belonged to one of *his* forebears, a certain Conte di Bellini. He was a somewhat dubious character who ran the Ridotto gaming salon here in Venice in the early 18th century and knew John Law.'

Now I'm confused. I can't decide whether the Count is a threat or completely plausible – or both. And since I'm quaffing it like water, the wine isn't helping. 'Diana says you've had the manuscript authenticated.'

'I have and of course I can provide you with the official report. It was confirmed as genuine – or at least it certainly dates from the period in question...'

He places his hands on the cream tablecloth – the whole place is exquisitely themed in cream and ochre – and leans across towards me, nailing me with that same pointed look. 'But Theo, this is not just about authenticating an antique object of some kind, as important as that is. It's also about an amazing story – a man who sets out to save the world and ends up corrupting it and himself. There's so much of interest in it, especially for someone in finance like yourself...'

Again, I get the impression that somewhere in what he's telling me is a warning.

Diana says: 'I take it you've had no chance to look at the copy I gave you, Theo.'

'I'm afraid not – Jo arrived earlier than expected and I had to er drop everything...' I look across at Jo, smile and take her hand. 'But now you've made me even more intrigued to read it, Piero.'

'Good – but please, let's leave the subject for now. I'd appreciate you coming to see the original before you return to London – perhaps tomorrow. If you'd allow me, I'd love to cook lunch for you all at my place.'

Diana interjects before I can reply: 'That's a rare and wonderful invitation, you two. Piero not only has one of the best views in Venice, he's just about the best cook in town too.'

'You flatter me, as always, Diana.'

'Well, it's not every day one's cooked for by a Count,' I say. 'I don't see how we can refuse – can we, Jo?'

'I don't think we can.' She looks across at Piero. 'That would be wonderful, thank you.'

'The pleasure will be all mine.'

And I'm left wondering what has brought the smile to her lips and the blush to her cheek. Is it the wine? Or is it the way he seems to be undressing her with those frisky blue eyes? Or am I just thoroughly pissed – in the British sense of the word?

*

I have finally receiv'd a reply from Katherine. Its arrival this morning was like a shaft of sunlight piercing the gloom of this winter day and yet it has taken me several hours to bring myself to open it. The seal remain'd intact until I return'd from the Ridotto and dismiss'd my servant Pietro for the night. Even then, after I had taken a little brandy, the blade hesitat'd over the wax, as if I was about to plunge it into some living, breathing thing.

What ridiculous fantasies have I concoct'd in the months since I last wrote to her! I picture her smuggling herself and Anne, and our paintings, out of France and coming to join me in Venice, just as she had in Rotterdam all those years ago. We are still estrang'd at first, circling each other like wild beasts, but then are reconcil'd in a headlong rush of physical desire. In the early evening, when the whole world is suffus'd in a golden light, we take a gondola along the canal. We walk to the Rialto and San Marco arm in arm. She smiles her glorious smile, as she did when we first met, so bright and warm, like the fire this winter's eve. Anne is thirteen years old and just budding into womanhood. She has fond memories of me and is happy to see her parents together again; she laughs constantly in our company. A gift'd singer, she attends one of the music schools – Maestro Vivaldi's, perhaps. With the money from the sale of our pictures – together with the proceeds from the Ridotto, for I am now gaming with renew'd vigour – we buy an old palazzo off the Grand Canal, and resume the content'd family life we had known in our early years in Paris...

Ridiculous fantasies, indeed – and now banish'd by the reality of her letter:

Paris

15th November 1728

Dear John,

Forgive me for not having replied sooner. Your proposal regarding the paintings came as a surprise to me and I need'd time to reflect on the matter. Furthermore, since I have become a 'celebrat'd' figure in Paris, somewhat in the manner of a circus freak or a person who is hideously deform'd, my life has been a great deal busier. Whereas it was fashionable to snub me and drop me, it has now become the thing to take me up. It seems to go with the latest style for even bigger wigs and stiffer stays and will not last long, I'm sure, so I must make hay. Even the King himself, still little more than a boy, has written to me, expressing sympathy for my situation and telling me that he and his ministers are considering my numerous requests to be allow'd to return to England. Meanwhile, I remain no more than a prisoner on a long chain, relying on my meagre pension and the charity of society, which is proving generous just now.

But such charity apart, I too can see little likelihood of providing for Anne in the longer term. Even if I cou'd secure capital from my family in England, which is extremely doubtful, my affairs remain under the closest scrutiny by the authorities and I am sure they wou'd lose no time in confiscating it. On the other hand, I wou'd do anything to avoid forcing our daughter into a marriage – or any other attachment - for the sake of money. I know only too well what unhappiness that can bring and am desperate to provide her with independent means, it being the only basis upon which a woman can sensibly negotiate the world. (But then, I hardly need to remind you of that fact of life...) In short, I cannot deny that your plan for the sale of our paintings and drawings is a good one, even if I have continued to cherish them as heirlooms rather than investments. Where I do have difficulty, John – and hence the need for careful consideration – is in trusting you.

Perhaps Anne's well-being and future happiness has now become a pressing concern of yours, and if so, I am thankful. But how can I be sure that it does not take second place to your compulsive desire to gamble everything one last time? Previously, when you were forc'd to make a choice between your family and your ambition, we both know which came first. You always want'd another throw of the dice, another round of cards. What you dress'd up as 'Money Science' and we turn'd into 'the System' was little more than the thrill of the wager for you, the gambler's implacable urge to win at all costs, and sadly it has ruin'd our lives. So, no, I cannot trust you, I cannot have faith in your proposal, and yet – and yet, I have no choice. Ironically, I must now take a gamble on you, but I have nothing to lose, for I can think of no other way of helping our daughter.

I will therefore undertake to send to you in Venice what I consider to be the most valuable pictures from the collection and will furnish you with all the details of its portage in due course, so that you may know when to expect arrival. Once the pictures are sold, I will expect immediate proof that the money has been deposit'd in a Venetian bank and details as to how Anne may obtain access to it. I will do this with all haste, because if your health is as poor as you suggest, we have – to be blunt – no time to lose.

Which brings me to the response to your second 'proposal': the marriage of our hearts, or some corner thereof, that transcends time and place and it seems, the dire consequences of your actions. This is some kind of sad delusion on your part, I assume, the product of a mind enfeebl'd by sickness and regret. If you thought to woo me once again, this time with words on the page

221

rather than dashing deeds, you are much mistaken. Even if you are now torment'd by thoughts of mortality and are comforting yourself with this sense of remorse, I remain unmov'd. It is shocking, I know, but much as I have tried, I cannot find it in myself to care whether you live or die, let alone reach out to you in forgiveness and reconciliation.

Today, I had a visit from Saint-Simon, who has continued to be my friend when I have been revil'd and reject'd in all other quarters. I think he has felt the loss of Philippe more profoundly than anyone and often talks of how he fail'd his friend in so many ways and now it is too late to atone. We shou'd never close the door on forgiveness, he says. We are all flaw'd and owe each other a great loyalty. Maybe he is right, but maybe he has never had his heart broken or his trust betray'd.

I have thought long and hard about putting all this in writing to you, but I finally decid'd that I had kept my pain and anger under lock and key for too long. My only hope is that its expression will not discourage you from doing the best for our daughter. She is the future, John; please accept that we are the past. Ruins are not fit for habitation.

Yours, Katherine

I doubt'd anything cou'd be more painful than Katherine telling me that she cou'd not bear to set eyes on me again, but I was wrong; 'I cannot find it in myself to care whether you live or die' was infinitely worse. I am sure it help'd bring on the several days of coughing and vomiting that follow'd, as well as the bloodied handkerchiefs and breathlessness I fear'd might put the truth of her bitter claim to the test. At first I intend'd to reply to her letter within days. I wou'd thank her for agreeing to send the paintings and make my act of contrition once again, imploring her to re-examine her feelings – to find that element of forgiveness in herself, no matter how small. Ridiculous, of course – opinions or arguments can be revis'd and reconsider'd, but emotion, genuinely felt, is what it is, and she

222

had express'd it bluntly and honestly. Nor did there seem any hope that, on reflection, she might take some responsibility for the distrust that sprang up like weeds between us and laid the ground for the estrangement that was to come. As far as Katherine was concern'd, the fault had been entirely mine, and in my current state of remorse, I accept that as the Gospel truth of it. I decide that any further petition to her wou'd be pointless.

In my despair, I even think to abandon this memoir. There seems little reason to carry on, to experience my failure afresh. On the other hand, I wish to understand exactly what happen'd in Paris: the cause and effect, the rights and wrongs – matters that can only be understood from a distance of years when the fog of engagement has clear'd. For this reason alone, the pain, both mental and physical, will have to be endur'd. I will take as much laudanum as necessary to numb it. I will drink more chocolate lac'd with cognac to raise my spirits. I will spend less time at the gaming table, so that I have more for writing. And in bringing all these events back to life, I will discover the truth about them. This is, after all, an experiment in Human Science as much as Money Science and I am its subject.

But despite this bold manifesto of mine, the next afternoon at the Ridotto finds me adrift on the same sea of gloom and despondency. Bellini appears on the piano nobile. He knows I have been hors de combat for a few days. He knows how eagerly I have been awaiting news from Paris, from Katherine. He senses my dejection and wears his best expression of sympathy and concern. (As a noble, his face <u>is</u> his mask and he always makes sure he wears the right one for each occasion.)

'Il Duce, forgive me for saying so, but rather than grieving for what we have lost, there is sometimes much to be said for taking a little pleasure in what we have.'

'And what if we have nothing, dear Count?'

'Then we are in that most privileged of positions, il Duce - we have nothing to lose. I have arrang'd a little treat for you. It will not take your pain away, but it may soothe it for a while, and it may well remind you that there are still things worth living for. A change of scene will help. Come – our gondola awaits…'

Somewhat reluctant to go anywhere but also to disappoint my host, I follow him down to the dock. 'And besides,' he says, 'I cannot afford to lose the Ridotto's greatest attraction to self-pity and despair.'

It is apparently a short journey in the gondola, which is good, because the weather is cold and overcast and the dark wet walls of the narrow canals rise up either side and oppress me like prison walls. We head into the San Marco area, behind the Ridotto – along the Rio del San Moise and into what is known as the Haberdasheries.

At first, I cannot think where he is taking me. But then, as we reach the Rio del Bareteri, I hazard a guess and decide that it must be the Venier gambling salon.

From what I have been told, for I have not been there, it is a much smaller version of the Ridotto, more discreet, one might say, yet beautifully, lavishly appoint'd. If I am right, I hardly think that playing at the table there amounts to the 'treat' Bellini has in mind. But then I remind myself that there are other diversions at the Venier and that its modest domestic façade conceals a pleasure palace within.

Once at the dock, it is only a short walk. Bellini takes two steps to my labour'd one but still makes swifter progress and I have to ask him to slow down.

'Ha! I am too eager to arrive,' he says. 'I find nothing enlivens a dull winter's afternoon like the cosy intimacy of the Venier casino.'

'I assum'd the Venier was our destination,' I say breathlessly.

'Of course, you did.'

'And why do I also assume that this visit will involve something other than a wager?'

'You of all people know there are many ways to place a wager, il Duce. Today my money is wager'd on your behalf and I have put it on a very beautiful woman – neither so young as to be ignorant of the subtleties of her art, nor so old as to have forgotten them. I am gambling on you finding her irresistible – or you must repay the cost, which I have to tell you is considerable.'

'What if I'm not strong enough to accept such a bet?' But I get no answer from the Count, for we have arriv'd at the dark portico of the Venier. We are immediately welcom'd into the vestibule by an apparition, a sight that wou'd have been arresting enough even had we been in the midst of Carnivale: a male midget wearing a woman's dress of satin, sequins and pearls that is singularly at odds with his beard and chest hair. Behind him looms a very large black man in flowing African robes, obviously there to discourage any undesirable visitors.

'My dear Count Bellini,' the apparition – or abomination, according to your taste – says in a manly baritone, 'how wonderful to see you. You are of course expect'd.'

Bellini seems unperturb'd by our doorman, as if a midget in a ball gown, accompanied by an African giant, was the most natural sight in the world. He is obviously a regular customer.

*

As I settle the bill at the Cipriani, the Count is going through another touchy-feely routine with Jo. 'I'm *very* much looking forward to entertaining you tomorrow, Joanna...I think you'll love the dish I have in mind, a great Venetian favourite...' etc.etc.

We take our leave of him and Diana and go to meet our guide at the dock. The weather has deteriorated and the rain is now so torrential that the maitre'd immediately rushes off to find us some umbrellas.

'*Complimenti della casa, signore.*'

I am drunk enough to try some very elementary Italian. '*Mille grazie, signore! Mille grazie!*'

'*Prego.*'

And drunk enough for the paranoia to take greater hold of me. Not only is every other person in Venice, including the Count, out to do me some serious harm, Jo's been having a torrid affair with him, and who knows what further mischief they're planning. I try in vain to convince myself that it's all complete nonsense.

The sight of Marisa and our launch somehow calms me. She too has an umbrella, a bright orange one, with water cascading off its rim. 'We planned our tour well,' she smiles, 'making the most of the sunshine this morning.'

'*You* planned our tour well,' I say, and for some reason, I'm moved to make a noise like the siren for *acqua alta.*

She laughs. 'That's very convincing, Theo.'

Jo and I climb down unsteadily onto the boat. The water around us roils and boils with the churn of the propellers and the heavy beating of the rain. 'As you may have guessed, Marisa, we've had a little too much wine at luncheon...'

'*We?*' laughs Jo.

'Don't worry. It's probably the right state of mind for the Venier,' says Marisa. 'I doubt its 18th century visitors were ever sober.'

As we pull away from the dock, we can hardly make out the other side of Giudecca and the Salute is completely lost to us. Our skipper proceeds with caution, steering a course away from the mouth of the Grand Canal.

'*Allora...*' Marisa nods in the direction. 'I thought we'd take another way into the city – just to show you the back of the tapestry, as it were, a side of Venice seldom seen by the tourists.'

'The *real* Venice?' asks Jo.

'As real as it gets...*Avanti...*'

The rain starts to ease off as we go round the old fortress and arsenal and make our way to the other side of the city. A little further on, Marisa points out the Isola de San Michele, the cemetery isle, shrouded in mystery and drizzle, mainly drizzle. As if I needed another *memento mori,* there it is, with its whitewashed tombs and gaunt crosses faintly visible through the gloom.

'Napoleon decided that burying corpses in the city had become a potential source of disease, so San Michele was designated as a burial ground. There's still some room if you're looking for a picturesque spot for yourselves.'

She laughs but I can only manage a tight smile.

'And by the way, Theo – your ancestor is not buried there. We'll get to his grave later.'

If I don't get to mine sooner, I tell myself.

We turn into one of the canals, which quickly narrows down to something not much wider than our launch. We've entered a backwater, what appears to be the remains of the old commercial area of the city. We're engulfed by the dark, damp walls of warehouses and workshops; the sounds of our voices and the purring of the launch reverberate eerily around us. I begin to feel even more vulnerable and exposed, in imminent danger of something, still as yet undefined but no less threatening. I literally start looking over my shoulder and am greatly relieved when the canal opens out into a wider, brighter area, where it immediately becomes apparent that the water level is again running very high. It can't be long until the real sirens start to sound.

There's a boatyard full of the carcasses of disused gondolas – a gondola graveyard and yet another *momento mori,* although some are undergoing repair. Mercifully the sound is not of gunshot, but of the hulls of vessels being hammered into better shape.

Further on, down more narrow canals and under bridges so low we feel we have to duck, we must negotiate our way past another launch coming from the other direction. It seems to have more room to manoeuvre than us, yet refuses to back off and keeps coming. Our skipper shakes his head at this poor canal etiquette. We are forced to back into a shallow niche in the slime-covered wall, which gives the other boat just enough room to get past. Two men in dark, hooded anoraks stand at its helm, like a pair of Franciscan friars.

As they edge past us they make no gesture of thanks or anything else, until one of them turns and looks directly at me. He's as pale-faced-and sad-eyed as a Pierrot clown. I'm convinced I see him raise his hand towards me, make a pistol of it and crook his thumb like a trigger. Then they're gone.

'Did you see that?'

'What?' says Jo.

'The guy pointing a gun...I mean, a finger at me...like a gun. Did you?'

The two women look puzzled, half-shake their heads.

'They're just canal inspectors,' says Marisa dismissively. 'But they should know how to behave better on the canal...'

227

Jo's expression has gone from puzzled to alarmed; I think she's expecting another meltdown from me.

'My mistake – I'm fine,' I say to her, but I don't think she's reassured.

A little further on and we're finally into a smarter part of the city – the Haberdasheries, says Marisa, the old garment district. The rain has more or less stopped – a mere pause, I'm sure. The temperature has dropped, and a thin layer of mist begins to rise off the water.

We glide quietly past the backs of crumbly old palazzos. Marisa almost whispers her well-rehearsed commentary. '*Allora*...imagine, 18th century Venice, a place where secret trysts and assignations are commonplace. They not only involve an endless supply of courtesans from all over Italy and Europe, but many respectable Venetian women leading duplicitous lives to rival those of their husbands. As one nobleman was quoted as saying, no husband would be caught dead with his own wife. The women come by gondola to the hidden entrances of their lovers' palazzos. They are always masked, the gondoliers sworn to secrecy – a lucrative business for them. On hot summer nights the canals must have reeked as much of infidelity as they did of human waste...'

We come to a major canal junction, stopping to allow a whole flotilla of gondolas to pass. They're full of Chinese tourists, who nod, smile or take our picture. Sitting together in the middle of one of the gondolas, as if summoned up by all this talk of infidelity, there's a Chinese bride and groom, with a photographer snapping away at them.

'Aaah...a wedding,' coos Jo.

Marisa smiles. 'They don't actually get married here – they just come to pose for the photos.'

I remember a banking colleague saying the Chinese pose in front of a famous European landmark one day and buy it the next. But at least none of them try to kill me.

'The tourist machine never stops,' Marisa adds, as if we're not part of it. 'Of course, I should be grateful,' she shrugs, but she doesn't sound it. '*Avanti*...'

*

Even before Bellini introduces me to the woman he has engag'd on my behalf, I feel a mounting sense of panic. It has been many years since I have indulg'd in the sexual act with anyone other than myself – not a fact of which I am necessarily proud, but after Paris I was unable to contemplate the alternative. There has of course been no shortage of opportunities at the Ridotto; many a handsome woman is attract'd to the heroes of the gaming room and not all of them for professional reasons. But regret for what I did to Katherine has acquir'd an uncomfortable association with the pleasures of the flesh, to the point that any lust I feel is trump'd by a crippling sense of guilt.

The interior of the Venier is even more exquisite than I was led to believe. The walls and ceilings are adorn'd with colourful frescoes and golden stuccowork. The til'd floor is as intricate as some Moorish mosaic. A quartet plays sedately at the far end of the room. A fire burns gaily in a hearth that is surround'd by a huge mantel of carv'd marble, the swirling pattern of which is as colourful as the frescoes. It seems surprisingly busy for a winter's afternoon, but then I tell myself that day and night there must be only degrees of busy-ness at the Venier. Concupiscence does not keep business hours.

At various tables sit an animat'd selection of Venetian grandees, indulging in social congress before or after the sexual kind – playing cards or just conversing with expensively dressed young women, all maquillage and décolletage, or tints and tits, as we us'd to say in London. The midget and other characters of indeterminate gender – the ever-popular castrati – ply to and fro between the tables, serving wine and cicchetti, when they're not occasioning much hilarity with their bawdy jokes. (If my basic – or base – Italian serves me correctly, I overhear the following snippet, or what is a loose interpretation of it: 'The Count's tool was so small' – I trust he is not referring to Bellini – 'that even though he'd been banging away in her bumhole for an age, she said, come, sir, insert your member and get on with it – you've only paid for half-an-hour...') I have to say that by comparison, the Ridotto has the atmosphere of a Lenten church, even though its congregation is no more likely to earn a place in Paradise.

But to return to my partner for the afternoon – or however long I choose to stay. Even were she sans the usual glamorous accoutrement of the courtesan, there is no doubt that she wou'd be exceedingly lovely, which only increases my anxiety, the more so because she has about her an air of the Parisian salon. It comes as no surprise, then, to learn that she is indeed French – a Mademoiselle de Valliere – specially import'd, I am sure, to bolster the sophisticat'd appeal of the Venier. (For the connoisseurs of the boudoir, it is a grace note that she bears the name of Louis XIV's first mistress.) With a smug, knowing look that says, 'See, il Duce, I told you this creature wou'd remind you that you still have a cock worth the sitting upon,' the Count takes his leave of us and no doubt goes off to have his own cock sat upon.

I think of making an immediate escape, but apart from the fact that this wou'd be ungracious in the extreme, the young woman starts to engage me in conversation. To my surprise, it actually feels good to be speaking French again, despite all its dire associations.

'I'm honour'd to finally meet the infamous John Law in person. I was a girl in Paris when you were at the height of your power, Monsieur.'

This is not what I expect'd. Bad enough that I shou'd have to face the sexual demon, but even worse that it shou'd be in the company of someone who wishes to speak about my time in France and looks as if she cou'd have been a guest at one of Orleans' orgiastic soirées.

'And from what a great height the mighty have fallen, Mademoiselle.' A gaudily dressed castrati brings wine and cicchetti.

'Please – call me Sabine.'

'And I am John.'

'Can you have fallen so low, John, if you're here in the Venier about to make love to me?' An ironic smile plays about her perfect lips. 'Many a gentleman wou'd give at least his right arm and most of his purse for a tilt at such pleasure.'

'It's true,' I concede with a smile, 'I am in that respect a most fortunate fellow.'

'*Yet you must have hurt yourself when you fell from that great height?*'

The last thing I want to appear is self-pitying and yet I find myself saying: '*A great deal, Sabine. I have never fully recover'd from the injury.*' *And having sipp'd my wine, I suffer a nasty coughing fit, as if to demonstrate how injur'd I still am. She reaches across and touches my hand. Hers is soft and warm; something like a jet of healing balm shoots through me as far as my loins.*

'*I wouldn't come near me, if I were you, Sabine. I might be bad for your health.*'

'*I am a professional – I have no choice. And anyway, how cou'd I pass up the opportunity of coupling with the richest man in the world? Or so the Count describes you.*'

'*The Count likes his little jokes.*'

'*But it was once the case.*'

'*I suppose at one time I qualified more than most for that distinction.*'

'*Did it bring you happiness?*'

'*Ha! Are any of us sure of the precise nature of that commodity? It certainly felt good, rather like winning at cards. For a moment you seem to hold the whole world in your hands...or hand.*'

I am not sure the joke works quite so well in French, but Sabine smiles indulgently. She leans across, as if to share an intimacy, enveloping us both in a wave of the best French perfume; her breath is all sweetness and wine. '*Come, John, I know it's early, but it's time to retire.*'

It is early, but I wonder if it is also too late. '*Look, Sabine, I do not think...*'

She places a delicate finger on my lips. '*That's right – do not think.*' *Her hand takes mine and squeezes it, before she stands and all but pulls me to my feet.* '*My, how tall you are, sir,*' *she says in passable English.* '*Is that the shape of things to come?*'

She laughs saucily, as we head up the white marble stairs. '*They'll bring our wine, and Genever, perhaps. It seems you may have need of some Dutch courage...*'

*

231

The Venier looks modest enough from the outside, certainly compared to Ca' Rezzonico. But inside, its rococo ceilings and frescoes have other, much grander ambitions, the kind of ostentation that Marisa says typifies Venice in its Age of Decadence.

'*Allora*...here, the city's three great pleasures were first brought together. 18th century Venetians of a certain class loved gambling, fornication and showing off – probably in that order. Here, they can do everything safely under one roof. This was a place dedicated to display – who could play at the best table, who could afford the most beautiful courtesan...'

For some reason – its sheer excess, perhaps – I think of my own attitude towards display and possessions. I realised a while ago that the need to acquire things and show them off is not what drives me. It's enough for me to be able to tell myself that I can have whatever material thing I want – no need to put theory into practice. In a world that's given over to mindless acquisition, the amassing of things – more an Age of Decadence than Venice's ever was – I've been content with simply counting the money; with seeing ten figures gather on the balance sheet like exotic birds on a wire. It may seem abstract, unreal even, but in fact it's as real as serious money gets. Not gold lying cold in a vault, but binary information on a screen that can move with the speed of thought to a better, more profitable place.

I wonder what my ancestor, John Law, would have made of it all, this quicksilver, electronic money. Billions and billions programmed to whizz around the globe at the whim of an algorithm, and in many instances with devastating consequences. Perhaps, he'd have done even more damage. (I might know more when I finally read the manuscript. I make a mental note to at least scan through it before we meet the Count again tomorrow.)

Anyway, whether it's e-wealth or any other kind, I'd have thought that rejecting the current fashion for flaunting it was something to be admired, rather than scorned. Not so. During the run-up to the divorce, Angela cited my obsession with 'keeping the financial score' as another measure of my 'fucked up' relationship with money. It came as something of a shock. I thought my relationship with money was fairly straightforward – I make as much as I can and do my best to hang on to it. But she reminded me that when we were together, she was the one who made every buying decision, from groceries to houses. It wasn't that I was 'tight' as such, but I had no real desire to buy anything, even things we actually needed. For her it made the way I earned such huge sums of money even sicker.

'All that criminal activity, so you could masturbate over a bank statement.'

'Would you rather I'd have masturbated over a Ferrari?'

So, suddenly I'm back on Angela and my M&D story, when I should be listening to what Marisa is saying about the Venier, which I'm sure is far more exciting. But I can't help myself. I'm drawn back to the particular conversation – the bitter exchange, more like – that partly explains how I got into this mess. There were several, but this is the one that sticks in my mind, keeps replaying, especially since I came off the anti-depressants.

After the painful scene at Boris' mansion, it was some time before Angela and I had a proper discussion about anything, let alone why she'd no alternative but to divorce me. (I wasn't content with the cause as stated in the divorce petition: 'irreconcilable differences'.) The day we did have that discussion, my reason for being at the Notting Hill house was ostensibly to visit Grace. She was being given her dinner at the kitchen table by the young Spanish nanny and – shock-horror – none other than Maggie, Angela's mother. Angela announced that Maggie was staying with them for a while.

'That's nice,' I said, with a strained smile.

Maggie actually looked well, I thought. She'd obviously been off the booze, her skin was less blotchy and she'd put on weight – she finally seemed to be eating more than she was drinking. She was dressed in clothes she hadn't slept in, recently acquired from M&S, from the look of them. How nice, how normal, how almost middle class.

'Watchya, Theo.' Her smile still had a hint of the sardonic, though. I think it was saying: 'What a turn up, eh? 'ere I am, all spic and span, back in Anj's good books, and there you are, out on yer fuckin' arse…'

'Mum and I are going shopping and leaving you to it.'

More M&S, I thought.

'Well, before you do, Angela, we need to speak.'

She was reluctant at first, but a look from her mother, her new mentor, perhaps – was it possible? – was enough to have her follow me upstairs to the sitting room. It was the first time we'd been alone together since the fateful weekend. I suddenly realised I didn't know where to start, so I tried a thumping great cliché.

'I think you still owe me an explanation.'

'For what?'

'What do you mean – for what? Let's start with why a previously happy, loving couple now have irreconcilable differences and are going through a divorce?'

'You know why. I told you that night. No matter what my feelings for you might be...'

'Then you do have some...'

'I can't live with someone who knowingly profits from other people's misery.'

'If you're talking about Boris' shady business dealings, you don't have any evidence.'

'I saw the evidence.'

'As shown to you by his embittered wife. She'll do or say anything to get at him.'

'His much abused wife. And don't think I didn't check it out – as you should have done. She warned you – and guess what? It's all true.'

'I couldn't find anything incriminating,' I lied.

'Then you didn't look very far.'

I tried another tack. 'Oh come on, Angela...grow up, *please*. Get off the moral high horse – you know the world we work in...'

'I don't work in it anymore...'

'But you profited handsomely from it when you did. The system is bent, rigged, *fucked* – you know that. If we scrutinised the ethical purity of every investment, every deal, every transaction, we wouldn't...'

'What?'

'Well...'

'What?'

'We wouldn't…do anything.' My words fell dead from my lips.

'Exactly. Exactly – especially when it clearly results in crimes against humanity.'

'Crimes against what? That's ridiculous.'

'Is it? How would you describe the things you've helped finance?'

'But I didn't know.'

'No – you *chose* not to know. That's different – and for that I can't forgive you. I don't want to be around you, Theo. I don't want to share my life with someone who can do that kind of thing without a second thought.'

'Oh, for fuck's sake!'

'And I don't want Grace to be part of it either – she's got enough to cope with.'

I looked down at the fine antique rug. For a Stepney girl, her taste was decidedly posh. She'd chosen everything in the house, of course – while I'd been masturbating over the bank statements.

'Are we done?' she asked, assuming me vanquished.

I looked back up at her – I realised I loved her more than ever. 'What can I do to change your mind?'

'Nothing you're capable of. Just count yourself lucky I haven't reported you to the authorities. It's only because I don't want Grace to have a father who's doing time – I know all about that.'

'And I'm not being punished enough, anyway?'

She didn't answer.

'How can I redeem myself? How can I make it up to you?'

'Have you even been listening to me, Theo?' She gave it her best Stepney for emphasis: 'It's never gonna fuckin 'appen. You disgust me. End of.'

*

As much as Sabine tries to put me at my ease, and as committ'd as I am in my head to a debauch'd afternoon in her company, it is not at first reflect'd in any urgent stirring of my

235

member. Having undress'd us both to our undergarments, she essays a couple of the usual methods for stimulating arousal – including fellatio – all to not much avail. Eventually, she fills my wine glass, then falls back upon the pillow next to me and a fresh round of conversation – '...to divert and relax you, John,' she says. 'You are trying too hard...'

We both laugh out loud at this, which goes some way to creating a more relax'd mood.

She starts by asking me more about my Paris years and how I became the most powerful man in France.

I demur: 'I was not the King, nor even the Regent.'

'No, but I was told you as good as own'd them both.'

'Only as long as it suit'd their purpose.'

'Nonetheless, John, a man in your position must have had enormous influence, particularly over women. I'm sure you were able to take your pick.'

'I had a wife' – which was true de facto if not de jure – 'with whom I was very much in love.'

'Just like many husbands – but in my experience it only seems to whet their appetite for more love.'

I do not know what to say to her. It is dangerous ground for me and cou'd well send me running from the boudoir in nothing but my undergarments.

She turns to me with a wry smile. 'Apart from your wife – with whom you were very much in love – who was your favourite?'

Again, I cannot answer.

She continues in hushed tones: 'How did you like to make love to her, John? Did you take her from behind? Did you prefer the back door?' (La porte de derriére, she says.) 'It is what most high-born Frenchmen like to do. It avoids the risk of any little bastards laying claim to their estates. You can bugger me if you like. With men like you, men I'm genuinely attract'd to, it gives me greater pleasure than the more conventional channel. It is the most intense experience. I surrender myself completely – which is beautiful in its way...'

Her provocative language is beginning to have the desir'd effect – especially as, all the while she speaks, she applies the

236

lightest of touches, the softest of fingertips to my penis. It is as if it is being brush'd by the wings of a butterfly.

'I am not a high-born Frenchman, Sabine. Buggery is not my preference.'

'That is not what your cock is telling me, John.' Her hand gently encloses its firmness. 'And what did you do before this considerable tool of yours found its final destination – in whichever port of entry that was? How did you get the lucky woman to open like a flower for you? I trust you are not a lazy lover, John – one who is only done to...*'*

Sabine wears only a short bodice of cream satin and is nak'd below her slender waist. She takes my hand and places it on the warm lips of her quim. She is already open like a flower; she already drips with nectar. She rubs my fingers against her moist folds and lifts them to my mouth and nose.

'Do you like the smell of me, John – my parfum de femme?' (There is no English expression that does this term justice.) I do, of course – it is a delightful nosegay and inflames me with a physical passion I no longer thought it possible to feel. Her hand, now on the back of my head, is some encouragement, but I hardly need it to guide me to the spot.

I was always fond of cunnilingus, as were those upon whom I perform'd it. Sabine is no exception. I realise that for all her regular plying of the trade, this is a rare treat. She grows excit'd, squirms beneath my attentions and wou'd have climax'd, I am sure, had she not drawn me up from her nether to her upper lips.

There is no dallying on my part now – quite the contrary. I fall upon her with the hungriest of kisses and a furious, breathless thrusting. In all too brief a session, our carnal natures run their course and we both find blissful release.

We lie there for some minutes, spent swimmers thrown upon a clement shore. I am surpris'd that I have manag'd such exertions without so much as a cough, a measure of how invigorating I found this love-making. For that is how it feels: an act of love rather than the grubby act of fornication I had envisag'd. Then she says, in a voice husky from her exertions:

'Well, John – what a revelation. I'm sure my mother must also have benefitt'd greatly from that skilful tongue of yours...'

It is a few moments before I register the word: '<u>Mother?</u>'

'Yes, we all have one.'

'Who is your mother, Sabine?'

'She <u>was</u> Madame Claudine de Tencin. I think you knew her. And my father was Cardinal Dubois. I think you knew him too, although she was never absolutely sure that he was the one – she was very busy that Christmastide. But whoever it was, he was certainly a high-born Frenchman, perhaps the highest, and, strangely, he preferr'd the more traditional channel...'

De Tencin. Dubois. The allusion to d'Orleans. The names send waves crashing down on me, as I lay on that now not so clement shore. There is a sudden convulsion in my chest and throat.

'John? Are you all right? John? <u>My God</u>!'

Even though she has deliberately set out to wound me, Sabine's voice strikes an almost apologetic note, when it is only I who have anything to apologise for.

*

I climb the Venier's marble stairs. During my painful recollection of the M&D, I have somehow become uncoupled from the others. Where have they got to? Have they abandoned me? And who could blame them if they have?

I suddenly feel panicked, like a lost child. I need to find Jo. I want to hold her, hug her, tell her how much she means to me – because, yes, I'm finally ready to exorcise Angela, to replace her in my affections. It may already be too late, but I decide Jo's the one who can get me through this – whatever this is. I can't do it without her.

At the top of the stairs, I open a door off the landing and find myself in a darkened room. There are closed shutters at one end, a large candelabra at the other. My eyes take a few moments to adjust to the flickering chiaroscuro before I make out the bed. It has cherubs – or are they cupids? – carved into the top of its large headboard; a man and woman lie entwined beneath them in a state of undress – period undress. He's wearing only a loose undershirt, she a short corset. His skinny backside gleams white as alabaster in the candlelight, as do her shapely legs, which he lies between. It's a tableau vivant minus the vivant; surely a couple of wax dummies, arranged in a coital embrace in what was once a bordello. More tourist fodder.

I move closer towards them, around the foot of the bed. I can see the young woman's breasts and pretty face. I'm startled when her lips move, but no sound emerges. I'm convinced they're both automata, but when he starts to move, when his body shakes and convulses, I change my mind – they're real, very real. The man raises his head from the pillow next to her. He appears to be choking, gasping for breath, but it's still a dumb show, I still can't hear anything. Not until he starts to cough up dark clots of blood that fall over her face and chest, and she emits a piercing scream.

Then they've gone, disappeared – the couple, the bed, the candelabra. I realise I'm in what looks like an office, listening to the wail of the siren that signals *acqua alta*.

Chapter 8

Venice, November 1728

A physician is summon'd, Dottore Allegri, the one who has visit'd me before at the Ridotto and prescrib'd retirement from the gaming table as a prerequisite for any remedy for my condition. He is a lugubrious character and hovers over me like the angel of death itself. He raises his giant eyebrows and shakes his grey bewigg'd head: 'And what exactly was a man in your condition thinking of, il Duce – cavorting in a whorehouse?'

'I wou'd have thought it was obvious, Dottore.'

He cannot suppress a smile. 'Well, then, you will doubtless be happy to stay here for a while. You are not to move from the bed for at least three days. Although' – he leans in closer, treating me to the aroma of tobacco mix'd with his garlicky dinner – 'I strongly recommend you not share the bed with anyone else just yet.' It is my turn to smile, albeit ruefully.

Calomel and herbal remedies are also prescrib'd, but I refuse the bleeding. 'Have I not shed enough of the stuff?'

Bellini lurks sheepishly in the background, wearing a mask of compassion mix'd with contrition, even if the latter is distinctly half-heart'd. 'Forgive me for saying so, il Duce, but it wou'd have been a glorious way to bid farewell to the world, wou'd it not?'

I am inclin'd to agree and had Sabine's shocking revelations not been the real cause of an almost fatal fit, I wou'd have tolerat'd her ministering to me as my nurse for as long as was necessary, expensive though that wou'd have been. Now at least, I can use the time more productively to work on my memoir. I send for my pen and papers from the Ridotto and order hot chocolate lac'd with brandy to make the taste of the remedies more palatable.

Before leaving, Bellini fusses around, making sure I am as comfortable as possible. He is not yet ready to lose his biggest attraction – especially not here at the Venier. Ideally, I must die at the tables of the Ridotto to help keep its notoriety alive and well. He urges me not to overtax myself. I tell him that writing my memoir is my best means of recovery.

'I live only to write,' I say.

'And I thought you liv'd only to wager.'

'It is a kind of wager. One stakes that most precious of commodities – time...'

And despite my weaken'd stake, I am soon able to wager some more time on my next chapter. In stark contrast to my 'cavorting' with Sabine in the Venier, the first thing I must report is that not long after Anne's birth, Katherine and I enter'd what was to be a prolong'd period of carnal abstinence. Which is to say that we made love less and less frequently and then not at all.

Although it was Katherine who initiat'd this move towards a more Platonic kind of love, I too felt a waning of the desire for physical contact, which I found perplexing in the extreme. Was it simply that our earlier passion had run its course or – as I have heard is often the case – that mutual attraction declin'd following child birth? Or was it that our difficult relations at the bank cast a shadow over our more intimate relations at home?

In all honesty, I cannot say for sure – it cou'd have been for any or all of these reasons. But if the cause was uncertain, the effect was clear: the cooling of our desire for each other creat'd a distance between us that began to curdle other aspects of our lives together. And it was made all the worse because we seem'd incapable of talking about it. We were ambush'd by other, more pressing events and, sadly, our attention was divert'd elsewhere.

On the business side, my insistence on our settling the two million in gold quickly paid off. If an increase in the number of customers is also a measure of confidence, then confidence in the bank increas'd at least tenfold. This was very satisfying, but it did not alter the fact that it cou'd not continue to be secur'd by coin alone. As was obvious – but Katherine continually point'd out to me, nonetheless – the increase in business actually made it worse: we were lending more money than ever

241

and so there was much more to secure, requiring far more gold than we cou'd ever accrue.

As a consequence, she thought it was high time we rais'd matters to the next level. We had to reveal the rest of the System to Orleans and gain his support for the establishment of a trading company.

'In fact,' she said, 'I've already been to see Noailles about that very subject.'

'You've seen Noailles? Why did you not tell me?'

'It didn't require both of us, John, and I can see how busy you are. Why didn't you tell me that the Mississippi trading rights were available for purchase?'

I mutter'd something about having meant to tell her but, yes, I had been very busy and it had slipp'd my mind.

I doubt she believ'd me, any more than I did her, but at least I knew my own reason for dissembling. Despite our reconciliation after the gold incident, I continued to resent what I saw as her interference in the running of the bank. By withholding news of the trading rights purchase, I was making a pathetic attempt to retain some control. Of course, I did not really intend to pursue the rights on my own – it was too big a step. As with everything else, we wou'd need Orleans' approval, and I knew only too well how much easier that wou'd be if Katherine were involv'd.

'We must write to Philippe immediately,' she said, 'explain the System to him, in all its glory – and make it clear that it's ours, not yours alone, John.'

Much as I want'd to, I cou'd not object. The System was indeed as much hers as mine and it wou'd only impress Philippe all the more for being so.

On October 10ᵗʰ 1718, I sent the following letter, written as the previous one, in Katherine's excellent and most persuasive French:

Your Royal Highness,

Shortly before the start of your Regency, you will recall that I wrote to you and outlin'd our plans for a National Bank of France. This Bank wou'd be empower'd to issue a paper currency that wou'd eventually replace the debas'd coinage, now in such short supply and hampering the development of French trade and commerce. In that letter I promis'd to reveal a work of Money Science that wou'd astound the world and make France the wealthiest and most powerful of nations. Now, bas'd on the success of our Banque Generale – which I have always regard'd as a forerunner to the National Bank – I can reveal these proposals, which Katherine and I have call'd our System. We hereby apply to the Crown for the official charters that will allow us to implement it.

As successful as the Banque Generale has been, recent events have to a degree expos'd its weakness: a dependence ultimately upon deposits of coin to guarantee its dealings. Our proposals will give the Bank the strongest of foundations and equip it for its role as a national institution, capable of financing major enterprises, as well as controlling the supply of French money.

It is my understanding that the Mississippi trading rights – which extend, I believe, three thousand miles northward from Louisiana, a considerable area of the Northern Americas – are no longer held by Monsieur Crozat and are available for purchase. As we know, trade and income from these and many other French territories overseas have remain'd relatively low, and the reason for this is plain: a chronic lack of investment. With the Crown's permission, it is our intention to purchase these rights and establish a joint stock company to fund the development of trade in America on the grandest scale.

We will issue 200,000 shares in this stock company – let us call it, the Mississippi Company – at a price of 500 livres per share: a total capitalisation of 100 million livres. We wou'd expect a sizeable percentage of these shares to be sold for billets d'etat, outstanding Crown debt which continues to be a crippling burden for the country. For these, the Company will charge a lower interest rate, thus saving the Crown considerable *amounts of money. And to ensure that the Company attracts investors, we will accept these devalued bonds at their <u>original</u> value.*

At the same time, I propose that the Crown take over ownership of the Banque Generale and begin, under our guidance, the wider issue and circulation of a paper currency – the value of which will eventually be guaranteed, not by coin nor by billets d'etat, but by the value and profits of the Mississippi Company! The success of one venture thus provides support for the other – and vice-versa. They stand firm as a gothic arch, with your government at the apex, and represent the perfect merger of public and commercial finance in one single trading and banking operation.

Imagine if you will, Your Royal Highness, the situation after our System of Money Science has been in place for several years. Through massive investment, as well as the direction and leadership that we will provide, trade in the North American colony will increase a thousandfold. The potential riches of the Mississippi region are well chronicl'd and the Company will help realise that potential in the way that Holland and Great Britain already benefit from their overseas territories. Profits from overseas trade will accrue to investors and to the Crown, enabling it to relieve the crippling burden of the National Debt. But they will also flow naturally into the French economy and combine with the flow of investment capital from the National Bank, to stimulate business throughout the country. Prosperity will increase and with it, the common weal. Public works of a monumental scale will be undertaken, monuments to French prowess, the like of which have not been seen since the early days of the Quartorze. In short, France will experience a new Golden Age, found'd, not on gold, but paper.

It goes without saying that Your Royal Highness has the wisdom and foresight to appreciate the virtue of our System of Money Science. But what you also possess in great measure is the power to persuade others of its virtue – your colleagues on the Regency Council whose support we will need if we are to realise this vision, with all its rich rewards for the Government and the people of France.

We eagerly await the Crown's first response to our proposals, in the most fervent hope that work on this significant public enterprise can begin as soon as the granting of Charters will allow.

We are yours etc.

Had we oversimplified the System or made it sound too complicat'd? Had we flatter'd Philippe or not been flattering enough? These were my worries over the next few days, although Katherine was convinc'd that the letter had struck exactly the right tone.

On the fifth day following its dispatch, a carriage bearing the Bourbon crest drew up outside the Bank. A small, portly fellow in an enormous wig enter'd with such pomp and accompanied by so many footmen that it might have been the Quartorze himself.

With the grand flourish of a large, lacey mouchoir, he bow'd as low as his belly wou'd allow and announc'd himself as Master of the Royal Office of Something, Chevalier of Somewhere and Philippe's Chief of Staff – or at least, that is what I think was meant by his immensely long and complicat'd title. 'His Royal Highness, the Prince Regent, requests that Monsieur John Law attend upon him at the Palais-Royal immediately.'

'Of course, Your Grace,' I said, somewhat amus'd by all this folderol. 'I will fetch Madame Law.'

'His Royal Highness requests that you come alone, Monsieur. Be so kind as to follow me forthwith…' And with that he turn'd on his high heels – how small he must he have been without them – and left with his entourage behind him. Meanwhile, I ask'd Monsieur Ginot to tell Katherine what had transpir'd and without donning either hat or topcoat, I follow'd after them.

Philippe was at his bureau when I arriv'd and look'd as business-like as I had ever seen him. I made to bow, but he stood up and cried: 'No, Monsieur Law, it is I who must bow to you!' And so he did, much lower than his Chief of Staff had manag'd.

'It is brilliant, absolutely brilliant. The scientist in me loves its reason and logic. The artist loves its elegant symmetry. Your System of Money Science is in all respects brilliant!'

'Thank you, Your Highness.'

'Don't thank me. I must thank you, Monsieur Law...and Madame Law, of course...'

'Of course...'

'Yes, I have the wisdom and foresight to appreciate it,' he said, quoting the letter, 'but nothing like the wisdom and foresight you have both display'd in dreaming it up. For it is a dream, is it not? But one that we can live...'

'It is,' I said.

He gestur'd for me to sit opposite him. Given his overwhelming enthusiasm, I was encourag'd to come straight to the point: 'So, you foresee no difficulty in granting the Charters, Your Highness.'

'I will need to persuade the Regency Council, many of whom, as you're aware, are not as well dispos'd towards you and your ideas as I am. However – how can I put this? – I am sure that if they are convinc'd your System is not only good for France, but also of benefit to themselves, they will approve it.'

'Such er benefits can easily be arrang'd as part of the setting up of the Company, I'm sure, Your Highness.'

'Excellent.' He shift'd uneasily in his seat, drew breath. 'But there is an even more delicate matter I must discuss with you, another kind of benefit that I require, Monsieur Law...and it is not of a financial nature...May I be extremely frank?'

'Of course...'

'As I think told you, Parabère and I have separat'd.'

'Yes, I remember.'

'And did I tell you why?'

'I believe you said that it was as if you had awoken from a spell and it meant you were no longer in her power...her slave, I think you said.'

'Yes - and shall I tell you the reason for that?'

'Please do.'

'It is because I have become the slave of another.'

I recall'd his puppy-like behaviour with Parabère and stifl'd a smile. 'Can I be bold enough to ask if you must always be a slave in love, Your Highness? Can you not be an equal?'

'An equal?' His expression cloud'd over. 'Monsieur Law, lovers cannot be <u>equals</u>. How dull and dreary wou'd that be! No – one of them must hold the power, one of them must be in control. That is what generates the excitement, the intensity, the passion between them. Or at least that is how it has always been for me...'

'And who now has this power over you, Your Highness?'

He held my gaze. 'Katherine,' he said, 'if I may call her by that name. It's one that has become birdsong to my ears...'

For some reason, when he first said the word 'Katherine', I did not think of Katherine, <u>my</u> Katherine. I thought it must be someone else in his circle, the first name of Madame de Tencin, perhaps. Then, as he went on, I chastis'd myself for not having realis'd how plain as day it was. Of course, you fool, I thought, he is obviously devot'd to Katherine and completely in her sway.

'I adore her. Ever since I first saw her that evening at Madame de Chateauneuf's, when you and she were first introduc'd to me. I liv'd for many years under the brilliance of the Sun King, but she is the Sun <u>Queen</u> – all other women are eclips'd by her. I've done my best to fight it, to resist my desire for her, but you know it's not my strongest suit, Monsieur Law. Desire always gets the better of me.'

'Why are you telling me this, Your Highness?' The question was partly rhetorical. I think I already had some idea where this conversation was leading and my stomach began to churn as it had done so when I stood, sword-in-hand, facing Beau Wickham.

'I think we're both agreed that your System can be the salvation of France. I just need to convince the Council – and to do that I need your permission...'

'My permission to speak to them, Your Highness?'

'No – your permission for me to pursue Katherine, your...partner.' At least he had resist'd calling her my mistress. 'To pursue her in the romantic sense, I mean...'

This was something I had not expect'd – _my permission?_ I cou'd not help but laugh. 'Have I understood the word permission correctly, Your Highness? Is this a kind of blessing – as if I were her father and you her young suitor?'

He had to laugh too. 'Yes, a little like that, Monsieur Law. It's not something I'm us'd to asking for in relation to women or anything else, for that matter. But it will make things much easier between us and I'm sure it will also help Katherine – to know that you are...in agreement.'

In agreement. To him making love to my 'wife'. I wonder'd at the brazenness of the man, even by French standards. But on the other hand, there was nothing surprising in any of this. He was a Bourbon and now Prince Regent. He was us'd to having whatever he want'd, especially as far as women were concern'd, and I think, rather than insulting me, he actually felt he was paying me the ultimate compliment with his talk of 'permission'.

What was surprising was my card-playing calm: instead of feeling outrag'd, I was quietly calculating how Katherine and I might turn this to our maximum advantage.

'With all due respect, Your Highness' – if respect is an appropriate word in the circumstances, I thought – 'what makes you think that my permission will have any effect on her. As I have explain'd, we are equals; Katherine is a free agent. She will do as she pleases, with whom she pleases.'

'And it will please her, I know, to return my love – or at least to give me hope of that possibility.'

Yes, of course, and how cou'd he think otherwise, with all the attention she had paid him these last few months, especially out at Marly? Wasn't that exactly the card we had play'd with him and had it not prov'd a winning one? Now, however, it was his turn to play a card and he had well and truly increas'd the stakes.

'I hope I have not offend'd you, Monsieur Law, but I wou'd not have dar'd approach you in this way if I had not sens'd something – how can I put this? – of the Machiavellian in you. '

248

'You think I will do whatever it takes to achieve my ambitions?'

He nodd'd. 'I sense – and I mean no offence to you, rather the opposite, for you will never be anyone's slave – that you are more of a gamester than you are a lover. And, if I may say so, I think Katherine knows it too...'

I ponder'd this for a moment. Even if it was calculat'd to offend, I was hardly in a position to react to it as such. 'You may well be right, Your Highness – we'll see. Meanwhile, I can do little more than convey your wishes to her.'

'And I can do little more than recommend the establishment of the Mississippi Company to the Regency Council. You have my full support, Monsieur Law...'

I did not respond with 'And you mine, Your Highness...'

*

It seems the office belongs to a bank that occupies the top floor of the Venier building. This being a Saturday, it's deserted – apart from me, and now the security guard who comes running in, *molto agitato*. Marisa translates for me when she arrives moments later: 'How did you get in here?' 'The door was locked.' 'Are you trying to rob the place?' 'Now please fuck off.' (*Please?*)

I have no answers, only apologies. I echo our skipper from earlier, when we were nearly rammed by the boat: '*Scusi...scusi tanto...scusi tanto...*'

I say to Marisa: 'The door was open, I promise you...' She translates this for the guard as he ushers us out, locking the door behind him and eyeing me suspiciously. '*Impossibile...impossibile,*' he mutters.

Jo meets us at the foot of the stairs. '*There* you are, Theo – where did you get to?'

'He was trying to rob the bank,' Marisa laughs.

'I thought there was some kind of exhibit in there...'

'What kind of exhibit?'

'You know...something to do with the history of the place. An 18th century couple going at it in a huge bed. It was all very

249

realistic...' My words trail away. Realistic? Maybe. *Real*? Probably not.

For the second time today, Jo and Marisa exchange sceptical glances. Marisa is still amused. 'Theo, I'm beginning to think you have a vivid imagination.'

'Certainly a lurid one,' says Jo.

I feign nonchalance with a shrug, as if I'm on top of things, which is far from the case. 'As I said before, too much vino at lunch...'

'Then what we need is some coffee,' says Marisa. 'Just as well our next stop is the Cafe Florian – the oldest coffee house in the world. Today it will be an adventure, because it's over by San Marco and it's *acqua alta*.'

As we leave, Jo puts an arm around me. (Isn't that what I wanted earlier – her protection?) There's more than a hint of seduction in her voice when she says: 'Are you sure you wouldn't rather go back to the hotel?' If I'm summoning up copulating couples out of thin air, she can be forgiven for thinking that's what I have in mind.

And indeed, the Moneyman is very keen. He's a hundred per cent sold on Jo, completely committed. She's his future. He can't wait. Let's go, he whispers.

But the Anarchist isn't interested. He's still Angela's man. He isn't ready to exorcise her, far from it. He's convinced he can win her back. Isn't that what this is all about, he says – winning Angela back?

Winning her back? scoffs the Moneyman. As if you'd lost her in a card game or something? Don't be ridiculous, Theo. Move on. Take the profit. Take Jo. Look at her – why would you *not*, for fuck's sake?

Yes, why would I not, for fuck's sake?

'Sounds like a plan, Jo, but let's have some coffee at the oldest café in the world first. At least we know it won't be Starbucks.'

'Oh, they probably bought it years ago and just kept the heritage brand.'

'No more need of the launch,' Marisa tells us. 'The Florian is a ten-minute walk from here at most, along the Calle

Spadaria. But I think you'll need your boots...' She looks down at her own smart rubber boots, which I notice for the first time.

The bags with our yellow galoshes are at the door, together with our umbrellas. We pull them on over our shoes before venturing out.

'*Avanti!*'

A light rain is falling. It's about 4.00pm and what little daylight has been contained by the dull afternoon is seeping away fast. Streams of water are beginning to flow into the alleyway that forms the Calle Spadaria, swirling around the feet of the puffa-jacketed tourists browsing the gaily-lit souvenir shops.

Jo and I share an umbrella. She puts her arm in mine and squeezes it as we walk. 'These are very stylish,' she laughs, looking down at the plastic goldons.

'Yes, very *alla moda*, as they say here.'

'His and Hers...'

We walk in silence for a few moments. 'I'm going to have to get tough with you, Theo. You really do need looking after.'

'You must think I've completely lost it.'

'Have you?' She looks genuinely worried. 'You were going to tell me what's going on.' She's continuing the conversation we were having outside the Cipriani, before Diana Leonard appeared.

'The bottom line is there's too much going on. I probably shouldn't have come – I mean, it's great being here with you, it really is, but...'

'I understand. It's not as though work's ever far from *my* mind.'

'No...'

'And I know these deals you do are hugely complicated.'

'Yes...' Complicated beyond belief, I want to say. Complicated like the most finely woven net that's closing in around me, tying me up, strangling me. I want to share some of those complications with her, unpick them together. Even the Anarchist would welcome some help.

'And this Vatican deal must be heavier than most...'

'Yes...' I want to tell her that heavy as it is, it's lightweight compared to what else I'm planning.

This doesn't stop the Moneyman taking the Vatican deal very seriously, of course. He sees it as his crowning glory. Not just for how lucrative it is, but for what it represents – the final triumph of Mammon: moneylenders not only in the temple of temples but buying it, lock, stock and barrel, turning it into a luxury apartment block and selling it at a vast profit.

The Anarchist, on the other hand, wants no part of it. He's moved on. He now sees himself as serving a higher purpose, call it a moral one, call it transcendent in some way or other. He's not clear on that yet – he's still working on it – but there's no denying the urge he feels to break with the past.

I'm actually ready to share some of this with Jo when suddenly there's a major diversion. Not Diana Leonard this time, but someone crashing into us, almost knocking us off our feet. At the same time, a hand slips into my coat pocket and I realise it's taken one of my phones – the hot line to my digital wizard. Still off-balance, I turn to see the receding back of a black hoody cleaving through the crowd. I'm immediately after him, the Anarchist urging me on, shouting in my ear: 'You must get it back!' No one knows it better than I do.

I'm not exactly a regular jogger anymore, but I was always a good sprinter and still play singles tennis, albeit without the same spring in my legs. I can't believe how quickly I move, especially as I'm wearing my ridiculous yellow boots. I manage to keep the hoody in sight, and start gaining on him, pushing people aside as I go, saying 'scusi...scusi tanto', which is ridiculous because none of them are Italian and anyway I should be shouting 'Stop the bastard! He stole my phone!' (I'm convinced it's one of the men from the launch that passed us on the canal, the 'shooter'.)

I see him take a left down an even narrower alleyway, only wide enough for single file. It's as if we're bullets rifling down its barrel and being shot out near an arched bridge over a canal. The water has spilled over the canal's banks and is inches deep. My quarry splashes through it and over the bridge into another shallow pond, where he slips and falls on his side. He's up and away again, but not before I'm across the bridge and almost upon him. He's within grabbing distance, when I'm surprised by the sight of my phone lying on the cobbles, just under the water. The bastard has dropped it!

I come to an abrupt halt, almost slipping over as well and toppling into the canal. 'Shit! *Shit!*'

I've got the phone back, though it's probably dead. I pick it up, shake it and dry it on my coat. My chest heaves painfully from running – I guess I'm not as fit as I thought. Then the damned thing rings. I stand there for a few seconds, the flood water lapping around me, half-way up my boots, before I answer it with a sheepish 'Hi.'

'Theo – that you?' I can hear it's my digital wizard – or the Spook, as he sometimes calls himself.

'Yes.'

'You sound...out-of-breath.'

'Yes...I mean...I am. I've been...running.'

'*Running*?'

'Yes...trying to catch a thief.' I try to catch my breath.

'Wow! You get 'im?'

'Sort of.'

'Congratulations. I just called to tell you we're good to go.'

I take a few moments to process this, breathing heavily all the while. 'Good to go?'

'That's what I said.'

'*Now*?'

'*Yes.*'

'You told me 48 hours.'

'I did – but you know what they say?'

'What do they say?'

'Under commit and over deliver...Do you wanna try sounding impressed?'

'I am impressed.'

'Good man – tell me when to push the button, Theo...'

*

When I recount'd my conversation with Philippe to Katherine, she seem'd more insult'd by the fact that two men had been discussing her as if she were 'a side of beef', as she put it, than by the substance of Orleans' proposal. In fact, I receiv'd the distinct impression that she was rather flatter'd by his reaction: firstly, by how successfully she had secur'd his devotion – she particularly lik'd being describ'd as the Sun Queen – and, secondly, that he had agreed to sponsor the Mississippi Company and the System.

'But isn't it a heavy price – to be his love object?'

She laugh'd, made light of it. 'Oh, there are worse things, I'm sure. I'll not let it go that far, John. I'll play him along, set him challenges. Perhaps, even send him on quests in the courtly love traditions of old. It will keep him at a safe distance until the Charters are issued and we have everything in place. If, as he says, he's now my slave it shou'dn't be too difficult to treat him as such.'

'Pauvre Philippe,' I smil'd.

'Pauvre Philippe? He'll enjoy every minute of it. As he told you, love isn't love unless it's wounding. He has to suffer.'

'What happens then?'

'Then, I'll find a way to disenchant him – or he will just lose interest, as Dukes and Princes do.'

I shou'd have said what a dangerous game I thought it was; that Philippe was not someone who was easily discourag'd; that her rejection of him cou'd make him even keener. But I said nothing. We both had everything to gain from this plan and Katherine was a very willing participant – who was I to persuade her otherwise?

Besides, I had been working on another plan of my own: how to get her away from day-to-day involvement with the Bank. Suddenly, it felt timely.

'It might help if you put some physical distance between yourself and Orleans.'

'How do you mean?'

'Well, perhaps, by leaving Paris for a while. I've been thinking that it's time we purchas'd an estate, not far from the city, but far enough for it to feel like an escape – our own little Versailles,' I laugh'd.

'I already have somewhere in mind: Chateau Gourmande, which is hardly so little. It's currently own'd by the usual penniless, over-mortgag'd nobleman, the duc de Berry, I think his name is. The estate is very large, the house very grand and

apparently the gardens are magnificent, if in need of some work...'

I thought the mention of the gardens alone wou'd be irresistible and I was right. If she had appear'd doubtful when I first broach'd the subject, she now threw her arms around me with girlish enthusiasm. 'It's a splendid idea, John – if you knew how long I've dreamt of being on estate. And it'll give me all sorts of excuses to keep Philippe at bay.'

She gave me a look of mock-alarm. 'But how wou'd you cope here without me?'

'Very badly, but I'll manage, somehow. We'll correspond every day. Anyway, haven't I got us this far?'

'Haven't we got us this far?'

'Yes - we have, Katherine.' And we kiss'd, so passionately that I thought it might lead further but she pull'd away.

'When can we see the place?' she ask'd.

'As soon as you like.'

'Tomorrow?'

'Tomorrow it is...'

*

I hadn't had any contact with Boris for some time, not since my separation from Angela and our last, painful conversation. Such radio silence wasn't unusual. What *was* unusual, if not unprecedented, was that when he did make contact with me, he did so over the phone.

'Is that you, Theo?'

I recognised the voice immediately from among my various Russian associates. It wasn't just the heavy accent. It was the underlying note of menace, as if you were being fitted up for a one-way ticket to the gulag. Given everything Angela had said, the menace seemed to come through more distinctly than ever. I had to make an effort to banish all those dark thoughts, to remind myself that this was business, nothing more or less.

'Boris?'

'Yes, Sorry to call you, Theo.' (An apology – now that was novel.) 'I know you don't encourage it, but it was the easiest way to reach you.'

'It's fine, Boris'

'I'm in London for a few days. I have a delicate matter to discuss with you.' On Boris' lips, the word 'delicate' sounded completely out of place, like an elephant wearing a tutu. 'I wondered if you might come and see me…'

He didn't wait for an answer, just gave me the address. 'Another substantial property I've recently acquired. You'll love the view.' We agreed a time for the next day and he signed off: 'By the way, we're in the penthouse.' *We*? Was he there with Gina? Or his loathsome accountant? Or was this the royal 'we' – more of His Lordship's airs and graces?

The substantial property turned out to be on the Thames near Vauxhall, and if not directly opposite the Houses of Parliament, it wasn't far upriver. Boris and I stood on the balcony, admiring the panoramic view of Westminster and the Thames at high tide, a picture postcard in the late September sunshine.

He gestured towards parliament and Big Ben with his tumbler of scotch – he was a great lover of the single malt – and gave a self-satisfied chuckle. 'Of course, I'd have bought that one if they'd have let me, Theo.'

As I sipped the gin and tonic I'd reluctantly accepted to keep him company, I couldn't help thinking that even though he hadn't got his hands on the actual physical structure, he'd almost certainly bought a few of the more influential politicians inside it. In fact, by joining the ever-swelling ranks of the conspicuous super-rich in London, Boris was fast becoming too visible a figure for my liking. (At the same time, I realised there was something to be said for hiding in plain sight.)

We retired inside to some uncomfortable over-designed chairs that still afforded a river view. From the garish abstract oils on the wall to the white marble floors and shiny glass tables, the whole place was like a set for a James Bond film – oozing style and opulence but soulless, forever unlived in.

'By the way, Theo' – Boris loved the BTW phrase, I realised; it was his way of signalling his main point – 'it's not just this apartment, I own the whole building. You may have noticed that all the other apartments are empty. I'll be – what's that American term? – *flipping* them, selling them on immediately.'

'You're becoming quite the property baron, Boris.'

He looked pleased with the description. 'Mainly in London at the moment. It's too good an opportunity to miss. I know you invest in several property funds on my behalf, but I rather enjoy being more...' He cast around for the English words.

'Hands-on?'

'Precisely...precisely...*hands-on.* It's more fun. By the way, Theo, it's one of the reasons I wanted to see you – to tell you that I'll be investing more money in these kinds of property assets for a while, diverting some of it from the fund – valuable to me as that is, of course.'

'Of course.' I sipped my G&T – somehow it tasted a little bitter after this news. 'These sound like considerable sums, Boris. I take it you're being careful.' I might have been talking to an adolescent about contraception – using the condom of a shell company when involved in a toxic transaction, so that the identity of the owner is disguised. 'I understand the British government is starting to police some of these foreign property deals.'

'Ha!' Again, he raised the tumbler towards Westminster. '*The British gov-ern-ment?*' He sounded out the word mockingly, shaking his head. 'It makes a lot of noise about stopping dirty money coming in, but then does nothing except round up a few petty criminals. And why would it do anything else? All it wants is to keep the billions flowing into London. It's not interested in knowing where they come from... But then I'm not telling you anything you don't already know, am I, Theo?'

'No...but we still need to be careful. With the Brits, it's all about being seen to do the proper thing – even if they know you're not.'

'Theo, please...don't worry. I'm not about to expose you or abandon you.'

'I'm glad to hear it.'

'In fact, as a demonstration of my good will I want to introduce you to yet another client, one that could be worth even more to you than I am. An associate in Africa. We jointly own a large tungsten mine in his country. And when I say *his* country, I mean one he more or less runs. I'll send you the details.'

'Thank you.'

'By the way, this is just – how do you say? – business-as-usual. It's not the delicate matter I wanted to discuss with you. That isn't so much about business.'

'Well, that's a relief,' I laughed. 'For a moment, I thought it might be something serious…'

I know for the most part I've portrayed Boris as a Russian stereotype – boorish, bullet-headed, rude, sardonic – and he was all of those things. Yet as I'd got to know him, I'd found other qualities. He did have a genuine sense of fun. He could be courteous, charming – as he'd been at his birthday bash – and even exude a certain degree of human warmth that was more in keeping with his stylish Italian suits and flamboyant open-necked shirts. He was, in part, a bit of a dandy, a rake, a rascal, which meant I almost warmed to him. Almost.

Suddenly, all these more positive attributes were gone and we were back to KGB frostiness.

He inclined towards me. 'But I'm afraid this *is* serious, Theo. Very serious. You probably don't know but Gina and I have separated.'

'I'm sorry.'

He shrugged as if it were a minor inconvenience. 'Our relationship had gone very – how do you say? – stale – and she is not a well woman, Theo.' He placed his forefinger on his temple and tapped it several times. 'Extremely disturbed. Extremely. She has had to be confined to a Swiss clinic – for her own good, you understand.'

'I understand.'

'But that is not the serious part, Theo.' He drank from the tumbler. 'The serious part is that she betrayed me.'

'Betrayed you? How? With other men?'

'No, no' – he waved his hand dismissively – 'far worse, far worse. You are also separated from your wife, are you not? What is her name? – Angela. A beautiful woman, by the way – and smart. Very smart. I liked her very much.'

'She got that impression.' I gave him a wry smile, but none was returned.

258

'I know the weekend at my party Gina told her all sorts of lies about me. She was intent on poisoning my reputation, doing me maximum personal damage. As I said, Gina is not right in the head. She suffers from – what's the word? – delusions, paranoia, that kind of thing. I'm almost certain she gave your wife some false information about me that supported her lies. On a memory fob – or whatever you call it.'

'I see. Well...if she did, I've certainly not seen anything of that nature. Nor has Angela said anything about it – not to me, anyway.'

'It's not you I'm worried about, Theo. Now you're estranged from your wife, I'm worried who else might see it. *You* should worry. In my experience angry ex-wives are a great liability.'

Even in the midst of this *very serious* situation, I smiled inwardly. Only Boris could have made such a statement. 'I don't think Angela qualifies – as an angry ex-wife, I mean.'

'I hope not. But just in case, I would like to issue a warning – and you should pass it on to her. The material must never be shared. *Never.*'

'If it exists, I can assure you it never will.'

'Good. *Good,* Theo – for both our sakes.' Finally, he managed a smile, albeit a wintry one. 'We wouldn't want the beautiful Angela to land up in a Swiss clinic too, would we? After all, who would look after your disabled daughter? Certainly not your alcoholic mother-in-law...'

Before I could respond or begin to ponder the deeply worrying implications of what he'd been saying – for a start, how the fuck did he know so much about my family? - I heard someone behind us.

Boris turned. 'Ah, Anna, you've finally woken up.'

'Am I interrupting you?' She may have woken up, but her sleepy voice was still back in bed.

'You could never be an interruption, darling Anna – and anyway, we are done here, aren't we, Theo?'

'We are.'

'Anna, you know Theo, I think?'

'Of course. How are you, Theo?' She treated me to a radiant smile, before falling down on the vast white sofa and folding her slender legs up under her and her short silky pink dressing gown. Her long fair hair was a masterwork of sexy disarray.

'I'm fine,' I said, doing my best to sound indifferent, as if I wasn't totally captivated by the pure, or rather, *im*pure sight of her.

'Well' – Boris stood – 'I must go. I have another meeting in the City.'

I also stood. 'Yes, and I should be on my way too.'

'Please, Theo,' he said, 'stay if you like. Keep Anna company for a while.'

I smiled at her. 'Much as I'd love to, I must head back to the office…'

I hoped my voice didn't betray my sense of panic. I knew I had to get out of there as quickly as possible, and if I'd only kept my eyes to myself, I'd have got clean away. But as I followed Boris across the room to the hallway, Anna held out a hand. 'Are you sure you won't stay?'

I took the hand, gently pressed it, and as I did so, the top of her gown fell open, revealing the considerable swell of her left breast. She shifted the silky material slowly back into place, fixed me with a classic come hither. *Oh dear.*

'I'm afraid I can't. Bye, Anna…'

Down on the street, Boris was collected by his driver. He offered to drop me somewhere, but I said it was out of his way – I'd call for a taxi.

Except I didn't. Once his car was out of sight, I went back into the building and straight up to the penthouse. Anna was expecting me, of course. The little lines of coke were already glistening invitingly on the glass coffee table.

*

Matters mov'd on apace. Katherine and I went out to Gourmande the next day. Some three hours south of Paris, the road took us to the top of a steep hill, from which we cou'd see a large turret'd chateau perch'd on the far side of the valley. She all but swoon'd when we alight'd from the carriage to take in the view. Much to her delight, the splendid gardens and woods slop'd gently down to the river, following the soft contours of nature in the new English style, rather than imposing on them with numerous parterres in the French. It seem'd we were overlooking a portion of Eden.

And so keen was His Grace, the duc de Berry, to get his hands on some cash – even our banknotes (with a little gold thrown in for a further discount) – and so keen was Katherine to get her hands on the estate that two weeks later it was <u>our</u> portion of Eden.

I cou'd not help but feel that the purchase had restor'd her to her true status; that she was once again the land'd aristocrat she had been born. When I put it to her, she did not disagree – unusual for her – and I knew that my plan had succeed'd; that despite her ambitions to be a New Woman, a woman of business affairs above all else, the beauty of Gourmande wou'd get the better of her and claim more and more of her attention.

Meanwhile, she wrote to Philippe, in terms that combin'd 'demur with allure', as she lik'd to say, 'stricture with hope'. She told him about her excitement in purchasing Gourmande, saying that she wou'd take up residence there for the time being and once certain necessary improvements were complet'd, she wou'd waste no time in inviting him to stay.

If he felt teas'd – and he probably did – it only seem'd to fire his desire to please her all the more. He wrote back to her almost immediately, promising to issue a lit de justice within the week, granting the Mississippi Company its Charter and transforming the Banque Generale into the Banque Royale, a National Bank. He add'd that he sincerely hop'd he might be allow'd to see Gourmande as a work in progress.

In fact, the lit de justice was issued by none other than the eight-year-old Louis himself. And adding to my surprise and delight was the fact that the proclamation took place at the Palace of Versailles in the Salon des Glaces. Both Katherine and I attend'd, before she left for Gourmande, together with the Regency Council and leading members of the Parlement. Even de Conti manag'd a bow in our direction, his hostility perhaps temper'd by the setting of Versailles and the moving sight of the young Louis – a small, fair, if rather sickly looking, boy weigh'd down by heavy regalia – presiding over this gathering of giants.

Afterwards, his young majesty was usher'd over to us by Philippe. Katherine execut'd her most perfect curtsey and, in order not to condescend to him, I sank to my knee and bow'd my head *(even so, I remain'd an inch taller). The boy made a short speech, obviously prepar'd for him by Orleans, but no less flattering for that.*

'My dear Monsieur and Madame Law,' he declar'd, in as regal a tone as a child's voice cou'd manage, 'we believe that your System of Money Science will bring glory to our reign and prosperity to our subjects. We wish you every success in this grand venture. Long live the Banque Royale and the Company of the Mississippi!'

'Long live, Your Majesty,' we replied and he smil'd and thank'd us.

There cou'd not have been a greater endorsement of the System; there cou'd not have been a better way of eclipsing the memory of my abortive audience with his young majesty's great grandfather, the Quartorze. All that was lacking was a peel of bells at Notre Dame, which, had we made the request, I am sure the Cardinal Dubois wou'd have arrang'd.

The only discordant note for me was the sense of sadness I felt when I watch'd Katherine with Philippe and saw the subtle, seductive web she was spinning, as if it were the most natural thing in the world. He had call'd me Machiavellian, said I was more of a gamester than a lover, but what he had not yet realis'd was that she was the same. It was the very quality that made us equals.

He hardly took his eyes off her throughout the proceedings and lavish'd more attention on her than he did his Royal ward. At one point, he usher'd her off to a corner of the Salon, where, she told me afterwards, he declar'd his love and plied her with invitations to private liaisons at the Palais-Royal and Marly. She graciously declin'd, while leaving the door of expectation ajar, as was the plan.

'I am deeply flatter'd and not a little overwhelm'd by Your Highness' attentions. But I am afraid I need some time to reflect. Meanwhile, please let us continue to correspond...'

It was as she had said. As long as he saw some glimmer of hope, the pain caus'd by her rebuff of him was an exquisite pleasure. La chasse was every bit as important as l'amour and she thought she cou'd play the game to advantage for some while yet. As it turn'd out, he ran out of patience sooner than we expect'd.

262

Chapter 9

Venice, November 1728

I am feeling much recover'd after my painful seizure at the
Venier, or as much recover'd as I will ever be. To Bellini's great
relief, I am back at the Ridotto and playing again at the table,
in better form than I have been for many months. My mind is
sharper, my memory clearer and my playing has taken on an
almost instinctive quality that I must exploit to the full while I
can, for I am sure these heighten'd powers will quickly pass.
Perhaps the bad news from Katherine has convinc'd me that
life permits no turning back; that there is no point in dwelling
on what might have been, on paths not taken, doors not open'd.
Such mental contortions are a waste of time. For better or
worse, I am where I am. Ironically, Katherine's final word – her
final judgement – has allow'd me to move on, to see the path
ahead more clearly, even if it leads to nowhere more
comfortable than a worm-ridden grave.

When the bell rings for what is called acqua alta – high
water – I am even inclin'd to walk out and experience it for
myself, rather than simply watch from the Ridotto's balcony.
The bell is usually only rung during the winter months, when
the high tide overflows the quays and floods part of the city,
including the Piazza San Marco. It does not happen every year;
it may not happen for many years and it is the first time it has
happened while I have been here, which is exciting in its way. I
am told it is to do with several constantly shifting factors: the
wind direction, the position of the moon, the amount of rainfall
and, of course, the fact that the city is slowly sinking into the
mud upon which it is built.

La Serinissima has long been in decline politically and
socially, but it is all too easy to overlook its physical decay.
Bellini says that its descent into the ooze mirrors the descent of
its public morals into fornication and pleasure-seeking on a
grand scale. He throws a theatrical hand towards the window

and the canal: 'Behold the creeping waters of decadence – isn't it marvellous?'

He laughs when I tell him that he is perhaps the city's greatest exponent of this moral decline.

I make the slow walk of the invalid out into the chilly dusk. I have decid'd that I will not play at the tables this evening. Instead, I will take in some of the sights of acqua alta and then return to my rooms to spend some of this freshly mint'd mental vigour on my memoir.

'Tread carefully, il Duce,' the Count calls after me.

Outside, the world has been transform'd disconcertingly into a lake that spreads out into the sea. I walk unsteadily upon rais'd boards, newly positioned for the purpose along the quayside and across the Piazza. There are a few others braving acqua alta and they cut shadowy figures against the flaming torches and their coruscations on the choppy surface of the water.

I head towards the Florian coffee house, which I only occasionally frequent, it being too noisy for the purposes of writing. (I am also no great lover of coffee and prefer my daily hot chocolate.) The gaily-lit Florian is open for business, but not nearly as busy as usual. Suddenly, from out of the evening stillness, there's a strong gust of wind that swirls around the square and extinguishes many of the torches. I am plung'd into darkness; I almost lose my footing and topple into the water.

As I steady myself, I see the silhouette of a figure coming towards me across the walkway. Suddenly – is it the extra chill in the air? – I am convinc'd it is the Wickham-like phantom, its first appearance to me in Venice, and I am petrified as it approaches. The wind blows more strongly, whipping the water up over the board upon which I stand, so that I am also scar'd of being swept off it. My boots and the bottom of my cloak are sodden. I struggle to turn round and, yes, run away from the apparition. As I do, someone grabs me from behind – I cry out from the shock of it.

'Sorry, il Duce, it's only me.' I turn to see Luigi, one of Bellini's manservants. 'The Count was worried about you and sent me to make sure you got home safely. Acqua alta can be *treacherous. One never knows where the walkway ends and the canal begins...'*

*

This stops right now, says the Moneyman.

I'm walking back to the Calle Spadaria in my goldons, retracing my steps along the narrow alleyway where I chased the pickpocket.

You can't go through with it, Theo. I won't let you. Call a halt now and save yourself a lot of misery. The whole thing is deluded, suicidal.

He's reading me the Riot Act, handing down the orders like some newly installed military dictator. He's drowning out any opposition, especially the Anarchist.

When you first decided to do this, you were in a very bad place. No one's denying it. But you're back on your feet. You've moved on. You're your own man again – a highly material man. What they used to call a Master of the Universe.

Is that so?

For sure.

Then why am I seeing things – why am I convinced they're real, when they're not? And why do I keep disappearing down black holes? This is not the mark of a man who's in control. I'm not behaving like someone who knows what he's doing, am I?

Before the Moneyman can respond, I emerge into the busy Spadaria. Jo and Marisa are there, still trying to work out where I've gone, looking this way and that.

Jo's much relieved. 'Theo! Are you okay? Did you catch him?'

I hold up the phone. 'No. I got this back, though.'

Marisa launches into an apology on behalf of the City of Venice. 'We've caught the Roman disease. There's more and more of it here...'

'It's not Venice. It's me. I'm attracting all sorts of crap at the moment.'

She shrugs, nods. Having witnessed several examples by now, she can't argue with that. 'Are you still okay for the Café Florian? Do you want to carry on?'

'Yes, but I may need something stiffer than coffee...'

Minutes later, the water has risen above our ankles and we come out into the flooded Piazza San Marco. Even though I saw it under water when I first arrived, it takes me by surprise in the dusky light: a lake, criss-crossed by duckboards raised on stilts, its surface shimmering with countless reflections. At the far side of the square, the illuminated façade of the basilica and the soaring campanile are a fairy tale palace floating on a shiny sea. We stand transfixed, watching the shadowy figures of tourists pick their ways across the boards.

Marisa pronounces: '*Allora*...people either think it's an architectural wonder or a failed marriage of the Italian and Byzantine styles. Personally, I think the wonder lies within – the gold mosaic ceilings and walls.'

'I don't suppose they're on the Decadence tour,' I say.

She laughs. 'They could be...but unfortunately *acqua alta* is so bad this year that for the first time I can remember the interior of San Marco is flooded as well as the square and they've had to close it.'

She points across the square. 'While we're here – in that far corner was the church of San Geminiano. It was demolished to make way for Napoleon's Palazzo Reale. Your ancestor, Theo, was originally buried there, but they were considerate enough to move his remains to the church of San Moise' – she points in the other direction – 'over towards the Rialto. I seem to remember that a descendant of Law's was a senior officer in the Napoleonic army and in charge of the operation.'

'You amaze me with your knowledge of Law.'

'I amaze myself,' she smiles. 'Perhaps your presence is inspiring me.'

'Perhaps it's *his* presence,' says Jo, a mock tremor in her voice.

'Ha! I can recommend a very good Ghosts Walking Tour, if you're interested – although I don't remember a sighting of John Law ever being reported. Anyway, San Moise will be our final stop, if you can bear it. But first the Florian. *Avanti...*'

She leads the way. We step onto the raised boards and make our way across the water to the colonnade on the other side of

266

the square. 'It first opened its doors in 1720, so John Law would have been a regular visitor, I'm sure...'

'We could always swim to it,' laughs Jo, who seems less concerned with whatever it is that's bugging me – for now, at least.

Much to Marisa's surprise, it turns out the inside of the Florian was also flooded earlier. They've drained the water between tidal surges, but there are signs it will once again breach the low plastic barriers across the front door. Despite this, the place is abuzz with tourists and with waiters going back and forth beneath the chandeliers and gilded ceilings. The walls are lined with engraved mirrors that multiply the frenetic scene many times over.

Marisa does her thing. '*Allora*...this is not the original interior. It was refurbished in the 19th century, but you can easily imagine how elegant it was in its early days. Venice was the first to introduce coffee to Europe. It came from Egypt and was almost as precious as gold. However, because it had Islamic origins, drinking it was originally thought sinful. Thankfully, ever pragmatic, the Venetian authorities decreed it was delicious enough to be a Christian beverage and it quickly became very popular – a stimulant not only of commercial and social discourse but creativity and, of course, romance. Casanova was a regular here.'

Marisa and Jo have some sinful coffee with cream; I have prosecco and am very glad of it. I finally get to breathe out, relax a bit. I take in the scene, take in Jo. She unzips her orange puffa. She's flushed from all the exertion; her hair's corkscrewing all over the place, out of control. I see her look in the nearest mirror and try to push it back into some kind of shape. It's not having it.

'I look a mess,' she says.

'You look beautiful.'

She smiles, reaches across the table and touches my hand.

'You see – as I said, it stimulates romance,' Marisa laughs.

'One thing that's intriguing me,' says Jo, 'is the role of women in this Age of Decadence. For the time, they seemed to have a lot of freedom and influence.'

Marisa's eyes light up; this is obviously a pet subject and she's impressive on it. '*Allora*...influence of a certain kind. Venice was still a patriarchy and women were not allowed to hold public office, so they had little political power. But socially, it was a different story. In the salon and the boudoir, they reigned supreme and this gave them huge confidence. Officially, a respectable noble or bourgeois woman wasn't supposed to be seen in public during the day, but this is where the Venetian fondness for masks and disguise came into its own. The wearing of a hat, mask and long cape meant it was impossible to tell a person's sex or social class. One could go abroad and mingle freely with...whomever. Now that *was* freedom! Casanova could entertain his mistresses in public, here or in the gaming rooms, and no one could be sure whether they were even female, let alone which Count they were married to. And, of course, this freedom of movement between sexes and classes reached its most intense expression during Carnivale, which as the century wore on became little short of an orgy.'

'So much for Swinging London,' says Jo.

'Yes, 18ᵗʰ century Venice was a *truly* permissive society.'

'But why here? Why Venice?'

'A good question – I have my own theory, of course.'

'Which is?'

'The building of a great trading empire requires lots of testerone, lots of strutting masculinity. Money and resources went into equipping ships and sailing them with great daring to the farthest ends of the earth. When that fell into decline, the money and resources went into something else: *pleasure* – music, theatre, gaming, socialising and *sex*, all born of the city's cosmopolitan sophistication. Venetian society became thoroughly feminised, which was further encouraged by the fact that unlike in the rest of Europe, when a husband died in Venice all of his estate went to his widow...'

Jo laughed. 'Which no doubt encouraged many premature deaths among the husbands!'

'No doubt!' Marisa echoed her laughter. 'The truth is this tour shouldn't be called the Age of Decadence but the Age of Women. For a while, we were in the ascendant. They called the shots – until Napoleon marched in and we were back to strutting masculinity.'

'But wasn't the permissiveness just another form of exploitation?' Jo asks.

'If you look further down the social order, yes. The area around the Rialto was one big brothel, where lower class prostitutes sold sexual favours for virtually nothing. But at another level, you could say there was a perfect trade-off – upper-class men handed over wealth and social influence for sex and conversation. In fact, men became more and more slaves to female sexuality – as the sad story of Casanova bears out. In many ways – what with the vast size of the porn industry today and the thousands of women who are trafficked around the world – I think there's more exploitation now...'

Is it the word 'trafficked' that sets off the Anarchist in me? Or just the prosecco that I'm guzzling down at an alarming rate? I'm looking out of the Florian, towards the flooded piazza. It's almost dark, but suddenly the scene turns almost to pitch black – except for a single, silhouetted figure, surrounded by a blazing white light that spills out over the surface of the water. The figure comes towards me, across the square. It wears a full-length cloak, secured at the front, and a large tricorne hat. Is it male, female – what is it? It's like some giant bat. I can't make it out its face or whether it's masked. This one *must* be a tourist show, surely – mustn't it, Marisa?

Neither she nor Jo are listening to me. They're still talking about women calling the shots and the feminised society, while I'm trapped in tunnel vision, watching this apparition – whoever it is, *what*ever it is – move towards me. And whatever it is isn't walking on the boards – the fucker is walking on water!

*

The purchase of Gourmande was the first of many of our portions of Eden, but the later ones were more acquisitions of mine than Katherine's. By the time the Banque Royale was in its second year, they includ'd the estates of Effiat, Chevalier, the Duchy of Marcourt and no less than five others, whose names escape me. We also bought up large swathes of Paris on both sides of the Seine.

Katherine had a romantic attachment to landed property, but even she felt I had become obsess'd with the acquiring of it, as did many of my French critics. Why was I not pouring money into the overseas ventures of the Company, as I was encouraging others to do? Why not invest in commerce rather than land?

There were several good reasons, although I cou'd not say so at the time. First, given that much of it was rundown, land was relatively cheap and wou'd be sure to appreciate quickly as the money supply increas'd; second, we were awash with liquidity and it was only one of many investments – I wou'd also invest much of our capital in the Company. And third – and most importantly – there was the matter of power and influence.

Even I, the champion of trade and commerce, had to accept that there was no better way for us to demonstrate our new social status than through the possession of land and property. But for me, it had a further significance that it cou'd never have for Katherine or the French nobility. It also symbolis'd achievement on the basis of merit. I was living proof that an individual – in this instance, both a foreigner and a commoner – cou'd ascend to the highest echelon of French society, not by virtue of his birth, but through a combination of ability and hard work. This idea was at the heart of the System and vital to its success. For if people were to improve their material lot, they had to believe that progress up the social ladder was within their grasp, despite the obvious barriers of privilege and prejudice. Alongside Katherine, I became the largest landowner in France, apart from the Crown – a fact that Philippe wou'd keep pointing out to me – and as such, I was a beacon for that progress.

Meanwhile, the final part of the System, its apex, so to speak, was put in place. Following the lit de justice, Noailles was dismiss'd as Financial-Controller, to plot and scheme resentfully in the shadows, and d'Argenson appoint'd in his place. At first, I felt a twinge of annoyance that I had not been offer'd the position, but Philippe was reassuring. Even though both Katherine and I had by then become French subjects, he

*thought the 'foreigner' factor still applied. Also, the
appointment of d'Argenson help'd placate certain parties – I
assum'd he meant de Conti. And furthermore, as the new
Financial-Controller knew nothing of finance, he wou'd rely
heavily on me for guidance. I cou'd expect to be Controller in
all but title.*

*In fact, with Katherine and Anne out at Gourmande, I was
happy to concentrate on the issue of a Prospectus for the sale of
Company shares, a short pamphlet that publicised the offer –
200,000 shares at an initial price of 500 livres each – to
potential investors. This was no easy matter, given that the joint
stock company was virtually unknown in France and
consider'd a strange, exotic brew that wou'd have many
turning up their long Gallic noses.*

*Louisiana held a certain allure, it is true, but even for those
in court circles, it was little more than a name on a map; few
had any real idea of where it was or what it was like. I must
admit that by then I knew too well of its deficiencies from
several eye-witness accounts and had already understood why
Crozat had invest'd so little in the place.*

*Far from it being the Eldorado I had allud'd to in my
description of the System, I had been reliably inform'd that the
colony was at best a mosquito infest'd swamp, that the town of
New Orleans – Philippe lov'd the name, of course – was a
rundown military camp; that both the native Indians and the
climate were hostile; that there were no known mineral deposits
of any description, let alone gold or diamonds; and that
exploration of the Mississippi River itself had so far result'd in
the disappearance of several large parties of settlers. Even
allowing for some morbid exaggeration on the part of my sea-
faring informants, it seem'd an uninspiring proposition for an
investor.*

*Yet I was not at all deterr'd and remind'd myself that the
Company was not selling Louisiana as it exist'd, but its
potential. If money and people could be attract'd to the place, I
was genuinely convinc'd that it wou'd develop rapidly. The
land of the interior was not only fertile but in plentiful supply
and there for the taking – unlike the 'interior' of France, which
had long ago been 'colonis'd' and mortgag'd to support its*

decrepit owners. Once settlers start'd to arrive in numbers, a vast new country wou'd develop whose trade and assets wou'd quickly grow in value and pay huge dividends. The trick was to make it seem as attractive as possible – and if I depict'd it as such, it was merely to anticipate a situation that I consider'd inevitable.

And I use the word 'depict'd' in a literal sense. The Prospectus contain'd maps and illustrations of grand ships on the high seas and intrepid settlers forging noble – and prosperous – lives in bucolic surroundings.

'Never has an investment opportunity exist'd on such a scale,' I wrote in the pamphlet, words that Katherine insist'd on checking from Gourmande. (She was right to do so and I was wrong to resent it, but I did.) 'For the first time that opportunity is open to anyone who is able to purchase shares. Great Britain, Spain and Holland have all prosper'd greatly from the development of their overseas possessions, and France now has the chance to dominate the great continent of North America from its base in Louisiana. In so doing, it will reinvigorate its own trade and commerce, and create wealth on an unprecedent'd scale, in which not only shareholders but the French people will share. The New World, as it is known, will be the re-making of the Old.'

*

How did I get here? How did I land up in such a desolate and dangerous place? You don't book these trips through Sandals or some luxury travel agency: a cruise around the Utterly Hopeless Islands, a trek in the Suicidal Mountains of Despair. You're forced onto them. You have no choice but to seek them out on some existential travel site of the soul – heartofdarkness.com or thedeadzone.co.uk. But the fact is you'd rather go anywhere else.

Yes, things were bad after Angela and I split. I desperately wanted her back and I probably wouldn't have survived on my own without the anti-depressants to keep me company. And yet, somehow I made my peace with it. (Peace? More a fragile cease-fire.) I still had those ten-figure sums on the balance sheet and my business was a huge success. I was still at the top of my game and I wanted to stay there. In fact, I wanted more of it. I wanted to go on racking up the high scores, and I wasn't about to toss it all away because Saint fucking Angela had climbed to the moral high ground and was looking down on me with disdain. No way. I was a winner before I met her and I'd continue to be a winner now she was gone. Does that sound like fighting talk? Well, it's meant to.

Yes, I know, it's not the whole story. If I'm honest, Boris's threats – to my family and by implication to me – had got me rattled. I was angry for a while, and I seriously considered cancelling all his business and telling him to go fuck himself – in the nicest possible way, of course. Anna, my Russian hooker, seemed to have taken a far more than professional interest in me and during our torrid afternoon together – which of course stretched well into the evening – she confessed to being yet another female victim of Boris' abuse. (Just think what it would have been like if she was married to him.) I knew she wouldn't have taken much persuasion to work for me on the inside and provide information I could use against him, should his threats continue. (Not that I needed more than the memory fob that was allegedly in Angela's possession.)

But then I came to my senses. Had I waved goodbye to Mr. Aronovsky, I'd have also parted company with considerable revenue. *Considerable* revenue. And besides, on another level, I was smart enough to realise that while he and I were still doing business, I posed little or no threat to *him*. We were in it together and I still had a large amount of skin in the game. But if I withdrew it, I'd have nothing to lose – and then he'd really start worrying about what might happen to that memory fob. In other words – and you don't have to be Einstein to figure it out – in wanting to maintain the status quo and keep everything sweet between us, I was motivated partly by profit, but also by fear.

And this uneasy truce, this shaky equilibrium may have continued indefinitely, but for two events that upset it.

The first was Maggie, to whom at the time I was still officially related. (The divorce was due to go through a few weeks later.) I could not have been more surprised when the receptionist told me that my mother-in-law had arrived. It made no sense for a few moments.

'My mother-in-law – as in *Maggie*?'

I heard the receptionist say: 'Excuse me, are you Maggie?'

And I heard Maggie reply: 'Yeah – why? 'ow many other mother-in-laws 'as 'e got?'

It was Maggie, all right. 'Please send her in…'

And in she came, still looking sober, well turned-out, and as relaxed as if this was a regular social visit. She certainly wasn't apologizing for dropping in completely out of the blue. 'Nice place for an office, Theo. Thought you'd be in the City - Mayfair's a bit more colourful, I s'pose?'

'*I* certainly prefer it.'

I was about to say how surprised I was to see her, when she said. 'Bet you're surprised to see me.'

'I am…but it's fine,' I said, trying and failing to sound like it was. 'Please…sit down.' I gestured towards the meeting area. She perched herself on the plush sofa, legs folded neatly, stylish handbag at her side, all very ladylike. I sat in one of the armchairs opposite.

She looked round, gave the place the once-over. 'Very nice, not as flash as I imagined. Bit understated – like you, eh Theo? Keep a low profile and carry on countin' the money.' She laughed. 'It's alright – don't worry, I'm not 'ere to ask you for any.' (It was disconcerting the way she read my mind.) 'Anj looks after me on that front – on every front, in fact. She's turned out to be a real goodun, that one, despite all the shit she went through.'

'Yes…a real goodun…'

'And I'm not gonna ask you if I can smoke either – somethin' else I've given up, along with men and the gargle. All very bad for you. *Very bad* – 'specially the men.'

'I'm impressed.'

'Not nearly as impressed as I am. Jesus, it's a borin' life I lead. I'll be takin' up fuckin' yoga next.'

It was my turn to laugh. 'Can I offer you some tea or coffee, then?'

'Only if you got some a' that Cinnamon and Ginger stuff.'

'Yes, we probably…'

'Just jokin', I'm fine. Ten minutes of your valuable time's all I want.'

'You have it and more, if necessary.'

She settled back on the sofa. ''ow you copin' on yer own, then, Theo? Or maybe you're not on yer own...'

'Yes, I am...I mean...for the most part...yes...'

She gave me her wicked fairy grin. ''andy bein' in Mayfair, then. I 'ad a coupla girlfriends used to do extremely well round 'ere. You 'ave to dress for the part, of course, invest in some expensive, designer gear, that kind of thing...'

'I'm sure you do.'

She gave another laugh. 'It's alright, I'm not 'ere to pimp for anyone either.'

'That's good to know. How's...er...Angela. Is *she* on her own?'

'Ha! She is – an' she isn't. She seems to 'ave gone right off men. In fact, she's got it together with Lola, the au pair. Turns out the Spanish girl's a bit of a carpet muncher. Never a'guessed it. Difficult to tell these days.'

'Right...a carpet muncher...' I echoed the term for want of anything more cogent to say.

'Well, she's always swung both ways, Anj. You must've known.'

'I suspected.'

'Look at it this way – whatever you were doing to 'er, she liked it enough to keep it nice an' straight for a while. Anj is 'specially screwed up when it comes to sex. 'ardly surprisin', is it? What with me as 'er mother and that fucker as 'er father.'

'Are you saying I should feel flattered, Maggie?'

'You should...which brings me on to the main point of my bein' 'ere. She says she's very 'appy with Lola. Just what the doctor ordered an' all that. But it's rubbish. I know what she really wants.'

'What's that?'

'She wants you back, Theo.'

'Me? I don't think so.'

'Well, she probably doesn't even know it 'erself yet. But I do. I know exactly. All she wants is an excuse, a reason to climb down off 'er 'igh 'orse.'

'What does that mean? What sort of excuse?'

'You makin' amends would be a good move.'

'How so?'

'Stop doin' what you're doin' – as in the business, I mean.'

'Is *that* all?' I made the phrase as heavily sarcastic as possible.

'I mean, it's not just a matter of you walkin' away from it…'

'You're damn right it isn't. It's not going to happen.'

'*No,* Theo. What I'm sayin' is you 'ave to do far *more* than walk away from it. You 'ave to make up for the wrong you've done by actually puttin' things right – in Anj's eyes, anyway.'

'*Putting things right?* And how do I do that?"

'I dunno. You'll figure it out – if you want to. Anyway, I'm not bein' entirely unselfish 'ere. I more than earn me keep with Anj. Much to my surprise, since you went, she's become very dependent on me, too fuckin' dependent – now there's a turn up for 'er alcoholic fuck up of a mother, eh? But it's not me, I'm afraid. I'm too much of an emotional cripple meself to support another one. And as for all this clean livin', that's not me, neither. At some point soon I know I'm gonna have to get down an' dirty again. I'm gonna need to go back on the streets, Theo – that's just the way I am. That's where I'm most at 'ome, a woman of my *chronic lack of self-esteem'.* She shook her head. 'Oh yeah, I've been doin' all that therapy shit, as prescribed by madam…but the point is when I do go, she's gonna need someone else to pick 'er up other than the Spanish au pair. Do you get what I'm sayin', Theo? You're gonna 'ave to win 'er back – for all our sakes. Hers, yours, mine – and let's not forget Grace. Let's not forget my lovely grand-daughter. All of us – it's down to you, Theo…'

*

As well as keeping up her correspondence with me from Gourmande, Katherine had to respond to a veritable bombardment of missives – let us call them 'billet doux' – from Philippe. So keen was he to see her that after a month of excuses to the effect that the chateau was not yet fit to host the Regent, she had little option but to agree to a visit from him.

If I was not surpris'd that she had conced'd on the matter, I was shock'd when she told me that she had chosen the occasion of Anne's third birthday to invite him. She thought that by making this a family affair, involving myself as well as Anne, it wou'd impose some restraint on the rampant Orleans.

But from the moment of his arrival, it was clear that he intend'd to set his own tone for the visit, one more akin to a drunken debauch than a child's birthday celebration. He came with a whole caravan of coaches that contain'd as odd an assortment of courtiers as I had seen, many of whom seem'd to have spent the journey from Paris drinking a great deal of wine and cognac. This motley band includ'd the tiresome d'Argenson, who wou'd no doubt take the opportunity to challenge me on the subject of the Company; the duc de Bourbon, who was more drunk than anyone and need'd the assistance of a footman to get from his carriage to the house; their respective courtesans, both looking highly flush'd and dishevell'd; at least six of the court musicians and their various instruments; and a whole retinue of servants, two of whom were unloading what look'd like a large painting beneath its protective shroud.

'John!' Philippe was as inebriat'd as the rest, which perhaps had something to do with the fact that he embrac'd me and call'd me by my Christian name for the first time. It may also have been a reflection of how pleas'd he was with his profits from the Banque Royale, not to mention what he probably regard'd as my support for his campaign to win Katherine's undying love.

He gestur'd towards the painting as it was carried past us. 'A small gift for the chateau...and, of course, we have many birthday gifts for your darling daughter...whose name escapes me...'

'Anne.'

'Anne...of course. I hope in some way they will compensate for this invasion of Gourmande. We were a party' – he made a *sweeping gesture towards the caravan and his companions –* *'and I cou'd not bear to break it up. I trust you are not inconvenienc'd, John.'*

'Not at all, Your Highness...'

He breath'd deeply of the country air and look'd around. 'And I can already see that this is as charming an estate as I have ever had the honour of visiting.'

'Thank you, Your Highness.'

Katherine appear'd beside me, brandishing Anne in her arms, like a shield. 'It is hardly as charming as it wou'd have been in a few months time, Your Highness - as I have told you repeatedly in my letters...'

With its absence of formal courtesies, there was a familiarity in Katherine's manner that was both endearing and worrying – endearing for Orleans, I am sure, and worrying for me that it had too much allure and not enough demur.

'Ah, Katherine, there you are!' Philippe lit up even more brightly, if that were possible. 'And pretty little Anne...' He lent in towards mother and daughter, took Anne's tiny hand in his bejewell'd fingers and smil'd at her. The child look'd on the verge of crying, but eventually manag'd a smile.

He spoke to Katherine: 'You know only too well, my dear, it is my hosts rather than any house that brings me all the way from the Palais-Royal...'

'Thank you, you are most gracious, Your Highness...is he not, Anne?'

It was then I caught sight of Madame de Tencin as she alight'd from the last carriage, and I understood the exact nature of Orleans' game. His sorry entourage was there to divert me, offer me some kind of consolation, while he devot'd himself to seducing Katherine. The musician's wou'd entertain me with their playing, D'Argenson wou'd engage me on public finances and de Tencin wou'd...well, speaking of seduction....

I had last seen her kneeling face down on the bed at the Palais-Royal, while Philippe plough'd into her from behind, but it did not seem to prevent us from greeting each other warmly and without embarrassment. The stage was set for an eventful visit, I thought, and so it prov'd from the start.

Upon entering the house, Philippe insist'd on unveiling the painting he had brought with him. It was one of his own, he said – more bacchanalia after Corregio, featuring a nak'd couple engag'd in the act of love beneath a sturdy laurel, while fauns and nymphs caper'd all around. I cannot say it was one

278

*of his best. Entwin'd in their carnal embrace, the limbs seem'd
out of proportion and the flesh tones too pink (especially that of
the woman's cleft, part of which was on garish display,
although thankfully the male genitalia were a little more
discreetly hidden).*

*This did not mean that we were any less gracious in
receiving the painting, however, just as it did not seem to
detract from Orleans' pleasure in giving it to us. One cou'd
hardly miss the mischievous gleam in his eye as he did so.
Meanwhile, Katherine was full of mock-horror and coquettish
smiles at the sight of it – 'Your Highness! You are incorrigible!'
She cover'd Anne's eyes and pass'd her to the nurse, who took
her off to the nursery. It was merely symbolic, but it seem'd to
me that Katherine was now without her shield.*

*

I don't know who said Hell is other people, but he or she
was wrong. Hell is being alone. Or rather, Hell is feeling
isolated, unable to connect with anyone or anything. Which is
why I'm so relieved to return to the present company – to Jo
and Marisa. How long have I been away? How long have I been
staring out on to the piazza, at someone who isn't there, yet
seems to have been watching me since I arrived in the city?
Each weird incident, natural or supernatural, real or surreal,
turns the screw a little tighter and leaves my grip on reality a
little looser. By comparison, the presence of these two women
takes on an almost cosy familiarity, as if we've been together
for months rather than barely a day. Whatever Hell is, I
increasingly realize that Heaven is the company of good
women.

Their conversation has moved on from Venice's history to
the more personal kind. Marisa is telling Jo about her life,
outside of being a guide. She's an academic – an English
teacher at an adult education college – and a translator. She was
born in Venice, but for years has lived across the causeway on
the mainland in Mestre, not far from the airport. It's much
cheaper and more practical than the historical centre, and even
if she had the choice, she thinks she'd find full-time Venice too

claustrophobic, too intense. As it is, she actually looks forward to doing these tours, especially the smaller, more intimate ones, when she can get to know people. It's a good antidote to fighting with her two teenage kids. She has a son of sixteen and a daughter of thirteen. The first is lazy, the second crazy, she laughs. She's been divorced for ten years and has no partner. Sometimes it's hard work being a single parent.

'My ex-husband was a professor at the university. He fell in love with one of his students and traded me in.' Again, the wry laugh. 'It was a terrible shock.'

'It must've been,' says Jo.

'Yes, but mainly because it was a young *male* student. I had no idea my husband was so inclined – and he had the nerve to tell me that he had no idea either! *Not till I met Gianfranco did I realise I was gay.* I didn't believe him.'

'I wouldn't have believed him either.'

'The worse thing is you live with someone for years. You think you know them and yet you can be spectacularly wrong.'

We all ponder this for a few moments and I have an even more depressing thought: we think we know *ourselves* and we also get that spectacularly wrong.

Marisa looks at each of us. '*Allora*...what about you two? You look like successful people who are' – she pauses, then goes for it – '*in love*!'

We obviously seem so embarrassed by the words that she quickly follows with: 'I'm sorry – how rude of me to suggest such a thing...'

'Not at all,' I say, before moving swiftly on. 'Jo's *very* successful, aren't you, Jo?'

'Well, in a very boring way – I'm a lawyer.'

'She's with one of the top law firms in London,' I add. 'And I know how good she is because she was once on the other side of a court, prosecuting me. That's how we met.'

Marisa smiles. 'It's an interesting way to meet someone.'

'I work such long hours,' says Jo, 'it's often the *only* way to meet someone. I've decided there's too much work in my life' – she looks fondly, hopelessly across at me – 'and not enough Theo.'

I reach out and touch her hand; our guide lets out a long sigh. 'See what I mean – *amore*! And what about you, Theo – are you successful?'

I finish off my drink and immediately want another. 'Not as far as marriage is concerned, no. I'm also divorced and funnily enough, my ex-wife now has a relationship with a woman.

Jo looks suprised; I hadn't told her about Angela's girlfriend.

'Ah, it's more common than I thought,' says Marisa.

'Apparently. But as for my working life, you could say I'm extremely successful. I'm an investment banker...'

'So you're also very rich.'

'In financial terms, yes, but in other ways...' I shrug. 'I've come to the conclusion that professional success is of little importance if you're a failure as a human being...'

'Are you a failure as a human being, Theo?'

'The jury's still out, as they say.' I look round for a waiter. 'Shall we have another drink? It must be time for a negroni, surely...'

Marisa looks at her watch. 'I'd love to but I have those two teenagers to get back for...*and* if you still want to go over to San Moise for our final stop on the tour...'

'Yes, we do. Don't we, Jo?'

'Yes, of course.'

'Then we'll postpone the negronis.'

'*Avanti*...'

As we leave, Jo squeezes my hand and gives me a smile that's a cross between the flirtatious and the consoling. I tell myself she's probably decided that Angela has had a damaging effect on my sexuality. If only it were that simple.

It's almost dark outside. The lightest of drizzle floats on the air, along with the briny scent of the sea. The piazza is still a large illuminated pool, the façade of San Marco even more dream-like. But far from feeling uplifted, I sink into a deep sense of dread. I look furtively around for spooks, assailants, pickpockets – whatever Venice is about to throw at me next. What will it be this time? What other torments lie in wait? But the only ones I'm aware of are more anoraked tourists, mostly Oriental, filing along the boards like soldiers on a routine manoeuvre. I stay close to Marisa and Jo, as much for psychological as physical protection.

'It's very near,' says our guide. 'Just along the Salazzada San Moise.' She points at a corner of the Piazza. 'It should be much drier…'

But it's not. The street is under a lot of water, creeping up towards the level of the boards, which we prefer to walk on where we can.

'I've never seen the water come up so high here,' says Marisa.

We soon come out onto a much smaller square, the Campo San Moise, which is also flooded. The elaborate façade of the church looms over it like a giant, heavily frosted wedding cake.

'This has never been one of my favourites,' says Marisa. 'Far too baroque for my taste. It was rebuilt in the late 17th century…'

The interior of the church is at a higher level than the square and is dry at least. It's sparingly lit, but enough to make out some serious paintings on the walls and a huge marble altar at the far end, another wedding cake, around which tiers of candles burn. Thankfully, the place looks deserted; my bristling antennae detect no threat.

I'm drawn towards the altar, but Marisa taps my shoulder and points to the floor, inside the entrance. '*Allora…*your ancestor's just there, Theo.'

We've walked right past – right over, in fact – the stone slab marking John Law's tomb. I can make out very little from the Latin inscription except 'John Alexander Law Lauriston'. Marisa translates: 'It basically says his remains were moved from San Germiniano and gives his dates, 1671 to 1729.'

It's something of an anti-climax – perhaps because I'd half-expected a ghost to appear, absurd as that sounds – but I'm glad to have seen it.

'Thank you for bringing us here, Marisa.'

'My pleasure. It's an important part of your pilgrimage.'

'Am I on a pilgrimage? It's not what I planned.'

Her hair glows scarlet in the light from a nearby sconce. There's something almost transfigured about her, like one of those many Renaissance images I've seen over the last few days. (Is that all it's been? My God.) 'You should know by now, Theo – the things we don't plan are often the most important things we do.'

I'm still pondering these wise words when a buzz in my pocket tells me I have an email, the first for some while. 'Excuse me…'

I take out the phone and see a whole batch have arrived at once. I scroll down and recognise a reply from Boris – or rather, something sent on his behalf, because he never sends me anything directly. I brace myself as I open it.

'Hi Theo. Sorry not to have come back to you sooner. I had trouble reaching one of the other investors. We are all very much up for the Vatican deal. It seems like a good place to park some funds in Europe for a while, certainly a more intriguing proposition than London property. Please proceed as per your proposal. We look forward to hearing how it progresses. Thanks.'

Bailing out one of the most venerable institutions in the world merely amounts to parking funds in Europe – I love it. But I'm thankful. It's as polite and business-like an email as I've ever had from Team Boris and just at that moment the Moneyman is happy to take it at face value.

Jo's at my side, suspecting trouble. 'More complications?'

'No,' I grin, 'things just became a whole lot simpler. Let's go have that negroni…'

*

In the brief time I had alone with Katherine that afternoon out at Gourmande – no more than five minutes in all – I ask'd her how she intend'd to deal with Orleans.

She look'd as if it was more of a chore than a challenge. 'Oh, I'll just have to make sure I'm never alone with him.'

'That won't be easy.'

'It will help if you're in the room.'

'That won't be easy either. He's come arm'd with diversions.'

'Ah, the infamous Madame de Tencin. I think you're more in danger of seduction than I am.'

She gave me one of her disarming smiles. 'Personally, John, I think the best we can do is make sure they all get even drunker than they are already...'

As ever, I admir'd her sang-froid in the situation; if she felt threaten'd by Philippe, nothing in her mood or demeanour indicat'd as much. And as for getting them all drunk to the point of impotence, this was worth a try, even if in Orleans' case, I knew what an insatiable appetite he had for a combination of women and wine. Along with the estate, we had purchas'd du Berry's vast wine cellar, whose further reaches I had not yet fully chart'd, though I had wander'd for some time among its racks of dusty bottles. I had many of its finest bottles brought up to the dining room and sang their praises loudly to the assembl'd company.

In fact, everyone seem'd to have become more sober during the course of the afternoon – apart from the duc de Bourbon, who was a lost cause – and the evening actually began in a highly civilis'd manner with our listening to the court musicians perform a chamber piece by Lully in the grand drawing room. For once, Philippe's attention seem'd to be less on Katherine and more on the music and de Tencin, the reason for which wou'd later become apparent.

We sat down to as sumptuous a dinner as it was possible to prepare with a staff we had only known for a matter of a month. Thankfully, du Berry had been us'd to entertaining in grand style – which had no doubt contribut'd to his bankruptcy – and while not exactly a state banquet, the meal was as fine as anything I had eaten at the Palais-Royal. And as we had hop'd, the quality of the wine meant that our guests soon regain'd the state of drunkenness in which they had arriv'd.

Katherine, of course, had no option but to sit next to Philippe; I sat next to de Tencin, who look'd especially ravishing even by her own standards; D'Argenson was opposite me, next to Bourbon's mistress.

'Monsieur and Madame Low, I must compliment you on the standard of your table,' said the Financial-Controller, tucking into a large plate of succulent duck. He was an unprepossessing specimen; a high-born ruffian, with a growl for a voice and a thin, straggling beard that failed to hide the ravages of an early

pox. As Chief of Police, he had obviously made a fine guard dog for the Royal family, but seem'd ill-equipp'd to be a minister of state. 'It seems your larder is as well stock'd with well-hung fowl as your bank with notes,' he add'd, much to the amusement of the table.

*'Your Grace flatters us,' I said. 'And it is not **my** bank – it is the Crown's.'*

He wash'd the duck down with a whole glass of wine and dabb'd at his thick greasy lips with a napkin. 'Whatever we're calling it, Monsieur Low, while we're on the subject, it seems to me that it's issuing far too many notes.'

'And how, in your professional opinion, is that a problem, Your Grace?' I gave the word 'professional' as heavy a sarcastic edge as I cou'd, but he had obviously had too much wine to notice.

'Because in my professional opinion the more there is of something, the less it is worth.' He tapp'd an empty decanter, which a servant then quickly remov'd. 'Otherwise we'd all be bottling air and selling it for a fortune.' There was more amusement all round, and I was about to respond to this impertinence when Katherine did it for me, in much greater style than I could have muster'd.

'With respect, Your Grace has perhaps overlook'd the point of the exercise,' she said. 'First, the Banque Royale is issuing notes to replace a debas'd coinage and increase the supply of money in a country where it is sadly lacking. Second, money in itself has no value – it is only worth what it can buy. And in France at the present time there is little to buy because there is little demand; and there is little demand because there is a shortage of money. Ergo, by increasing the supply of money, the supply of goods will increase and the value of money will rise accordingly because you will be able to buy more with it.'

At this point, the servant brought another bottle and replenish'd our guest's glass. 'This theory is amply demonstrat'd by Your Grace's consumption of wine,' she add'd with a modest smile. 'The more you drink, the more you seem to have in your glass...'

Orleans laugh'd out loud and clapp'd his hands in appreciation, while d'Argenson look'd like an old guard dog that had lost its bone. He was not, however, deterr'd from seeking another: 'Well, let's hope the theory is born out by the practice, shall we? But as I understand it, everything depends on the success of the Mississippi Company.'

'And have you any reason to doubt the Company's success?' I ask'd him.

'I have every reason to doubt that the shares are selling as fast as you had expect'd, Monsieur Low – unless of course you didn't expect to sell any at all...' Again, there was general amusement.

'I think Your Grace may have misunderstood my expectations – just as you have often misunderstood my intentions at the card table.' It was not a bad riposte and drew some plaudits of its own, but it did not stop me admitting to myself that there was some truth in his remark: we had not sold as many shares in the Company as I had hop'd and I was looking at ways of publicising the issue more widely. One of my main worries was that those who had the means to buy substantial numbers of shares were already aware of the offer, but had been slow in taking it up.

Orleans, who had been content to sit looking admiringly at Katherine, decid'd it was time to mediate: 'If the sale of shares is indeed slow, I have a suggestion to make. The prince de Conti and the duc de Bourbon came to see me earlier this week, regarding matters of pubic finance.' He look'd up the table at Bourbon, who cou'd barely sit upright, let alone discuss the topic. 'I think I can persuade them to buy many more shares than they currently own – and where they put **their** money, other money will certainly do likewise.'

'That wou'd be most helpful of Your Highness,' said Katherine. 'Thank you.'

'Anything for my good friends...' He smil'd at us both, before extending a hand along the table and placing it over hers. 'But for now' – he made a sweeping gesture with the other hand – 'enough of such matters. Let's on with something more pleasurable. After the syllabubs, I wou'd ask you all to indulge me, while I show off my latest accomplishment...'

I had no idea what to expect – a juggling act, perhaps, a naked séance – but it was soon apparent that there was another reason for his bringing along the court musicians: so that he cou'd play his viol with them. Whether this wou'd result in 'something pleasurable' for the audience, remain'd to be seen, or rather heard. And yet, from his infectious enthusiasm in talking of this newly discover'd passion, it was obvious that Philippe was determin'd to add the role of 'musician' to that of 'scientist' and 'artist'.

While the instruments underwent a lengthy tuning process, we again took our places in the grand drawing room. At first, they play'd a piece by Marais, which I recognis'd from the labyrinth at Versailles, the day we had visit'd the Quartorze. It was call'd 'La Musette' and had the jaunty rhythm of a dance. After this, Philippe announc'd that they wou'd accompany – to my great surprise – Madame de Tencin, who wou'd sing the Dolorosa from a Stabat Mater by the young Italian composer, Antonio Vivaldi.

Given the absence of Roman or any other religion from my life, I was unfamiliar with the Stabat Mater, although I quickly gather'd that it was a Latin hymn expressing the grief of the Virgin Mary as she stands at the foot of the cross. Suffice it to say, that at first I was astonish'd to see Orleans and de Tencin performing such a hymn when I had associat'd them more readily with the performance of acts of obscenity. Nonetheless, to close one's eyes and listen to de Tencin one wou'd think an angel had descend'd briefly to Earth to regale us with the most heavenly music.

Philippe's playing was technically flawless, whilst her voice was full of feeling and curiously affecting, as if she genuinely experience'd the Holy Mother's sorrow. When I open'd my eyes and look'd at her, I realis'd that not since my first encounter with Katherine had a woman so excit'd me. (The fact that I also pictur'd her coupling with Orleans and had done little or no coupling myself for many months may have also influenc'd my reaction.)

At one point, I look'd across at Katherine and saw her watching Orleans intently – and it was hardly a look of displeasure. It seem'd the sudden unveiling of these more serious, sensitive souls had taken us both by surprise, as if two of the most lurid carnival masks had been remov'd to reveal the *fairest of human faces. Was there no limit to Philippe's talents? If so, as far as I knew, it lay only in the region of gaming.*

Speaking of which, following the recital, we play'd cards with the ladies for a while and there was much drinking and high spirits, especially when d'Argenson and Bourbon start'd drooling over their mistresses, who squeal'd at their every lame attempt at wit. Philippe was pair'd with Katherine and together they prov'd a formidable combination, winning hand after hand. Both during and after the game, he paid her much attention, lavishing compliments on her and telling her how lucky at cards she was for him.

Meanwhile, lacking the attentions of Philippe, de Tencin sat down at my side and engag'd me more directly in conversation.

She prais'd the house and its hostess; she agreed with Philippe that Katherine outshone every woman in Paris. I felt oblig'd to say – and it was not entirely a lie - that it was only true with the exception of herself. I prais'd her singing and its emotional intensity; it was as if she too were grieving for the loss of a child, I said.

She was almost coy in manner – not a word one normally associates with the most brazen of courtesans – and spoke softly, her large liquid eyes fixing me one moment and darting away self-consciously the next.

'Sometimes, Monsieur Law, one is forc'd to do things as a woman that one wou'd not necessarily choose to do - things that one considers not just immoral, but evil.'

'Evil is a heavy word, Madame.'

'I always weigh my words carefully, Monsieur.'

'What of men?' I ask'd. 'Are they not fac'd with moral choices?'

She replied without hesitation: 'They do not face them so much as define them. Men set the rules; women only do their best to follow them...'

Prompt'd by that particular notion, I look'd towards the far end of the drawing room where Philippe and Katherine had sat talking. To my surprise, they were no longer there. In fact, they were no longer in the room and I ask'd if anyone knew where they had gone.

D'Argenson shook his head, but Bourbon look'd up briefly from his mistress's breasts and manag'd a crook'd, drunken smile: 'I believe that Madame Law is showing His Royal Highness a painting of some kind...Women will go to any lengths to get the Regent alone, you know...'

Had Bourbon been less drunk and I less concern'd about what might be happening between Katherine and Philippe, I wou'd have told him in no uncertain terms just who was keen to get whom alone. As it was, I made my excuses to Madame de Tencin and set off to find them, which in itself prov'd difficult enough, as the house was very large and I was still unfamiliar with it.

Eventually, when I had search'd various bedrooms, including our own, a servant direct'd me to the library, where I knew we had display'd one of our favourite paintings, a portrait by Titian.

'Katherine?' I call'd .

There was a sudden whispering in response, as I walk'd slowly into the book-lin'd room, anxious what I might find wrong and, yes, allowing time enough for it to be right'd. At its far end, a large reading lamp illuminat'd both of them: Philippe standing and turn'd away from me, adjusting his clothes and looking up at the Titian; Katherine sitting on the chaise, smoothing down her skirts, and looking decidedly flush'd.

'John' – she stood up – 'you must have wonder'd what had become of us...'

Philippe span round, unruffl'd and all smiles. 'Katherine has been introducing me to this work by the artist Titian. His use of colour, the way he captures the character of the sitter - truly humbling, isn't it, John? Truly humbling...'

'Humbling indeed.' I said, betraying little emotion.

Philippe met my level gaze with his own, which simply said: was this not our deal, <u>John</u>? You get the Company, I get Katherine.

'Well, I really shou'd be returning to Madame de Tencin. She will be feeling terribly neglect'd...' And with his usual effortless poise, he nodd'd to us both, stepp'd past me and was quickly out of the room.

289

But for the lonely hoot of an owl in the gardens, there was silence until I spoke: 'I thought you were going to avoid being alone with him.'

'I was.'

'Well?'

'He seem'd relax'd, harmless even, while we were speaking in the drawing room. He spoke about his life as a child in the Royal family, his love of music and painting... I thought lechery was the last thing on his mind. When he ask'd to see the Titian, I was sure it was an innocent request...'

'Katherine...'

'I know...it was stupid of me...I dropp'd my guard.'

'What happen'd?

'Do you really want to know?'

'We have to be honest with each other...' Or we will land up being nothing to each other, I want'd to add.

She shrugg'd. 'Well, we were looking at the painting and talking about Titian and then, before I knew it, he was telling me how I drove him insane with desire and he start'd forcing himself on me. I manag'd to restrain him, but on the condition that I wou'd...' She stopp'd.

'That you wou'd what?'

'Give His Royal Highness...a measure of satisfaction.'

'Which was what?'

She took a deep breath. 'If you must know, John, I brought him to a climax with my hand, which I have always found the best way of dealing with over-eager little boys like Philippe.'

She held out the front of her dress, a turquoise silk, and gestur'd at a livid patch in the middle. 'You see – that's as far as the Royal juices went...and it's as far as they'll ever go. I think it's time I reject'd His Royal Highness' advances in no uncertain terms...'

*

The second event that fundamentally changed my relationship with Boris was my visit to a certain Central African country. You may recall that when I'd seen him at his London penthouse, he'd offered to put me in touch with an extremely wealthy business associate, his partner in an African tungsten mine. (I suspect this was partly compensation for then threatening to 'off' my family, a nicely God-like gesture: He giveth and He taketh away.)

Well, he did put me in touch, and no sooner had he done so than it was arranged for me to go there and meet with this prospective client. I protested/suggested that this was not really necessary. If the client – I still didn't know his name – needed a face-to-face meeting, we could easily do it via a secure video link. This was the usual approach, I told the intermediary – a youngish, posh-sounding Englishman, called Willliam Penfold (solid name + solid accent = hollow words, in my experience) – with whom I had an email exchange and then a brief phone call. But he had other ideas. He insisted that I 'forego the usual approach on this occasion' and that a meeting in the flesh was more appropriate.

'And why is that?' I asked. He didn't answer directly. He just said he was sure I'd find the visit very rewarding on several levels. 'To be candid, Theo – if I may call you Theo – it might be a bit outside your comfort zone, but I can guarantee it will be great fun...'

Given all this covert behaviour in foreign parts, it sounded like it would also be straight out of John Le Carre – or was that Graham Greene? And anyway, who was 'Penfold' to make assumptions about my comfort zone? Did he think that all I did all day was sit in front of a laptop, moving money around? Yes, said the Moneyman, and he's right. But what the hell, what does it matter? As long as it's *financially* rewarding, we should go.

And 'we' did, and it certainly began well. I was picked up by an extremely luxurious limo, plus escort – a beautiful, designer-clad African lady, who introduced herself as Sanyo and was so poised and elegant that my own status felt instantly elevated by association. I was ambassadorial, presidential even. As the only passenger, I was whisked seamlessly through customs – no passport check required – and onto a waiting Air Force One-style jet that was primed for take-off and all but revving its engines. I think it qualified as the peak transport experience of my career. Very VVIP.

My elegant companion, together with a handsome male steward, spoilt me rotten during the flight, plying me with fine food, champagne and movies. (The latter were actually less fine.) Try as I might to get information from her on my prospective client, she was determined to be as discreet as she was poised. All she would say was that I'd be meeting with Mr. Penfold at the Ministry – 'The Ministry?' 'The Ministry of the Interior' – followed by a meeting outside the capital. She insisted it was all she knew, which meant it was all she was prepared to tell me. 'More of the vintage Krug, Mr. Law?' If she'd said 'Mr.Bond', it wouldn't have seemed out of place.

When we landed, there was, of course, another luxurious limo waiting for us on the tarmac – same colour and model of Merc as the previous one – along with a truckload of soldiers, our armed escort. Only the lack of a military band stopped it from being the full, foreign dignitary treatment.

Sirens wailing, we sped off along a palm-lined, six-lane highway that took us straight into the city centre, past a lake so vast it might have been the ocean had the country not been land-locked. If you averted your eyes from the corrugated slums that lurked behind the huge hoardings for smart phones and bank loans, there were just enough shiny glass towers around the spruced up colonial buildings to convince you that this was a thriving, modern metropolis.

It was only my second time in sub-Saharan Africa. (My first had been at a 5-star safari park in South Africa, so I'm not sure it counts.) So far, I'd gone from air-conditioned plane to air-conditioned car and was about to enter an air-conditioned building. But in between, even though it was late afternoon, I was acutely aware of the searing tropical heat and that distinctive, not unpleasant African aroma - a kind of steamy, musky earthiness that's always present, no matter how man-made the environment. It certainly pervaded the whitewashed halls of the Ministry building, where I was taken for my 'orientation' meeting with Penfold.

'Orientation? Are we heading off into the jungle?' I asked Sanyo.

'Anything is possible, Mr. Law.' (I *knew* she knew more than she'd let on.)

We entered a small anteroom and then a much larger, more palatial one whose teak furniture and whirring ceiling fan hailed from another era. *Very* Graham Greene, I thought.

Which could not be said of Penfold when he arrived a few minutes later. In contrast to the rumpled, broken down characters of Greene's stories, he was streamlined and sleekly contemporary. A suit of creamy linen, somehow creased in all the right places and snugly tailored around an athletic build; a shirt of impeccable sky blue; a red and gold striped tie in a bold Windsor knot; a sharp haircut and horn-rimmed specs that were fashionably retro. He was a mixture of CIA, SAS, MCC and Harry Potter. I was impressed, but couldn't help wondering what the fuck he was doing there. I would find out soon enough.

Sanyo wordlessly withdrew. Penfold and I exchanged pleasantries – 'Trust you were well looked after on the journey down…Vintage bubbly to your liking? It's a favourite here…' etc. etc. But he was not the sort of chap to waste too much time on small talk and we went swiftly onto 'matters more germane'.

'Our Russian friend, Mr. Aronovksy, can't recommend you highly enough, Theo – which for a man who's very rude about, and *to,* most people is praise indeed.'

'Thank you, Willliam.' Will we ever be on 'Will' terms? I wondered. (He was certainly no 'Bill'.)

'I'm told that among your many attributes is your total discretion.'

It's funny how this particular compliment never fails to come across as a thinly veiled threat. 'It is'

'Good. Well' — he spread his arms in priestly fashion – 'let me start by giving you some idea of *my* role in all this. The gentleman you'll be meeting – Charles Okello – is Minister of the Interior. He's the President's righthand man, his enforcer, if you like, which means he more or less runs everything here – including, if I'm honest, the President. It is Mr. Okello who has need of your services, but I'll let him tell you all about that. I am his chief advisor, mainly on matters to do with security – which are pressing, given the rebel force that controls the north of the country and various other insurgents, jihadists, refugees and raiders who make regular incursions across the border. And that's before we get to the Chinese, who want to buy up anything and everything. It keeps me extremely busy.'

'I'm sure it does. I take it you don't represent the British government?'

'No, not guilty. I'm well-connected, of course – to the Brits and the Americans' – a wry smile – '*and* the Russians, but I represent no government.'

So who *did* he represent was the next logical question, but he anticipated that. 'I represent certain *commercial* interests, shall we say.'

'Excluding the Chinese.'

'Yes.'

'And *in*cluding Boris.'

'*In*cluding Mr. Aronovsky, yes, and others investing in the long-term future of this country. You'll appreciate that it's difficult to conduct business of any scale in an atmosphere of unrest.'

If I knew Boris, 'investing in the long-term future of this country' meant some form of rape and pillage, probably of its natural resources, for starters. However, I was very much being treated as 'one-of–us' – and, of course, at that point I was – so it was politic not to say as much.

'So you help maintain a business-friendly environment.'

'Precisely, Theo, that's an excellent way of putting it.' While bestowing a patronizing smile on me, he also contrived to look quite proud of himself, as if the violent suppression of a large part of the population was an act of heroism.

'Anyway, to continue with the arrangements for your visit – the immediate plan is for us to head out of town tomorrow to Mr. Okolllo's estate further down the lake. We'll go via the chopper, so it should only take an hour or so. Sanyo will collect you from your hotel at around 1400, if that's okay?'

'Of course.'

'A heads-up, by the way. It's worth at this stage mentioning one or two of the Minister's...idiosyncrasies. He can be a bit...irascible at times, a bit up and down. Don't worry – the moods pass very quickly. Once he's had the offender shot, he usually calms down.'

He was most amused to see that I might be taking him seriously. 'Sorry, Theo – my idea of a joke.'

'Right. You mean he *doesn't* usually calm down after he's had the offender shot.'

'*Yes...touché.*' His smile broadened. 'Another thing is that the Minister loves to party, especially in the company of as many white women as he can lay his hands on, so to speak. So don't be too surprised if you trip over the odd tart or two while you're down there. You never know, you might get lucky...'

More amusement on William's part. He dipped his voice, which was naturally rather loud. 'Between ourselves, that's another of my little jobs - keeping him supplied with the wherewithal to party, though I tend to delegate it.'

I couldn't help thinking that Mr. Aronovsky was probably a handy contact for that particular wherewithal. This was obviously the 'fun' bit of my visit that Penfold had mentioned on the phone.

'I see. So as well as being his security advisor, William, you double as his pimp and dealer.'

'You could say that...' He managed another chuckle, but this time it sounded more hollow.

*

If I found it difficult to express my feelings to Katherine about what had happen'd out at Gourmande, it was because I found it difficult to express them to myself. I was thrown into a state of confusion that left me uncertain as to how I shou'd react.

Part of me was angry that Orleans had forc'd himself upon her. Another part regrett'd that Katherine and I had led him on. Another felt she had gone too far in giving him some kind of 'satisfaction'. (I knew she had done so under great duress, but I cou'd not help wondering if she was secretly attract'd to him and had actually enjoy'd it!) Yet another part – yes, the male pride part that Katherine had so often disparag'd – told me that my honour had been impugn'd and that I shou'd seek my own kind of satisfaction in the form of a duel. On the other hand, I knew only too well that I had made that mistake once before and I had no intention of ever repeating ti.

Then there was a final card staring up at me from the table, an Ace of Spades that might trump all others in the high stakes' game we were playing: for the System to succeed, we still need'd Orleans' support, to which Katherine's relationship with him was critical.

Nor did her reaction help settle my mind. Despite her sang-froid at the time, she admitt'd to me after our guests had depart'd that she had been extremely shock'd by Orleans' behaviour; the way he had gone from charmant to mechant, from cultur'd gentleman to rapacious villain, was offensive in the extreme. Romantic ardour she cou'd bear, but she wou'd not countenance physical violence. She blam'd herself for having agreed to encourage him in his infatuation – it had been a terrible mistake – and she want'd nothing more to do with him, certainly not on any intimate level.

I took her in my arms, but cou'd feel her tense against me, as if I was Orleans. 'I understand, of course...but we need to be careful. You know as well as I do what's at stake...'

'You don't need to remind me, John. I'm all too aware of it and I'll let him down gently, I promise. But it has to stop...you do agree, don't you?'

'Of course, I agree...'

But then, over the next few days, it became apparent that de Conti and Bourbon had bought large numbers of shares between them. This, in turn, initiat'd a whole host of purchases by others, so that by the end of the week the sale of our first issue of shares was complete. Orleans may have behav'd very badly towards Katherine, but he had been as good as his word as far as the Company of the Mississippi was concern'd.

I tried lightening the mood: 'At least, you didn't ruin your dress in vain...'

She was not amus'd, nor was she impress'd by Philippe having interced'd on our behalf. Instead, she told me that she had not bother'd to open a letter he had sent to her out at Gourmande two days earlier.

'Is that letting him down gently?' I ask'd.

'No, it's letting him stew in his own juices for a while...' (I'm not sure she intend'd any pun, but I cou'd never be sure with Katherine.)

I was considering what diplomatic measures I might take in this difficult situation, when I receiv'd a note from Saint-Simon, asking if he might visit me at the Banque Royale – 'in order to discuss a matter of some delicacy regarding His Royal Highness...'

*

William apologised for not being able to join me for dinner at the hotel. 'Best food in town, which isn't saying much. I have a finance meeting that's bound to run on. Not my favourite subject, Theo, I must admit – hey, perhaps you should take it! Just joking...'

I was beginning to realise he was often *just joking*, this security advisor who displayed signs of deep insecurity along with insufferable smugness. I couldn't help thinking that it was largely the result of an English public school education. Never had I been more grateful that part of my own education had taken place in America – or was that insufferably smug of *me*?

'But you get an even better option,' he went on. 'I insist on Sanyo keeping you company instead. Not a bad substitute, eh? I did say *sub*stitute, by the way...

Please, William, *enough* with the 'jokes', I should have said. Instead, I protested that I really didn't need any company and anyway I had some work to do.

But he wasn't hearing of it. Sanyo was duly summoned and instructed to take me to dinner, a task she accepted with what I already recognised as her trademark graciousness. When I said, 'Seriously, I'm sure you've got better things to do. It's really not necessary', she was also deaf to my entreaties, which was fine. After all, who in their right mind would have passed up the chance to have dinner with Sanyo?

'Have a good evening,' Penfold said, as I left. 'Oh, and if you're tempted to go for a wander, stay close to the hotel. In fact, delete that – stay *in* the hotel. Or call me and I'll send a bodyguard to look after you...'

The hotel was a silver monolith amid tropical landscaping, replete with tennis courts and a large pool, fed by waterfalls - a jungle paradise kind of thing. All of it was deserted, hardly surprising given that the early evening was still heavy with heat and humidity. Within the cool interior, there seemed to be more staff than guests, the former behaving like actors who hadn't quite learned their script. Indeed, I got the impression that the whole place was one big stage set, a pop-up just for visiting VVIPs that otherwise disappeared into the bush like some Central African Brigadoon.

This certainly seemed to be the case when Sanyo and I met in the restaurant. Apart from two portly gentlemen in traditional African dress – who looked like they'd been specially positioned in the background to add a touch of authenticity – we appeared to be the only diners.

'Quiet tonight,' I said, as we sat down and at least four waiters instantly buzzed around us.

'It's never thronging, Mr. Law.'

'Please…Theo will do…'

'*Theo.*' She looked around and smiled. 'Except with waiters. As you see, the good thing is we get a lot of attention. And what will you have to drink?'

I'd had enough Krug for one day, so we opted for one of the finest French reds on the surprisingly long list. She guided me through the menu: the International offerings were mediocre, the local dishes were better, but best of all was the Chinese. The chef was from Szechuan and if I liked spicy food, his 'specials' were to die for. So that was quickly settled.

Even just days before, I would never have expected to be sitting in a luxury hotel in the middle of Africa, drinking one of the best wines and eating the best Chinese food I'd ever tasted, all in the company of a charming, intelligent, ebony beauty. Nor could I ever have anticipated the turn our conversation would take.

Sanyo quickly dropped the mask of polite formality, which surprised me, and we were soon exchanging bon mots and biographical details. I told her about my Anglo-American background, my failed marriage – why did I mention that except, sadly, to signal that I was available? – and gave her a sanitised version of my life in finance. She told me she was the daughter of a local politician, now deceased; that she'd been educated at an English-style boarding school in the capital and then done degrees in London and New York, both of which stints had been a real eye-opener and had a profound effect on her. And yet, strangely enough, as extraordinary as that experience was, it had only made her want to return to her native country.

'Why's that?' I asked.

'To try to improve things for the ordinary people here, Theo, to work in their interest – as my father did.'

'Is that why you're working for William Penfold?'

'Would it surprise you if I said yes?'

'Frankly, it would.'

'Why?'

I gave a nervous laugh. I wasn't quite sure how far, as 'one-of-us', I should be going with this. 'Because...well...and you probably don't need me to tell you...Mr. Penfold only appears to be serving the interests of a very small group of people here – and they're certainly not *ordinary*.'

She threw her head back and laughed a beautiful, half-mocking laugh. 'Then why are *you* working for him?'

'Strictly speaking, I'm not. I might do some work for his boss, Charles Okello.'

'Which is the same thing – why have anything to do with either of them?'

'Because it's what I do, it's my job.'

'And that is?'

I had been disarmed by her charm; now I was being skewered by some colder, more clinical side of her nature. And I had no clue as yet where she was going with it, or whose interests *she* was serving.

'Well...I'm what's called a wealth manager. I look after very rich people's money.'

'And make yourself very rich in the process.'

'Yes, to some degree...but...it's more complicated than that.'

'Is it?' She raised an eyebrow, a teacher patiently waiting for her pupil to come up with an answer, preferably the right one.

'Yes. Look, how can I put it? As well off as I am, and I'm very well off, I'm not the same sort of creature as my super-rich clients. Yes, I'm reasonably comfortable around them. I get on with them when I have to. But I don't take on their values or share their world view.'

Part of me was obviously desperate to impress this woman with my own superior values, but she all but scoffed at the attempt. 'And how does *that* work, Theo? How are you not taken over by their world view?'

'Well' – I had to think about it – 'let me give you a small but significant example.' And I began to recount an experience with one of my Russians, who like Okello had insisted on a face-to-face meeting: "Say, if I was out with one of those clients of mine, and he – it's usually a he – is rude to someone, like a waiter in a restaurant, for instance, as these sorts of people often are. I'll sympathise with his petty grievance, share a joke about it. But I'll also make sure I discreetly apologise to that waiter afterwards and give her – it's usually her – a very big tip. Do you see?'

'I do. You're saying you're a nice guy at heart, no matter how nasty your clients are.'

'Sort of...yes...I mean...I'm simply doing a job...I'm a dedicated professional offering a niche financial service...' *Dedicated professional? Niche financial service?* What was that shit? I was wriggling away like a worm on a hook, while still not sure where she was coming from. Maybe I'd got it all wrong and she'd been tasked with finding out if I really was 'one-of-us'. Maybe I'd blown it and I'd be sent home the next day.

She looked around, waited till all the waiters were out of earshot. 'You asked me how I can work for William Penfold *and* serve the interests of ordinary people. Well, this is how – and I'm exposing myself to all sorts of risk here, Theo, I'm appealing to the *nice guy* in you, the guy who apologises to the waiter. I'm an impostor, a spy. I use my position to oppose what Okello and his cronies are doing to this country with every means at my disposal. When you go down to his estate tomorrow, I'm sure you'll get some idea of what I mean, of the kind of crimes that are being committed, the kind of exploitation that's taking place here. I think you'll be appalled by it and I think you'll want to help me.'

I finished my wine. 'Well, I'm flattered you feel you can take such a risk with me. But what if I decide I can't or don't want to help you, Sanyo, for whatever reason?'

'Then I hope I can trust you to say nothing about this - and simply get on with being a *dedicated professional.*' The last couple of words were said with more than a hint of sarcasm.

*

I always look'd forward to seeing Saint-Simon, no matter what the occasion. I was entirely comfortable in his gentle presence and as much myself as I was with anyone in Paris, including Katherine by that time.

As soon as he arriv'd, I gave him a tour of the new Banque Royale offices and banking hall, with its grand marble columns and dom'd ceiling.

'It is conceiv'd as a temple,' I said, with a flourish of hands towards the roof. 'I intend to commission the painting of a tableau of epic proportions. It will depict the triumph of Trade and Commerce, with His young Majesty, at its centre, surround'd by the spirits of Credit and Enterprise and so forth. I have in mind the Venetian artist Pellegrini, who is more us'd to adorning cathedrals than banks. What do you think, Louis?' ('Vous' had become 'tu'; we were now on first name terms.)

'I think that mere money has never risen to such celestial heights,' he smil'd wryly.

We retir'd to my newly appoint'd office. The walls were hung with several fine Flemish landscapes and interiors, one of which wou'd soon be replac'd by my own recently commission'd portrait; a huge mahogany desk and several throne-like leather chairs stood astride the swirling meditations of a Persian carpet; above them gleam'd the largest crystal chandelier the room cou'd bear. Secretly, it was not just a temple I was evoking – I want'd it to feel like the inner sanctum of a Royal court.

Saint-Simon seem'd genuinely interest'd in the fortunes of the System, even if I knew public finance was hardly his favourite subject. I told him that we had sold our first issue of shares and that we were planning to make a second. I ask'd if I cou'd set aside five hundred of the new issue as a gift for him, but he respectfully declin'd. Just as he avoid'd gaming, he said, so it wou'd be unwise for him to involve himself in another kind of financial speculation – it wou'd bring, he was sure, bad luck to the whole enterprise.

'I prefer to save all my good fortune for love, John – which brings me on to the reason for my visit...'

'An affair of the heart.'

'Indeed – Philippe's heart...' He shook his head and sigh'd. 'Between ourselves, I sometimes wish that he didn't confide in me. The ins and outs, so to speak, of his relationship with Parabère both embarrass'd and exhaust'd me and that's only one more recent example. I think he relishes my discomfort more than my opinion – although in the long run he usually admits I'm right.'

He look'd as if he was suffering a little discomfort even as he spoke. 'His latest liaison, however, is far more complicat'd and challenging...as you know, John...'

'What has he told you?'

'I'll set it out as plainly as I can. That he is in love with Madame Law – the Sun Queen, as he calls her – and wishes to be permanently in her company. That she, to some degree, reciprocates those feelings. That he has sought your approval in wooing her – again, his words – and that you have agreed to this on certain conditions. He didn't tell me what they were. That his passionate nature got the better of him when he was visiting you at Gourmande and that he foolishly tried to force himself physically upon Madame Law...'

He shook his head again. 'He thinks he has ruin'd any chance he might have of securing her affection. Finally, he wishes me to approach you and ask you to speak to Madame Law – to apologise on his behalf and restore him to her favour. He says he has written to her repeatedly expressing as much himself but she has not replied to him.

'So here I am, John, doing my friend's bidding. Please tell me if any of this is true – and I must add that it wou'd be a great relief to me if it was a complete fantasy on his part...'

I decid'd I need'd cognac and offer'd some to Louis. He did not normally partake during the day, he said, but on this occasion he wou'd make an exception.

I pour'd each of us a large measure. 'Cognac aside,' I said, 'I'm afraid I can't offer you much relief, Louis. Apart from my questioning to what exact degree Katherine does return his affection, everything is as he told you.'

He took a moment to digest this. 'As I'm sure you're aware, Philippe is a man of great appetite, carnal and otherwise, so while I'm disappoint'd by his behaviour in that regard I'm not altogether surpis'd by it. What I find harder to understand, John, is that you agreed to his seeking to…<u>woo</u> Madame Law in the first place. That does surprise me, very much so. You and she have seem'd to be so close, so much in love with each other…'

I down'd the cognac in one and pour'd some more. Confiding in Louis might help me clarify my own feelings on these matters, I decid'd. And anyway, who else cou'd I talk to? Who else cou'd I trust? 'If I can speak in absolute confidence, Louis – this must not go back to Philippe…'

He wav'd my concern away. 'You have my word, John…'

'The situation is complicat'd, to say the least. To be honest, I've come to the conclusion that despite appearances to the contrary, Katherine and I are now more business partners than we are lovers.'

'I'm sorry to hear that.'

'Don't be, Louis. It seems to have happen'd quite naturally – we have grown apart somewhat. But we are still close and what we still share, more than anything else – apart from our daughter – is a deep commitment to the success of the Banque Royale and the financial system we've establish'd here in Paris. To realise this dream, we've need'd – and may well continue to need – Philippe's support. There is no other way to make it work. We have many enemies in Paris and his sponsorship is vital…'

'Yes, I'm aware of how important he is to the whole enterprise.'

'Indeed…so, when he express'd an interest in Katherine, she and I decid'd – and I emphasise that it was a joint decision,

Louis – that she wou'd encourage him in his affections and thus in his support for the Mississippi Company.' I sipp'd some more cognac. 'It seem'd manageable at the time, but I'm afraid his desire for her has proven a little too...'

'Urgent?'

'Urgent, yes - the mot juste,' I smil'd. 'She was appall'd by his behaviour and will have nothing more to do with him...'

Now it was Louis' turn to down the cognac. 'As you say, a complicat'd situation, John.'

'Far too complicat'd for me. What do I do?'

'You have no choice. You have to respect Madame Law's wishes. You must tell Philippe that you have to withdraw from your...arrangement. He is feeling contrite. He knows he has gone too far. He will not like it, but he will understand.'

'But we risk losing his support.'

'That's a risk worth taking, isn't it, John? Surely the virtue of your System speaks for itself. Philippe keeps proudly declaiming how much he and the country is benefitting from it – and he thinks I'm a fool not to invest it myself. I am happy to remind him of this when I go back to him with your answer.'

'You will speak to him?'

'That's why I'm here – to be the go-between.'

'Thank you, Louis.'

'But I wou'd offer you one piece of advice, as I have Philippe.'

'What is that?'

'Affairs of state and affairs of the heart do not mix – and where they do it will always end in tears...always...'

*

If I'd been closer to home, in my more natural habitat, Sanyo's revelations would've turned the world on its head. I may have been on the anti-depressants by then, but the paranoia would still have run amok. I'd have felt like the victim of some kind of Boris-led conspiracy that had set me up to fail. Or worse – to *die*.

But there in my pretend luxury hotel it was different. I was in a John Le Carre novel. (Or was it Graham Greene, or Ian

Fleming, even?) Nothing was real, so anything was possible. Anything that gave the plot an unforeseen twist or heightened the tension was fine by me, since it wasn't really happening anyway. Which is probably why, instead of lying awake in an air-conditioned sweat, I slept very well. Having looked at a spread sheet and answered some emails, I slipped easily from what had been a bizarre waking dream to the more traditional, sleeping one, in which nice things happened: I lay upon soft grass; a woman cradled me in her arms, whispered sweet nothings and stroked my cock – some consolation for a lack of regular sex. Not even the thought of what horrors might await me at Okello's pleasure palace kept me awake for more than a few minutes. I was, after all, just a good old, dedicated professional, there to ply his trade and enjoy the sleep of the just. Or, in my case, the sleep of the just having made another couple of million US that day and hardly having opened a laptop.

And while I sat in the palatial breakfast room the next morning, alone again but for the waiting staff, the calmness and complacency continued. I opted for the Szechuan breakfast special – why change a winning formula? – and sat pondering the huge water feature that was gushing out of the wall. It cascaded over rocks, ran in a torrent through the middle of the room and disappeared into the floor, before re-emerging to feed the pool just beyond the terrace. Along with the delicious dim sum and hot sauce, it was a grand start to the day.

But what to do with the morning? Go for a swim in the jungle pool, check out the spa and return to the laptop? *Yes,* would have been the sensible answer. But it was the feeling of infallibility and unreality, combined with Penfold's warning not to stray from the hotel without someone *to look after me,* that decided me otherwise. I would not be patronised. I would show *him* who was comfortable outside of his comfort zone. I would do something revolutionary in its simplicity – I would go for a walk.

I dressed down for the occasion, left the Rolex, phone – I could hardly bear the separation - and wallet in my room, and stuffed some US dollars in my pocket. The tiny concierge, wearing a hotel uniform that was at least two sizes too big for him, looked a little surprised when I said, no, I wasn't being picked up and, no, I didn't need a taxi – I was going for a walk. I asked him if he had a map of the area, which, after much rummaging in his desk, he eventually produced. He pointed out the immediate vicinity around the hotel – 'Good for walking here, sah.' Then a bit farther afield, where he indicated there was a large market 'But be careful of your wallet here, sah.'

'Thank you.'

'Welcome, sah.' It was my first conversation with a local – although I suppose Sanyo qualified in that respect.

As I was leaving, he said, 'Wait, please, sah.' He shot off and returned minutes later with a bottle of water and a panama hat. 'Please, sah...'

I tried on the hat; it fitted perfectly. 'Thank you. That's very kind.' I offered him a few dollars, but he waved them away.

'Welcome, sah.'

Outside, I was hit by a blistering sun and a vicious wave of humidity. This was not going to be a stroll in the park, no matter how slowly I strolled. It probably explained why there were only a few pedestrians on the streets – the men in ties and shirtsleeves, the women in tight black skirts and high heels. The immediate area was smart enough, a modern commercial district of nondescript office blocks and shops featuring expensive brands that could have been anywhere. But it quickly tapered off into something less smart, with a lot more local flavor and texture. The sidewalks began to break up; the buildings crumbled away like broken biscuits. The dapper dresscode of the business district gave way to a general shabbiness among the men, but dazzling, traditional dresses for many of the women, some with baskets on their heads and babies on their backs. Swathed head to foot in brightly coloured fabrics, they looked like giant butterflies and treated me to smiles as big as their derrieres. This alone made my trudge through the heat more than worth it.

Indeed, with the air-conned sanctuary of the hotel a mere memory, I was actually beginning to adjust to the conditions. And my spirits were further lifted as I rounded a corner where road and sidewalk merged into a dusty track and I stood overlooking the vast outdoor market. Encircled by crude concrete buildings of no more than two stories, hundreds of plastic and umbrella covered stalls lined the shallow valley floor, spread out like some giant picnic blanket.

Having had my glimpse of the real world, I suppose I should have stopped there and gone back to the hotel. But even though I was already being hassled by a crowd of half-naked hawkers in filthy shorts, keen to sell me CDs and cigarette lighters, the buzz and energy of the market itself drew me on. It was irresistible. I politely declined all offers and headed towards the maze of stalls, followed by my new fans.

This was that special kind of market, the kind where there was nothing you would ever want to buy. Instead, you could just consume the experience of the world's largest and scrappiest boot sale. There was junk everywhere, most of it stuff the rich world had no doubt dumped here and most of it in bits – radios, tvs, stereos, steam irons, iron pots and pans, circuit boards, computers, phones, car engines, mopeds, motorbikes, bicycles, used shoes – many of them odd – clothing – from rags (literally) to three-piece pin-striped suits, Savile Row style. This was all mixed in with food stalls, piled high with technicolor fruit and dusty vegetables I didn't recognise, plus the charred remains of small scrawny creatures on improvised barbecue grills. Add to this the garbage – mountains of it, mainly plastic bottles, bags and other packaging – and the overwhelming impression was of a colourful but abject squalor as far as you could see.

And then there was the noise. I can't forget the noise. Everyone shouting. Those who weren't shouting at me, waving their arms and trying to attract my attention, were shouting at each other. It was a deafening babble that quickly morphed into more of a commotion, as if a vast flock of pigeons was taking off. Farther into the market I could see people moving their stalls and wares in a single great wave, as if tightly choreographed. In short order, the commotion was superseded by the sound of a shrill whistle or siren and the unmistakable clatter of what I realised was an approaching train. It suddenly dawned on me that there was a railway track running right through the centre of the market. For a good few minutes the train whistled and rumbled its way through the throng, while everyone stood to one side or the other. No sooner had it passed through than all the pitches were promptly moved back into place and the deafening babble resumed as if nothing remarkable had happened – certainly nothing more remarkable than my presence at the market.

I was still marvelling at it all when a young man, tidier looking than any other there, strode purposefully towards me. I remember thinking: what are *you* trying to sell me? But the thought had hardly been had before I saw the blade in his hand and realised he was about more than hawking tat. He meant me some serious harm.

There was further commotion, as four or more soldiers came from nowhere, bursting through the crowd, strong-arming my would-be assailant and dragging him away. Another grabbed me, a little more delicately, and escorted me briskly towards a very large, black Jeep, its dark windows flashing in the sun. The door glided open. Penfold sat in the back. He didn't look in the mood for joking.

'Good morning, Theo. What did I say about *not* going out alone?'

Chapter 10

Penfold was not pleased with me. As if to a four-year-old, he explained that the attack had not been random – 'Do you understand?' It wasn't someone trying to mug me but kill me – 'Do you understand?' They knew who I was, why I was in the country and they wanted to stop me from meeting Okello. If they can't hurt him physically, they'll hurt him financially – 'Do you understand?'

'I think I've got the idea, William. And who are *they*?'

'Prime suspects are the rebels, but there are several possibilities. He has enemies closer to home – who obviously know about you...'

Sanyo, I thought, but *she* wouldn't have sent someone to take me out – would she?

'We'll know better after your attacker has been questioned.'

I winced inwardly at what that might mean.

'Now, *please*, Theo, stay in the hotel until we come and get you. That's not a request, it's an order. I'm posting a guard outside your door – do you understand?'

On the one hand, I was flattered by all the fuss and the fact that it added yet another 'V' to my already VVIP status. On the other, it was deeply depressing. Enough with the plot twists - with John le Carre, Graham Greene or whoever. If I'd had the choice, I'd have headed back to London immediately rather than board the chopper to the pleasure palace. But I didn't have the choice, at least not without the risk of suffering acute embarrassment and, worse still, incurring Boris' wrath.

The flight down to Okello's place took under an hour. We followed the shore of the lake, passing over several small towns and villages but little by way of what you'd call modern infrastructure – highways, railways, industrial areas and so forth. Meanwhile, over the cans that cancelled out the thumping din of the engine, Penfold provided detailed commentary on the region's various 'security issues'. If I hadn't realised it before, I knew by then that this was a country on a major war footing.

The rest of the terrain passing beneath us was a scrubby variety of bush that became thick jungle towards the end of the flight. The estate itself appeared to be carved out of it: a huge landscaped area, within a high perimeter fence, complete with watchtowers and several large armoured vehicles that included a rocket launcher. Charles obviously wasn't taking any chances.

We dropped down and followed an avenue of lofty palms until the main house came into view. 'Quite something, eh?' said Penfold, as if it was his very own.

I nodded, although whether it was quite something good or bad, I wasn't sure. It was certainly massive and massively white, a combination of domed Mogul palace and Deep South plantation house – *Gone with the Wind* meets *The Raj Quartet* and settles down in Las Vegas. There were also several large outbuildings, a huge satellite dish, more of those deserted clay courts, a swimming pool of the bluest hue – with someone actually swimming in it – and, a little way off, a couple of helipads, one of which was occupied when we landed. If all else failed, Charles had his own chopper waiting to airlift him to safety.

I think it's fair to say that by then I'd more or less made up my mind that I wouldn't be doing business with Mr. Okello – whether or not what Sanyo had told me turned out to be true. While I could convince myself that dealing with Russian oligarchs in country mansions and London penthouses was a relatively civilised business, furthering the interests of someone who was well on his way to becoming a military dictator was not something for which I had an appetite. All that was left to decide was the delicate issue of how I could extricate myself from the situation without causing offence and avoid being seduced by the enormous financial incentives that would inevitably be on offer.

In fact, when I actually met Okello, my resolve, such as it was, almost faltered. I was expecting a monster, a mobster, a warlord, and what I got was more the male equivalent of Sanyo. He was younger than I expected, better looking, better dressed – posh English threads in the Penfold vein, not the military fatigues I'd envisaged – and very charming, very much the genial host. At that point, there was none of the fabled volatility; the surface of his personality was calm, serene even. It was a clear case of the devil getting the best tunes and he almost had me dancing to them – or at least to the musical cadence of his voice. 'Trust in me, trust in me...' sang Kaa the python to Mowgli in *The Jungle Book*. I felt as spellbound.

The interior of the house certainly combined scale with opulence – Louis-Quinze-goes-on-Safari is my best shot at describing it, with the mounted heads of much big game in evidence. Yet it too seemed relatively blameless. Plenty of smartly dressed young men went about their business – soldiers in civvies, I decided – but there was no sign of the white, mischievous women or orgiastic excess. I was mildly disappointed. But then it was still very early in the evening when I was summoned to one of the large reception rooms to meet my host.

Penfold made the introduction and left us to it. Okello looked me straight in the eye and gave my hand an honest shake. As it was almost that hour, he offered me a sundowner, but I declined. If he didn't mind, I said, sparkling water would do until we'd talked business.

'But please, don't let me stop you.'

'Oh, you won't,' he replied, lighting up the room with his smile and getting one of his young men to pour him a large scotch. Having told me I should call him Charles – he was definitely no Charlie – he got straight down to business.

'First of all, I must thank you for making the journey, Theo. It's a long way from London in *every* sense. However, this is business of such *magnitude*' – he pronounced the word in a magnitudinous way – 'that I thought it *absolutely essential* that we meet in person. I can only assure you, as I am certain Mr. Penfold already has, that it will be very worth your while financially – as I am trusting it will be mine...'

I meant to say, in that terribly polite British manner that masks many a slight: 'Well, actually, Charles, before we go any further, I must apologise for putting you to so much trouble, but I really don't think this is my glass of Pimms...' The words would not come, however. They were already being stifled at birth by the sheer weight of his charisma.

'I need one or two things done and my good friend Boris Aaronovsky says you're the only man for the job. There is no one else in all the whole wide world, he says, who can work this kind of magic like your good self.' (At least he didn't go on about the need for discretion etc. – but then when you've got a rocket launcher in your backyard, you don't have to.)

'Oh, *you know Boris*,' I said, 'everything's larger than life.'

'No, no, I trust his judgement on this – and I also have good instincts myself. I know instantly whether I can work with someone, and I already know I can work with you, Theo.'

'Thank you, Charles.' The question is can I work with *you*? I thought, but the fact that I was even asking meant it was still a possibility.

'So…the first thing I need is to begin moving substantial sums of money offshore – or at least *further* offshore. Much of it is currently in Mauritius, where I have some good connections.' He looked exceedingly pleased with himself in having achieved that much, but he must have known it was the relatively easy bit.

'How substantial?'

'I would say in the region of *two billion US dollars*.' He was obviously expecting some eye popping and jaw dropping on my part and at least I gave him the satisfaction of a small nod of acknowledgement. After all, it was an impressive sum to put in your back pocket, even if all those 'security issues' meant that people had noticed the bulge. 'And that is just for starters, my friend…'

'And may I ask why you want to move it now?'

'You may, Theo, but it is *absolutely between ourselves*. I have decided to spend more time abroad…in Europe and the United States. I need to build a life for myself outside of this country, while still maintaining a presence here – so as to safeguard my interests, you understand.'

I understood that he wanted to go on plundering it for as long as he could. 'And the other thing?'

'The other thing?'

'The other thing you need me to do.'

'Ah yes, it is perhaps more challenging, the other thing. As a country, as a *government,* we need to raise a substantial amount of money. Call it an investment – through a bond, perhaps. If we go to the usual Western sources – or even, say, to the Chinese – it will come with all sorts of *unwelcome* strings attached.'

'Roughly how much?'

'I estimate around a billion US.'

'And for what purpose?'

'Let us call it…a transport system.'

'But what is it really for?'

'Does anyone *really* need to know, Theo?'

'I do – it will help me make those strings more welcome.'

'Ha! I like your style, my friend. If you must know, it is for arms – and the men to use them.' His expression grew more serious. 'In terms of weapons, you can easily spend a billion dollars and get very little for your money. However, if we do business with the right people, we will get what we need to crush these rebels and the other sources of opposition before they ruin all the good work we are doing here. And we will also be able to guarantee handsome returns to our investors.'

I wanted to ask about those other sources of opposition and what good work he was referring to, but I thought it better to stick to the business in hand. So we talked more about the assets in Mauritius, what kind of terms his government could offer through a bond and the timescale he had in mind for both projects. 'Yesterday,' he laughed.

I told him what I told most of my clients as this stage: if I was to proceed swiftly, I would need full access to the relevant data and the total co-operation of his finance people – both his personal and the government teams. Full disclosure from trusted sources was essential.

He assured me I would have it. 'I will put them in touch with you immediately. They will do everything they can to support you.'

'Thank you.'

'And let me do something else. Let me take you up to the mine tomorrow. We can fly over it before you head back to London.' He smiled. 'Just to show you that it really exists.'

I thought this was more about showing off than any other kind of showing, but what the hell, it'd be good to actually see the scene of the crime. I smiled back. 'Reassuring to know there's nothing fraudulent involved.'

'Ha! *Of course* – we are all honest fellows here! I look forward to a long and prosperous relationship, Theo. I am very excited by the prospect. *Very* excited, *my friend*. I trust you implicitly...' There was a pause, while the old paranoia kicked in again and in my head I heard: 'Do *not* betray that trust.'

'*Now* - will you have that drink?'

'I will, yes.'

'Some of this fine scotch whisky? Or I have a good bourbon for the American in you.'

'I'd prefer a gin and tonic – for the Englishman in me.'

'Ha! Of course!' He summoned a boy. 'What do you think of this little bolt-hole of mine?'

'I think it's...quite something...'

*

Venice, December 1728

Dottore Allegri, my physician, can sometimes look so close to death's door himself that it hardly inspires confidence in his ability to cure his patients. On the other hand, perhaps it uniquely qualifies him to minister to those who share his hopeless situation.

For I am having severe trouble with my breathing again this morning and after examining me and spending some time with his ear press'd against my chest – when I think at one point he nodd'd off – he announces that I must leave the infernal dampness of Venice immediately. As with many Italians his hands are his most expressive feature. He manages to wave them with more vigour than he moves any other part of himself, except perhaps his shoulders, which he shrugs in time with his gesticulations. He advises me to decamp to the South. Or preferably North Africa – if I can abide the deplorable moor, he says – but somewhere as warm and dry as possible. And as quickly as possible.

'Maestro, it is that or laudanum.'

'Then it must be laudanum,' I say, after a hearty coughing fit.

As cold, damp and downright miserable as this winter in Venice has become, I cannot find the physical strength to leave, and anyway, I feel sure that the benefit of going wou'd be more than cancell'd out by the effort of getting there. Strangely enough, later that day, the weather turns clear and mild, the canals dance with sunlight, and it is as if we are suddenly in the gentle embrace of an early spring. (Alas, it lasts only a day before the slate grey skies return.)

Following the Dottore's cheerful diagnosis, I receive a visitor, although at first I am reluctant to have him interrupt my writing. I am at the Ridotto in the morning, when the conte de Bellini hands me the calling card. (Bellini continues to make much of me, even though I am playing less and less at the tables just now. He has taken to bringing mask'd players to the door of the piano nobile and gesturing in my direction: 'And there he sits — the famous John Law, once the richest man in the world and certainly its most successful gambler...' It is the equivalent of Katherine's freak show experience among Parisian society and I wou'd not be surpris'd if the Conte is charging them for the pleasure.)

The calling card reads 'Baron Charles Secondat de Montesquieu'. It seems odd that he has come to see me. He and Voltaire were among my most savage critics in Paris, although they possess the redeeming feature of also being the cleverest. For even if one does not share another's views, one can take pleasure in the intelligence that expresses them, and I have gone as far as to commit some of their finer barbs to memory. When the Company shares had reach'd their highest value and money fever was rife, Voltaire, who was a constant gadfly, wrote:

'Is this reality? Is this a chimera? Has half the nation found the philosopher's stone in the paper mills? Is Law a god, a rogue or a charlatan who is poisoning himself with a drug he is distributing to everyone?'

315

No doubt because of his own aristocratic background, Baron de Montesquieu had to be subtler with his broadsides. He did not publish until just after I left Paris in 1721 – a book entitl'd 'Persian Letters', in which two Turkish gentlemen visit Paris and describe their experiences in a series of letters home. Philippe and I are portray'd as a pair of black magicians who have cast an evil spell over the city. It sinks in an ooze of decadence, given over to nothing but hedonistic excess and the pursuit of paper. I am parodied in great style:

'You think yourselves rich because you have silver and gold. Your delusion is pitiable. Take my advice: leave the land of worthless metal and enter the realms of the imagination, and I promise you such riches as you will be astonish'd.'

Montesquieu is shown into the piano nobile. He is a youngish man in his mid-thirties, modestly dress'd, not the gouty, gilt-edg'd noble I had imagin'd. In perfect English he says he is deeply honour'd to meet me and thanks me for granting him an audience.

I tell him he is right to feel honour'd, for he has enjoy'd much success at my expense.

He laughs. 'If you are referring to 'Persian Letters', I am very much in your debt, Monsieur Law, it is true.' He pronounces it 'Low', as did Dubois and others. 'But I am primarily a philosophical and political essayist, and that's what brings me to Venice. I have been touring Europe, gathering material for a series of essays that explore the possibilities for political reform. I have long been an admirer of the English parliament.' (Hence the good English, I assume.) 'If you will permit me, I would take two hours of your time to discuss these matters. Few people have your experience of government at the highest level.'

'And live to tell the tale,' I add.

'Indeed,' he smiles.

'Then you are not after money or vengeance?' I say. 'You wou'd be the first Frenchman in seven years who wasn't.'

'Not at all.' The smile has turn'd faintly ironic. 'Unless it is painful for you to talk of such things – that might well qualify as vengeance.'

316

He is nothing if not charming, this Montesquieu, but he also has some iron in him, which I like. I set aside my writing and order us some hot chocolate, mine with more than a dash of cognac, the better to speak of French affairs. I warn him that at any moment I may be overtaken by a fit of coughing and apologise in advance; I am far from well.

He is very sorry that I am less robust than when he last saw me, which was in Paris, trading shares on the Rue de Quincampoix.

'Ah, Baron,' I reply, instantly engulfed by nostalgia, 'then when you last saw me, I was at my best...'

We start off gently enough, speaking of the French and British systems of government, although I confess to him that of late, I have had little direct contact with London. 'Of course, it is the English attitude to money that makes the difference,' I say. 'The simple practice of using credit to stimulate trade has had a profound effect on the country – although not even the English cou'd fully comprehend the wonders of my System. The South Sea Company, which arose around the same time in London, was a very poor imitation of the Mississippi. You may remember it.'

'I do,' he says, 'and I also remember it suffer'd a similar fate.'

I smile and shake my head; the System is often dismiss'd as just another financial scandal and my response is always the same. 'Both companies collaps'd, I cannot deny it, but you must understand, my dear Baron, that the South Sea Company was an out-and-out deception, a fraud right from the start. It never had a single ship to its name, never trad'd a single cargo. The Mississippi, on the other hand, was well supplied, own'd its own fleet and was part of a coherent system of what I call economic management, which can and will form the basis of a new rational society. It was undone, not by any inherent flaw in its structure or operation, but by the betrayal of the French government itself...'

As the conversation turns to the System, Montesquieu's manner turns cooler. Suddenly, for all his charm and expressions of sympathy, he seems determin'd to wound me and lets fly a whole salvo of accusations:

'But, of course, your System was inherently flaw'd, Monsieur Law – it spread corruption at every level of French society...In order to enrich yourself, you encourag'd greed instead of reform...The failure of your System has condemn'd France to poverty for generations...It is new philosophies that bring about change in the world, not the pursuit of money...'

I cou'd easily grow angry at these charges, but instead I relish their repudiation. I decide to put Montesquieu's half-bak'd ideas back in the oven, so to speak, and give them a good roasting.

'My dear Baron,' I reply, 'you seem like a man who has spent too much time in the salon and not enough in the street. As Reason has deduc'd and Science will demonstrate, we humans are animals, driven by basic needs – food, shelter, the instinct to procreate; this is the way we all live – yes, even the supine aristocracy, and the men of letters and ideas. Therefore, the great driver of change and progress is that which directly answers those basic needs – the economic and financial system. Everything else – religion, art, philosophy etc. – is so much froth and artifice, a means of disguising the material dominance of a particular class or legitimising its rule, be it a priesthood or a royal family. Certainly, I was guilty of wanting to change the world - as are you - but I knew that the only way to do it was to change it at its most fundamental level. My enrichment was a result of the System I devis'd to do that, it was never its purpose...'

I pause, partly to draw breath, partly to appreciate how liberating it feels to speak a sophisticated form of English and partly to tell myself that I have not once mention'd Katherine's involvement in all of this. (But then it was never common knowledge that she <u>was</u> involv'd in it, certainly not as far as the likes of Montesquieu was concern'd. I bore the brunt of the opprobrium; I will enjoy my brief self-acclaim.) I sip my hot chocolate.

'Money,' I continue, 'paper or metal, is only a means to an end. If distributed widely enough, it acts as a purgative that breaks down and removes the barriers to social progress. By stimulating trade and production, it helps create a society in which people succeed on the basis of merit, not birth or

*position. The greatest number benefit, not the privileg'd few.
Unfortunately, the System did not last long enough to see this
happen. Money became the raison d'être, the end in itself.
Speculation, not productivity increas'd...'*

*The Baron cuts in at this point; he has been lectur'd enough.
'But, Monsieur Low, it was you who encourag'd speculation.
You creat'd the market. You controll'd it – at first. You push'd
up the price of the shares. You let the beast out of its cage and it
destroy'd everything you'd work'd for. The French government
– and your friend the Regent – merely stood by and watch'd
whilst the System collaps'd of its own accord. There was no
lasting reform; nothing really chang'd at all, except that
everyone got poorer and more cynical, which is to say poorer in
spirit. And now we must start the process again – not through
the power of money this time, but through the power of Ideas...'*

*Montesquieu smiles his ironic smile and then the coughing
fit is upon me. I want to say, fool, don't you see, in one sense
Voltaire was right: money is the philosopher's stone, the
substance that transforms base metal into gold and your
precious ideas into action – unless you understand that, the
future will be tyranny and oppression. I want to mount another
defence of the System, of its scope and brilliance, of the
injustice I suffer'd, but I have not got the breath. Instead, as the
taste of blood and bile rises in my mouth, I can only cough and
spit and think these things.*

*It must make an unpleasant spectacle, but he waits until I
recover, extending a comforting hand and placing it on my arm.
When the storm has pass'd, he gets up to leave.*

*'I shou'd go, Monsieur Low. Much as I have enjoy'd our
conversation, I fear it has overexcit'd you and aggravat'd your
condition, as you said it might. Thank you. It alone was worth
my visit to Venice.' The ironic smile is back. 'May I convey your
greetings to any one in Paris?'*

*Still short of breath, I shake my head. Then as he makes to
go, I find some words. 'Please...if you see him, give my
warmest regards to the duc de Saint-Simon...'*

*The Baron nods. 'Saint-Simon and I do not often cross
paths, as you will appreciate. But I will make sure he gets your
message...'*

319

*

The spirit is willing, but the flesh is weak – isn't that how the biblical quote goes? Well, I made my peace with my spineless resolve by telling myself that once back in London I'd find some excuse for not proceeding. Some insurmountable obstacle would prevent me from working my magic for Mr. Okello. Boris would be disappointed, but so be it. Magic I can do, I'd tell him, but miracles are something else. The trouble was I knew the flesh would go on being weak even then, especially if he started threatening the family again. As estranged as I was from them, I'd still have no option but to start washing Okello's grubby money. Meanwhile, just the thought of having an escape route was enough to allow me some brief diversion and to get on with enjoying the evening, if that was possible.

And it turned out there was plenty of diversion on offer. The dining room alone was a diverting spectacle. Charles had obviously read the Boris book of lavish dining experiences, except that instead of Palladian splendour he'd gone for the Disneyland safari lodge, as devised by Vincent Price. Three of the adobe walls were hung with garish tapestries depicting traditional hunting scenes, bloody enough in themselves but punctuated by more stuffed animal heads – among them a gazelle, a rhino, a wildebeest and, incredibly, an elephant, each one scarily lit by flaming sconces. But that was by no means it for the big game: at one end a stuffed giraffe – a smallish one, it's true, but still a giraffe – stood between two lions that were poised to attack; at the other, was a large antelope, between two crouching leopards. The long dining table – made of some rare hard wood, I'm sure – sported massive candelabra, coated in volcanic folds of candle wax and assembled from a combination of elephant tusks and what looked like monkey skulls – at least I *think* they were monkey skulls. The dark stone floor was covered with a mixture of zebra and other animal skins.

I was still taking all this in when Penfold caught my eye and pointed a finger upwards. A flock of stuffed birds, wings spread in full flight, were suspended invisibly from the glass dome above. They were a combination of many-coloured macaws and large black vultures with pink faces. Beneath them, several red-bottomed baboons swung from leafy branches that spanned the base of the dome. Most of the fourth wall consisted of huge folding glass doors. These opened onto a covered terrace that overlooked the pool and was lit by more flaming torches. At its far end was a giant barbecue where boys were grilling what turned out to be a variety of exotic meats. Ostrich, crocodile, wild pig, antelope, zebra, giraffe, wildebeest and lion (*yes, lion*), were all on the menu. That which had been stuffed would now stuff us. There didn't seem to be a vegan option.

The mood was informal. We were joined by a group of African men, whom Penfold described as local dignitaries and several other white men, more consultant types like myself, I assumed. Everyone was dressed down, even Penfold, who wore a short-sleeved shirt with swirling jungle patterns and now looked like a drug dealer (which, of course, we knew he was). Copious drink flowed, mostly fine South African wines. The boys served the meat on skewers as long as lances and used machete-like knives to slice it off in great slabs that landed heavily on the plate. A range of pepper sauces, mild to scorching, and some fried yam did the rounds. 'I'll have a crocodile sandwich and make it snappy,' I told the lad who served me. (I'd always wanted to say it in a restaurant and would never have a better opportunity.) His broad smile was fixed and had nothing to do with my joke – if you can call it that – but he did return with the skewered crocodile, which tasted surprisingly like chicken.

Penfold introduced the white men, who seemed to be a mixture of American and Russian, some of military bearing, others more geeky. We were all getting acquainted, when more 'meat' suddenly appeared, this time alive and strutting. Had these women just been flown in? Or had they been lurking in some remote part of the house, or one of the outside chalets, where I was staying? If so, I hadn't seen them. With their slick make-up, scanty cocktail dresses and killer heels, they looked like they'd come from working some smart casino. It reminded me of that scene in the film *Apocalypse Now*, when the strippers are airlifted into the Vietnamese jungle for a special performance for the troops. The entrance of these ladies wasn't quite as dramatic and their reception not quite as raucous, but I for one was very distracted by their arrival. (That weak flesh again…) They were all beautiful, a mixture of slender, high-cheek-boned Slavs and small-but-perfectly-formed Orientals. Charles took them in hand and sprinkled them liberally around the party. Penfold gave me a look that said: see, Theo, now the fun really begins. Then the coke arrived. The flesh was about to get even weaker.

But to my surprise, I quickly found I wasn't into any of it. One line and I was done. (To be honest, it wasn't the best stuff, anyway.) Perhaps the anti-depressants were having their wicked way with me instead, dampening my usual ardour. The oriental woman I was speaking to was undeniably gorgeous – and no mean English conversationalist either – but I felt no great urge to sleep with her, just a leaden tiredness, which was most unlike me.

And then, out of the blue, there was a mood-changing moment. Okello was out on the terrace, laughing and joking with one of the girls. I saw a boy go over and refill his glass with red wine, which he somehow managed to spill down the front of Charles' milk white shirt. At first, I thought he'd laugh it off and certainly he held his broad grin for a few moments. Then he flew into a monstrous rage, like some crazy war dance. Eyes bulging, arms waving, feet stamping, he roared at the boy in what must have been the local language.

The boy stood there, head bowed and suffered the tirade for what seemed like several minutes. At one point I thought his boss was going to strike him, but he didn't. Instead, he pointed to the floor and the boy immediately got down on his hands and knees and started to…to what? To beg for mercy? No, it wasn't that. It became apparent that Okello was making him lick the wine off the tiled floor.

'It's floor lickin' good,' a voice said in my ear. It was one of the Americans I hadn't been introduced to, one of the geeks. He seemed to have taken the place of my lovely oriental lady.

'Saves on the cleaning bill,' I said.

'Every night the big chief throws a little tantrum over something. It's usually one of these beautiful ladies of the night he chews out. Gives him an excuse to punish someone.'

'I've heard he can be a bit volatile.'

'Is that what you call it? He's a bona fide sadist more like – and I'm Al Feinstein, by the way.'

'I'm Theo Law.'

We shook hands.

'I know. I've been waiting to talk to you.'

*

I am tir'd and not a little depress'd after Montesquieu's visit. His words keep returning to me: 'You let the beast out of its cage and it destroy'd all you'd work'd for.' In light of what happen'd when the System collaps'd and the mob turn'd savage, I cannot deny that the beast was unleash'd abroad. But worse still was that it was also unleash'd within me, where, if I am honest, it had almost certainly lurk'd since I was a child. In its essence, it is a mean, hostile creature that I somehow manag'd to turn to advantage at the gaming table. It pitches one against the world and makes of it an enemy, fit only for conquering and subjugation. It is incapable of giving and cares only for itself. It lets no one and nothing come near; its snapping and snarling keeps all at bay.

Miraculously, for a brief, exhilarating period, it was put to sleep. It was tam'd and chain'd by Katherine – on her own at first, and then with the help of Anne. We thought, felt and act'd as one. I possess'd a strength I had never known before. I was protect'd by my family. No harm cou'd befall me; there was nothing I cou'd not do. My bond with her and Anne became a bond with life itself.

And then that bond was broken and the beast awoke once more, as wild and angry as ever. I fell again into my pit of isolation, where I have brood'd ever since, with only the hideous creature for company. Here in Venice, the jokes with Bellini, the visitors, the, flirtations, the occasional game of Pharo and even the music of Maestro Vivaldi do little to relieve the situation. In fact, it is more acute than ever. For now, I am not even divert'd by action and the affairs of the world. All I have are these recollections, ghost-like memories that I cling to in the hope of finding the comfort of some kind of truth and being forgiven by the only person who can redeem me: Katherine.

Bellini appears in the doorway, accompanied by a young woman, who is wearing a mask. For a bizarre moment I think she is Katherine, as she was when we first met. Every visible feature resembles her: the height, the shoulders, the colour of her hair, her elegant bearing, and I am briefly fill'd with the most intense longing; not just physical but – how may I say it? – 'with every fibre of my being'. I soon come to my senses. Bellini nods and smiles; she, rather touchingly, curtsies. I am merely on show again as the former richest man in the world and the greatest gambler of all time, earning his keep. They withdraw. I order more hot chocolate, lac'd with cognac, and continue with my writing...

Following my meeting with Saint-Simon at the Banque Royale, I wish'd only to throw myself into my work at the Company and try to put all other matters aside. At first, this was far from easy. Katherine, who remain'd out at Gourmande, told me that she had finally written back to Philippe. She had inform'd him of how hurt and insult'd she had been by his actions and made it clear that she had no wish to see him 'until the pain of their encounter had heal'd'.

How long wou'd that be? he had ask'd. She cou'd not say – 'I have no experience of nursing such an injury' – but she thought it might be wise for him to seek a new object of affection, someone who cou'd afford him the kind of satisfaction he desir'd.

It was typically shrewd of her. She had both cut him off and yet somehow left him hanging by a thread of hope.

Meanwhile, Saint-Simon wrote to me with news of his 'discussion' with Philippe. As he had expect'd, Orleans deeply regrett'd his actions and accept'd their consequences. He also reassur'd me that that there was no indication that His Royal Highness remain'd anything other than positive in his attitude towards the Bank and the Company and that it retain'd his full support. However, on the less positive side, he felt he need'd to *warn me. He was of the opinion that despite Katherine's rejection of him, Philippe wou'd continue to harbour strong feelings for her. 'He can perhaps control his actions, he told me, but his emotions are their own master...'*

Both of these reports were somewhat reassuring in their way and yet I cou'd not help thinking that I need'd to drive the Company forward as quickly as I cou'd while the road was still clear. It was hard to predict from whence the next obstacle to progress might appear, but I knew there must be one.

Demand for the first issue of shares – the 'Mother' shares, as I call'd them – was now running so high that I was encourag'd to launch the second issue – the 'Daughters' – sooner than I had agreed with Katherine. Far from depressing the share price, it rose within a week to 1000 livres, twice its original price.

I publicis'd widely the equipping of more trading vessels, bound for Louisiana, as well as an expedition of four ships that I had financ'd privately to stake land claims for tobacco and silk plantations and prospect for gold, silver and diamonds. The day they sail'd from La Rochelle – which was done amid great rejoicing and distribution of banknotes in the streets around the Company offices – I made much of the fact that when gold was found, it wou'd not be sold to the Mint for the making of louis d'or, but us'd only to decorate our buildings and our women. In this new age of paper money, I announc'd to the crowd, coins of any description wou'd soon be redundant.

With all the Mothers and Daughters sold, shares now began to change hands between shareholders more rapidly. People began to realise that they cou'd make a tidy profit just by selling them on, which push'd up the price even further. A month later, I decid'd to make a third issue. When I arose early that June morning and look'd across the jumble of rooftops to the twin towers of Notre Dame, still slumbering in the haze, I can remember the words that toll'd like the cathedral bells in my head: 'France, you are asleep, but I will wake you and make you dance to the music of money...'

From that day, I threw myself into the affairs of the Company and the Bank Royale with even greater vigour. A week after the third share issue, the price leapt from 1000 to 3500 *livres, and shares began changing hands with even greater alacrity. Dealing took place on the Company premises at first, but as the number of dealers and buyers grew, it spill'd into a narrow street nearby, known as the Rue de Quincampoix. Personally I favour'd this more public location, for it made a spectacle of the share dealing and help'd generate excitement throughout the city. It thrill'd me to see that people from different levels of society, male and female, were already rubbing shoulders in order to buy and sell shares – not just nobles and the wealthier merchants, but trades people, artisans and even servants, many of whom came to buy on behalf of their masters and mistresses and decid'd to invest a little for themselves.*

I began to go amongst the crowd in the street, selling shares, buying them back and then selling them on again at a higher price. I offer'd discounts to many, especially to those of more modest means, and gave away paper currency, as long as it was us'd for the purchase of shares. It all help'd promote their sale and distribution, which in turn push'd up the price. And what was more I enjoy'd it thoroughly – the hustle and bustle, the buying and selling, the sense that every exchange chang'd the world and increas'd everyone's wealth, including my own. It was also good to see a growing number of Englishmen on the street, which meant that word of the System's success had cross'd the Channel and was drawing them over to Paris.

I was less pleas'd, however, to see the burly figure d'Argenson, topp'd with an absurdly heavy peruke for such a fine summer's day. Half-a-dozen Crown guards accompanied him, as if he had resum'd his role as Chief of Police. Perhaps he had, I thought, and I wou'd be summon'd to replace him as Minister for Finance. It cou'd not happen too soon.

'Has Your Grace come to arrest me?' I smil'd, knowing full well that he wou'd enjoy nothing more.

'One needs to have all the protection one can among this rabble,' he replied in the familiar gravely voice.

I look'd around. Nearby was a duc, a marquis and several comtesses, all jostling with members of the lower orders to purchase shares.

'Hardly a rabble, Your Grace. More a worthy cross-section of His Majesty's subjects – as well as some of his family relations, I wou'd hazard. They are all engag'd in the noble pursuit of share dealing, of investing in the greatest trading enterprise the world has ever known...'

'Yes...yes,' he scowl'd with impatience, 'and it's about that very same trading enterprise that I've come to see you. Shall we retire to the Company offices and discuss these matters in less public surroundings? I'm sure you'd prefer that, Monsieur Law.'

I was glad that I had never underestimat'd d'Argenson or assum'd that he cou'd be as easily push'd aside as Noailles. Something – his guard dog nature perhaps – had alert'd me to a tenacious cunning and his next move came as no surprise.

Once we were seat'd in my office at the Company – a far less grand affair than the one at the Bank – he was straight to the point.

'Have you heard of a Captain Lescaut?' he ask'd.

I shook my head.

'He is a traveller and explorer of some reputation and has just return'd from Louisiana, where he has been operating outside the jurisdiction of the Mississippi Company.' He spoke these last two words as if they left an unpleasant taste in his mouth. 'The point is that he has done an extensive survey of the area, mapping and so forth, and surprisingly enough has found it to be...'

'A wasteland?' I cut in, smiling. 'A disease-ridden swamp?'

He frown'd at my ready concurrence. 'Those were...some of his words, yes...'

'Well, God forbid that it shou'd be anything else at this point,' I said brightly. 'If it already bustl'd like Marseilles or was as cultivat'd as the Loire, we cou'd not add value to it. The Company is selling potential, Your Grace. Much is still to be done to develop Louisiana – but with the money rais'd from the share issues, plus my own investment, it will be done and very quickly, as I have said before.'

D'Argenson tried another tack. 'It sounds like a noble plan, Monsieur Law. But apparently, according to the dear Captain, there's no one there to execute it. You have led us to believe that

New Orleans is already a thriving port, a firm base from which a trading empire can be forg'd, not a few miserable hovels where a handful of wretches barely scratch a living...'

'Yes, it's most unfortunate,' I replied. 'I too have been disappoint'd by the Frenchman's natural aversion to migrating to the colonies. The English, the Scots, the Irish, even the Dutch cannot leave their native lands fast enough, but the French seem tied to the apron strings of Mother France. I don't know why exactly. It exploits and impoverishes them more than any other. Why wou'd they not want to bid the place adieu? Do they simply lack a spirit of adventure?'

His Grace's pock-mark'd complexion grew very flush'd.

'It is for this reason,' I went on, 'that as part of the development of Louisiana, the Company will be instigating a series of measures to encourage emigration...'

'Encourage emigration? It is the first I've heard of it,' he said – and the first I've heard of it too, I thought, much to my own amusement. He look'd most upset. 'What kind of measures?'

'Some involve incentives and others...a degree of coercion. _Encourage_ may have to mean _enforce_ in certain instances. Carrot and stick, I think it is term'd.'

D'Argenson cou'd not now contain his anger. He stood up, full of menace, and leant forward, placing his hands on the desk in front of me. His less than pretty face was inches from mine. I cou'd see the heavy wine and tobacco stains on his yellow teeth. His breath was rank.

'How long do you think you can go on peddling illusion, Law?' he snarl'd. 'You cannot base a country's future on a wasteland.' He nodd'd towards the window. 'Those poor fools out there are buying into nothing. They might as well throw their money in the Seine, as put it in your _Mississippi Company_. You and I know it's a farce and as Financial-Controller, I intend to put a stop to it.'

Card-playing calm was very much the order of the day. I stay'd seat'd, look'd him in the rheumy eye and call'd his bluff. 'Those poor fools, as you call them, include many members of the Regency Council, the Regent himself – and, of course, you, Your Grace...'

His expression harden'd further; a hint of panic crept into his eyes. It was only a calculat'd guess on my part, but I knew he was too close to de Conti not to have his snout in the same trough. He wou'd simply have made sure that his shares were sold at a profit before his revelations began to damage the System. Or so he thought. Having caught him off-balance, I drove home the advantage.

'Crow all you like about conditions in Louisiana and the lack of settlers but it will be drown'd out by the clamour for more shares from your colleagues – and the sound of my exposing your arrant hypocrisy. How wou'd that affect your standing as Financial-Controller?'

He straighten'd up and back'd away from the desk, eyeing me warily. The dog knew his master.

'I trust when we next meet,' I add'd, 'you will have far more flattering things to say about the System that has already enrich'd you considerably. And I sincerely hope you will endorse my new emigration measures. Good day, Your Grace...'

And so he withdrew, muttering curses, swearing to destroy me, even see me hang'd. It was gratifying that he thought I warrant'd such loathing.

Meanwhile, I sat amaz'd at my own ability to invent policy on the hoof – and all without Katherine at my side, to advise me. Indeed, I decid'd that I was far more effective when I operat'd alone and cou'd make my own decisions. I was so taken – I wou'd now say unhing'd – by this notion that I even convinc'd myself there and then that far from helping me, Katherine was actually holding me back.

Cou'd she have risen so quickly to this challenge and been so radical in her thinking? I doubt'd it. Although I was aware of the paltry numbers of migrants going out to the Americas, I had given it little thought until d'Argenson rais'd the issue. Yet the door was hardly clos'd behind him before I had formulat'd in my head the bold measures requir'd to remedy the situation.

How exhilarating, I thought. And how quickly that feeling ebb'd away when I realis'd that the measures I was contemplating were so radical, they wou'd need the approval of *the Crown before I cou'd implement them. I was once again reliant on Philippe's support.*

*

Al Feinstein had my attention. Why had he waited to speak to me? How did he even know I was coming? He'd tell me, he said, but he wasn't saying anything till he'd had a cigarette. He was dying for one. At least one, maybe more. He'd been trying to cut down, but this wasn't the time or place.

'Can we go outside, get out of the Rain Forest Café?'

Okello had gone from the terrace – apparently to change his shirt – but the hapless waiter still had his face pressed to the ground, terrified to move until his master gave him permission. We stretched out on recliners by the blue neon glow of the pool, as far from the house as we could get. Giant insects, flying piranhas, flitted round the lamps, and I was glad I'd applied some of the repellent provided in the room; the sounds of other creatures pierced the outer darkness. It felt hotter and stickier than in the dining room, but it was a relief to be outside, to look up at the dense tapestry of the stars, rather than a bunch of stuffed birds and monkeys.

'Amazing sight,' I said.

'Yep – best thing about the place.'

Feinstein offered me a 'straight', as we stoners used to call them, and although I'd not smoked one for years, I took it. I needed it. I hadn't realised how on edge I'd been since I arrived in this country – and I probably should have guessed that it was about to get edgier.

My first drag tasted good. 'So…you seem to know more about me than I do you.'

'I know you're the moneyman. One of the best.'

'Ha!' I scoffed at both descriptions, but they weren't completely wrong.

'All the billions in the world are of no use to Okello if he can't spend 'em, right? Isn't that where you come in?'

'It is…yes…'

He blew a cloud of smoke towards the stars. If you were casting a mad genius, you could do worse than cast Feinstein.

Aquiline Jewish profile, big boffin glasses, a head of dark spiral curls framing the dome of a forehead, inside which radically inventive solutions were a dime a dozen – or was that too much invention on my part?

'So what are you doing in the jungle?' I asked.

'Crudely speaking, social control.'

'*Social control.*'

'Yep.'

'Forgive me, Al, but you don't seem like the security type.'

'You're not wrong. I seem like a geek, right? I am a geek. I – and my team – employ psychology rather than brute force.'

'Psy Ops, as they call it.'

'Sort of, except that sounds very US government and we're not working for the government. We're working for the same guys you're working for.'

'Well, I'm not actually working for any of those same guys as yet...' What was I saying? I already worked for Boris and he was certainly one of the same guys. 'Who exactly are they anyway?'

'You really don't know?'

'Not entirely.'

He looked back at the house, made sure we were alone. 'They're a loose affiliation of millionaires and billionaires – isn't that how the song goes? – except you can take out the millionaires. Their aim is to ensure our busted system stays bust and they go on getting richer.'

'And how do they do that?'

'By making sure the right people get elected around the world, or at least stay in power. That's where *I* come in. I use cyber technology as a tool of persuasion. Did I say tool? I meant weapon – a weapon of mass persuasion. Ha! How about that?'

'I wouldn't have thought there was much cyber anything in this part of the world.'

'You'd be surprised. Cheap cell phones, given away, more or less, the ubiquitous satellite dish. We're here advising Okello's people, as a favour from your friend Boris. It's basic stuff. Some of it even involves good old-fashioned billboards – and a little military back-up. But it's working, as it does in many places – you may have noticed. Have you ever known so many turkeys voting for Thanksgiving? So many people ignoring issues that are of vital importance to them? There's a pandemic of self-harm out there.'

'You don't sound particularly happy about it.'

'I'm not. You're one of the world's great moneymen, right? I'm one of the world's great hackers. I was known as the Spook. I broke into some high security systems, stole some big data, analysed it and sold it to the highest bidder – and no one ever knew I was there. Not that I did it for the money, you understand. I did it for the hell of it, because I could. I was what they now call a talented disruptor, a maverick, an anarchist. Then I tried to sell something to *these* guys – very stupid of me. They not only bought it, they asked me to work for them. Made me a very impressive offer.'

'Why was that stupid?'

'Because it was only the carrot – there was also a stick. If I didn't join them, they'd shop me to the Feds…'

He stubbed his cigarette out on the ground and immediately lit another; I followed suit. 'So now I'm *their* talented disruptor.'

I took yet another satisfying drag. 'What do you want, Al? With me, I mean.'

'I'm told you could be up for joining a good cause.'

'Sanyo?'

He nodded. 'Personally, I agree with her.'

'What's the cause?'

He sat upright, leaned in towards me. 'I really don't like these people or what they're doing, Theo – may I call you Theo?'

'You may.'

'And I'd like us to take them down.'

'*Us?*'

'Yep. You're essential to the enterprise. Can't happen without you.'

'And how are *we* going to do that?'

'Put simply, by perpetrating the biggest heist in history. And no one will ever know we were there…'

But then Penfold was there, looming over us, like a spook himself. Where had *he* come from?

'Everything okay, gentlemen?'

'Yes,' I said. 'Just taking the night air – mixed with some cigarette smoke.' I looked up. 'Nice sky you have.'

'Quite something, isn't it?' Just for a moment and for the first time since I'd met him, he gave off a genuine air of menace. 'The girls not to your liking then? I thought throwing some Chinese into the mix might *spice* things up a bit.' Another unfunny Penfold joke.

'Nothing wrong with the girls,' said Feinstein. 'They're all gorgeous.'

Penfold looked mollified, a proud pimp. Even so there was an awkward silence, until I pushed myself up off the recliner and said: 'Well, gorgeous as they are, I'm afraid I'm gong to hit the sack, on my own…'

'Yep, me too,' said Feinstein.

'Well, you two are the party poopers, aren't you?' said Penfold.

We all three walked back towards the house and the sound of music and conversation. Dinner had turned into a full-blown party. Several of the guests were dancing with the women out on terrace, some in tight embrace, others doing a slow jiving, laughing, twirling around each other. They looked like they were actually having a good time; I almost envied them.

I said my good nights and headed off down the tunnel-like path through heavy shrubbery that led to the chalets. The musky smell of the earth and the high-pitched cries of night creatures intensified, but they were underscored, I realised, by a more human noise the low throaty moan of someone experiencing either pain or pleasure – or both.

I peered through the bushes, fully expecting to see one of the girls hard at work. Instead, I made out Okello in his clean white shirt, standing with his back against the trunk of a tree. He was the source of the moaning and someone – the boy who'd spilled the wine, it looked like – was on his knees in front of him. Charles was holding the closely shaven head with his right hand and moving it slowly, rhythmically back and forth, the better to ensure that the boy sucked the whole length of his large cock.

In his other hand, he held a pistol pressed against the boy's temple.

Then someone was behind me, Penfold again, making me start. He put a finger to his lips before whispering in my ear: 'Seems Mr. Okello isn't keen on the girls tonight either. Best leave him to it. Sleep well, Theo.' He turned and slipped silently into a dark pool of shadow, like a man who was used to night manoeuvres.

*

With Katherine out at Gourmande and seemingly taking less and less interest in the affairs of the Bank and Company, I ask'd myself how much I shou'd I tell her about these latest developments. The answer was clear: nothing, until I had to. Where speed was of the essence, sharing my plans with her might only bring delay. She knew nothing of the third issue of shares, the 'Grand-daughters'; and, as for my proposals for increasing emigration, only I and, to some extent, D'Argenson were aware of them. The next to know wou'd be Philippe, not Katherine. That evening, I wrote to him, employing all the rhetorical guile and fine French I had learnt from her.

I start'd by praising the achievements of the Company in terms of Money Science, which I knew he wou'd appreciate. The number of shares issued: 200,000, valued at some 80 million livres. The amount of new money in circulation: no less than 400 million livres. The number of Company ships designat'd for trade in Louisiana: a fleet of thirty – twenty of which were already in service and ten in the process of being fitt'd out.

But even more significant was the impact of all this on French commerce. My research show'd an estimat'd tenfold increase in the number of commercial transactions since April, which had meant a huge demand for craftsmen and artisans of every description: blacksmiths, goldsmiths, silversmiths, carpenters, chandlers, ferriers, gilders, builders, masons, cabinetmakers, clockmakers, weavers, tailors, dyers, shipwrights and cartwrights – the business of every trade had been invigorat'd. The same was true for the suppliers of raw materials – wood, stone, metal, wool, silk, linen. And of course, food – the more men work, the more they need feeding. The farmer was selling more of his crops and livestock, and he was selling them at a higher price. Even the lowliest peasant, the meanest tiller of the soil, was feeling the benefit of the System.

Indeed, so heavy had the demand for craftsmen and tradesmen become that France was rapidly exceeding her own supply and was importing them from England...

'Think of it, Your Royal Highness,' I wrote, 'armies of Englishmen, not fighting on French soil, but employ'd to restore France's great chateaux or build new ones. Or participating in the many public works that were now embark'd upon, the largest programme since Colbert: schools, roads, bridges, canals and of course, palaces and gardens – like the Tuileries, the renovation of which has been a project close to your heart. France is awakening as sure as trees burst into leaf in April – the System is unfolding exactly as I had foreseen...'

'As I am not' – I refrain'd from adding the word 'yet' – 'Financial-Controller, I cannot speak with absolute authority on the subject of the public purse. However, I think it is reasonable to assume that this growth in commercial activity will result in much higher tax revenues – which will in turn contribute to a reduction in the National Debt that has proven to be such a heavy burden on the country. This, after all, is the ultimate objective of the System – the restoration of French finances – and after only a few months, we are well on the way to achieving it...'

And now I came to the main point of the missive – that which might put all these monumental gains in jeopardy. There was one area where progress had been disappointing, I told him, and that was to do with a shortage of settlers in Louisiana and the slow rate of emigration from France. Unless we address'd this situation, the colony wou'd be unlikely to thrive. Although I had done my best to promote America as a place where dreams cou'd be realis'd and fortunes made, the French *currently preferr'd to make their fortunes in the Rue de Quincampoix. I cou'd not entirely blame them for this. In fact, I had actively encourag'd it and we had all benefitt'd from the trade in shares. However, the time had come for us to direct our efforts towards increasing the trade in goods from the colony across the Atlantic...*

'*As I have just describ'd, more people in France than ever are productively employ'd; I propose to encourage emigration among those who are not – the jobless, the vagabonds, the criminals, the prostitutes, the orphans. We will release them from a life that is blight'd here and offer them the hope of a new life in America...*'

Of course, I add'd, I did not expect this underclass to suddenly rise up en masse and head for La Rochelle of their own accord. They wou'd need a more immediate incentive. I suggest'd a sum of money be given to each man and woman who volunteer'd for transportation to New Orleans – where, incidentally, the garrison wou'd be strengthen'd to help maintain law and order.

For those who did not see the attractions of such an arrangement, a degree of coercion might be necessary. A new militia wou'd be form'd to apprehend any able-bodied lawbreakers and offer them the opportunity of being deport'd to America as an alternative to detention in a prison or poor house. They wou'd have the choice between the incarceration they wou'd anyway suffer and a new life in Louisiana – and I cou'd guess which most of them wou'd choose. I end'd on a high note...

'*The result will have an exquisite symmetry: France will rid herself of some of her less desirable subjects and Louisiana will gain thousands of new settlers, who will contribute to its development and the enrichment of the Motherland!*'

I found the very setting down of these plans on paper exciting in itself, even without the certain prospect of their execution. There were many more details I cou'd have includ'd, but I felt this was enough to convince Orleans of their necessity. Even if this was not entirely the case, it did have the effect of gaining me immediate audience.

The morning after sending the letter, I was treat'd to a second visit from his ceremonious Chief of Staff and was again swept off to the Palais-Royal, with hardly a moment to powder my peruke.

What was different this time was the state in which I found Philippe. If he had appear'd formal, elegant and business-like before, he was now wigless, dishevell'd and – my heart fell – the worse for drink, even at this relatively early hour. He sat, not at his desk, but sprawl'd upon a large chaise longue, clutching a goblet of wine, like some debauch'd Roman Emperor. My letter sprawl'd on the floor beneath him.

I went to bow, but he gave a dismissive wave of his hand – or rather, the fine lacy cuff of his sleeve. His shirt hung loosely about him and was undone to the chest. In fact, he seem'd altogether undone, as I had never seen him before.

'Let's dispense with the formalities, John, shall we? Take off your wig, sit down and share a glass of wine with me. And do not say it is too early – I will have you escort'd home immediately...'

Two servants came from nowhere. One mov'd a chair closer to the Regent, before gathering up my letter from the floor and handing it to him; the other pour'd me a glass of wine. They were dismiss'd with another brusque wave of perfum'd lace.

He did his best to focus on the letter. 'Now, let me see...yes, here it is, here...you say that prostitutes are among those who are not being productively employed...'

'I do, Your Highness.'

'But who is more productive than a whore, tell me that? There can never be enough of them, as far as I'm concern'd...certainly of the prettier variety. Their work is essential to the well-being of France...you can't just ship them off to the colonies and leave us without this important national resource...'

I laugh'd. 'Well, we won't ship all of them, Your Highness, you have my word. I'm sure there will be enough left - and many of them pretty - to maintain France's <u>well-being</u>...'

'I'm reliev'd to hear it, John...' He check'd the letter again. 'But more seriously...whores aside, how do you expect us to build a thriving Louisiana with criminals, vagabonds and the rest of the ne'er-do-wells? It will be little more than a penal colony – hardly the foundation of a great trading empire!'

He took a sip of wine and bade me do the same, which I duly did.

'At first glance, I wou'd agree, Your Highness...but think on it, if you will. It is a fact that most colonies – be they Spanish, Portuguese, Dutch or British – have been develop'd on such a basis. We wou'd wait a long time for the rich and powerful to seek their fortunes when they are already in possession of them. No, it's invariably the poor and dispossess'd who strive to build new lives in a new land.'

He nodd'd slowly at this. 'Yes, I agree...the settlers may not be rich and powerful...but surely a degree of honesty and decency might be useful?'

'And who is to say they won't be honest and decent, Your Highness? Those we call criminals are often so because of their circumstances. Evil does not so much reside in them as the conditions in which they find themselves. Change those conditions, add the magic ingredients of money and opportunity and you do have the stuff of which empires are made. Moreover, there is every reason to assume, human nature being what it is, that these pioneers will quickly engender a whole host of children. A new generation – innocent, free and industrious – will populate the New World and bring glory and prosperity to France.'

He look'd me more directly in the eye. I felt I had finally broken through the vinous haze that surround'd him. I press'd on: 'It is for this reason that we will offer the incentive of extra currency – let us call it a dowry – to those who consent to marry before they leave France and are transport'd as couples. To inaugurate and make public this new legislation, the Company wou'd stage a unique event. A mass public wedding wou'd take place between a hundred young women of ill-repute and a hundr'd young male criminals, who wou'd then parade through the streets of Paris on their way to La Rochelle and transportation to America. They wou'd be a living symbol of the success of the Company and the French colony of Louisiana.'

His face broke into a broad smile. He drank some more wine. 'You speak well, John, very well...and all in very acceptable French...'

'Thank you, Your Highness...'

'Your arguments are very persuasive...certainly I am persuad'd. It is an extremely bold undertaking...but I understand it is something we have to do. We cannot have a colony without settlers...'

'I'm glad you agree, Your Highness.'

'I will announce these measures at the next Council meeting. There will be some objections, I'm sure, but they will be overcome. In the end, the members of the Council care nothing for the poor and everything for their own enrichment, which your emigration policy undoubtedly helps to guarantee...'

'Thank you, Your Highness.'

'I will also make another announcement at the meeting of the Council. I am planning a major public celebration, a grand pyrotechnic display for the opening of the restor'd Tuileries, which will be His Majesty the King's new home after his move from Versailles. I think you'll agree, John, it is a fitting symbol of our newfound prosperity.'

'Very much so, Your Highness.'

'And I think it is also only fitting that you and Katherine be His Majesty's guests of honour on the night.'

I took a deep breath. 'That is indeed an honour, Your Highness...' My smile may have seem'd a little forc'd.

'I know, I know...she will be reluctant to come, John, of course, she will...but you must persuade her – as part of our arrangement... You are, as I have said, good at persuasion...'

'I thought Saint-Simon told you...'

He became agitat'd. 'I know what Saint-Simon told me! But can't you see how I am without the prospect of being with her? Can't you see what it's doing to me, how the lack of her is eating away at me like a canker? It cannot go on in this way, John. I know she cares for me, I'm certain of it... Despite *my…behaviour towards her, I think we can be reconcil'd. You must see to it, John – and I will see to your programme of forc'd emigration.'*

His genial aspect return'd. He put my letter aside, held up his glass. 'Long live the Mississippi Company! Long live His Majesty!'

'Yes, long live His Majesty…'

*

I was exhausted, but it took me a while to get to sleep. Apart from all the Feinstein stuff rattling round my head, there were the jangling effects of that single line of coke or whatever it was. I even thought I heard gunshot later in the night, but it could have been a drug-addled dream. I definitely heard at least one of my fellow guests returning to his chalet with a companion – giggling, shushing each other, giggling some more. Thankfully, the chalets were completely separate, so I didn't have to suffer the sounds of them making out.

I saw Feinstein only briefly in the morning, as I grabbed some breakfast. (I was relieved to see the unfortunate waiter from the night before serving at table. He looked a little sheepish, puffy-eyed – *quelle surprise* – but at least he still had his head on his shoulders.)

Feinstein said he had a meeting and I'd be gone by the time he was done. So was it okay to contact me?

'Please do,' I said, without hesitation. 'I'll give you my details.'

'Already have 'em.' It was a good example of the laconic style that was to be his trademark, and probably one of the things that would help harness me to his plan. He would make the whole preposterous enterprise seem so effortless, so simple, so destined to succeed.

Just then, though, when I saw Okello to take my leave, the very thought of the preposterous enterprise made me shudder. He seemed remarkably upbeat and the charisma count was running high. (Being sucked off by a young man obviously agreed with him.) He thanked me effusively for making the

340

journey and looked forward to seeing me in London or New York.

I said I looked forward to that too and that I'd be in touch very soon. Before my conversation with Feinstein, it would have been a lie on both counts. Now, the more access I had to the finances of people like Okello, the bigger the 'heist' would be – wasn't that where we were heading with this? *Oh my God.* I felt I'd deserted the ranks of the 'dedicated professionals' and signed up to the disruptors, minus the talent.

Finally, despite my insisting I really didn't need to see the mine, that I was happy to take his word for its existence, Okello insisted the chopper fly over it on the way back to the capital.

'It is really worth seeing, my friend. It is very, very impressive, believe me.' Then he caught me off guard, by throwing his arms round me and giving me one of those big man hugs that seem to double for a formal handshake nowadays and mean about as much. (Or perhaps that's the stiff Brit in me speaking.) I couldn't help thinking that when I last saw those hands now thumping my back, one had been rocking that boy's head to and fro and the other had held a gun to it.

Penfold was to accompany me, of course. I got the impression he couldn't get back to the capital soon enough. He got very agitated when there was a delay in our taking off. He started shouting and made some less than flattering remarks about the work ethic of the locals that made him sound more the vile, blustering colonialist than ever.

'These people need a good kick up the arse sometimes,' he muttered. 'Delete that – a bullet in the head more like...'

On our way up to the mine, he resumed commentary mode. 'Sparsely populated...big risk of rebel incursion...patrolling the border to the east is a nightmare...not much to look at...'

However, there was soon lots to look at it, once we got to the mountains. Huge volcanic cones rose majestically above the steamy tree-line and floated on a sea of mist. We flew over this breathtakingly beautiful landscape for some fifteen minutes, following a wide muddy river that snaked its way between the peaks.

'Quite something, eh?' said Penfold.

'Amazing...'

'By the way, Theo, I forgot to mention it – I spoke to my team back at base. The gentleman who attacked you? Turns out he was working for Namono, the rebel leader. He was acting on information from a manager at the hotel, who somehow knew you were coming and why.'

'Did he er…volunteer the information…?'

He laughed. 'Or did we torture him, are you asking?'

'Yes.' Did it actually start then, the new era of me owning up to my responsibility and beginning to feel…what? Remorse? Compassion even? Surely not.

'Not unless you count as torture offering him more money than he was paid by Namono – no we didn't. I would like to say your conscience can rest easy – except I can't. Once we got what we needed, they were both shot.'

He obviously enjoyed telling me this, watching me blanch. 'No other way, I'm afraid, Theo. It's war – of a sort. They'd only go back to the rebels and be shooting at us out in the bush somewhere. Heart of Darkness stuff, eh? You'll be glad to get back to London.'

While we were speaking, I'd noticed the chopper starting its descent. We rounded a large rocky outcrop, followed a broad sweep of the river and there, some distance ahead, was the mine.

There may have been a difference between what I saw and what I thought I saw. The latter was obviously influenced by the contrast with the unsullied natural beauty I'd just witnessed. Now the human footprint came down with an extra heavy stamp and seemed all the worse for it.

Penfold picked up the commentary again: 'It's been a huge challenge developing somewhere so remote. Most things had to be airlifted in at first and the river made navigable, so they could get the ore downstream to a point where it could be transported by road. There's also a railway under construction to take it all the way to the coast. The Chinese are doing it for a slice of the action. *But* – it's worth it. It so happens that what we have here is one of the richest deposits of tungsten anywhere on the planet. Do you know much about tungsten, Theo?

'Not really.'

'Apparently, it's the hardest of metals. No one can make weapons or tools or cell phones or computers or anything that underpins our modern industrial economies without it. And there's only so much of it out there.'

'A great asset for the country, then.'

He gave a wry smile. 'Indeed.'

What he didn't tell me at the time – and what I subsequently discovered – was that because tungsten is so hard, its ore has to be refined chemically, some of it on the spot. This may have explained why the rust-coloured river took on a much darker hue downstream of the mine – just one aspect of the general pollution and disfigurement of the landscape it had caused. The guts of the mountain seemed to have been torn out by quarries and tunnels. A vast area had been cleared of trees and scrub, a scorching of the earth. There were numerous processing plants emitting a mixture of steam and sulphurous smoke. Accommodation and service blocks were scattered around like so much industrial Lego. A line of cranes loaded a fleet of barges at a concrete dock. Trucks the size of houses, piled high with rubble, lumbered across the site. Giant diggers gouged away at the mountainside. On the one hand, it was standard stuff – the rape of poor old Mother Earth that has gone on for centuries. On the other, seen here in this virgin land, that rape seemed to be compounded by child abuse.

As we approached, we flew over a heavily fortified fence, topped with razor wire like some high security prison. Armed guards were much in evidence.

'There's nearly 2000 workers on site including the soldiers. There's a lack of local mining skills, of course, so we've had to ship a lot of them in from South Africa. Bit of a bugger, really. They're used to much higher standards – pushes your costs up...'

The pilot looked over at him and gestured at one of the gauges. '*Right.*' Penfold turned to me. 'We're going to have to land and refuel, I'm afraid. You might as well get out and stretch your legs for a while.' It was unfortunate, but at least he wasn't threatening to give me a tour of the place.

We put down on a pad near several other choppers, adjacent to a short airstrip. I got out and strolled over to the small terminal building to use the bathroom.

At first, with all the different industrial noises around, I didn't register the gunfire. It was only when the rockets came screaming and crashing in, that I realised the place was under attack. One landed dangerously close to the choppers, another a guard post. I looked round in a panic. Penfold had instantly morphed into a field commander in a Savile Row suit, gathering his troops, barking orders. I stood there paralysed – partly by fear, but more by not knowing where it was safe to go.

He ran over to me. He was actually smiling and I realised he loved all the action – he was a pig-in-shit. 'It's okay, just a little local difficulty, as they say. We'll soon have it under control.' As he said this, another rocket flew over our heads, on its way towards the processing plants. It fell well short. 'Meanwhile, I think we should get you out of here, don't you? We'll get your stuff into another chopper and you can take off immediately.'

'Won't we be a target?' I asked.

He laughed. 'No, no, they'll never hit anything with those duds. Cheap cast-offs from Syria or somewhere. Bark's much worse than their bite.'

After a few more terrifying minutes, as the sound of the gunfire increased and those 'duds' continued to be lobbed into the site, he and another guard escorted me to the relative safety of the terminal and then out to the second, waiting chopper.

Penfold shouted over the sound of the whirling blades and general din. 'I promised you it'd be fun, didn't I?'

'You did.'

'I have a favour to ask, Theo.'

'What's that?'

'Can you shift some money for me – from this shit-hole to somewhere a little more er congenial?'

I climbed up into my seat in the chopper; he stood on the ground looking up at me. 'In case you're wondering if it's worth your while, I'm afraid it's nowhere near the scale of Okello's stash, but it's still in the millions.'

I pretended to give it some consideration, the impression I was doing him a favour. 'Of course, William. Send me all the details.'

'I will. Thanks. Have a safe trip...' The door was closed and locked and we took off, leaving him to the joy of his little local difficulty.

*

I do not know why I thought that Philippe wou'd endorse my emigration plans solely on their own merits, but I did. Perhaps, I had become so intoxicat'd with my powers of rhetoric and reasoning – all deliver'd in 'acceptable French' – that I thought he was too.

And perhaps he was. But he was also in the grips of something even more intoxicating: his desire for Katherine. No matter how brilliant my argument and how much it appeal'd to his material self-interest, it cou'd not outshine the attractions of the Sun Queen. Unless he was given another chance to bathe in the warm glow of her presence, I knew my plans wou'd come to nought; if the Company founder'd as a result, he wou'd simply shrug and say, so be it.

I also knew that if my powers of persuasion had been at their best on the subject of emigration, they wou'd have to be even more effective if I was to convince Katherine to attend the public celebration and shine upon His Royal Highness.

That task was made even harder when I receiv'd a letter from her a week later. An extremely disturbing situation had come to her attention, she said. Philippe had written to her inviting her to the Tuileries celebration as guest of honour – which was disturbing enough – but then in passing, he'd also mention'd the Company's third share issue and something about a forc'd emigration policy, both of which he had assum'd she was party to. He was very pleas'd to see the Company doing so well, he said, and look'd forward to discussing its progress with her when they met.

Her letter to me end'd: 'I think you need to explain yourself, John. Come out to Gourmande at the earliest opportunity. It cannot be too soon...'

It cou'd not be put off long enough for me, but nor cou'd it be avoid'd. I went out the next day, pondering my arguments and options – what I want'd to gain, what I was prepar'd to lose.

As I arriv'd at Gourmande, I also arriv'd at a shocking conclusion: that the situation was somewhat similar to my plans for the migrants to Louisiana. If Katherine cou'd not be persuad'd, then she might need to be coerc'd – but where wou'd that leave the two of us and our partnership?

*

Back in London, it felt as if my African adventure had never happened. It was one of those life-and-death dreams that are wildly graphic at the time but fade to nothing when you wake. At least, I wished it'd had that fleeting quality. Numerous things contrived to keep it real: a recurring image of the beautiful Sanyo, who'd sadly not been around when I'd returned to the capital; a note from Boris asking how the trip to Africa had gone; the nagging thought that I should make contact with Okello sooner rather than later; a telephone conversation with Feinstein.

Did Feinstein exist, I wondered, or was he just a character in the same racy novel I dreamed I was in? No, he very much existed. He was very much alive and well and back in San Francisco, plotting the biggest ever heist or sting or whatever it was that I may have tacitly agreed to be part of. And he was very much on the phone asking me to send him the details of Boris' accounts, so he could investigate the 'access possibilities' and start to 'scope out' the grand plan.

But could I trust him? How did I know whether his grand plan added up to anything more than hacking into Boris' accounts, ripping him off big time and disappearing back into cyberspace, leaving me to take the rap and pick up the pieces?

I didn't say this. I said: 'Let me think about it.'

'You don't trust me, Theo.'

When I didn't answer, he said: 'What can I do to make you trust me?'

'You can't. Just let me think about it.' I rang off and my only think was 'who needs this, anyway?' But the fact was I was sold on it and he knew it. He'd planted the idea in my brain and it was growing with the speed of bamboo, overrunning the walls of all resistance.

Having said that, I might still have resisted it, had I not seen Angela when I'd gone to pick up Grace for a paternal visit. I'm ashamed to say I'd skipped a couple of these visits for work reasons and been given a warning by her mother of the use-it-or-lose-it variety. Not that she'd have been able to do anything without legal action. But her response was a measure of how angry she continued to be with me and I didn't want to provoke her any further.

She usually made sure she wasn't around when I went to the house. She'd leave our, by then, four-year old daughter with the Spanish girlfriend and/or Maggie. But that morning was a first – no one else was there. Angela and Grace came to the door, Grace standing proudly upright in her new walker, Angela smiling proudly down at her. Grace was unable to walk without the aid of a frame, but she could move remarkably quickly. I watched her beetle back up the hallway, hunched over its handles like a cyclist, her blond curls bouncing round her face. I couldn't help thinking she was looking more and more like me, poor thing. Indeed, Maggie had told me that one of Angela's 'dykey friends' – as my ex-mother-in-law referred to them – had called Grace 'Theo-in-a-Dress', much to 'Anj's dismay.

Grace was heartbreakingly happy to see me; she always seemed to enjoy our time together, even though I wasn't always the best of company. She immediately became all forlorn in the exaggerated way of kids, creasing her brow and sticking out her bottom lip.

'Mummy's very sad, Daddy – Maggie's gone away...' (Maggie didn't permit use of the 'Granny' word.)

I looked at Angela, who'd hardly spoken since I arrived; she burst into tears. What do I do? I thought. My immediate reaction was to want to put my arms round her but I held back.

I spoke to Grace: 'Do we know where she's gone, darling?'

'We don't know, do we Mummy?' She reached for Angela's hand. She was being so grown up, I wanted to cry too.

347

Mummy still wasn't saying anything. She was doing her best to stifle the tears and seemed uncomfortable at having to share this raw moment with me.

I remembered my conversation with Maggie. 'Has she gone walkabout again?'

Angela shrugged, sighed.

'Is there anything I can do? I could go and have a look in the usual places.'

She sniffed, ran the back of her hand across her eyes. 'I've looked. She's gone somewhere else, maybe left London, I don't know. I don't think she wants to be found.'

'Would she do that to you?'

'She did it to me for most of my life.'

She started crying again. This time I couldn't restrain myself. I spontaneously threw one arm around her, the other around Grace and pulled us all gently together. Surprisingly, Angela didn't resist.

'She'll be all right, Mummy,' said Grace, and then my eyes really did well up. There were a few blissful moments of sheer togetherness. For a few moments we felt like a family again – until Angela pulled away and quickly pulled herself together, resuming the usual chilly demeanour.

'You better get going, Theo.' She looked down at Grace. 'Is your bag all packed, darling?'

'It's upstairs.'

'I'll get it for you.'

She went to leave. '*Look*, Angela...I...'

'Theo, *please* – I'm just upset over Mum. Nothing else has changed...'

'But it has, a lot's changed.'

'Like what?'

I issued the press release before I'd even approved it myself. 'I'm getting out of the business – and in the process I'm taking down Boris and his whole rotten operation. I'm going to ruin him.'

I couldn't be sure but I thought a milder expression passed briefly across her face before the frost returned. 'It's good to know, Theo...but it doesn't make any difference to us. We've moved on.'

'I don't think we have.'

'You're wrong.'

During the African experience the anti-depressants had kept the abyss at bay. But just then, as Angela turned away from me – in slow-motion, it seemed – a black hole beckoned. It was all I could do to resist its gravitational pull.

And it wasn't her saying I was wrong that almost made me lose it, but the sense that *she* was wrong and that by demonstrating I'd finally found my moral compass, there was a chance I could win her back.

*

The balmy summer breeze in the gardens of Gourmande was at odds with Katherine's wintry mood. She greet'd me amid the roses with a froideur that might have taken off their bloom had she stood too close to them. I had half-expect'd it, yet nonetheless, I found it deeply disturbing.

There was no sign of Anne. I was told she was asleep, although I suspect'd she was being kept from me as part of my chastisement. I had been ask'd there 'to explain' myself, but it seem'd any explanation wou'd prove futile; Katherine had already decid'd that I was guilty.

She left me to take some refreshment and shake off the dust of the road, and we arrang'd to meet later in the library, which she also referr'd to as her 'office'. She seem'd to be making it clear that whatever took place between us while I was there, it wou'd fall strictly under the category of 'Company business' and nothing else. For all the warmth and affection we show'd each other, we might have been two perfect strangers engag'd in the driest and most formal of business meetings.

Much to my surprise, however, when we did come together again and were seat'd at a table in the library, I found myself feeling more than a faint stirring of desire for her; a sense that if we cou'd only return to our original status as lovers and forego any involvement in affairs of business, all wou'd be well.

But then again, I wonder'd if we were ever exclusively lovers, even at the very beginning of our liaison. It had always been as much a commercial venture, as an amorous one. The two had gone hand-in-hand and now it appear'd that one had outgrown the other.

'Philippe made an excellent job of insulting me, but you seem to have gone one better...' Her opening gambit brought an abrupt end to my musings.

'I beg your pardon, Madam?' The more formal manner of address seem'd only fitting in the circumstances.

'A *third* share issue, <u>Sir</u>? <u>Forc'd</u> emigration to Louisiana, <u>Sir</u>? All done without the slightest attempt to consult me.'

'I had to act quickly.'

'You are suppose'd to act in accordance with the terms of our business partnership. And if you had done so, I wou'd have advis'd caution. By increasing the market for shares too quickly you risk driving up the price to a level that cannot as yet be sustain'd by the Company's profits. The two things must be in step. You must know that, <u>Sir</u>.'

'I know that once demand for the shares took off, I need'd to maintain its momentum. You are not in Paris, <u>Madam</u>. You cannot judge the mood. The more people purchase shares, the more popular the Company becomes. It needs the widest public support – not just the support of Philippe's courtiers and cronies.'

'Of course, it does...but over time, not overnight, <u>Sir</u>. Steady rain brings growth, torrential downpours cause floods.'

Oh dear, no matter how much I tried to brazen it out, I knew that even in the heat of argument, her combination of intelligence and eloquence was formidable. I felt my solid conviction begin to crumble under the pressure of it.

She went on: 'But if issuing shares too quickly was merely rash, <u>Sir</u>, the policy of forc'd emigration is utterly wronghead'd and damn'd foolish. It will ruin everything we've achiev'd so far.'

'What will ruin everything, <u>Madam</u>, is a lack of colonists. No colonists equals no colony. If the French won't go to the Americas voluntarily, they must be made to go – and who better to be made to go than those who fulfil no useful role here...and what's more, are in no position to resist such a measure...'

She scoff'd at this: 'Whether they have any value or influence is of no consequence – although I for one find it cruel in the extreme to ship someone off three thousand miles against their will. Bad enough if they were African slaves, <u>Sir</u>, but the fact is they are <u>French</u>. Can you not see beyond your preening self-regard?' (That remark stung me.) 'Can you not see how our – <u>your</u> enemies, for <u>your</u> name is on it – will use this against you, if not now then at some later date? They will accuse you of enslaving the French people – you, a foreigner. I can hear the jeering in the streets now. I can hear them asking for <u>you</u> to be sent to the colonies – in chains...'

'Ha! They are more likely to exalt me, <u>Madam</u>! I too am guest of honour at the Tuileries. I too am much celebrat'd. I hold all Paris in the palm of my hand is the truth – and this policy will only increase my grip on it. Anyone sent to Louisiana will be thanking me for it. They leave a life of misery here and have the chance of a fresh start in a new world. They are not slaves – they are settlers!' I calm'd down, lower'd my voice. 'Besides, the Regent himself is in full support of my policy...'

'Because he wants to <u>fuck me, Sir!</u>'

'Please, <u>Madam</u>...'

'Oh, does my language offend you? I do apologise, but the truth often offends. And here's some more of it – even if he does support it, he will distance himself from you, the moment opinion turns...'

'What you don't realise is that opinion will turn, whatever we do, it is the way of the world – and the Company must be in the strongest possible position when it does. As well as being effective, these measures will be a public demonstration of that strength, the more so because they will be endors'd by the Regent and the Council...' I took a breath. 'Or at least they will be...as long as...'

'As long as I pander to Philippe and accept his invitation.'

'Yes – he's desperate to see you. He doesn't expect anything more.'

She shook her beautiful head, gave a wry laugh. 'I've told you what he expects and I thought I withdrew from that arrangement.'

'His Royal Highness seems to think he can win back your favour.'

'Well, he's wrong. Why wou'd I go back on my decision – especially for something I think as misguid'd as your plans for forc'd emigration? No, <u>Sir</u>, you will have to find another way of securing support for them. You decid'd to act alone and that's what you can do now. I'll have no part of it.'

I wish'd I did not treat every encounter as if it were a game of cards. I wish'd my desire for Katherine at the time had overcome my desire to win that game, whatever the cost. I wish'd it then, and I wish it again now... But as we all of us discover early in life, wishing does not make it so.

I stood up and glar'd down at her. I hop'd I might have a menacing air, but if I did, her face did not register as much. 'I see no point in continuing this conversation, but before I go I wou'd ask you to think on this. Your rights to our financial assets do not exist in French law – and that law takes precedent over any private contractual agreement you and I might have. As a wife, you own nothing. Everything belongs to me, and I will assert my rights to it immediately – if you do not accept Philippe's invitation.'

'You forget, <u>Sir</u>, I am not your wife.'

'No – but you are someone's – Sir William Gregg's...which puts you in an even weaker position. If you wou'd be so kind as to let me have your decision within twenty-four hours, I wou'd be most grateful... Good day to you, <u>Madam</u>...'

*

I trace the birth of my dual personality to that day at Angela's. It was the day I embraced the Anarchist in myself, not only because I thought it would bring me redemption in her eyes, but because I wanted it in my own. I never thought I'd ever admit it, but part of me had become ashamed of aiding and enriching the already mega-rich, even if I enriched myself in the process. I'd come to accept Angela's argument one hundred per cent. These people were criminals, and for one to knowingly be the agent of a criminal – even as the most 'dedicated professional' – was to be a criminal oneself. End of story.

But. *But.* I was a mega-rich criminal too. I was the Moneyman, remember? Money mattered to me more than anything else. I couldn't just turn off the supply and call it a day. It wasn't going to happen. And when it came to redemption, the Moneyman in me thought it was a joke, an insult to my true nature. Redeemed from what? From doing what I did best? From being perfectly adapted to the system that had created me? I don't think so.

This same fault line spread across the whole landscape of my life. Given the new possibility of winning Angela back, something in me decided I needed to be faithful to her. But the Moneyman had other ideas. He was more than ready to come off the anti-depressants and start partying again – or at least to start having lots of sex. Notching up sexual conquests was like adding noughts to a bonus – it meant you were a winner; staying faithful to anyone or anything other than the urge to make money meant you were a loser. Which was why within a month or so of the birth of my split personality, I had no compunction about hooking up with the beautiful Jo de Vere, even as I entertained dreams of getting back with Angela and had agreed to join forces with Feinstein so there was a chance it would happen.

It makes little sense and yet it's all the sense there is. Most of us spend our lives in conflict with ourselves. We struggle between self-love and self-loathing. We flick through different versions of ourselves like pages on the web. We lose ourselves in a maze of contradictions, in a world grown too complicated for our understanding. It's all part of our Age of Unreason. And yet it can have a positive side. It can mean that to understand who we are, to fully explore our humanity we have to embrace these contradictions – to go beyond the binary, the light and shadow, and see what emerges, what evolves. A personal dialectic, if you like: thesis, antithesis, synthesis – and/or redemption. It could mean that. We'll see.

Meanwhile, I agreed to Feinstein scoping out the grand plan. He set up some hyper-secure links between us; I sent him the contact details he needed, not just for Boris but for all the other big clients of mine, including Okello and, of course, my old friend Penfold.

Within days he came back to me, full of a geeky kind of enthusiasm.

'It's better than I thought.'

'How so?'

'I managed to hack my way undetected into Aronovsky's whole contact book as well as his accounts. The Spook hasn't lost his touch. We can do some serious damage to the world's billionaire community.'

I loved the use of the word 'community' in this context, applied to those who serve only their own interests. I imagined them on the tarmac, waving to each other from their private jets, or tying up their super yachts together at Cannes. 'When you say 'damage' what do you mean? What are we actually doing here?'

'I'm still scoping it out, Theo.'

'I know you are, Al. But indulge me with some broad strokes.'

'My thinking at the moment is that we fabricate requests for transfers of funds from the target accounts. We won't get everything – but we'll get a large percentage of what's on deposit. We'll then make it disappear by laundering it through your magical networks.'

'What happens to it then?'

'To be decided. It can be kept. It can be pissed away – although it's hard to see how you'd manage that with *so* many billions. Or it can be passed on in a way that doesn't attract too much attention. Or a mixture of all the above. It's up to us.'

'Passed on? You mean given away?'

'Redistributed. Call it a Robin Hood tax.'

The Moneyman suddenly perked up. Like the old Sheriff of Nottingham, he said: 'Let's take out Robin Hood. I like the sound of *It can be kept*'. The Keptomaniac. He imagined an addition of multiple zeros, like a string of priceless pearls, like a tsunami of coins from a slot machine, an avalanche of jackpots. They temporarily blinded him to the risks involved, and he withdrew his veto of the heist: 'Let's go for it, Theo.' And so we went for it.

The genius Feinstein went on with his scoping, promising to submit a fully detailed plan within a month. This would be followed by the lengthier business of writing and testing all the software that would enable him to proceed to 'execution', as he put it. (I wished he hadn't.)

I went on with business as usual with all my clients and I also messaged Angela. It was form of communication we used for practical arrangements, like picking up Grace. I was direct and to the point, as was she.

'Hi Angela. I believe Boris' wife Gina gave you a memory stick. I'd be grateful if you'd pass it on to me.'

'Hi Theo, why should I do that? I don't trust you.'

'So you do have the memory stick?'

No reply.

'Boris knows you have it and while I'm his friend that's fine.' Pause 'When I do what I told you I'd do and he knows it's me who did it, that will change. He could come after you.' Pause. 'And Grace.'

No reply.

'I can use the information on that stick to protect you both.'

Pause.

'I still don't trust you, Theo.'

'You don't have to trust me. Are you familiar with the stick's contents?'

Pause. 'Yes.'

'Is there anything on it that might upset the Kremlin? Has Boris been cheating on the Russian government in some way?'

Pause. 'Yes – a lot yes.' Pause. 'Gina told me it was where he was most vulnerable.' Pause. 'She said the Godfather in the Kremlin would be very unhappy.'

'Good. That's all I need to know. Keep it safe.'

Pause. 'Theo.' Pause. 'Is it enough to protect you too?'

Pause. 'The more I have on him, the safer I am. But yes, I hope it is.'

I also hoped that Angela had understood the implication: that the reason I'd stayed loyal to Boris was to protect her and Grace. It wasn't the whole truth, but I deserved some credit. And even if she didn't, I had a sense that she actually *cared* whether I was protecting myself. A sense of it, but I couldn't say for sure.

I ended our conversation both excited and terrified by my commitment to the project and its possible consequences. Since then I've been looking at the future through my fingers, as if it were that subtler kind of horror film in which you get only intimations of menace but dread it all the more.

In the three months that followed I hardly saw Angela and she seemed to have gone back to avoiding me. But for one occasion, when she was at the house when I arrived. She told me there was still no sign of Maggie and that the next time she saw her mother she fully expected her be on a slab in some mortuary somewhere.

It was obvious that her feelings had hardened since I'd last seen her, but I still made lots of sympathetic noises,

There were a few moments of awkward silence. 'So how's it going, Theo?'

'What?'

'Your big project.'

'Oh that. It's going. I'm told we're not far off now.'

'Look…please don't do this because you think we might get back together again. I've told you it will never happen.'

'You have and I'm not.' It was only partly a lie.

'And *please*, don't put any of us at risk because of it. It's really not worth it.'

'You and Grace will both be safe – safer than you are now. I promise. I wouldn't do it unless I was sure. That's why the information on that stick is so important.'

'You know it's not just about me and Grace…'

'Do I? I mean, yes…I do.' I said the words with the solemnity of a marriage vow, as if the truth of it were self-evident. But of course, I hadn't been sure until that moment.

And it was confirmed just before I left for Rome, when a package arrived containing the memory stick and a note: 'Good luck, Theo. It's the right thing to do. Ax.' Yes, she did care, she really did.

'Bullshit!' said the Moneyman. 'Bull*shit*!'

*

I manag'd to control myself, to maintain the usual card-playing calm, until I was in the carriage and on my way back to Paris. Then, as soon as Gourmande was out of sight, I broke down. Tears well'd in my eyes, my hands began to shake; I felt a

pain across my chest as if my heart was contracting – perhaps it was, given what I had done in my blind rage. I had cut myself off from the person who had been my mentor, my lover, my greatest friend and ally. And I had done so in a way that was most calculat'd to offend – a man asserting his legal rights over a woman, making her and all she owned <u>his</u> property. Nothing cou'd be more repugnant to Katherine, I knew that. Nothing cou'd be more of a betrayal of everything she held dear.

For several minutes, I thought about having the carriage turnaround and go back to Gourmande. I wou'd go down on my knees, pour out abject apologies, beg her forgiveness. We wou'd be reconcil'd. We wou'd rekindle those early flames of passion, a passion that cou'd overcome any obstacle life threw in its way. I wou'd restore her to her role in the business. I wou'd act on her advice...

But I said nothing to the coachman, except 'Don't spare the horses. I want to be back in Paris before dusk....' (The roads into the city were even more dangerous after dark.) Meanwhile, I recover'd myself somewhat by shining the light of reason where there had been panic and hysteria.

The breakdown of my relationship with Katherine had not just happen'd out at Gourmande; it had been a long, cumulative process, the build up of silt in a river that cou'd not be easily remov'd. My direction was set, not only on the road to Paris, but in life. The truth was that I did not want to be a 'partner' any longer. I want'd to be my own person, singular and free to do exactly as I pleas'd when it pleas'd me; I want'd to be master of my own destiny. I remember actually saying the words to myself, as I sway'd back and forth in the fast-moving carriage, watching the trees in full leaf rush by: <u>master of my own destiny</u>. That is how drunk I was on my own – what were her words? – 'preening self-regard'. At the time, they went on stinging me, those words, and the rage return'd. Katherine may be the Sun Queen for Philippe, but for me she was now nothing more than a sacrificial pawn.

And so I wait'd for her response. And if I thought I had made the last decisive play of the game, I was mistaken. When it came a day later, it was as waspish and cunning as ever.

She wou'd accept Philippe's invitation and do what was requir'd of her to ensure his immediate support for the Company. But securing her share of the business – which she regard'd as rightfully hers, whatever the circumstances – was not enough in return. She want'd no further part of the Bank or the Company, because she had no faith in my ability to manage them. In her opinion, their future was in severe jeopardy and she relinquish'd all her interests in them.

She, therefore, wish'd to receive another kind of compensation. She want'd full ownership of Gourmande and its contents – which meant most of our picture collection – plus regular contributions to its upkeep, together with a lump sum of 1 million livres – not in paper, not in Company shares, not in government bonds, but in gold. Only gold – there cou'd be no other form of payment. If I refus'd, I shou'd be in no doubt as to the consequences: she wou'd leave France for England immediately and crawl back to Gregg, taking – and this was an add'd twist of the knife, a sting in the tail – Anne with her.

Chapter 11

The visit to San Moise marks the end of our Age of Decadence tour. It also leaves us not far from our hotel and, as seems only fitting, the site of the Ridotto. We've come full circle and Marisa delivers a final commentary as we head towards the Monaco.

'*Allora*...one last word on our tour – an epilogue, if you like...'

I'll miss her narrative. It's provided me with a welcome distraction from having to make an extremely painful decision. Only Jo now stands between it and me.

'The Ridotto eventually became a victim of its own success. The city fathers thought it was not only a source of moral corruption but that it also impoverished the local gentry. In 1774, they took the decision to close it down. The *poor* gentry were so addicted to the wager, however, that their immediate response was to set up gaming rooms in their own houses – *casa* in Italian and the derivation of *casino*, the word that in many ways defines our own Age of Decadence.'

We give her a round of applause; she takes a mock bow. I pull out all the Euros I have and hand them to her as a tip, probably around 300.

'Please, Theo, it's too much.'

'It's too little. You've been marvellous, Marisa. Thank you.'

We each give her a hug. 'For when you're next in Venice,' she says, handing us both a business card, 'you can come to me directly.'

Jo and I give her our cards. 'For when you're next in London,' Jo says. 'Come and see us.' She makes it all sound so cosy, as if we've set up home together.

It's only then I realise the waters have receded. We're standing on dry-ish ground and the banks of the canals are no longer submerged.

I gesture round excitedly. Somehow, I feel I've had a miraculous hand in this, like Moses parting the waters. 'Lo and behold, no more *acqua alta.*'

'It just means it's low tide,' Marisa laughs. 'It'll be back – you haven't heard the last of the sirens, I'm afraid…'

We bid our final farewells. As she heads off towards a water taxi, I spontaneously put my arm round Jo. Our guide turns back to us once more and laughs. 'See!' she shouts. '*Amore!*'

'*Avanti!*' I shout back to her.

*

Venice, December 1728

The sicker I become, the harder it is to focus on the present, let alone unravel the past. The laudanum – as well as the hot chocolate – eases the pain in my chest and lightens my mood. But it also makes it harder for me to recall the past with any great accuracy. Or indeed to know if what I recall is the result of memory or imagination. What I think I remember – through the mist that now swirls as much in my head as it does along the canals – is that after I agreed to Katherine's terms, events seem'd to move more quickly; to rush headlong towards a conclusion that I did everything in my power to change, but cou'd not avoid. It was as if the outcome was, yes, my destiny, but certainly not one of which I was the master.

Katherine's response to my cruel, heavy-hand'd threat was equally cruel and heavy-hand'd. Her loss of faith in my stewardship of the Bank and the Company and her insistence on payment in gold cut me to the quick. However, with the future of Louisiana on a knife's edge, I felt I had no choice but to give her all she want'd. I consol'd myself with two thoughts: first, that I wou'd not have to deal with her again as a business partner (although why not having to deal with someone who had given me nothing but sage advice shou'd be a consolation, I do not now know); and, second, that it was my intention, in due course, to make a compulsory recall of all the gold coinage in circulation and exchange it for banknotes. The game was far from over.

And so to the celebration at the Tuileries. Having receiv'd Katherine's acceptance of his invitation, Philippe was as wildly enthusiastic about the arrangements for the evening as I was about those for the emigrants' weddings. Both wou'd be spectacular theatrical events on the grandest scale. Both wou'd enhance the power and influence of the Company, and take me a few steps closer to assuming the role of Financial-Controller. I was already picturing the disgruntl'd look on d'Argenson's face.

Up until the evening at the Tuileries, my only proper contact with Katherine had been over the legal confirmation of our agreement and the conditions for fulfilling it – the transfer of the ownership of Gourmande to her, the handing over of the deeds, the setting up of a regular maintenance payment and the single payment of the 1 million livres, all of which she want'd done post-haste. She wou'd not hear of her gold remaining on deposit in the vaults of the Bank, even though it wou'd earn interest and she cou'd have had full access to it at any time. I was therefore reduc'd to dispatching a heavily armour'd wagon, load'd with louis d'or out to the estate.

Nor wou'd she reply in full to my repeat'd enquiries about my seeing Anne and my suggestion that the child spend some time with me at Louis le Grand. All she wou'd say was that she herself did not intend to stay at the house ever again and that she wou'd prefer that Anne was kept well away from Paris for now. I felt I had little choice, but to raise the subject when I saw her at the Tuileries, not a prospect I relish'd.

An hour or so before dusk, an enormous crowd, which seem'd to include every member of Parisian Society who cou'd walk, gather'd in the newly plant'd gardens, while beyond the walls, the rest of Paris jostl'd and press'd to catch a glimpse of all this pomp and splendour. Amid the broad parterres and exotic shrubbery was a shifting sea of powder'd perukes and periwigs, of the fanciest frock coats and ball gowns I had seen assembl'd since our arrival in Paris. There were reams of the finest lace, every hue of silk and satin imaginable, and a display of countless cleavages that amount'd to at least an acre of expos'd female flesh of every vintage. And still they arriv'd – by swarms of gild'd carriages at the gates, by brightly colour'd boat at the river moorings. All overlook'd by the old Tuileries palace, whose crumbling façade had been clean'd and repair'd, so that it appear'd more like Catherine de Medici's grand original.

Much of the interior had also been restor'd, I notic'd, as in the company of Saint-Simon and his wife, I made my way up the broad sweeping staircase to the ballroom on the first floor where Philippe was holding a reception for his distinguish'd guests and guests of honour.

'May I enquire as to the whereabouts of Madame Law?' Saint-Simon ask'd. 'I trust she is not unwell?'

'No, she's very well, Louis, and I believe she'll be arriving presently.' And 'separately' I was about to add, but thought better of it. I did not wish to advertise our estrangement, even to him. It might only detract from the Company's general show of strength and stability.

We found Philippe, already flush'd by wine and the heat of the evening, among a crowd of doting courtiers.

He welcom'd us warmly and declaim'd to the room: '...Monsieur Law! After His young Majesty – and Madame Law, of course' – he rais'd an enquiring eyebrow in my direction – 'the greatest gift that God has bestow'd upon France!' He was swift in taking me aside; there was a note of panic in his voice. 'Where is she? She promis'd me she wou'd be here...'

'And she will be here, very soon, Your Highness. Our daughter was taken sick this afternoon and she delay'd her departure to make sure the child was settl'd.' Why I bother'd to say this, when he was bound to find out it was untrue, I am not sure. Anne was very much on my mind and it was probably also part of the same game of pretence – an utterly futile one, as I wou'd soon discover.

He gave a wry smile. 'She is a devot'd mother as well as a wife.'.

'She is, Your Highness...'

While Philippe welcom'd another of his guests, it was Saint-Simon's turn to draw me aside. He spoke softly in my ear: 'I was told the Duchesse might put in a rare appearance: Francoise-Louise, Philippe's long-suffering wife...'

He nodd'd towards a woman of brood-mare proportions with what might have been an open, attractive face, had she allow'd herself to smile. Instead, she was obviously less than comfortable in public. She stood apart from the crowd with her female companion and gaz'd upon everyone with a sullen disdain that only emphasis'd her plainness.

'Philippe increasingly refers to her as Madame Lucifer,' he add'd. 'She's usually shut up at Saint-Cloud, the family estate, but apparently she adores pyrotechnic displays and wou'd not be kept away. Expect him to misbehave even more than usual this evening.'

'You mean, we've even more pyrotechnics to look forward to.' We both laugh'd and, at that moment, Katherine enter'd from stage left.

I wou'd not have thought it possible, but she look'd more radiant than ever. I was immediately transport'd back to when I had first seen her at Argyll's. I had been unable to take my eyes off her then and the same was true as she swept into the Tuileries that evening. And, yes, that same bolt of physical desire for her was back again, except what shou'd have been a pleasurable sensation was more a sword point pressed against my flesh.

Was her beauty enhanc'd by the fact that she was now beyond my reach? Was it because I had lost her that I want'd her again, there and then? Was that why I felt more than a twinge of jealousy as I watch'd her face light up for Orleans, in the same way it had once lit up for me?

They seem'd to go on laughing and talking for the longest time, but it was likely no more than a few minutes before she took his arm and they all but float'd across to us on a cloud of bonhomie.

'It seems that Anne is completely recover'd!' Philippe exclaim'd to me.

I look'd at Katherine. 'I'm greatly reliev'd to hear it.'

'No more than I am,' said the Sun Queen archly. 'It leaves me completely free to enjoy the evening with His Royal Highness...'

His Royal Highness look'd like the cat that had not only got the cream but finally caught the mouse he had been chasing for a while. 'Now, now, John,' he jok'd, 'you mustn't stand here gossiping with Saint-Simon all night. You're like a pair of old dowagers. Come with us...'

Was I being over-sensitive or did he wish for me to be an eye-witness to how much he was enjoying Katherine's company and, more to the point, how she was enjoying his? And did he also wish me to see that all his distinguish'd guests were witnessing it too?

Whatever, I did as I was bid and join'd them, as he proceed'd to effect formal introductions to various dignitaries around the room, most of whom I had already met. Once we had complet'd this tedious round, he announc'd to the company that the King wou'd soon arrive for the start of the display.

It had not occurr'd to me that the young Louis wou'd attend and yet it made perfect sense. The Tuileries was his new home and pyrotechnics appeal'd as much to children, even Royal children, as they did to adults.

A few minutes later, the King enter'd the room to a flurry of bows and curtseys. Then, the extraordinary happen'd. (I did not realise quite how extraordinary until that great observer of court protocol, Saint-Simon, inform'd me a little later.) In any other circumstances, Philippe wou'd have been join'd by Francoise-Louise at this point in the proceedings and together they wou'd have escort'd the King to the grand balcony, overlooking the gardens. Instead, Orleans and Katherine escort'd the King and left his wife, the Duchesse, to trail along behind them like a handmaid.

As the other guest of honour, I was invit'd to join them. Everyone else sought other balconies and windows or went swiftly downstairs to the gardens in order to watch the display.

Dusk had fallen and the gardens were etch'd by the light of a dozen giant torches. The drone of conversation rose on the soft evening breeze, mix'd with the sinuous strains of a string quartet. All grew hush'd as the King appear'd on the balcony with Philippe and the Duchesse. Suddenly, there was cheering and shouts of 'Long live the King!' 'Long live the Regent!' which then became 'Long live Monsieur and Madame Law!' when Katherine and I appear'd.

As the cheering continued, the young Louis turn'd to me. 'Thank you, Monsieur Law, for making France rich again.'

'It's my pleasure, Your Majesty.'

'I shou'd very much like to visit you some day at the Rue de Quincampoix. It sounds very exciting.'

'And I very much look forward to receiving you there, Your Majesty.'

What made this so affecting was not just the fact that Louis XV, as he wou'd be crown'd at his majority, thank'd me for my services – the very thought of him on the Quincampoix was both amusing and thrilling – but that he did so in his own words rather than those of Philippe. If it hadn't been for Philippe's and Katherine's unbecoming antics, my sense of triumph wou'd have been complete. As it was, an evening that shou'd have had the character of the finest vintage wine had taken on that of lemonade – <u>bittersweet</u>.

We did not have long to wait for the pyrotechnics. The torches were soon extinguish'd. We were plung'd briefly into darkness, and the quartet began to play again. From the back of the gardens, in the central parterre, there came a series of sharp explosions. Great fountains of coloured light – red, blue, yellow and green – gushed into the air, higher and higher, as if rising to the music. After a time, these eventually gave way to what seemed to be flaming arrows or 'rockets' as they are known. They shot into the heavens and explod'd into a myriad of stars that fell in sparkling cascades.

I had seen such fireworks – to use the English word – in London, at Southwark by the Thames, but they were nothing by comparison. I stole a look at the others on the balcony. Katherine, Philippe and Francoise-Louise stood with rapt expressions, marvelling at each shower of falling stars. The young Louis was agape and wide-ey'd with wonder, as if the Lord himself and a host of angels had descend'd from the clouds to anoint him.

Then, with a final flourish and crescendo that seem'd to set the whole canopy of the sky ablaze, it was over. The last few stars fad'd into oblivion and another great cheer went up from the crowd.

The torches and the lamps were re-lit. I turn'd to Katherine – but she was gone. And Philippe too, I realis'd. I look'd back into the ballroom, but cou'd see no sign of them.

'I think that pyrotechnics are my most favourite thing in the world,' said Louis with a broad smile. And then: 'Where is the Regent?'

The Duchesse inclin'd towards him. 'As so often happens, Your Majesty, he has had to attend to a pressing matter of state.' She dart'd a poisonous look in my direction. 'He apologises and has ask'd me to escort you and your entourage back to the Royal apartments.'

The King wav'd adieu to the still cheering crowds, bade me good night and withdrew, leaving me alone on the balcony.

What was I to do? I cou'd not run through the palace, as I had done at Gourmande, trying to prevent a liaison that I had condon'd. And yet, why had they made such a public display of it? Katherine had done far more than simply attend the event to keep Philippe happy – she had flaunt'd herself, behav'd like a strumpet. The whole of Paris wou'd soon know about the affair and I wou'd be left humiliat'd. Instead of the man who runs France, I wou'd be seen as Orleans' dupe.

I wonder'd if this was how Francoise-Louise felt or whether she was beyond caring about such things as love and fidelity. I had thought that I was indifferent, but I had been fooling myself, judging from the churning knot in my stomach and the searing pain in my chest. (I trace the origins of the malady in my lungs to this time.)

After the display, the crowd began to gather again in the ballroom and it seem'd to me that word had already spread of Katherine's and Philippe's less than secret tryst. I cou'd have sworn there were knowing looks and whispers behind every hand and fan, but perhaps that was only normal practice for courtiers. I ask'd several if they had seen them, but none had. One came up to me, with a fawning smile that verg'd on a smirk. A footman had told him that His Royal Highness the Regent and 'Madame Low' had been seen leaving the Tuileries.

'Did he know where they were going?' I ask'd.

'He believ'd the Palais-Royal, but who can say for sure, Monsieur Low' – there was a saucy gleam in his eye – 'on an *evening such as this a romantic trip down the Seine might be the thing...'*

I want'd desperately to slap the man's roug'd cheek and make it even rouger. I also want'd desperately to confide in Saint-Simon, but the dancing had begun and he was partner'd with his wife at the far end of the room. Only an hour before, I had deliberately given him the impression that Katherine and I were still together and jok'd about how Philippe might behave in front of the Duchesse. I had not thought that the joke wou'd be at my expense.

My mood turn'd wretch'd and foul. I cou'd no longer behave as a 'guest of honour'. I summon'd my carriage and return'd to Louis le Grand.

But neither was there comfort there. It was desert'd. The servants had all gone to the Tuileries and were doubtless party to gossip about the Regent's latest mistress. I cou'd not bear the thought. Nor cou'd I bear the sight of the rooms where Katherine had once sat nursing Anne. My Madonna and Child were now a conspicuous absence that brought tears to my eyes, as sure as if they had been dead. They were to me.

I took a bottle of cognac, went up to my study and sat drinking at my desk. I thought to write to Katherine, but after several false starts abandon'd the idea and push'd the paper and quill aside. Half the cognac had gone when I saw 'him' appear in the room – the phantom whom I had not seen since our early days in Paris and had almost forgotten. He gave me his most piteous look; the blood from his chest wound seep'd through his strange fustian jacket. He reach'd out the other hand, as if to warn me of something, some danger – and was gone.

*

For the first time since breakfast, Jo and I are alone. It feels awkward for me and I'm sure it's the same for her. We can't get a drink quickly enough. I think we're hoping to re-establish an intimacy that seems have been lost as the day's worn on.

We're sitting in Harry's Bar, once frequented by the glitterati, now a pricey tourist trap, full of chattering Chinese and burly Germans off the cruise liners. We're there, partly because it's famous but mainly because it's a stone's throw from the hotel, on a corner by the Grand Canal. Not that you'd know once you're inside. The windows are small and shut out the world: it's a Venetian snug.

I remember reading somewhere that the original owners of the bar – the Ciprianis, the same ones who used to own the hotel where we had lunch – were fined millions of dollars by the US authorities for tax evasion and offloaded the loss-making bar to a Luxembourg-based investment company. Harry's Bar – from the haunt of Hollywood stars to a tax write-off. What would Marisa and Diana Lennon have to say about that?

We sit at the bar at first and watch the young, white-coated barman prepare our negronis – equal measures of sweet vermouth, Campari and gin, with a twist of orange. It's a heavy hit but we need it. He says the bar's speciality has always been a bellini, but he can do a very fine negroni for us, one of the best. As he pours, he tells Jo he's sure he recognises her from somewhere – an American film, perhaps.

She says she's so dressed down she thought no one would recognise her. She puts her finger to her lips, looks around and asks him to keep it to himself.

He smiles wryly. 'Your secret's safe with me, Signorina.'

'Signora.'

'*Signora.*' Waytogo, Jo. Fight BS with BS.

We order some *cicchetti*, take our drinks and retire to a corner table. It's extraordinary how with a new relationship you're acutely aware of every minor shift in mood, of the most minute change in the emotional weather, even though you don't have enough experience of each other to know what it means or if it's actually happening at all. Maybe it's only happening inside your head as you project one insecurity after another onto this relative stranger. I've forgotten what these rooky relationships are like. The longer you're together, the more you learn to ignore the weather. Isn't that why I didn't see what happened with Angela coming? Isn't that why I didn't realise that her heinous background, far from disposing her toward the criminal, had created disgust for it of a visceral nature?

And speaking of relative strangers, that's what Jo and I amount to, don't we? I've done it again, the classic man thing – spent time getting to know a woman's body and ignored most other things about her. Now I have little idea who's sitting across the table from me – although I *do* know enough to recognise two sides to her nature: the tender, concerned girlfriend and the hard-nosed lawyer; the solicitous and the solicitor. It's the latter she now unleashes on me, catching me off-guard.

She takes a hit of the negroni before she pitches in: 'So Theo.'

'So Jo.'

'Can I be honest with you?'

'Please do.'

'I'm struggling to get through this weekend. I've tried backing off, not taking it too seriously, giving you room to go through whatever it is you're going through. It's a side to you I haven't seen before, but I've done my best to accommodate it.'

'You've been great. I'm sorry.'

She shrugs, breathes deeply. 'I'm afraid I'm done with it. It's left me feeling…used, abused even. Apart from anything else, it's very depressing.'

'God, that's terrible. *Abused?* It's a strong word.'

'It's how I feel.'

'I didn't mean to…'

'I know, Theo. At least I think I do, but the end result's the same.'

'I'm *really* sorry.'

'Coming here with you has obviously been a mistake. I'm going to head back first thing tomorrow.'

'Are you sure?'

'Yes.' We both take large, desperate hits of our drinks.

'What can I do? How can I convince you it's not been a mistake?'

'I don't think you can.'

'Please – if this is a test, I don't want to fail it.'

'It's not a *test*. I'm not trying to catch you out. I just want you to be honest with me, that's all.' Another sip of her drink, another deep breath. She's showing distinct signs of irritation.

'It would be good to know what's going on with you. Let me in a little is all I'm asking.' She looks away. 'Not that it matters anymore.'

'Of course, it matters. It matters very much.'

Suddenly I find myself placing my hand on hers, leaning across and kissing her gently on the lips. She doesn't pull away and it's as good as a hit of the negroni.

'I'm sorry,' I say, 'this has been all about me.' As if it might signal that I'm now only interested in her, I look with what I hope is a longing into her eyes. It's the first time I've really appreciated their colour – deepest, darkest brown, almost black. 'I want to know more about you. I want to get closer to you, not push you further away.'

She looks a combination of confused and heart-achingly lovely.

'I mean it,' I say. 'I'm being straight with you, Jo.'

'Okay…' She deliberates for what seems an age. 'If that's the case, you tell me your big secret – and I'll tell you mine.'

*

I fully expect'd to hear from Katherine following her disappearance with Orleans. Just as she had demand'd an explanation for my behaviour, I felt she now ow'd me one for hers. But after some three days of my shutting myself up in the house, it finally dawn'd on me that we were now free agents, without obligation to each other, and that apart from allowing me time with Anne, she ow'd me nothing whatsoever. Nor I her.

Moreover, I cou'd not go on living in fear of the opinions of servants or society. If I was seen as some sort of cuckold, then so be it. Compar'd to my position as head of the Bank and the Company – and the power I increasingly wield'd in wider French society – it was nothing. Philippe had what he want'd, and so did I, which meant that I need'd to get on with doing the thing I lov'd. I head'd straight to the Rue de Quincampoix, where I found that the hustle and bustle and sheer excitement of trading quickly banish'd my despondency.

The news of the emigration policy had push'd up the share price and brought praise for my prudent approach to the management of the Bank and the Company. The street itself was busier than ever. The volume of share dealing had virtually doubl'd and I was petition'd on all sides by potential investors from every walk of life and level of society. Nobody want'd to know what was going on between the Regent and my 'wife'; everybody want'd to know when there wou'd be another share issue – 'When will we meet the Great Grand-daughters?' they cried. 'Soon,' I said. But even I didn't realise how soon.

Suddenly d'Argenson was standing before me, but this time he was without his arm'd guards and sounding – dare I say it? – less of an attack dog and more of a lap cat.

'I know you're busy, Monsieur Law,' he purr'd, 'but cou'd you possibly spare me a few moments?'

His more clement attitude was a welcome surprise and not a little suspicious, but once we were sitting in my office and he reveal'd the reason for his visit, I felt he rather shou'd have crawl'd to me on all fours!

'I am sent by the Regent to discuss the National Debt with you.'

'That is a big subject.'

'It is.'

'How big?' I ask'd. He retreat'd into sullen silence. 'If you want to discuss the subject in any meaningful way, I need to know how much it is – within a few million or so.'

He revert'd to his characteristic growl – he had obviously come under much duress. 'If you must know, Law, it is some...1.2 billion livres... But it's not increasing, at least. And we have been able to service it...just...'

'Nor is it reducing.'

'No.'

'And the Regent thinks it shou'd be.'

'He's got the idea into his head that there shou'd be much greater tax revenue to offset it.'

'And so there shou'd...'

He shrugg'd and look'd uncomfortable. 'There's something else, though, something far more pressing...'

'Is that possible?'

'Oh, yes. A number of big foreign lenders are calling in their debts, waging financial war on us, I call it. I wou'd tell them to

go sing for their money, but as the Regent says, who wou'd lend to us in the future? As it is, it puts us more on the verge of bankruptcy than ever...'

I let that statement hang in the air for several seconds. Meanwhile, a solution to the problem sprang immediately to mind. As with the emigration policy, it came fully form'd, capable of running and jumping before it cou'd even crawl. I almost had to catch my breath from the excitement of it.

'Please tell the Regent, I will visit him at the Palais-Royal this afternoon to discuss a solution.'

D'Argenson was obviously disappoint'd at not being the bearer of more dramatic tidings himself, but there cou'd be only one hero in this story, and it wou'd not be him.

As I return'd to the hubbub of the street, I told myself that this was the chance I had been waiting for – the chance to teach the French Monarchy the true meaning of absolute power.

*

'Who's going first?' I ask.

'You are.'

I genuinely want to tell her everything; to stop us being strangers and show her how much I care. But there's another, more practical reason – and it's why the Moneyman is screaming in my ear: *Don't you dare, you fucking prick!* He's very coarse at times, ruthless, Stalinesque. He knows it could well mean I cross a line. Once it's all out there, I may have nothing to lose – I'd be committed to the heist. The sheer articulation of it will make it a reality and the Anarchist will have won.

So, I'm probably trying to placate the Moneyman in some sense when I say: 'Whatever I tell you is strictly between us, Jo. I must be able to trust you.'

'Of course. Isn't that what this is all about – trusting each other?'

Now she leans across and kisses *me* on the lips. 'I realise there's a lot of fall-out from the marriage. I'm not stupid.'

'Yes, that's part of it, certainly...' And I'm off talking about me again. I pitch into the history of my depression after the break-up, the panic attacks, the opening up of those black holes, the migraines. 'Nothing surprising about any of that,' I say. 'All the usual self-pitiful stuff you'd expect from the *hurt party*.'

'It doesn't matter that it's the usual stuff – it still hurts.'

'Yes. But there's a much bigger problem and it pre-dates the marriage. In fact, it was the cause of the break-up. It's about what I do for a living.'

What I do for a living. Now there's a euphemism. *What I do to promote dying.* 'Which means it's about who I am.'

'And who are you, Theo?'

'You must have had some inkling when you were involved in that court case.'

'I knew you were working for a fairly unsavoury character, but so was I. If we only worked for the good guys…'

'Yes, I know. But providing a legitimate professional service, within the law' – I almost said being a *dedicated professional* – 'doesn't make you a criminal.'

'Some might argue it makes me an accessory.'

'They might, but I'm something different. I *am* a criminal, categorically, on a grand scale. There's no argument. For many years, I've laundered large amounts of dirty money for characters like that one. Worse than him, in fact, much worse. And in doing that, I've not only broken the law myself, I've enabled *their* crimes. I've helped them exploit people, destroy people, destroy whole countries, I've realised. Of course, I pretended I didn't know. Found all sorts of ways to make it seem acceptable. But I did know and it's not acceptable. I hid it from myself as I hid it from Angela – and when she found out she decided I was a different person, not someone she wanted to go on sharing her life with – or even continue to be the father of our child…'

Saying all this is painful, but it's also good, cathartic: the purging power of the confessional. I don't know why I haven't done it before – and I haven't even got to the really important bit.

'Is that what's giving you the nightmares, that sense of guilt?'

'I wish it were that simple.' I drain my glass, she drains hers and we order two more negronis. (We haven't yet touched the antipasti; mainlining alcohol has been our first priority.)

'It's one thing to admit you're guilty of a crime,' I say, 'but something else to atone for it.'

'Atone? That's as strong a word as abuse.'

'It's what I'm planning to do – at least I think I am.'

'How?'

'By taking down the criminals I've helped – and probably myself in the process.'

She flinches at the thought. 'Sounds very risky.'

'It is. I'm doing my best to limit the risks – but it is. I don't think those near accidents while I've been here are so accidental. They might be on to me.'

'*Theo*...I'm sorry...' As the fresh drinks arrive, she leans across and kisses me again, this time more firmly.

The waiter waits for us to finish. '*Scusi...*' He smiles and gives me the classic nod and wink.

'When is all this supposed to happen?' she asks.

'When I say so. Anytime. I just have to give the word.' We embark on our second negronis of the evening. '*But* – and this is a very big but – I haven't finally made up my mind to do it – that's the truth of it. That's where the nightmares come in. I keep asking myself: am I actually going to do this?'

She's clearly shocked and trying to gather her thoughts. If she hasn't had the thought already, I'm sure she's thinking now that it's not a great idea to be hanging out with this person. 'And what is *it*? What are you going to do – expose these people in some way?'

'Yes, but also something much worse. They can buy their way out of any exposure. It happens all the time. What I've set up is a massive cybertheft – except I'm not stealing data, I'm stealing something that's more precious to them – billions of dollars, at the touch of a button – or rather the entry of particular codes. I don't begin to understand most of it.'

'Wow! And what will you do with all these billions?'

'Give them away – along with my own billion. I've identified several deserving causes.'

'You're Robin Hood,' she smiles.

'Does that make you my Maid Marian?' The Moneyman is in my ear again – *what the fuck, Theo?*

She laughs. 'But you haven't made up your mind yet.'

'No.'

'What's stopping you?'

'Fear. Partly for what might happen to Angela and Grace – although I'm sure I've got that covered – and for what could happen to me, if I'm honest. I don't think there's any way I can protect myself from the wrath of Boris.'

'Boris?'

'Boris Aronovsky – the chief victim of the sting, the big bad guy...' I break off. 'Listen, Jo – it's so good to speak about these things. You wouldn't believe how good it feels.'

'I'm glad it's helping.'

'Of course, it is.' *It* and the negronis. 'I've just been locked inside my head for so long, going round in circles with this. You begin to wonder what's real and what isn't. And there's always this nagging sense that I can't change, that it's impossible, because I'm stuck with who I am – the Moneyman. Period.'

The Moneyman punches the air. *Finally! Thank fuck for that!*

'Maybe you are stuck with being the Moneyman, Theo – but maybe you can be another kind, the kind that spreads the money around to those who deserve it.' *Noooo!*

*

We met in d'Argenson's office. Two things caught my attention: the chaos of the Financial-Controller's desk – how cou'd he determine the day of the week, let alone the size of the National Debt? – and the fact that Philippe seem'd, by his own standards, extremely ill at ease. Was it the looming financial crisis or the fact that he hadn't seen me since that evening at the Tuileries and now felt somewhat embarrassed by the whole business? It was difficult to say.

D'Argenson also appear'd uncomfortable, more so than when I had seen him earlier. Perhaps, he thought I wou'd start the discussion by suggesting that I replace him as Financial-

Controller. But as much as I want'd that to happen, there were other priorities on this occasion.

We dispens'd with pleasantries and I pitch'd straight into my main theme: 'It seems that there are two separate but inextricably link'd problems here, gentlemen. The first is the corrupt and inefficient method of tax collection, which sits like a parasite on the body politic; the second is the unsustainable level of the National Debt. Each of them is bad enough, but together they are much worse and must be dealt with as quickly as possible. If they are not, they will undermine all the efforts of the Bank and the Company to revitalise France and will eventually bring the whole edifice of the State and the Monarchy itself crashing down...'

D'Argenson look'd as if I had blasphem'd or utter'd a heresy; Orleans respond'd with a series of nods. Certainly he must have known I spoke the truth – why else wou'd he have sent for my help?

I push'd on: 'As far as tax collection is concern'd, I believe that the rights to collect are currently held by the General Receivers for direct taxation and the Farmers General for indirect. I wish to acquire the rights for both and see to it that they are properly administer'd. This will have an immediately favourable effect on the Exchequer.'

'But the rights are held by a group of private individuals,' our Controller moan'd, 'not government officers.'

'I know who holds them,' I replied. 'Indeed, I suspect I know many of them personally, as do you. It shou'd make it easier to arrange.'

I look'd at Philippe. I knew how close to him this axe wou'd fall and that it might even deal him a glancing blow, so hand-in-glove was the higher nobility with the corrupt revenue system.

'How much might you pay for these rights?' he ask'd. D'Argenson seem'd surpris'd that he was pursuing the topic.

'I wou'd have to look more closely at the public accounts' – I pointedly eyed the chaos of the Controller's desk – 'but given what I already know and the estimat'd yield, I wou'd say around sixty million livres...'

376

He nodd'd again. 'A considerable sum, John – but then it wou'd need to be to get them to agree to it. And how do we solve the problem of the National Debt and the creditors who are baying at our heels?'

'The Company will agree to pay it off.'

It was the only time I ever saw Philippe's jaw literally drop – a singularly inelegant expression for His Royal visage.

'More precisely,' I went on, 'the Company will lend the Crown 1.2 billion livres to redeem its debts. It will become the Crown's sole creditor, offering it far better terms than have ever exist'd before.'

He struggl'd to regain his composure. 'The Company has 1.2 billion livres?'

'It will do – after the next share issue.'

He ponder'd this for a moment. D'Argenson's unease was palpable; he cou'd have sat upon it and ridden it around the room.

'John,' he said finally. 'Why don't you and I take a walk together around the grounds?' He turn'd to the Controller. 'If you will excuse us, Sir?'

D'Argenson bow'd low. 'Of course, Your Royal Highness...'

Philippe and I said very little until we had left the palace and were outside among the parterres.

'Firstly, John, I want to apologise for my behaviour at the Tuileries. Katherine and I shou'd not have left as we did.'

I acknowledg'd his apology with a terse nod. I was in no mood to indulge him; it seem'd just then that he need'd me more than I need'd him. 'Perhaps you shou'd not have left at all.'

'Perhaps, not...'

'Then why did you?'

'Because Katherine insist'd upon it. It was her idea that we leave.'

'I don't understand.'

'Neither did I. At first, we were enjoying the evening perfectly well together and I was extremely content just to be in her company. But then, to my surprise, she grew more forward with me – one might almost say coquettish – and I grew more and more excit'd. Truth be told, I was like a dog on heat. I not only had an ache my heart, but a much worse one in my balls...'

I rais'd an eyebrow. 'Pardon me, John – but I want you to understand the power she has over me. She has treat'd me like her slave from the start, but it has only increas'd my desire for her. In my over-eagerness to have her, I can't deny that I caus'd her great offence out at Gourmande, but I thought she had forgiven me. Ha! Some forgiveness...

'When we got to the Palais-Royal, she chang'd completely. She went from Venus to Gorgon in the twinkling of those beautiful eyes. We stood in the hall and there, in front of the servants – who, incidentally, gasp'd throughout her monologue – she told me she found me repellent. I was a pathetic creature on every level – incontinent as a lover and incompetent as a ruler, the latter mainly because I listen'd to you. She said she had nothing but contempt for me and never want'd to see or hear from me again. Any of my letters wou'd be return'd unopen'd.'

He look'd pain'd at the very thought. 'Finally, she told me she had a carriage and arm'd guards waiting outside to take her back to Gourmande, and she left. She had only come to the Tuileries to punish me...'

'If this is true...'

'It _is_ true, John, I swear it...'

'If it is, then she want'd to punish both of us. I was left to look a fool and a cuckold...'

'And I was left...with a large dent in my pride – and an even more severe pain in my balls.'

I could not help but smile. He was encourag'd to go on: 'You know, I am always being told by women – by women like Madame de Tencin, for instance – how men hold all the power, all the cards, and they, the poor wives and mistresses, are merely our puppets and playthings. Yet, as a man – and here's an irony, John – as one of the most powerful men on Earth – in relation to every woman I have ever bedd'd, I have always found _myself_ to be the puppet. We are in the most pitiful position, are we not? We may hold all the cards, but we haven't a clue how to play them, except by putting our cocks to the fore...'

378

*Before I cou'd tell him how well Katherine had play'd her
hand with me, he said: 'And here's another irony – how do you
think I feel after being treat'd so badly by her?'*

'That you want her all the more.'

'Of course!'

*We walk'd on in a broody silence that was broken only by
the birdsong drifting on the breeze. Then, he turn'd to me as if
to a new chapter: 'I'll see to it that you can take over the
collection of taxes, John, and, if you really think you can raise
the money with a further share issue, I will strongly recommend
that the Company pay off the National Debt. There will be much
protest, especially from d'Argenson, but they will all do as
they're told. They will be made to understand that there is no
alternative and that it is all in the best interests of France – and
the King.'*

'Thank you, Your Highness.'

'John – once again, the gratitude is all mine.'

*'In that case,' I laugh'd, 'speaking of d'Argenson, I have one
more request...'*

'That you be made Financial-Controller...'

'We are speaking each other's minds today.'

*He smil'd – it felt as if Katherine was long forgotten.
'Indeed, we are, John. But strangely enough, out of all the
requests that one is the hardest to arrange, harder than
anything else we have achiev'd.' I was both amus'd and
gratified by his use of the word 'we'. 'Your appointment as a
foreigner, albeit one who is now a French subject, to such a
high office of state will cause outrage in certain quarters.
However' – he stopp'd walking, as did I; he reach'd out and put
a hand on my shoulder – 'if you pull off the trick with the
National Debt, we shou'd be able to arrange it very soon...'*

*

More tourists press into the bar, driven inside by heavy rain,
judging from their dripping anoraks and umbrellas. We were
thinking to move on, but now decide to stay a bit longer, at least
until it stops raining.

Should we have another negroni? I'm game, but Jo's had enough of them. 'Anymore and you'll have to carry me out.' She opts for a glass of Brunello. She's heard it's one of the best Italian reds.

And we're suddenly hungry. We scoff down the *cicchetti* and order some more.

The volume in the bar has shot up and Jo has to raise her voice: 'Tell me something, Theo – and please be honest.'

'I'm trying my best.'

'In attempting this amazing stunt, are you atoning for your crimes or trying to win Angela back?'

The sharp City lawyer has put her finger on it. 'I don't expect to win Angela back.'

'That's not what I asked.'

I pause for thought. 'It's a bit of both.'

'I think I hear you. At least I know where I stand.'

'Do you? I wish *I* did. The real truth is I haven't a clue. I'm lost, Jo.'

'The real truth is, Theo, you need to reinvent yourself. When your truth is shattered, you need to recreate it.'

I smile. 'All very profound for one so young. Anyone would think you're speaking from experience.'

'I am – bitter experience. That's *my* big secret – I'm an expert in reinvention.'

It's as if someone's been drawing Jo and just added a single, defining line that's brought her image to life. Her voice takes on a new sharpness too.

'Who do *you* think I am, Theo? I mean, I know you haven't gone out of your way to find out. You've been too caught up in your own stuff.'

'For which I sincerely apologise... I think you're a whole host of wonderful things, Jo – smart, attractive, ambitious, but not to the point of ruthlessness.'

'And where do you think I'm from?'

'I only know what you've told me. You moved around a lot as a kid, went to several international schools. You have a fairly privileged background. The person I see reflects all of that. You're self-assured, accomplished – obviously a product of a comfortable upbringing. Now I think about it, though, I can't exactly say where you're from. You yourself said everywhere and nowhere, and you have one of those unplaceable international accents...how am I doing?'

'Not badly. Except I lied – I'm very much from somewhere. Do you want to know where? You may find it shocking.'

'I'll risk it.'

'My mother was Romanian, although her family was from Georgia originally. I look very Georgian, apparently – the pale skin and black hair. I don't know who my father was. He could have been one of many. But he certainly wasn't an international oil executive, and my mother wasn't the corporate wife I described to you, running an immaculate home, organising dinner parties and suchlike. She was a prostitute working in the town of Deva, in Transylvania, where I was born. You see, Theo, I'm not only from somewhere, I'm from somewhere famous – for vampires. The economy was bad in the Eighties, but it got a lot worse after the fall of Ceausescu. My mother was desperate to leave. We moved to Bucharest, where she paid an official a lot of money to get a passport, so we could leave the country and start a new life that didn't involve prostitution. He took the money – then he and his cronies took her, violently, and trafficked her along with many other women, to brothels in various foreign cities. I was four years old and they were going to send me to one of those dreadful orphanages you may remember reading about at the time.'

I nod – it's all I can manage.

'But my mother begged them to let me go with her. Maybe because she was very beautiful and very good at what she did, they finally let us stay together. God knows, what she had to do to get them to agree. A week later we emerged from the truck that had transported us across Europe to find ourselves in the glorious city of Manchester. My home for a while was a brothel in a shabby suburb, where, at a tender age, I became increasingly aware of how badly my mother was treated by her captors – how many men she was forced to have sex with every day and how all the money she made was taken away from her – partly, they said, to pay for the drugs they plied her with. As soon as she could, she got me out of that hellhole and sent me to live with a relative, an aunt, in London – Harlesden, to be precise. It wasn't exactly the smartest part of town, but it was heaven by comparison – except of course I was separated from my mother. I saw her only once after that. My aunt and I paid her a visit about a year later. She'd lost her beauty. She looked very ill, dangerously thin. She kept coughing and I noticed that under the make-up one side of her face was badly bruised. About six months later, when we tried to contact her again, we were told she'd left the house in Manchester. My aunt got on to the local police and eventually it turned out her body had been found in a park on the other side of the city. Just another illegal immigrant of no fixed address. The police said she'd died of heart failure, probably brought on by a drug overdose. There were no signs of foul play – she even had money in her purse, together with her Romanian passport. My aunt thought about telling the police about how she came to be in the UK in the first place, but in the end, she was persuaded to keep quiet for fear of reprisals. The trafficking operation was organised by some very dangerous men who wouldn't have thought twice about silencing a witness – *permanently*.

'The rest is the tale of my reinvention. I had to be made official in the UK. My aunt told the authorities the truth, more or less. I was her niece and she'd become my guardian when my mother died. She herself had been granted residency, and I was too. In due course, I'd be able to apply for citizenship – how times have changed. I was enrolled at a local school and once I'd learnt English, there was no stopping me. I turned out to be relatively bright. Despite being brought up in a brothel or two and a sink estate, I became a straight A student. But I wanted more. I wanted to be a well-spoken, middle class English girl, bordering on the posh even. I'm not sure where I got my role models. There certainly weren't many around Harlesden. I think it must have been all those BBC costume dramas or the young Joanna Lumley. Anyway, I made a conscious effort to lose my accent, which as you noticed, wasn't entirely successful. *Although compared to this'* – she briefly affects a heavy guttural Eastern European accent – 'it's really quite refined. I even dyed my hair a mousey blond at one point, but instead of making me look like an English rose, it made me look like a tart – or what do we say these days? Sex

worker. I got to a decent university, got a first in Law and of
course changed my name. Illeana Angelescu became Joanna de
Vere – the Joanna in homage to you know who and the de Vere
to add a degree of poshness. I blagged my way into a top law
firm, where I've just been made a Junior Partner, the most
junior they've ever had, I was told. And here I am, in Venice, in
Harry's Bar, with you – someone who, coincidentally, down the
years, has perhaps done much to support the kind of
international criminal that traffics women from Eastern Europe,
and many other places besides.'

She takes a sip of her wine. 'You too can reinvent yourself,
Theo – and it's good that you wish to atone for your sins or
whatever it is you want to do. But it sounds like you need to do
it soon, before someone stops you doing anything at all...'

My stomach began to turn when she started her account and
it has gone on turning, probably encouraged by the third
negroni. In fact, I need to throw up is the truth. I need to get to
the washroom as soon as possible. I say nothing. I clamp my
hand over my mouth, jump up and start to edge my way
through the throng. I make it to the washroom just in time,
where I'm violently sick. I can't remember when it last
happened to me and I've forgotten what a God-awful business
it is. The head craning over the bowl, the vomiting, the painful
retching, the foul taste and smell. Twice I think I'm done, but
there's more to come. The purging that is Hell.

I clean myself up, which takes a while, and go back through
a thinned out throng. (The rain must have stopped.) Jo's
disappeared – I can't see her anywhere – and a group of
Chinese are sitting at what was our table.

*

*No sooner had so many hurdles been clear'd than another
appear'd. The day after my meeting with Philippe, I receiv'd a
letter from the Abbè Dubois, Orleans' wily old Foreign Minister
and perhaps his closest advisor in government. Saint-Simon
had told me that Dubois increasingly saw the System as a threat
to his propos'd alliance with Britain – which if achiev'd cou'd
well bring him the Cardinal's hat – and, by extension, myself as*

a threat to him. Sure enough, he wrote to me about the need for us 'to moderate its effects on London, without damaging the interests of France.'

My immediate reply was that unfortunately the two things were incompatible. The company stock markets that had been establish'd in London and Paris were much in competition. As in Isaac Newton's universe, so in the world of finance: the larger the mass of interest payable, the greater its gravitational pull. 'These are Laws of Financial Motion,' I observ'd 'and if they work in favour of Paris, London will inevitably be the loser...'

Within the hour, he had sent back to me, asking that the two of us meet at his apartments 'to discuss the diplomatic aspects of this affair.'

There were many other matters I need'd to attend to, but I knew his opposition cou'd prove troublesome and felt oblig'd to indulge him.

Dubois' palatial rooms were in the Louvre, which, like the Tuileries before its refurbishment, had been neglect'd by the Quartouze and seen better days. It was a fine evening and in the more fragrant parts of Paris the air still possess'd the balminess of high summer. Dusk had fallen by the time I made my way into the echoing courtyard and the torches and lamps were being lit. The cloak'd figure of a woman reced'd down the arcade, and as the light of a lamp caught her, I realis'd it was Madame de Tencin. I doubt'd that she had been visiting the Abbé on a purely ecclesiastical errand, even as the Cardinal's sister. After all, Dubois' appetite for women was legendary, as indeed was that of many clerics. What an obscene and wonderful whirligig it was, I thought, and all increasingly driven by the circulation of paper!

The Abbè start'd by expounding on 'the momentous prospect of an alliance between France and your own country, which wou'd prove an invincible combination in Europe, if not the world.'

'My dear Abbé,' I said, 'I do not regard Great Britain as <u>my own</u> country. Firstly, I am now a French subject and secondly, I believe that Scotland shou'd never have gone into union with England.'

Dubois wav'd this away. 'Whatever one's patriotic feelings, Monsieur Low – and patriotism is a noble sentiment,' he said, trying to appear as conciliatory as his hawkish features wou'd allow, 'the fact remains that Great Britain is a sovereign state and one with which France is keen to ally – a policy incidentally that has the full support of the Regent and the Council. However, apart from the rivalry of many past centuries – which we can overcome, I think – there is one stubborn obstacle to this alliance. As you know, the sale of Mississippi shares is drawing large amounts of money out of London, so I am merely seeking a compromise in the interests of diplomacy. The trading in Mississippi shares cou'd be temper'd to accommodate the South Sea for a short period. Cordial relations with London wou'd be restor'd and the alliance wou'd proceed.'

'Yes, that may be the case,' I said, 'but I'm not sure I want France to be allied with Great Britain.'

The Abbé arch'd his eyebrows. 'Forgive me for saying so, but it's hardly your place to want it or not. You speak as if you govern France, Monsieur...'

'Indeed, there's something in that,' I replied. 'Whoever controls France's money goes a long way to controlling France.'

He fix'd me with a piercing look. 'Does he? Or is it that whoever controls the Regent's heart – or perhaps another part of his anatomy – _thinks_ he controls France?'

Suddenly I had lost my patience with Dubois. 'And if you think the Mississippi Company is attracting too much money from London now,' I said, as I took my abrupt leave, 'I wou'd ask you to wait a week or two. Far from depressing the sales of shares, I intend to boost them.' And the devil take your alliance, I thought.

There is no doubt that I had act'd rashly in telling Dubois that I intend'd a further share issue. But it was less out of spite and more to do with the gamester's urge to trump his opponent; to see that look of dejection on his face, just when he thought he had me beaten.

Chapter 12

My immediate thought is that Jo must have returned to the hotel. I'm out of the bar and all but running in that direction before I realise how lightheaded I feel – or is that just plain drunk? If a black hole, or any other kind of hole, opens up, I'll topple into it, for sure.

But there's no black hole; there's only solid ground. Very wet in places, but free of floodwater now the tide has receded, and solid, probably more solid than anything I've known for a long time. It seems my 'confession' to Jo has helped me resolve my dilemma. I'm actually committed to a course of action and – can you believe it? – the Moneyman is saying nothing about it. He's gone suspiciously quiet, at least for now. It's a huge relief, but it comes at a price. I've driven Jo away and it's hardly surprising. Even without her own startling revelations, even had she really been the daughter of an oil executive, a child of plenty, and not of a Romanian prostitute who'd been trafficked and enslaved, I'm sure she'd have left. And yet I don't want to let her go. It's important that she, or someone, is here to bear witness to my – what? – to my *atonement,* if I can use that word and keep a straight face; to my settling once and for all the moral account. If I'm left on my own, it may never happen.

I'm breathless by the time I get to the hotel. There's a crowd at the elevator and it's taking an age. So I head up four flights of stairs, which leaves me even more breathless. When I get to the room, she's not there and more worryingly all her things are gone too.

I go down to the front desk. Have they seen her? Did she order a water taxi? They haven't, she didn't. I dash outside. The canal front is there in all its evening glory: the naked torches, the moored boats, the illuminated palazzos – an ancient Disneyland in full swing. What should I do? Where should I go? Then, in the half-light, I think I see her, or the back of her – her orange jacket, her shock of dark hair. She's standing with her bag on her shoulder, way off down by the mooring. And I think she sees me, because she suddenly turns and takes off away from the canal, through a group of tourists. The group blocks my path briefly, obscures my view, but it's enough time for her to get some way ahead of me. She's going back towards the San Moise church, home of John Law's remains. At least she is before I lose sight of her.

Now I do break into a run, shouting 'Jo!' at the top of my voice, so that people turn round and wonder what's going on. (Join the club.) Which way has she gone? I catch sight of her again, to my left, crossing the canal that runs by San Moise. I run faster, shout louder. 'Jo...*please*...*Jo!*' And now she too starts to run, down a long broad street, turning right and approaching a bridge across another canal. Suddenly, there are more people and they're all going in my direction. I slalom between them. I'm gaining on her – she's carrying that bag, remember.

I follow her across the bridge, down a narrower street and out into a small, crowded plaza, with the illuminated façade of a grand Palladian building at one end.

And then I catch up with her. '*Jo – for God's sake!*' I grab her by the arm, turn her round towards me – and realise it's not her. She, whoever she is, screams at me in Italian, a torrent of expletives, I'm sure. But worse, she also flails at me, catching me an eye-watering blow with the flat of her hand across the bridge of my nose. As she moves away, she turns back and treats me to some more filthy Italian. I'm bent over, clutching my painful nose, which is already dripping blood.

'*Fuck! Shit! **Fuck!***'

'Theo?' says a female voice.

I look up and find myself squinting at Diana Lennon.

*

I press'd on with my plans apace. The mass wedding of whores and criminals was arrang'd for September 4th. It was such a dramatic demonstration of the Company's support for Louisiana that I decid'd the share issue shou'd take place the following day. The nuptials were conduct'd at the Basilica of

Saint-Denis, with the blessing of Cardinal de Tencin. The Company's Board of Directors was present and I gave a speech to the Regency Council, in which I describ'd the great opportunities awaiting the settlers in America and their future children and grandchildren. They shou'd feel extremely proud, I said, for they were helping to build the foundations of a French Empire that wou'd stretch magnificently from the Mississippi delta in the south to the Great Lakes in the north.

In fact, many look'd less than proud of their involvement in this venture and seem'd to want little to do with the Great Lakes or the Mississippi delta, no matter how magnificent. What was more, they were all extremely unhappy with their respective partners. It was necessary to take the precaution of shackling each couple together and posting a large company of guards to ensure that no fighting took place between them. Even with this degree of coercion, however, when the bells of Saint-Denis rang out and a hundred newly wedd'd couples were parad'd through the streets, many in the large crowd of on-lookers were visibly mov'd by the occasion.

De Conti was particularly impress'd. 'My dear Monsieur Law, your ingenuity amazes me. And to think I had set myself against you. How profoundly wrong I was...'

There was something about this benign version of my corpulent colleague that made me squirm, so much so that at times I long'd for a return of the malignant Prince. 'And this little spectacle,' he continued, 'acts as a grand prelude to the share issue – very clever, Monsieur Law, very clever...'

He had every reason to be pleas'd. He wou'd no doubt make another fortune, if the issue was successful – and it seem'd likely that it wou'd be. Yes, there had been some general rumbles and grumbles from the Council, but with Philippe's firm support, the main reaction to my proposals had been – as it had been with Orleans himself – jaw-dropping amazement rather than outrage. If de Conti and his friends were in any way oppos'd to my plans, they appear'd to have been won over by the prospect of huge financial gain. Nonetheless, I decid'd not to inflame opposition unnecessarily. In all my communications with the Council members, I understat'd the issue of reform and made much of the benefits to the Exchequer.

And so, following the launch of the Company's emigration campaign, the stage was set for the largest issue of shares in the short history of stock-jobbery. To realise my plans, I knew it wou'd first be necessary to draw as much money as possible – in whatever form it came – into the Company stock. I began with an issue of 100,000 shares, pric'd initially at 5000 livres, and follow'd this with two more issues of 100,000 and another of 24,000, all within weeks of each other. At the same time, I announc'd that the holders of billet d'etats – the National Debt – wou'd be given an incentive to convert their bonds to shares – or take annuities of 3%, which was 1% below what they were getting. Generous bank loans wou'd also be made available for share purchase and the printing presses at the Mint were put on full alert. In addition, I made it clear that a down payment of 10% of the price wou'd be sufficient to secure a share purchase. And finally – and perhaps most importantly – I declar'd that the purchase was open to everyone, not just owners of Meres, Filles and Petite-filles.

The effect was spectacular. From the first day of issue, the movement into shares was like a river in full flood – and my experience of it was like being drawn along by the swiftest of currents.

I have said it before and I say it again – I was never happier or more excit'd than when I was trading shares in the rue Quincampoix and, as I sit writing these words, I find myself in Paris once again: rained upon, up to my ankles in fetid mud, besieg'd by crowds of prospective buyers, but wearing a perpetual smile, whilst devising the most complex of transactions as naturally as drawing breath.

As much as my fast fading powers of description will allow, let me paint the picture.

Stock dealing, as well as a general exchange of political and financial news, was now well-establish'd in the Quincampoix. But what had been a busy scene now began to throng to an almost frenzied pitch. From the first, I did my best to impose a semblance of order. Carriages were bann'd within a week. A morning and evening bell was sound'd to signal the beginning and end of the day's trading. And gates were erect'd at each end in an attempt to temper the flow of people into the street – one entrance for the nobility and gentry, another for the rest. Suffice it to say, however, that the gatekeepers were easily brib'd to keep the gates open, and every class and type of person was jostl'd and jumbl'd together in their frantic determination to buy shares.

And buy they did – not just from the Company's representatives, but from the many independent dealers who set up stalls in the street. The latter bought shares in volume, sold them at a profit, bought them back again and sold them on for even more. Indeed, everyone seem'd to become a dealer of sorts, buying and then selling their shares at a higher price – which was what I had expect'd, nay, encourag'd. In this way, more and more money was circulat'd and the price rose rapidly. By mid-October it was 7500; by November 8500; and by Christmas 10,000 livres!

So quickly did things change that the very ground beneath my feet seem'd to move. And yet, there I stood each day, firmly at the centre of this swirling mass, mobb'd by members of all classes, implor'd by them to part with shares on generous terms – and doing my best to accommodate everyone.

At first, maids and footmen were sent in droves by their masters and mistresses. Then, as the stakes grew higher and profits increas'd, the 'gentles' essay'd the hurly-burly themselves, not trusting their employees to deal in such large sums of money.

Most voracious of all were the poorer ranks of the nobility, those who knew only too well what money cou'd bring and lack of it deny. They wou'd often elbow each other aside, grabbing at finery and pulling off periwigs in order to establish a prime position before me, breathless in their desperation to acquire shares.

'Monsieur Law, I beg you – I have sold every bit of silver.'

'I have sold my last field.'

'...my last cow.'

'...my last pig.'

'...my wife.'

'...my children.'

'...my wife <u>and</u> my children.'

'Quick, Monsieur Law, while the price still rises, the deeds of my estate are yours...' And a cesspit it was too, like many of them. Nonetheless, I took his deeds and within the hour he was worth more than six estates! They all were.

Even more shocking was the behaviour of the highborn women. (So much for the gentler sex.) Many wou'd bite and scratch their ways into gaining audience, whilst the pulling of prettily coiff'd hair and wigs and the tearing of satin dresses became a commonplace.

I cou'd have had an army of mistresses, all of them keen to open their legs for me there and then; hefty breasts were thrust at me from every direction, like weapons of war. Once I was thus under siege from three fine baronesses and was desperate to go and pee. They form'd a circle around me: I must part with the shares before they wou'd let me go. 'But my dear Baronesses, I must take a piss!' I cried.

'Then piss away all you like, Sir,' replied one of them. 'We are not letting you out of our sight until a sale is agreed...' To the amusement of many and the disgust of some, I turn'd and reliev'd myself on the spot, while the ladies continued to talk terms.

The next day was even busier. So many people press'd into the street that I hardly had room to sign any share certificates – and certainly none to piss! There was a great deal of pushing and jostling, and several brawls erupt'd over who had secur'd deals and who had not. Two challenges were issued and accept'd; the duels were fought outside the gates, with the winners coming to claim the losers' shares. It was all so exhilarating, I forgot about Katherine, Philippe, Dubois, d'Argenson, de Tencin, de Conti and all the other dramatis personae to whom I had been subject during my time in Paris. I even forgot about my daughter, whom Katherine seem'd to have decid'd I shou'd never see again. I simply allow'd myself for a brief time – all too brief – to be completely immers'd in the business of trading.

Over the next few days and weeks the share price wou'd rise rapidly, fall back as some dealers tried to undercut others, and then leap upwards again. People from every class came forward with whatever currency or denomination they cou'd *muster. The state bondholders were my primary target, but I happily took paper currency, promissory notes and, of course, louis d'or and other coinage. Much as I had tried to rid the world of metal, it was still in circulation and now it was finding its way to me almost naturally, as a river runs to the sea. I gave special discounts for gold and silver – many brought their cutlery and candlesticks, which I was less inclin'd to accept – and most of the dealers were happy to off-load their metal to me, not least because they had nowhere else to store it in the Quincampoix. As a 'great favour' to them, I took it off their hands in return for shares or paper, and transport'd it immediately to the Bank's vaults.*

What stories began to filter through to us – of rags to riches, of unbridl'd luxury, as the newly rich indulg'd in every kind of ludicrous excess: carriages so heavily gild'd that not enough horses cou'd be found to pull them; feasting of such magnitude that the guests wou'd be at the table for days and have to be carried to their beds; suits and dresses so encrust'd with jewels that their wearers cou'd not walk around in them; and commoners paying ancient, arthritic nobles many thousands of livres to marry their young daughters.

One afternoon, on my way from the Company's offices to the Bank, I witness'd the most remarkable and amusing of scenes. Many servants still came to the street to buy shares on their masters' behalf, usually at an agreed rate on the morning. One particular footman found the share price had risen so much while he was there that he could sell at a higher rate and pocket a considerable difference. By the end of the morning, he had trad'd this into a fortune and bought himself a stylish carriage. When he came to be driven away, instead of getting inside, he took up his customary position on the back!

The crowd who had witness'd the transaction stood laughing. One of them – a severe-looking gentleman clad all in black, who I later discover'd to be the notorious Voltaire – turn'd to me and smil'd sardonically. 'Monsieur Law, see how you have stood our world on its head. No one knows his place anymore – quite literally.'

I continued on my way. 'Indeed, Monsieur,' I replied, without a backward glance, 'and that is the greatest cause for celebration.'

And for all its absurdity, I truly believ'd it was. Everything I had hop'd for had come to pass. I coin'd a special term for this nouveau riche. I call'd them Millionaires – Mississippi Millionaires. They were heroes from the battlefield of the Quincampoix and they deserv'd to be award'd their medals of money and status. Servants really were becoming masters. Wealth was being distribut'd throughout society as never before; more and more paper circulat'd at a faster rate; and every form of craft and trade was stimulat'd into profitable activity. The new age of commerce and enterprise was upon us, and France, at last, was wide awake.

*

'Looks like you're in the wars again.'

Diana pulls a hanky from her bag and passes it to me. Several people have gathered round, looking like they may want to make a citizen's arrest rather than offer any sympathy. But they quickly disperse once they see justice has been done and I'm the one who's come off worse.

I struggle to staunch the flow of blood and salvage a little dignity from the situation. 'When I'm not behaving like a teenager,' I say through a pinched nose, 'I'm behaving like a hooligan. Very embarrassing...'

There's a woman standing next to Diana – younger, prettier, very Italian, very stylish.

'Oh, this is Francesca. You would have met her tomorrow at Orsini's, but...well, you're meeting her now.' She turns to the woman. 'I think I told you about Theo Law and his beautiful girlfriend.'

'You did. Hi Theo – are you okay?' Her accent is heavily Italian, but it all adds to her charm.

I nod my head in her direction and hold up a bloody paw. 'Forgive me for not shaking hands.'

'Francesca's my – how do we describe us these days, Fran? Girlfriends? Partners? Yes, *partner.*' She and Diana gaze at each

393

other with puppy dog eyes as if they're in the first flush of romance, which perhaps they are and perhaps that's why Diana wants the world to know. Either that or she's clearly signalling that this is not someone I should even think about laying my male hand on, bloody or not.

There's a pause and a definite sense that we're avoiding talking about *what-the-fuck* I was doing chasing that woman across the square and having a stand-up fight with her, when the last time Diana saw me I was with a perfectly good woman – and beautiful, to boot – who doted on me and hung on my every word. Those were the days. In fact, that was earlier today, would you believe? How can things have changed so quickly? And is it barely more than a day I've been in Venice? Incredible.

Diana breaks the awkward silence. 'Why don't you come and have a drink with us, Theo? Recover from your ordeal. We're actually on our way to La Fenice, the opera house.' She indicates the grand building on the other side of the piazza. 'There's a performance of Mozart's Requiem this evening. I always think it's good to get a requiem or two under your belt at this time of year and La Fenice is such a wonderful place to hang out. We've got a little time before the start.'

Embarrassing as the situation is, I can't deny I feel fortunate to have run into Diana, the alternative being my own company. 'Thank you,' I honk.

Once there, Diana's all for ordering negronis, but I say I overdosed earlier and blame her for turning me on to them in the first place. I order a glass of Prosecco, instead.

La Fenice is indeed a wonderful place, if a bit too ruched and gilded for my taste. As I'm still not volunteering an explanation for the sordid scene they just witnessed, Diana and Fran wax all Marisa-like on the subject of the theatre – how since the 18th century it has burnt down three times. (The third time was arson, apparently.). Little did anyone realise that when they named the first rebuild The Phoenix, it would rise from the ashes twice more. The latest building is a rather kitsch copy of the 19th century version, but they love it nonetheless.

There's another awkward silence until Diana can't resist flexing her crime writer muscle any longer. 'So, Theo, I take it you were chasing that woman across the piazza because you thought she was Jo? Keep the hanky, by the way.'

'Thank you.' My nose has finally stopped bleeding and I'm left contemplating the rag as a symbol of the bloody mess that is my life.

'That's more or less what happened, yes. We had a...difference of opinion – she went off in a bit of a strop. Later, I caught sight of that other woman and chased after her, thinking she was Jo – which as you saw didn't go down too well.'

'Jo will be back, I'm sure.'

'I doubt it. She's taken her things from the hotel. I'm sure she's on her way to the airport, as we speak.'

'I'm sorry.'

I shrug. I almost want to tell them how it's the least of my problems, but one open can of worms is enough.

'Will you still come to lunch tomorrow? By the way, I must text you the address.'

'Yes, of course. And as I've little else to do this evening, I might even go back to the hotel and read the first chapters of that manuscript.'

'Ah, the manuscript. I feel as though I've caused you all sorts of problems, dragging you to Venice for that.'

'You did it in good faith, I'm sure.'

'Well, if I'm honest I did it to make a sale, but, yes, I wanted it to go to a good home and I thought you might genuinely want to acquire it.'

'Which I may yet do.'

'As you're on your own, Theo,' Francesca chips in, 'why don't you join us for the concert? There are still tickets.'

I want to say that requiems aren't my thing; that I'd rather stick my head down that toilet bowl again, but I don't want to appear ungrateful or the philistine finance man I am.

'I feel as though I've imposed on you two enough...'

'You haven't – has he, Diana?'

'Not at all.'

'There you are.'

'Well...in that case, I suppose I can put off reading that manuscript a while longer...'

Francesca goes off to get me a ticket.

Diana beams after her. 'Isn't she a wonder?'

'She certainly is.' My nose may have stopped bleeding, but it hasn't stopped hurting, throbbing even. I touch it lightly. It's tender and swollen.

'I feel very lucky to have found her. She's kind, beautiful, smart, *young*' – she dwelt on the word knowing it would resonate with yours truly – 'what more could a clapped out old dame like me wish for? She's a dealer in religious art, by the way, one of the most successful in the country, has galleries here and in Paris. I think of her as an angel who's just stepped out of one of those Renaissance paintings...oh, Theo, I'm so sorry. Here I am going on about how in love I am and you're...'

'In pain, yes. How does the nose look?'

'Red...and a little swollen.'

'Do you think it's broken?'

'I'm no expert – but I think you should be able to move it if it's broken.'

'*Please...*' The very thought makes me shiver. 'As I said to you when we first met, for a museum Venice is a dangerous place.' She starts to laugh. 'I'm glad you find it so amusing, Diana.'

'I don't mean to be amused, but there's nothing like a man's wounded vanity to set me off – and you do look rather sorry for yourself, Theo.'

'I'm *feeling* sorry for myself.' And for some reason, I start laughing too.

Francesca returns, waving the ticket in triumph. 'I managed to get a seat next to us...'

As we go through to the auditorium, Diana whispers in my ear. 'Bear up, Theo. You'll get through this, I promise.'

Through what? Through the break up with Jo? She must know it's not *that* tragic. Or does she mean something else? Does she *know* something else – and how can she be in a position to promise anything?

*

396

By mid-October, as the leaves turn'd the colour of louis d'or, I was able to inform Orleans that the Company was now in a position to complete the cancellation of France's National Debt. I was surpris'd not to hear back from him immediately, but instead he sent his own special messenger.

I was completing a deal in the busiest quarter of the street, utilising of all things the hump of a hunchback upon which to write out the agreement. (The enterprising fellow had already earn'd a small fortune by hiring himself out as a mobile escritoire and investing the proceeds in shares.) A Company official push'd his way through the crowd to tell me that I had a visitor at the offices. Cou'd I come at once? It was the duc de Saint-Simon.

I conclud'd the share agreement, but a large crowd still jostl'd for my attention, blocking my exit from the street. In desperation, I took out a handful of paper money and threw it in the air, so that it scatter'd behind me like so many rose petals. The crowd dispers'd in its pursuit of the notes and my path was clear.

Saint-Simon sat waiting in my office. His face lit up when he saw me. 'John, my apologies for dragging you from your business. I cou'd not face the tumult in the street.' The raucous sounds of trading came from below, a jarring accompaniment to our conversation.

'It's no place for a gentleman,' I smil'd wryly, knowing that the wildest behaviour usually emanat'd from the so-call'd 'gentles'. 'Have you come to purchase some shares?'

'Ha! Not at all. I'm here on Philippe's behalf. He wou'd have come himself but he thinks it wise if he stays away from the Quincampoix, and a mere letter to you wou'd not suffice. I must be his unworthy emissary, I'm afraid.'

'You are the best of all emissaries, Louis. And how is His Royal Highness?'

'In all truth...sad.'

'How so?'

His eyes widen'd and invit'd me to supply my own answer. 'Katherine?'

'Of course. He still loves her, he says, he still yearns for her. But the longer he goes without seeing her and the more of his

397

letters she returns, the more I fear his love turns to anger. In some ways, it is better that he doesn't see her. I am not sure how he wou'd behave. He claims to be a slave to love, but the fact is he is a slave who is us'd to getting his own way...' He gave a great sigh.

'But on a happier note that is not what I came here to tell you, John, not at all. He wants me to congratulate you on the success of the share issue and to thank you most sincerely for the cancellation of the Debt and taking on the collection of taxes. You shou'd know that the whole court is abuzz with it and speaks of nothing else but John Law and his Mississippi Company and the Millionaires he creates everyday. Surely, they say, he is the richest man in France, if not the whole world.'

'The country of France grows rich – that's what's important,' I said.

'Of course, John, but everyone knows it's because of you. To most of us, you're a hero. The only detractors I've heard are Dubois, who resents the damage you do to London – but you knew that – and Philippe's mother, Madame, who thinks that France has become unhealthily obsess'd with money and will go to the Devil. Orleans finds this most amusing, since in another breath she's urging him to purchase shares for her.' He laugh'd.

'And what do you think, Louis?' I ask'd.

'About what?'

'This...scramble for money.'

'I've said it many times before: I've no understanding of financial affairs.'

'But what of human affairs, are you not more expert there?'

He look'd away absently. 'As you know, I'm deeply suspicious of change of any kind, yet I know how much France suffer'd under the Quartorze. A country that is subject to the extravagant whims of one man can never be at peace with itself. Something new is requir'd, something to give people hope, of that I'm sure.' He paus'd. 'However...'

He look'd down at his gold signet ring, as large as a louis d'or, and started to turn it on his finger, as if turning over his thoughts. 'How to put this...I think the beast is running out of

398

control. I have not said as much to Philippe, but I believe it's time to rein it in before it gets away from you.'

'You think I will lose control?' I ask'd.

'I think there's that possibility, yes.'

'That's a serious charge, Louis,' I said with mock sternness.

He look'd up at me, wary of my reaction. 'And one I agree with,' I add'd. 'The beast must be rein'd in – but not just yet. It still has a little farther to run. Trust me. I've start'd all this and I'll know when to end it.'

He smil'd faintly. 'I've little reason not to trust you, John. You've brought us this far – even if it does mean respectable men bawling and brawling in the street.'

'Even with that, yes, but it won't go on forever. At some point soon, the share price will stabilise and the brawling men – and women – will become respectable again. So, if you're going to buy shares, buy them now, please...'

Again, he wav'd the idea away. 'To come to the main reason for my visit – Philippe also ask'd me to tell you that your appointment as Financial-Controller is imminent and in anticipation of that, arrangements have been made for your instruction.'

'My _instruction_?'

He smil'd. 'Yes – for your conversion to the Roman faith.'

It undoubtedly had its humorous aspect for him – a grown heathen like myself having to submit to the rule of the Church – but I did not immediately appreciate the joke. 'It is a condition of your appointment to an office of state that you become a Roman Catholic, John, and so important is it that the Cardinal himself has consent'd to instruct you – just two hours a day for a week, follow'd by a ceremony and mass at Notre Dame. Philippe knows how busy you are – and anyway, it's longer than Dubois spent studying to become a priest, from what I recall. He proposes a banquet afterwards to celebrate your official elevation to the position of Financial-Controller.' He was still smiling. 'Think of it as one of your business deals, John – a little bit to God for a large amount from Mammon.'

Finally, I was smiling too. 'Now it's making sense. And when will this take place?'

'Next week, if it suits you.'

'The sooner, the better. France cannot afford to leave d'Argenson in the job much longer. Thank you, Louis, for being the bearer of such good news.'

I took out the share certificates that I always kept about my person. 'If I cou'd ask one more favour of you? I wou'd be grateful if you wou'd pass these on for me. '

I wrote out a certificate for 2000 shares to Cardinal de Tencin and sign'd it: '...for the trouble of instructing me in the one true Faith...' And 5000 to the Regent's mother, Madame: '...that she may benefit personally from this obsession with money...'

He took them, frowning. 'Are you sure? Should the charm'd circle stretch so far?'

I laugh'd, by then full of bravado. 'An important law of gambling, Louis: once someone starts playing the game, win or lose, they will almost certainly want to play again – and the more people play, the more secure the System becomes...'

How pompous and arrogant these words seem to me now, but at the time I felt truly invincible, unstoppable. I was completely in step with the march of history and other such fanciful notions that in a more rational frame of mind, informed by the laws of chance and mathematics, I wou'd never have entertain'd.

*

The auditorium is only half-full but no less impressive for that. As we take our seats in the stalls, I look up at five balconied tiers, dripping with gilt. They rise to a celestial ceiling with a vast sun-like chandelier at its centre. Beneath it, on and around the stage, the assembled ranks of the choir and orchestra seem to exceed the size of the audience.

'Are you familiar with this piece of music?' Diana asks me.

'Not at all. I don't really do classical music, certainly not the religious stuff. I apologise in advance if I nod off.'

She smiles what I now recognise as her patronising smile. 'Oh, I think this'll keep you awake, Theo. In my opinion, there's little more exhilarating than Mozart's Requiem. It's designed to raise the dead rather than bury them.'

And I have to admit, if not exhilarated by it – I doubt anything can have that effect on me right now – I'm certainly finding the soaring crescendos of the choir very pleasing when I realise I haven't turned off my phone. Fortunately, the ring tone is set low, although not so low that Diana doesn't shoot me a disapproving glance. I take a discreet look and see it's Jo - thank God. I mime an apology to Diana and Fran, and the other half dozen people in the row I have to squeeze past before I can rush out to the entrance hall.

'Jo?' No answer. '*Jo?*' Between pounding waves of requiem, I gradually make out airport sounds – an echoing flight announcement, muffled people noises.

'*Jo?*' The phone must have gone off accidentally in her pocket or bag and although we may not actually be speaking, it's telling me one thing loud and clear: it's confirming she's at the airport. Any remote hope – yes, I know, pathetic – that she'll be back at the hotel when I get there, keen to pour the oil of sexual congress on the troubled waters of our relationship, is dashed. She's a gone girl, no question.

I ring off. Do I text her, make one last desperate plea for her to return? I'm pondering this, pacing the exquisitely tiled floor, under yet another huge chandelier, when my other phone rings. The hot line.

'Theo?' It's Feinstein. 'You okay?'

'Yep – why?'

'You were right.'

'About what?'

'I think they *are* on to us. Some signs of incursion this end. They may have found our footprint, traced it back. They're good, these Russians.'

'*Shit!*'

'Just wanted to warn you.'

'Thanks.'

'One plus, though – I managed to gain access to a whole new network via Boris. Seems he has a lot of friends in the City of London. We'll be cleaning them out too.'

'Good to know...'

'At least we *will* as soon as you push the button, Theo – do it soon, will you?' *While you still can* is implied.

'I will.'

'When?'

'Very soon.'

'How about now?'

'I need another few hours.'

He goes quiet. 'Al?'

'*Yes,* Theo' – a note of impatience – 'you're still the boss.'

'Thank you.'

'Be careful out there.'

'I will.'

I assumed the men in dark suits were ushers. Now I'm not so sure. Now they're watching me and seem more sinister. I imagine them grabbing me and beating the shit out of me until I reveal our plan. Not that it will help them – I know little of the critical technical detail, which means they think I'm withholding it and go on beating me. I see them drag me outside, dump my limp body in the canal.

It makes sense to go back into the theatre, seek the safety of the crowd, of Diana. So why do I decide it's better to escape into the night and throw off any pursuers? Sheer panic, perhaps. Or perhaps I'm also trying to escape the black hole that's rapidly engulfing me, that familiar sinking feeling. And I thought I was way beyond all that.

*

As a means of my assuming the role I had long covet'd, I actually began to look forward to my 'instruction'. Religion was for me the most fanciful of all notions, but when harness'd to some practical benefit or advantage, I found the prospect of it almost attractive. I wou'd freely and solemnly submit to whatever outlandish articles of faith were necessary – the Trinity, the Transubstantiation, the spiritual sovereignty of His Holiness the Pope – in order to establish my own sovereignty. All of this I was prepar'd for – and yet even I found myself shocked by the nature of the instruction that I actually receiv'd.

On the first day, I was summon'd to a seclud'd chapel behind Notre Dame, known as the Chapel of the Crucifixion and set aside for the Cardinal's own private devotion. (It no doubt help'd concentrate His Eminence's mind on the subject of pain and sacrifice, with which, I guess'd, he had little natural affinity.)

My carriage took me – from the money lenders to the temple, as it were – through the crowd'd streets by the Louvre to Notre Dame. As we made our way with glacial haste through a mêlée of carriages, each more gild'd than the other, I curs'd myself for having made too many people prosperous enough to buy them. All those who recognis'd me wav'd and cheer'd, and many ask'd for shares or money. If they look'd deserving enough, I oblig'd.

Even with these delays, however, I was almost on time, and at the appoint'd hour I strode through the cloisters of Notre Dame, taking in the crisp air and the shafts of golden autumn sunlight, as if they were long draughts of wine. By contrast, the chapel itself was gloomy and airless, like a family vault or the Bastille even, lit only by a high narrow window and a small bank of candles. I was greet'd by a young fresh-fac'd friar, who bade me cross myself with holy water and kneel at a prie-dieu before the altar. Over this, illuminat'd by the candles, loom'd a large wooden crucifix, with the broken body of Christ nail'd upon it, blood dripping from every wound and a large golden halo setting off the vicious crown of thorns. His blood-streak'd face was upturn'd in a rictus of pain and desperation. 'My God, my God, why hast thou forsaken me?' I recall'd from the story of the Crucifixion.

The friar inform'd me that the instruction wou'd begin with a meditation on Our Lord's Passion. I shou'd begin this on my own, as best I cou'd, and His Eminence wou'd join me presently. The young man bow'd, genuflect'd before the altar and withdrew, his modest sandals padding softly as he mov'd across the stone floor.

Silence – but for the sound of my own breathing, barely comforting enough. My first sight of the macabre crucifix had been enough contemplation for me. My mind was already wandering, marvelling at the wood carver's art – the bony contours of the Christ figure, the delicate folds of its impossibly position'd loin cloth – when I heard the majestic tread, not of sandals, but expensive boots. His Eminence had arriv'd. I did my best to strike an attitude of pious contemplation, resisting the urge to look behind me. The steps drew nearer. A hand fell upon my shoulder.

A voice said, 'Well, Monsieur Law, what a picture of piety you are. I'm sure you'll make a very fine Catholic.' And I turn'd to find, not Cardinal de Tencin, but his sister.

*

The next thing I know I'm standing in the square, outside the theatre. I've got my coat on, but don't remember collecting it from the cloakroom. My head's spinning, my nose is throbbing again. The air feels cooler, but at least it's not raining.

I decide to walk – where to exactly, I don't know, as long as I get away. I realise I'm running out on Diana, but I'll text her to apologise, say I'll see her tomorrow. Or will I? I'm not really sure what I'll do. Maybe I need to head for the airport too.

I tell myself I shouldn't go back to the hotel right now – my pursuers could well be there waiting for me. In fact, I'm sure one of them, a man-in-black from the theatre, is already following me. I slip down one of the alleyways off the square and quicken my pace. I cross a tiny bridge and continue down another narrow street, in amongst the shadows and the tall, silhouetted buildings. It's as if I want the ancient city to swallow me up, protect me, but it's not that kind of place. I've never known anywhere like it. One moment, you're in toy town and the only danger is getting overcharged for an espresso or a gelato. The next, you're in a horror movie. Someone's trying to mug you down a dark, deserted street, silent as the grave, except for the echo of footsteps, not your own. You're feeling a sense of dread; death is stalking you.

Which is how I'm feeling now. Someone *is* stalking me, I'm sure of it. Not for the first time during this very long day, I break into a trot that becomes a gallop. (Who'd have thought I'd get so much exercise on this trip?) The street twists and turns and takes me over another canal. And all time the footsteps of whoever is behind me grow louder, closer. The path takes another turn to the right and eventually widens out into a small square, a dead end. I'm a rat in a trap. Dripping with

404

sweat, chest heaving, I come to a breathless, bedraggled halt. Ahead of me is a tower that appears to spiral into the sky. Above it, floating in a crystal sky is the pale, silver disc of a full moon – don't they call it a hunter's moon? And then I see the hunter – not the man behind, rapidly gaining on me, but another one. Another man-in-black, from what I can make out, standing at the top of the tower, pointing something at me – a gun, a rifle? Yes, he's got a rifle! I can see his long hair and face, luminous as that moon. I can even see someone beside him in the shadows, a woman, I think.

I freeze – not just in the sense of being unable to move, even reach for my phone to call Feinstein. But in the sense that the hot beads of sweat on the back of my neck have turned very, very cold, because I'm convinced that the man in the tower is going to shoot me.

*

I am in Paris with Madame de Tencin, undergoing instruction. Suddenly we are aware of someone entering the chapel, of approaching footsteps. We break off from our love-making and turn to see a tall figure silhouett'd against the arch'd window. Is it the Cardinal come to check on my progress? Or Philippe reclaiming his old mistress? A face floats into view; a voice says, 'Il Duce?'

I have been asleep and dreaming, sweet, erotic dreams, wou'd you believe? I am in the Ridotto and Bellini is standing over me.

'Il Duce,' he says again, more gently.

'Il Conte…' I must have slept for most of the afternoon. The winter light is fading; a lamp has been lit. I rouse myself, sit up and see that several pages from my manuscript have slipp'd to the floor. Bellini gathers them up, places them on my lap.

'I'm sorry to wake you, il Duce, but there's someone who wants to meet with you.'

No doubt another ghoul from France come to haunt me. 'Who?' I ask.

'You will see.' I look beyond him, expecting this person to appear. 'Not here,' he says. 'Come – if you feel strong enough, I've arrang'd for you to meet at the palazzo.'

'The palazzo?'

With a flourish of the hand, he enunciates the words in ascending scale and volume: '<u>The Palazzo Contarini del Bovolo!</u>'

Ah, yes, he has been wanting to show off his latest acquisition to me for some time. (I cannot help thinking of Gourmande, among many French chateaus I once own'd – now there was something <u>worth</u> the showing off!) The Contarini del Bovolo is a small palazzo, north of San Marco, in which Bellini has invest'd some of the profits from the Ridotto – much of it money that I have likely made for him. As the name suggests, it belong'd to the old noble family of Contarini, reduc'd to near penury and desperate for cash – an increasingly familiar tale in Venice where old money has evaporat'd along with the city's trading prowess.

Bellini is looking very pleas'd with himself. 'It is beautiful, a gem, you will see.'

He has told me that 'Bovolo' means 'spiral' and refers to the spectacular spiral staircase that climbs to a loggia, from where one can look out across the whole city. Bellini is very impress'd with it, as well as with himself for having got his hands on it – and at a very good price too, he tells me.

'We can take a gondola along the Rio del Barcoli to Campo Manin. It's a short walk from there – but only if you feel up to it, il Duce.' He thinks that if he keeps alluding to my physical weakness, he will goad me into going with him. He is right, of course. When he offers me a silver-tipp'd cane, I almost refuse it, just to show him that I have no need of such an aid.

But I am very glad of it as we go down to the landing and board the gondola. I am already breathless from my exertions and happy to be row'd most of the way to our rendezvous – though the narrow canal feels oppressive in the dying light and with the mist rising off the water. The dankness, the eerie silence – but for the gentle plashing of the oars – is like death itself. I shiver, pull my cloak more closely around me.

From Manin, we walk across to the small, quiet calle where the del Bovolo is situat'd. It is a modest setting for a grand architectural feature like the spiral staircase, hous'd as it is in an external tower of many arches that seem to ascend to the Heavens. (A picture of the famous Tower of Pisa, without the leaning, will give you some idea of its appearance.)

Bellini gestures proudly. 'Spettacolare! Eighty steps up to the belvedere!' And I have to admit my spirits rise at the sight of it. Even my breathing becomes a little easier.

Inside, the house is all cosy medieval charm, none of the grandiose spaces of later palazzos. We settle in the main reception room, and a servant brings us wine and chicetti, just as the mystery guest appears. She is wearing a long hood'd cape – for it is a she – and fleetingly, stupidly I think it might be Katherine. My pulse quickens as she throws back her hood to reveal a mask, the kind frequently worn by genteel women going abroad in Venice. When she removes it, I realise it is Sabine de Valliere.

Has Bellini arrang'd another of his carnal treats? If so, there is nothing I am less in the mood for. As if reading my mind, he whispers in my ear, 'It is not what you think, il Duce.'

'Welcome, Mademoiselle de Valliere,' he says in his stage French, 'you have arrived along with the refreshments – what a double delight!'

She treats Bellini's unctuous blather with the demur it deserves.

'Forgive me if I leave you briefly to your own devices. I must attend to the workmen who are making some repairs to the building. Please – make yourselves comfortable...' As he leaves, he gives me a sly nod and smile, and I have difficulty not smiling back at the Master of Mischief.

Sabine shakes her head and waits until he is out of earshot. 'Bellini – Venice wou'd be a sadder place without him.'

'It wou'd indeed...'

She takes a seat at a discreet distance. 'Thank you for seeing me.'

'To be honest, Sabine, I didn't know who I was seeing, but I'm glad it's you...'

'As opposed to some bitter French creditor,' she smiles. As with all the best courtesans, her tongue is as quick as her manoeuvres between the sheets. *'I'll get straight to the point, John. I want'd to tell you I am expecting your child.'*

For a moment, I think my hearing is failing me, along with all my other physical faculties. Either that or my French has grown extremely rusty. *'I'm sorry, I must have misheard, Sabine. I thought you said you were expecting my child?'*

'I did.'

There is a pregnant silence. *'Are you sure?'*

'It's not been long, it's true, but yes…'

'That it's my child, I mean.'

'Yes.'

I laugh. *'With great respect, Sabine, given your profession as …'*

'A whore, yes – how cou'd I possibly know whose child it is?'

'…Yes.'

'Well, in this instance, it is very clear. Most of my clients are old men who drink themselves into a stupor and rarely consummate. The only one who did so during the period in question used the…er…alternative route I remember discussing with you. It has to be you, John.'

For once, I am render'd speechless, not least by Sabine's matter-of-fact account. *'And now you are probably thinking I am here for money,'* she adds.

'I don't know what I'm thinking.'

'Apart from conceiving your child, I have had a second stroke of good fortune. It turns out I am not the daughter of the Abbè DuBois…'

'That must come as a relief. I am very happy for you.'

'Thank you. I am happy too, because it turns out that I am the daughter of Philippe, duc d'Orleans.'

I fear my jaw must have dropp'd so far that I was gaping at Sabine like a village idiot, because she suddenly starts to laugh. *'Oh, John, I'm sure it is all too much for you and yet it is all too true. I received a letter from the duc du Saint-Simon, a great friend of yours, I believe.'*

'Once upon a time, yes…'

'He informed me that amongst Philippe's effects was a letter to my mother – she must have died before he cou'd send it. In it, he acknowledges me as his daughter and agrees to set aside a considerable legacy for me in his will – which he duly did. It is ironic, John, is it not? The money he made from the Mississippi Company has come to me...and much of it will, I hope, go to your – _our_ child. I will never more have to be a whore.'

The words do not rhyme in French, but I think the phrase in English is fitting for what cannot be described as anything other than poetic justice.

Bellini returns, all smiles. Does he know about Sabine? Surely, she wou'd not miss the opportunity to impress him with the news of her Bourbon bloodline? His fawning over her will become the greater for it, God forbid, and he will say that she can play at the Ridotto without a mask. The thought of it amuses me and, indeed, now that I am over the initial shock, the thought of the child – _our_ child – gives me greater pleasure than I have felt for a long time. To think that I am to be a father again, and thus relat'd to the Bourbons. These are invigorating thoughts, so much so that when Bellini asks if Sabine wou'd like to tour the house and ascend the spiral staircase, I say that I wou'd like to go too.

Bellini is genuinely concern'd that I will expire while climbing his eighty steps. 'Are you sure, il Duce? I thought in your condition...'

'I am,' I say with great enthusiasm.

Sabine beams at me, happy that I am happy. 'Come, John' – she stands and holds out her hand – 'let's climb the stairs together.'

Bellini leads the way through the house, pointing out various features, as we go. We ascend the staircase very slowly, pausing several times. I am grateful for the cane on one side and for the support of Sabine on the other. Even so, by the time we reach the belvedere, I am left exhaust'd and breathless, but it is worth it to look out across the city – La Serenissima, indeed! Everything is illuminat'd by the full moon, silver tipp'd, like the cane I point at it

'Let us make a wish for our child,' I say, 'for his future happiness.'

She laughs. 'You are so sure it's a son?'

'I am.'

'If you're right, I will name him John. And whether it's a girl or boy, their family name will be Law.'

We squeeze each other's hand. Bellini, as if out of respect for our intimacy, stands quietly in the shadows. Even he realises that the view speaks for itself.

Suddenly, on the ground, something moves, appears from nowhere. At first, I think it is a mere passer-by, but then I see exactly what it is – the same apparition I have seen repeatedly down the years; the same ghostly features, wracked with pain, the same wound on his chest, a bloody rose. But how corporeal, how real he seems this time. Surely it cannot just be me who sees him?

I point the cane towards him; he stands there staring up at us. The excitement, the joy, the good mood drains out of me to be replac'd by a profound dread.

'Do you see him?'

'Who, John?'

'Down there, where I'm pointing. He's looking up at us.'

'I can't see anyone.'

'There! Look more closely, Sabine! <u>There!</u>'

'There is no one, John...'

She turns to Bellini. 'Il Conte, please...'

He has heard the note of alarm in my voice and thinks I am having one of my fits. He comes up beside me, places a comforting hand on my shoulder and looks down below, where I am pointing.

'Sabine is right, il Duce. There is no one there.'

*

The man-in-black with the rifle is no longer there. No shot as been fired. I'm still standing and the other man-in-black is there beside me, sweating heavily and out of breath. He's no fitter than I am, but does he have a gun?

'*Signore...*' he finally manages.

I do my best to sound annoyed, when really I'm just relieved I'm not dead. 'What do you want? Why are you following me?'

He holds up what I instantly recognise as my wallet and hands it to me. 'You dropped it at the theatre, signor…when you were collecting your coat.'

I must have pulled it out with my ticket, when I was in the black hole.

'Thank you…I didn't realise, I'm sorry…' I open it and go to pull out a note that I realise I don't have – I gave them all to Marisa. Just as well, he waves it away.

'Please, no, *signore*' – deep breath – 'it was good to get the exercise. *Buonanotte.*'

'*Buonanotte…*'

Chapter 13

I look up at the moon and start to laugh, which, seeing as I've been behaving like a madman of late, is much better than howling at it. I laugh at my paranoia, at how terrified I was of the men-in-black. I laugh at the idea that a Master of the Universe, like myself – so said the Moneyman – has, in the last few days, been reduced to behaving like its slave, feeling entirely subject to forces outside his control. I laugh at what an asshole I am. I laugh at the fact that I'm still alive and in charge of my own destiny – that I can still do what the fuck I like. *Yes!*

I've also come over all tired and hungry. In my newly elated state, I tell myself that nobody's after me, it's all in my imagination. I can return to the hotel and tend to my most pressing needs – eating and sleeping.

I take out my phone to check where I am. There's a text from Diana: 'What happened, Theo? Are you ok? D.'

I text her back: 'Everything's fine. Sorry, had an important business call and needed to return to the hotel. Thanks for looking after me. I was enjoying the requiem. T.'

She responds immediately: 'Good. Take care of that nose. See you tomorrow, for lunch. Ca'Alvisi, 1600 Grand Canal. Staggering distance from your hotel. Around 1.00. D.'

Yes, tomorrow, of course. I have a lunch date, like any normal, sociable person. It's all okay. Everything really *is* fine. I'm just on a long – a very long – weekend in Venice, taking some time out from a busy schedule. That's all I'm doing. Okay, it didn't exactly work out with Jo but, hey, that wasn't going to last anyway. It helped get me off the anti-depressants. It got me through the worst of those black holes and panic attacks and, most importantly, it got me making love again. (Sort of.) What more can I expect?

I head for the hotel. I'm soon back in the tourist crowd, feeling safety in Chinese numbers. I really haven't felt this light-headed, this happy – yes, *happy* – for a long time. In fact, I ask myself, when *was* that? When did I last feel happy? In the first flush of romance with Angela? During that period of hottest lift-hopping sex? They were heady times, all right, but surely a little too out-of-control to be happy. Or was it when I first started ratcheting up those noughts, earning those first big bonuses and realising that I was actually quite good at this money business, that I was a winner? It was certainly a peak experience, but it was always accompanied by a peak level of stress. It was too adrenalin-fuelled to be happy. And anyway, I was quickly looking to add more noughts, and realising, sadly, that no matter how many there were, there would never be enough of them.

No, I would have to go back further – but how much further? My parents split up when I was nine. Before that I was aware of how *un*happy they were, and although it hadn't been all-out war, the skirmishes hardly made for a happy family life. Afterwards, I felt the anxiety and guilt of being torn between them and, as an only child, was never able to share the experience.

Then I remember the sand dunes. Yes, of course, *the sand dunes*. After my parents' separation, I went back to the US with my mother for a while. My father eventually insisted that I was sent to a boarding school in England, but for that period in America, I was very happy to be with my mother. I had most of her attention and watched her become much happier herself, as she shed what I later came to realise was the crippling burden of the marriage.

She returned to her hometown of Ann Arbour, Michigan and we spent summers on the lake, up in the north, near what are known as the Sleeping Bear Dunes. As I pass the church of San Moise once again, I am back, standing at the top of one those huge dunes. I'm in my new red swimming trunks. I can feel the hot sun on my back and head, the hot sand beneath my feet. Below me is the turquoise expanse of the great lake and on the narrow shore, my mother sitting on the towel and waving up at me.

I kick off like a ski jumper and start to run down the dune. The softly baked crust of the sand gives way with each step. I run faster and faster until, about half-way down, I'm running so fast I lose my footing and tumble forward, rolling over and over down the rest of the dune, lost in an ecstasy of sun, sand and laughter and knowing I'll arrive to find my mother and a big hug. The place where freedom meets security – pure happiness. Or does that sound too much like an ad for a pension plan?

I think I actually have a smile on my face as I enter the hotel and pass the reception desk.

'Signor Low!' One of the women on reception hails me. I go over to her – is there finally a message from Jo?

'Signor Low...' She gestures across to a suited and booted couple – him my age and thick set, her younger and slimmer. They were seated in the lobby but are now walking towards me. 'This is Inspector Brunelli from Europol and his assistant' – she looks down at her notepad – 'Signora Paulo. They've been waiting to speak to you...'

*

Venice, January 1729

Such a fine week I had of it during my instruction at the hands of Madame de Tencin! The excitement of share trading in the morning, of watching the price rise continually; the sheer pleasure of love-making with her in the afternoon, where my manhood became a phallic barometer of the Company's stock. I realis'd how much I had miss'd that pleasure; how all too ready I was to resume an intimate physical relationship, and how natural it seem'd for that to happen with de Tencin.

Philippe was right: she was indeed the most expert, the most passionate of lovers. And there was no better demonstration than the fact that during my time with her, I spar'd scarcely a thought for Katherine, or made any comparison between the two women. The smell, shape and texture of their bodies, the way they cried out at the height of their passion, the words they whisper'd to me during mine – these might have form'd columns of debit and credit in my head. But no, I was completely immers'd in the sensuality of the present; neither the past nor the future were of any concern.

Each day we met in the chapel and immediately retir'd to her apartments on the île St. Louis. She herself was a city, full of architectural splendours, and I left no part of it unexplor'd. Nor did it detract from my pleasure to know that Philippe, that most season'd of carnal travellers, had been there before me. On the contrary, there was an add'd excitement, a strange kind of quid pro quo for his lusting after Katherine. Indeed, given that several other members of government had also roam'd these streets, it seem'd as if I was participating in some Society rite of passage, an essential part of my conversion to Rome, you might say. Madame de Tencin was in fact performing a public service.

Between bouts of love-making, we lay in a nest of eiderdown and pillows, and talk'd – or rather, she did: astonishing tales of how she had been rais'd and educat'd in a convent and was to become a nun; of her escape; of her love for Philippe – which was finally over; of her life as a courtesan and of the sacrifices she had made to be one. She told me of pregnances lost, of children she had born, but never rais'd: a boy, adopt'd by a prominent family, with whom she had had no contact; a girl, left at a church door, albeit her brother's, so that she was able to maintain some kind of relationship with her.

I express'd the fervent hope that there wou'd be no further offspring to find homes for among the clergy.

'No, my child-bearing days are over. My daughter very nearly died and I nearly died with her...' And suddenly her eyes moisten'd and she look'd as sad and pitiful as it was possible to look in the company of someone as full of good cheer as I was.

I squeez'd her hand.

She shrugg'd and quickly compos'd herself, ready to resume the task in hand: 'So, Monsieur Law, what tragedies have you known in life?'

'None compar'd with yours, Madame – mere disappointments.'

'But what of the end of a great love affair – isn't that a tragedy of sorts?' She smil'd archly. 'I think we all know the identity of Philippe's new mistress...'

I thought for a moment that I might tell her what had actually happen'd between Katherine and Orleans. Instead I summon'd as much nonchalance as I cou'd. 'I have merely adopt'd the ways of my compatriots, Madame. My wife has become a mistress – and I have taken a mistress. What cou'd be more French?'

She shook her head. 'You shou'd know that the Frenchman is a spendthrift with love. Then he finds his heart is bankrupt and spends the rest of his life regretting it.'

I laugh'd this off. 'Madame, rest assur'd – I will never be a bankrupt, neither of the heart nor the pocket.'

'You know that you have many enemies.'

'I'd be insult'd if I didn't.'

'But there's one who's working very hard to damage you.'

'You mean Dubois?'

She nodd'd. 'He's constantly urging Philippe to abandon the Bank and repeal the Company charter. He's a great danger to you.'

'And he'd be even more dangerous, if he knew that I was here with *his* mistress.'

De Tencin was incapable of blushing, but I thought there was the faintest flicker of embarrassment. 'I'm one of several,' she replied.

'But his favourite, no doubt.'

'Perhaps – but it doesn't alter my warning.'

'And thank you for it,' I said. 'To show my gratitude, I have a gift for you.'

I leant across to my to topcoat, which had been hastily abandon'd on the floor, and pull'd out a share certificate that I had already prepar'd.

'Have you acquir'd any Mississippi shares?'

Again, the flicker of embarrassment. 'Philippe kindly gave me some.'

'Have you sold them?' She shook her head. 'Good – the price will continue to rise for a while. These' – I hand'd her a certificate for two hundred shares – 'are worth a lot even now, but they'll be worth even more in a few weeks' time.'

On the seventh day we rest'd. She told me that it wou'd not be her but the Cardinal who wou'd meet me in the chapel. He wou'd hear my confession in order to prepare me for the High Mass that wou'd include my official conversion; I wou'd be expect'd to receive Holy Communion, the bread and wine turn'd into the body and blood of Christ, for which I must be *the purest of vessels. During the confession, I wou'd have to make a short act of contrition, she said, which she was kind enough to teach me, as we both lay sat'd and exhaust'd by our coupling.*

Still I did not believe that His Eminence wou'd appear, until he did, resplendent in red, full of thanks for my gift of shares, 'the proceeds of which will mostly find their ways into the hands of the poor,' he assur'd me.

No mention was made of his sister or the miss'd instruction of the previous week. He gave me a short lecture on 'the forgiveness of sins' and the 'sacr'd mystery of the Transubstantiation – the daily miracle that is Christ's presence in the consecrat'd bread and wine'. He conclud'd by announcing that Catholicism was the one true religion, that all others were an abomination, and that His Holiness the Pope was Christ's one true representative on Earth. He then usher'd me into a small box in the corner of the chapel – not far from his splendidly upholster'd chair – where, he said, he wou'd hear the confession of my 'mortal sins': those that were serious enough to consign my soul to Hell, shou'd they go unshriven.

Despite the threat of Hell's fire, however, a frank admission of such serious transgressions to someone as closely connect'd to my enemies as the Cardinal seem'd ill-advis'd. So I quickly resolv'd to give my confessor an account of those relating only to fornication. No names were mention'd, but when it came to my describing my time with 'a certain courtesan', he seem'd to become more curious. The shadowy outline of his cardinal's hat inclin'd towards the wooden grill and he ask'd for more details: how many times, where, in what circumstances and then, to my astonishment, what positions we adopt'd. As his voice grew more excit'd, I thought that he was deriving almost as much pleasure from hearing me describe these unholy acts as I had performing them. If this was the case, it was perverse beyond belief: the sister engag'd in all kinds of lechery; the brother a voyeur of it in his imagination!

Then, there was my act of contrition, follow'd by penance. To atone for so many impure acts, His Eminence propos'd the giving of alms to the poor – shares in the Mississippi, perhaps, that he himself would ensure were distribut'd to deserving beneficiaries. Finally, he mumbl'd the Absolution of my sins 'in nomine patre et filio et spiritu sancto. Amen.' I was thus deem'd fit to become a Roman Catholic.

Speaking of my sins – if not my contrition and certainly not my Absolution – throughout this period, with all its dramas and excitements, I had kept up a fitful correspondence with Katherine. I want'd her to know about my taking on the tax collection and the Company taking over the National Debt; about how quickly the fourth issue was selling and the stock price rising:

> *The new share issues have been an even greater success than I anticipat'd, with investors literally fighting each other in the Quincampoix to buy them. My critics say that 'Mississippi Madness' has gripp'd the city, but for me it is a benign affliction. More money is coursing through France's veins than ever; I am now in a position to assume the tax raising powers and pay off the National Debt; and the System reigns supreme…*

In other words, I was full of braggadocio, although I did not think of it in that way at the time. I want'd her to know that I was right and, by implication, that she was wrong. I also continued to ask – and then to demand – that I see Anne.

For her part, she made the odd scornful reply, to the effect that I was both overweening and overreaching; that the fourth issue wou'd push up the share price to an unsustainable level, and that the whole enterprise wou'd come crashing down around my ears. Regarding Anne, I was told no more than she was well.

Finally, I wrote to inform her of the occasion of my appointment as Financial-Controller of France, the pinnacle of my ambition, and of the pomp and circumstance involv'd: the conversion to Rome, the ceremony at Notre Dame and the banquet. She was, of course, invit'd, I said, but I did not expect her to attend. However, I very much want'd Anne to be there, and I trust'd that wou'd be acceptable to her. Her response came five days' later:

So, make the most of your Divinely sanction'd elevation, John. What a dreadfully sad day it is – for you and for France. Your acquisitiveness and lust for power knows no limits. You will control everything – and everything will suffer because of it.

But let me make one thing clear: you will not control me nor have any power whatsoever over me. Perhaps, I shou'd not be telling you this, but I must concede that as Anne's father you do have some right to know: before the deluge that will drown us all, I am leaving France and taking Anne with me. This means that she will not be attending your Beatification, or whatever it is call'd, because on that day we will be departing for the Low Countries. Both I and my gold will feel much safer there. I will head to the Hague in the first instance and then have the more valuable contents of the house shipp'd on to me once I am in residence.

You shou'd know that despite all that has occurr'd between us, for Anne's sake, and for no other reason, I wou'd tolerate a visit from you. Indeed, if all unfolds as I think it will, you may well be seeking sanctuary there, even if, as I remember, you are not popular in that country.

I wou'd ask you not to tell a soul of my departure, especially not Philippe. He is so sick with wound'd pride and self-love – which he mistakenly thinks is love for me – there is no telling what he might do…

For some reason, I found this letter more shocking and disheartening than any other communication I had receiv'd from her, perhaps because of its cold-heart'd sense of purpose and finality. It was enough for me to let the page drop from my hand and fall onto my favourite rug; to stare for some time at the most vibrantly colour'd painting of a vase full of tulips and see only the fallen, fad'd petals.

I was at home – 'home'? where was home for me? I did not feel I had one. I was at the house in Louis le Grand, taking a short recess from the exhausting demands of the Quincampoix. The ceremony in Notre Dame was meant to be the next day, but *just at that moment, I felt like cancelling my conversion, refusing my appointment as Financial-Controller and resigning from the Bank and the Company. If Katherine cou'd be persuad'd to take me back, I was ready to join her and Anne on the journey to the Netherlands.*

And if Philippe had not appear'd at my door a few minutes later, I may well have done so.

*

The detective inspector and his assistant flash their Europol IDs at me. In fluent, if somewhat formal English, he is full of apologies for intruding on my Saturday night and what he is sure is my enjoyable visit to Venice. *However*, it is a matter of some urgency that they speak to me. He asks if we can find a quiet spot in the bar. Or if I prefer, we can retire to my room. The other option is the police station, which is some way across the city.

'Yes, of course, we'll find somewhere in the bar.' My euphoria has all but evaporated. My main concern is that I don't look as much of a disreputable mess as I feel. I'm already aware of them checking out the cut on my forehead and my swollen nose, and of my feeling more defensive i.e. guilty, than I want to appear. Strange what a sudden encounter with the forces of law and order will do.

We find a moody corner of the bar, which like so many hotel bars in a tourist town, isn't what you'd call busy. They decline the offer of a drink, so I decide against the glass of wine I had in mind and opt for – now here's a first for a Saturday night – sparkling water instead.

We exchange a few uncomfortable pleasantries, on the subject of *acqua alta* and the perils of negotiating the walkways. The inspector gestures towards my wounds and asks if that is how I injured myself.

I jump at the opportunity to lie about it. 'Yes, I slipped and fell near San Marco. Dangerous place, Venice – for a museum.' I laugh nervously. He smiles; his assistant remains poker-faced.

'Yes,' says the inspector. 'You must be careful, Signor Low. Sometimes it is difficult to know where the walkway ends and the canal begins.' (Now where did I hear that before?)

More nervous laughter on my part. Then more seriously: 'So...what's this all about, what's so urgent?'

The inspector clears his throat, gets down to business. 'You are we believe, a business associate of a Russian gentleman, Boris Aronovsky. Is that in fact the case?'

'It is in fact the case, yes.' I speak to them both, doing my best to wrest a more sympathetic expression from Assistant Paulo. If they're playing good cop, bad cop, there's no doubt which one the badass is.

'And what kind of business are you in, Signor Low?'

'I'm an investment banker. Mr. Aronovsky is one of my clients. I manage some of his funds.'

'Which are considerable? Many millions of Euros?'

'Which are, yes...in that sort of region...'

'And may I ask you, Signor Low, when you last had contact with Signor Aronovsky?'

'I had an email from him...er...today, in fact.' (Was it really only today?)

'Today?'

'Yes – why?'

'And when did you last *see* Signor Aronovsky?'

'See him?'

'*Si*...I mean, *yes. See him.*

'It would have been many weeks ago. I'd have to look in my calendar. We don't actually meet up that often.'

'And why did you meet on that occasion?'

'He was keen to show me a new property he'd acquired in London. Show it *off,* you might say.' I try another modest smile in Paulo's direction to no avail. I didn't think it worth mentioning the main reason for our meeting: that Boris wanted to intimidate me into to returning a certain memory stick.

'And – how can I put it? – did he seem in any way concerned for his safety?'

'His safety? Er...no, I don't think so.' It was more a case of me being concerned for *my* safety. 'Why? Has something happened to Signor Aronovsky?'

There's an exchange of glances between them before he says: 'Yes. Last Thursday, he was found dead at his London apartment. He had been stabbed in the chest' – he placed a hand on his own chest – 'to be precise, through the heart.' (Pronounced 'art-a', it somehow made the whole thing more graphic.) 'So, I would have to say that the email you received today could not have been sent by him.'

'Unless the delivery to your mailbox was delayed for some reason,' a sombre Signora Paulo chips in. 'Or it was sent by someone else.'

Surprise that she can actually speak defuses the shock of the news about Boris. 'Yes, that's true,' I say, somehow wanting to encourage her.

The inspector moves quickly on. 'You arrived here in Venice on Friday, I believe.'

'Yes, but I was in Rome, on business, the day Mr. Aronovsky was killed.'

He shakes his head. 'It is okay, Signor Low, we are aware that you were not in the UK that day.'

Were you? How were you? *Why* were you? He reads my thoughts. 'We are not suggesting that you were responsible for the death of Signor Aronovsky. At least not' – he gives me a wry little smile – 'at first hand, so to speak.'

'That's good to know…'

'*However*, I must tell you that Mr. Aronovsky has been – *was* – the subject of a Europol investigation for some time.'

'Investigation? For what?'

'The list is long, but top of it are people and drug trafficking. The fact is, Signor Low, as an important business associate of Boris Aronovsky, you are also a subject of that investigation.'

I must look even more deflated by this news, because Assistant Paulo's features relax, as though she is finally experiencing a degree of job satisfaction.

*

'His Royal Highness, the Regent', a footman announc'd, and suddenly, there he was, sweeping into my study, like a ship

in full sail, reeking of wine and attar of roses. I went to get up; he gestur'd for me to remain seat'd.

'My God, John – you look as miserable as I feel. I can tell I'm in the right company...'

'It's good to see you, Your Royal Highness.'

'I'm sure it's no such thing. Please forgive this intrusion, but I had to speak to you. I'm at my wits end.'

'I'm sorry to hear it.'

'Katherine is of course to blame.'

'You've heard from her?'

'No – that's why she is to blame. She returns all my letters.'

'But you told me yourself that she said she wou'd, that she never want'd to see you again, that you were...'

'Repellent to her. Yes, I know, John, I don't need reminding... But I liv'd in hope, you see, hope that it was just part of a...game she was playing with me...'

I affect'd my most sympathetic expression. 'Well, I think she's stopp'd playing games with you, Your Highness. I think the best you can do is let her go – as I have done.'

'But I can't let her go. I really can't...'

As I watch'd the tears roll down his roug'd cheeks, I realis'd two things: that it wou'd be a terrible mistake for me to leave France when the country was crying out for my help; and that if Katherine thought the game she and I had been playing was over, she was wrong – it was still mine to win.

'Your Highness, I have to tell you – she is leaving France.'

'Leaving France?' He was dabbing at his cheek with a large mouchoir. 'What do you mean? Where is she going?'

'To the Netherlands.'

'Why wou'd she go to the Netherlands? What cou'd there possibly be for her in that drab little country?'

'She says she will be safer there.'

'Safer from what – from me?'

'And me, perhaps.'

He sat down for the first time since he had arriv'd. What little wind was left in his sails had all been taken out. 'And when is she going?'

'Tomorrow.'

He shook his head. 'This is the most dreadful news...dreadful... She's leaving from Gourmande?'

'Yes, I believe so.'

He look'd about him as if for an answer. 'She can't do this to me. She can't leave me...'

I was not for me to tell him that you cou'd not be left by someone you had never been with, but I did say: 'Perhaps, you shou'd not allow it, Your Highness...'

He star'd blankly at me for several seconds and stood up. 'Thank you, John. Thank you for telling me. I very much appreciate it.'

I stood too and inclin'd my head. 'Thank *you*, Your Highness.'

He manag'd a wry smile. 'Tomorrow is a big day. I must leave you to learn your Catechism, a profoundly rewarding exercise, if I remember rightly. I will see you at Notre Dame...at noon...'

'Yes...Notre Dame...at noon...'

However, when, at noon the next day, I look'd out across the nave of Notre Dame from my singular position in front of the high altar, there was no sign of Philippe. There were many of the Great and not-so-Good, including most of the Regency Council – even Dubois was present, which surpris'd me – and the more prominent members of the Court and the Nobility, among whom I was pleas'd to see Saint-Simon. But there was no Philippe.

The Mass got underway and as I listen'd to the singing of the choir, saw the great rose window ablaze with pure winter light and inhal'd the sweet-smelling incense that float'd in clouds around the altar, I must admit to being so taken up with the sensuous beauty of the scene that I gave his absence not a second thought. Until, at the beginning of the Gloria, when he did appear and then I cou'd think of nothing else – for he was in the company of Katherine and Anne.

I was shock'd to see them, but what was more shocking was Katherine's appearance: her usual proud, upright demeanour was reduc'd almost to a slouch; those bright, emerald eyes of hers, usually so direct and challenging, were downcast. She *was the walking wound'd in retreat from the field of battle, desperately clasping Anne's hand, as if for physical support.*

If she wou'd not meet my eye, Orleans caught it immediately, with a look of huge smugness. He was showing off his power over her, however that had been achiev'd. The cat had not only caught the mouse, he had dropp'd its mutilat'd body at my feet for my appreciation.

But I cou'd not indulge him with any response. I was plung'd into inner turmoil. Suddenly, my heart went out to Katherine. I cou'd only imagine what Orleans might have done or threaten'd to do to get her to come with him, she who I knew from bitter experience wou'd bow to no man's will, bend to no man's purpose unless it suit'd her own. The very thought pain'd me and what worsen'd that pain was the knowledge that I was responsible. I had sent Philippe to her to prevent her from leaving. I had unleash'd him on her, without any concern for the ultimate consequences. All I cou'd think of was how she had reject'd me and all I stood for; how she had somehow got the better of me, got away from me – with a million in gold and with Anne.

Well, I had stopp'd her – and yet there was no satisfaction in it. Far from it. I did not believe in the need for Contrition or Absolution or in that Almighty Judge in Heaven who dictat'd their terms. But at that moment, as I took in the piteous sight of Katherine and my daughter, I felt the weight of sin fall like a millstone upon me, a burden that was only increas'd by a deep sense of remorse and the knowledge that there was no human or divine agency that wou'd forgive me. In Christian terms – in any terms – I was beyond redemption – and the look of bitter disappointment on Saint-Simon's face confirm'd as much. Either Philippe had told him what had happen'd or, as a close observer of human character, he had simply work'd it out for himself.

The rest of the ceremony and the subsequent celebration pass'd off as if it were a bad dream, the saturnine mood of which cou'd not be lighten'd, no matter how uplifting it wou'd have been in other, more felicitous circumstances.

I did not see the going of Katherine and Anne from Notre Dame. I knelt before the Cardinal and the high altar to receive the Body of Christ – my first and last communion – and when I turn'd back they were gone.

I only got the chance to ask Philippe of their whereabouts when I stood with him at my side, greeting each guest at the Palais-Royal. He wav'd the question away, said he wou'd explain later and promptly introduc'd the Papal Nuncio – the grey-hair'd, Jesuit Silvo Vittorio. Orleans had already told me that his presence was a great tribute in itself, a measure of how seriously I was taken in Rome.

When I thank'd the Nuncio for attending, he lent into my ear, as if we were in the confessional, and spoke in a soft accent'd English that wou'd have charm'd contrition from the most harden'd of sinners: 'When one of the most powerful and influential men in Europe joins our Holy Mother the Church, we are honour'd to attend.' And to the amazement of all, he bent and kiss'd the large gold signet ring that I wore on my right hand. Lips that only kiss'd the hands of Cardinals and His Holiness himself freely made such a gesture for me, John Law, maker of Millionaires and Financial-Controller of France.

Saint-Simon did not appear at the banquet, which was another sign of his disapproval. It was a tame affair by Palais-Royal standards, perhaps because there were so few women present, although the lavishness of the meal itself exceed'd anything I had experience'd there before. Philippe look'd particularly pleas'd as each new course was brought on, accompanied by yet another wine. The game had been good that season, and with Christmastide approaching, we were treat'd to a roast'd, pott'd, pickl'd and stuff'd selection of everything that ran, swam or flew around the Royal estates – or at least used to. Now it was all prettily display'd on the great dining table: trout, salmon, hare, venison, duck, quail, peacock, swan and suckling pig, dressed in such animat'd attitudes that they might have been about to flap or run away. And as for the selection of syllabubs, there were more exotic fruits than I had names for, mix'd with the finest ports, rums, brandies and, it seem'd, the sugar of ten plantations. I cou'd eat and drink very little and what I did tast'd sour to me.

Afterwards, several speeches were made in my honour, including a by then familiar one from Philippe about my being

*the saviour of France. They might as well have been the jeers of
a hostile rabble or the words of that monstrous judge in
London, sentencing me to death by hanging.*

*

Boris stabbed through the art-a? The full shock of it finally
reaches me, like the aftershock of a major earthquake, bringing
down more buildings that are already on the verge of collapse.
I'm stunned. I don't hear what the inspector and his assistant
are saying to me. For all I know, they're reading me my rights
and about to arrest me.

'Signor Low…*Signor Low?*'

They bring me back to what they're actually saying and it's
no less depressing. The important thing for them now is to
identify those who have taken over Boris Aronovsky's criminal
operations and will undoubtedly be in contact with me. They,
the police, know what a critical role I've played in Boris'
affairs. They've had me under surveillance for a while, both
online and in person. Most recently, for instance, they know
that my cuts and bruises are not due to my slipping in San
Marco. My swollen nose is the result of a blow from a woman I
mistook for my girlfriend, Joanna de Vere, who walked out on
me in Harry's Bar. That surveillance will continue, although
they already have enough evidence to prosecute me on several
very serious charges.

However, things will be much easier for me – lighter
sentences and fines, less confiscations – if I help them with
tracking down Boris' successors. I should go back to London as
planned and await further instructions.

'You will be working for us for a while, Signor Low. Do we
have an agreement?'

I've gone very quiet. I can hardly breathe; it's as if my chest
has caved in. The sensation is beyond falling into black holes –
that's child's play. I'm inside one of those collapsed buildings,
buried alive under tons of rubble and no one's ever going to
find me, no matter how sensitive their detectors.

'*Signor Low? Do we have an agreement?*'

427

I take a very deep breath. 'It's an offer I can't refuse – isn't that what you say to the Cosa Nostra?'

They both permit themselves a smile at this. (At least I've got something right today.)

The inspector takes out his card and hands it to me. 'Meanwhile, if any of Boris' people make contact, please let me know – day or night.'

They stand up. 'And Signor Low, one more thing. I am sure you are aware from the repeated attacks on your person that Boris Aronovsky's successors – and likely assassins – do not have your best interests at heart.' (There he goes again with his 'art-a'.) 'They are engaged in a campaign of intimidation. You are almost certainly in grave danger and we will be doing all we can to protect you.'

'Thank you.'

'It is our pleasure. *Buonanotte.*'

I watch them leave the bar. *Signor Low, in other words, you are well and truly fucked.* Did that really just happen? Did the gleaming tower of my life really just come crashing down on me, each and every steel and concrete floor of it? *Yes, well and truly fucked.*

I decide I need some major self-medication. I order a maximo gin with minimo tonic and try to work out what to do next – other than sit here and get completely shit-faced. If I was hardly capable of thinking straight before my encounter with Europol, I'm even less capable of it now. More than ever, I'll be prey to panic and self-delusion.

Silenced earlier, the Moneyman now seizes his chance and pipes up again. You have a special account for such emergencies, he says, you know that, Theo. Transfer as much money as you can to it and make a dash to a non-extradition country, somewhere they can't get to you.

Which would be where exactly? Russia? I don't think so. And besides, since they seem to know when I fart and go to the bathroom, they might just be aware of when I'm boarding an international flight; I won't even make it out of Venice airport.

Then hire a jet, Theo. *Buy* a fucking jet! Leave from a private airfield. Think big, you asshole. Think like a billionaire.

428

Think like a Master of the Universe. This is a life or death situation. You can't just give up and roll over without a fight.

You're right, I can't. So the answer is to do what I should have done already: go out in a blaze of glory. No more shilly-shallying, no more beating around the bush – and no more Moneyman. *Ever.* The Anarchist will call Feinstein and give him the green light.

But then, as ever, my resolve goes limp. I start to worry that the police are aware of *Feinstein's* activities. Were *they* – not the Russians – responsible for the 'incursion' he mentioned? Do they have him under surveillance too?

No, impossible, I tell myself, he's too smart, too many steps ahead of them. And even if they have got to some of Boris' accounts and frozen them – which they probably have – they won't have found the ones only I know about, the ones that are buried deep within the deep, dark web. The biggest heist in history can still happen.

*

After the banquet was over and the last guest had depart'd, Philippe told me that Katherine and Anne had return'd to Gourmande and that they wou'd not be travelling to the Netherlands or anywhere else.

'How can you be sure?'

He look'd uncomfortable. 'Because, for the present, they are...under guard...'

'They're your prisoners...'

'Wards of the State, John, shall we say...' Then words pour'd out of him in a churning torrent: 'I only want'd to stop her leaving France, that is all, and I've tried every other form of persuasion, starting with gentle, coaxing words. I plead'd with her, declar'd my love for her, all to no avail. Nor did my authority as Regent of France have much effect. When I order'd her not to leave the country, she laugh'd in my face, said authority had more to do with strength of character than any official status and I had little of the former... I even offer'd her money, as much as she want'd...' He drain'd his wine glass. 'But it turns out she has no need of it. She has more than

enough and all in gold, she said, which she chose in preference to paper because it will still be worth something when <u>your</u> System collapses...' He gave a rueful smile at this. 'So I had to resort to a degree of...force...'

'But, Your Highness...'

'I know, John, I know...you cannot force love out of someone, it's impossible...but what else am I to do?'

I had no answer for him. I need'd to sleep, I need'd time to think, and I knew that the two things wou'd compete against each other.

'We'll speak more on this tomorrow,' I said. 'I promise.'

He shrugg'd as if there was no more to be said. 'Your first day as Financial-Controller. Will I see you in your new office?'

'After I have paid my usual visit to the Quincampoix.'

'Of course. More than ever you need to keep your finger on the pulse...'

I went to take my leave. '<u>John</u>?'

'Your Highness?'

'Is Katherine right – will the System collapse?'

'The System will go from strength to strength.'

'I'm greatly reliev'd to hear it.'

I left him, alone at the table but for another glass of wine.

The next day, I did not make it to my new office in the Palais-Royal. In fact, I rarely went there, unless I had to. Nor did I have another conversation with Philippe about Katherine, at least not for some weeks; nor did I attempt to contact her myself or go out to Gourmande to see her. This was partly due to my sense of shame at what had happen'd and partly because I was reluctant to face the inevitable confrontation with her and all the complications that wou'd arise from that. But it was mostly because I was completely overtaken by events in Paris.

The word 'Millionaire' possess'd great potency, and by early December everyone seem'd driven by the desire to become one. The share price had risen to 10,000 livres, and despite the cold weather, trading in the Quincampoix had reach'd an even more frenzied level. Skirmishes became commonplace, but none had more serious consequences than when a young Marquis stabb'd a fellow bidder for shares through the heart, killing him on the spot.

This felt like an ominous sign on my first day as Controller of Finance. I was at the other end of the street when it happen'd, and during the hue and cry that ensued I made my way to the scene of the crime and supervis'd the arrest of the young man. He was not at all asham'd of his actions and wav'd his share certificate around in joyful triumph, proclaiming that he was now a Millionaire and cou'd save the family estate from ruin.

He was tried within days by the local Paris court and sentenc'd to be broken on the wheel, a particularly grim form of execution and unusual for a man of his social rank. Despite appeals by his family – who blam'd 'the rabid money madness that has infect'd every level of society from the highest to the lowest' – he was publicly execut'd a week later; every bone in his body was broken with iron bars and he took some nine agonising hours to die. It was hardly a great tribute to the System and left Paris subdued for days.

As brutal and repellent as this spectacle was, however, it might have had little effect on the level of trading, had it not coincid'd with bad news from Louisiana. Rumours had start'd to circulate that there had been virtually no increase in the volume of trade with the American colony since the Company had begun its programme of investment and enforc'd emigration. Much as I tried to discourage these notions – which were more or less true – they began to spread like wildfire, the more so when coupl'd with reports that the emigration militias had start'd to behave like press gangs in some areas. Far from deportation being an alternative to imprisonment for a crime, honest subjects were finding themselves cudgel'd and pack'd off to the Americas. (Several respectable burghers of towns as far apart as Lille and Marseilles had apparently suffer'd this indignity.) The overall result was a wave of riots against the measures and the colony itself, while Katherine's prophetic warning on the subject rang in my ears.

In fact, 10,000 livres was as high as I wish'd the price of shares to go. So when in early January, it became clear that trading was beginning to diminish, I was not unduly worried. At a meeting of the Council I turn'd it to good advantage in the face of much disgruntlement. D'Argenson – back to his old role

431

as watchdog – was stirring up trouble again, this time over the appalling state of the Quincampoix, which had become seedy in the extreme and a source of shame to its more genteel residents. (The fact that the majority of Parisians liv'd in the most squalid and wretched of conditions seem'd to have escap'd his notice.) De Conti appear'd twitchy and restless and was much concern'd about prices, which had risen some 25% in the last two months. And in a rare moment of sober lucidity, Bourbon stat'd that according to his own information, Louisiana was as profitable as a dung hill and about as fragrant. Even I had to smile at this, before rising confidently to my feet and addressing every issue as if it were routine business for the Controller of Finance.

First, I conced'd that with the recent murder, trading in the Quincampoix had indeed become a danger and a disgrace. I had therefore decid'd to restrict share dealing to the Company's offices and to those authoris'd by the Company. (This was privately a great disappointment to me, of course, but there was a more important reason than the need to restore order to the street. Worried by the apparent slow down, many traders were planning to push up the share price to an unsustainable 15,000 livres by offering special purchase schemes, mostly learnt from yours truly. The time had come to exert a greater discipline than the imperative of pure greed.)

As for rising prices, I assur'd the Council that they were the result of the large increase of paper money in circulation and that they wou'd soon level out, as the price of shares stabilis'd.

And finally, on the subject of Louisiana, I announc'd that although it was still too early to expect large returns on such an investment, the Company wou'd be paying a dividend of 200 livres, so confident was it of the colony's future prosperity. Meanwhile, the emigration measures had fulfill'd their objective of increasing the flow of settlers to the colony and cou'd now be repeal'd.

But if Philippe and the Council seem'd happy enough with this, the salons and streets were less convinc'd. Despite the fact that these announcements were widely publicis'd – particularly the news of the share dividend – I began to sense an ebbing of general confidence. All I requir'd was that the share price remain'd stable, and yet it seem'd that something compell'd it to move in one direction or another; if not up then it must go down. No matter how much I reassur'd investors, the price continued to fall. Each day an increasing number of shares were sold, mostly to the Bank or the Company, and the paper convert'd to gold, silver and diamonds.

It was my worst fear – a loss of confidence in paper and a consequent demand for metal that the Bank cou'd not sustain. Over the next few weeks, I watch'd the price of shares fall steadily, while the price of everything else continued to rise. Finally, a report from customs officials in the Channel ports persuad'd me to take action: large amounts of metal were leaving the country for London, where they were being invest'd in the South Sea Company! I had made the Mississippi shares as attractive as possible with the carrot of a large dividend; now the only other method of keeping money in shares was to apply the stick and restrict the use of metal by law. In this way, I wou'd demonstrate the Government's absolute confidence in paper.

Did I think to seek Philippe's agreement before passing this law? Indeed not. As Financial-Controller, I was within my jurisdiction, and anyway it was not something I thought he wou'd object to – paper had made him much richer than gold ever cou'd. Furthermore, it was an opportunity for me to display the kind of bold, decisive action that was necessary to protect everything the country had gain'd from the System.

The next day at the Palais-Royal, I issued an edict discouraging the use of metal. It was made unlawful to take gold and silver coins out of the country or use them for any transaction over 100 livres. To this bitter medicine, I add'd the sugar of allowing coins to be exchang'd for paper at a favourable rate.

From the Palais-Royal I then return'd to the Bank's offices to authorise the necessary increase in the supply of paper money. Whilst there, I cou'd not resist taking the opportunity to view the progress of Pellegrini's ceiling – France's Sistine Chapel, as I call'd it, with Pellegrini as my Michelangelo. (Did this make me his Pope Julius? I hop'd not.) Indeed, I was becoming at least as interest'd in the unfolding tableau as I was in matters financial. I must have stood for some while beneath the vault, watching the master at work, when I heard a woman's voice: 'And why, John, do you not come to visit me anymore? Have you become such a devout Catholic?'

It was deTencin – or Claudine, as she now insist'd I call her. She look'd ravishing, and it caus'd an immediate rush of blood to the groin. This being the case, I ask'd myself why in fact I had not visit'd her, but the answer was simple: she like everything and everyone else – including Saint-Simon – had taken second place to the financial crisis.

Yes, I had been a model of piety and chastity, since our blissful week of instruction together and my conversion. I begg'd forgiveness for having neglect'd her and told her how dull my life had been without her. How I had miss'd her, how I had struggl'd. (How facile the beast of lust makes us once it has its prey in sight!)

Of course, the wonderful thing about de Tencin, was that she did not believe a word of it – and nor did that seem to bother her. We retir'd to my office; I ask'd for us not to be disturb'd, as we had much business to discuss. Within minutes, we were pleasuring each other as we had in the chapel. Several piles of important state documents were scatter'd to the winds by our passionate exertions; quills and ink were knock'd to the floor, spilling on to the fine Persian carpet. In my final convulsions, I toppl'd forward into her arms.

'Well, here we are at the Banque Royale, Monsieur Law,' she laugh'd, 'and you seem to have made yet another deposit.'

'I trust you pay a decent rate of interest,' I replied, breathless.

'The best in Paris,' she said. 'And speaking of which – shou'd I sell my shares, as many seem to be doing? The price is falling, I'm told...'

'No, it will rise again,' I replied, regarding my now limp member, 'I promise you.'

She laugh'd again and then grew more sombre. 'John, you will visit me, won't you? Or must I always come to fetch you?'

'Of course, I will visit you, Claudine,' I said to the sound of sharp knocking on the door.

Having quickly made my appearance more business-like – I subsequently realised that part of my shirt hung out of my breeches and my periwig was badly askew – I open'd the door to a messenger from the Palais-Royal; one of my own clerks mouth'd apologies behind him.

'Monsieur Law, if you cou'd possibly tear yourself away from your pressing duties,' the messenger said, in a manner intend'd to convey the terse tone of the original, 'the Regent requests your immediate attendance at the palace.'

'I am somewhat press'd,' I replied, with remarkable calm. 'Does His Royal Highness say for what reason?'

He shook his head, thoroughly enjoying the arrogant display. 'Only that it is of the utmost importance that you come now.'

And so, deploring the demands of office, I apologis'd to Claudine for the interruption of our 'discussions' and bade her adieu. It was the last time I ever saw her.

*

I'm suddenly struck – not by a woman this time, but by the sheer absurdity of what passes for money in our crazy world: Boris' money, my money, money in general. What is this thing that I've put above all else, upon whose altar I've sacrificed everything? This is a time for action, of course, not for waxing philosophical, but I can't help myself. It's like that scene in the film *The Matrix* when the Keanu Reeves character – Neo, I think his name is – comes to understand that his material reality, his whole world, is nothing but a stream of binary data.

And now, I'm watching my own reality, the thing that's held me spellbound for so long, melt before my eyes, fade to nothing. Feinstein will capture nothing but electronic data, bits and bytes, from Boris and the others, but in doing so he can make himself a god, a true Master of the Universe. He can destroy worlds and create them. *How is that possible?* And it goes on all the time, all over the planet. Data, mere numbers – things you can't touch or feel – blessing some lives and shattering others. They open the door to vast opportunity for the few and slam it shut for the many. *How the fuck is that possible?* I'll tell you how – through the illusion that money is real; the willingness of people to buy into the idea that when the magician pulls the rabbit out of the hat, he's not just performing a trick – he's really, actually conjuring something out of nothing.

I order another large g & t and call Feinstein on the hotline. Let's do it, I'm finally going to tell him, let's wreak havoc. But the call doesn't connect. I try again – still no connection. And again. And again. The battery and signal levels are okay, but there's nothing. Nada. A silence as resounding as any I've heard: someone has got to us. The Russians? The police? *Someone.*

I put off full-scale panic by emailing him: 'Everything all right? Hotline is down.' I have various addresses for him. I try them all. Then I think how stupid I'm being. If we *are* under surveillance, it's probably not a good idea to be emailing him at all. But it doesn't matter. They all bounce back. Undeliverable. Address not valid.

The wise man knows when to call it a day. I down my drink in one and go up to the room. I had planned to order some food, but I'm not hungry anymore. I hang up my waterproof, take off my shoes and socks. (I've left my yellow boots in a box for the purpose by the hotel entrance.) The room's been made up since I was here. The drawn curtains shut out the beautiful view of the canal, but that's fine because I want no part of it just now. The king size bed's been made; the covers turned down on both sides and chocolate mints placed on the pillows. (Is there anything more ludicrous than the 'turn-down' service?) There's a complimentary bottle of wine with two glasses on the main table, and two sets of bathrobes and slippers have been laid out at the foot of the bed. They make a sad sight. In the bathroom, my toiletries have been tidied, the lotions and potions set out in a soldierly line. From my wash bag, I take a small pack of sleeping pills – or sleep aids, as they seem to call them these days, perhaps because you're less likely to OD on an aid. (No, that isn't where this is going.) I may not want to eat, but I do very much want to sleep, and as exhausted as I am, I know I need to take a pill. I raid the well-stocked minibar, pour a couple of gins into a glass and wash it down.

I was going to undress, but I find myself lying fully clothed on the bed. I look at the time: 10.10pm. Still early. There's a small side table by one of the armchairs and perched on it, reproachfully, is the manuscript – *the* manuscript.

I have the crazy notion that now is a good time to start reading it. I force myself to get up and grab it and fall back on the bed. I manage the first couple of sentences:

'Venice, October 1728

> *Let me begin by making one thing clear. If I have my way – and in the more important matters it has often been the case – I will carry on playing at the tables until the very end, until they carry me out and lay me in my Venetian tomb...'*

The rest is a tomb-like darkness.

*

I was greet'd by Philippe in his large office. The walls were adorn'd by several Corregios – more flamboyant nudes in sylvan landscapes. The afternoon light flood'd in through a broad bow window that look'd out on to the parterre below. In one corner sat the silver-hair'd Dubois, like a puppet master in the shadows, pois'd to pull Orleans' strings. I had wonder'd if Katherine was to be the subject of this discussion, but the moment I enter'd the room and saw Dubois, I knew it had to do with my edict on metal.

Philippe had obviously been drinking. 'What is the meaning of this edict, John?' he ask'd without ceremony. 'Surely it's something that the Council and I shou'd have approv'd...' He had only once adopt'd such a hostile manner with me – when I had accus'd him of soliciting financial favours for his mistress, Parabère.

'Your Highness, I saw no reason to involve anyone else. The measure is in keeping with my stat'd policy of moving the currency almost entirely to paper. It has simply happen'd a little sooner than I anticipat'd.'

'It is unacceptable. Any restrictions on the movement or use of metal run counter to France's wider interests.' It was a line learnt from a tutor.

I look'd sidelong at Dubois. 'Or counter to certain narrow vest'd interests,' I said.

The Abbé had been waiting for the chance to challenge me. 'Come, come, Monsieur Low, if your System were robust enough, you wou'd not fear a little gold changing hands – or even leaving the country. Anyway, you cannot hope to make such a law work.'

'It will work,' I replied. 'With the Government's support.'

He gave me one of his thinnest smiles. 'And do you have that support?'

I turn'd to Philippe. 'Much as I value the Abbé's opinion, Your Highness, I'd be grateful if I cou'd be grant'd a separate audience with you.'

He nodd'd towards Dubois, who rose slowly from his chair. 'I think I've express'd my opinion with sufficient clarity,' the latter said. He made a curt bow to us both and left.

Philippe stood looking out at the gardens that stretch'd away towards the Tuileries. 'Your Highness...' I start'd, but he cut me off, abruptly.

'You cannot assume that you have my unqualified support on all these issues, John. There are other considerations, as you know.'

'With respect, Your Highness, it has not been the case until now. You've support'd me throughout – may I ask what has chang'd?'

'Nothing has chang'd, except there are many who will not tolerate restrictions on metal. Giving them the option of paper is one thing; penalising them for not taking it is another.' He turn'd and fac'd me. 'You wish'd to be Financial Controller and you are. I will now judge each issue on its merit. Dubois and others feel very strongly about metal.'

'And this has nothing to do with how you feel about Katherine?'

He look'd as if this were the most unreasonable question in the world. 'My feelings for Katherine have no bearing on this.'

'May I ask if you've seen her?'

'You may – but for now I have nothing to say on the subject. Let us speak only of the edict.'

'Very well, Your Highness. Let us speak of that. If Dubois and the others get their way it will jeopardise the System and the prosperity of all of us. Is that what you want? And if it is, as your Financial-Controller, I wou'd respectfully ask that you think about how greatly you have benefit'd from it – some might say, too greatly, perhaps. And if the Bank were to collapse, it's likely that everyone wou'd discover how much.'

Our eyes met; expressions harden'd. Not for the first time I had the impression that I was lock'd in a duel of sorts with Orleans; I had to take the fight to him or be overwhelm'd – a dangerous move, but a necessary one.

'Are you threatening the Regent, John?'

'It is a threatening situation for all concern'd. I am merely offering advice...Your Highness.'

'Then here's some for you – even if I do support you in this, there are others who will be ruthless in their opposition to it – you must realise that.'

'I do, but together we can resist them and protect the System. And good things are worth protecting, are they not?'

He did not answer but return'd to looking out of the window. After some moments, he said: 'I'll think on it, John, and contact you tomorrow.'

Sure enough, his answer came in a note the next morning. I was at the Company offices, contemplating the falling share price – down to 8000 – and the latest dire reports from Louisiana – another settlement lost to Indians and all attempts at tobacco and sugar cultivation bedevill'd by water-logg'd soil. Thankfully, the news from Philippe was better. He agreed that the protection and maintenance of the System was our first priority. He wou'd fully support me in my efforts to control the use of metal – and duly inform Dubois of his decision.

I was much reliev'd. My edict remain'd in force and within a week the situation had improv'd: there was a large exchange of gold for paper and the share price recover'd to 8500. Any protests were ignor'd; it was unsettl'd February weather, but I was sure it wou'd pass. I was wrong.

I was at the Bank, when I had an unexpect'd visit from the Prince de Conti. He arriv'd with a company of guards and several large wagons, as well as his own heavily gild'd carriage. (He was not to be outdone by the 'Mississippi Millionaires'.)

Standing under the Bank's ceiling, admiring Pellegrini's progress, I was unaware that the Prince had come arm'd with malicious intent and greet'd him as a respect'd colleague. To my horror, he was once again the snarling creature I had known before my offer of vast wealth had tam'd him. Now, he still want'd the wealth, but was not for taming, it seem'd.

'You won't like why I'm here, Law' – his crude form of address said as much – 'but I have little alternative. The situation in Louisiana has made it impossible for me to trust in the value of all this paper.'

He look'd contemptuously at the large boxes of bank notes being carried in by his guards; I guess'd where this was leading.

'But Your Grace knows that the Bank guarantees the value of each and every note.' I made every effort to sound patronising.

He laugh'd dismissively. 'And we both know the Bank's ability to guarantee anything depends on the value of Mississippi shares...'

'Which is very high,' I said.

'Only because you've restrict'd the use of metal, Law. I think it will fall again very soon. That's why I want all these notes exchang'd for coin.'

'But as Your Grace just said, its use is restrict'd.'

'Well, that's something I will have to bear. I still require the full amount to be exchang'd – right now, if you will...'

It was the very same act of war that he had perpetrat'd in the early days of the Bank Generale, only this time there was no intermediary. I inwardly curs'd myself for being caught so flat-foot'd and defenceless. I shou'd have foreseen this turn of events, but had thought de Conti still had more to gain from supporting me. I wonder'd what had happened to change that and whether other powerful allies were similarly disaffect'd.

Unfortunately, it was difficult to use my previous ploy and stall him: as a Council member, he had a good idea of how much coin the Bank had taken in and that it was stor'd in the vaults. I cou'd only resort to reason, which was not a commodity that appeal'd to him.

'As you know, this is highly irresponsible of Your Grace. It will damage confidence in the Company and the currency.'

'My prime concern is my investment, Law – metal is a safer place for it than paper in any shape or form. You understand that, don't you? After all, isn't that what your System is found'd upon – self-interest?'

'Only in as much as it benefits the whole – this action of yours could destroy it.'

His gloating expression indicat'd that this was exactly his intention. 'Is there any reason that you can't convert the notes? Or don't you have enough gold?'

If I cou'd not dissuade him from converting to metal, I wou'd at least convince him that the Bank had more than enough to underwrite its operations, irrespective of the value of Mississippi shares. 'How much does Your Grace require?'

He nodd'd towards the boxes, as a guard plac'd yet another on the stack. 'There are roughly 50 million livres in these.' It was like the slow insertion of a stiletto into my stomach – now he gave it a sharp twist: '20 million of it is from my sale of Mississippi shares this morning, Law.' This was indeed a declaration of war.

'You can have the amount in full today,' I said without hesitation, 'but we will of course need time to count it before it can be exchang'd. Wou'd Your Grace care to return a little later?'

'No, I'll wait here until the transaction is complet'd...' And he eas'd his upholster'd bulk into one of the upholster'd chairs in the Salle de Mississippi.

His servants brought him wine, tobacco and reading material; various associates came to call, as if he had set up court. Occasionally, he look'd up at Pelligrini and his team at work on the ceiling. After three hours, both notes and coins were count'd and exchang'd, and we watch'd as the guards struggl'd to load the tens of boxes of coins on to his wagons.

441

When the last one had been carried out, he got up and follow'd, waddling and wheezing as he went, leaning heavily on his cane. He stopp'd and rais'd it towards the roof. 'Blasphemy, I call it! Why decorate a bank like a church?' he growl'd.

'Because men worship money as much as they do the Lord,' I smil'd woodenly, 'especially those of infinite greed, like yourself...Your Grace.'

He laugh'd. 'Thank you, Law. I'm glad you've lost none of your sense of humour...if you've lost much else today. This game is mine, I think. Please feel free to visit me any time and try to win some of it back.' He had a further chuckle to himself and left.

Never had I felt as angry, and yet it was more important than ever that I kept my card-playing calm. Monsieur Ginot and the rest of the Bank's staff stood listless and long-fac'd, as if at a graveside. And as much as I tried to make light of what had happen'd, claiming it help'd maintain confidence in the Bank, we soon had another reason to mourn. Within half-an-hour there was a second unexpect'd visitor: the duc de Bourbon.

He was far too drunk to get out of his carriage – which was also at the head of several wagons – so he sent his retainer with a prepar'd script. The man was obviously very nervous and kept apologising for the situation, but the message was clear. His Grace was profoundly disappoint'd with the Company and the rising prices throughout the country and had decid'd to convert all his paper, shares as well as currency, to coin. In all, it totall'd 30 million livres (less than I expect'd, but perhaps he had already consum'd the rest in wine).

While the Duc wait'd in his carriage, plying himself with drink and fondling his mistress, more boxes of notes were brought into the Bank, count'd and exchang'd for coin. Again, I maintain'd a placid surface, but beneath it I felt more and more incens'd at being outmanoeuvr'd, and I vow'd immediate revenge. Even so, I am still convinc'd that my next move was a logical one and not the result of panic born of desperation, as some have suggest'd.

The consequences of Bourbon's and de Conti's actions were wholly predictable. Over the next few days there was a headlong rush for gold and silver, as never before. Quite *simply, if two of the richest men in France – as they certainly were now – had chosen to dump paper, then it was very much the thing to do. Shares were sold in their thousands; the Bank was besieg'd by investors of all hues wanting to convert to coin, so many that we had to lock its doors and summon the guard to control the crowd. At the same time, this riotous atmosphere was intensified by a rapid rise in prices due to the flood of paper I had releas'd in order to displace coin. Before the week was out, protests were report'd on the streets of every major town in France, while Parlement, for so long cow'd by Philippe, had begun its mischief and was baying for my blood.*

My response was swift. To offset the rise in prices, I instantly reliev'd the burden on the poor by repealing the clutter of archaic taxes on commodities with a single edict and replacing them with a property and income tax on the well-off. This provok'd further outcry from Parlement, but was popular among the mass of people and begun to calm the general situation. Unfortunately, it did not stop the run on shares or the scramble for metal. To do that, I wou'd yet again require Philippe's support.

*

There's nothing but oblivion till I wake, in desperate need of a pee and to a wailing sound from outside. At first, I think it's a fire alarm; I've forgotten all about the siren for *acqua alta*. Daylight is leaking in around the curtains. The clock at my bedside says 9.58. I appear to have slept for nearly twelve hours. Even with a sleep aid or any other kind of drug, I don't know when I last did such a thing, probably when I was a teenager.

And like a teenager, I feel I could go on for another twelve hours. It takes me a good while to gather my senses. Who am I? Where am I? What's my situation? The first two answers come easily; the third's a little trickier.

I take in the fact that the pages of a document are scattered around me, like giant fallen leaves; that I've slept in my clothes and am probably in need of the valet service. The events of yesterday slowly unspool in my head, and what a large spool it is: my strange behaviour through the night and into yesterday morning, Marisa and the Decadence tour, the threatening email, the near accident on the water, the lunch at the Cipriani, the ghostly lovers upstairs in the Venier, the ghostly figure in the square, the attempted mugging, the painful exchange with Jo, her departure, the incident with the woman I thought was her – I touch my nose; it's still sore – the meeting with Diana and her same sex partner – I didn't expect a *same sex partner* – Mozart's Requiem – I didn't expect to like it – the men-in-black, the police, the news of Boris' death, the news – or is that confirmation? – that there's a serious threat to my own life…

My God, it gets darker and darker. I feel like I'm deep inside a cave and my torch is on the blink. I'm trapped in a labyrinth of narrow, twisting tunnels leading nowhere and back again. It's not a question of me having lost my way – more that I didn't know where I was going in the first place. And now, I'm not only confused, I'm scared shitless. I hear the snarls and growls of the Minotaur as it moves ever closer.

Then I remember the contact with Feinstein – and the lack of contact with Feinstein. I reach for my phones, only to find they're both out of battery. I put them on charge, but they're so dead, it'll take a few minutes before I can use them.

The effects of the sleeping pill are finally wearing off and I'm beginning to feel very hungry. I think about ordering some breakfast but decide to make myself some coffee in the room instead and wait for lunch.

Because, yes, a reminder of my lunch date has dropped into my mental inbox – lunch at Count Orsini's and the purchase of the manuscript. *Remember?* That's what the document spread around me is – the reason I came here in the first place. I gather up all the pages, before pulling back the curtains to reveal that wonderful view. The grey sky is shot through with shafts of golden sunshine, but darker clouds loom in the distance and the water level is on the rise again. It feels like another calm before the storm.

I settle back down on the bed with the strongest coffee I can muster and the manuscript. I'm not going anywhere just yet, so if I can stay awake, I may be able to get through it before the lunch. It doesn't have to be a good read for me to buy it for some outrageous price. But it would be nice if it were.

*

News had come through to me that Orleans was unwell – a sickness of the stomach that show'd no signs of abating. Twice he was indispos'd when I call'd upon him at the Palais-Royal, and I began to think that I wou'd have to proceed without his approval. The third time I was far more insistent and permitt'd to visit him in his bedchamber. There I found him suitless and bootless – although still wearing a peruke – and sitting on a large commode, his face a study in discomfiture. A doctor and several nurses were in attendance, while two servants spray'd attar of roses round the room to counteract the foul fumes wafting from the chair. He dismiss'd them all when I arriv'd and spent several minutes cursing his condition.

'It has plagued me for no less than five days,' he croak'd, mopping at his fever'd brow with a large lace handkerchief, 'in which time not a morsel of meat or drop of wine has pass'd my lips.' I doubt'd the latter. 'I've had broth to the gills – and I hate broth. Can't you see what a wretch'd fellow I am, John? Is this matter of yours so urgent?'

Looking back now, I realise that I underestimat'd his disillusionment with both myself and the System, attributing his bad mood solely to sickness. 'I fear it is, Your Highness, although it pains me to see you so afflict'd.'

'It pains me all the more,' he groan'd, 'almost as much as hearing the news of rioting and general discontent. Even Parlement is on my back again. I will not stand to be made unpopular, John - aren't you suppos'd to be putting matters right?' And he clutch'd his stomach and groan'd again. 'Blast these rotten guts of mine!'

'Indeed, I am, Your Highness. But de Conti and Bourbon have deliberately sabotag'd my efforts – by insisting on exchanging all their paper for coin. A sum of 80 million livres. The exchequer cannot stand to make too many such payments.'

He looked away; I was not sure whether he already knew this or not. 'I warn'd you. They will not be controll'd.'

'I can control them, Your Highness – with your support.'

He rais'd an eyebrow. 'In what way?'

'I intend to ban not only the use of all gold as currency, but its possession in any form.'

'Any form?'

'Down to the display of it upon the person – necklaces, rings, brooches etc. I cannot take the risk that it will be melt'd down and us'd as currency.'

But for the rumbling of his stomach, Philippe was stunn'd into silence for some moments. 'It cannot work,' he said finally. 'Our wives and mistresses will never tolerate it.'

'Then let them wear diamonds, Your Highness. But I must ensure that people stay in paper, whether shares or notes. At the moment the option of metal seems too attractive.'

Orleans stomach suddenly let out a growl; there was a spurting and spluttering sound, like that of an old pump. He winc'd with pain. 'Surely there's nothing left inside me,' he moan'd, 'it must be my very innards!' Then, when he had recover'd somewhat: 'What of Louisiana? What of the great wealth you promis'd from our Royal colony?'

'It will come, Your Highness. The foundations of prosperity are being laid, but it will take time. Meanwhile, we must keep people in paper. It's the only way.'

Oddly enough, I felt that I too was a doctor of sorts, one who prescribes an unpleasant but unavoidable course of treatment: the surgical knife – gold and silver must be cut out of the body of France!

He seem'd too weak to put up a fight; he clos'd his eyes, as if a great weariness had come over him. 'Very well, John, if you must. We will try it for a month...but you will find it extremely difficult to enforce.'

'Indeed,' I replied. 'Which is why I will make an example of one or two more prominent figures – in order to encourage the others...'

Another severe bout of pain brought our meeting to a swift conclusion. Having thank'd him and wish'd him a speedy recovery, I summon'd back the doctors and hurried off to my office in the Palais-Royal. There was much to arrange if I was to issue the edict before the end of the day – an act made even more urgent by a message I receiv'd later that afternoon. The share price had fallen below 5000 and an angry crowd of investors was gathering outside the Company office.

Once again, soldiers were dispatch'd to the scene and I follow'd on, fully intending to speak to the crowd and remind them of the solid value of their shares and the prospect of the next dividend payment. As I was soon to discover, however, I had grown so us'd to the public's adulation that I had quite forgotten how cruel and fickle a mob cou'd be. There were nobles, merchants, artisans, servants – men and women – all jostling and jeering in the Quincampoix. They had broken down the gates and were surging towards the offices. What had been the scene of so many triumphs soon became one of humiliation. My intention was to speak to them from the Company steps, but once my carriage had been spott'd, they became more and more rabid, such that even the mount'd militia had difficulty restraining them. Missiles – stones, rotten vegetables, lumps of wood – were thrown at the carriage. There were shouts of vile abuse, especially from the women, and cries of 'Give us back our gold!' and 'Fuck off back to England, you thieving foreign bastard!'

I was not encourag'd to get out and appeal to reason. My only recourse was to withdraw – to Louis le Grand, I thought, it being nearer than the Palais-Royal – while ordering in the cavalry to disperse them. Many actually follow'd the carriage, attempting to jump aboard. Fortunately, a company of guards afford'd me enough protection and then station'd themselves outside the house, where another crowd was beginning to gather.

It was several days before the city felt calm enough for me to set foot outside the house, which was mainly because the general reaction to my new edict was at first one of stunn'd silence – as it had been with Philippe. It also had the immediate effect of halting the rush into metal, even if the share price continued to fall. Above all, I need'd to demonstrate my resolve on the question of gold. I organis'd a special militia around the country, charg'd with confiscating louis d'or and jewellery where they had not been officially surrender'd for their equivalent in paper. At the same time, rewards were offer'd for information leading to such confiscations.

There was the inevitable flurry of protests, but this was more than outweigh'd by the initial clamour for rewards and the favourable rate of exchange for notes. Searches were instigat'd where it was thought that gold was being hoard'd, and I personally led one such mission to the house of a prime offender, the Prince de Conti. Somewhere he had stor'd away 50 million, mostly in gold coin, and while I did not expect to recover it all, I thought at least to intimidate and make an example of him.

I went with a contingent of guards to his large hôtel in the Faubourg Saint-Germain. He had just complet'd his levee and was sitting down to a breakfast of foie gras and quails' eggs. Outrag'd by my 'gross intrusion', he struggl'd to his feet and demand'd to know on whose authority I cou'd force my way into the home of a Prince of the Blood. He wou'd personally ensure that I was prosecut'd by the Crown and sent to the Bastille etc.etc.

'It's on the Crown's authority that I do this, Your Grace,' I cut in. 'As a member of the Council you shou'd be aware of the new law prohibiting the use and possession of gold.'

'I am aware of it,' he bluster'd, 'but naturally I assum'd that it did not apply to me or anyone of my class.'

'It very much applies to you. I've every reason to suspect that Your Grace is breaking that law. And anyway' – I smil'd wryly – 'you did invite me to try to win back some of the Bank's coin. I have simply chosen to play a game other than Pharo or Piquet.'

'So that's it, Law, is it? Well, go ahead and play your silly games, if it makes you happy.' He sat back down to his breakfast and I gestur'd for the guards to start their search. 'You'll find little gold here,' he shout'd after them. 'Much of it has already gone to my partner in crime.'

'If you mean Bourbon, I'll be paying him a visit too...'

'No, I mean my good <u>blood</u> relation, Orleans.'

My face must have register'd disbelief.

'Yes, Law, the Regent – your great sponsor and supporter.'

'And why wou'd it have gone to His Royal Highness?' I ask'd. 'So that it can be return'd to the exchequer, I hope...'

He scoff'd at this. 'Why do you think? It was he who initiat'd our raid, as he term'd it, being fond of military manoeuvres. He's greedier than the rest of us, you know – and has probably lost more to you at cards. As a rule, Bourbons hate to be losers.'

I had seen prize-fighters in England, men of singular strength, so confident of victory they had lower'd their guard as they press'd home their advantage. Suddenly they had been caught by an unexpect'd blow and fell'd like a tree. Inwardly, I was like such a man. I had been knock'd almost senseless and lay on the ground, struggling to comprehend what had taken place.

Outwardly, however, I was all bravado. I derid'd the idea that Philippe had been involv'd with de Conti in his act of sabotage. I even chid'd the Prince for his malicious tongue and the fact that he was always attempting to undermine his cousin.

'You'll see soon enough,' he said. 'It is he who wou'd undermine everyone else.' And he continued with his foie gras and eggs.

A few moments later, some of the guards return'd with several bags of gold coin; I reckon'd around 2000 louis d'or, a small sum in the circumstances. These wou'd be confiscated by the Crown, I told de Conti. But as a token of my good will, I insist'd he take paper in exchange, and count'd it out for him on to the table. He pick'd it up and tore it to pieces, throwing it back in my face. ''Good will?' he sneer'd. 'It's worth little now, Law – it'll soon be worth nothing at all!'

Having inform'd him that his chateau near Paris was also being search'd for gold, I bade him good day and left. It was later report'd to me that a few bags of coin had been found there, but little more than wou'd be need'd for the daily running of a large estate.

I left de Conti's in a daze and return'd to Louis le Grand under arm'd escort. Crowds were once again gather'd on the street and I was booed and jeer'd whenever my carriage was recognis'd. As I watch'd the mounting anger and ponder'd the implications of de Conti's remarks, my sense of panic and

449

confusion grew. Shou'd I go straight to Philippe and confront him with these startling allegations? Or shou'd I first seek out Saint-Simon? Somehow, Louis always knew his friend's heart better than anyone, including Orleans himself; he wou'd know whether de Conti's claims had any truth in them. However, after what had happen'd at Notre Dame, I felt no more certain of a warm reception from Louis than I did from anyone in the jeering crowd. As it turn'd out, confirmation of Orleans' betrayal came via another channel.

In my frantic search for gold, I had start'd to cast my net in any and every direction, including Katherine's. I sent the militia on to Gourmande to confiscate the large amount of coin I knew to be there, instructing them to exchange it for twice the value in paper – as if she wou'd see that as any kind of compensation – and not to confiscate any jewellery.

The officer in charge return'd to me in the evening, having ridden all the way back to Paris post-haste. Desperate for news of Katherine, I immediately plied the exhaust'd fellow – who was by no means a young man - with many urgent questions.

Were there any of the Regent's guards present? There were not – although the servants inform'd them that several had left a few days before. Had his own men confiscat'd any gold? They had not – Madame Law had assur'd them that there was not a gold coin on the estate, and after a thorough search, they were able to confirm that this was true. How did Madame Law behave? She seem'd calm an compos'd when they first arriv'd, but she later became distraught and often broke down and wept. Did she send any word to me, any message at all? Yes, she had written out a short letter while he wait'd to leave and had ask'd him to deliver it to me in person – which he duly did.

I opened it and read it on the spot, wincing inwardly all the while:

Dear Financial-Controller,

Are there no lengths to which you will not go to control _my_ finances? Like so many of your recent actions, this one is beneath you, and even more futile than usual.

I am afraid that you have been outflank'd by His Royal Highness, Philippe, duc d'Orleans, Regent of France. He has already 'confiscate'd' my pot of gold, and he did so without going through the charade of offering me soon-to-be worthless paper in exchange. For a man who is no better than a common criminal, this at least bespeaks some degree of honesty on his part. You wou'd appear to have none.

Anne and I are no longer his prisoners here at Gourmand, which is to say his guards have left us. However, with barely a sous to our name and all the freedom that affords, we might as well be lock'd in the Bastille. We are unable to go to the Netherlands, or anywhere else for that matter, and remain confin'd to the estate.

Nor, I must tell you, is this the worst of Orleans' crimes against me. There are others, so vile that I cannot bring myself to put them in writing.

Where did we go wrong, John? How did we allow ourselves to stoop so low and pick up so little? On the one hand, I am compell'd to ponder these painful questions. On the other, I do my best to put them out of my mind; to forget that we ever came to France, that we were ever lovers and partners and that you are the father of my daughter.

I thank'd the officer and let him go to his bed. He hesitat'd as he went to leave; he had one more message to deliver: 'Forgive me, Sir, perhaps I shou'd not be saying this. In my many years as a soldier, I have been witness to much grief and sadness. But never have I seen a woman in a more sorrowful state than Madame Law...a woman as sorely us'd as she is beautiful...'

*

It turns out the manuscript *is* a good read, in my humble opinion – or it is for the first 120 pages or so. My ancestor's financial wizardry and disastrous personal life is an even more impressive combination than my own and just as destined to end badly – his more spectacularly, but who knows? My end hasn't ended yet. I'm so engrossed in his exploits that I'm oblivious to the time and my ravenous hunger. I also let most of my coffee get cold and forget about trying to call Feinstein.

Then I get to the part where Law goes to the Venier gaming salon we visited with our guide, Marisa, and lands up in bed with Sabine de Valliere, a French courtesan. It verges on the pornographic and as sex scenes go, in my limited experience of reading such things, it's hot. But it freezes me in my tracks or, more accurately, sends a chill up my spine and puts me in a cold sweat. The ghostly lovers I imagined I saw at the Venier, the ones I thought at first were some sort of tableau or automata, the ones that *disappeared, are in his story, for fuck's sake! I know it's crazy, but it's them!*

How is that possible? If I only just found out about them when I read the manuscript, how could I have conjured them up yesterday? There's no rational explanation but I'm desperate to find one. The only thing that makes sense is that it's some kind of weird coincidence and my reading about it somehow affects my memory of it. I'm convinced I saw this raunchy scene – most likely a trick of the light or the product of sheer horniness – and then I read a detailed account of something similar in the manuscript that influences what I *think* I remember about it: a kind of retrofit memory. Indeed, isn't that what some experts say about memory? That we don't return to the original. We actually recreate it each time and how we think of it may change according to our circumstances. So, my mother and the dunes in Michigan are as much a product of my imagination as of my memory and they're different each time I recall them – as is that scene at the Venier.

For the next 20 pages, the cold sweat and chill up my spine are gone. But when I get to the bit where Law visits the Palazzo Cantarini del Bovolo and climbs the spiral staircase, they return with a vengeance. He points his cane – the 'rifle' – at the moon, then sees a man with a chest wound down in the square and points it at him. Or rather, at *me*. Because that was, *is me* – there, looking up at him, thinking he's about to shoot me.

My God! There's no way this one can be a weird coincidence too. It's impossible. Forget that memory and imagination crap, someone is seriously fucking with my head, pulling some extremely elaborate stunt; somehow creating these illusions *and* planting them in the so-called memoir, which must be an out-and-out fake.

It's either that – but, let's face it, who would go to such trouble and why? – or I *am* being haunted. In some ways, it's the more likely scenario. And, what's even stranger, and even more worrying, Law is/was being haunted too – not by the ghost of his friend Beau Wickham, *but by me. I'm* the man who keeps appearing to him – the man with the rose-like wound on his chest!

*

Contrary to all reason, I discover'd that when so many serious troubles bear down upon you and press for your attention, sometimes the only thing to do is to ignore them. The next morning at the Bank, after a long, sleepless night, I was like a drowning man who finally gives up all resistance to the waves dragging him under and realises that he is borne up by them, albeit briefly.

Pellegrini approach'd me as soon as I arriv'd. He too had been up most of the night, but his time had been spent more productively. He had complet'd the ceiling and was keen to show it to me. He wou'd not hear that I had other pressing business, and quite rightly so – nothing was more important at that moment than the ceiling of the Salle de Mississippi.

The scaffolding and covers that still obscur'd the last section were remov'd and for the first time I had an unhinder'd view of the whole panorama. It was nothing short of magnificent. Winds blew, ships sail'd to and from the fecund Americas; the Angels of Money and Credit herald'd an age of joy and prosperity. France had become the most powerful nation on Earth, a land of plenty bath'd in the golden light of a new Sun King – the young Louis XV, whose happy reign was bas'd on the solid foundations of the System. It was just as I

453

had envision'd: the triumph of Trade and Commerce – the new religion of Man emblazon'd across the heavens!

Pellegrini saw the sheer pleasure writ large across my face. I thank'd him warmly and we stood there together, smiling up at his work – 'our work,' he insist'd generously. For a few blissful moments, my worries were forgotten.

But only for a few. Monsieur Ginot soon demand'd my attention, his face etch'd with deep contours of concern. (The poor man had ag'd considerably over the last few weeks, as had I.) The share price had fallen below a thousand livres, he said feverishly. There were reports of renew'd rioting around the Quincampoix and the Palais-Royal. They were shouting for the Regent's head, as well as my own, and Parlement had call'd for my immediate removal and arrest. He was sure that it wou'd not be long before a crowd gather'd at the Bank.

To add to these sorry tales was another that was even more disturbing. Two of the Company's biggest investors, Mississippi Millionaires many times over, had apparently lost everything since the fall in share price. That morning they had made their way to the front of the crowd at the Palais-Royal and run upon their swords in the Roman style, bleeding to death on the spot. There were also several stories of bankrupts jumping from upper windows onto the cobbl'd streets below, while others had actually set fire to themselves and their houses upon receiving news of the share collapse.

My assistant wou'd have continued with this litany of woe, had I not cut him off. 'Thank you, Monsieur Ginot,' I said. 'I think that's enough tragedy for one morning, don't you?'

'Yes, Sir – except that there is one other matter I feel I shou'd report to you.'

'Which is?'

'Madame de Tencin call'd to see you yesterday afternoon. She want'd your advice on her shares. She doesn't know what to do in the situation. She knows there are so many demands on your time, but if you cou'd spare an hour to visit her at her apartments or at least send word, she'd be most grateful... I thought you wou'd want to know, Sir.'

'Thank you, Monsieur Ginot. You were right to tell me.' I turn'd to the rest of the staff, who were standing around in *fretful clusters. 'Meanwhile, let's celebrate the completion of our wonderful ceiling. Bring food – meats, fruits and cheeses. And musicians. Bring them all. We'll have a banquet...'*

Ginot looked puzzl'd. 'Surely, Monsieur Law, this is no time for celebrations?'

'This is exactly the time,' I replied. 'There is little more we can do today. My edicts will act as a medicine over time, I can assure you.'

And I stood up and rose to my full height, determin'd to restore confidence. The food and drink were brought and plac'd on counting tables in the banking hall; the Bank's doors were clos'd and all the staff invit'd to join the celebration. Outside the crowd gather'd. as Ginot had predict'd, and grew rowdier by the minute. It was only constrain'd by a cordon of heavily-arm'd guards. I feign'd unconcern. I made speeches; I laugh'd and jok'd with Pellegrini; I toast'd him and his ceiling a dozen times, and inwardly resolv'd to do two things: I wou'd reinforce the edicts by contriving some 'good news' from Louisiana in the hope that it wou'd boost the share price, and I wou'd go to see Claudine.

The first was easy enough. I retir'd briefly to my office and wrote out instructions to one of the more trustworthy clerks at the Company. Several of the largest ships in the Mississippi's fleet were due into La Rochelle that evening. I told him to announce that their cargoes had greatly increas'd in value over previous shipments, and that several tobacco and sugar plantations had been successfully establish'd and wou'd be producing a yield within the year. In fact, I had no idea what to expect of this most recent shipment from Louisiana and the next day it wou'd come as an enormous relief to me to hear that it was truly larger and more profitable than ever before. Sadly, it was to make little difference to the Company's ultimate fate.

The second task was harder, not least because my leaving the Bank was bound to attract hostile attention from the mob. Fortunately, the wine had not only rais'd our morale, it had given me a large infusion of courage. As the quartet began to play and our impromptu gathering grew more animat'd, I quietly took my leave of it and order'd up an unmarked carriage to take me to the île Saint-Louis.

De Tencin's apartments were on the third and fourth floors of a grand hôtel that overlook'd the Seine at the island's southernmost tip. I left the carriage at the end of the narrow street and walk'd the rest of the way, pausing at the entrance to allow two men – servants, from their appearance – to hurry past me. As I climb'd the winding stair to her rooms, another man pass'd me on his way down. He stopp'd and turn'd.

'Monsieur Law?' I nodd'd. 'I'm Doctor Lescaut.' He made a small bow. He was an elderly fellow, thin of lip and solemn in manner, better suited to burying people than keeping them alive, I thought. 'I lately attend'd His Royal Highness, the Regent, at the Palais-Royal.'

'Ah yes, I remember you,' I said, although I did not.

'Forgive me for asking, but are you here to see Madame de Tencin?'

'I am – why, is she not at home?'

'Yes and no. She is dead, Monsieur. I was summon'd to the house and told she was sick, but I have just confirm'd that she passed away some hours ago.'

My breathing grew shallow once again; I struggl'd to take in the shocking news. 'How did it happen?'

He came back up the steps, leant in towards me and lower'd his voice. 'Suicide, Monsieur – an extremely lethal dose of poison, definitely self-administer'd.'

I felt even greater constriction in my chest. 'Was there a note?'

He shook his head. 'Not that I found, but I spoke to her maid – simply to help confirm the cause of death, you understand.'

'I understand.'

'She said that Madame was greatly distress'd, having lost everything in the Mississippi, Monsieur. Thank God that some of us were a little more cautious - if you don't mind my saying.'

'Not at all…I wish there were more like you…'

I made to go up the stairs, but he had not finish'd with me. 'Monsieur Law?' I turn'd back. 'I shou'd warn you. The poison was very powerful – Madame de Tencin died in severe pain. You may find her appearance…quite disturbing.'

We nodd'd to each other. He turn'd and continued down the stairs, I continued on up. But after several steps and some deliberation, a terrible breathlessness came over me and I decid'd I cou'd not bear to see her. In fact, I was physically unable to proceed. It was all I cou'd do to get myself down the stairs and out into the street. From there, I immediately made my way to the river bank and despite the air's pungency, took great gulps of it as it blew off the water.

How long I stood there exactly, I cannot say. I was stunn'd and numb'd by the news of de Tencin's suicide and my part in bringing her to that point. For the first time, perhaps, I became fully aware of the sheer havoc that had been unleash'd by the failing system and its tragic consequences. For the first time, I ceas'd considering how I might save it and instead consider'd how I might save myself. I knew that if Philippe had not only withdrawn his support, but was actively plotting to undermine me, my position had indeed become untenable.

Eventually I return'd to the waiting carriage and set off for the Bank. The crowds had swollen. As well as protests around the Palais-Royal and other public buildings, gangs had begun marauding through the streets, stealing from shops and accosting passers-by. It seem'd that only weeks before Paris was a thriving centre of commerce, a city of the future in which many had perform'd the miracle of making a fortune and ascending the social ladder. Now it had dissolv'd into barbarous chaos, and a hideous mixture of thievery, begging and bullying had overtaken legitimate social discourse.

Later, I was to learn that Parlement and others had stirr'd up unrest where it did not exist and suppress'd any good news from the Bank and the Company. At the time, however, I was puzzl'd as to why the general populace had not been a little mollified by my various measures, including those on taxation. It was as if the whole world had risen up against me in equal and opposite reaction to the popularity I had enjoy'd before becoming Controller. I had jok'd about it with Dubois, but was there really some inexorable Newtonian principle at work here, I wonder'd – the social as well as financial equivalent of his laws of motion? Even more fearful for my safety than when I had set out from the Bank, I pull'd down the blind and shrank back into the carriage and myself.

Given the need to avoid the turbulent crowds, it took me hours to return to the Bank. At one point, I thought we wou'd have to abandon the attempt, but I was not sure where else I might safely go. At least, I knew it was well-defend'd.

By the time I did return, only Pellegrini and a solitary violinist were left in the Salle de Mississippi. The musician play'd a soft adagio; the artist was amiably the worse for wine. He sprawl'd in a chair, staring up at his ceiling, which he had illuminat'd in part with many lamps and candles. The visual effect was most church-like; the keening violin add'd a note of deepest melancholy.

I pick'd at the remains of the food, took up a bottle and join'd him. We both gaz'd at the ceiling. The flickering, dancing shadows leant it an entirely different quality to that of daylight: the figures seem'd sinister and full of menace.

'Maestro, I'm very proud of our ceiling,' he said.

'As am I, Pellegrini.'

'Yet you seem so sad.'

'There are the small matters of a financial crisis and the crowd baying for my blood.'

'Of course,' he shrugg'd, 'but that's not why you are sad.'

'No,' I replied. 'There are other reasons – betrayal, for instance.'

'Ah, Maestro! I have found it's the same in life as in painting: you can put your faith in no one but God...'

Pellegrini was drunk – and of course a Catholic – but for some reason I expect'd less of the Christian piety from him. While he talk'd of the great commissions he had execut'd by virtue of his trust in the Lord, the violin play'd on and I decid'd that I wou'd confront Philippe with his betrayal, no matter how sick he was. I finish'd the bottle and start'd another. I lay looking up at the ceiling until the musician had finish'd his last adagio, Pellegrini had talk'd himself into oblivion and the lamps had died, leaving me in sepulchral darkness.

*

Now I do notice the time: almost 1.00pm. Any hope of radically smartening myself up for the lunch is gone. No time to shower. I won't even get to shave, which, combined with my swollen nose and grazed forehead, makes for a mess. (Maybe I can at least pass as raffish.) On the plus side, I do have a clean shirt – I always pack an extra one or two – and my trousers seem to have un-crumpled themselves while I've been sitting reading. *Whatever* – appearance is the least of my concerns.

As I go down to the lobby, something else from the scene at the Palazzo Cantarini occurs to me. According to the family tree, I'm supposed to be descended from John Law via an unbroken male line. Given that he had a daughter with Katherine, it means Sabine must have given birth to a son, whom she named after Law. Which in turn, means I'm descended from a prostitute and the Bourbon kings of France – if the memoir is genuine. It's an amusing thought and this dead-man-walking – for that's what I've decided I am - almost cracks a smile as he passes the concierge.

'*Buongiorno*, Signor Law.' (He knows my name – I've probably become notorious since the police visit.) He gives me directions to Ca'Alvisi, plus the yellow boots and umbrella again, as he did Friday evening. A lifetime ago.

'*Grazie mille.*'

'*Prego.*'

And again, I'm very glad of those yellow boots. Ca'Alvisi may be within staggering distance, but the waters have risen and the walk along the Grand Canal is a soggy one. On the way, I stop and try to contact Feinstein, but there's still no response, and it's nearer 1.30 by the time I get to Orsini's.

I apologise when he greets me on the *piano nobile*. He's dressed more casually than yesterday, in designer jeans and a shirt of pale peach. If he's noticed my new war wound, he doesn't remark on it. He waves away my apologies, shakes his well-groomed, silver head – a stark contrast to my own – and says how profoundly sorry *he* is that the beautiful Joanna has had to leave at such short notice. He hopes her mother will make a full recovery.

Diana sits regally on a chair of gilt and red velvet, cradling a glass of bright orange-coloured liquid, too bright orange-coloured and too early in the day to be a negroni. She catches my eye. 'Hi Theo. I told Piero that Jo had to dash back to London to be with her sick mother.'

'Yes,' I say. 'Apparently, it's very serious.'

'I'm sorry.' Diana wouldn't know but the reference to 'Jo's mother' makes me feel a little sick too.

'Well, we're glad *you* were able to stay, Theo,' says Orsini. 'My lunch party would have been all the poorer without you – wouldn't it, Diana?'

'It would.' His old-world charm is ramped up to the max. God knows what heights it would have reached had Jo still been with me.

He does the introductions – first, to Diana's partner, Francesca. '...I think you've already met at the opera house.' (I'm assuming he didn't get the full embarrassing story.)

'Yes,' she says. '*Ciao*, Theo, how are you today?'

'Fine, thank you – and you?'

She smiles and raises her glass.

Then he summons his 'close friend, Paolo' from the kitchen. '...He's also my co-chef on this occasion.'

'Almost as good a cook as Piero,' says Diana

'Oh, he's better,' Orsini laughs, 'much better...'

Paolo duly emerges from the kitchen. He's wearing a blue and white chef's apron and bearing another of those orange-coloured drinks.

'Greetings, Theo,' he says as if he were *my* close friend. 'We're serving bellinis to bring a little summer into our lives. I took the liberty of making you one, but I can fix you something else, if you like...'

Paolo is an exquisite young man, much younger than Piero. He has a head of thick black curls, the widest and whitest of smiles and is more than a little camp. So much for my idea that Orsini and Diana were once lovers, although you can never rule out any permutation these days. Maybe I'll be next to come out. Given the way things are going, it's hardly out of the question.

'The bellini's good,' I say.

'Made with the best Venetian Prosecco,' Orsini adds. 'Today's lunch is all Venetian specialities.'

'Can't wait...' Which is no exaggeration. Despite being – or perhaps, *because* I'm a dead-man-walking – I could eat and drink anything, Venetian speciality or not. I start by falling upon the olives that Paolo offers round.

We're gathered at one end of a long, high-ceilinged room, where a fire burns in a large marble fireplace. The other end is an elegant dining room, in the high baroque style, with the table fully laid for lunch. The crystal pear drops of a large chandelier glisten overhead; the walls are hung with some serious paintings, a vast rococo mirror and, nearest to us, an array of carnival masks, several of them crowned with colourful plumage. Beyond the table is a set of arched French doors – or should I say Italian doors? Their tall, gilded frames are ornately carved and open onto a broad balcony. In a different season, we'd have been sitting out there, I'm sure.

Orsini sees me looking in that direction. He jumps up. 'Ah, Theo, let me show you our famous view. Bring your drink...'

As we cross the room, he draws my attention to the masks and the intricacy of their design. 'I'm particularly proud of the collection. They date back to some of the earliest carnivals. Such fine craftsmanship...they're mostly made in China now...'

He opens the huge doors and leads me out onto the balcony. It feels chilly after the warmth of the room, but even in the flat, grey light and with a film of mist on the water, the view across the mouth of the canal is magical.

Orsini gestures towards the basilica. 'The *Santa Maria della Salute,* as described by many great writers and painted by many great artists – but you already know what it is, I'm sure.'

'I only just learnt – I'm almost a Venice virgin, remember. The view from my room at the hotel is similar, but from here everything seems closer.'

'Yes, it would have been very like the view from the *piano nobile* at the hotel when it was the Ridotto – until they built in front of it, of course. For such a beautiful building, the Salute had rather morbid beginnings. It was built after a terrible outbreak of the plague carried off over a third of Venice's population. Salute means 'health' and inside there are many references to the Black Death, which it seeks to deliver us from.' He smiles. 'There's been many outbreaks of *la peste* since then, so I'm not sure how much it has worked.'

461

'And now there's the worst ever *acqua alta* to deal with.'

'Yes, *acqua alta. And* a plague of tourists. Venice is forever under siege.' He turns to me. 'Diana is always talking about the air of death and decay about the city, of how deeply melancholic it is. I'm of a different mind. The original white masks worn by the plague doctors to prevent them breathing in the infection' – he pretends to pull at his nose, as if to draw out its length – 'had long beaks that made them look like ghouls feeding on the dead. I take consolation in the fact that they somehow mutated into the carnival masks you just saw. The Venetians took death and turned it into a party – I love that. *Salute*, Theo!'

'*Salute!*' We drink and ponder the view for a few moments.

'And speaking of the Ridotto,' he says, 'did you have a chance to look at the manuscript?'

'I did – I didn't quite finish it.'

'How far did you get?'

'As far as his visit to the Palazzo Cantarini. I only broke off to come here. What did I miss?'

'I'll let you finish it for yourself, but as you can imagine, it's not a happy ending.'

'Is it ever?'

'Probably not - unless you believe in Paradise.' He gives me a wry smile. 'But I can't help feeling that the manuscript is unfinished. It doesn't get to Law's final months here. It ends rather abruptly with him receiving an invitation from' – he holds up his glass – 'Bellini to come to the Ridotto.'

'Perhaps, he was too ill to write anymore.'

'Or perhaps, the last chapter is missing.'

We weren't aware that Diana had come out onto the balcony. She was suddenly standing there between us. 'Or perhaps it's still to be written,' she says.

Orsini turns and laughs. 'If that's case, I know just the person to write it…'

*

Daylight return'd. My body was cramp'd from sleeping in the chair, my head ach'd from the wine, but I was up quickly

462

and ready to do business by the time the staff arriv'd. (Pellegrini slept on soundly, the sleep of those who trust in the Lord, no doubt. Two of us carried him through to one of the back offices, where he continued snoring quite happily.)

By nine o'clock the crowd was once again like a mad dog at our door. By ten, the din had increas'd to the point where the tellers cou'd hardly hear themselves count. And then there was more bad news: the share price had dropp'd below 500 livres and was continuing to fall – a significant point in that it was now lower than the opening price of the universal share issue.

An hour or so later, a liveried messenger from Orleans arriv'd, demanding my immediate presence at the Palais-Royal. 'Gladly,' I thought, 'gladly...' It was a meeting I had anticipat'd with relish.

I knew that I was bound to be recognis'd in travelling from the Bank to the Palais, so an extra guard was summon'd. From the long faces of my colleagues, it was as if I were about to ascend to the gibbet. A speech seem'd in order – or some further attempt to restore morale – but I resist'd the temptation and left on the instant.

The journey was short but hazardous. The crowds jeer'd and chant'd their abuse; many threw themselves against the carriage, pounding on the doors in an attempt to break in, before being repuls'd by the mount'd guards. If I had not been intent on the purpose of my journey, I might have taken fright and order'd a return to the Bank.

Once inside the Palais-Royal, I head'd straight for Orleans' office. Each servant and secretary I pass'd was unusually sombre in his greeting, and although I expect'd to find Doctor Lescaut and other attendants hovering around Philippe's door, there was only a solitary footman. I enter'd to find a dark figure silhouett'd against the window, looking out at the gardens. When he turn'd to face me, I realis'd it was not Philippe at all, but the Abbé Dubois.

'Monsieur Low, welcome. Please sit down...' He gather'd up his long clerical robes and sat in the throne-like chair, crown'd with the Bourbon crest – Philippe's chair – gesturing for me to sit opposite him. I was to be grant'd a royal audience, it seem'd, but without the presence of His Royal Highness.

463

'The Regent apologises that he is unable to see you. Alas, his health has not improv'd, so he has decid'd to retire to the peace of Marly to help effect a cure. I'm sure you'd agree that Paris has become a little uncomfortable of late.'

I nodd'd. 'Let us pray that His Royal Highness makes a speedy recovery.'

'Yes, prayers are always of benefit,' he said, with priestly solemnity. 'It means, however, that I have a somewhat difficult task to perform on his behalf.' His eyes narrow'd; he leant forward towards me. 'You, more than anyone, Monsieur Low, must be aware of the many problems that beset our country at the moment, especially as they all relate to the domain of finance. In case you're in any doubt, let me list them for you.' He began to count on his fingers, like a school teacher: 'The colony of Louisiana is a disaster...the Company share price has fallen away to nothing...many thousands are left bankrupt...the prices of all goods, from bread to a lace chemise, have doubl'd in as many weeks...your paper currency is virtually worthless, but you have bann'd the use of all coinage... the streets of Paris and other cities are in turmoil...the general populace has erupted in protest – they have my sympathy: by your actions, their lives have been made even more miserable than they already were.'

He sat back magisterially. 'My conclusion is, Monsieur Law, that your System lies in ruins – it and you are a failure, and on the Regent's and the Council's behalf, I have no alternative but to dismiss you as Financial-Controller.'

I breath'd deeply and wrestl'd with the urge to strike him. It was fruitless to try to refute each allegation in turn, so I went straight to the heart of the matter. 'If I am a failure, Sir, you are a liar and a hypocrite. Along with others – including, I believe, the Regent – you have deliberately set out to undermine both myself and the System for your own material and political gain. The measures I set in place wou'd have ensur'd its survival, had they been allow'd to work. How dare you speak of the misery of the general populace when you've contribut'd to it as much as anyone.'

His expression grew even more hawk-like; the set of his jaw was implacable. 'These are serious allegations, Monsieur Law

– treasonable even! I urge you to be very careful. You seem to want to blame everyone but yourself for the collapse of the System and yet it is entirely your responsibility. Most of us want you to rot in the Bastille for it. The mob want you hang'd; Parlement and the former tax farmers think that's too good for you and want you broken on the wheel. However, His Royal Highness, the Regent, has argued strongly for immediate exile and the Council has reluctantly agreed.'

As the full meaning of his words sunk, my resolve began to falter. Even so, I remain'd on the attack.

'The System was destabilis'd by de Conti's and Bourbon's exchanging shares and paper currency for gold. You know that, Dubois. The Regent support'd them and benefit'd directly – as did you, no doubt.'

He smil'd his most sardonic smile yet, and I had certainly seen many such from him. *'For which he wou'd wish me to convey his deepest gratitude. If your System did nothing else, it ensur'd that much of the country's metal resides in the Bank, where it can be legitimately requisition'd. That institution, together with the Company, will now be clos'd down and there will be a return to coin and the traditional methods of state finance. The Paris brothers are already drawing up plans. Our country will no longer be indebt'd to you – if it ever really was.'*

I made to object once more, to demand an audience with Philippe himself, but he cut me off.

'I see no reason to continue this conversation. Good day to you, Sir. I suggest you make haste before the Council prevails upon a sick Regent to change his mind on the subject of your exile. The guards who are protecting you from the mob are also charg'd with ensuring that you leave the country immediately.'

I can honestly say that I have rarely if ever been roundly beaten at cards, yet here was the experience of being so in the most dramatic terms.

I got up to leave. *'There is such a thing as the rule of law, Dubois, even when it's abus'd by scoundrels like you. As far as I'm concern'd, the state is still deeply indebt'd to me and will pay me eventually.'*

'Yes,' he sneer'd, *'with your worthless currency, perhaps.'*

'Perhaps – and also through the disgrace of the entire Government. Mark my words, the Crown will never recover from this.'

He wav'd me away and shook his head. 'Please, Monsieur Low – you're arrogant enough to think you can bring down governments? If you persist you'll have me weeping with laughter. Good day to you, Low – and goodbye.'

We talk of 'blind rage' and this was a most apt description of my state. I saw nothing as I left the Palais-Royal – not the hallways, by then so familiar to me, not the secretaries and servants, who until that day had always given me a warm welcome, not the soldiers who met me at the gate, my escort turn'd turnkeys. Nothing – until several ruffians came running at me, brandishing clubs.

How they manag'd to get through the Palais' gates as I walk'd towards my carriage, I will never know. My guess is that the guards deliberately let them through on Dubois' orders to intimidate me further. If so, it had the desir'd effect.

One of them caught me on the temple and drew blood, another hit me across the shoulders before the guards manag'd to restrain them.

There was a cacophony of shouting and abuse. 'You thieving bastard, Law! We'll hang you!' 'You've stolen our gold, you shit head!' 'You fucker! Where's my money? You've ruin'd me.' 'You've brought the plague upon us, you filthy, stinking foreigner! Almighty God himself has curs'd us because of you!'

I was genuinely puzzl'd by this final barb – how cou'd I have brought the plague? – and anyway the blow to my head had left me somewhat daz'd. As my attackers continued snarling, I hurried breathlessly to the carriage, as if it were the sanctuary of the Church itself. I felt the fall in temperature as soon as I clos'd the door. There, in the opposite corner, was a visitor I had not receiv'd for some time – ghastly and ghostly, pale as linen; eyes looking through me, blood dripping from his chest. Whoever, whatever it was, it seem'd to be telling me one thing before it quickly melt'd into the air: my System was dead and unless I was supremely careful, I wou'd soon be dead too.

*

Orsini says he'll show me the original manuscript later, but first, those Venetian specialities. Without more ado – thank God, I'm almost faint from hunger – we begin with *sarde in soar*: an *agrodulce,* Paolo says, or sweet-sour dish of marinated sardine fillets. They're delicious. I can't get enough of them, and I'm not usually that keen on fish. More bellinis are on offer, but I choose to move onto a local white wine, Orisini's favourite Soave Classico. I want to drink litres of the stuff and down the first, large glass in short order. It's immediately refilled.

My lunch companions seem very familiar and relaxed with one another, and the conversation, like the bellinis and the Soave, flows freely. It turns out Paolo – whose surname is Levi – is a Professor of Cognitive Psychology at the University of Bologna. The oldest university in the world and the most distinguished in Italy, says Orsini proudly, as if Paolo were his son, which is not such a wild notion, given their age difference. His specialisation is Artificial Intelligence. He works with some of the world's top neuroscientists – mostly American – looking at how the processes of the human brain can be replicated in robots. 'It's where bio meets tech,' says Paolo.

Would you believe it? There I was thinking there'd be more talk about *acqua alta* and the death of Venice and suchlike, and suddenly we're plunged into an animated discussion about the death of the Self, or certainly of the Soul – and mostly in English, for my benefit. There seems to be an ongoing debate between Diana, who doesn't accept that the workings of the mind can be reduced to a complex series of algorithms, and Paolo, who thinks this the inevitable outcome of current research. Orsini takes over from him in the kitchen, so he can continue to hold up his end of the discussion.

Diana insists that '*Professor* Levi's model' cannot account for creativity of even the most basic kind. She says that the characters she creates in her novels are more 'alive' than any robot could ever be. They live in the imagination, which is what defines the human mind – the ghost in the machine, the creative spark that burns in all of us, even if it lies dormant most of the time. Paolo dismisses this as quaint Romanticism. It's only a matter of time before all these neural processes, including the

467

so-called creative ones, are mapped and replicated in artificial terms, especially with the introduction of the new quantum computers.

Nobody wants to get into that one, so Diana asks me about the implications of AI for the world of finance. 'Don't you use algorithms to make many investment decisions these days, Theo?'

'I don't personally, but some do.'

'And hasn't it caused all sorts of havoc?'

'It has. There've been things like flashcrashes, as they're known, caused by algorithms going rogue. But then as we've seen down the years, humans are just as capable of making monumental cock-ups when it comes to finance. My ancestor, John Law, would seem to be a prime example.'

'Yes, that man went rogue, for sure. Good job they didn't have the worldwide web in his day...'

In fact, the most pressing issue for me is not AI or John Law but the next course. I look wistfully towards the kitchen. 'Anyway,' I smile, 'the question is whether there will ever be a time when a robot will cook our gourmet lunch.'

'Exactly my point,' says Diana. 'It'll never happen – they'll never get the seasoning right.'

'Oh, robots will soon be cooking and writing novels at the same time,' Paolo laughs. 'But I agree the food will never taste as good as Piero's.'

Right on cue, Orsini exits the kitchen bearing two plates of a jet-black concoction that looks like it's been soaked in sump oil. '*Risotto al nero di seppia! Squid risotto!*' he cries. 'It's the squid ink that gives the rice its colour.' I can't say I like the sound or the look of it, and my face must have registered as much.

'At first sight, it can be a little off-putting,' says Orsini, 'but wait till you taste it.'

The others wait till I summon up the courage to sample a forkful. 'You're right, it's delicious,' I say and get a round of applause. I can't resist a lame joke: 'It must be a favourite of the Black Nobility.'

'Ha! I've never thought of it in that way.' He pours more wine for everyone and settles down to eat. 'But it does bring me onto my next subject, Theo.'

'Which is?'

'His Holiness the Pope.'

'That could be as heavy a subject as AI.' I smile at Paolo. The wine is taking over and for a dead-man-drinking, I'm having a great time.

'Oh, this is a far heavier subject.' And Orsini's expression takes a heavy turn to match. It's as if he's suddenly sucked all the fun out of the air.

*

I was treat'd as a prisoner, a criminal. I was not allow'd to return to the Bank or the Company offices, so I was unable to gather any paper evidence that wou'd incriminate others and exonerate myself. I was permitt'd to visit Louis le Grand and that only to collect clothes and some personal affects. (Among these were several large bags of gold, the very ones I took to the gaming rooms when we first came to Paris; also, a money belt, full of louis d'or, that I secret'd about my person.)

Perhaps the fact of my exile had not sunk in. Perhaps I felt that I wou'd soon be ask'd to return and rescue France from the financial turmoil I knew wou'd follow the collapse of the System. Whatever the reason, I took the minimum for a short journey, without thinking what I might need for the rest of my life.

I ask'd the Captain of the guard where we were bound, but he refus'd to say. I bluster'd with righteous indignation. 'How dare you treat me in this manner! How dare you prevent me from going to the Bank and the Company offices! Do you know who I am?'

The Captain - very much the haughty aristocrat – manag'd a strain'd smile: 'I know precisely who you are, Monsieur Law – or rather who you were – and for that reason alone you are lucky not to be receiving worse treatment...'

I continued my rant. Whatever our destination, I demand'd that we go via Gourmande, so that I cou'd see my wife and child. Again, he shook his head; he had been given strict orders to the contrary. However, if I car'd to write a letter, he wou'd see that it was deliver'd.

I tried pleading with him, offering him a large inducement – not that the 'richest man in the world' had much at his disposal by then – at which point he grew angry. 'So, you still think that money can buy you anything? I've seen the misery you've caus'd, the many people ruin'd by your actions. France will be well rid of you and if I had my way, Monsieur, it wou'd be at the end of a rope rather than through exile!'

And so it was that I was unceremoniously 'escort'd' out of France – without a chance to settle my affairs or even pack a dress coat or a spare periwig. I wince even now at the thought of what I left behind: the Company; the Bank; all my financial assets – apart from the bags of gold and the money belt; a dozen or more estates; streets of properties in Paris; a collection of paintings and drawings; my favourite Persian carpets; the ceiling of the Salle de Mississippi; and – most precious of all, although I had not even begun to realise how much so – Katherine and Anne.

Our merry party travell'd north of Paris, stopping at a wayside inn, where I consider'd and reject'd the idea of escaping from 'custody'. Once again, I told myself that this was only a temporary set back; that I wou'd soon return in glory and that it wou'd be unwise to become a true outlaw (which I was, anyway). At one point I thought we were heading for the channel ports and fear'd that I might be forc'd to return to England, where I was certain the two Governments wou'd collude in my persecution. Thankfully, we continued due north and I realis'd that the Netherlands was the more likely destination. (I like to think that Philippe at least had some hand in this; he cou'd not have known that my reputation was as poor in Rotterdam as it was in London.)

At a border crossing near Mons, there was a final humiliation. In searching the carriage for contraband, one of the border guards discover'd the bags of gold.

'I'll have to confiscate them, Monsieur Law,' he said with a wry grin. 'Surely you, of all people, shou'd know that the

possession and export of gold is strictly forbidden – by Royal edict?'

My shock'd expression must have add'd to their fun. Everyone except me join'd in the laughter and doubtless had a share in my first winnings from the gaming tables of Paris. Without the money belt, the 'richest man in the world' wou'd have been left a beggar by the side of the road. Indeed, by the time he reach'd Rotterdam and ask'd the authorities for an asylum they wou'd not grant, that is more or less what he had become.

*

As Orsini explains the unholy situation with His Holiness, I find myself eating less of the squid risotto, delicious though it is, and drinking a lot more of the wine.

He tells me that the Pope has made it one of his priorities to root out corruption within the Vatican. There are few people in his inner circle whom he can trust, least of all Cardinal Mancini. So he's turned to Orsini and other members of the Black Nobility to help him achieve this.

'Three weeks ago, Theo, we learnt that Mancini had invited you to the Vatican to discuss a loan that would in effect cover up a huge scandal at the bank and support the forces of corruption. We knew the nature of your business and therefore where the money would be coming from. Forgive us, but we decided the Russian Mafia could not be allowed to take over the Vatican.'

I feign a smile. 'Yes, it's probably best to stick with the home grown variety...'

He's not amused. 'We agreed that we would have to stop you whatever it took. Once we got you here, we started by trying to scare you.'

One hand goes to the cut on my temple; I take a nerve-steadying gulp of wine with the other. 'Did that happen to involve a near-accident on the way to the hotel?'

Diana nods. 'It did. It also involved a near-accident on the way to the Cipriani...'

I make a gun with my hand and shoot myself in the head. 'And the hooded men on the barge?'

'And the attempted theft of your phone...' says Francesca.

'It was all down to you guys?'

'It was all down to us,' says Paolo. The distinguished professor's doesn't seem the Papist type, but perhaps he's just taking a professional interest in all those neural processes. Either that or he's a robot himself.

'Well, mission accomplished – you scared the shit out of me. What about the email? Was that one of yours?'

'The *email*?' says Orsini.

'The one saying Venice was a good place for me to die.'

'No, we stuck to good old-fashioned physical intimidation, Theo – that definitely wasn't us. You must have some other enemies.'

Well, he's not wrong there. I don't even bother asking if they had anything to do with those ghostly appearances of John Law. They already have a low enough opinion of me, without me telling them I'm being pursued by ghosts.

'I'm sorry,' says Diana, 'but we had to make sure we had your attention.'

'And you have it – and you have the result you wanted too. I can promise you I won't be arranging any deals for the Vatican Bank, not now, not ever.'

Orsini looks surprised. 'Just like that, Theo? Can we really trust you?'

'Yes, just like that. I'm sorry you didn't get to use the thumbscrews or whatever the Inquisition's favourite form of persuasion was.' (Orsini *is* amused this time.) 'You can absolutely trust me. It won't happen, and it has nothing to do with the near-accidents, I just have other plans. I'm in the process of withdrawing from all my business activities. It's time for me to move on.

'Diana, you could have saved us all a whole lot of trouble and simply spoken to me about this on Friday evening over my first negroni...' I drink more wine.

She smiles her knowing smile. 'It's less than 48 hours, Theo, but I think you've become more amenable since then. And besides, it's been kind of fun, don't you think?'

Fun? For her maybe, a writer of crime fiction.

'And the manuscript?' I say. 'That's a fake, right?'

Orsini smiles and looks around at his friends. 'No, we are the only fakes here, luring you to Venice under false pretences. From what we can tell, the manuscript is genuine. As I think I told you, it comes from a reliable source and it's been in my family's possession for many years. When your name came up in relation to the Vatican Bank, we did some research on you, of course, and we became aware of an extraordinary coincidence – that you are descended from its author. In fact, I think Diana found an article your father had written on John Law for an economics journal. It was entitled *Reaping the Whirlwind.* Have you ever read it?'

'I've never even heard of it. In fact, I'd forgotten all about the family's notorious forebear until Diana's text reminded me.'

'Well, once we'd established the connection, our efforts to stop you felt…not so much fated, as divinely ordained.'

'You had God on your side.'

'Something like that…'

We all seem to dwell on that notion for a few moments, until I say: 'At least it means I'm descended from the Bourbon kings. And more importantly, I'd like to offer you a million Euros for the manuscript I think it's the right sort of price for the work of a man who invented the word *millionaire.*'

Orsini shakes his snowy head. 'That won't be necessary, Theo. I'm giving it to you, as a token of our appreciation for not pursuing the loan with Mancini.' He has visibly relaxed – they all have. The job's done and it's been easier than expected.

Paolo starts to clear away the plates; Orsini fills our glasses and I raise mine. '*Grazie mille*, Pietro.'

He raises his. '*Prego.*'

I realise I need to try Feinstein again.

'Anyway, I should make a call – to kill the Vatican deal. Do excuse me…' I hold up my phone and nod towards the balcony. 'May I?'

'Of course.

I go outside and take a very deep breath. The beauty of the view strikes me again. The waters have receded a little. There are now more people along the banks of the canal, more vessels plying back and forth. The cloud has thinned and the sun is making a brave attempt to break through.

I could own this view, I tell myself, or one very like it. I could buy a palazzo on the canal, somewhere near here. I could help the police in their investigations and salvage a lot of my money in exchange for dishing the dirt. Then I'd retire here, like John Law, happy in a hopeless, abstract kind of way, pondering lovers lost and deals undone, while sipping negronis and watching the sun disappear behind the Salute. I could even make friends of these people, even though they threatened my life. We could have regular dinner parties, go on discussing the death of the Self, whether the human being is programmable and other philosophical questions. I could do all that. I could still choose to live.

I stand there enjoying the thought, as the sun finally does break through. A bright golden arrow of it strikes the statue of the Virgin that stands on the crest of the Salute: God's spotlight. It brings a genuine smile to my wounded face. It takes everything to a higher, more mystical level – to the level of the sacred or the sublime, or whatever it is they call it. I wouldn't know. I'm just a humble ex-Moneyman. But I do know what it's telling me: that such beauty is beyond measure and can never be owned by anyone.

*

Venice, February 1729

The frosty Dutchmen gave me a week to find an alternative refuge and I had to all but beg on my knees for that. After five days, I still had no firm idea of where I shou'd go; where I might find any true welcome, as oppos'd to one that was ultimately about punishing me or trying to extort the millions of livres they thought I might have hidden away. It was then that I receiv'd a letter from the conte di Bellini at the Ridotto gaming salon in Venice:

Dear Sir,

Please forgive the fact that this letter is not penn'd by my own hand. My written English is poor (although I speak it reasonably well), my French is not much better, and I may be doing you a disservice, but I assume that you speak no Italian. I have, therefore, ask'd a certain gentleman of my acquaintance to be my scribe and to write to you on my behalf. He is an English aristocrat of impeccable taste and integrity, so I can be confident that his language is of the highest order.

As a connoisseur of the gaming table, I know I speak to another. I have follow'd your brilliant career with great interest: from your days at the tables in London to the heady heights of your time as Financial-Controller of France. Unlike many, I do not value you for what wealth you may or may not possess, but for your skill at cards, your mastery of the wager and your profound insight into the characters of those who sit across from you at the table. What I have ascertain'd from many eye-witness accounts, together with your extraordinary reputation, is that your gaming prowess is second to none in this world and cannot be better'd in the next – which is to say, you are the best there has ever been.

To come now to the specific point of this missive. It is my belief that you are in need of profitable engagement and a safe haven that affords every comfort and luxury – not just the proverbial port in a storm, but somewhere you can come to think of as home. Shou'd that be true, it wou'd give me the greatest pleasure if you were to join me here at the Ridotto and be a professional player at our tables, our very own Banker-in-residence, so to speak. There is no shortage of men with large purses and vanity to match, who wou'd traverse the continent to play cards with the best card player of them all. They will come like bees to the flower – the more so because he is also known to have been – and, many think, still is – the richest man in the world.

I cannot pretend that this position will offer you anything like the wealth and prestige you acquired in Paris – until more recently, anyway – but I am sure that we can negotiate a financial arrangement that is to our mutual satisfaction.

Sir, I beseech you to give this offer your most serious consideration. Your talents at the table are too immense to languish in disuse for much longer.

I look forward to your earliest reply.

Yours sincerely and in hopeful anticipation etc.

*

I try the hotline again. This time it rings and Feinstein answers immediately. 'Theo?'

'What's going on? Where have you been?'

'We've been under cyberattack, my friend. I had to shut everything down.'

'*Fuck!* It's got to be connected with what's happening here.'

'What's happening there?'

'I had a visit from the police – not the local kind, the serious, international crime kind...'

'Shit!'

'They're targeting me – I've been under surveillance for a while. Boris has been assassinated and they're forcing me to help them get to the people who've taken over from him. It's either that or I spend a long time in jail and come out very poor – if I ever come out.'

'Wow! Aronovsky's dead?

'That's what they told me. They also told me that whoever's taken Boris out will be coming after me...'

'That's...*heavy.*'

'*Very* – and with all that shit whizzing around, it wouldn't be surprising if some of it was coming your way.'

'Ha! I can deal with it. I just need a little more time is all. I've been getting into some heavy stuff this end too. I keep breaking into more and more networks. I've gone right to the top of the Russian pyramid. I mean, *right to the top. And* I've hacked into London again. As well as Russians, Arabs, Chinese, I've got to some very big Americans. *Very big...*'

I've never heard Feinstein so excited. 'You should see what these fuckers control, Theo. We're gonna turn the world upside down. We're gonna take out most of the world's biggest players...'

'If they don't take us out first...'

'They won't. Give me another coupla hours and we'll be good to go – you're still up for this, aren't you?'

'Couldn't be more so.'

'Good to know *you're* now the one who's hot to trot. Hang in there, buddy.'

'Call me as soon as you're done...'

I ring off, worried that Feinstein is over-reaching himself, to put it mildly; that the whole project has become far too ambitious. What started as a plan to redistribute Boris' wealth, has taken on a vast, global dimension – who knows what the fuck will happen once Feinstein releases his bug?

Orsini joins me on the balcony. 'Is it done?'

For a moment, I wonder what he means – *oh, the Vatican bank.* 'Yes, it's done. And you know what? I'm not sure they were that bothered. Other frontiers beckon.'

'And the Vatican Bank is, after all, a very small frontier.' He smiles and gestures for me to go inside. 'Please...the *dolce* course awaits...'

'You know, I'm not sure I can eat any more. Perhaps, another drink...

Orisini pours me more wine, while Paolo serves *fritole,* deep-fried pastry balls dusted in sugar. They're a favourite during the period of *Carnevale,* he says, but we don't need to wait till then. I don't think of myself as having a sweet tooth, but I love these.

'I have something else for you, Theo,' says Orsini.

'Not more food, I hope.'

'No...' He goes over to where the masks are displayed and takes one down. 'This is one of the oldest in the collection, and perhaps my favourite.'

It's a full-face mask of white and gold, with exquisite red embroidery, crowned with a jester's red coxcomb and many golden bells. He has me stand in front of the huge Venetian mirror. 'I'd like you to have it, as well as the manuscript.'

He puts it on me, ties it at the back of my head. Given the state of my face, it's probably an improvement, but I'm not sure whether it makes me look glorious or absurd – perhaps a bit of both.

Suddenly, the others gather round me. They stand looking in the mirror too, while each of them puts on one of the masks from the wall. I start to feel a little giddy. Am I about to topple into a black hole? It's been a while, but this feels different. Was it something in the *fritole*?

From somewhere, there's music – dance music, it seems, in the baroque style. And there's the sound of people's voices, a crowd of people, singing, shouting down in the street. I want to go out on the balcony to see them, but I can't move. I'm paralysed. All I can do is stare into the mirror, watching the room slowly descend into darkness, and the others melt into the background until they disappear completely. I'm left alone, listening to the music and the singing and shouting of the crowd, as it grows louder…and louder…and louder…

Chapter 14

Carnival was reaching its heady climax. As if in recognition, the mist had cleared quickly off the water and the sun had shone for most of the day. Now it was dusk and masqueraders were everywhere around the city, sporting their anonymity and enjoying the sheer sense of abandon that makes this the Venetians' favourite time of year. From the *piano nobile,* he could see crowds of them across the canal. They wove in long dancing lines between the great torches that flashed and shimmered in the dark water. He could hear the strains of viols and horns and the beating of drums; the men were shouting, the women squealing with laughter. They celebrated the dawn of another year, the return of light and life by throwing off the shackles that held them in the greatest thrall: not the Church, not the State, but themselves – their own identities.

How easily John Law used to play this game; to slip off one metaphorical mask in exchange for another; to be whomever he wanted, whenever it served his purpose. But it seems that such play-acting is a conceit of the young. As we grow older, our masks grow heavier and more difficult to remove. We realise, for better or worse, that character is not so much written on our faces as in our bones. It dictates all that we become, no matter what outward appearance we contrive.

And what has he become? Sick, unbearably sick – he was almost completely defined by it. The stabbing pain in his chest grew more acute; his coughing was relentless; the handkerchief much bloodier. Perhaps his body has become inured to the laudanum. The large tinctures seemed to have made little difference to the pain and left him feeling tired and confused. He struggled to concentrate on his writing; each word was a burden, each sentence a sentence, eased only by the fact that the Ridotto was now deserted. Everyone was at the masquerade, but the peace would be short lived. After the fireworks, they would return to play at the tables and continue with the celebrations, all in their carnival masks, nobles as well as commoners.

He suddenly heard voices in the next room – were they back already? No, it was Bellini and several servants making final preparations for when they did return. He stood smiling in the doorway.

'Il Duce, why are you not out there chasing the women?' The Conte loved his little jokes – he knew Law could hardly stand, let alone join in the dance.

'It's time the women chased *me*, Your Grace.'

'I'm sure they always did,' he laughed. 'You will play later, I hope? We have missed you at the tables – a game for *Carnevale*, perhaps.'

'Perhaps,' Law smiled and returned to his manuscript. But although he told himself that he must press on with his memoir, something else was distracting him: on the table – a letter from Katherine.

It had been delivered that morning, much to his surprise, but he could not bring himself to open it for fear of what it might contain: recriminations, accusations, expressions of loathing and disgust. He had neither the strength nor the courage to confront those unwelcome visitors, and yet he wanted to know what she said – or rather, to read the words that evoked her lovely voice, her beautiful face; the person he'd missed so much those past eight years.

Outside, the crowd still flowed in a torrent along the banks of the canal and carried with it – bobbing, twisting, turning, jostled and confused – was Theo Law, a man out of time, in every sense. People, mainly women, complimented him on his mask and strange attire, although he hardly understood their eighteenth century Italian any more than the twenty-first century version.

Where the *fuck* was he? How did he get here? What were all these people doing in period dress? With a huge stretch of his cognitive faculties, he gradually got his bearings. He could see the Saluté and San Marco, but there were no cruise ships, no motor launches, no electric streetlights, no neon, only flaming torches, scores of them. And there was no Monaco Hotel.

Instead, there were several houses on the quay, set back from the canal, one of which surely had to be the Ridotto.

He decided he was in an elaborate theme park or a dream. Either that, or the Age of Decadence tour had taken a very weird turn indeed and he was actually back in eighteenth century Venice – which was *beyond insane.*

The mental impasse brought him to an abrupt physical halt. He became so rigidly rooted to the spot, like a rock in the stream of the crowd, that instead of crashing into him, people went round him, staring at him curiously, as *he* stared up at the Ridotto's *piano nobile.*

Then another crazy notion occurred to him – in this Alice-in-Wonderland world, could he, John Law, be up there? And if he was, could he, Theo Law, meet him, speak with him, a man who'd been dead for almost three centuries? Of course, it was as nonsensical as everything else, but then he'd already abandoned all sense, all reason. Which was probably why another crazy notion popped into his head: that he and Law would both somehow benefit from such a meeting; that it would be an act of love across those centuries.

As she passed him, a young woman, her breasts spilling out of her sequined gown, threw her arms around his neck and drew him to her. She wore a black half-mask and planted a lingering kiss on the permanently smiling lips of his full one. Meanwhile, her hand wandered to his crotch and teased him into an erection.

She said something in Italian. It sounded like an endearment, but he couldn't have known the exact meaning: 'My poor Fool', she whispered, as she tinkled one of his bells, as well as his balls, 'I'm afraid you're doomed…' She laughed out loud, and her male companion pulled her away, leaving Theo still looking up at the Ridotto – *could Law actually be there*? There was only one way to find out.

*

Bellini looked in on him again. Perhaps he thought he'd expired on the *piano nobile* in the middle of the latest bloody coughing fit. Perhaps he couldn't wait to appropriate the moneybags that he'd stowed for il Duce in the Ridotto's vaults.

The fact was that in his memoir John had been less than forthcoming about the income he'd derived from his time there. As Bellini's letter of invitation had indicated, for all his kind words and little jokes, he hadn't brought Law to Venice just for the fun of it. According to their financial arrangement, which had taken a while to negotiate, half of Law's monthly earnings in gold coin had gone to the Ridotto, the other half Law had kept. The richest man in the world had more than paid his way, both as an attraction and a customer, and his own hoard, relatively small by his Paris standards, was their secret. As a devotee of the wager himself, Bellini had understood perfectly what it meant to il Duce, without having to discuss it: that he was still a player, still in the game – and in that respect, it was his one source of happiness.

There were more shouts from the revellers outside. He was again tempted to open the letter and might have done so, had he not been seized by another terrible fit. So breathless and icy cold did it leave him that he feared he wouldn't survive it.

Finally, when he opened his eyes, the room appeared to shift, as if the Earth itself had shuddered, and when it settled down, a dark figure appeared in the doorway. At first, it was difficult to make him out in the lamplight: was it Bellini again or one of the revellers returning early? He wore a red and gold Fool's mask and a style of suit Law didn't recognise, plain but strangely exotic.

'Sir, can I help you?' Law spoke in his best Italian.

'I'm looking for Mr. John Law,' the other replied in English.

Why the sound of his mother tongue was so reassuring, Law didn't know. Maybe he'd missed London more than he knew. Maybe it simply brought Katherine to mind, although the man's accent had more the ring of the American colonies, he thought, than the English drawing room.

'Who is looking for him?'

'An admirer,' said Theo.

'Well, you're a rare breed these days. I am John Law. I take it you've come to play?'

'Play?'

482

'At cards. It's usually why people come to see me. If you have, Sir, you're out of luck before you've even started. I've retired from gaming.'

'They were right, then...' The bells on Theo's cap jingled as he went over to where John was sitting. 'May I take a seat for a few minutes, Mr. Law? My feet are killing me from all the dancing...'

John gave him a weary, wary nod. 'For a few minutes, you may, yes. We mustn't allow a man to be killed by his feet... Who were right?' he asked, as Theo pulled up a chair opposite him at the table.

'I beg your pardon?'

'You said *they were right, then.* Who were right?'

'Ah yes – some people in London. A crowd I used to run with, to my shame. Gamblers and reprobates – all gentlemen, of course. You know the sort.'

'I do. London abounds with them. What did they say?'

'They told me that you'd retired...'

'Due to my being in poor health?'

'Due to your being...*poor*, Mr. Law – bankrupt, in fact. They said that you'd suffered a series of heavy losses, that you'd not only lost the will to play, but the gold to play with.'

Law was silent for a moment. 'You've been misinformed, Sir. If there's one thing I'm not lacking, it is the gold to play cards.' And he bent over, picked up a full moneybag from under his chair and dropped it with a thud onto the table's green baize.

'And you, Sir, where is your gold? Or have you just come to taunt me with your' – he looked at Theo's cap and bells – 'jests. Are you no more than a jester, Sir?'

'Then you are prepared to play with me?'

'If you have something worth my taking from you, yes...'

In the short time Theo had been speaking to him, he noticed that a certain gleam had appeared in Law's eyes and his breathing had become easier. The prospect of the wager was clearly medicine to il Duce.

Theo had no cash on him. He'd given it all to the guide, Marisa, as we know, and anyway, it would've held no value for Mr Law, though he'd have doubtless been thrilled by the idea of a European currency and its banknotes and maybe seen it as some kind of great vindication. Nor – and Theo smiled to himself – was there much chance of his accepting a credit card, even a gold American Express.

Now he thought about it, however, he did have some real gold about his person. His wedding ring may have long gone from his finger, but he still had the 18ct gold Rolex that Angela had given him as a wedding present.

He took it off and passed it to Law, who looked at it with a mixture of admiration and curiosity. 'It's mostly gold,' said Theo. 'Oh, and its internal movement contains 17 jewels, I believe.'

'I've never seen anything like it – it's worn upon the wrist?'

'The first of its kind. Made in Switzerland.'

'Switzerland? Good pocket clocks are usually made in Saxony.'

'The er *Saxon* part of Switzerland.'

Law turned it back and forth, trying to make sense of it. 'How does one wind it?'

'It er winds itself. It's known as an *automatic.*'

'*Automatic.* I've not heard the word, but then I'm out of touch with my mother tongue. It's a remarkable piece of work, Sir, and something I'd be proud to own.'

'Thank you, Mr. Law…would you like to make me an offer? It's worth a small fortune.'

'How much did you pay for it?'

'Around…10,000…' Theo didn't know exactly how much it had cost Angela, but it was of that order.

'*Guineas?*' Law said before Theo could say pounds.

'Yes. *Guineas…*'

Even the richest man in the world couldn't disguise the fact that he was impressed by the cost. He began to take out gold coins from the bag on the table until he'd counted out fifty, about half.

'That's way below its value,' said Theo.

'Let's not debate value, Sir, which you and I know is almost entirely governed by circumstance. It is merely a loan, after all – I will be taking it back presently.'

Theo smiled wryly to himself under the mask. 'Well, in that case, it's all I'll need…'

Law gathered up the papers of his manuscript and put it and the quill and ink to one side. From a drawer beneath the tabletop, he took out a pack of cards. A colourful crest with the sun-in-splendour adorned their back, the Bellini family crest. 'You're familiar with the game of Piquet, I assume?'

'I may need a little refreshing on the rules. It's a been a while since I played...'

The word 'hustler' was not in Law's vocabulary, but that didn't stop him ignoring this kind of talk, designed as it was to seduce the opponent into a state of over-confidence.

He shuffled the cards, as he recapped the rules for Theo. Piquet was not Law's favourite game, but it was one he excelled at, and it was ideally suited to two players. Each player was dealt seven cards from the pack and had to make up certain combinations of cards or 'tricks' – three of a kind, a run of consecutive numbers, several of the same suit etc. He then wagered that they were worth more than his opponent's. At least three of each player's cards had to be displayed at all times and no more than four cards could be exchanged from the pack at each turn before a bet was placed. Theo thought it bore a strong resemblance to Texas Hold 'em. Then it occurred to him that 'piquet' was probably the derivation of the word 'poker' and it all made perfect sense. Maybe he wouldn't be at such a disadvantage, after all.

'By the way, you have my permission to remove your mask, Sir.'

'Thank you, Mr. Law, that's kind of you. But to be honest, I've heard that you're capable of reading a fellow's face as if it were a book. So I'll stick to the house rules for commoners, if you don't mind, and keep my mask on.'

'As you wish.' Law knew how people thought it was a particular skill of his to see a hand in a face, so to speak, and he'd deliberately encouraged the notion to give his masked opponents a false sense of security. In reality, there was more to be gained from counting cards than watching faces.

'However, I would crave another indulgence from you, Mr. Law.' (Theo was warming to the more elevated eighteenth century idiom.)

'And what would that be?'

'To play a wild card.'

'A *wild* card?'

'A card that can be any card you like. For instance, if Jacks are wild and you need an Ace, it can be an Ace.' Law stared at him. 'As well as a Jack, of course.' Law still made no response. 'In my country, a wild card is also known as a Joker. I find it adds a little...'

'I am beginning to think that you really are the joker here, Sir. I cannot begin to imagine what country you are from, nor do I care to find out. *Nor*, for that matter, do I wish to see your face or know your name. I've never heard of your wild card, but we can allow it and Jacks are fine with me. It will make little difference to the outcome. Let us just *play*, shall we?'

And so they did – no talking, except in relation to the wager, just playing – and yes, Law immediately realised just how much he'd missed the gaming table. How could he have spent so long away? No wonder his condition had worsened, for now it had instantly improved. His coughing had stopped, and the chest pain was better than it had been for many months. Bellini would be pleased.

To mirror the feeling, Theo also realised how much *he'd* missed gaming, and Law quickly discovered that, despite the jester's mask, his opponent was a seriously skilled card player.

Law quickly won the first four tricks, but Theo won the next half-dozen – several of them using the wild card – and so easily that il Duce began to think he *had* been lured into feeling over-confident. To his relief, he managed to take the odd trick, but before he knew it, Theo had raised the stakes so high that Law's stack of gold florins had migrated to his opponent's side of the table and Law was seeing the bottom of the bag.

It must be the effects of the laudanum, Law told himself. The cards he anticipated did not appear; the odds stubbornly refused to work in his favour, and he began to wonder if his calculations were incorrect. He needed to clear his head and called for some strong coffee to help sharpen his senses. He also called for Bellini and asked him to bring more gold from the vault.

Il Conte looked at Law in surprise; this was the first time he'd ever made such a request. Nonetheless, he fetched him another bag, and it was not a moment too soon – as they finished the round, Law lost the last of his coins.

'Are you feeling all right, Il Duce?' Bellini sounded worried.

'Better than I have felt for a long time,' he said, which at that point was true.

Bellini gave them both a curious look and went back to shepherding the servants.

'Another round?' Law said.

Theo nodded, and they began again.

Within minutes, Law's excitement had become a mild state of panic, a feeling he had rarely if ever experienced in relation to gaming. He lost no less than ten tricks in a row! Now, the laughter from the crowds of revellers outside seemed more like jeers aimed at himself. He shuddered to think how it reminded him of the public derision he'd experienced in his final days in Paris.

John wondered if it had anything to do with the wild card, but how? He was sure he hadn't missed any or failed to count them. His opponent, on the other hand, seemed able to predict the lay of every card. He had raised the stakes even higher and the round was far from over, when Law was forced to send for Bellini again and ask him to bring more bags of gold. 'Please make it three this time,' he said.

'Il Duce, is that wise – to have so much money lying around at Carnival time?'

'Yes, Bellini,' he said impatiently. 'Just do as I ask!' An exchange between them had never been less good humoured. Bellini disappeared, shaking his head in dismay, and took his time returning with the bags.

'I seem to be having quite a run of luck, Mr. Law,' said Theo, as if he knew Law's views on subject of 'luck' and was seeking to taunt him.

'Then if it's only luck, Sir, I trust it will run its course...'

But it did not – far from it. Theo's winning streak continued unbroken and Law's panic intensified. He struggled to maintain his card-playing calm; the coughing and the pain were back. He began to feel cold again, yet sweat poured down his face and dripped onto the cards. Many rounds were played; many times Bellini was despatched for gold – half-a-dozen at least, until he threw up his hands in desperation. 'Il Duce, there are no more bags!'

Law looked at him indignantly. 'Are you sure? What has happened to them?'

'You have all of them at the table.'

'*All of them?* Impossible.'

'Do you think I'm lying to you? Do you think I've been stealing them?' There was more waving of hands. He stamped his feet and flounced out, uttering a stream of colourful Italian curses as he went.

'The conte de Bellini,' Law said. 'He's very excitable in that Italian way.'

'Indeed,' Theo replied. 'But he's right to worry – if this *is* your last bag.'

Law won one more trick but was soon down to his last stack of coins. For this, he played what he thought was an invincible three Queens, which Theo trumped with three Jacks become Kings. A violent coughing fit ensued.

Law glared at the mask; the mask smiled back. If he'd had the strength he'd have torn it off and exposed his tormentor, but that would hardly have been decorous.

'Is there no more gold?' Theo asked. The other shook his head. 'A shame, Mr. Law – I think you're finally getting into your stride. Is there nothing else you can wager?'

'Nothing,' he said, when he finally got his breath. 'You have everything.'

Theo leant forward. 'Everything? No, surely there's more – some paintings, I believe, sent to you from France.

So this was it, this was his game – not Piquet but betrayal! His so-called creditors – or one of their henchmen – had finally cornered him. The French government had sent this man, he was sure of it. How else could he have known about the paintings?

'Who *are* you?' Law asked.

'I have told you – an admirer.'

'A villain more like, come to persecute me.'

Theo shook his head. 'Come to play you at cards, as you've seen – and what of the paintings?'

'They are not negotiable assets, Sir.'

'Oh, I think they are,' he replied. 'Everything is – you of all people know that, Mr. Law. Why won't you wager them?' He gestured at the array of bags and coins on the table in front of him. 'I'll wager all this against the paintings – *on one last trick.*'

Law didn't know what to do. The paintings were all he had left, and yet…he thought he could win. If he could just muster his failing powers of concentration, with one last effort, he was *sure* he could win. There was one hand left in the pack and he knew the cards.

He nodded slowly in agreement. Theo asked him to deal – to avoid any possibility of his being accused of cheating, Law assumed, though he'd watched Theo carefully throughout the game and thought it was impossible, at least by any natural means.

There were two small exchanges of cards before they were ready to lay down the trick, and yes, Law was sure he had him beaten. If it had been physically possible, he would have danced a jig of victory at that point. He laid down four Kings, only one of which had been displayed. These could only be trumped by a run of all seven cards in the same suit, and although Theo had only Spades displayed, they were the two, four and five, and Law was certain that the Seven had gone. *Absolutely certain.*

He turned over his three other Kings. Theo drew breath – out of shock, Law thought – and showed the rest of his cards: a motley collection, not a pair among them. And then Law realised, to his horror – *all seven cards formed a run, with the Jack of Diamonds at their head!*

Law's would-be jig was club-footed. 'But the Jack of Diamonds is gone, Sir,' he said.

'Evidently not.'

Law grabbed the discard pile, ran through it in a trice – at the bottom, a Jack of *Hearts.*

'It was Diamonds, I'm sure of it!'

'You are mistaken.'

'I said *I'm sure of it!*'

'John Law – are you calling me a cheat?'

Who had said that to Law before? His friend Beau Wickham, of course, but he was certain this man wasn't Beau. He was an unnatural being, but he was not the ghost of Beau Wickham. Suddenly, Law grew colder and started to cough again; the blood and phlegm rose from his tormented lungs like hot lava. He tried to stem the flow with his handkerchief, but some of it spilled on the table and the Kings became speckled with dark blood.

The mask smiled on implacably.

'I'm not calling you a cheat, Sir,' Law said breathlessly. 'You're right. I *was* mistaken. Now, please...whoever you are, take your gold and leave me in peace.'

'But you persisted in accusing your friend Beau of being a cheat, didn't you, John? Even though you knew he wasn't, you went on accusing him – because you wanted to kill him.'

Law stared at the Fool's mask. 'I don't know how you know. I'm not sure of anything anymore, but yes,' he said, 'I hate to lose. I was in a rage. I was insanely jealous of what he'd done...defying every law of chance, of nature. Such a run of so-called luck was as impossible a feat then as it was tonight – and I've regretted my reaction ever since. We fear what we cannot understand, Sir...'

'Then understand this, John Law. You thought you could command the world with your *Money Science*; that you could put everything in your purse – as you've tried to do ever since. And you killed your friend because he showed you it wasn't possible and you sold out the woman you loved because she was even better at it than you were. And how do I know you've done all this? Because I've tried, for most of my life, to do the same thing. I had to be the winner and take it all, to put it all in my purse – and in doing so, I've been responsible for *many* deaths, for the losses and the loss of many of my fellow human beings...'

'Who *are* you, Sir?'

Theo took off the mask. 'My name is *Theo* Law, John, and I am the future. A distant descendant of yours, an inheritor of your legacy – from a time when your legacy, your vision has been fully realised – when money is nothing, not even paper, completely without substance, mere figures in the air. And yet when it is *everything*, when it is the ruler and measure of everything, of everything human and natural. When it has taken on a monstrous life of its own that destroys the Earth, as it destroys its people. That's what we've come to, John. The end of days.'

A look of recognition spreads across Law's face. 'You're the one who's haunted me all these years – not Beau.'

'I suppose I am – and I suppose I've come to tell you that you must do what I will do. You must let it all go, give it all away – and get back yourself in return.'

'Ha! I have nothing to give away...'

'Oh, you do, John.' And Theo pushed all the moneybags and coins back across the table.

'Truly?'

'Yes, take it all. It's yours.'

For a moment, Law thought this was another jest, but then he understood what was to happen. 'Then please, this is yours...' He handed over Theo's Rolex to him.

'Thank you.' He slipped the watch back on his wrist. 'Its only value to me is sentimental, you understand.'

'I understand.'

Theo stood up to go and as he did so, a small dark patch appeared on his shirt and spread quickly across his chest. His face was already contorted with pain and he was tumbling forward into the familiar black hole, when he disappeared.

'*Theo*?' Law looked around. He was alone in the room, surrounded by his moneybags, with the Fool's mask smiling up at him from the table.

*

Theo woke up – Where was he? *When* was he? People came into focus. None of them looked like John Law, but he did recognise Orsini and Diana Lennon. The faces that had been wearing carnival masks when he last saw them now hovered over him, wearing expressions of concern. He realised he was in a large, comfortable armchair in Orsini's beautiful drawing room. His whole body felt leaden, as if someone or something was pressing down on him. He might have drifted off to sleep again if Orsini hadn't spoken to him.

'Are you okay, Theo? You passed out – you've been unconscious for a while. We've called for a doctor…'

Francesca appeared. 'Is he all right?' Paolo was behind her.

'We're not sure,' said Diana. 'How are you doing, Theo? We were worried you might've had a stroke or a heart attack or something.' (This from someone who'd recently threatened him with all sorts of physical injury.)

'I'm fine…I think…' He could speak, at least, he had no chest pain and he could definitely feel the rest of his body. 'I'm sorry…I don't know what happened…'

Fragments of his dream, or whatever it was, floated to the surface: handing Law his Rolex (he was relieved to find it was still on his wrist); the shock-horror that spread across Law's face when he realised he'd lost everything; telling Law to give everything away. *Everything.* (He *must* speak to Feinstein as soon as possible.)

'I suspect too much wine and too little sleep,' he said.

'You gave us a scare,' said Diana.

'Do we still need the doctor?' Paolo asked.

'No…no, thank you. I'll be okay…' Theo eased himself up and out of the chair. Some of the lights were on in the room. Out beyond the balcony, the sky had darkened. A storm had blown up and gusts of wind were shot-blasting the rain against the window. 'I really must be going – I've some things to do.'

'If you're sure you're well enough,' Orsini said. 'It's not pleasant out there. Please, stay as long as you like.'

'I'm actually fine, Pietro…just very embarrassed.' He managed a smile. 'I can assure you it had nothing to do with the risotto – which was delicious, as was everything else…'

'You're too kind,' said Orsini. 'And just to re-iterate, we're very grateful for your change of heart. His Holiness would want to thank you too, I'm sure.'

'Well, that's good to know. Just so long as there are no more *near-accidents.*'

Orsini laughed. 'If there are, they certainly won't have anything to do with us – will they, Diana?'

'They won't – although, as I've said, Theo, *acqua alta* can be treacherous and it's getting worse. You still have to tread carefully...'

It seemed you only had to whisper the *a*-words and the siren sounded. 'And there it goes again, right on cue.' Diana rolled her eyes. 'I've really had it with these high tides...'

'Don't worry,' Francesca laughed. 'MOSES, the great flood barrier, will soon part the waters and it will all be fine.'

'*No* - MOSES will only make it worse...'

Theo went across to the large mirror, where he winced at the sight of himself. Battered, puffy-eyed, he ran his hand through his hair and adjusted his shirt collar in a lame attempt at grooming. An image of the others standing around him in their masks flashed through his head, making him look across at the mask collection on the wall – only his, the Fool's, was missing.

'Ah, yes,' said Orsini, 'you must not forget your mask.' He picked it up from the floor next to where Theo had been sitting.

'And you must also take the manuscript,' said Diana. She went over to a bureau in a corner of the room and took out a large leather pouch. She opened it and showed Theo the contents – a large sheaf of yellowed pages, tied together with what liked black ribbon.

'You see, Theo – it's for real. Looks like parchment, doesn't it, but the paper was actually made of rags in those days and the writing was all done with a goose quill pen...'

'Let's find something to put them in,' said Orsini.

'I'll get a couple of bags,' said Paolo, who disappeared into the kitchen and returned immediately with two black cotton bags, each displaying the words: *Internationale d'Arte Cinematografica della Biennale della Venezia'*– Venice Film Festival.

Theo took a closer look at the manuscript. 'Are you sure you want to part with it?'

'It's all yours...' said Orsini. He put it and the mask in the bags and presented them to him.

Theo made his farewells. It was hugs and kisses all round, as if they were genuinely old friends – or at least, all on the same team. He still wasn't sure what that team was, but he was convinced it had little to do with devotion to 'His Holiness'. What it did have to do with, he didn't care to know at this stage. It didn't matter.

Diana hugged him like she meant it. She looked into his bloodshot eyes. 'Be careful, Theo.'

'How could I forget? *You never know where the walkway ends, and the canal begins*' – right?'

'*Right.*'

Outside, he was relieved to find it was the twenty-first century again, albeit the living museum version. The water level was rising rapidly, and he headed straight back to the hotel along one of the raised walkways. He decided there was only one place he should go – the room on the *piano nobile* that was originally the Ridotto and now used as a general function room. Fortunately, there was no function going on; it was deserted, but for a baby grand piano at one end and a few random chairs. He settled in the most comfortable one, throwing off his damp coat and letting it drop to the floor, alongside the bags containing the mask and the manuscript.

There were more flashbacks to his eighteenth century experience of the room. John Law sat at a table by the window that would have looked out on the canal, his moneybags piled in front of him. Theo was about to speak to him when the hotline rang. It was Feinstein.

'Still hangin' in there, Theo?'

'Just about. Some very weird things have been happening to me.'

'Such as?'

'Such as I think I got transported back to the eighteenth century – and met an ancestor of mine…'

'O-**kay**…'

'And now I'm back in the twenty-first century, I've been helping the Pope root out corruption in the Vatican and I'm caught in the worst *acqua alta* Venice has ever known. The place is *drowning…*'

'O-**kay**…*surreal - I get it*…Just remember you've been under a lot of stress – we both have. Meanwhile, we're ready to roll.'

'*We're all set?*'

'Yep.'

'Then let's do it.'

'Is that finally the green light, Theo?'

'It is…just one last thing…'

494

'There had to be *just one last thing…*'

'I'll be honest with you. I always had a sneaking suspicion you intended to rip me off. I thought you'd clean Boris and me out and keep the money for yourself.'

There was what seemed a long silence before Feinstein said: 'And *I'll* be honest with you, Theo, the thought has occurred to me – and I could already have done it.'

'But you didn't.'

'And I won't. A deal's a deal. This is strictly Robin Hood – redistribution, not theft – plus a little for ourselves to cover expenses. That was always the plan. It's just on a grander scale than we thought.'

'Can't be grand enough, as far as I'm concerned.'

'You'll get a stream of data on your phone – did I say stream? I meant torrent. It'll show you where the money's coming from and going to. It won't be in real time, but it'll be as near as I can make it.'

'You're a genius, Mr. Feinstein.'

'I know – a compression of Fucking Einstein, right? And with your help, Theo, I'm about to come up with a new Theory of Relativity. This one's to do with the relative levels of wealth in certain quarters. See you on the other side.'

'Yes, see you on the other side…'

Or not, thought Theo, at least not in the way you're thinking, Mr. Feinstein. Someone was bound to come after both of them, he knew that – either the police, or the criminal victims of this mega-crime they were about to commit.

Such morbid thoughts prompted those of Angela and Grace. He reached for his other phone. He knew he had to make contact before anything happened – to him or them – but he was surprised to find that Angela had beaten him to it. She'd just sent him an email, a rare event over the last few years, but there it was, with uncanny timing:

Hi Theo

I don't think we're due to see you until the weekend after next, but I thought you might want to hear this news before then. Maggie was found dead yesterday, on the street in

Stepney where we used to live, literally lying in the gutter. She'd probably died some time during the night.

She went on yet another of her walkabouts over two weeks ago and I'd not been able to track her down. There were no signs of foul play, apart from what she'd done to herself with the booze and whatever else she'd been taking. Apparently, she died of heart failure, although I'd call it a very badly broken heart.

I can't believe how hard it's hit me. I can't believe how the pathetic, fucked-up creature I am came to be so dependent on the pathetic, fucked-up creature she was. It turns out she meant more to me than I ever realised. Even after we had our big reconciliation and she was Maggie rather than Mum, I still didn't realise how close we'd become. Can you believe it? I despise the very thought of her for years and years and we land up best buddies.

I'm so sad, so miserable, and yet I can't seem to cry, to let it all out. Poor Grace is upset too but, bless her, she's doing her 6-year-old best to comfort her mother when it's supposed to be the other way round.

I don't know where to turn, so this is probably why I'm turning to you. I should be picking up the phone and speaking to you directly, but maybe I think you won't want to hear from me, and maybe I can understand that. I haven't exactly done much to encourage our relationship over the last few years.

Anyway, Theo, if you can be bothered anymore, please let me know how you are, where you are. I'd very much like you to come to the funeral. Suddenly I realise how few people there are in the world I really care about and you're definitely one of them – as Maggie kept reminding me.

AngelaX.

Theo called her in a hot second.

'Theo?'

'*Anj*?' It was a very poor imitation of Maggie, and she didn't laugh exactly, but he could almost hear the ear-to-ear grin.

'Yes, it's *Anj*,' she said and promptly burst into tears. She cried for a full minute at least, then wiped her nose and took a deep breath. '…I'm sorry…'

'What are you sorry about?'

'Where do you want to start? *Sorry* I cut her out of my life for so long and blamed her for everything. *Sorry* I didn't have more time with her. *Sorry* I turned my self-loathing into a rejection of you and all you stood for.'

'Sounds like you've been in some very expensive therapy. Don't be sorry about any of it, Angela, and especially not the last part. I deserved it. You were right – and what's more it woke me up to who I am and what I've been doing with my life. Some serious things have happened, *are* happening.'

'What sort of things?'

'The police are on to me. They have been for a long time…'

'It wasn't me. I didn't tell them…'

'I know, I know. They were investigating Boris and it led them to me… Either I play ball with them or I lose everything *and* go away for a very long time…'

'Theo…'

'But it gets worse. The fact is I'm fucked anyway. Boris is dead, murdered, and his killers, the new Russian lot, will inevitably come after me.'

'Where are you? Are you in London?'

'I'm in Venice.'

'*Venice?*'

'Don't ask – it doesn't matter where I am. They'll still get to me.'

'*Christ!* Well, don't just sit there waiting for it to happen. At least come back here, so you can be with us. *Please.*'

'That may not be a good idea. I want to keep you and Grace as far away from this as possible. In fact, you should probably disappear for a while and not have any contact with me. I'll deal with it one way or another, I promise.'

'Theo, no…'

'But there's something else I really want you to know. Before I heard from the police or knew any of this, I'd decided to get out of the business and give all the bad money away to some good causes. But not just *my* bad money – all my clients' bad money too, and many others' besides.'

'I take it they're not making a donation.'

'No. I'm doing it for them. Robbing the robbers. Clipping the wings of the kleptos. Billions and billions of dollars snatched from their on-line accounts and redistributed to the deserving...'

'Theo, stop! What are you talking about? What kind of madness is this? I can't begin to think how you're attempting such a thing, or how dangerous it must be. For fuck's sake, I hope you're not doing it for me. I just want you back, that's all. The unreformed version is fine. We can work it out from there...' She started to cry again.

'It's good to know, Angela, but you'll be getting a new, improved version, whether you like it or not.'

She spoke through her tears. 'Get back here, please. Come back as soon as you can. I don't care about the danger to us – we'll get police protection, surely.'

'You know we can't rely on that...'

He heard her turn away from the phone. 'Grace...come here, Grace...speak to Daddy...*Theo*? Grace is here. She wants to speak to you...'

'*Daddy?*'

He tried to perk up. 'Hi, darling – how are you?'

'I'm sad. We're all sad because Maggie's dead. Mummy's not well, Daddy. We need you here to help make her better. We want you to come back.'

'I know darling and I want to come back too. I'll do my best, I promise.'

'Please, Daddy, come home...'

As they were speaking, another email appeared. It had no sender's name on it, but he recognised the same format as the one that told him Venice was a good place to die – the shouty upper case:

498

WE HAVE YOUR GIRLFRIEND. DO NOT IGNORE THIS IF YOU WANT TO SEE HER ALIVE AGAIN. MEET US AT THE CHURCH OF SAN MOISE NOW. MAKE SURE YOU'RE NOT FOLLOWED.

'*Theo*?' Angela was back on the line.

'I should go. Look, I'm really sorry about Maggie. I was very fond of her. I hope you realised that.'

'I did, of course, I did. *Please be careful* – come home. I love you. *We* love you.'

'I love you too.'

He rang off. Mr. Law was back, staring at him from behind his moneybags, but he had no time to engage in conversation. 'Fuck...Fuck...***FUCK***!' was about all he could manage. Poor Jo, he told himself, she was an innocent victim in all of this and he had no choice but to try to save her.

*

John Law got up, walked to the large windows that overlooked the canal and opened them. Instantly, he felt the chill of the evening rush into the *piano nobile*. He stepped outside onto the balcony and stood looking out over the throng of masqueraders on the quayside below. He went back to the table, took up two of the bags of gold and carried them, one in each hand, out to the balcony. He shouted in Italian to the revellers below: 'People of Venice – here is something to help you celebrate *Carnevale*!' With that, he opened the bags and showered the gold coins down onto the crowd beneath.

There was a wild commotion, a glorious uproar, as they realised what was happening and started to scramble for the coins. Law took the rest of the bags, two at a time, and did the same thing; each time the din grew louder and the commotion wilder.

A few moments later, Bellini burst into the room, accompanied by two servants. 'Il Duce, have you gone completely mad? What are you doing? Raining gold coins down on the crowd? This is a gaming salon, not an almshouse! Or worse, a madhouse!'

'My dear Conte, I had no choice. I was instructed to do so by my…friend…'

'Your *friend*, il Duce? What *friend*?'

'The man I've been playing cards with, the man who won everything from me…everything…and then gave it back to me…'

'But you've been alone all day.'

Suddenly Law was exhausted and the pain in his lung had redoubled in intensity, as if some sharp-toothed creature were burrowing deeper and deeper inside him. He must return to his lodgings, he thought. He could not die there, in the Ridotto. It might be appropriate, but it would not be seemly.

With as much strength as he could summon, he stood and gathered up his manuscript and Katherine's letter; he left the playing cards on the table, the empty moneybags on the floor.

'My dear Conte,' he said, 'I must join in the celebrations.'

Bellini's concerned expression was restored; he was again Law's protector. 'You're hardly well enough, il Duce.'

'I'll be fine. I've never felt better,' he said, almost toppling forward. They went to help him, but he motioned them away and steadied himself. 'Thank you…I'll be fine…'

Bellini picked up Theo's mask from the table. 'You will need your mask for *Carnevale*, il Duce. It's a very fine mask, one of the best I've seen.'

Law went to tell him that it wasn't his, but instead he said: 'Yes…thank you, a good idea. Would you be so kind as to help me with it?' Bellini picked up the mask, placed it on Law's face and tied it at the back.

'Now you are ready for the masquerade.'

'And the ladies,' said Law. The mask made him look full of that sort of mischief.

'And the ladies,' Bellini laughed. 'Good night, il Duce.'

'Good night, my dear Conte…and thank you, all of you, thank you…*a domani*…' He bowed to them and left.

'*A domani*, il Duce.'

Outside, in his mask, he wasn't recognised as the man who had disbursed such largesse from the balcony. The masqueraders, all of them high on wine and gold, danced around him, hugged him and shook him by the hand. Briefly, it brought back memories of the frenzied Quincumpoix.

It took him an age to make his way through the crowd. At times he felt so weak and faint he was only held upright by those around him, leading him in a dance, it seemed. As Theo had been earlier, he was carried along on a tidal flow of masked revellers, while he clung to the manuscript and Katherine's letter, precious salvage that buoyed him up.

And the noise was deafening. As well as the shouts of the crowd and from the large gondolas drifting by, full of musicians and revellers, the fireworks had begun. Launched from the square of San Marco, they flashed like sheet lightening and crashed like thunder, as he struggled to find his way to the Rialto and his lodgings. Bellini would have been amused to know that Law was right about the ladies chasing him. Liberated by their carnival masks from their usual, more modest demeanour, they had become nothing short of predatory. They hunted in packs, whispering seduction in a fellow's ear, then grabbing and squeezing his balls and running off, laughing. And his Fool's mask seemed to attract them all the more. Three times he narrowly escaped this dubious pleasure, before finally making it to his lodgings and collapsing breathless inside the door.

Pietro, his manservant, was out at the revels, of course – doubtless pretending to be a duke – but at least he had left several lamps burning and the embers of a fire. Law was determined to reach his bed, but remained on the floor, propped up against the wall for some minutes, before he attempted the stairs. It was an arduous climb and he paused many times, thinking he might collapse again. Eventually, he fell onto the bed, still clutching the manuscript and the letter, and still wearing Theo's mask, he realised, which made him smile. He was all smiles.

As he removed it, he suffered his worst coughing fit since he'd left the Ridotto. Only when it stopped, was he finally able to open and read Katherine's letter. Afterwards, he intended to place it at the back of his memoir, so that it formed its final pages. But a burden of tiredness fell upon him, such that he had never experienced, and as he slipped from consciousness, the letter slipped from his hand and fell under the bed. When Bellini came to take away il Duce's corpse and few belongings, he must have missed it.

Paris

February 1729

Dear John,

Although it may never be possible, I wou'd be greatly reliev'd to know that you had actually read this letter. I have had reports from a certain Conte de Bellini at the Ridotto in Venice, who says he is your greatest friend and admirer and thought that I wou'd want to know of your condition. He paint'd such a grim picture of your physical health that I am finally mov'd to write to you about matters that we shou'd have discuss'd long ago. Only now, at this eleventh hour, can I bring myself to tell you these things and I pray God that I am not too late to do so.

First, there is a practical matter – and unfortunately, it is not good news. I have receiv'd word from the company that was charg'd with the carriage of our paintings to Venice that there has been a tragic accident. Apparently, as they were being transport'd across the Isere at Valence, a freak flooding of the river occurr'd – most unusual this early in the year – destroying the bridge and taking the wagon containing our precious cargo with it. What was not swept away in the floodwaters was damag'd beyond repair. I am very sorry, John, but the wonderful drawings and paintings that were to have provid'd an inheritance for Anne are lost.

Only yesterday I was in such despair over this that I cou'd not refrain from sharing it with Saint-Simon. He has heard so much of my bad news these last few years, yet somehow he always manages to find the words to comfort me. Yesterday was no exception, for it was then that he inform'd me of a plan he had had in mind for

502

some time and it seem'd an appropriate moment to unveil it. He has always claim'd to be unskill'd in financial matters and yet early in the rise of the Mississippi, he purchas'd a considerable number of shares – with your encouragement, he says, although he never told you at the time – sold them at their height and convert'd everything to gold. He has always felt guilty for making a fortune from something that was disastrous for so many, including ourselves. It will therefore give him the greatest pleasure, he assures me, to settle the whole fortune on Anne. When she comes of age, she will be a very wealthy young woman and financially secure for the rest of her life – assuming that she does not squander it on the wrong man or invest it in the wrong enterprise!

All of which brings me somewhat awkwardly to us. As I said in my last letter, it is a subject I never thought to revisit, a subject that has become abhorrent to me, and yet here I am once again trying to work out how it went so badly wrong. It is a futile exercise, but one I am nonetheless driven to perform.

More than I realis'd at the time, our rivalry certainly play'd a part. I shou'd have known that as a hero of the gaming table, you wou'd treat our every encounter as if it were a card game. The rights and wrongs of any situation seem to have taken second place to your winning, whatever the cost or consequence. But if it came as no surprise to know that <u>you</u> always had to walk away with the largest purse, I was shock'd to discover that I was similarly afflict'd with the will to win.

Nor did I fully realise how threaten'd you felt by my need to be involv'd in the running of the bank, especially as I genuinely thought that I was a great help to you; indeed, that I had a much better grasp of what need'd to be done – which I now see only increas'd your resentment. (Obviously, I do not have to remind you of what happen'd once you chose to ignore my advice.)

Moreover, I must admit that I behav'd very badly when I was pregnant with Anne, the worst part of which was that I lost all physical desire for you and cou'd not

503

recover it afterwards, no matter how much I tried. From then on, I became aware, as I am sure you did too, of a growing distance between us – and how easy it is for distance to turn to distrust! Unfortunately, my distrust of men in general alight'd upon on a particular man, a man I had once lov'd, and your cruel behaviour towards me only deepen'd it. Had you been more forgiving, so might I. Instead, ever the gamester, you rais'd the stakes on our mutual enmity even higher.

Which, of course – inevitably, unavoidably – raises the most difficult subject of all: Philippe. More confessions on my part: I did find him tolerably attractive, and I do take full responsibility for electing to play him like a fish on a line – which, I wou'd remind you, was in both our interests. That was <u>my</u> game, if you like, and how foolish and damaging it turn'd out to be, since in the end Orleans was better at playing us than we him. By the time I had grown tir'd of it and want'd nothing more than to leave the game, he was just warming to his quest.

And his quest became a conquest. The day Anne and I were due to leave for the Netherlands and you sent him out to me at Gourmande was the worst day of my life. When I reject'd his advances in the strongest terms, his charm turn'd to belligerence, even more so than it had before. He scream'd at me: I was a cold English bitch who had teas'd, tantalis'd and insult'd him for long enough. He hit me several times across the face, threw me to the floor and while I was all but unconscious, commit'd the most violent rape. I was soon to discover that this had been witness'd by Anne from an adjoining room, and it was only when she rush'd in, frantic and tearful, poor darling, that he was oblig'd to stop.

I am still sicken'd by the thought of what happen'd that day – which was compound'd by his dragging us to Notre Dame and stealing my gold – and I think of it often, as much as I try not to. As a man, you cannot appreciate the total devastation that is wrought upon a woman by such an act, the worst of it being that the sense of violation, humiliation and shame she feels makes her despise herself as much as her oppressor.

And how much sadder is it that this is a common experience for so many women, and not just in the most literal, physical sense. We are abus'd and rap'd every day by the whole social and political system, with little hope of any change in sight. (As you can tell, my thinking has only grown more radical and cynical down the years.)

Of course, I had every reason to blame you as well as myself, and I have continued to blame you ever since. Now, eight years later, something has suddenly chang'd, and I am not sure exactly why. Perhaps, Bellini's description of your pitiable condition has affect'd me. I still see you swaggering around the gaming salons with your bags of gold or in our bedroom in Rotterdam the day I join'd you from Scotland or on the night of Anne's birth, when we felt bless'd and the world seem'd ours to command. And then I think of us now – angry, embittered and alone.

There was a time, a short time ago, when I wou'd have rejoic'd in the pain of your sickness, John, but now for some reason it pains me. Cou'd it be the nagging thought of what we had and how we lost it; how we were ensnar'd by greed and ambition; how we were caught up in a web of intrigue that we never fully understood and how it brought out the very worst in our natures? What happen'd to the best in us? Is it there, buried deep beneath those layers of bitterness, resentment and regret? If it is, there is only one way to draw it to the surface. You begg'd forgiveness from me and I refus'd it. Now, I not only grant that forgiveness, but ask it from you.

These last few days, I have even thought of rushing to join you in Venice. I still cannot leave France officially, but it cou'd be arrang'd with Saint-Simon's help, now that my notoriety has fad'd and I am somewhat restor'd in status. Maybe I will. Maybe I will follow this letter. Maybe I will not be too late. But for now, this cold February night, I can only reach out to you and try to *comfort you in my imagination. And who knows, perhaps it is better that way: together in spirit, without the distractions of the flesh.*

Rest in peace, John.

Katherine

*

Theo decided to take the mask with him. There was no time to leave it in the room and, anyway, it did feel like a bit of a talisman. Against all odds, he'd managed to win a fortune when he wore it, even if it was in a dream, and now the odds were more stacked against him. As for the manuscript, he left it at reception.

'Would you please put it somewhere secure?'

'Si, Signor Law, it will go in our safe.' He'd gone before she could give him a receipt.

There was a crowd at the front of the foyer, and it was only when he'd edged his way through it and got to the front door he realised why. The doormen were advising people not to go out. The water level was still rising; they were laying sandbags, three-deep across the front of the hotel. To anybody like Theo who ignored the advice, they were offering the yellow boots and umbrellas, but he was in too much of a hurry and declined the offer.

Outside, the wind was stronger, the rain even harder, the sky a darker shade of inky black. He made it to the nearest raised walkway, which itself was only just above the high-water level. The flooding had left the Grand Canal much grander. It had burst its banks and become an extension of the sea, lapping around the Salute and the nearby buildings across from the hotel, which appeared to be floating off into the lagoon.

The Europol officer on surveillance duty had seen Theo come down to the reception but missed him leaving. He went outside just in time to see him taking a right turn into the Calle Ridotto, a narrow, deserted passage that led up to San Moise.

He made to follow but slipped and fell headlong into the water. Several concerned Chinese tourists helped fish him out.

The walkway in the alley was completely submerged but only by a few inches, so Theo was able to scramble along it until he reached the back of the church. From there, he made his way round to where the façade overlooked the piazza that was now a swimming pool.

He stopped by the church and surveyed the scene from the walkway. It led to a bowed bridge that stood clear of the water, over what was once a canal but now formed part of a large pool of floodwater, stretching across to the buildings on the far bank. The wind and rain raked the pool's surface and the reflections of the streetlights. He was drenched through and began to shiver – from fear or cold or both, he wasn't sure. He was alone, with only the sound of the wind and rain for company. Oddly, it was as peaceful a moment as he'd known all weekend. He was neither Moneyman nor Anarchist. He was just little Theo running down the dunes in total abandon into the arms of his mother.

What the fuck, he thought, none of it mattered in the great cosmic scheme of things. Bring it all on...

There was a buzzing in his pocket and he pulled out the Feinstein hotline. Data, most of it indecipherable, was cascading down the screen, a torrent, as Feinstein had said. The biggest heist in history was happening – and billions were being redistributed to lots of good causes. To name a few: help for trafficked women and drug addiction, domestic violence charities, educational and environmental charities in the developing world (a large chunk went to the African country he'd visited); cerebral palsy research and anti-fascist political campaigns (including the one run by Sanyo in that same African country.)

But he barely had time to take all this in before he glimpsed a flash of bright orange, like an exotic bird swooping through his peripheral vision: the slender figure of a woman was moving quickly away from him on the far side of the bridge. As she moved in and out of the shadows, he recognised the puffa jacket and yellow boots before anything else. It was Jo.

'*Jo!*'

He took off after her . 'It's me – ***Theo!***'

What was she doing? Was she trying to escape from her captors? Had she not seen him?

'*It's me!*'

She kept running as best she could across the walkway. He made it over the bridge, as she disappeared down a narrow passage that led away from the canal. It was dark and there was no walkway, but the water was only ankle deep and he was able to pick up speed. As they came out of the alley and onto what he assumed – he couldn't tell for sure – was the bank of another flooded canal, he'd almost caught up with her.

'Jo! For fuck's sake! *It's me!*'

They'd emerged into the streetlight, when she suddenly stopped and turned to him. She was half in shadow. Rain streamed down her face; her gravity-defying mane hung in rat's tails. She looked terrified.

'It's me. It's Theo.'

'Thank God. I was so scared.'

He didn't wait to be asked. He waded over to her – the water was now almost over his knees – and letting go of the bag with the mask, threw his arms around her.

'Jo, you poor thing. I'm so sorry. It's me they're after – what happened?'

He felt the Feinstein phone buzzing away in his pocket again – another torrent of data, of mega-money. Then he felt something else – a searing pain in his chest. He pulled away from her and looked down at the knife she was holding, its narrow blade sheathed in blood.

Theo put his hand to his chest, felt the warm, damp patch that wasn't water and saw the dusky bloom of the rose, like in his dream. John Law was there once again, staring at him, accusing him of being the man who'd haunted him down the years.

*

Knee-deep in water, knife-in-hand – a knife she'd bought in Venice on her way to the hotel that first night – Jo stood watching the mortally wounded Theo. She watched him with a weird sense of detachment, as if none of it was actually happening, as if time had come to a virtual halt.

Instead, the real action took place inside her head. The events that had brought her to this point coursed through her mind, like that churning of data on Theo's phone: how she'd tracked down Boris as the man behind the gang that had trafficked her mother and been responsible for her death; how she'd identified Theo as the person who'd enabled him to keep on operating and grow super-rich from it; how she'd decided that both of them had to die; how she'd found her way into Boris's legal team and then his affections; how she'd agreed to find out what had happened to that memory stick; how she'd realised there was only one sure-fire way of doing that and become Theo's lover too.

And that was when things got complicated. Boris made her flesh creep and taking revenge on him was relatively easy. But Theo made her flesh cry out for more of him. Despite her best efforts, there was some powerful chemistry between them.

She'd killed Boris on the Thursday, as he drew her to him and pressed his hardening cock against her. On Friday, before she travelled, she'd sent the delayed messages to Theo: the anonymous DEATH IN VENICE note and the one telling him to proceed with the Vatican deal – a kind of gaslighting by email. However, she was not convinced she could go through with the second execution.

And on Saturday – yesterday, was it only yesterday? – even when he'd actually confessed his guilt and talked about his need to atone, she still had her misgivings, especially when he'd told her about the biggest heist in history.

She'd decided to fly back to London, to put Theo out of reach. She'd even tried calling him from the airport, telling him everything was fine – she just needed some space, some time to reflect.

But the words refused to come. Or at least, they were pre-empted by the sight of an attractive young woman with long dark hair who reminded her of her mother, of herself even.

She watched the woman run across the concourse, sweep her little daughter into her arms and smother her with kisses. Suddenly, she knew that it was not only her mother and the many other victims of the gang who had to be avenged, but the loss of her own childhood and any chance she might have had of happiness in her life. She had to be straight with herself: she was just too fatally flawed, too terminally damaged for anything other than the settling of scores.

Tears welled in her eyes, blurring the scene before her; anger rose from the pit of her stomach, up through her chest to the centre of her brain, cauterising all sense of compassion. Boris's life was not enough. None of these crimes could be committed without the help of the Moneyman. Nothing ever happened without the Moneyman. The Moneyman had to pay – and, yes, it was a great shame, but giving all his money away to good causes was not a high enough price.

And now, here he was, looking up at her, clutching his chest. His expression asked her why, but surely he could work it out for himself. In fact, wasn't that a faint smile forming on his lips, as he sensed, almost tasted the sweet justice of it all? His debt to her and many others repaid; her risk rewarded: the perfect deal. *Game over.*

She continued to watch him, while he desperately tried to staunch the flow of blood. She was concerned, not by the fact that he was in pain, but that he wasn't fighting for breath as Boris had done; that he wasn't already dead. Had she somehow missed the mark – the heart or a major artery? Did her knife know more about her own heart than she did?

Whatever. She needed to finish the job.

'Sorry, Theo…'

*

As she came at him, he still had the strength to grab the arm wielding the knife and push her away. Neither of them realised how close they were to the edge of the flooded canal. Jo lost her footing in the struggle and fell into the deeper water, hitting her head hard against the submerged stone bank as she went down.

He was unaware of this. He'd passed out and toppled forward into the dark water, his final black hole. He was as likely to die from drowning as he was from the wound in his chest leaking his lifeblood.

Minutes later, the police patrol boat carrying the Europol officer who'd been trying to tail Theo arrived on the scene, flashing its green, white and red lights, like an illuminated Italian flag. The flooding had enabled it to reach parts of the canal system where it could not have gone in normal circumstances. It's an ill wind - or wind, rain and an extra-high tide, in this case.

The officer who pulled Theo out of the water found him still breathing and bleeding. Meanwhile, the boat's spotlight fell upon an orange object floating in the shadows. Was it a buoy? No, a girl. It was Jo. Unfortunately, she wasn't breathing; she'd drowned after bashing her head as she fell into the canal. The smiling face of the Fool floated next to her.

*

Although much of the redistribution took place off grid, under the radar of the mainstream markets, it still gave rise to some serious wobbles. There were panics when some very, very rich people looked at their secret deposit accounts and realised they weren't as rich any more. This caused several flashcrashes that would push the fragile global financial system further towards a final, fatal meltdown, the palpitations that are often forerunners to a massive heart attack. Theo would say it was an indication of how much the 'shadow of the shadow system', as he called it, underpinned the official one – the ship of all that appears clean and legitimate floating on a rising tide of dirty money.

*

And speaking of rising tides, Marisa had come into Venice on Sunday evening, partly to meet a friend for dinner, partly to see the extent of the worst flooding La Serenissima had ever known. They were down by the Rialto Bridge when they heard the siren.

'Is it for *acqua alta*?' her friend asked.

'No, it's a police boat...' They watched it rush past them, its wash breaking against the facades of the palazzos as it disappeared around the bend of an even grander canal, heading for the hospital.

'*Allora...*'

'*Avanti...*'

Theo Law, London 2019

511

Printed in Great Britain
by Amazon

48122843R00295